CW00482329

ROMANTIC DRAMA

Drama in the Romantic period underwent radical changes affecting theatre performance, acting, and audience. Theatres were rebuilt and expanded to accommodate larger audiences, and consequently acting styles and the plays themselves evolved to meet the expectations of the new audiences. This book examines manifestations of change in acting, stage design, setting, and the new forms of drama. Actors exercised a persistent habit of stepping out of their roles, whether scripted or not. Burwick traces the radical shifts in acting style from Garrick to Kemble and Siddons, and to Kean and Macready, adding a new dimension to understanding the shift in cultural sensibility from early to later Romantic literature. Eye-witness accounts by theatre-goers and critics attending plays at the major playhouses of London, the provinces, and on the Continent are provided, allowing readers to identify with the experience of being in the theatre during this tumultuous period.

FREDERICK BURWICK is Emeritus Professor of English Literature at the University of California, Los Angeles. He is the author of over twenty-five books, and his research is dedicated to problems of perception, illusion, and delusion in literary representation and theatrical performance. In 1997 he was awarded the Barricelli Award for Outstanding Book of the Year, for *Poetic Madness and the Romantic Imagination*. He has been named Distinguished Scholar by both the British Academy (1992) and the Keats–Shelley Association (1998).

ROMANTIC DRAMA

Acting and Reacting

FREDERICK BURWICK

CAMBRIDGE
UNIVERSITY PRESS

CAMBRIDGE UNIVERSITY PRESS
Cambridge, New York, Melbourne, Madrid, Cape Town, Singapore, São Paulo, Delhi

Cambridge University Press
The Edinburgh Building, Cambridge CB2 8RU, UK

Published in the United States of America by Cambridge University Press, New York

www.cambridge.org
Information on this title: www.cambridge.org/9780521889674

First published 2009

Printed in the United Kingdom at the University Press, Cambridge

A catalogue record for this publication is available from the British Library

ISBN 978-0-521-88967-4 hardback

Contents

List of illustrations   *page* vi
Acknowledgments   vii

Introduction   1

1   Periscopes into the theatre   14

2   Nationalism and national character   33

3   Genre: the realism of fantasy, the fantasy of realism   56

4   Acting: histrionics, and dissimulation   80

5   Transvestites, lovers, monsters: character and sexuality   115

6   Setting: where and elsewhere   151

7   Gothic and anti-Gothic: comedy and horror   170

8   Blue-Beard's castle: mischief and misogyny   202

9   Vampires in kilts   230

Notes   258
Bibliography   296
Index   328

Illustrations

1 Apprehension, *Hamlet*.   *page* 84
2 Painful Recollection, *King Lear*.   86
3 John James Halls, Edmund Kean as Richard III.   87
4 James Northcote, John Philip Kemble as Richard III.   88
5 Benjamin West, *King Lear*.   90
6 Benjamin West, *Hamlet*.   91
7 Camilla in *Les Horaces*.   93
8 Odoardo in *Emilia Galotti*.   94
9 Odoardo in *Emilia Galotti*.   95
10 Henry Tresham, *Antony and Cleopatra*.   96
11 William Hamilton, *Much Ado About Nothing*.   98
12 The smith hears of Prince Arthur's death. *King John*.   99

Acknowledgments

For the approach and ideas developed in this book my debts are large and vast. Scholars who work on the drama of the Romantic period are an especially generous and collegial group. We gather together at conferences to share our concerns in exploring this still largely uncharted field. I thank the many whom I have consulted, and I wish to name especially Betsy Bolton, Jacqueline Bratton, Catherine Burroughs, Gilli Bush-Bailey, Julie Carlson, Jeffrey Cox, Lila Maria Crisafulli, Thomas Crochunis, Stuart Curran, Tracy Davis, Ellen Donkin, Michael Gamer, Terence Allan Hoagwood, Diane Hoeveler, Jane Moody, Daniel O'Quinn, Marjean Purinton, Charles Rzepka, Diego Saglia, and Daniel P. Watkins.

In thanking the students in my courses on Romanticism and Romantic Drama: Performance and Production, I owe a practical debt – the discovery of the transmutations that occur when a play is rehearsed for weeks and then performed on stage with a live audience. Among those players who returned year after year to perform in my revival productions of Romantic plays, I am grateful to the dedication and talents of William Bibiani, Veronica Bitz, Lauren Cheak, Greg Cragg, Kristin Crawford, Brian Hayden, Schuyler Hudak, Charles Maas, Nicolas Moreno, Jenna Pinkham, A. J. Rodriguez, Rebecca Wyrostek, and Daniel Zamani. We were also joined in performance by Thomas Wheatley, Professor of Theatre Arts at UCLA. Brian Holmes, Professor of Musicology at San José State University, provided original scores and instrumental adaptations of period scores. For four years Jong-Ling Wu was lead member of the music ensemble. Among the graduate students who joined in the performances were Julian Knox, J. D. Lopez, and Kathryn Tucker. Stephen Pu and Holley Replogel commenced working with me as undergraduates and continued to assist as graduate students.

While many discoveries about the drama can occur only in the process of rehearsal and performance, other discoveries take place at the opposite end of the spectrum – in library archives. For research on this project

I have been especially blessed by having access to major collections. The plays submitted to the Lord Chamberlain for licensing from from 1737 to January, 1824, are in the Huntington Library, San Marino, California. Those submitted for licensing from 1824 to 1968 are in the British Library Manuscript Collections. I am grateful to the librarians at both facilities for their assistance. I have also relied extensively on the journals and letters of John Waldie, D. Litt., of Hendersyde Park, Kelso, Scotland. This collection (UCLA MSS 169; MC4973228), spanning the years 1799 to 1864, consists of seventy-four journal volumes, eleven volumes on travels transcribed from the journals, and a volume of passports. Thanks to the assistance of Victoria Steele and Lucinda Newsome, UCLA Special Collections, I have been able to edit an extensive selection with commentaries on over a thousand performances: *The Journal of John Waldie, Theatre Commentaries, 1798–1830*, eScholarship Repository, California Digital Library.

Introduction

The poet, John Keats insisted in his letter to Richard Woodhouse (October 27, 1818), has no self, no character, no identity, but is ever ready to assume identity and enter into a role:

As to the poetical Character . . . it has no self – it is everything and nothing – It has no character – it enjoys light and shade; it lives in gusto, be it foul or fair, high or low, mean or elevated. It has as much delight in conceiving an Iago as an Imogen. What shocks the virtuous philosopher, delights the camelion Poet. It does no harm from its relish of the dark side of things any more than its taste for the bright one; because they both end in speculation. A Poet is the most unpoetical of anything in existence because he has no Identity; he is continually in for and filling some other Body.[1]

To describe how the poetic imagination moves from nonentity to identity, Keats introduces contrasting Shakespearean characters: the innocent Imogen, the evil Iago. Whatever their moral difference, both have equal affective value because "both end in speculation." The poet is always ready for such role-playing, "continually in for and filling some other Body." Keats's theatrical metaphor for entering into character might seem to apply broadly to the assumptions about acting in the period. The successful performer, a Sarah Siddons or a John Philip Kemble, is presumably one who can enter convincingly into role and become that character for the duration of the play. The efficacy of the performance is measured by the degree to which the audience, too, participates in the illusion, identifies with a character's pleasures or pains.

This Romantic dictum of imaginative identification with character is countered by playwrights, actors, and critics alike. Identification with character may be one prevailing proposition, but maintaining an aloof distance is certainly a strong corollary. In *Illusion and the Drama* (1991), I identified an abundance of negative counter trends, political and social as well as aesthetic, at work in the very exposition of illusionist theory.[2] Illusionism, yes, but with anti-illusionism riding tandem. In an era of virtuoso performance, audiences went to the theatre not to see *Macbeth*, but to see John Philip Kemble play Macbeth and Sarah Siddons play Lady Macbeth.

In the ensuing pages of the introduction, I describe changes taking place in performance, in theatres and audiences, and in the kind of plays that gained popularity. I also anticipate my intentions in the chapters to follow, where I argue that all aspects of theatre and performance were interrelated, and that each aspect involved a fundamental duality or bifurcation. In the first chapter, concerned with audience response, I privilege those eye-witnesses who may be the least representative, the critics. They are unavoidable because they report what they experience. So do the players in their memoirs. Critics disagree, but weighing one report against another may give us a broader and more accurate understanding of performance. This is especially true in the political arena when international events may distort both the representation of, and response to, foreigners on the stage. More than liberal vs. conservative bias, the split is informed by a complex interplay of cultural tradition and translation. Another arena of duality arises from the contrary demands of realism and fantasy, tugging some playwrights into the indulgence of melodrama, others into a documentary fidelity to historical facts. A similar kind of tug-of-war occurred in the very art of acting, the extremes of tempered restraint as opposed to flamboyant histrionics. Furthermore, actors exercised a persistent habit of stepping out of their roles, whether scripted or not. A significant and complex factor in an actor putting on character was the way in which sexual identity might be problematized, especially in comedies that delighted in cross-dressing, and Gothic tragedies that presented villains as perverted sexual predators. Not just character, but also setting was marked by studied displacement, inviting the audience to recognize domestic or national relevance in far-flung places. Another crucial aspect of duality occurred in bridging the traditional distinction between comedy and tragedy. Even as Gothic melodrama gained dominance on the stage, it was riddled with anti-Gothic elements. Horror was accompanied by alternating scenes of comedy. The final two chapters, on the arch-villains Blue-Beard and the Vampire, examine themes of misogyny and domestic violence brought under scrutiny on the Romantic stage as fantasies arising from facts and fears.

In consequence of the prevailing "star" system of the period, actors were inclined to rush through dialogue in order to grandstand with a powerful monologue: Kemble as Penruddick, contemplating his revenge on Woodville,[3] or Siddons as Mrs. Haller, revealing her pangs of guilt upon receiving the letter announcing the visit of the Count and

Countess.[4] With interest focused on the performer, the way was open for the novelty performer, such as Robert "Romeo" Coates, an incredibly bad actor whose performances were so ridiculous that audiences flocked to see him mangle his roles with his wildly garish costumes, flamboyant gestures, fumbled and ad-libbed lines. When he took over from Robert William Elliston the part of Lothario in Nicholas Rowe's *The Fair Penitent* (Haymarket, December 9, 1811), the theatre had to turn away thousands who had lined up to see the mawkish performance. Coates was clever enough to realize that if audiences were laughing at his bad acting he could exploit his natural talent for buffoonery in all of his roles. Charles Mathews mimicked Coates in such comic routines as the "Dissertation on Hobbies, in humble imitation of the celebrated Amateur of Fashion" (Bath, April 28, 1814).[5]

Also rising to fame as a novelty player was William Henry West Betty, "the Infant Roscius" who maintained his success as a child actor from ages twelve to seventeen, after which he outgrew the novelty. Master Betty did not play child roles; rather he appeared on stage in leading adult roles. With a stage debut as Osman in Aaron Hill's *Zara* (Belfast, August 19, 1803), he went on to play Douglas, Rolla, Romeo, and Hamlet in the theatres of Dublin and Cork. The following year, at age thirteen, he had invitations to play in Glasgow and Edinburgh. In London he appeared first as Achmet in John Brown's *Barbarossa* (Covent Garden, December 1, 1804), a role that had originally been played by David Garrick in 1753. He then commenced an engagement in the title role of Home's *Douglas* (Drury Lane, December 10, 1803). For his twenty-eight nights the box-office brought in the unprecedented sum of £17,000.[6] I will return to Master Betty in Chapter 7 to examine his performance as Osmond, the vicious sexual predator of *The Castle Spectre*.

Another theatrical phenomenon of the age was the one-man show, a virtuoso comic performance in which the skilled mimic and quick-change artist would shift rapidly from one role to another. The three great masters of this sort of comic routine were John Bannister (1760–1836), Charles Mathews (1776–1835), and Joseph Grimaldi (1778–1837).[7] Bannister was given an opportunity to develop his skills as a solo performer in George Colman's *New Hay at the Old Market* (Haymarket, June 9, 1795). In this metatheatrical spoof on the London theatres, Bannister played an out-of-work actor, Sylvester Daggerwood, who tries to convince the would-be playwright and the theatre manager of his talents. He sings and mimics a variety of performers. Playing alongside of Bannister in subsequent performances, John Caufield, in the role of Apewell, also showed off his uncanny skill in mimicking other actors. Bannister's role as Daggerwood gradually evolved into a one-man show, *Bannister's Budget* (Drury Lane, 1807), in which he played a dozen different parts.[8]

Charles Mathews, the most popular of the solo performers, displayed incredible versatility as an impersonator. His performances in *At Home* began at the Lyceum theatre in 1808. It had no fixed plot or cast of characters, but in all of its variations Mathews played every character, carrying on dialogue between two, three, and four characters. Although the performances involved rapid changes of costume, he also could rely simply on his changes in voice to become a different personality. Mathews' repertory for *At Home* not only featured a multitude of characters; it also combined mimicry, storytelling, recitations, improvisation, quick-change artistry, and comic song.[9]

Another master of the one-man show was Joseph Grimaldi, the most celebrated of English clowns. Very different from those of either Bannister or Mathews, Grimaldi's pantomime performances drew from the old tradition of *commedia dell'arte* and exploited the current popularity of Harlequinades. His fiabesque *Harlequin and Mother Goose; or the Golden Egg* (Covent Garden, 1806) was often revived and adapted throughout his career.[10] In spite of the marked differences in their performances, all three solo performers invited the audience to watch the subtleties of role-playing, the acting ingenuity of the self putting on other identities, other personalities. Watching the actor acting was a common response to all performance in the period, whether of Kemble, Siddons, Coates, Master Betty, or Mathews. The audience who came to Mrs. Webb's benefit (Haymarket, July 21, 1786) were less interested in watching *Henry IV, Part I*, than in watching Mrs. Webb play Falstaff. As is well known, when Sarah Siddons performed her signature role as Lady Macbeth for her farewell to the stage (Covent Garden, June 29, 1812), the curtain was dropped at the close of her mad scene (v.i). This was the finale that the audience had come to see, and they refused to allow the play to continue.

In spite of a new attention to historical accuracy in costumes and stage design, and a new emphasis on special effects to enhance stage illusion, there was also a relentless exposure of both the art and artifice of performance. Hanna Cowley, in the preface to her comedy *The Town Before You* (Covent Garden, December 6, 1794), complained that audiences no longer cared for the development of character in a play. They wanted the instant gratification of comic antics: "The patient developement of character, the repeated touches which colour it up to Nature, and swell it into identity and existence (and which gave celebrity to Congreve), we have now no relish for."[11] A century had passed since Congreve's day. What had changed? Everything – audience, acting, stage design and costumes, the plays, and the theatre itself. Each of the changes was inextricably entangled with all the others. The major factor was the huge growth in the London population. By 1750 the population of London had reached almost 700,000, and by 1800 over a million. It had become the largest city in the world. By 1821, 1,378,947 were crowded into London's urban area. Industrialization and the rising middle class had their inevitable impact on the theatres of London. While melodrama, novelty acts, spectacle, and special effects on stage entertained and distracted, prostitutes and pickpockets were at work in the audience. Patrons of the Haymarket and the Adelphi theatres were wise to be especially wary.[12] In addition to thieves and prostitutes inside the theatre, beggars flocked round the entrance. The Royal Coburg, built in 1818 on the Waterloo Road in the dangerous neighborhood of New Cut, south of the Thames, attracted patrons willing to exercise necessary caution.[13]

New theatres were built and old theatres were refurbished, and with every modification more and more seats were added. When David Garrick performed at Drury Lane, he could elicit a roar of laughter from the audience by arching an eyebrow. Under Richard Brinsley Sheridan's ownership, Drury Lane was demolished and rebuilt (1791–4). When it reopened, on 12 March 1794, technical difficulties with the stage had not yet been resolved; a programme of sacred music was offered on opening night. Another month passed before the first dramatic performance could be offered. The play was *Macbeth*, with John Philip Kemble and Sarah Siddons in the leading roles (April 21, 1794). The new Drury Lane was a cavernous theatre, accommodating more than 3,600 spectators.[14] Sarah Siddons called it "a wilderness of a place." The size was not designed for superior reception of dramatic performance, but only for larger audience and larger box office revenue.[15] Sturdy iron columns supported five tiers of galleries. The stage was 83 feet wide and 92 feet deep, flanked by sixteen boxes, four within the proscenium arch on either side, and four more above the stage doors left and right. James Boaden did not consider the vastness discomforting. He argued that it could easily manage a full house, bringing in "a nightly receipt of £700," but that the audience could be well distributed so that the house did not "look deserted on a thin night."[16] More especially, Boaden was pleased with stage machinery that could accomplish all the wonders of special effects, with "vast and beautiful" scenery that "rose from below the stage or descended thither." Even the costume wardrobe had been richly augmented.[17]

Other theatre-goers were less sanguine than Boaden about the huge size of the new Drury. John Byng was among those who lamented the "warm close observant seats of Old Drury." Byng attended *The Siege of Belgrade* (May 6, 1794), a comic opera by James Cobb and Stephen Storace, and found that much of the dialogue could not be heard.[18] Not entirely vanquished, but seriously challenged, was the sense of intimacy between performer and audience. The consequences were inevitable. No longer able to rely on subtle gesture and vocal nuance, acting style had to employ broader histrionics and maintain volume in its vocal projection. Productions tended more toward spectacle and pantomime.

Such a spectacle was Kemble's *Lodoiska* (June 9, 1794).[19] At the opening of Act II, Lodoiska, played by Anna Maria Crouch, looks out from a tower upon the "streams, that round my prison creep" (II.i), hoping to be rescued by her lover, Count Floreski, played by Michael Kelly. From rooftop tanks, water flowed down a rocky stream into a wide expanse traversed by a draw-bridge. In spite of the great attention Kemble had given to the stage design, Kelly reported that the final scene almost ended in disaster:

[W]hen Mrs. Crouch was in the burning castle, the wind blew the flames close to her; but she still had sufficient fortitude not to move from her situation; – seeing her in such peril I ran up the bridge, which was at a great height from the ground, towards the tower, in order to rescue her; just as I was quitting the platform, a carpenter, prematurely, took out one of its supporters, down I fell; and at the same moment, the fiery tower, in which was Mrs. Crouch, sank down in a blaze, with a violent crash; she uttered a scream of terror. Providently I was not hurt by the fall, and catching her in my arms, scarcely knowing what I was doing, I carried her to the front of the stage, a considerable distance from the place where we fell. The applause was loud and continued. In fact, had we rehearsed the scene as it happened, it could not have appeared half so natural, or produced half so great an effect. – I always afterwards carried her to the front of the stage, and it never failed to produce great applause, – Such are, at times, the effects of accident.[20]

The accident turned out to be a spectacular *coup de théâtre*, but it might have left Kelly and Crouch with broken bones and third-degree burns. The stage of the new Drury was equipped with a metal curtain that could be dropped to stop the spread of fire, and the roof-top water tanks also had a practical purpose in dousing fires. As the production of *Lodoiska* made evident, even without the accident, the audience was treated to startling special effects.[21] Most importantly, it was a huge audience. With a full house of 3,600 spectators, fewer than half would have been able to see and hear clearly. But they would see the peril of the lady in the burning tower and be thrilled by the heroic rescue. Acting utilized the same sort of dumb-show gestures that were later characteristic of the silent movie era. A large part of the new audience were from the mercantile and working class. This was an audience who welcomed spectacle and melodrama.

Neither the water tanks nor the metal curtains were of any help in halting the fire that destroyed Drury Lane on February 24, 1809. Financially ruined, Sheridan relinquished management of the theatre to Samuel Whitbread, who oversaw the rebuilding. Designed by Benjamin Dean Wyatt, Drury Lane reopened with a production of *Hamlet* (October 10, 1812) with Robert Elliston in the title role.[22] The new theatre seated 3,060 people, about 550 fewer than the previous building, but the only concession toward intimacy was not in the size, but in the increase in box seating, intended to bring in more revenue. Still an extremely large theatre, Drury Lane's productions continued to rely more on scenery and effects than on dialogue and acting.

Covent Garden had been the smaller of the two patent theatres, but when it burnt down on September 20, 1808, its new architectural design by Robert Smirke increased its capacity by over 1,100, so that when it reopened on September 18, 1809, it seated over 3,000 people, almost as many as Drury Lane.[23] Just as he had fifteen years earlier at Drury Lane, the actor-manager John Philip Kemble opened with a performance of *Macbeth*. He also raised seat prices to help recoup the cost of rebuilding. The new prices were vehemently opposed, and the audiences disrupted performances. The Old Price Riots lasted over two months, until the management finally acquiesced and restored the lower rates.

From the 1790s through the 1820s theatre performances adjusted to the expectations of the larger middle-class audiences. The period saw the rise of melodrama and a pervasive musical presence. Historical costumes and elaborate set designs provided a new verisimilitude. Stage illusions were enhanced by innovative mechanical devices. Phantom images projected by the *laterna magica* and the virtual images reflected by giant parabolic mirrors were made possible by advances in lighting technology, which progressed rapidly during the era: the Argand lamp of 1780; the Clegg lamp of 1809; the gas lamps of 1815; the intense illumination of oxygen- and hydrogen-fed lamps of 1819; and, by the 1830s, the lime light.[24] Equipped with a tank measuring 40 × 100 feet, holding 8,000 cubic feet of water, Sadler's Wells was able to offer scenes of shipwrecks and maritime battles, such as *The Siege of Gibraltar* (April 2, 1804). Astley's Amphitheatre featured a ring for the performance of equestrian melodrama.[25]

In the ensuing nine chapters, I give primary attention to the varied dynamics of performance and audience response, beginning by establishing an entrance into the theatre through the critic and dedicated affecionado. Chapter 1, "Periscopes into the theatre," introduces John Waldie, a prolific theatre critic who not only published his reviews in newspapers and theatre journals of the period, but also kept an extensive journal of his attendance at the theatres with accounts of hundreds of plays. Waldie often saw the same popular play many times, and each time he noted the differences. Although his focus was on British theatre, he traveled extensively and was familiar with the theatres in France, Germany, Italy, and Spain. He was especially alert to foreign plays and foreign players on the British stage. As a proprietor of the Theatre Royal in Newcastle, he was familiar with the performances in the provinces as well as in London. His eye-witness accounts, alongside those of Leigh Hunt, William Hazlitt, and other critics, documented the paradoxical response of enthralled engagement and aloof detachment that was presumably experienced by a large portion of the audience and mirrored, as well, the peculiarities in the acting of many of the most successful performers of the era.

Chapter 2, "Nationalism and national character," examines the opposing tensions of Francophilia and Francophobia in plays of the period. London theatre, which had strong ties to France during the preceding centuries, now turned increasingly to Germany, and also to Spain and Italy, for its dramatic matter. Even as performances began to reveal more and more importation – from the Germany of Kotzebue and Schiller; from the Italy of Goldoni, Gozzi, and the revival of *commedia dell'arte* – French sources and the representation of French characters fell under the sway of the factional responses in Britain to the French Revolution, the Terror, the rise and fall of Napoleon, and the Bourbon Restoration. The representation of French character on the British stage between 1790 and 1830 was complicated by the continued popularity of French playwrights and the success of Parisian actors and actresses in London. Critical attention has been given by other recent critics to the ways in which the theatre in Paris responded to the political issues of the Revolution, and to how the theatre in London monitored and mediated the political events in France. Moving beyond these earlier studies, the present chapter examines the performance of French character, and representation of the emotional, intellectual, moral, and ideological attributes of French national identity, male and female.

Chapter 3, "Genre: the realism of fantasy, the fantasy of realism," studies the contrasting functions of the heightened illusionism of the age. On the occasion of his production of *King John* (Covent Garden, March 3, 1823), John Philip Kemble recalled his earlier production (Covent Garden, February 24, 1804) with the boast that he was a major instigator of the movement toward historical accuracy in costume and design.[26] In addition to period costumes, that "accuracy" was wrought by a series of magnificent flats painted with landscapes, camp scenes, and battlefields, as well as architecturally detailed renditions of the walls of Angiers (Act II), the gates of the castle (IV.iv), and Swinstead Abbey (v.vii). "The catastrophe took place in a night scene, lighted by torches, within *The Orchard at Swinstead Abbey*, and the final curtain fell to a 'Grand Symphony in the Orchestra'."[27] Even in the effort to conjure a realistic historical setting, Kemble and other theatre managers could not resist displaying the showmanship involved. The illusionism made itself equally apparent alongside the realism. As examples of the intermixing of the contraries in plays of fantasy as well as in documentary drama, this chapter will examine Edward Fitzball's *The Flying Dutchman* (Adelphi, January 1, 1827) and William Thomas Moncrieff's *The Shipwreck of Medusa* (Royal Coburg, June 19, 1820).

In *Hamlet*, Polonius introduces the players with praise of their ability to perform in any genre: "The best Actors in the world, either for Tragedie, Comedie, Historie, Pastorall: Pastorall–Comicall–Historicall–Pastorall: Tragicall–Historicall: Tragicall–Comicall–Historicall–Pastorall: Scene individable, or Poem unlimited. *Seneca* cannot be too heavy, nor *Plautus* too light. For the law of Writ, and the Liberty, these are the only men" (*Hamlet*, II.ii). Shakespeare's jest, of course, concerns the mixing of dramatic forms. More extreme than the combinations imagined by Polonius were the mixed forms that actually evolved during the Romantic era. For example, James Robinson Planché identified his production of *Blue Beard* as "A Grand Musical, Comi-Tragical, Melo-Dramatic, Burlesque Burletta."[28] The mixing of realism and illusionism, tragic and comic, had become the norm.

Chapter 4, "Acting: histrionics, and dissimulation," traces the radical shifts in acting style from Garrick to Kemble and Siddons, and again to Kean and Macready. Bringing together the actors' own descriptions of their performance (from memoirs and diaries), the stage directions in prompt-books, the poses in contemporary theatre paintings, the gesture and body movement prescribed in books on acting and oratorical delivery, this chapter examines how the norms of behavior are established and then broken in fits of rage or madness. The transgression of sanity into madness, the comforts of pleasure into pain, are studied especially in

the acting style of Sarah Siddons. The dynamics of gesture are complicated in the dishonesty of the villain, in the hypocrisy of the unfaithful
lover. Acts of dissembling and duplicity raise special problems in the
covert/overt art of telling lies with body language: as in Iago's deception
of Othello, the audience must discern what the immediate auditor on the
stage fails to perceive. Over the course of the Romantic period, the
histrionics of dissimulation became less subtle and covert; villainy was
painted in broader strokes. Machiavellian cunning lost its polish and
became more blatant.

Following the elucidation in the previous chapter of the language of
gesture in enacting truth vs. falsehood, lapses of sanity, normal vs.
abnormal behavior, Chapter 5 on "Transvestites, lovers, monsters: character and sexuality" continues to examine acts of dissimulation in terms of
trans-sexual disguises, sexual identity, and motivation. Shakespearean
characters, as August Wilhelm Schlegel observed, are frequently required
to put on disguise (*Verkleiden*) or to pretend to some beliefs or feelings
not their own (*Verstellen*).[29] The duplicity is literally a doubling, in which
both self and other are revealed in the role-playing, with boundary-
crossing juxtapositions of gender, race, or rank. With all female roles
played by men, Elizabethan playwrights had abundant occasion to
introduce jests of sexual identity. This practice of transvestite casting was
further complicated by the frequent stage ploy of a man playing a woman
playing a man: Rosalind becomes Ganymede, Viola becomes Cesario,
Imogen becomes Fidele.[30] Following the Restoration, when women were
allowed to play the female roles, the cross-dressing did not cease, but took
on new dimensions of titillation and exploration of sexual identity. The
disguise of females dressed as males coexisted with the representation of
males of compromised masculinity. The fop and preening dandy were
stock characters in comedy.[31] By the end of the eighteenth century, the
manners of the voluptuary and the homosexual had acquired a new
psychological dimension. Having begun with a survey of the dramatic
function of cross-dressing – male-as-female, the more frequent female-as-
male, and the representation of ambiguous sexual identity – this chapter
also discusses the "love or money" dilemma in comedy, then turns to the
representation of sexual malevolence, and the psychological motivation
for those melodramatic villains relentless in their acts of perversion, rape,
and excess. It considers too the extent to which character may confirm or
oppose misogynist and homophobic attitudes.

Chapter 6, "Setting: where and elsewhere," examines not the dissembling of character but the dissembling of the stage and setting. With its

picture-book and art gallery décor, the stage itself was transgressive, always converting then to now, here to there, there to here. While similar displacement belongs to drama of all periods, in the Romantic period relocating time and place was sometimes a maneuver necessary to circumvent the constraints of cautious censorship. Audiences, however, had learned to see identity in alterity, and to discover a critique on the figures of contemporary politics masquerading in the historical disguise of other times or places. The multiple refractions of then and now, there and here, amid the representational matrices of Romantic drama provide yet another strategy of transgression. The plays discussed in this chapter demonstrate that the "elsewhere" of the Romantic stage was historically and geographically wide-ranging. In *Pizarro*, the Peruvian struggle against the Conquistadores was recognized as the British resisting Napoleonic invasion. In *Sardanapalus*, Byron developed his oriental version of the effete king, transposing the dramatic prototype of Marlowe's *Edward II* and Shakespeare's *Richard II* to ancient Assyria.[32]

Comic scenes amidst Gothic horror may well be considered as examples of the grotesque as defined in the latter eighteenth century,[33] but Chapter 7, "Gothic and anti-Gothic: comedy and horror," seeks to investigate what purposes that dubious and duplicitous aesthetic might be made to serve in theatrical performance. Since the influence of the Marquis de Sade was first examined in Mario Praz's *The Romantic Agony*,[34] his presence in Britain has been recognized in Matthew Gregory Lewis' Gothic novel, *The Monk* (1796); in his Gothic melodrama, *The Castle Spectre* (Drury Lane, December 14, 1797); and pervasively in the character of the Gothic villain throughout the period. Not always fully recognized in commentary on the staging of the Gothic are the reliance on music and comedy to heighten the dramatic effects. Sade's own use of music and comedy is evident in his *La tour enchantée* (1788). Seven years before *The Monk*, *La tour enchantée* had already been adapted for the London stage as *The Haunted Tower* (Drury Lane, November 24, 1789), and had been welcomed with stunning box-office success. With attention to comic character in *The Castle Spectre*, to comic situation in *The Haunted Tower*, and to the "clumsy juggling" of "comic and tragic plots in *The Iron Chest* (Drury Lane, March 12, 1796), this chapter examines how humor may function, or fail, to mediate the transgressive sexual themes of Gothic horror; how the songs and musical score may be integrated into, or intrude upon, emotional context and action. Arguing that the songs and the comic subplots contribute an anti-Gothic dynamism to the dramatic exposition of Gothic terror, this chapter goes on to examine Stephen Storace's music in Cobb's *The Haunted Tower* and *The Siege of Belgrade* (Drury Lane, January 1, 1791) and in John Philip Kemble's *Lodoiska* (Drury Lane, June 9, 1794). George Colman's *The Iron Chest* presents a rather different case precisely for the reason that the comic subplot and Michael Kelly's songs seem interposed rather than integrated, leaving the Gothic and anti-Gothic at cross-purposes.

Further ramifications of the Gothic and anti-Gothic are studied in Chapter 8, "Blue-Beard's castle: mischief and misogyny." Recollecting from the previous chapter that the Marquis de Sade, incarcerated in the Bastille, was at work on *La tour enchantée* at the very time that Jean Michel Sédaine was composing *Raoul, Barbe Bleue*, this chapter points out that both Sade and Sédaine turned to the historical record of Gilles de Rais (1404–40) in constructing the character of libertine depravity. A century early, the notorious crimes of Gilles had already influenced Charles Perrault's tale of "Barbe-bleue": none of the previous tales of the notorious beheader of wives located his castle in the East. George Colman's Turkish setting provides an opportunity for the sort of stage opulence discussed in Chapter 6, but it also conveniently distances the violence. The music, too, contributed to a more light-hearted reception. Continuing, from Chapter 7, the attention to music, this chapter examines the lyrics of Michael Kelly's songs. *Blue-Beard; or, Female Curiosity!*, as Cox and Gamer observe, "challenges us to think about the ramifications of this fairy-tale of misogyny – where a tyrannical husband kills his wives when they inevitably display an essentialized 'female curiosity'." They go on to suggest that "Colman's play could be seen either as re-enacting masculine stereotypes or as using conventional orientalist imagery to decry the subjugation of women to oppressive men."[35] It is necessary, therefore, to question why Blue-Beard's castle is removed far from its usual European setting. As in the several versions of the folk tale, the present bride is rescued, even in the face of gory evidence that previous brides have been brutally tortured and killed. If Coleman is to be defended against the charge of misogyny, then the defense must take its evidence from the intelligence and integrity he has lent his women to counterbalance their emotional whims.

As first depicted on the stage, the vampire lurked in dark, dank, legend-haunted Fingal's Cave. In the figure of the sophisticated vampire, sexual transgressions were blended in with the Sadistic themes of the sexual liberties of a decadent aristocracy. Chapter 9, "Vampires in kilts," examines the stage vampire as a Byronic descendent of Ossianic legends of the North. John Polidori's novel *The Vampyre* (1819) was based on the fragment originally conceived by Lord Byron at the Villa Diodati near Geneva in April, 1816, as one of the "ghost stories" told by Percy Bysshe Shelley, Mary Shelley, and John Polidori. When Mary Shelley published her story, *Frankenstein* (1818), Polidori, who had abandoned his own tale of "a skull-headed lady," decided to revamp Byron's story. *The Vampyre* was published anonymously, but reviewers recognized the vampire as a typical "Byronic hero" and assumed that Byron was the author. It was immediately adapted for the stage, first in Paris and then in London. The vampire, whom Polidori named Lord Ruthven, was staged as if he were Lord Byron, "mad, bad, and dangerous to know." Concluding with attention to the belated advent of the female vampire on stage, this chapter provides an opportunity to discuss the presumptions of transgressive theatre: not simply to reveal the trespasses of established norms, but to provoke an audience response of either repudiation or participation.

Romantic drama, as reviewed in these chapters, is a drama of dichotomies and contrarieties, persistently exposing its own strategies. Actors seem to step out of their roles, not just in the tradition of Aristophanic parabasis, but in a self-conscious revelation of their own identity. The Shakespearean strategies of characters exchanging roles (Falstaff and Prince Hal), or switching genders (Viola and Cesario), serve a new dimension of testing and resisting social status and behavioral limits. Nationalism is likewise bifurcated and politically factionalized: now encouraging, now denouncing social reform; now lauding, now condemning events in France. The doubleness extends even to the imagination and audience response, for as the players would step in and out of their roles, so too the audience responded to the theatrical tensions of realism and illusionism, engagement in the action and detached observation.

CHAPTER I

Periscopes into the theatre

An exhibition, *Theatrum mundi: die Welt als Bühne* (*Theatrum mundi: the World as Stage*), was on display in Munich at the Haus der Kunst, May 24 to September 21, 2003. The occasion for the exhibition, curated by Ulf Küster, was the 350th Anniversary of the Bavarian State Opera. With an historical emphasis on the seventeenth and eighteenth centuries, the collection included portraits of performers, theatre paintings of performances, historical costumes, stage settings, mechanical devices for a variety of special effects, and architectural plans for many of the great playhouses of Europe. Along with the architectural plans were exhibited scale models of the theatres. Protected in plastic cases, these models were not only open-roofed, so that spectators could peer into the interior; they were also equipped with periscopes, which provided the viewer with an interior perspective, as if occupying one of the best seats and able, with a turn of the periscope, to peer about in all directions.[1]

To achieve a similar periscopic view into the theatre of the Romantic Era, the present and ensuing chapters on Romantic drama draw on the eye-witness reports of several theatre critics, most persistently on the observations of John Waldie (1781–1865). Already smitten with the theatre in early youth at the family estate at Hendersyde Park, Kelso, Roxburghshire, Waldie attended as a young boy the French theatre at the Kelso inn, the Cross-Keys, where officers among the French prisoners performed.[2] In January, 1799, he commenced his studies at the University of Edinburgh. Eagerly anticipating events to come, he put his pen to the first blank page of his journal and began with a flourish, "The Adventures of John Waldie." Not until 1864 did Waldie, ill and near death, set aside his journal without further adding to the long collection of daily entries. Much in the sixty-five-years of his journal falls short of the adventurous excitement anticipated in 1799, but Waldie traveled extensively and recorded faithfully what he observed in the greater and lesser theatres of Europe.

There is good reason to peer through many different periscopes, for each discloses a distinctive view. The perspective on the acting of

John Bannister provided by Leigh Hunt is not the same as that of William Hazlitt, nor of Charles Lamb. Hunt wrote: "Mr. Bannister is the first low comedian on the stage. Let an author present him with a humorous idea, whether it be of jollity, or ludicrous distress, or of grave indifference, whether it be mock heroic, burlesque, or mimicry, and he embodies it with instantaneous felicity."[3] Hazlitt asserted that "Bannister did not go out of himself to take possession of his part, but put it on over his ordinary dress, like a *surtout*, snug, warm, and comfortable. He let his personal character appear through; and it was one great charm of his acting."[4] For Hunt, Bannister *embodied* a role. For Hazlitt, Bannister *wore* a role, but only as a partial cloak over his "ordinary dress," letting his "personal character appear through." Lamb is much closer to Hazlitt in his appraisal, but he also comments on the effect of Bannister's maintaining "a perpetual subinsinuation" in his roles. Jack Bannister was always able to step in and out of character with a mastery of the "aside":

Jack had two voices, both plausible, hypocritical, and insinuating; but his secondary or supplemental voice still more decisively histrionic than his common one. It was reserved for the spectator; and the *dramatis personae* were supposed to know nothing at all about it. The *lies* of Young Wilding, and the *sentiments* in Joseph Surface, were thus marked out in a sort of italics to the audience.[5]

The differences may expose particular characteristics of the periscope. While several views are better than one, it is also an advantage to understand the nature of the lens.

Among the many actors' memoirs, Michael Kelly's *Reminiscences* are particularly revealing about the production and performance of *The Haunted Tower* (Drury Lane, November 24, 1789), *Blue-Beard* (Covent Garden, January 23, 1798), and dozens of other plays of the period.[6] With her insight as actress and as playwright, Elizabeth Inchbald was alert to more in a play than an inexperienced viewer might be. In her commentary on *The Road to Ruin* (Covent Garden, February 18, 1792), for example, she observed that the scenes between Dornton, a respectable banker, and Harry, his profligate and dissipated son, are less "like scenes in a play," and more like occurrences of distress and embarrassment in many actual households. She praised Joseph Shepherd Munden's ability to maintain the comedy of Dornton's role without sacrificing the pathos of his predicament, and she was able to see that William Thomas Lewis transformed his role as Goldfinch into more than the low comedy character that Holcroft had written.[7]

John Philip Kemble's prompt-books allow us to see how rehearsals were conducted; how scene changes, entrances and exits, upstage and downstage movements were managed; not just for two dozen Shakespearean productions, but also for such plays of the period as *The Wheel of Fortune* (Drury Lane, February 28, 1795), in which Kemble played Penruddock, or *The Stranger* (Drury Lane, March 24, 1798), in which Kemble had the title role opposite Sarah Siddons as Mrs. Haller, or *Pizarro* (Drury Lane, May 24, 1799), in which Kemble played Rolla.[8] Hunt, in his theatre criticism, candidly reveals which of Kemble's mannerisms, gesture, and speech he found particularly annoying.[9] Hazlitt, in his reviews, effectively conjures the energetic, sometimes erratic acting of Edmund Kean.[10] James Boaden enables readers to reconstruct in the mind's eye the scenes of Sarah Siddons on stage.[11] In addition to contemporary reviews and theatre criticism, further periscopic views can be found in stage histories and biographies of popular performers.[12]

Although a collective resolution is not possible, there is nevertheless an advantage of multiple vantages, for they provide cumulatively a richer sense of prevailing tastes. Each member of the audience, in identifying with the characters on stage, replays her or his own version of the paradox of identity and alterity that the actors themselves are performing. The audience still sees the familiar player, even as that player enters into and strives to become the character in the play. The experience remains paradoxical because alterity is never fully resolved into identity. Participation shifts into alienation, attraction into repulsion, involvement into estrangement. What Coleridge famously called a "willing suspension of disbelief for the moment" operates only "for the moment."[13]

The stage fictions may be accepted as an alternate reality, but that acceptance is seldom, if ever, sustained – except, of course, as a meta-theatrical element in the fictions themselves. Stendahl, for example, tells of the sentry posted in a Baltimore theatre during a performance of *Othello*. The sentry becomes so convinced of the reality of the illusion that he fires his gun at Othello in the act of murdering Desdemona, shattering the actor's arm.[14] Similarly, Achim von Arnim tells of a love triangle that has developed among a troupe of players, so that when they are on stage performing their roles as Maria, Leicester, and Mortimer in Friedrich Schiller's *Maria Stuart*, the parallel rivalry in the play drives the actor in the role of Mortimer to stab himself in what was supposed to be only a stage suicide.[15] In their fictions Stendahl and Arnim push the intense response that may well be experienced by audience or players into a realm of delusion well beyond the normal limits of dramatic illusion.[16] When suspended disbelief is transformed into sustained belief, psychological intensity becomes pathological. When critics report on the emotional intensity of performance, an audience filled with screaming and fainting women is the recurrent trope.

Waldie's student notes on Dugald Stewart's lectures in philosophy and Alexander Tytler's lectures on cultural history indicate the intellectual background informing the mode of criticism and the aesthetic perspective that he exercised in his published reviews.[17] In his journal, by contrast, he eschewed formal pretense and candidly recorded his likes and dislikes. Although it never pretends to be more than an habitué's personal view of the theatre, Waldie's journal provides insights into performances in Edinburgh and Newcastle, but also in London and throughout Europe: Paris, Vienna, Rome, and Naples, as well as contingent reference to performances in virtually every other major center, from Berlin to Barcelona. An avid theatre-goer, he shared the tastes of the landed gentry and middle-class audience of his day. Yet few were as compulsive in their theatre attendance as Waldie, and certainly that very compulsion informed how and what he witnessed on stage.

After receiving his D.Litt., Waldie enjoyed an adequate income from the Waldie estate. Taking over his father's investment as a corporation share-holder of the Theatre Royal in Newcastle, he served on the Theatre Commission during the successive management of Stephen Kemble (1791–1806), William Macready (1806–18), and Vincent De Camp (1818–24). Disinclined to take an active role in the family business, Waldie left the management of the collieries and the glass factory to the "more competent" and lived the life of a gentleman of leisure. Identified in the journal only by his first name, Giacomo was hired as his servant but soon became Waldie's constant companion at home and abroad. Shortly before the death of his father, George Waldie, in 1826, he assumed administration of Hendersyde Park. The estate came to the Waldie family through the marriage of John Waldie's grandfather to Jean Ormston, eldest daughter of Charles Ormston, Esq., of Hendersyde. Sir Walter Scott fondly recalled "the good Lady Waldie of Hendersyde" who placed the "library at my disposal when I was a boy at Kelso" (June 8, 1831).[18] George Waldie had also married into the Ormston family; his marriage to Ann, eldest daughter of Jonathan Ormston, Esq., of Newcastle-on-Tyne, was recorded at Kelso in 1779. John Waldie, the eldest son, remained a bachelor, but all three of his sisters married: Maria Jane to Richard Griffeth, Esq., of Dublin; Charlotte Ann to Stephen Eaton, Esq., of Stamford; and Jane to Captain (afterwards Rear Admiral) George Edward Watts. John's younger brother William was killed in a duel.[19]

Both Charlotte and Jane published accounts of their travels. Charlotte Waldie's *Narrative of a Residence in Belgium, during the Campaign of 1815* (London, 1817) was popularly received and twice revived later in the century (*The Days of Battle* [1853], and *Waterloo Days* [1888]). After the grand tour of 1818–20, Charlotte published, in three volumes, *Rome in the Nineteenth Century* (Edinburgh, 1820). In spite of its numerous inaccuracies, this work was long popular as a travel-guide and went through six subsequent editions by 1860. Under her married name as Charlotte Eaton, she also wrote two novels based on travels with her brother: *Continental Adventures* (3 volumes, London, 1826) and *At Home and Abroad* (3 volumes, London, 1831). Jane Waldie, who had many of her paintings exhibited at the Royal Academy and the British Gallery, had her panoramic sketch of the battlefield of Waterloo published with a prose description, *Waterloo, by a near Observer* (London, 1817), which enjoyed ten editions within a few months. Jane's *Sketches Descriptive of Italy in 1816–1817* (4 volumes, London, 1820) was less successful than Charlotte's work, and it prompted from Lord Byron a denunciatory tirade before he discovered, "(*horresco referens*) that it is written by a WOMAN!!!"[20]

Although John Waldie was more observant and more meticulously attentive than either of his sisters, he kept his journal, as he occasionally remarks, for his own amusement and the pleasure of friends who browsed in his library. Waldie's artistic aspirations were modest: he was an accomplished tenor, and often performed at various private musical entertainments, where on many occasions he sang with such professionals as the great Angelica Catalani, John Braham, and Michael Kelly. But Waldie prided himself most in matters of taste, and he had hoped his reviews of drama and music would command attention.

By 1809 Waldie had begun to grow somewhat disillusioned: "I have certainly a great deal of enjoyment, but I fear no lasting benefit to myself is to result from it: – the ground I wished to occupy, being, I have too much reason to fear, preoccupied. Something however I hope may cast up for me in my profession."[21] Just the week before, at the opening of Samuel Arnold's English Opera at the Lyceum Theatre, Waldie met "Mr. Hunt of the Examiner . . . a very clever & entertaining man."[22] Acknowledging that the place he sought was "preoccupied," he still felt that his criticism could influence a few artists or guide a local theatre audience. In his review of the season at Newcastle for *The Monthly Mirror*,[23] he praised the talent of twenty-year-old newcomer, William Augustus Conway, who that very summer at Bath also attracted the attention of the elderly widow, Hester

Lynch Piozzi.[24] As is evident in Conway's letter to Waldie, the actor was pleased with the encouraging review:

Your critique in the *Mirror* I think very elegantly written and critically correct, tho' somewhat severe to McCready [*sic*]. With regard to myself as mention'd in the same, I will not affect modesty, but simply offer my thanks for your favorable opinion (I – tho' I fear it is too sanguine – however if I am blessed with health & favor'd with your advice, I will endeavor to realize your expectation by every effort in my power . . .)[25]

As Conway's letter also makes clear, Waldie used this, and every other, opportunity to condemn Macready for appearing drunk on stage and for his mismanagement of the theatre. Conway's homosexuality aroused Hazlitt's harsh criticism when he dared to pervert the role of Romeo opposite Eliza O'Neill's Juliet. Conway's size (he was over six feet tall), gestures, and voice reveal, in Hazlitt's view, a fundamental deformity. Hazlitt then glosses Conway's role as Romeo with the words from *Love's Labour's Lost*, in which Biron, having forsworn all contact with women, defines himself as "love's whip; / A very beadle to an amorous sigh" (iii.i.176–7).

Of Mr. Conway's Romeo, we cannot speak with patience. He bestrides the stage like a Colossus, throws his arms into the air like the sails of a windmill, and his motion is as unwieldy as that of a young elephant. His voice breaks in thunder on the ear like Gargantua's, but when he pleases to be soft, he is "the very beadle to an amorous sigh" . . . – *Quere*, Why does he not marry?[26]

Waldie's defense of Conway failed to protect him from homophobic critics. After accepting an engagement in New York, where he performed successfully for four years, Conway committed suicide by leaping from a ship in the Charleston harbor.[27]

Waldie did not abandon his "profession," but his published reviews became more a matter of special interest in a particular performer, and much less dedicated to forming or reforming popular taste. Because his reviews appeared anonymously, or signed only with a "W" that might have been used by many, Waldie's published reviews are difficult to trace, unless the phrasing echoes the journal. The later reviews, however, depart considerably in language from the journal entries. His journal, for example, contains only a bald account of Braham's six performances at the Newcastle Theatre in January, 1822, but his "Musical Report" for the *Newcastle Chronicle* gives an eloquent defense of Braham, whose "amazing powers have now been the delight of England and Italy for upwards of

twenty years, yet they still remain undiminished."[28] Waldie's vast collection of commentaries on performances of the period remain available
in this extensive private journal.

As he grows increasingly familiar with the theatre his commentaries
gain the assurance of experience, but even the naïve accounts from his
student days in Edinburgh have their periscopic value. In June, 1799, he
traveled from Edinburgh to Newcastle expecting the arrival of John
Philip Kemble, Sarah Siddons, and the troupe from Drury Lane, only to
discover that they had been held over in London "on account of the great
run of Pizarro."[29] During the fifteen years of Stephen Kemble's management (1791–1806), John Philip Kemble and Sarah Siddons regularly
performed in Newcastle and Edinburgh. The family connection with
Edinburgh was continued by Sarah Siddons' son Henry, who was there
from 1809 until his death in 1815, with his wife as his leading lady.
Although the young Waldie tells us little that cannot be found in James
Boaden's biography, it is obvious that these are the effusions of an
eighteen-year-old enthusiast. Sarah Siddons performed four of her most
successful show pieces, as Lady Randolph in *Douglas*, as Mrs. Beverly in
The Gamester, as Isabella in *The Fatal Marriage*, and as Jane Shore in
Rowe's play of the same name. In John Home's play, Waldie was especially moved by "the circumstance of Lady Randolph & Douglas being
really Mother & Son." So "impassioned" was her suffering in Edward
Moore's play, that Waldie declared that if "all gamesters had been
there . . . it would surely have cured them of their passion for gaming."
Waldie concludes with a retrospect on how much his theatrical sensibility
has matured since he was a fourteen-year-old and saw her perform in 1795
as Desdemona (*Othello*), Sara (*The Mourning Bride*), and Euphrasia (*The
Grecian Daughter*). Jane Shore, Belvidera (*Venice Preserv'd*), Palmira
(*Mahomet*), and Katherine (*Taming of the Shrew*): "I was old enough to be
much affected by seeing most of them, yet I was not old enough to
perceive her many excellencies" (July 4–8, 1799 [IV: 54–64]).

Six months later, with the theatre troupe from London expected to
arrive on January 25 for a series of performances in Edinburgh, Waldie
was eager to be among those on hand to greet the players. He raced from
the University along Princes' Street to the theatre in Shakespere Square
only to discover that heavy snows had delayed some of their party. Well
on his way to becoming a thoroughly obsessed theatre habitué, Waldie
was not content to await for the theatre to open. Instead he made a
personal call on Elizabeth Satchell Kemble. The seeming presumption of
Waldie's visit requires some explanation, for even granting that actresses

in this period surrendered much privacy, a young man's unannounced call might seem a trespass. As already noted, the senior Waldie was one of the proprietors of the Newcastle theatre, and therefore an employer. His son would also have been a familiar visitor. Mrs. Kemble is certainly at ease with his company. Entertaining the daughter of Madame Frederick, the popular dancer of the Edinburgh stage,[30] Elizabeth Kemble is arranging her collection of scripts:

[F]ound her in her parlour with Madame Frederick's little girl, whom she has brought with her. The Room was very elegant – hung with pictures of John Kemble, Mrs. Siddons, Stephen & Mrs. Kemble, Miss Fanny, & all the family, & also – Garrick, Shakespeare &c. All very fine prints, and a fine medallion as large as life of John Kemble in Coriolanus, moulded by Mrs. Siddons. I sat about half an hour, & talked of Newcastle &c. – she said John Kemble will not be here till Summer, to my sorrow. She is a very pleasant woman, & had a bundle of papers by her on the floor – of an immense size – which she told me were all the parts she had acted – & she was looking for one of Lisette in Animal Magnetism which she has to act tomorrow night. Mr. Kemble will be here in 10 days – . . . Mrs. Kemble is a very pleasant, conversable woman, & looked very well, for she was neatly drest. She said – she & the rest had had a most dreadful journey thro' the snow – the Mail stuck fast & was detained all night – in the road from Alnwick to Felton. She in a chaise was forced to stay it Alnwick two days. (January 27, 1800 [IV: 149])

Presumptuous, too, and even more brash, were the anonymous letters sent to Miss Perry and Miss Biggs, two younger actresses in the troupe. The events of the ensuing week reveal habits of Waldie's youth still in need of further maturation, but nevertheless characteristic of his latter obsession with acting. Waldie found a vicarious life among the performers. After the delay in their arrival the troupe open with a production of Richard Cumberland's *The Brothers*.[31] The two young ladies had the leading female roles: Miranda Biggs as Lady Dove, wife to the henpecked Sir Benjamin Dove, played by the masterful comedian Thomas Quick; and Mary Perry as Sophia Dove, Sir Benjamin's daughter by a former wife. Waldie has nothing but praise for Quick, but is critical of Biggs and Perry:

Miss Biggs played Lady Dove very well – pity she had not a stronger voice, & a more commanding figure – she is too young for those characters, but does them with great judgement. Miss Perry is 6 feet high, good looking, & of a most elegant figure – she is sprightly & may be a good actress, but she does not speak distinct. (January 27, 1800 [IV: 149–50])

The comedy is followed by a farce, *The Miser*, in which "Miss Biggs did Lappet with great spirit – better suited for her than Lady Dove, which requires more weight"; and "Miss Perry looked handsomer in Mariana than in Sophia" (IV: 151).

The following day, Waldie received a letter from his parents, delivered personally by Miss Perry. When he saw her again that night as Julia Faulkner in Thomas Morton's *The Way to Get Married* (Covent Garden, January 23, 1796), he declared that she "played with great feeling, & spoke better than last night." He also praised "the pathetic scenes between her & her father," played by Daniel Egerton: "much better than I expected." The farce was Elizabeth Inchbald's *Animal Magnetism* (1788), with Quick as the Doctor; Macready, "who seems to act everything well," as the Valet La Fleur; and Egerton as the Marquis. Mary Perry played Constance, the Doctor's ward, and Elizabeth Kemble her maid, Lisette. Because this was Elizabeth Kemble's first appearance of the season, she was received "with great applause." She was "sprightly" as Lisette and performed "in her usual charming manner" (January 28, 1800 [IV: 152–3]).

Waldie's meetings with Mary Perry become more frequent. The next afternoon he spent an hour with her talking of the theatre season at Newcastle. "She is really a sensible girl," he writes, "& of elegant manners, & very modest in her behaviour" (January 29, 1800 [IV: 154]). He was reluctant, however, to accept her invitations to dine: "did not stay supper, tho' she asked me, as I thought it as well, not" (February 10, 1800 [IV: 171]). Soon he is more comfortable in her company, dining at her room in Shakespere Square, accompanying her to the theatre on her non-performing evenings, and often singing with her. His male theatre companion was another student, Fullerton. "I like to have somebody to make my observations to, and hear theirs," Waldie says of the need for a theatre companion. With Fullerton, he adds, "I have struck up a great intimacy at the Play, as we have twice sat next each other in the Pit . . . He is a good theatrical judge (at least I think so, as his sentiments agree with mine)" (January 30–1, 1800 [VIII: 156–7]). Sending anonymous letters to Mary Perry and Mariana Biggs with suggestions on how they might improve their acting was not Waldie's idea but Fullerton's.

Waldie had expressed his disappointment in Mary Perry's poor showing in Arthur Murphy's *The Way to Keep Him*. "I wish I could say much for Miss Perry's Widow Bellmour, but she has not that genteel air necessary – & in everything, the defective & low manner of her speaking & articulation are much against her. She sang a song sweetly & with taste, but she has no power or compass of voice, tho' a sweetly modulated one" (February 1, 1800 [IV: 150]). He is seated again with Fullerton for the performance of George Farquhar's *The Beaux' Stratagem*. "I was afraid for Miss Perry in Mrs. Sullen," he confessed, "for she spoiled the Widow Bellmour by speaking too low." Mrs. Sullen is an even more demanding role, and Waldie is impressed by her improvement: "she spoke a great deal better – & I had not the least difficulty in hearing her – indeed she went thro' the part with a spirit & gay vivacity I didn't think she possessed so much of: – her manner of speaking was so much improved I was quite astonished." Fullerton then revealed that, realizing his friend's concern with Miss Perry's acting, he had written her "an anonymous letter, desiring her to mend that fault, &c. – & she has taken the hint." Waldie is all the more impressed with Miss Perry's interpretation of Mrs. Sullen, because *The Beaux' Stratagem* "is a very licentious play," addressing matrimonial unhappiness and marital separation. Mr. Sullen was played by George Frederick Cooke. Perhaps because his real-life marriage to the actress Miss Daniels lasted scarcely a year before she divorced him, Cooke "made Sullen into tragedy." Miss Perry gave Mrs. Sullen a bright disposition to contrast with her distempered husband. "Most shocking" to Waldie was the scene in which Sullen gives his wife to Archer, simply as property to be disposed of, without the proper divorce to protect her reputation. Fortunately Macready "made a very good Archer – in the lively scenes with Cherry he was excellent – & did it very well" (February 5, 1800 [IV: 164]).

Waldie confided to Fullerton his intent to call on Miss Perry to see if she said anything about the anonymous letter. At their next meeting just three days later, "she showed me Fullerton's anonymous Epistle to her, at hearing of which I appeared very much astonished." Even if the nineteen-year-old Waldie did not possess enough acting skill to bring off his ruse of surprise, Mary Perry was sufficiently in command of her acting skills to convince him that she thought his feigned surprise was genuine. Waldie acknowledged that the anonymous Fullerton had written a judicious "critique on the faults of her acting." Mary Perry then said that "she was much obliged to the Author, whoever he was" (February 8, 1800 [IV: 168]).

Now convinced that anonymous epistles are a benign and effective way to promote the improvement of the players, Waldie and Fullerton agreed that each of them would address letters to Mariana Diggs. Their particular motivation was that on the very next day she was to act the part of Miranda in Susanna Centlivre's *Busy Body*: "tho' it won't prevent her from acting, as now too late to be changed, will warn her for the future." In his letter, Waldie "expressed [his] surprise at her taking the part – supposed it was forced upon her as [he] never could believe that a Lady who so much excelled in other walks of the drama, should wish to leave them for a line in which she was so incapacitated, as that of genteel comedy" (February 12, 1800 [IV: 175]).

As he pursued the "profession" that began in naïve but importunate meddling, Waldie managed to develop into a more urbane and forthright critic. Even in his later reviews and journal commentaries, however, his focus remained more upon the performer and ensemble than upon the plot. He provides a periscope that directs our attention to the players.

Richard Cumberland kept up his popularity as a playwright by adapting to changing audiences and changing social issues. As already noted, Waldie saw Cumberland's *The Brothers* (Covent Garden, December 2, 1769) when it was performed on the Edinburgh stage (January 27, 1800). Cumberland's *The Wheel of Fortune* (Drury Lane, February 28, 1795) was very much a play of the 1790s.[32] With the premise that sympathy is powerful moral force, Coleridge, in *Osorio* (1797; first performed as *Remorse*, Drury Lane, January 23, 1813), showed villainy and the lust for revenge softened by sympathy. Penruddock, a rough, uncouth, misanthropic solitary, displays much more than a receptivity to sympathy: he is transformed by it and rises to noble benevolence. With the integrity of a Wordsworthian rustic, he is uncorrupted by sudden wealth. For John Philip Kemble the role of Penruddock was one of the most successful and often repeated of his career. "There is a character in it that will do something for me," Kemble told Michael Kelly, "at least I feel that I can do something with it."[33] William Hazlitt praised Kemble's portrayal of Penruddock as "one of his most correct and interesting performances and one of the most perfect on the modern stage."[34] "Perfect" is the term that Leigh Hunt also uses when he says that Penruddock is Kemble's "greatest performance, and I believe it to be a perfect one."[35] In Elizabeth Inchbald's judgment, the entire drama is invested in Penruddock, and Penruddock is what Kemble makes him:

Kemble, in Penruddock, stands forth another Atlas with the whole *Dramatis Personae* on his shoulders; and sure enough they are a heavy load – yet, he moves steadily, firmly, and triumphantly under the burthen. Perhaps, in no one character he performs, does Kemble evince himself a more complete master of his art than in Penruddock. The dignity of mind and mien, which appears under his old coarse clothes, and the tenderness of his love, beneath the roughest manners, are so wonderfully impressive, that an audience (without admiration for the personal or intellectual endowments of the object of his affection) commiserate his passion, and feel its power in every fibre with himself.[36]

Inchbald suggests that as a playwright Cumberland had to resist giving Arabella a larger part. She has, after all, left Penruddock to marry the villainous Woodville, and she returns to beg his help only after Woodville has lost his fortune in gambling.

Waldie saw *The Wheel of Fortune* in Newcastle, just six months after his anonymous letter to Mariana Biggs. His comments precede Mrs. Inchbald's by eight years, but his opinion is much the same, although expressed more bluntly. "The play," he wrote in his journal, "was very stupid, and execrably acted except Mr. Kemble, whose Penruddock is a very fine piece of acting." Waldie, as did other critics, ignored the rest of the cast and focused on Kemble:

He . . . shews what was intended to be character, yet sometimes impatient & testy. His eye is so calm & yet resigned that it is delightful to see him – he looks so noble & truly great in the shabby dress of Penruddock. It is an easier character than Hamlet. But how different he plays it from his brother Stephen, who bellows & rails away with the voice of an ass as he is, at least when he acts such characters. John K. is all calmness, fortitude, & resignation – there is a peculiar mildness in his manner which is very pleasant, yet one sees at once that he is in distress. (August 12, 1800 [IV: 328])

Waldie often came to the defense of Stephen Kemble as manager of the Theatre Royal in Newcastle, but he had no praise for his ability as an actor in serious roles. Not until he saw Robert William Elliston in the lead role at Drury Lane did he recognize that *The Wheel of Fortune* need not be a one-man show. In praising the performance as ensemble, he acknowledged precisely what Inchbald had doubted: Mrs. Woodville could indeed be portrayed sympathetically. She is, after all, a mother pleading not for herself but her son. The sympathy gained by Arabella, played by Mrs. Powell, did not subtract proportionately from the sympathy for Penruddock; it merely shifted the interest. The minor comic action, Waldie conceded, is meagre (April 2, 1805 [XI: 33–4].

Cumberland took the idea for *The Wheel of Fortune* from a review of August von Kotzebue's *Menschenhaß und Reue* (Schauspielhaus Berlin, June 3, 1789): "Never was there one play taken from another," Inchbald wrote, "with such ingenuity, such nice art, and so little injury to either."[37] Cumberland took the motivation of sympathy and remorse, but left the plot and character to be translated by Benjamin Thompson as *The Stranger* (Drury Lane, March 24, 1798).[38] Between 1799 and 1820, Waldie attended ten productions of *The Stranger*. As an Edinburgh student, he was enthralled by Sarah Siddons in the role of Mrs. Haller (January 19, 1799 [IV: 6]; January 28, 1799 [IV: 8]; June 24, 1799 [IV: 50]). When he saw the play a year later, it again featured Kemble and Siddons in the lead roles, but not the same Kemble and Siddons. Elizabeth Kemble played Mrs. Haller and Henry Siddons, Sarah's now twenty-five-year-old son, appeared as the Stranger. The year before, Waldie had seen Henry Siddons in the role of Douglas opposite his mother as Lady Randolph (July 4, 1799 [IV: 56]). Waldie was fully aware that theatre in the provinces was not the same as theatre in London, but he argued the value of the local cast and production. He also appreciated that the younger players saw themselves in training for a move to London. He commenced his report with a comparison of the present and previous year's cast, with the note that the changes were "on the whole for the better." He liked Egerton in the role of Steinfort, and he now applauded Mary Perry as the Countess and Mariana Biggs as Charlotte.

The main problem with the casting that Waldie might have addressed, but chose to ignore, was that Henry Siddons was too young for the role of the Stranger. To correct the age difference, Elizabeth Kemble had transformed her part into a younger Mrs. Haller, "as she is supposed to be only 19 years old." To a British audience, Kotzebue might well have been seen as too tolerant of adultery.[39] Cumberland alleviated the problem by having the villain seduce not Penruddock's wife, but the young lady whom he hoped was his wife to be; in *The Stranger*, Mrs. Haller forsakes her husband and children in her adultery. There is a corresponding difference in the character of Penruddock and the Stranger. The effect of sympathy begins immediately to smooth away Penruddock's hatred and desire for revenge. The Stranger, by contrast, persists in his anger at the wrong that has been done to him. Not until the final scene does he forgive his errant wife. The painful forestalling of their reconciliation prompted Genest to complain of the "sad number of scenes, which do not forward the plot."[40] But the very prolonging of her guilty sorrow and self-recriminations made Mrs. Haller a more substantial part.

Siddons, I think, is greatly improved, even since last Winter – he grows more and more like John Kemble . . . – he plays this character with great judgement & spirit, & it is not beyond the power of his voice . . . – his Scene with Steinfort & the last Scene were most admirable – he pays the greatest attention to his part, & never loses sight of it an instant. This shews how much may be done by study, for he has few natural requisites for the Stage. Mrs. Kemble, tho' much has been said against her Mrs. Haller, is, I think, excellent in it – it does not require that great power of voice, nor majesty of figure, which Mrs. Siddons has . . . indeed it is almost all the pathetic, in which Mrs. Kemble so much excels – her voice may be too monotonous for some impassioned scenes, but she does them with great justice & whatever faults may be found with either her or Siddons in this play, they act so as to reach the heart – & that was what was by the author intended. (February 22, 1800 [IV: 188–9])

The debate over the play's immorality seemed to be stirred less by the wife's adultery than by the husband's forgiving her, for the forgiveness might seem an encouragement to "go and sin some more." As summarized in one account of the reception history, "One party maintained that the forgiveness of the adulteress was abhorrent to human nature and if persisted in would shatter the foundations of society. The other held with equal vigour that he who refused forgiveness to the repentant was an inhuman wretch."[41] Waldie argued that Mrs. Haller's sufferings make the play a moral corrective: "I think any woman of common sensibility who has erred like Mrs. Haller need only to see this play to bring her to repentance – tho' perhaps the impression might not be very lasting."[42]

The last clause, that "the impression might not be very lasting," may seem to undermine the moral corrective, but that is precisely Waldie's position on the presumed morality or immorality of the drama, and indeed of its entire range of emotional and aesthetic effects. They may be very powerful in the moment, but none are very long lasting. A play may move the observer, but it cannot appreciably alter her or his character. Nevertheless, the audience needed moral reassurances about the improvement of Mrs. Haller's character, so that was provided in an epilogue: "Mrs. Kemble spoke an appropriate Epilogue, written by someone in Edinburgh, which was a kind of moral, or apology for the correlation – it was well written & she read it with propriety" (February 22, 1800 [IV: 187–9]).

When *The Stranger* was performed at Edinburgh again six months later, the cast was the same, with the exception that Henry Siddons had returned to London, and the lead was played by Stephen Kemble:

his Stranger is a most admirable character, and well calculated to shew off his acting. He has so much nature & feeling, & so little rant & affectation – his looks are so pale, so woe be gone, & yet he is torn by passions of every kind – he acts in every motion of his face or body – one forgets they are in a theatre. Mrs. Kemble seemed animated in an unusual degree and did her character in her best style, which is, I think, as well as it can be done, tho' many people cavil at it – but she is charming to me in Tragedy, comedy & farce, & even Opera. (August 13, 1800 [IV: 330])

On what he recalled as the twentieth occasion of seeing *The Stranger*, Waldie was visiting the Theatre Royal in Bristol at the invitation of Charles Charlton, the acting manager. In 1800 "the centre portion of the Upper Circle, hitherto the Gallery, was converted into Boxes, and an extra gallery tier was built above it."[43] Because the theatre was small, the boxes over the stage were soon warmed by the stage lamps. With a full house, Waldie noted, it became uncomfortably hot. Also, because of the small theatre, the acting of John Philip Kemble, accustomed to performing in much larger theatres, seemed all the more powerful.[44] The intimacy of the small theatre, lost with the expansion of Covent Garden and Drury Lane, would have been felt affectively by any audience member, especially one as responsive as John Waldie.

The house was very full – but at the end of the play we got downstairs where we had very good seats: – & above we saw the play perfectly well in the box above the stage door tho' it was very hot. The Play was the Stranger. Great as John Kemble is in this part & often as I have seen him act it, I never saw him to such advantage: the settled melancholy & misery at the beginning, & the recital of his misfortunes to Steinfort, & the conflicting emotions of love, pity, & sorrow in the last scene were admirable. Mrs. Johnston is an excellent actress, & possesses forcibly the power of exciting the feelings; in her story related to the countess, & in her last scene, she was very affecting; her figure is good & her action graceful – her face is expressive tho' not handsome: her voice in the lower tones reminded me much of Mrs. Siddons; she feels the part very strongly, & upon the whole performed it very well indeed: – tho' in a character of more passion, I can easily see, that she would be apt to be too violent. Tho' I have seen the play twenty times, I could not help again watering it with tears; I never saw it make a stronger impression. (April 16, 1803 [vii: 106–7])

Married to Henry Erskine Johnstone, with whom she often performed, Mrs. Johnstone was known to Waldie as Nannette Parker during her earlier days on the stage in Edinburgh. For Waldie, her feminine beauty and grace were a disadvantage, especially in comparison to Sarah Siddons whose features were handsome, not beautiful; whose voice had a deeper resonance; and whose movements seemed governed by stoic endurance and restraint.[45] Waldie was concerned that Nannette's passions might give way to unbridled excess.

In 1815 Waldie records a completely different interpretation of the repentant adulteress, one who turns her suffering inwards. Eliza O'Neill gave to Mrs. Haller a suffering in silence.

Charlotte, Jane, & I went to C. G. Theatre to Lady Collingwood's box . . . very full house. *The Stranger*. Young hard & cold in the Stranger – Solomon, Emery – Peter, Simmons Steinfort, Barrymore – the Count, Hamerton – the Countess, Mrs. Egerton – Charlotte, Mrs. Gibbs – Annette, Mrs. Liston & Mrs. Haller, Miss O'Neill – a most lovely & striking representation – all depressed quiet, softness, & elegance – fine conception – in some parts she might have been more violent – but her distress thro' quiet is so natural, affecting, evident, & great that one feels every line – she was in this part on the whole equal to Mrs. Siddons – far below her in expression of face, but in manner & accent more retiring, soft, modest, & conscious, yet in the scene where she sends her message to her husband she was very inferior – her best scenes were her story to the Countess & her last scene – tho' in some parts of the last she might have done more – yet her power by quietness of drawing tears is astonishing – & altogether her acting in Mrs. Haller is admirably conceived & most delightfully expressed, & draws tears from every eye. There were several times such choruses of tears & handkerchiefs as I have not heard for long. (June 1, 1815 [XXXII: 78–9])

According to Hazlitt, "her style of acting was smooth, round, polished, and classical, like a marble statue."[46] Achieving that external bearing, as Winkelmann phrased it, of "noble simplicity and calm grandeur,"[47] she nevertheless communicated to the audience a stoic effort in concealing her intense feelings. Playing opposite such male actors as Edmund Kean or Charles Young, neither of whom used subtleties of constraint and calm in their acting, O'Neill's quiet suppression of intense feelings worked all the more powerfully. No actress of the period used silence more effectively, and Waldie is right in referring to "her power by quietness of drawing tears."

Waldie was fluent in French and Italian and had a traveler's command of conversational German. He was keenly interested in the differences in Continental theatres and acting styles, and also the differences in which the same plays were performed in different countries. The very first play that he saw on his first tour abroad, shortly after arriving in Rotterdam, was a performance of Kotzebue's *Joanna of Montfauçon*, which Waldie knew from the English adaptation by Cumberland (Covent Garden, January 16, 1800). On his twenty-first birthday (May 1, 1802), he visited his first foreign theatre and made the most remarkable discovery of a significant difference in the stage. In Britain there was no prompter's box; the prompter's cues were given from the wings. During the first performance, Waldie grew curious about the strange box front and center, at which the players seemed to stare repeatedly. As soon as the performance was over, Waldie rushed onto the stage and peered into the box, frightening a bald-headed man who dropped his sheaf of papers. The prompter's box, Waldie decided, is a Continental innovation that should be kept on the Continent. In his first impressions, Waldie judged British theatre superior in acting and in morality.

[W]e found a very crowded audience, and the piece just begun; however, we easily got our places, which are never taken by those who have none secured, as they are marked by a piece of white paper put on the seat with a pin thro' it. The

play was a translation from Kotzebue's *Joanna of Montfaucon*, and was . . .
tolerably acted: tho' many of the actors were clumsy and uncouth, and often
ranted dreadfully, making most discordant sounds. Joanna was acted by a Dutch
woman of the name of Oswald, who elegant in her person, and very interesting,
had she not contracted the habit of making her breast heave constantly, of which
the continual exhibition is both ridiculous and disgusting. The performers were
all well dressed, the Music was tolerable, and the Scenery good. The Prompter
sits with his head up thro' a trap door in the centre of the stage, behind the stage
lamps, and concealed from the audience by a little screen – but this is the custom
all over the Continent. The wings, and roof scenes were remarkably correct and
neat, and managed so as to give the stage exactly the appearance of what was
intended to be represented, which is too often neglected in England. On each
side of the Stage, instead of stage doors, are figures of Thalia and Melpomene
with their different attributes, and very well executed in white marble. The house
is neat, tho' in a heavy style, and not so large as ours in Newcastle. The pit is the
largest part of the house, and goes entirely under the boxes, of which there is but
one row, and above them a gallery goes round exactly the same size. They never
changed the scene in presence of the audience, but always dropped the curtain,
let down at the end of the acts for at least five minutes, so that the play was
divided into 10 or 12 acts, and took above four hours and a half in representation.
There was no after piece, which is never given when a full piece is acted; which
indeed I do not wonder at, as they are so long and tedious . . . Adjoining to the
Theatre there is a Coffee room, where there are tea and coffee, cakes, orangeade,
lemonade, &c., and these are continually brought into the Theatre during the
play, to the great interruption of the performance. The Company were a most
curious set – genteel and shabby, were scarcely to be distinguished as they were
all very grotesque. (May 1, 1802 [v: 34–6])

In the theatres of London, Waldie was accustomed to seeing prostitutes,
but in Rotterdam he could not distinguish, either in dress or in manners,
the proper ladies from the improper ones.

Among the many performances that Waldie saw of Kotzebue's *The
Stranger*, was an Italian translation of *Menschenhaß und Reue* as
Misantropia e pentimento, which he saw many years later in Mantua:

[T]he Theatre, which is in the Palace . . . was built by Pierparini – it is 5 tiers
high but too deep for its breadth, tho' very handsomely gilded and fitted up –
however it is in too remote a situation – and tho' it is large and handsome, and
Mantua contains about 25,000 people, another on the plan of that at Cremona
and by Canonical, the same architect, is now erecting in the Corso. We got good
places in the orchestra at 15 sous each – the pit is 10 sous. We saw the play of
Misantropia e Pentimento (our *Stranger*), very well acted by the 2 principal
characters and not ill by the rest. Mrs. Haller was a very lovely woman, young
and with some feeling – but little sense. The Stranger was a plain man, but with
much feeling and good conception. Their last scene had a great effect – but I am

sorry to say the Italians have little taste for plays beyond Melodrame and Spectacle, for they were often talking in the most interesting parts, and last night at Cremona the vilest trash of Melodrame was received with thunders of applause. On the whole I was very much pleased, especially with the Stranger – some of his points were well imagined and new – and to-night the Prompter was pretty quiet on the whole, at least in the best scenes – it spoils every piece to see the Prompter with his body out of his box turning first to one and then to another and bawling out the piece as fast as the actors – without leaving out a word. (November 4, 1819 [IXLIV: 344–5])

In spite of several extended trips, and an experience in European theatres almost extensive as his experience in Britain, Waldie still retained a strong British bias and a discomfort with foreign culture.

Whether home or abroad, Waldie had revisited familiar plays again and again in new and different settings. Waldie was thus able to enrich his commentaries with comparisons, not only of plays that he had seen repeatedly, but also similarities between old plays and new ones. For example, when he saw *Wallace*, the historical tragedy by Charles Edward Walker,[48] he was reminded of Richard Brinsley Sheridan's *Pizarro* (Drury Lane, May 24, 1799). *Wallace* had opened at Covent Garden (November 14, 1820). Waldie saw it four months later in Newcastle. As a Scotsman, Waldie thought that "a great deal might have been made" of the tragedy of Wallace's betrayal. The play opens with Wallace's defeat by the English troops under Edward I at the Battle of Falkirk. The opening acts are more narrative than dramatic. "As it is, the last act is very affecting – and his refusal to live, with the despair of his wife . . . is fine, but the language and ideas are poor – yet the characters of Wallace, Douglas, & Helen are well conceived." Pizarro, of course, was a foreign invader. Wallace was betrayed by one of his own people, the Scots knight Sir John De Monteith, who turned him over to the English. Walker had collapsed the roles of Elvira, Pizarro's mistress, and Cora, beloved by Rolla but taken as wife by Alonzo, into the character of Wallace's wife, Helen. The problem was not the alteration in Helen's character; rather the compromised character of Monteith, "a bad villain's part, a Pizarro in love." Waldie saw the resemblance to *Pizarro* not in plot, but rather "in business & situations" (March 12, 1821 [XLVII: 409]).

Because he seldom critically probed the complexities of character, Waldie's commentaries lack the depth of Hunt's or Hazlitt's. As in Genest's entries, he typically listed the cast, summarized the plot, and provided a brief evaluation. He was far from the belief that there was one definitive performance. He read the popular plays, occasionally commenting on variances from text to performance. He often read, too, the adaptations from foreign plays – such as Kotzebue or Pixérécourt – in their original German or French. His perspective remained conditioned, not so much by the prevailing nationalism of the period, but rather by a cautious xenophobia. Accustomed to the need of role-playing among his homophobic contemporaries, he was much more comfortable with the otherness of the stage than with the otherness of national politics and prevailing social mores. Even in his response to a performance he revealed contrary impulses of fascination and trepidation in the very act of audience voyeurism.

Although he readily declared his emotional response, he never betrayed anything further of the self. Waldie commented on the love conflicts and cross-dressing escapades of contemporary comedy without exposing his own homosexuality. In the opening sentence of *Goodbye to Berlin* (1939), Christopher Isherwood described his role as an observer: "I am a camera with its shutter open, quite passive, recording, not thinking." Waldie was not a passive observer, for memory and emotion were among the recorded details, yet he seemed content to give primacy to the alterity of the stage over any affective introspection.

From Alain-René Lesage's *Le diable boiteux* (1707), Joanna Baillie borrowed in her "Introductory Discourse" to *Plays of the Passions* (1798) the metaphor of removing the roof to peer into a private scene. This is similar to the metaphor that I borrowed from the *Theatrum mundi* exhibition in Munich. The comparison of the stage to a room with one wall removed has perpetuated the equation of audience experience with voyeurism. In basing her theory of the drama not on Aristotle's *katharsis* but on a "sympathetick propensity," Joanna Baillie added a more important dimension to what otherwise might seem to lapse into a prurient curiosity and reduce the drama to mere peep-show. For Baillie, the desire to witness the effects of strong emotions in others is driven by the need to understand the human condition.

Waldie adhered to a very similar tenet, supplemented by his attention to the performative. Because he recorded what he saw and experienced alongside other members of the audience, Waldie allows us to see the performance with him. While he is very much a representative theatre-goer of the period, his peculiar obsession, his need to be in the theatre night after night, sets him apart. More than idle entertainment or aesthetic indulgence, theatre for him had become an addiction. He needed the entropic exchange that only the theatre could provide. His "profession" became the very essence of his being.

CHAPTER 2

Nationalism and national character

Foremost among the charges assigned to John Larpent, Examiner of Plays from 1778 until 1824, was to protect Church and State from demeaning references to clergy, monarchy, or aristocracy.[1] Other groups, however, might be ridiculed with impunity. The worst sort of assaults, from our contemporary perspective, were directed toward foreigners and minorities. National and ethnic stereotypes were appropriated blatantly as stock characters: negro, Jew, Scotsman, Irishman, Frenchman, German, Italian were often prefabricated from prejudice.

There were, of course, attempts to break down the prevailing xenophobia. George Colman's *Inkle and Yarico* (Haymarket, August 4, 1787) lent support to the abolitionist movement.[2] Ira Aldridge, the negro actor who performed in anti-slavery plays as well as in the title roles of both *Hamlet* and *Othello*, contributed significantly to a broader public understanding of racial identity.[3] Amidst a horde of stage Jews as comic caricatures and cunning villains, Edmund Kean attempted a sympathetic portrayal of Shylock.[4] John Braham, lead cantor of the Great Synagogue of London, had also established himself as the leading stage tenor of the age. Similarly, Isaac Nathan found success as a Jewish composer through his collaboration with Lord Byron on the *Hebrew Melodies* (1815–16), and then with James Kenney on *Sweethearts and Wives* (Haymarket, July 27, 1823) and *The Alcaid* (Haymarket, August 10, 1824).[5] Among the national, cultural, racial, and ethnic characters appearing in the plays of the Romantic period, representation of the French occurred under unique circumstances of political and ideological conflict.

The factional response in Britain to the *ancien régime*, the storming of the Bastille, the Terror, the rise and fall of Napoleon, and the Bourbon Restoration directly influenced the representation of French character on the British stage between 1780 and 1830. The reception was complicated by the continued popularity of French playwrights and the success of Parisian actors and actresses in London. Critical attention has been given to the ways in which the theatre in Paris responded to the political issues of the Revolution and to how the theatre in London monitored and mediated the political events in France.[6] Moving beyond earlier studies, the present chapter examines the performance of French character and representation of the emotional, intellectual, moral, and ideological attributes of French national identity, male and female.

Theatrical representation mirrors contemporary socio-political debate among the pro- and anti-French factions. Sympathizers with the revolutionary effort in France to secure *Liberté, égalité, fraternité* through a new constitutional government were vehemently opposed by those who saw the effort as dangerous to the stability of British institutions. The arguments of those opposing factions are well articulated in Edmund Burke's *Reflections on the Revolution in France* (1790) and Mary Wollstonecraft's reply in *A Vindication of the Rights of Men* (1790).[7] Similar divisions arose with the rise of Napoleon, seen by some as liberator and by others as tyrant.[8] The British love–hate relationship with the French informs the Francophilia and Francophobia of stage representation. The stage may be a mirror of social opinions, but it is a distorting mirror, turning character into caricature, idealizing or demonizing in order to dramatize. To ridicule or vilify the French on the stage was simultaneously to critique the same elements in domestic culture. The plays of the period thus gave rise to a paradox of attraction and repulsion, or of identity and alterity in representing French otherness.

The most vehement vilifications of the French were addressed against the crimes of the *ancien régime*. In the comedies of Miles Peter Andrews, performed during the early 1780s, those crimes were reduced to petty affectations. When Napoleon was advancing his empire throughout Europe in the early 1800s, Frederic Reynolds found occasion in his comedies to deflate French monsters, their poisons, and the threat of invasion. Even after the Bourbon Restoration, John Poole, in the 1820s, aroused audience laughter with his stereotypes of a French gentleman, a French lady, or a French merchant. Major evidence of Francophilia existed in the abiding presence of French drama on the English stage. Several of the most popular British playwrights – among them Elizabeth Inchbald, Thomas Holcroft, and John Howard Payne – enhanced their box-office record with their successful French adaptations. Many of the French playwrights were themselves critical of the vices and atrocities within their own country. Pro-French sentiments were seldom unmixed with anti-French censure.

The English reception of playwright and revolutionary Pierre-Augustin Beaumarchais, for example, was certainly enhanced by the fact that he was twice imprisoned because of his conflicts with the French aristocracy. He was also known as an active supporter of the American Revolution, founder of a commercial enterprise to supply the American rebels with weapons, munitions, clothes, and provisions. His three Figaro plays, *Le barbier de Séville* (1775), *Le mariage de Figaro* (1781), and *La mère coupable* (1792), depict a traditional master–servant rivalry, with the important difference that the commoner, Figaro, proves superior in all respects to the aristocrat, Count Almaviva. In spite of the fact that Beaumarchais was careful to set the events in Spain rather than in France, Louis XVI banned the performance of the second of these plays because the ridicule of the aristocracy became too pointed. It was, of course, in the second play, *Le mariage*, that Figaro and the Count become rivals for the beautiful Suzanne. Louis XVI was not mistaken in seeing in these characters an expression of the class struggle, even then nearing revolutionary volatility. Promptly after the King was finally persuaded to lift the ban, *La folle journée, ou Le mariage de Figaro* opened at the Théâtre de l'Odéon (April 27, 1784).

With news of the play's tremendous success, Thomas Holcroft traveled to Paris to secure a copy for performance at Covent Garden. Never was a script more closely guarded. Dazincourt (Joseph-Jean-Baptiste Albouy, 1747–1809), who played the original Figaro, refused to allow the script to be published or a copy to leave the theatre. He was probably more concerned with stifling any rival production than he was that Beaumarchais' text would be exploited as political fodder. Holcroft's only recourse was to attend performances night after night with "a young Frenchman his friend," make notes, and memorize as many lines as possible.[9]

For the opening performance of *The Follies of a Day* (Covent Garden, December 14, 1784),[10] Holcroft himself appeared as Figaro. On subsequent nights the role was returned to the gifted comic actor, Charles Bonnor.[11] William Thomas Lewis played Count Almaviva.[12] Holcroft certainly earned his "right of the first night," for he had struggled against seemingly impossible obstacles to reconstruct the script. Holcroft's joke was apparently lost on most of the audience, although it ought to have been obvious. The plot, after all, hangs upon the Count's insistence upon enforcing the *jus primae noctis*. Figaro's bride Susan is to spend her wedding night in the Count's bed. But it was not a common English practice, in spite of John Dryden's jest that the

> monarch after Heaven's own heart,
> His vigorous warmth did variously impart
> To wives and slaves, and, wide as his command,
> Scattered his Maker's image through the land.[13]

Among the causes of Wallace's rebellion against Edward I, Frederick Engels cited the assumed right of an overlord to demand that the bridegroom surrender his bride on their wedding night.[14] In eighteenth-century Britain the context had shifted to accounts of the gentleman of a wealthy estate preying upon his female servants, as in Richardson's *Pamela*.[15] In the latter half of the nineteenth century, confirming Engels' account of the historical trajectory of misusing women of the lower classes, the context shifted again to the factory owner molesting his female workers. In the present day, the problem is addressed as the persistence of sexual harassment.[16]

On the Continent, the fears prevailed that the local petty tyrant might still attempt to exercise the *droit de seigneur* (also called the *droit de cuissage*, *droit de jambage*, or, in Count Almaviva's Seville, *el derecho de pernada*).[17] Voltaire wrote the comedy *Le droit du seigneur ou l'écueil du sage* in 1762, performed in 1779 after his death.[18] François-Georges Desfontaines-Lavallée made the sanction of aristocratic lechery the subject of his comedy, *Le droit du Seigneur* (Paris, 1783), which was immediately adapted as a comic opera, with the same title, by the French–German composer, Jean Paul Egide Martini.[19] Because the *jus primae noctis* was a blatant example of the misuse of power, it became a repeated theme in the pre-revolutionary theatre. Christian August Vulpius used it in *Rinaldo Rinaldini, der Räuber-Hauptmann* (1799–1801).[20] In *Wilhelm Tell* (1804), Friedrich Schiller named it as a factor in the Swiss rebellion.[21]

Not only did the audience miss the point of Holcroft's first-night jest, they missed all references to assumed rights and empowerment that make up the comedy. According to John Genest, the scenes with Dr. Bartholo and Marcelina, who turn out to be Figaro's parents, appeared dull and uninteresting. Nor does Genest even mention the *jus primae noctis* as the crux of the plot.[22] The fault was not Holcroft's, for he has Susan make the Count's presumptions very clear:

SUSAN.   Thou knowest how our *generous* Count when he by thy help obtained
           Rosina's hand, and made her Countess of Almaviva, during the
           first transports of love abolished a certain gothic right –
FIGARO.   Of sleeping the first night with every Bride.
SUSAN.   Which as Lord of the Manor he could claim.
FIGARO.   Know it! – To be sure I do, or I would not have married even my
           charming Susan in his Domain.
SUSAN.   Tired of prowling among the rustic beauties of the neighbourhood
           he returned to the Castle –
FIGARO.   And his wife.
SUSAN.   And *thy* wife – [*Figaro stares*] – Dost thou understand me?

FIGARO.   Perfectly!
SUSAN.   And endeavours, once more, secretly to purchase from her, a right
which he now most sincerely repents he ever parted with.[23]

Equally clear in Holcroft's version is Figaro's counterplot "to turn the tables on this Poacher, make him pay for a delicious morsel he shall never taste, infect him with fears for his own honor" (1.i, p. 4). Beaumarchais's French audience would have been alert to the carefully couched critique against the abuse of the lower classes. That critique was utterly lost on the English audience, who saw in the comedy only a rather conventional seduction plot. What might have been imported from France as a significant proto-revolutionary play was bereft of its political thrust.[24]

Jean Nicolas Bouilly brought to the Parisian stage daring dramatizations of the intrigue and atrocity of the French Revolution and the rise of Napoleon. His *Léonore, ou L'amour conjugal* (1798) was adapted as the libretto of Beethoven's *Leonore* (1805, later reworked as *Fidelio* [1814]). Holcroft's *Deaf and Dumb* (1801) was translated from Bouilly's *L'Abbé de l'Épée* (1800). Melodrama is seldom a genre of subtleties: the political significance of this play was imported fully intact across the channel. Abbé Charles Michel de l'Épée (1712–89) founded in 1755 the first free school for deaf people. De l'Épée developed and taught a system of signs that enabled deaf people to communicate through a language of conventional gestures, hand symbols and finger-spelling. He died at the outset of the Revolution in 1789. Ten years later, in 1799, the Institution Nationale des Sourds-Muets à Paris, founded by de l'Épée, was granted government funding, and a monument was erected in his memory. This was the occasion for Bouilly's dramatic tribute. As Holcroft recognized, the play is pro-French in honoring a dedicated benefactor of those deprived of speech, but simultaneously it also depicts members of the upper class as ruthless in their exploitation of the unfortunate.

To argue that Bouilly's play is therefore anti-French would be as specious as to declare that Shakespeare's *Richard III* is anti-English because of its royal villain. Bouilly emphasizes that social change is underway. A new spirit of compassion and benevolence is replacing the corrupt principles of the *ancien régime*. Holcroft made the most of a plot in which generous philanthropy is pitted against cruelty and greed. Heir to the late Count of Hancour, the deaf mute Julio was to be reared by his uncle. Motivated by greed, Darlemont dressed his nephew in rags and abandoned him in the Paris slums. With his confederate Dupré, Darlemont then claimed his brother's estate for himself. Rescuing the boy from the streets, the Abbé de l'Epée named him Theodore and taught him to communicate in signs. Not alone in his opposition to Darlemont's villainy, de l'Epeé is aided by the Advocate Franval, who advances the boy's legal claims. Franval's mother and sister marvel at the boy's intelligence and are quick to provide the family comforts he had been denied.

John Larpent, who served as Examiner of Plays from 1778 until 1824, was followed, from 1824 to 1836, by George Colman the Younger. His career as playwright and manager of the Haymarket might have made him a sympathetic and tolerant reader of the plays submitted to his office. In fact, his treatment of manuscripts was notoriously harsh. When Mary Russell Mitford submitted the manuscript for *Charles I* in 1825, Colman refused the play a license. The play was not performed until July 2, 1834, when it opened at the Victoria Theatre. A similar encounter with Colman's censorship was experienced by Richard John Raymond, whose *The Castle of Paluzzi; or, the Extorted Oath* (1818) and *The State Prisoner* (1819) had received Larpent's approval. Because of Colman's objections, performance of Raymond's *The Old Oak Tree* was delayed several years until it opened at the English Opera House (August 24, 1835). Raymond announced that his play was "Founded on the incidents of the escape of de Latude from the Bastille." Raymond's Latude was closer in character to Epée; the real Latude was closer to Figaro, closer yet to Macheath in John Gay's *Beggars' Opera* (1728).

Henri Masers de Latude (1725–1805), a rogue, charlatan, con man, and escape artist, was the sort of Frenchman who might well delight an English audience – on stage though not in reality. Abandoning the military career for which he was trained, Latude infiltrated aristocratic circles and plotted "get rich quick" schemes. Attempting to win the favor of Madame de Pompadour, he had secretly delivered to her a box of poison, which he then intended to intercept, pretending that he had foiled a plot against her life. Unfortunately Latude's stratagem was exposed, and Madame de Pompadour had Latude condemned to the Bastille, to which he was delivered on May 1, 1749. Latude was to spend the greater part of the next thirty-five years in prison, in the Bastille and in Vincennes. Three times he escaped: first in 1750, again in 1756, and yet again in 1765. Each time he was tracked down and returned to guarded confinement. He was transferred to the insane asylum in Malesherbes in 1775. With the condition that he return to Montagnac in Gascony, his birthplace, he was discharged in 1777. As on the earlier occasions of being recaptured, Latude could not resist his desire to join the social whirl of Paris. Once again he was returned to prison.

Rather than devising a new plan to escape, Latude now sought to gain public attention by writing his *Memoirs*. Latude himself relates how Madame Legros read an installment of his *Memoirs*, became interested in his plight, and managed to secure his release in 1784.[25] His supreme performance as a con artist was in crafting a new identity in his *Memoirs*, where he now introduced himself as the son of the Marquis de la Tude, a military officer and engineer, who had become a target in one of Madame de Pompadour's intrigues.[26] With her considerable political power, she issued the *lettres de cachet* that brought about his arrest and imprisonment. Representing himself as a victim of the old aristocracy, Latude was honored as citizen and hero of the Republic and granted a pension. In 1793 the National Convention compelled the heirs of Madame de Pompadour to pay him 60,000 francs' restitution.[27]

Taking his plot and character from Latude's self-promoting *Memoirs*,[28] in *The Old Oak Tree* Raymond enhanced the fiction of Latude as self-sacrificing hero in the vanguard of the Revolution. The role of Latude was played by Thomas James Serle (1798–1889), a playwright and actor who had played the lead role in his own adaptation from Alexander Dumas's *The Man in the Iron Mask; or, The Secrets of the Bastille* (Royal Coburg, January 16, 1832). The villain Mouchard was played by O. Smith, another playwright and actor, who performed the title role as the cruel French pirate in his own melodrama, *Lolonois; or, The Buccaniers of 1660* (Royal Coburg, August 6, 1818).[29] *The Old Oak Tree* opens in a small chamber. Mariette reads the note that she has written to Latude expressing her despair at his captivity, her hopes that he may regain his liberty. At her garret window, she sends the note by pigeon to the high wall of the Bastille. Her neighbor, Dame Bouval, observes her actions, cautions her of the risk that she is taking. Mariette explains how she was rescued from her poverty by the kind intervention of Latude shortly before he fell victim to the cruelty of Madame de Pompadour, who had Latude arrested by means of the dreadful *lettres de cachet*. Mariette and her neighbor are interrupted by a knocking at the door. It is the porter who warns that the police are in the street watching the room. Dame Bouval insists that she and Mariette trade rooms. Before the trade can be managed, the police are pounding at the door. Mariette hides in a closet, Dame Bouval calmly deals with the suspicious and aggressive Mouchard, who has observed the pigeon sent to and from the garret window. Dame Bouval is able to dodge his accusations, but it is clear that no more messages may be sent by carrier pigeon.

That fact is made evident in the next scene, Latude's cell in the Bastille. His jailer tosses him the dead pigeon, which he had just sent off with his last message to Mariette. For the past seven years of his incarceration he has been making a rope-ladder for his escape. It is now 180 feet long, the length needed to descend the wall of the Bastille. He keeps it concealed beneath the floorboards of his cell. From below he hears a scraping of mortar and the removal of stones. It is the prisoner from the cell below, also seeking to escape. Latude helps him climb through, and recognizes an old friend, Florville, also arrested for having penned a lampoon about Madame de Pompadour, "that female devil incarnate."[30] Latude reveals his scheme, and the two plan to escape together. Florville is supposed to inform Mariette, and all three are to travel separately and meet in Amsterdam.

Determined to find Latude, Mouchard stops at an inn on the road to Amsterdam, where he meets, but does not recognize, Florville. In a dramatically clumsy aside to the audience, Mouchard confesses his earlier criminal career for which he was "condemned to the gallies at Toulon." Together with another prisoner, Antoine Clouson, he escaped from Toulon, then Antoine was falsely arrested in Lyon for a robbery committed by Mouchard (II.i, p. 24). Although it is introduced awkwardly and belatedly, Raymond needed this "confession" for his dénouement. In Amsterdam Latude is employed as secretary to Van Dunk, who entrusted him with a large sum of money. Latude has won the friendship of Van Dunk's workers, especially the morose loner, Bertrand. Florville arrives in company with Mouchard; Mariette has made her way separately. Mouchard sees his opportunity to steal the money placed in Latude's care, then cast the blame for the theft on Latude in the very moment when Mouchard arrests him as escaped prisoner and Mariette as conspirator. Bertrand, however, secretly witnesses Mouchard stealing the money and hiding it in the hollow of an old oak tree. When Mouchard makes his arrest and accusation, Bertrand steps forward to reveal the truth, also identifying himself as Clouson, victim of Mouchard's betrayal.

Raymond, like Holcroft, brought to the stage a totally benevolent and humanitarian character. The French did not fare as well in the representations by Andrews, Reynolds, or Poole. In Andrews' comedies, *Fire and Water!* (Haymarket, July 8, 1780) and *Dissipation* (Drury Lane, March 9, 1781), the jokes were often at the expense of French manners and customs.[31] Andrews' humor was largely directed at perceived trespasses against proper British decorum.[32] "Andrews was a witty man," recalled John Bernard, "but his sayings were like fireworks; – they startled you one moment, to leave you in utter darkness the next. You always admired what he said, and yet you never could remember it."[33] The "fireworks" metaphor for Andrews' wit was often repeated because his family wealth derived from the manufacture of gunpowder. Andrews was often called upon by other playwrights to compose their prologues and epilogues, which were always shrewd in satirizing the "follies of the day."[34]

Defending himself against the charge that *Dissipation* was a comedy without a plot, Andrews claimed that the bother of a plot would be too fatiguing. His aim was

to draw a lively picture of the manners of high life, characterized by an easy indifference to the vicissitudes of fortune, and a kind of indolent acceptance of every fashionable enjoyment; he therefore imagined an intricacy of plot would ill accord with the delineation of personages, who would not themselves undergo the fatigue of engaging in a multiplicity of business, to promote either their dearest interests, or their fondest pleasures.[35]

Andrews introduces an ambitious Frenchman, Coquin, as servant to the household of Lord and Lady Rentless. As first performed at Drury Lane, the Frenchman was played by an actual Frenchman, Monsieur La Mash. According to Bernard, La Mash was always cast as the fop–servant in comedies because he was "naturally a fop, though not a polished one." As Bernard explains, "he could not assume the gentleman, but the gentleman's gentleman suited him like his clothes." He thus always appeared on the stage as himself, "his acting was the counterpart of his deportment, and not the result of minute observation."[36] Bernard's argument was not that Coquin was a stage stereotype for the French servant, rather that the actor La Mash was such a stereotype in real life. The dialogue in the opening scene, quoted here in its entirety, develops the contrast between Coquin, the French servant with Trusty, the English servant:

COQUIN.   Ah, Maistre Trusty, vel met, vere be you going so fast?
TRUSTY.   Business, business, must be minded, Monsieur, Coq – Coq – what the Devil is your hard name? I always forget it.
COQUIN.   Oh, fidon, Maistre Trusty! vat, forget your ver good friend, Oh, for shame!
TRUSTY.   Forgive me, Monsieur. You still live with my Lord Rentless, I suppose. What capacity are you now in?
COQUIN.   Capacité, ma foi; I cannot answer dat question. Me be ver ready to do any ting at all.
TRUSTY.   Or nothing at all, just at happens.
COQUIN.   Ha! ha! ha! you be one drole negotiant, Maistre Trusty, tho'en verité de famille, no know wat to call me.
TRUSTY.   [*Aside.*] That's a pity, indeed. I think I could tell them.

COQUIN.   Oh! I recollect, de parlement d'Angleterre, have invent one title exprès, and I am charge in de tax bill, as Maitre d'Hotel to my Lord.

TRUSTY.   Upon my word, our nobility are much oblig'd to the parliament for taking the trouble to distinguish their servants: but if I mistake not, this means master of the house, and that's a strange employment surely for a French – you understand me, in the service of an English peer.

COQUIN.   Pardonez moi, my Lor love de jeu, de quinze, de hazard, he hate account, he love bon vivant, good eat, good drink, he hate de tought, de reflection; in a word, he love plaisir, and he hate trouble, so he give it up to me, dat's all; he love de prett girl, and he –

TRUSTY.   And he hates his wife: does he give her up too?

COQUIN.   Oh, que non! he love dem both ma foi; but your master de Alderman, do just de same tin, he leave to you de commerce, no more preserve mango, and sweet oil for de customer, 'tis all blood and wounds for de foe.

TRUSTY.   Aye, times are sadly changed; formerly, indeed, a day in the artillery ground once a year, and a review of the orange regiment, with a march to dinner, was quite sufficient for a sober citizen; but now my master is stark staring mad, and has been lock'd up three hours a day for these two months past, to learn to salute; at his years to learn to salute.

COQUIN.   Certainement! never too late for dat!

TRUSTY.   And worse still, since your lord has thought proper to appoint him to a light infantry company in his own regiment; he has totally discarded his sober snuff-colour'd frock, grey silk stockings, and smooth powder'd bob, for a short jacket, loose boots, and a little helmet.

COQUIN.   What, would you not have de good citizen defend his country?

TRUSTY.   Undoubtedly, at a proper time of life, nothing can be more honourable or praiseworthy; but I would not have my old master run about making anticks, when he should be thinking only of making his will. Then Miss Maria –

COQUIN.   Mademoiselle Maria, ver sweet creature, vat of her?

TRUSTY.   Why, she's always in regimentals too, prancing about the streets on horseback, or firing pistols at our goods in the shop; I dare say she has shot a dozen red-herrings thro' the head within these ten days.

COQUIN.   Ah! la jolie militaire!

TRUSTY.   But I must be gone, so I wish you a good morning.

COQUIN.   Attendez! Will you do me de faveur to give one little card des complimens to Mademoiselle Maria?

TRUSTY.   That's not quite in my way, Monsieur!

COQUIN.　　Oh, fidon! no harm, upon my vord.

TRUSTY.　　Well, give it me, I'll save you the trouble, as you seem to be so
　　　　　　hard work'd. Your servant, good Mr. Coquin. [*Aside.*] What a
　　　　　　hypocritical French rascal.

COQUIN.　　Adieu, mon cher ami, my ver dear friend. [*Aside.*] Quel vulgaire
　　　　　　Englis brute! (1.i, pp. 1–3)

Gossipy servants are commonplace in social comedy. But Andrews is
more concerned in setting forth the national differences. While Trusty
reveals only his concern that his master, the Alderman Uniform, is too
old to be actively engaged in leading a military home guard to protect
against French invasion, Coquin exposes details of Lord Rentless' gambling and his sexual affairs that ought to be kept confidential. Moreover,
Coquin pretends to a higher social class, not just insisting upon his title as
Maitre d'Hotel but also in taking the liberty as a suitor to call upon the
Alderman's daughter, Miss Maria Uniform. Coquin's overtures are
misdirected not simply in terms of social class, but also because of
Alderman Uniform's vigorous opposition to the French.

Quite in character as Coquin, as Bernard also observed, La Mash was
an irrepressible ladies' man:

Whilst at Drury Lane, Kitty Frederick flopped her affections on him, (he was the
most elegantly made man I ever saw,) and had run after him to Dublin. I could
not, however, but express my surprise, that a person of notoriously expensive
habits should have quitted the scene of her resources to join a penniless comedian. "Whay, ay," said he, "eet ees vary remarkable, but eet ees varry true; all the
warld theenks there ees but one Frederick, and she theenks – ha! ha! – there ees
but one La Mash." He took a pinch of snuff in saying this, and his tone and
manner under other circumstances, I am sure, would have obtained him a round
of applause.[37]

Considered one of the most beautiful women of her day,[38] Kitty Frederick
soon discovered that La Mash was driven by the same delusions of
grandeur as Coquin and the many stage characters whom he played.
Bernard ends his account by relating that Kitty left him, but only after he
had emptied her purse. La Mash was jailed in Edinburgh, but managed to
charm the jailer's daughter, whom he then married for the convenience of
release from jail.[39] La Mash's character as Coquin involves him in a predicament almost as complex. Realizing that his title as Maitre d'Hotel does
not lend him the social prestige that he needs as suitor to Miss Uniform,
he pretends to be a French nobleman, a role that is sure to arouse
Alderman Uniform's most hostile suspicions. Also endeavoring to seduce
Miss Uniform, Lord Rentless has persuaded her to accompany him to a

hotel. Lady Rentless arrives at the same hotel to meet Ephraim Labradore, a Jewish money-lender, and reclaim from him the jewels that her husband has pawned to finance his sexual exploits. With no chance of approaching the otherwise preoccupied Alderman's daughter, Coquin, disguised as a French nobleman, offers his attentions to Labradore's daughter, who is quite responsive. While she aspires to a life of quality, Coquin is after her money – much like La Mash in his real-life pursuits.

DAUGHTER.   But come, vid your glass of wine, eat a piece of our cakes. Eigh, what wou'd my father say, if he saw me give de Jewish cake to de dear littel Christian?
COQUIN.   Ah! ah! But vat vil he say when he find de dear little Christian has run away vid his daughter, as well as his cake?
DAUGHTER.   Aye; he does not know how true and disinterested our love is.
COQUIN.   Disinterested! Certainement! à-propos, Have you secure de littel bijoux, de jewel, de bond, and de argent, just to amuse till I go vid you to my own country.
DAUGHTER.   Yesh; here they are all safe. Oh, how I long to be a French noblewomansh of quality! To see the king and queen at supper, and sit up all night at cards. (IV.i, pp. 47–8)

At this juncture the maid reports that Labradore is returning home. Coquin must don another disguise:

DAUGHTER.   I have it. Here is one of our Rabbi's dresses which has luckily been left here. Suppose you put it on. Quick, quick; it will deceive my father.
COQUIN.   De tout mon cœur – Vid all my heart; any ting to deceive your father.
DAUGHTER.   [*Helping him to dress.*] There, take this flapt hat.
COQUIN.   What! all dat hat?
DAUGHTER.   Yesh, yesh, my Lord. Your Lordship must affect to be sick, and your Lordship must try to speak in our dialect.
COQUIN.   [*Disguising himself.*] My Lordship! my Lordship! By gar, my Lordship shall try to do any ting. Mon Dieu! I am Jewish Abbé. (IV.i, p. 49)

There is no contemporary report on how well La Mash could shift from his natural French to an assumed Hebrew dialect. For the purpose of the comic action, he succeeded well enough to fool the father, who realizes too late that his daughter has "gone off with a cursed French Lord, and taken jewels, monies and all my moveables along with them – Oh, my papers! my bonds! my deeds! Oh! Oh!" (v.v, p. 77). Labradore seems to echo Shylock, but only for a brief moment, for Coquin reappears to return the missing property and to declare that Labradore's daughter is now Coquin's wife.

COQUIN. Ah! mon chere, papa, don't make so noise – here are de papiers dat Mademoiselle, your daughter, my wife give to me.
LABRADORE. Your wife!
COQUIN. Yes, I am de French nobleman, and one of de goodsh short de poor sick Rabbi, dat your daughter married out of disinterested love. (v.v, p. 77)

While it may be argued that Andrews has thus redeemed his Frenchman by having Coquin return the property, the fact that he intends to rely on his father-in-law's future beneficence renders him no less an opportunist.

In *Fire and Water!* (Haymarket, July 8, 1780), Andrews introduces a scurrilous French adventurer, Fripon, who like Coquin also passes himself off as a nobleman. This earlier comedy featured yet another, far more insidious French character, Ambuscade. In contrast to *Dissipation*, this piece had a strong political context. Set in Portsmouth at the time of the French Invasion of October, 1779, *Fire and Water!* deals with the French assault on Portsmouth and the Isle of Wight. In the final scene, traitors are apprehended in the act of setting fire to the harbor storehouse. The play opens in the shipyard of Launch, ship-builder to the King, keeper of the Royal storehouse, and vigorous opponent of the French. "If the French should come," he warns his workers, "they'll take your wives away from you."[40] Nancy, his daughter, is in love with Frederick, Midshipman in the Royal Navy, and son of the Portsmouth Mayor. Tremor, the Mayor, is more afraid of his own capture than he is of the French occupation of the harbor: "the French would be very glad to catch me, no doubt; well, what a dangerous thing it is to be in power! I should certainly be thrown into the Bastille, they would take no ransom for such a precious captive" (1.ii). The villain of this piece is Ambuscade, a French fencing-master, secretly spying for the French, and at the same time attempting to gain Launch's permission to marry his daughter and also to gain access to the storehouse. Ambuscade is aided by three co-conspirators: Sulphur, "a mongrel American" and mixer of explosives; Firebrand, an arsonist; and San Benito, a Spanish Jesuit, who attempts to persuade the local Catholics to support the French. In describing Sulphur's occupation, Andrews alludes to the jest about his family wealth from the manufacturing of gunpowder. Tremor says of Sulphur "He's a train of gunpowder, a walking firework" (11.iii).

Fripon, a French adventurer, and Commode, a French milliner, arrive in Portsmouth having fled their creditors in London, where Commode procured "Les jolies fillies for de gentlemen, and de smuggled good for de ladi" and Fripon exercised his scams as "de Grand Seigneur de Marquis François" (ii.i). As he proudly declares, he lives at "de expence of my creditors," keeping "les domestiques and give no wage," occupying "les grands appartements, and pay no rent," participating in London highlife "exactement like a man of qualité, vidout being suspect" (ii.i). Commode was played by Mrs. Webb, an actress who could use her corpulence to advantage.[41] Fripon was played by Ralph Wewitzer, a Jewish jeweller-turned-comic and, as a French scholar, particularly adept at French characters. Accompanying his portrait in the Garrick Club is the following verse by Anthony Pasquin:

> His Caius and clowns we may see and admire
> And his Bellair, like glass, is engendered by fire,
> His Frenchmen are free from unpleasant grimace,
> And his Jews you would swear were all born in Dukes Place.[42]

Fripon and Commode agree to supply family references for Ambuscade to support his request to Launch to marry his daughter. Ambuscade introduces them as Marchioness de Grenouille (frog, or trollop) and Marquis de Crapaud (toad, or ugly person). In describing Launch's response to this presumed French nobility, Andrews rehearses the paradox of Francophilia/Francophobia. He has the supremely patriotic ship-builder recognize that his own anti-French convictions, fully justified at this time of national peril, exist within a culture in which French arts and manners hold strong sway: "won't it look odd in me tho' to entertain foreigners at these times? No, not in the least; all people of consequence do the same. French ways and French plays are quite the fashion now-a-days" (ii.i). Frederick offers another version of the paradox when he reassures his father, "never fear the French; they may talk of invading us, but, believe me, they will never do it effectually but with their vices" (ii.iii). Frederick exposes Ambuscade's treason, and the play concludes when Launch gives him his blessings to marry his daughter.

Pitting the generous humanitarianism of the hero against the cruelty and greed of the villain – the Abbé de l'Épée vs. Darlemont; Latude vs. Mouchard – Holcroft and Raymond gave their representations of French character alternative if not balanced perspectives. Their heroes were not chosen from the distant historical past, but from recent events; their characters were fictionalized, but nevertheless presented as participants in events actually taking place in France. Andrews moved considerably further away from real people and real events, even when his subject-matter was as immediate as the French raid on Portsmouth. His characters – Coquin, Fripon, Commode, Ambuscade – are modeled not on actual French persons, but are created out of popular prejudices about French character. That La Mash played the same foppish character whether on stage or off may well have derived from the fact, as Bernard surmised, that it was his "natural" character, but it is equally probable that he adopted that stereotypical role off stage precisely because it was what the public expected of him.

In Frederic Reynolds' *Notoriety* (Covent Garden, November 5, 1791), there are no French characters, only French affectations. Nominal and his Irish servant, O'Whack, have just returned from a tour of France. As a result of "living entirely with English abroad," Nominal's manners have become second-hand French. For his part, O'Whack has lived among French servants, and now exercises a hybrid French–Irish impudence, and "to his brogue has joined a smattering of French" (I.i).[43] The jumbled ingredients jostle rather than blend. The French, the Irish, Scot, and Jew were all adopted as popular comic characters during the period. The character of Coquin, as noted above, was called upon to layer his identity as a Frenchman disguised as a Rabbi. O'Whack, played by Irish-born John Henry Johnstone, presents a similar comic compound as a French-speaking Irishman. O'Whack explains how he serves Nominal, his master: "he is toujours wanting to get into notice, and between our three selves, he keeps me as his Valet, Frisseur, and all that, only because I perplex, make a noise, and am quite au fait at botheration wherever I go!" (I.ii, pp. 8–9). To establish "notoriety," Nominal has himself carried in a chair into the dressing room of Lady Acid (played by Mrs. Webb, who played Commode). This outrage leads to a sham duel with Lord Jargon. Nominal's "singularity" attracts the affections of Sophia Strangeways, authoress and private actress, who knows that public censure is more valuable than public praise. As she tells Lady Acid, writing morally does not pay. "I had made a sum of money by a Novel called 'Seduction,' and I lost it all by writing 'An Essay on Charity'!" (III.i, p. 36). Nominal recognizes that Sophia shares his predilections for private acting and public reputation: "there's a pair of us, and if we elope, we shall alarm all Europe" (v.i, p. 51). Genest observes that in depicting Nominal's relationship to his guardian, Colonel Hubbub, Reynolds has borrowed the father–son relationship from John Fletcher's comedy, *Monsieur Thomas* (1639), in which Thomas indulges "his mad-cap follies," yet toward his father – who wishes to relive his own younger years in witnessing his son sowing his wild oats – pretends to be "a studious and grave young man."[44] In the antics of Nominal and the speech of O'Whack, Reynolds mocks French affectations. Not the French, but those mimicking the French are the object of ridicule.

Eleven years later, in *Delays and Blunders* (Covent Garden, October 30, 1802), Reynolds has altered his jokes, now at the expense of the legal system. Returning from service with the French in America, Lieutenant St. Orme finds himself accused of killing his father-in-law, Sir Frederick Delauney, who had opposed his daughter Lauretta's marriage. Her father died of natural causes, but her uncle, Sir Edward Delauney, has trumped up the charges against St. Orme. If Lauretta loses her claim to her father's estate, then it will pass to her uncle. The lawyer whom Sir Edward secures to prosecute St. Orme is Paul Postpone, whose name also explains the title of this comedy. It does not matter whether St. Orme is found guilty of the false charges; as long as he is kept in prison, Sir Edward can take possession of the estate and keep his niece confined. The "little ugly French monster" is no threatening villain but Lady Sensitive's lap-dog (1.iii, p. 14).[45] When Captain O'Sash elopes with her in a chaise, the servant, Robert, reports with a slightly distorted sense of geography that they have gone to "a French foreign place call'd Tipperary" (v.ii, p. 67). The principals in the subplot, Lady Sensitive and her Irish lover Captain O'Sash, never appear on the stage, but they are "much talked of."[46] The Epilogue is written by Andrews, who finds his metaphor for the current fashion of scandalous "French" behaviour in the recent Parisian attraction of flights in a hot air balloon.[47]

> Balloons are now the hobbies that engage;
> Certain criterion of a *soaring* age.
> The flighty heroine, and the dashing fair,
> Whose characters are rather worse for wear,
> May scorn dull squeamish prudes, stiff laced and curl'd,
> Mount a Balloon, and rise above the world. (Epilogue, p. 75)

The balloon-flight metaphor suits, as well, the notion of a husband pursuing an adventure abroad and returning to find his wife pregnant:

> "Good Mounshur Flyaway! do let me out;
> "Dickens! what's duck and journeyman about?
> "The compter's left – spouse does so love to chat –
> "She'll now do nothing else." – "No fear of dat.
> "Allons – de French philosophie you learn –

"Leave journeyman – he manage your concern."
Off goes Balloon – all cares are out of sight:
Down in a marsh drops Giles in hapless plight,
And finds himself a happy man e'er night. (Epilogue, p. 75)

But what wife, Andrews asks, will want to stay at home when France offers such novelties:

If France in novelties must still have sway,
What dainty dame at home will bear to stay?
Sir John, a simple knight, nor more nor less,
Dubb'd for his township's, not his own address;
Thinks all but Paris now is low and silly;
So wife, son, self – are cramm'd into the dilly. (Epilogue, pp. 75–6)

Once in France, the English adopt the French language and speak it no better than the Irishman O'Whack:

On shore, my lady cries, "Now, dear, d'ye see,"
Don't you parley – but leave the French to me!
"Here, Mounsur Waiter! *porter* me some beer.
"*Plait il, madame?* I say – *Ontong* – d'ye hear?
"*Porter de dinné.* Is Paris far? *Bien loin.*"
"That's right, my lady – Porter and sirloin,"
"*Teeray* Sir John. Zounds, mother! change that strain,
"Speak in the vulgar tongue, and you'll speak plain.
"*Fi donc*! with English we shall not advance:
"Plain English truths are not the taste in France." (Epilogue, p. 76)

In *The Blind Bargain* (Covent Garden, October 24, 1804), Reynolds has one character wonder whether "the curst French dishes had poison'd me" (I.i), and another discuss "new meanings against the French admiral's head; – and talk of invasion" (V.i).[48] But these are only incidental references in an improbable plot about a baby stolen by a gypsy, the torment of the parents, and a scam played upon the foster father by the greedy Dr. Pliable.[49]

Although French–English relations had become more cordial during the 1820s, ridicule of French characters persisted with the perpetuation of old stereotypes. This is certainly the case in John Poole's *Simpson and Co.* (Drury Lane, January 4, 1823). Mary Ann Orger played Madame La Trappe,[50] a character similar to Mrs. Webb's Commode, also in the same occupation of procuring "Les jolies fillies for de gentlemen, and de smuggled good for de ladi." The "*and Co.*" of Poole's title is Bromley, junior partner of Simpson. Bromley attempted an elicit affair with an attractive widow whom met at the Opera. From Madame La Trappe he purchased smuggled lace to be delivered to the young widow. As payment when the gift was delivered to her, he gave the widow a promissory note from his business partner, Simpson. The comic plot commences when La Trappe appears at the Simpson house, attempting to sell lace to Bromley's wife and to collect on the note from Simpson. Mrs. Simpson and Mrs. Bromley are together when Madame La Trappe is introduced:

MAD. L.   Mi ledi, I have the honneur to salute you. I will to speak wid mi ledi Bromley.
MRS B.   If you mean, Mistress Bromley, madam, I am the person.
MAD. L.   Mistress I am your servant – Madame La Trappe, from Paris: – [*Looking cautiously about.*] I sell de littel contraband – I smuggle de littel marchandize from Paris. – I am recommend to you from mi ledi Ledger, over de vay – I have de advantage to sell to her many littel ting vat I smuggle, and I sall be proud to take the advantage of you.
MRS B.   Pray, ma'am, don't give yourself the trouble –
MAD. L.   Trouble; O mon Dieu! Mon Dieu! is no trouble for so amiable ledi – [*turning and curtseying to Mrs. Simpson.*] for so amiable two ledi – and some lace which was make for Madame La Duchesse.[51]

La Trappe claims to offer the lace cheaply because she has already made her profit: "it was a *sentiment* one great *mi lord* buy for two hundred guinea for Mam'selle Pirouette, of de Grand Opera. – Ha! ha! ha! Dat poor mi lord! he give it her to-day; to-morrow she sell it to me, and yesterday I sall sell it to every body else" (1.i, p. 10). When the ladies again attempt to dismiss La Trappe, she reveals that she has come to collect on Simpson's note: "I come to-day, because I have to receive fifty pound in de bureau – de counting-house down de stair" (1.i, p.10). She explains that she has received the note from "one very pretty ledi, beautiful, who buy of me some lace – Madame, Madame – I forget her name, but she live in Harley-street" (1.i, p. 10). Simpson is thus accused of the infidelity of his partner, and Bromely hopes that he can thus manage to keep his wayward affair concealed. When Bromley finally acknowledges his guilt, he persuades Simpson and Mrs. Simpson to keep the truth concealed from Mrs. Bromley.

Poole's introduction of La Trappe was the sole feature that distinguished his infidelity plot from dozens of other comedies. The role of the French procuress and peddler of smuggled goods was a recognizable stock character, but one that a good comic actress could make effective. Poole's *'Twould Puzzle a Conjuror!* (Haymarket, September 11, 1824), is another comedy that relies on national stereotypes. As Genest has noted, the play is borrowed "with slight alterations" from Reynolds' *The Burgomaster of Saardam; or, the Two Peters* (Covent Garden, September 23, 1818).[52] The plot is loosely based on Voltaire's account of the younger years of Peter the Great (1682–1725).[53] Peter was said to have gained his knowledge of European ship-building and mercantile trade while living abroad among workers. In this piece by Reynolds and Poole, Peter is working in the shipyards of Holland, but his identity has been discovered and his life is in danger. Although the plot might have allowed occasion for a critique of European politics, that possibility is totally subverted by stock comic representations of national character. The cast of characters includes three Russians: Czar Peter; his military aide Admiral Varensloff; and Peter Stanmitz, a deserter from the Russian army who works as a laborer in the shipyard in Holland. The French Ambassador, Count de Marville, played by Coveney,[54] and the German commander, Baron Von Clump, played by Younger, both plan a coup against Russia by taking Czar Peter as prisoner. Van Dunder, played by John Liston,[55] is the head of the shipyard and local burgomaster. He is requested by the government to sequester the incognito Czar, but he mistakes the two Peters, and a comedy of errors ensues, until the true Czar is recued. By Genest's account, the strength of this production was in Liston's acting as the dunderheaded Dutch burgomaster. The French Ambassador is cautious and wily with the gentlemen and a flirt with Bertha, the burgomaster's daughter.

In the company of Coquin, Fripon, Ambuscade, Commode, and La Trappe, Poole's French Ambassador achieves no distinction. Nor do any of the characters represent a vehement or vituperative vilification of the French. Even the villainy of Mouchard and Darlemont do not push against the extreme limits of evil. If George Colman had left his Blue-Beard in France, as in André Ernest Modeste Grétry's *Raoul Barbe-bleue* (March 2, 1789), then the historical presence of the murderous sexual predator Gilles de Rais (1404–40) might have continued to haunt the castle with its secret chamber of beheaded wives. But Colman, in *Blue-Beard; or, Female Curiosity* (Covent Garden, January 23, 1798) moved the entire spectacle to Turkey. Similar geographical displacement occurs in James Robinson Planché's *The Vampire* (1820). The ultimate source was John Polidori's prose tale, *The Vampyre* (1819), but vampires first gained their stage popularity in France. A sequel to Polidori's tale was Cyprien Bérard, *Lord Ruthven ou les Vampires* (1820). Adapting the novel to the stage, Charles Nodier's *Le Vampire* was performed at the Théâtre de la

Porte-Saint-Martin on June 13, 1820.[56] Planché's version is from the French adaptation that had already appeared on the Parisian stage. Themes of dark eroticism and demonic seduction wore a supernatural disguise. In the figure of the sophisticated vampire, sexual transgressions were blended in with the Sadistic themes of the sexual liberties of a decadent aristocracy. It all might well have been another indictment of the *ancien régime*. But Nodier's version and Planché's English adaptation moved the setting to the Scottish North, and the vampire's lair to Fingal's Cave.

Other than the fact that Matthew Gregory Lewis' source for *Venoni* (Drury Lane, December 1, 1808) was the French melodrama, *Les victimes cloîtrées*, the play has no reference to the French. As in Lewis' novel *The Monk*, the evil is Catholic. On the eve of her marriage to Venoni, Josepha, at the urging of Coelistino her confessor, agrees to spend an intervening year in the convent of St. Ursula. Coelistino, who intends to debauch Josepha in her captivity, informs Venoni that she has died. In his grief, Venoni is then persuaded by the evil Coelistino to enter the monastery of St. Mark. With both the groom and the bride as his prisoners, Coelistino is at liberty to pursue his perverted desires, even enlisting an Abbess of the convent "to assist him in the debauching of Josepha." Genest, who considered this action "improper for representation on the stage," reports that "this disgusting scene . . . was tolerated by the audience" only because of Lewis' language.[57]

The contemporary French author whose plays were most often adapted for the British stage was René Charles Guilbert de Pixérécourt, "le Corneille du genre mélodramatique." Observing the extraordinary interest excited in Paris by Pixérécourt's *Valentine, ou la séduction* (Théâtre de la Gaîté, December 13, 1821), John Howard Payne, an American who pursued his career as actor and playwright in London, lost no time in bringing to the London stage his version, *Adeline, the Victim of Seduction* (Drury Lane, February 9, 1822). In his prefatory advertisement to the play, Robert Elliston asserted that "the only liberty taken since its arrival in England, has been the alteration of a few phrases, and a partial, but certainly an effective, deviation in the catastrophe."[58] It was in fact the "deviation in the catastrophe" that aroused Genest's complaint that this play, too, ended with a scene that is "horrid and disgusting."[59] In the opening scene, the distraught Adeline runs out of Remberg's house having just discovered, too late, that she had been duped by a sham marriage. Fabian, the young artist whom she thought she had married, was the deceitful seducer – Count Wilhelm – already married to Countess Blanche. In the final scene, believing herself betrayed by all whom she had loved and trusted, she leaps from a bridge at the back of stage into the river below. As Genest observes, her "suicide takes off vastly from the pity which her sufferings had previously excited – she had been disobedient to her father, and shamefully deceived by Wilhelm, but it is only by her own act, that she became guilty of any serious crime."[60]

Payne's attempt to present a play based on the intrigues of the duc de Richelieu was stifled by Colman's censorship. He published in New York an edition of the original *Richelieu*, but it was only a much altered version, *The French Libertine* (Covent Garden, February 11, 1826), that was allowed on stage in London. Payne acknowledged that his play was adapted from Alexandre Duval's *La jeunesse du duc de Richelieu ou Le Lovelace français* (1796). The Richelieu who was the object of this exposé was not the cardinal and duc de Richelieu (1585–1642), but the grand-nephew of the cardinal, Louis François Armand du Plessis, duc de Richelieu (1696–1788), who served as marshal of France during the years leading up to the French Revolution. His character as libertine is defined in the opening scene:

He is the universal lover and betrayer; – princesses and peasants, ladies of the court and ladies of the city; maids of honour, milk maids or nursery maids, or maids of any kind, – 'faith, 'tis all alike to him – he woos and wins and abandons them by turns with an impartiality that makes him wonderfully popular! Oh, trust me, my good dame, Richelieu is a man to make an epoch in history.[61]

Payne openly declared that his intentions in this indictment of Richelieu as a heartless libertine was meant to be "a faithful picture of high life in France at the time in which the scene is placed – a state of manners and morals which led to all the subsequent sufferings of that country, and especially of that class."[62] Payne states that "the opposition to it in the office of the Lord Chamberlain has been strong and unexplained," but he also makes it clear to his American readers that the "objections of the licensers" were for "political reasons which cannot prevail in America."[63] The alterations, in which Payne himself had no hand, were the work of Charles Kemble, who played the lead role as the licentious Duke. The principle change was to remove Payne's insistence on historical validity. No longer identified with the infamous Richelieu, the character becomes a fictional ducs de Rougemont. There was indeed a historical line of Rougemont among the ducs de of Bourgogne, but the change in name muted if not eradicated the historical reference.

Because of its presence in Jane Austen's *Mansfield Park* (1814), *Lovers'*
Vows (Covent Garden, October 11, 1798), adapted from August von
Kotzebue's *Das Kind der Liebe* (1790), has received more critical attention
than Elizabeth Inchbald's other plays.[64] Just as the plays of Pixérécourt
were more frequently adapted to the London stage than any other French
playwright, so too among the German authors the plays of Kotzebue held
prominence. But in most cases of importing plays from the Continent,
adaptation prevailed over translation. Such was certainly the case in
Inchbald's *Lovers' Vows*.[65] Recognizing her own hand in transforming her
sources must also be a part of examining Inchbald's many adaptations
from the French.[66] A major characteristic of her French adaptations is
that, rather than emphasizing foreign manners, she allows them to
evaporate. No matter when and where the setting, she seeks to reveal
English ways and manners.[67] The feminist themes of her social satire and
domestic comedy establish her as a somewhat more ribald contemporary
of Mary Wollstonecraft. Her *Animal Magnetism* (Covent Garden, April
29, 1788) – to be examined more closely in Chapter 6 – is set in France,
but the assertive independence of Constance and her maid Lisette sets
them in sharp contrast to their counterparts, Isabelle and Aglaé, in *Les*
docteurs modernes (1784). In *The Child of Nature* (Covent Garden,
November 28, 1788), from Countess de Genlis' *Zélie ou l'ingénue*,
Inchbald has moved the setting to Spain, but again in her female characters – the Marchioness Merida and her maid Amanthis – Inchbald
holds to the conventions of English domestic comedy, and in the matter
of marriage she gives the last word to the Marchioness.[68] The Epilogue,
the last word after the last word, is another example of Andrews' mastery
of that genre. Andrews wisely chooses to confirm Inchbald's argument
on the superiority of women: "**Men** are strange things – 'twere happy
cou'd we scout 'em, / Make up our minds, and fairly do without 'em"
(lines 1–2; bold in original).

This broad sampling of plays by Holcroft, Raymond, Andrews, Reynolds, Poole, Lewis, Payne, and Inchbald provides only a few significant
markers of the representation of French character on the British stage. By
no means a complete taxonomy of the theatrical workings of Francophilia
and Francophobia from 1780 to 1830, the plays discussed here document
the prevailing stereotypes in representations of national character and the
prominent political issues in English–French relationships. Andrews was
quite right when he had Launch comment on the dominance of "French
ways and French plays." The debt to both is obvious in the dramatic
works of the period. Even before Pixérécourt commanded extensive

popularity on the British stage, French adaptations had achieved a well-established place. These adaptations reveal how extensively the French playwrights themselves contributed to the trends of Francophilia and Francophobia in England, even in nurturing the stereotypes of French character.

CHAPTER 3

Genre: the realism of fantasy, the fantasy of realism

Never in the history of the drama was "a willing suspension of disbelief" more essential to sustaining dramatic illusion, nor more operative in representing the magical and marvelous: not just the mixture of comedy and tragedy, but of pantomime and song in melodrama, of domestic realism and supernaturalism in Gothic romance. Audiences of the period delighted in plays that were richly embellished in song, that combined the thrills of adventure romance and the terrors of Gothic villainy, with a full indulgence of sentimental and the moral righting of wrongs necessary to a "happy ending." The combinatory experimentation with dramatic form compromises any attempt at strict categorization. The anti-Gothic becomes a feature of the Gothic. The spectrum from fantasy to documentary is not linear, but rather a snake biting its tail. This chapter will challenge the presumed opposition between fantasy and realism by attending to the efforts to make the fantastic appear "real" on the stage. It will proceed to argue that documentary drama is equally committed to the theatrics of illusionism.

The optical metaphor of the periscope, introduced in Chapter 1, was intended to conjure the experience of joining an audience in the theatre and seeing a performance from that unique vantage of time and place. As an optical metaphor for what the audience saw unfolding on the stage, I propose "Pepper's Ghost." This simple but effective illusion was developed by Henry Dircks and introduced by John Henry Pepper at the Royal Polytechnic (1862). Wrought by placing a large pane of glass diagonally across the stage from upstage center to downstage left, a skeleton in a coffin upstage left appeared to transform into a ghostly figure. The trick involved dimming the light upon the coffin, and casting a bright light on a person in the wings, whose reflection would appear on the glass pane exactly superimposed upon the skeleton behind the pane. This manipulation of reflection and refraction created stunning visual effects, which Pepper brought to the stage in a production of Charles Dickens'

The Haunted Man at the New Adelphi (1863).[1] Although "Pepper's Ghost" was relatively late in making its stage debut, the phenomenon of super-imposed reflected and refracted images was no doubt as old, and as familiar, as window glass. Samuel Taylor Coleridge, in a passage written at Greta Hall, describes himself staring out the window at dusk, observing how the reflection of the interior of the room seemed to blend with the scene outside the window.[2] For Coleridge that optical phenomenon served as an apt metaphor for how the mind projected its own images as apparitions into the exterior world.[3]

Superimposed reflected and refracted images might also serve as a metaphor for the double-perception experienced by a theatre audience in beholding, if not simultaneously then at least in an easy alternation, the actor and the character, the illusion and the stage. This chapter will trace such superimposed perception as operative in Romantic melodrama, in the irony of Romantic metadrama, and in the depiction of contemporary events in documentary drama. With an audience of frequent theatre-goers who were alert to familiar tropes and situations, playwrights could easily engage in a conspiracy of allusions, knowing that many would perceive the cross-references and layering of sources. The term "conspiracy" is not out of place, because allusion operates on a covert level, making it pos-sible to skirt those themes apt to be censored by John Larpent, Examiner of Plays, engaging them indirectly through reference to plays of another time or place. Treading upon the forbidden grounds of Church or State, clergy or aristocracy, could be obscured when thus smuggled rather than openly imported.

In *Romanticism and the Forms of Ruin*, Thomas McFarland distin-guished between the mimetic (representation of things that are there) and the meontic (representation of things that are not there). Because McFarland's terms displace the more obvious antonyms (mimetic and non-mimetic, ontic and meontic), it is necessary to realign what McFarland refers to as the "rudimentary terms" expressed by Keats in his endeavor to distinguish his poetry from Byron's: "There is a great difference between us. He describes what he sees – I describe what I imagine."[4] The representation of "what is there" and "what is not there" becomes more complex with the shift in literary genre from the descriptive to the performative.[5] The descriptive strategies of conjuring visual pres-ence for nonexistent objects in poetry, as in Keats' "Grecian Urn" or Coleridge's "The Picture," function quite differently in drama. It might well be presumed that drama prioritizes "seeing" and poetry "imagining." This division, however, is problematic, for often the dramatic action is made to depend on "what is not there," and the audience may, or may not, participate consciously in the conjuring.

Victor Hugo, in his Preface to *Cromwell*, complains about the reliance on offstage events:

[E]verything that is too characteristic, too intimate, too local, to happen in the ante-chamber, or on the street corner – that is to say, the whole drama – takes place in the wings. We see on the stage only the elbows of the plot, so to speak; its hands are somewhere else. Instead of scenes we have narratives; instead of tableaux, descriptions. Solemn-faced characters, placed, as in the old chorus, between the drama and ourselves, tell us what is going on in the temple, in the palace, on the public square, until we are tempted many a time to call out to them: "Indeed, then take us there! It must be very entertaining – a fine sight!"[6]

Hugo argues against those who fear that the dignity of the drama would be compromised if violence or vice were permitted on stage. It might also be argued, however, that the unseen actions may engender their own peculiar excitement, enhancing rather than halting the action on stage. In conjuring a visual presence for the unseen, whether off stage or on stage, the playwrights, no less than the poets, are complicit in strategies of the meontic. The "fine sight" that remains hidden may nevertheless excite or titillate even in its concealment.

Wordsworth, poet of invisible spirits and powers at work in nature, laughed at the theatrical attempts to mimic invisibility:

> The champion, Jack the Giant-killer: lo!
> He dons his coat of darkness, on the stage
> Walks, and achieves his wonders, from the eye
> Of living mortal safe as the moon
> 'Hid in her vacant interlunar cave'.
> Delusion bold! – and faith must needs be coy –
> How is it wrought? His garb is black, the word
> 'Invisible' flames forth upon his chest.[7]

Even in confessing that theatres "were then my delight," Wordsworth admits that his senses were "easily pleased" and his imagination provided the needed "animation" to "all the mean upholstery of the place" as well as to "the living figures on the stage" (VII.437–65). For Wordsworth, the mimetic efforts could not overcome the artifice of performance, and the meontic pretenses lapsed into ludicrous sham.

Gothic drama, such as Matthew Gregory Lewis' *The Castle Spectre* (1797), provided a prime occasion for conjuring visible transformations of the invisible fears haunting the guilty or superstitious mind. Gothic

spoofs, such as James C. Cross' *The Apparition* (1794), invited the audience
to be suspicious of the merely rumored ghost. In his over-protective
fatherly zeal, the Baron Fitz-Allen has sought to protect his daughter, Lady
Lauretta, from the importunate overtures of potential suitors. He has kept
her under lock and key. Lady Lauretta, however, is in love with Earl
Egbert, who seeks to rescue her. When the lovers are discovered alone in
the garden, the enraged father draws his sword. Presumed to have been
mortally wounded in the ensuing swordfight, the Baron is gone, and a
relative, the wicked Glanville, assumes his title to the castle and endeavors
to force Lauretta to marry him. To rescue his beloved from the villain's
clutches, Egbert enlists the assistance of Chearly. For his part, Chearly is in
love with Polly, a servant to Lauretta and daughter to Hubert, faithful
servant to the Baron. Elinor, another servant, maintains a lively rivalry
between two of her admirers, Peter and Larry, the comic characters who
also report evidence of the haunting.[8] Larry's accounts are typically a
tangle of contradictions, as when he first reveals to Elinor that he has held
watch at the "ruinous haunted old hole of a Tower":

ELINOR.   Haunted, why I thought you always –
LARRY.   You may think what you please, but if there ar'n't spirits as naturally
           alive as you and I are in those old ivy walls I'll –
ELINOR.   Bless me! spirits!
LARRY.   Yes, you may stare, but if I didn't see 'em invisible my own self, I was
           fast asleep all the time I was waking, that's all – a jolly old
           ghost of a fat friar and my poor deceased good looking master
           as natural as life. (1.ii, p. 14)

Seeing the invisible or sleeping while awake, Larry confirms the presence
of ghosts "naturally alive" and "as natural as life." To be sure, Larry's
speech is always caught in paradoxical inconsistencies, as when he con-
templates spying on Lady Lauretta: "to take a peep thro' the bushes, to
see if I could hear what she was thinking about" (1.ii). While Larry's
double-speak of material immaterialities alerts the audience to the
subterfuge of a fake haunting, it also infects the fears of the susceptible
non-believer:

GLANVILLE.   Be trebly observant on your post, and should a stranger's foot
              approach the castle, give instant intimation.
LARRY.   Fait! then a brace of strangers, without either feet, stockings,
              shoes or shoulders, made their approach here last night.
GLANVILLE.   What mean you?
LARRY.   I mean that a couple of ghostesses –

GLANVILLE.   Folly! these superstitious menials give body to the phantoms
which their fears have raised. (1.ii, p. 15)

Forcing Lady Lauretta to marry him so that he may thus secure a legal
claim to the Baron's estate, Glanville has reason enough to succumb to
guilty fears. He nevertheless vanquishes both Chearly and Egbert and is
prepared to execute his enemies when the Baron appears, rescues them,
then gives his blessing to the marriage of his daughter to Egbert.

Dismissed by John Genest as "a strange piece . . . calculated for a Minor
theatre,"[9] Edward Fitzball's *The Flying Dutchman* found an enthusiastic
audience when it opened at the Adelphi on New Year's Day, 1827.[10] By no
means as powerful as the score composed by Richard Wagner for his own
adaptation of the legend, which premiered in 1843 at the Semper Opera
House in Dresden, the music by George Rodwell, director of the Adelphi,
nevertheless provided stirring accompaniment to Fitzball's melodrama.
Genest's disappointment in the performance at Bath (March 24, 1829)
may well have been due to the inadequate attention to staging. The
enchantment of the melodrama was enhanced through its clever illusionism: surging tides, sinking ships, flickering flames, sudden appearances and disappearances. Fitzball created more than just a showcase for
stage magic and startling special effects. He also crafted a well-integrated
dialogue between onstage and offstage action, avoiding the lapse into mere
narrative to which Hugo had rightly objected.

Fitzball's *The Flying Dutchman* opens with a conjuring scene that is a
counterpart to the scene that opens James Robinson Planché's *The
Vampire* (1820). In Planché's melodrama, Unda and Ariel meet in Fingal's
Cave and call forth the vampire, who has twenty-four hours in which to
take a bride and drink her blood in order to prolong his life. Fitzball's
play opens in a similar cavern scene. A backstage magic lantern projects
an image of a moonlit seascape on the upstage dropcloth, eerie blue
flames are reflected on the tinsel-covered rocks, and a red-yellow flame
flickers on a prominent rock center stage. The stage is otherwise dark-
ened. Rockalda, Evil Spirit of the Deep, is discovered seated on her
Grotto Throne, stage right, with a Neptunian trident as her scepter. Eight
grotesque little Water Imps enter two by two, alternately from right and
left, to dance before Rockalda's throne. During a flourish of demonic
music the imps depart, and she rises and circles the stage. With the sound
of a gong, she returns to her throne, and Vanderdecken – long-drowned
captain of the phantom ship, *The Flying Dutchman* – appears from the
waves amidst blue flames. Pale and haggard, he bears a black flag, the

Jolly Roger. Placing the flag at her feet, he kneels in submission to her will.

VANDERDECKEN.   Mighty genius of the deep, behold me at thy feet. My century having expired, I come to claim its renewal, according to thy promise – give me, once more, to revisit my native earth invulnerable, and, if I please, invisible, to increase the number of thy victims; and name thy own conditions.

Rockalda grants his wish, gives him a cloak of invisibility, and a touch to render him invulnerable in mortal combat. Vanderdecken has this one day each century to claim a bride, but he must do so under an oath of silence:

ROCKALDA.   And now go seek a bride to share thy stormy fate. Rockalda's fatal death-book make her sign, and become my slave. She's thine, and thou shalt renew thy present respite when another century has expired; but, remember, on earth, as the shadow of man is silent, so must thou be. Voice is denied thee 'till thy return; lest, in thy treachery, thou disclose to human ear the secrets of the deep.[11]

The site of the ghostly Vanderdecken's quest for a mortal bride is revealed in the next scene.

Lestelle Vanhelm, niece to Captain Peppercoal, is confined with Lucy, her attendant, in a chamber of the Fortress at the Cape of Good Hope. A telling detail in this chamber, later to attract attention, is the large painting of a ship under sail, bearing a date one century earlier, 1727. It represents the fatal voyage of Vanderdecken's ship, *The Flying Dutchman*, reputedly "still seen in the Cape seas in foul weather."[12] The two young ladies are in the midst of an animated discussion about their lovers. Captain Peppercoal has arranged a marriage between his niece and Mynheer Peter Von Bummel, a "Dabbler" in Law. Lestelle, however, is in love with the dashing Lieutenant Mowdrey who has contrived a way to hide from the vigilant uncle by crossing the river at the back of the fortress, climbing the lattice for his secret trysts in Lestelle's chamber. And his gentleman's gentleman, Toby Varnish, a marine painter, has found his interest in Lucy conveniently reciprocated.

The secret visits to Lestelle's chamber coincide with the return of the ghostly Vanderdecken, who sees in Lestelle a reincarnation of his lost bride and who intends to sail off with her on *The Flying Dutchman*. Another eager visitor to Lestelle's chamber is Peter Von Bummel, to whom Captain Peppercoal has offered his niece in marriage. The intrigue of comings and goings in the chamber, by stealth and by magic, are further complicated by a ruse of many disguises. Lestelle's chamber has a painting of *The Flying Dutchman*; the adjacent turret chamber has two portraits, also from the year 1727: one of Captain Vanderdecken, the other of his bride dressed as a shepherdess. When Vanderdecken magically appears in the turret chamber, he transforms his portrait into the likeness of Peter so that the Captain's men will mistake the suitor for the ghostly pirate. Mowdrey, who knows the legend of *The Flying Dutchman*, himself pretends to be the pirate in order to frighten off the Captain's men so that he may elope with Lestelle. Toby Varnish, whom the uncle would recognize, dons a bear costume and pretends to be the pirate's trained pet. It soon becomes obvious that bear is no bear, and the Captain holds him hostage. Vanderdecken's trunk, which has remained for the past century beneath the portraits in the turret chamber, contains the shepherdess dress that belonged to Vanderdecken's lost wife. When Peter arrives he intercepts Lucy's letter intended for Mowdrey, and therefore also disguises himself as Vanderdecken.

The central plot of Vanderdecken's quest for a bride thus takes place amidst a mad scramble of disguises, mistaken identities, and supernatural trickery. The Adelphi provided Fitzball with all the stage accoutrements to accomplish his special effects: the house light in the Adelphi was provided by a gas luster hanging from the ceiling.[13] The gas footlights were in a float that could be raised and lowered to darken the stage and to exchange colored lenses. The stage was equipped with a "devil's trap" that allowed for Vanderdecken's magical appearances and disappearances; there was also a concealed panel through which he could vanish. His costume – "Green old-fashioned dress, with white sugar loaf buttons – belt – high boots – old English hat – red feather"[14] – would on appropriate occasions be bathed in the blue light from a Clegg lamp in the fly gallery, so that he seemed engulfed in a ghostly aura. For his magical gestures, he palmed a small mirror, which would reflect an offstage beam, so that a colored flash of light seemed to dart from his hand. This trick is used with the exploding letter at the end of Act 1. When he changed his own portrait into the likeness of Von Bummel (11.ii), the electric bolt that seemed to pass from his finger tip to the painting was actually the arc of a concealed voltaic pile. The long arc appeared when Vanderdecken slowly separated a positive carbon electrode from the negative electrode attached to the frame. Further trickery is involved when the painting of *The Flying Dutchman* becomes illumined with crimson fire as an omen that Vanderdecken approaches. The sliding wings depicted the two interior chambers: when they were withdrawn the stage seemed to open into an expanse of moonlit ocean. The rearstage dropcloth was backlit by a magic lantern and the illusion of the crashing and receding waves was accomplished by moving the lantern forward and backward on its trolly tracks.[15]

The dialogue between Lestelle, Lucy, and Peppercoal provides the necessary background. As Lucy realizes that their quarters in the gloomy fortress are "haunted by the Flying Dutchman, who comes here once in a century to visit his old habitation, and to carry off poor young maidens by stealth to his den under the sea," Peppercoal scoffs at the superstition: "I don't believe a word of it; though they do tell me, that the old lady that's painted in the turret chamber, with a long marlinspike in her fist, with a crook at the end of it, was the dead Dutchman's dead wife; and that the old sea-trunk that stands under the window contains the clothes in which he last beheld her" (1.ii, p. 14).

Act 1, Scene iii takes place on the ship's deck of the *Enterprise*, with a projected backdrop of sea and setting sun. Tom Willis, looking through a mariner's telescope, cries out a sighting of land in the wings, stage left. Peter Von Bummel, on his voyage from London to meet his new bride at the Cape, has suffered sea-sickness and is heartened by the news that land is in sight. Tom looks again through his telescope and declares that the land has vanished. Looking for the third time, he sights the approach of the *The Flying Dutchman*. The ship appears as a projected phantasmagoria then vanishes; Vanderdecken clambers wet from the sea over the railing. He attempts to distribute letters of fatal contract to the sailors who refuse to accept them. The stage direction explains the action:

Peter attempts to snatch the letter, when it explodes – a sailor is about to seize Vanderdecken, who eludes his grasp, and vanishes through the deck – Tom Willis fires on R., Von Swiggs on L. – a Sailor falls dead on the deck – Vanderdecken, with a demoniac laugh, rises from the sea in blue fire, amidst violent thunder – at that instant the Phantom Ship appears in the sky behind – Vanderdecken and the Crew in consternation exclaim "Ah! Vanderdecken! Vanderdecken!" (p. 19)

The curtain falls, ending Act 1.

Act 11 commences with a similar scene of gazing into the wings, stage right. From the seacoast, Mowdrey gazes across the river to the fortress for a sign of Lestelle. The unseen shadows in the wings take on substance and

shape for the audience. Mowdrey confirms what he beholds: "There she is
again! ... I'm sure 'tis Lestelle at the lattice, yonder ... She waves her
handkerchief ... That was to have been the signal." Although the
audience has presumably accepted the truth of Mowdrey's sighting,
Fitzball has Varnish undermine confidence in what can be seen among
the shadows in the wings. He mimics Mowdrey's action by staring
intently into the wings stage left: "Eh! ah! what do I see? ... Can I believe
my eyes? ... O, sir! I spy nothing less than Chancery Lane, Lincoln's Inn,
and the Court of Equity, running a race through the back woods of
Africa." The joke, Fitzball's injection of counter-illusionist irony, concerns the current colonial investments.

Having discovered Mowdrey's plan to disguise himself as the resurrected Vanderdecken so that he can elope with Lestelle, Captain Peppercoal has captured Varnish and sits with him awaiting Mowdrey's
arrival in disguise. In the meantime Peter, too, has disguised himself as
Vanderdecken. What is stunning about the stagecraft in this scene is the
interaction with the characters in the wings. The fortress chambers have
no exterior doors, so the entrances of Mowdrey and Peter can be
accomplished only by crawling through a window. Vanderdecken, of
course, can simply materialize where he wants. Peter knocks loudly at the
window. Varnish knows that it cannot be Mowdrey, so he fears that it is
the ghost himself. He drops trembling to his knees:

CAPT. P.   [*Laughing.*] Ha, ha, ha! Well, sir, why don't you hoist your sail, and
           open the window to his ghost ship.
VAR.   [*Imploringly.*] N – o! no, sir!
           [*Captain Peppercoal snatches up a pistol.*]
CAPT. P.   But I say yes; yes, blubber, open the window, sir, or I'll pop a bullet
           through your topmast, I will.
VAR.   Ye – ye – yes, sir! O – h! o – h! I see his cloven foot through the –
           I smell brimstone – I! o – h!
           [*Captain Peppercoal presents the pistol.*]
           Yes, sir.
           [*Varnish opens the window and falls, as Peter, with an enormous mask,
           hat, and feathers, presents himself at the window in flat – a dark
           lantern in his hand.*]
PET.   [*In a gruff voice.*] B – oo!
CAPT. P.   [*Throws the candle and candlestick and fires a pistol at Peter.*] Miss'd
           him, by Jupiter.
           [*Peter runs out, stage left. – Varnish gets behind the screen.*]
CAPT. P.   [*Calling without, stage left.*] Smutta, get a blunderbuss; give him a
           raking fire at his stern, and blow away the gingerbread work!

PET.   [*Through the window.*] What am I to do? They smoke the plot below –
         twenty of 'em at my heels – here's a reception for a lover: I –
         [*Pistol fires without; Peter tumbles in at the window and overturns the*
           table, &c.]
         I'm shot! o – h!
         [*His mask falls off.*]

VAR.   [*Throwing down the screen.*] Spare all I have, and take my life. (II.iv,
         pp. 34–5)

Varnish and Peter recognize each other as old friends, but there is no time for reunion; Peppercoal is returning with his men. Varnish escapes through the window, but the rope-ladder gives away. Peter is trapped in the chamber and has no other place to hide than Vanderdecken's trunk.

PET.   [*Getting up and putting on his mask the hind part before.*] Toby! my
         Toby. Oh!

VAR.   Peter, my Peter, oh!
         [*Noise.*]
         They return; what's to be done – they've taken away the ladder!
         [*Looking out of the window.*]
         Ah! the rope ladder – here it is; follow me; but first lock that door.
         [*He flings the rope ladder out of the window and escapes, while Peter*
           locks the door.]

PET.   Don't go without me.

VAR.   [*Behind the flat.*] Hollo! the rope ladder has given way.

PET.   The ladder given way! what am I to do?
         [*Noise at L. D.*]
         No closet, no outlet; a chest – fast! confusion!
         [*Snatches a knife from the table and forces the lock open.*]
         Devil take the knife, I've cut my finger; I'll tie it up with old
         Peppercoal's table-cloth.

CAPT. P.   [*Without.*] Bear a hand.

PET.   They're coming; box open, in I go! I fancy myself in England, – I've
         got a private box all to myself.
         [*Gets into the box, R. – A crash without.*] (II.iv, p. 35)

All those who would come to Lestelle's aid become entangled in their own plots, thus leaving Vanderdecken free to abduct her. His invisibility, invulnerability, and magical powers seem to render him unstoppable. Even Mowdrey is helpless. The sentinel, posted by Peppercoal to guard Lestelle's chamber, is easily driven off. Vanderdecken enters stealthily stage right, crosses unperceived to the sentinel stage left. Lestelle appears on the veranda, she starts at the sight of the threatened sentinel. With a wave of his hand Vanderdecken causes a small rose-colored flame to descend on the sentinel's gun. A wick of burning phosphorus suspended on a fine wire enables Vanderdecken to send the flame in pursuit of the sentinel who retreats in terror. When Mowdrey returns, Lestelle begs him to protect her. Even as he folds her in his embrace, Vanderdecken, invisible to Mowdrey, comes from behind them and touches Lestelle:

LES.   How is this? A sudden chillness rushes through my veins – I faint – I
         die! Ah, Mowdrey, see, that horrid spectre! – support me.
         [*Swoons in Mowdrey's arms.*]
MOW.   Lestelle, Lestelle! All here I behold – the trees, the fortress – nothing
         more. Ah, this cold hand – her bosom, too, no longer palpitates. I
         dare not call for aid – the water – in the hollow of my hand –
         [**Music**. *– He supports Lestelle in his arms to a bank, and hurries towards
         the water. In the meantime, Vanderdecken covers her with his
         mantle, and Lestelle vanishes. – Exit Vanderdecken.*]
MOW.   [*Returning.*] Lestelle! my love, my life! my – horror! – lost, lost! Help,
         help!
         [*Falls.*]

Act II comes to a close with a phantasmagoria depicting Vanderdecken's successful abduction:

[Storm. – A mist begins to arise, through which Vanderdecken is seen crossing the sea in an open boat with Lestelle, – the storm rages violently – the boat is dashed about upon the waves – it sinks suddenly with Vanderdecken and Lestelle – the Phantom Ship appears (a la phantasmagorie) in a peal of thunder. – The stage and audience part of the Theatre in total darkness. (II.vi, pp. 38–9)

The comedy of errors continues in the opening of Act III. Baffled by his violent reception, Peter has hidden in the trunk. When Smutta returns with the Captain's men, he has the idea of taking the valuables from the trunk, but is frightened away when Peter pops out in his pirate costume. Peter escapes and takes with him the dress as his second disguise. Varnish, still trying to escape from the Captain, returns to the turret chamber and also hides in the trunk. Smutta and crew come to expose the fake Vanderdecken only to discover Varnish in his bear costume. Varnish tosses them coins, and makes his escape while they scramble for the money. Just then Peter returns, now disguised as the shepherdess.

This comic scene is followed by a semi-darkened scene in the sea cave. At the rear rises a gigantic cliff, down which the sea is rolling with terrific violence carrying with it rocks and seaweed. The cave appears to be sinking ever deeper into the ocean. Vanderdecken enters with Lestelle in his arms. He places her on the bank, then listens for pursuers to arrive from the wings. When Lestelle revives, he gestures that she must now sign the fatal book as his eternal bride. In Act III, Scene iv, Mowdrey arrives at the cave to rescue Lestelle. He is, of course, no match against Vanderdecken's supernatural powers. Lestelle has again refused to sign the magic book. Vanderdecken grasps her hand in the attempt to force her signature. Lestelle screams and sinks at the base of the rock. Footsteps from off stage loudly echo. As Vanderdecken listens, Mowdrey emerges from behind a rock. Laughing at this mortal's futile attempt, Vanderdecken draws his sword. Although repeatedly stabbed by Mowdrey, the ghostly pirate is unfazed by the blows. Vanderdecken lifts his foe on high and furiously throws him down. Exulting in his victory, Vander-decken shouts out "Mortal, die!" A thunder blast is heard, and the pirate immediately realizes that he has broken the vow of silence, and with it the spell that has resurrected him.

The spell which admits my stay on earth is destroyed with my silence. I must be gone to my phantom ship again, to the deep and howling waters; but ye, the victims of my love and fury, yours is a dreadful fate – a hundred years here, in torpid life, to lie entombed till my return. Behold!

Vanderdecken points to the magic book and explains its power: "Seest thou this magic book: its mystic pages, consumed by the hand of a sailor's son, on ocean born, would set ye free; but never can that be accomplished, for in Vanderdecken's absence 'tis denied that human footstep e'er seek this cavern, or pierce those flinty walls." This hopeless impasse is quickly resolved by the resourceful Varnish, who snatches up a torch and sets fire to the mystic book, shouting triumphantly " 'Tis done! 'Tis done!"

Romantic drama exhibited a persistent fascination with beings and objects that seem to belong to a supernatural rather than a natural world. Sir David Brewster was among the wizards of optics who were called upon to provide the "natural magic" of physical science.[16] Although the representation of "what is not there," as opposed to "what is there," was by no means the exclusive preoccupation of Fitzball, he was, even among contemporary practitioners of the Gothic, especially adept at integrating special effects and managing offstage–onstage dialogue.

Again with a musical score by Rodwell, Fitzball's *The Devil's Elixir; or, the Shadowless Man* (Covent Garden, April 20, 1829) was adapted freely from Hoffmann and mixed in a measure of Chamisso.[17] Brother Francesco, renamed from Hoffmann's Brother Medardus, covets the beautiful Aurelia, his brother's bride-to-be. With a swallow of the elixir the monk takes on the physical appearance of his brother, but as a shadowless *Doppelgänger*. As in *The Flying Dutchman*, this play, too, involves a vividly active engagement of offstage action and an ingenious repertory of onstage conjurations. After delineating the special effects involved in the trial to see which of the look-alike brothers casts a shadow, and the scene in which the Demon of the Elixir attempts to enter the cell of the repentant monk and is struck with a thunderbolt, Genest declared that "the foundation is better than superstructure."[18] Waldie, who judged the piece "silly & stupid," was nevertheless impressed with the "most splendid effects of changes & scenes." In his estimation, the performance was carried by the comic acting of Robert Keeley, as Nicholas the bell-toller, and Mary Ann Goward, as a "sprightly" Ulrika, maid to Aurelia.[19] During his visits to Covent Garden in 1829, Waldie repeatedly expressed his admiration for Keeley and Goward as a comic team.[20]

From the illusionist staging of "what is not there" to representations of events very much "there" in current news would seem to be a shift to the opposite end of the spectrum. Documentary drama requires realism and the aura of authenticity. Not surprisingly in the context of radical experimentation with dramatic forms, documentary was as effective as fantasy in commanding audience attention. Both, of course, relied on the artifices of stage illusion. There were several different modes of docu-drama during the later eighteenth and early nineteenth centuries. In addition to the staging of sensational crimes (the Ratcliff Street murders, Burke and Hare) and political plots (the Cato Street Conspiracy), there were national and international events. Some of the plays responded to events in the newly established United States and to the continuing political tensions with Britain.

If there were a hanging in the square, would the audience stay in the theatre to witness a make-believe execution on stage? Defined as a room with the fourth wall missing, the stage may invite a voyeuristic curiosity about the events exposed within that room. Indeed, Joanna Baillie, in her "Introductory Discourse" to the *Plays of the Passions* (1798) makes that curiosity the motivating impulse in her theory of drama.[21] One popular anecdote, repeated by Denis Diderot and several critics of the eighteenth century, supposes a stranger from a remote culture brought for the first time within a theatre, and informed that when the curtain is raised, according to local custom, the King's chambers will be exposed and will reveal the actual events in court. Would the stranger believe such a fiction? Not likely, answers Diderot, for even the most naïve stranger would not fail to see the mannerisms and artifice that distinguish performance from reality.[22]

Even the sort of docu-drama that gained popularity in the Romantic period is marked by the inherent difference of the performative act. Wordsworth, as he related in *The Prelude* (1805, VII.316–59), attended a performance of Charles Dibdin's *Edward and Susan, or The Beauty of Buttermere* (Sadler's Wells, April 11, 1803). This "operatic piece in rhyme" brought to the stage a scandalous seduction that had occurred in Wordsworth's native Lakes six months earlier. Coleridge had reported the event in five articles for the *Morning Post*.[23] John Hatfield, a notorious swindler, had seduced a nobleman's natural daughter, who bore him three daughters, and married his jailer's daughter, who helped obtain his release. Then, in the Fall of 1802, calling himself "The Hon. Augustus Hope, M. P." – supposedly a brother to the Earl of Hopetown – he arrived in Buttermere, met Mary Robinson, the innkeeper's daughter, and persuaded her to marry him. Hatfield's identity, his swindling schemes, and his bigamy were exposed. With his production of *The Beauty of Buttermere*, Dibdin sought to make the most of the scandal before the case even went to court. With no denigration of Dibdin's theatrical exploitation, Wordsworth simply declared that it shows

> . . . how the spoiler came "a bold bad man,"
> To God unfaithful, children, wife, and home,
> And wooed the artless maiden of the hills.
> And wedded her, in cruel mockery
> Of love and marriage bonds. (*The Prelude*, III.321–6)

Yet Wordsworth also implied that the very theatrical transformation made an artifice of sentiment, and thus taught us "to slight the crimes / And sorrows of the world." He recollected the fate of Mary Robinson, the real Maid of Buttermere, whose infant, conceived in false wedlock, had died at birth and was buried in the village churchyard. From the actress who performed her role on stage, he looked into the audience and saw a young mother, carrying her small child with her through the theatre, as she plied her trade as a prostitute (III.363–411). Were the emotions aroused by the theatrical representation not utterly shallow and ephemeral, there would be none in the audience who would not perceive the young mother as the victim of like betrayal.

Another sensational documentary was *The Gamblers* (Royal Coburg, November 17, 1823),[24] which brought onto the stage an exposé of an actual murder that had occurred on October 24, and only fourteen days after the murderer, John Thurtell, had been apprehended. Thurtell, who lost a large sum in gambling with William Weare, invited him to a country house, and robbed and murdered him en route. The dramatization followed blow by blow the events in the crime. To insure the utmost realism, the coach and horse that the murderer had used to transport his victim were brought on stage in the appropriate scene. The set designers duplicated with utmost verisimilitude the gambling house, the inn where they stopped, the byway where the murder was committed, and the country house to which the corpse was delivered. In the final scene, *We are not yet dead*, Weare revived long enough to accuse his murderer. This scene, the reviewer reports, was a deviation necessary to bring the play to a close, for in the actual case the accused was still on trial.[25]

The question that must be asked of *The Beauty of Buttermere* and *The Gamblers* – indeed of any documentary then or now – is not simply the extent to which the representation deviates from what is represented, but rather the extent to which that deviation is also a displacement of the social and ethical ground. What prevails in the theatre is the very opposite of Immanuel Kant's postulation of an aesthetics of disinterest.[26] Box-office success is predicated on taking full advantage of whatever stirs popular interest. Aestheticization as dramatic performance does not eliminate the various attributes of *interest* – morbid or libidinous curiosity, desire or fear. Instead, interests are rendered "other," no longer constrained by the moral censorship and taboos that govern personal actions. The dramatization of John Thurtell's crimes plays to much the same interests that were addressed by Thomas De Quincey in his several essays on "Murder Considered as a Fine Art."[27] De Quincey repeatedly urged the principle of *idem in alio* – identity in alterity, sameness in difference – as crucial to artistic representation.[28] In the enactment of *idem in alio* there resides a doubleness, a two-way interaction. What is familiar is rendered strange; what is strange is rendered familiar.

As examples of the broad range of "otherness," *The Beauty of Buttermere* and *The Gamblers* provide reminders of how "otherness," as Freud says of the *Unheimlich*,[29] begins at home. A young woman deluded by a rakish swindler, doubtless not a rare occurrence in actual domestic life, had been featured in numerous sentimental melodramas of the period. Dibdin, of course, had taken a case that was currently in the newspaper headlines. The documentary facts were well known to everyone in his audience. Dibdin's choice was to heighten the emotional impact of his subject by transforming Mary Robinson into an operatic heroine, pouring out the passion of her love and the agony of her betrayal in song.

In the opening scene of *The Gamblers*, Thurtell is shown at the gaming table with Weare; then there is a scene with fellow gambler William Probert, who agrees to Thurtell's plot to invite Weare to a country cottage, ostensibly for a weekend of gambling. In Act II, Thurtell's horse and gig are brought onto the stage in front of a façade of the Wagon and Horses Inn. The murder scene was gruesome in its detail: a pistol was fired at the victim's head, and there was a copious use of stage blood as the wounded Weare struggled to escape. The bullet had not killed him, so Thurtell now set about slitting Weare's throat, then clubbing him with the muzzle of the gun. The final act, at Probert's cottage, depicted the murderer and his friend, attempting to dispose of the body by throwing it into a pond, when Weare rose up with a final cry of accusation before he died. Crafted in haste to bring the dramatization before an audience while interest in the murder still captured the public imagination, William Thomas Moncrieff, the manager at the Coburg, sought the utmost realism in depicting the crime in all its gory details. The audience wept at Weare's agonies and applauded Thurtell's capture at the end. In spite of the "realism," it was a show, and the audience responded accordingly, fully aware that what they had witnessed was "other," a transformation of the actual crime.

As Michel Foucault has argued, the attributes of performance and spectacle transform even the reality of public executions.[30] When Thurtell was brought to London for his hanging on January 9, 1824, the event was played out as a public act of expiation: as the prison bells tolled twelve noon, James Foxen, the hangman, led the prisoner from his cell to the gallows. Thurtell, for his part, was "elegantly attired in a brown great coat with a black velvet collar, light breeches and gaiters, and a fashionable waistcoat with gilt buttons." The prison chaplain read the burial service. Thurtell mounted the five steps of the gallows and positioned himself on the trap. As Foxen removed his cravat and loosened his collar, Thurtell prayed. Then Foxen placed the noose around his neck. Wilson, Governor of Hertford Gaol, shook hands with him and said "Good bye Mr. Thurtell, may God Almighty bless you," to which Thurtell replied "God bless you, Mr Wilson, God bless you." Wilson asked, "Do you consider that the laws of your country have been dealt to you fairly and justly?" Thurtell answered, "I admit that justice has been done me – I am perfectly satisfied." Foxen drew the bolts and Thurtell dropped through the trap with a crash. It was reported that his neck broke "with a sound like a pistol shot," as if an echo of the crime.[31] The hanging of Thurtell clearly substantiates Foucault's argument that public executions were ritualized.

Ritual distances the immediate and lends a symbolic "otherness." But even then, the performative value was not yet exhausted: a lifelike effigy of Thurtell was exhibited in Madame Tussaud's wax works.

These first two examples of *idem in alio* were selected precisely because the *idem* seems to be so powerfully present: real events, local events, currently occurring events.[32] Not even the distance of place or time puts *The Beauty of Buttermere* or *The Gamblers* at a distance from audience; nevertheless, the distance is there. The stage asserts representation *in alio*. Moncrieff's audience, no less than Dibdin's audience, is gathered at the accustomed site of artifice. Moncrieff's Thurtell, no less than Madame Tussaud's, is a representation wrought for display. And to grant Foucault his argument, even the Thurtell who is brought to public execution is no longer Thurtell the gambler, Thurtell the murderer, but a performer in a scripted act.

International news was also a rich source for dramatic representation, and more likely to escape the strictures of censorship. Docu-drama, like all forms of reportage, always held a potential for propaganda. The revolution in the American Colonies gave rise to such plays as Hugh Henry Brackenridge's *The Death of General Montgomery, in Storming the City of Quebec* (1777), an American play with strong anti-British polemic. In Chapter 2, examples of docu-drama were cited for the representation of French character: Thomas Holcroft's *Deaf and Dumb* (1801), adapted from Jean Nicolas Bouilly's tribute to L'Abbé de l'Épée; Richard John Raymond's *The Old Oak Tree* (1835), based on Latude's own memoirs of his escape from the Bastille. Docu-drama draws power from the interests, passions, and political fervor of the audience. Its theatrical success depends upon the degree in which it succeeds in simulating real people involved in real events. In fantasy spectaculars like George Colman's *Blue-Beard* (1798) or Fitzball's *The Flying Dutchman* (1827) the audience has no limited preconceptions of characters and costumes. But in documentary, the audience may have very specific notions about appearance, dress, manners, and gesture. These and other details of place and circumstance may well have been reported in the newspapers. Theatrical re-enactments, however, must avoid the principal constraints of actual events, for reality is always too little and too much. Too little, because its plot and dialogue want efficiency and organization; reality is haphazard and scattershot, and needs tighter control, more focused interest, more dramatic conversation and spicier wit. Too much, because it is always engulfed in an incomprehensible superfluity of detail; reality has no censorship to block out discomfiting, painful, disgusting elements.

The boundaries defining the limits of what may be tolerated on the stage have shifted again and again in the history of the drama. Immanuel Kant, in his *Critique of Judgment*, famously asked how a beautiful sickness, a beautiful rape, and beautiful death might be possible.[33] The performance on the stage offers the audience not reality but an alternate reality that maintains its illusion as the "real" real.

Moncrieff considered it his obligation as playwright to make sure that true events are dramatically exciting. Thus even the "reality" of the documentary must be heightened, yet at the same time given its clear moral resolution. Moncrieff typically simplified the story, allowed the most extreme brutality to occur off stage, and presented the characters as more consistently either good or evil. In the course of imposing such changes, he often found himself altering the reality so that it conformed to his own concepts of how he would like that reality to be, or how he thought his audience wanted to see reality.

Though he began losing his sight in 1835 and was blind by 1843, Moncrieff continued to write until his death in 1857, producing hundreds of theatrical pieces, as well as theatre criticism and poetry.[34] Though many of his plays document sensational events in England, in *The Shipwreck of the Medusa, or The Fatal Raft!* (Royal Coburg, June 19, 1820)[35] Moncrieff turned to an international maritime scandal. The public was well aware of the infamous aftermath of the shipwreck: the betrayal of the crew by the officers and the cannibalism among the starving survivors.[36] Moncrieff may be charged with having altered the tragic tale by removing the most grisly details and adding, "for the purposes of dramatic effect," a sentimental scene of reconciliation, a patriotic voice introduced by the addition to the crew of an English sailor, and a bit of romance with a cross-dressed female sailor. *The Shipwreck of the Medusa* presents the raft as the stage on which the drama of human suffering and survival is to be performed.

In late June, 1816, the *Medusa* set sail from France for Senegal to bring troops, supplies and the new governor to St. Louis, the capital. Senegal had been traded back and forth with Britain for more than fifty years, and, after negotiations by Talleyrand, the colony was returned to the French after the Napoleonic Wars.[37] Somehow, owing to the incompetence of the crew and those in charge, the *Medusa* ran aground on a reef and was stranded on July 2, and, with the tide sinking, the ship had to be abandoned. Of the four hundred passengers and crew members, all but seventeen abandoned ship. One-hundred-and-fifty survivors boarded a makeshift raft constructed from the wreckage. The boats took off in a straight line with tow ropes connecting them. Then, one by one, each boat threw off the tow line. The last boat, which was connected to the raft, carried the new governor, who gave the order to loosen the line. As a result, the raft of the *Medusa* was set adrift with little food and water. During the second night, some of the men stole the wine, became drunk and tried to revolt by killing the officers. The mutiny was put down, but on the fourth night, there was another mutiny. Only twenty-seven were left by the fifth day. Of those, twelve were seriously wounded, and it was decided that instead of making them suffer starvation, the healthy would put them out of their misery. Thus they were thrown into the ocean and left to drown. The fifteen remaining, with no other alternative, survived on the flesh of those killed in the mutiny.

The raft, cast off on the orders of the governor, was discovered not four, as in Moncrieff's version, but thirteen days later, by a vessel sent to recover items from the *Medusa* and to look for the raft along the way. The governor visited those whom he had once cruelly abandoned while they were in the hospital. He promised to help them but never followed through. Of the fifteen rescued, only ten lived; the other five perished from exposure and malnutrition. The governor's wife and daughter, who should have been sympathetic, not only ignored them but hated them, and could not be "in the presence of these men without feeling a sentiment of indignation."[38] When Savigny went to the government to tell of the governor's negligence, he was ignored and even put on trial for his statements. Following his testimony, a proclamation was ordered by the governor to cover up his actions, and those still in the hospital were forced to sign the statement or be denied permission to return to France. Frustrated with their treatment and determined to expose the truth, Savigny and Corréard wrote their *Narrative of a Voyage to Senegal* (1818). The *Narrative* sold well and was immediately translated into German and English. In France, the painter Géricault interviewed the two authors and began his famous painting, *The Raft of the Medusa* (1819). Because it was a visual reminder of the cruelty of French authorities at the time of the Bourbon Restoration, Géricault's painting was not well received in France. Géricault took it to London in 1820 where it was received with acclaim. In June of the same year, capitalizing on the sensational response to Géricault's painting, Moncrieff opened his play at the Royal Coburg Theatre.

The curtain rises on the preparations for the *Medusa* to set sail for Senegal. The officers are confronting a problem with deserters. Loyalty is completely lacking among the French sailors. Jack is found in a French pub, where the German sailor Jan Kobold has gone to look for replacements for the deserters. Upon Jan's entrance, Jack decides to "speak vessel with him." When Jan asks him to join the crew of the *Medusa*, Jack responds as a true patriot, "what! Desert my king and country, you shark? – never! I've fought and bled for old England . . . damn me if I'll ever desert her."[39] Jack assumes that the *Medusa* is set to head off to Senegal to fight the British for the land, but when Jan assures him that they are simply taking supplies to the new French colony, Jack agrees, and because he is English Jan gives him double wages. The French crew are thus characterized as deserters, drunks, and dangerous rowdies. Two of the characters, Constant and Adolphe, engage in a vicious fight, fire guns at each other, and, missing their mark, turn to sword fighting. Eugene, in love with Constant, tries to stop the fight and is assisted by the old widow Gabrielle. After Constant and Adolphe are sent to the *Medusa*, Eugene decides to join her beloved. With the help of Gabrielle, she sneaks aboard the *Medusa* dressed as a boy.

The romance between Eugene and Constant is countered by the jealous obsession of Adolphe, whose love for Eugene rankles into hate for Constant and lust for vengeance against both. Adolphe's "fatal passion" is meant not only to "unman a sailor's heart," but also to become a contributing cause of the calamity that befalls the entire crew. When the *Medusa* runs into a reef, the passengers and crew are forced to abandon ship. As there are not enough lifeboats, a raft is constructed from the wreck. Adolphe is put in charge of the longboat that will tow the raft ashore. In Moncrieff's version it is Adolphe, not the governor, who casts off the rope and lets the raft drift off to meet its fate. Thus abandoned, those on the raft are left to their own resources. Moncrieff depicts the prevailing mood of the castaways as fear. It is Jack, the English sailor, who rallies the crew and persuades them to support one another. A watch must be kept at night to guard the dwindling store of food and drink and to keep a look-out for land or rescue ships.

During her turn at watch, Gabrielle falls asleep. Jan takes advantage of the situation: "I think dey are all asleep now, and Ich can get some of der brandy" (p. 32). After awakening Francois by accident, Jan threatens to kill him if he makes a noise. In his drunken stupor, Jan plots to put the others out of their misery. "Poor fellows! Dey are fast asleep – we had better kill dem at once and let dem remain so, or dey will want some of der brandy when dey wake, and we shall not have enough for all." At this point François, a trusty crewman, musters enough courage to alert the crew. At the alarm, Jack leaps up shouting "Damme, a mutiny! – give up the stores, you swabs, or you shall have a belly full of cold steel and warm lead!" to which Jan responds "Nein, nein! we have got possession of der brandy and we'll fight like der lion for it." A stage direction describes the action: "A desperate struggle ensues – the mutineers are destroyed, and thrown into the ocean" (p. 33).

The mutiny stifled, Constant laments "they have destroyed themselves and us," to which the captain responds, "we are like men upon destruction's brink, growing giddy with apprehension, and toppling untimely to our fate" (p. 33). As they face starvation, the captain suggests, "will it not be better one should die to save the rest, than all should perish?" (p. 34). The cannibalism that actually did take place is introduced by Moncrieff only as a desperate last measure. The captain offers to be sacrificed, but the governor proposes that they "cast lots – let fate decide it" (p. 34). After Jack prepares the lots, the victims are chosen: Eugene is to die, and her father, the Captain, to strike the blow. Accepting her fate, Eugene feels compelled to reveal her true identity. Thus exposed, a variety of exchanges are proposed: the Captain or Constant for Eugene. But Jack, ever the voice of reason and loyalty, stops the conversation, reminding them, "we are desperate – we are desolate – dying men; but we have the hearts of human beings, and we must act up to them" (p. 34). Thus inspired, the forsaken decide to reject cannibalism in favor of human decency, agreeing that "when the worst comes to the worst, and hope and chance are gone, damme, we'll cut the lashings – scuttle the raft and all take our passage to heaven together" (p. 35). Luckily at that moment a turtle floats by the raft, which Jack catches, providing them with one more meal.

The passengers on the real raft were not so lucky. Faced with starvation they decided to eat the flesh of those already dead. They too were offered some relief by catching a few flying fish, but it was not enough. The truth – real cannibalism – was horrendous; Moncrieff's fiction allowed an affirmation of benign humanity. Adolphe, who had acted with hate against the crew, is met with hate among the Moors of Senegal where he has reached harbor. Just as the sailors were betrayed by Adolphe, the Moors were betrayed by the white man, who, in their quest to expand their territories, caused destruction among the Moorish people. The Moors, led by King Zaide, want revenge against the "pale infidel." When Zaide discovers his daughter missing he vows that he will kill his victim with the fury of a tiger (p. 39). Held as a slave of the Moorish princess Liralie, Adolphe begins to realize his mistakes. He remembers a note given to him by the disguised Eugene. Reading the note, Adolphe learns that Eugene was the boy who had given him the letter. Realizing that she was among those whom he left to perish at sea, Adolphe becomes tormented by "demons of guilt and vengeance!" (pp. 35–6). His sufferings are only made worse by the advances of Liralie. Unable to respond to her desires, Adolphe confesses, "I am a fiend – a murderer! – better it were to hold communion with a rank demon! Than one so foul, so hideous as I am!" (p. 36). As her favored slave, he begs Liralie to grant him a boat and freedom, promising to return once he has found the raft (p. 37). The woman to whom he is enslaved has fallen in love with him and agrees to help. Disobeying her father, they procure a boat and head out to sea to rescue the abandoned raft. Near death, Eugene looks off into the distance and cries "what do I see? – it is! – hold! hold! a boat! – a boat! – a boat!" Jack responds " 'tis but a delusion lady" (p. 38). Adolphe, pulling the boat alongside the raft, announces, "the penitent Adolphe brings preservation for atonement" (p. 38). Even Constant, who had sworn vengeance against Adolphe, is grateful to the rescuer: "thou know'st our hearts, ask not for thanks! Adolphe, thou hast redeemed all" (p. 38).

After Adolphe and Liralie return with the rescued castaways, they are brought before King Zaide, who threatens to kill them in punishment for Liralie's disappearance. Finding his daughter safe, Zaide's anger is calmed. "You Christians call me a barbarian! – a heathen! – call me what you will, I feel I am a man! – a father! You give me back my child, take life in recompense," to which Liralie adds her own plea, "and liberty, dear sire?" Zaide, without hesitating, answers "ask not too much"; after all, they are still the enemy, and Zaide believes that if the tables were turned he would have fared no better (p. 40). The Captain, desperate to preserve his freedom, cries, "spare us! – save us! We come not to usurp or to destroy, but to make peace, and enter into bonds of mutual interest and unity" (p. 40). Jack declares the practice of his own land would assure Zaide's people of liberty: "if you were in our condition, and were cast ashore in my country, old England, whether you were friend or foe, there isn't the poorest cottager there that wouldn't open his doors to receive you . . . his heart to cherish you, and his arms to protect you" (p. 40). Zaide's mind is changed. The people he was ready to commit to slavery become guests of his hospitality. Zaide remarks, "revenge and hospitality are our ruling passions" (p. 41). The Moors accept their European guests and the play ends with a bond of peace. As the curtain falls, Eugene is joined with Constant, Adolphe with Liralie.

Jack's unrestrained chauvinism is much the same as that touted by the English soldier Robinson in Moncrieff's *The Cataract of the Ganges!* (Drury Lane, October 27, 1823), a play that will be mentioned in Chapter 6. In *The Cataract*, the Rajah praised the "Generous Britons." Jack Gallant and King Zaide similarly become spokespersons for the benefits of colonization and empire.[40] Precisely because it would have undermined his celebration of colonial expansion, Moncrieff does not allow his *Shipwreck of the Medusa* to become an indictment of the criminal actions of the French officers and the Governor of the French colony of Senegal. He transforms the actual events of the betrayal into a love-triangle between Adolphe, Constant, and Eugene. An heroic Jack and a repentant Adolphe save the day. The horror of the starvation and death of hundreds is glossed over in a drama of romance adventure. And the play ends with rousing patriotic confirmation that Moncrieff knew would please his audience. Documentary, as often happens, gives way to propaganda.

Having drastically altered the truth, Moncrieff might be expected to comment on his changes. He does so in an introduction written ten years after the play was first performed. Moncrieff affirms that the "drama is founded on facts" (p. vii). In discussing the *Narrative of a Voyage to Senegal*, Moncrieff notes that "The Quarterly Reviewers, in their notice of this work, make the following just remarks: – 'This well-authenticated little volume presents the details of a scene of horror, that can scarcely be conceived to have taken place among men in a state of civilized society'" (p. vii). Moncrieff informs the reader that "it will be seen the author of this drama has deviated materially, in some instances, from his text, for the purpose of dramatic effect; but the main circumstances have been adhered to as closely as possible." If the "main circumstances" were that the *Medusa* was shipwrecked and someone cast the survivors adrift on a raft, then yes, Moncrieff has adhered to the facts of his source (p. viii). To demonstrate "how far the author has been enabled to adhere to facts," Moncrieff summarizes the true story of the *Medusa*, but here too details are altered (p. vii).

Water, rather than fact, was what Moncrieff considered the important ingredient of his play: "with the novelty of the subject and the striking interest of the raft, it was more than commonly successful in repre-sentation, and led the way for a new species of drama: – the nautical drama, that has since been highly popular" (p. viii). Moncrieff had taken over the management of the Royal Coburg in 1819, and he might rightly claim that one year later his *Shipwreck of the Medusa* "led the way" for nautical melodrama at that theatre. But shipwrecks and battles at sea had been the attraction at Sadler's Wells since 1804, when the theatre was equipped with a shallow tank, 100 × 40 feet.[41] The success of *The Siege of Gibraltar* as an aquatic spectacular was the true trend-setter; not even Sadler's Wells was the first. Ten years earlier, as may be recalled from my comments in the Introduction on Kemble's *Lodoiska* (Drury Lane, June 8, 1794), water tanks were already in use to create waterfalls and rivers, and "the piece concluded with a grand sea-fight."[42] Other London theatres had also installed tanks to produce similar aquatic effects.[43] What Moncrieff could rightly claim as his contribution was the effective conjuration of "reality" through the documentary pretense of representing the most scandalous sea disaster of the period.

CHAPTER 4

Acting: histrionics, and dissimulation

In the period from David Garrick (1717–79), through Sarah Siddons (1755–1831) and John Philip Kemble (1757–1823), the use and under-standing of gesture underwent radical changes affecting conventions in acting. Classical works on gesture discussed ways in which movement of the body and hands, tilt of the head, gait, and movement of legs and feet display attributes of gender, of age or state of health, of social class and profession. Studies of chironomia had, from Elizabethan times, replicated the same description of arm and hand gestures with the same prescription for their rhetorical use. During the latter half of the eighteenth century there was a growing recognition of how gesture revealed or defined character. Gesture in acting too was seen to have other implications beyond expressing thought or feeling. It enabled a character to construct the very space upon the stage. With the point of a finger or the sweep of an arm, height, depth, direction, motion are defined. Books on gesture began to deliberate on more complex instincts and motives influencing the body movement. Corresponding changes were taking place in figure painting and acting.

Michael William Sharp's "Essay on Gesture," delivered as a lecture to the Philosophical Society at Norwich in 1820, makes the case that gestures not only reveal emotions; they also reveal even those emotions that a person might strive to conceal.[1] Sharp's point is that gesture is an instinctively honest language, often exposing a truth that a speaker may attempt to deny or disguise. Thirty-five years before Sharp, Johann Jacob Engel introduced the discrimination of true and false gesture in his *Ideen zu einer Mimik* (1785). As "Adapted to the English Drama" in *Practical illustrations of rhetorical gesture and action* (1807; 2nd edn. 1822), Henry Siddons retained Engel's critique of false or feigned gestures as opposed to "natural" gestures.[2] By augmenting Engel's commentary with cross-references to the English stage and numerous examples drawn from the acting of his uncle and his mother – John Philip Kemble and Sarah

Siddons – he provided a correction to the formulaic presentation of acting style in Gilbert Austin's *Chironomia*,[3] which was published just the year before Henry Siddons brought out his first edition.[4]

In addition to beholding an actor acting a character, the audience was expected to perceive as well when that character commenced another dimension of role-playing. It is as if "Pepper's Ghost," as introduced in Chapter 3, was no longer merely a confounding of superimposed reflected and refracted images, but those images had begun to perform contrary to one another, much as De Quincey described the "Brocken spectre" as a disobedient shadow making motions of it is own.[5] Whether a spectator could distinguish a natural from a feigned gesture was a crux implicated by Denis Diderot in *Le paradoxe sur le comédien* (1773).[6] During the eighteenth century, dramatic illusion was generally defined as the heightening of emotional response to the point that the reason is overwhelmed.[7] The spectator is then affected by the dramatic imitation as if it were reality. Illusion in these circumstances is often attributed directly to the success of the actor. The actor, so it seems, ceases to be himself and becomes the character he plays. In examining how this apparent transfer is wrought, critics argued the same distinction between reason and emotion in acting that they used to address the problem of audience response. But in explaining the success in acting, the argument took the opposite turn. The idea of artistic control conflicted with the notion of "feeling" the part.

If actually caught up in the throes of emotion, Diderot argued in *Paradoxe*, the player would lose all rational command of mime, gesture, and elocution. Thus to create the illusion of powerful emotions affecting a character, an actor must play the role with studied deliberation. Total constraint enables the actor to concentrate artistic training and skill to performing the very extremes of passion.[8] Should an actor actually surrender himself to the sway of feelings, the performance will become awkward and uneven. The paradox thus has a positive and negative aspect: if the spectator ceases to behold the actor and sees only the character caught up in emotional agitation, then it is certain that the actor has repressed emotion to achieve the effect; contrarily, if the spectator becomes aware of the actor's inconsistent performance, the fault may well lie in the actor having been affected by the emotional conditions of the role. The emotional response is excited in the audience when it is only mediated, not felt, by the actor.

Seen merely in the terms described, it may seem that Diderot expected the actor to be cold and dispassionate. The opposite is true; it is not insensibility but extreme sensibility that belongs to the psychological nature of the actor.[9] The actor must be a keen observer of human behavior and have the capacity to understand the expressions of passions that she or he may never have personally endured. May the role of a woman whose husband is killed be played only by a widow? No, but it must be played by one who has witnessed human grief and can imitate its effects, who can mime the physical convulsions of the passions without actually suffering them on the stage. Because acting a passion is distinguished from feeling a passion, this theory of the drama considers all stage gestures counterfeit. The body language is merely mimicked. Successful acting, of course, requires that the gestures be successfully replicated so that the audience does not perceive the artifice.

In *Wilhelm Meister's Apprenticeship* (1795–6), Wolfgang von Goethe has his title character propose a method of acting that requires that the actor recreate in his own mind the circumstances and experiences that brought the dramatic character to the situation confronted in the play.[10] The player must nurture her or his own "memory" of the events, which presumably belong to the character's life. In recounting her experiences on the Weimar stage under Goethe's direction, Karoline Jagemann stated that entering into a character's memories and emotions was an exercise to be conducted in rehearsing a role, so that in the actual performance the emotional intensity could be controlled as remembered re-enactment.[11] The psychological and emotional aspects of acting were, however, subsequently stressed even further by such influential theorists as William Archer (1856–1924), Konstantin Stanislavski (1863–1938), Jacques Copeau (1879–1949), and Béatrix Dussane (1888–1969). The efforts to create genuine emotion by constructing a fictional "memory" and fabricating a psychological "identity" were aimed at reconciling the difference between acting a passion and feeling a passion, thus overcoming the crux of Diderot's paradox. The theorists succeeded in internalizing the mimicry, giving it a subjective or psychological center. Yet even these new approaches recognized that body movements corresponded to emotional states. Therefore the player must still master the body language of the emotions even before attempting to master the lines of a play.

If all stage gestures are essentially false, and the players are merely feigning emotions, how might a player then proceed to play a character who is feigning an emotion? It is one thing to feign an emotion, another to feign the feigning of an emotion. The purpose of this chapter is to analyze the revelations and artful deceptions of body language as crucial attributes of acting. Performances of Shakespeare, and engravings of them, are important references for the analysis. What subtle deviation does an actor or actress employ to portray a scene of deception? The task is easier if the playwright has alerted the audience to expect dissimulation. Iago, for example, announces in the opening scene, "I will wear my heart upon my sleeve, . . . I am not what I am" (I.i.64–5). If he is to succeed in convincing Cassio, Roderigo, and Othello to accept his reports and advice, he cannot always appear lurking with dark malignancy in a corner. In his monologue on "the winter of our discontent," Richard III reveals his scheme, and then proceeds to gain power precisely through his skill in dissimulation. In playing Richard, Kemble made the most of vile hypocrisy wearing the disguise of piety. Iago and Richard provide occasions for an actor to assume the role of a character disguising not their outward garb, but their motives and the verity of their words.

Within the last two decades, the popular book trade has seen a number of books promising to reveal how to read body language for signals of insecurity or dishonesty, and how to use the body to communicate sincerity even in situations where truth might be distorted. One title announces clues for detecting "Deceit in the Marketplace, Politics, and Marriage"; another offers skills in interpreting and using body language to attain "Love, Wealth and Happiness."[12] Engel's attempt to distinguish natural from false gesture anticipates the study of body movement that two centuries later became a major subject of behavioral research.[13]

A shift toward a more scientific method of analyzing gesture was already evident during the latter half of the eighteenth century. Handbooks on chirologia and chironomia were being superseded by studies of gesture and expression that endeavored to establish a typology and to interpret observations of body movement in terms of a physiology of musculature and the nervous system. The earlier work of Charles Le Brun, *A Method to Learn to Design the Passions* (1734), is dismissed by Engel as partaking "too much of caricature" to be useful as a guide.[14] Johann Caspar Lavater's *Physiognomische fragmente* (1775–80), translated into English as *Essays on Physiognomy* (1789–98) with illustrations by Lavater's former pupil Johann Heinrich Fuseli, argued a relationship between psychological character and the formation of facial expression.[15] Lavater's typology was uninformed by scientific knowledge of anatomy; the first scientifically grounded study was Charles Bell's *The Anatomy and Philosophy of Expression* (1806). Bell's detailed understanding of the nervous system and the facial muscles made it possible for him to show the actual effects of nervous disorders and certain mental conditions on the muscles of the face. Engel proffered a very different argument by insisting on an active strategy of counterfeiting emotions and using body language to deceive.

Figure 1 Apprehension, *Hamlet*. Siddons, *Practical illustrations*, Plate 10.

Engel distinguished five provinces of gestural communication: to mime is to act out a situation; to pantomime is to act out words as in a parlor game of charades; to mimic is to copy the movements or expressions of another person. Representation can be mimetic, concerned with reacting to and interacting with the external world; but it can also be mimismetic, revealing the internal process of discovery or realization. The pace and the movement of arms are synchronized with the movement of the mind: now moving slowly, now irregular, now agitated and quick.

The moment that a difficulty presents itself, the play of the hands entirely ceases – the eye, which, as well as the head, had a gentle and placid motion, while the thought was easy, and unfolded itself without labour, . . . in this new situation looks straight forward, and the load falls on the heart, until, after the first shock of doubt . . . suspended activity resumes its former walk. (p. 60)

Henry Siddons modifies Engel's account of "Doubt" and "Apprehension" to describe John Philip Kemble's performance of Hamlet's soliloquy (see Figure 1).

Hamlet's reflections bring him to a crux: "To die, to sleep; / To sleep, perchance to dream." Hamlet comes to a full halt, pauses a moment, then exclaims "ay, there's the rub" (iii.i.64–5) and at the same moment should give the exterior sign of that which his interior penetration alone has enabled him to discover.[16] Another example of the mimismetic is Lear's recollection of the unworthy treatment he has experienced from his daughters (see Figure 2).

Again the pace, the tilt of head, the agitation of the hands and arms, must undergo a transformation. As if he catches himself, he stops still, changes his tones, and suddenly exclaims, "That way madness lies" (iii.iv.21).

Even though he must appear as "honest Iago," Shakespeare's villain is given frequent occasions to reassert his dark purpose. An audience expecting a stronger display of passion found it in 1814, when, as Leigh Hunt expressed it, Edmund Kean (1787–1833) did "extinguish Kemble," or at least hastened his going out.

Kean played Richard III, that "foul bunch-backed toad" (*Richard III*, iv.iv.81), preying upon his victims with Satanic cunning (see Figure 3). "Kean's manner of acting this part," William Hazlitt claimed, "is entirely his own, without any traces of imitation of any other actor." Yet two characteristics common to the acting of the period were also evident in Kean's Richard III. The first was the tendency to play the part as a series of self-conscious poses, the second was to provide frequent reminders that his character – Richard, Duke of Gloucester – was simply acting the roles necessary to transform himself into King Richard III. These two characteristics are both manifestations of the reflection/refraction doubleness informing performance throughout the period, but Hazlitt notes them as especially pronounced in Kean's movement upon the stage. His acting, Hazlitt states, "presents a perpetual succession of striking pictures" and supplies "the best Shakespeare Gallery we have had." The doubleness of his performance was crucial to the scene with Lady Anne (i.ii): "Richard

Figure 2 Painful Recollection, *King Lear*. Siddons, *Practical illustrations*, Plate 11.

should woo not as a lover, but as an actor – to shew his mental superiority, and power to make others the playthings of will." To reveal his character to the audience as consummate hypocrite, Kean's acting must reveal Richard's acting.[17]

John Philip Kemble kept Richard's limp, but avoided a display of physical deformity. He internalized Richard's villainy and rendered it most obvious by playing with icy aloofness the scenes of outrageous hypocrisy.

Figure 3 John James Halls, Edmund Kean as Richard III. Act iv, Scene iv (Drury Lane, February 14, 1814). Engraved by Charles Turner (1814).

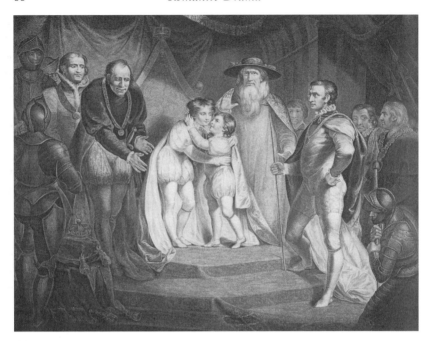

Figure 4 James Northcote, John Philip Kemble as Richard III. Act III, Scene i. Engraved by Robert Thew (1791). Pape and Burwick, eds., *The Boydell Shakespeare Gallery*, Vol. II, Plate 22.

When James Northcote invited Kemble to his studio to pose for the scene depicted in Figure 4, he complained that Kemble displayed little emotion and did not seem to enter into the part. Kemble responded by telling Northcote to come to the theatre and watch him in the role.[18] In fact, restraint was the key factor in Kemble's performance of Richard. Kean would subsequently play this scene with a lurid display of false affection in welcoming the princes. Kemble's Richard, however, maintains an apparently passive unconcern even as he plans their imprisonment and murder. Act III opens with the arrival of the young princes and concludes with the appearance of Richard upon the balcony with two bishops who have been attending his pious devotions. In playing Richard, Kemble made the most of vile hypocrisy wearing the disguise of piety. No less than Kean, Kemble saw it as an occasion for an actor to assume the role of an actor. When Kemble retired from the stage in 1817, Kean had already gained considerable prominence. Kean's passionate intensity presented audiences with a striking contrast to the studied precision of Kemble's style; there was nothing of the cold, calculating aloofness in

Kean's rendition of Richard III. Like Kemble, Kean was a poser, but his poses were more varied and rapidly modulated. In Hazlitt's account, Kean played the scene with Lady Anne as the Serpent confident of his seduction of Eve. "His attitude in leaning against the side of the stage before he comes forward," Hazlitt writes, "was one of the most graceful and striking we remember to have seen." As he approached and spoke to Lady Anne, his body language involved gradual transitions in a series of pictorial attitudes: "smooth and smiling villainy," "wily adulation," "encroaching humility."[19]

In the latter eighteenth and early nineteenth centuries, Gotthold Ephraim Lessing and August Wilhelm Schlegel gave detailed attention to dissimulation in dramatic plot and character.[20] When dramatic intrigue calls for a character to disguise her or his actual motives, the player must presumably reveal to the audience the very deceit and cunning that is concealed from other characters in the play. Certainly this poses a special problem for the use of gesture in acting, but it raises an even greater challenge for the visual artist. Can the artist capture in the frozen moment of a single scene the nuances of body language by which the deception might be conveyed? As an example of dissimulation (*Verstellung*) in the drama, Lessing discusses Francesco Scipioni di Maffei's *Merope* (1713), drawn from the *Fabulae* of Hyginus.

Telephontes, the son of Merope, returns to Messenia where Polyphontes has usurped the throne by killing Telephontes' father. Polyphontes has offered a reward for the murder of Telephontes, and Telephontes himself comes to claim that reward as a way of gaining audience with Polyphontes and possibly finding a way to avenge his father. Suspicious of duplicity, Polyphontes tells Merope that he has given hospitality to her son's murderer. Merope enters his chamber with an ax intending to kill him. His true identity is revealed just in time, and together they plot their revenge. Merope pretends that she has forgiven Polyphontes. Telephontes, still in his guise as the stranger come to collect the reward, is called upon to slaughter a sacrificial animal before the throne to celebrate the reconciliation and forthcoming marriage. Instead, he kills the usurper and reclaims the kingdom for himself. All three principal characters are implicated in dissimulation. Noting Maffei's clumsiness in representing the dissimulation of Polyphontes and Merope, as they each pretend, with different motives, to believe in the dissimulation of Telephontes, Lessing comes to the conclusion that such an elaborate game of pretense loses credibility and becomes ill-suited to tragedy: "It is more permissible for the writer of comedy thus to pit conception against conception, because to arouse our laughter does not

Figure 5 Benjamin West, *King Lear*. Act III, Scene iv. Engraved by William Sharpe
(1793). Pape and Burwick, eds., *The Boydell Shakespeare Gallery*, Vol. II, Plate 39.

require the same degree of illusion that is necessary to arouse our
sympathy."[21] Dissimulation can be effective in tragedy. But Lessing cautions
against allowing it to turn into a complex comedy of errors. He also points
out that dissimulation may demean the dignity of the hero. Boxing
someone's ear may be suited to comedy, but not to tragedy. It is the
unhappy consequence of the dissimulation in John Banks' *The Earl of Essex;
or, The Unhappy Favourite* (1682): "Without dissimulation the character is
lost; with the dissimulation the character's dignity is lost."[22]

In his *Hamburgische dramaturgie* (1767–8), Lessing endeavors to define
the respective limits for dissimulation in comedy and tragedy. August
Wilhelm Schlegel, in his *Vorlesungen über dramatische Kunst und Literatur*
(1809–11), is concerned, rather, with the way in which dissimulation adds
depth to the spectator's perception of character. When Shakespeare has a
character assume another identity, or disguise his or her actual motives, the
audience must exercise a dual perception of the character, constantly
adjusting the words and action of the revealed character in order to fathom
the concealed character. The dual perception is not merely a complication
of dramatic illusion, as Lessing argued; it repeats the primary engagement

Figure 6 Benjamin West, *Hamlet*. Act IV, Scene V. Elsinore. King, Queen, Laertes, Ophelia, &c. Engraved by Francis Legat (1802). Pape and Burwick, eds., *The Boydell Shakespeare Gallery*, Vol. II, Plate 45.

of illusion. We see a replication of the actor playing a character, as that character plays another character.[23]

In addition to the duality of dissimulation, there is another duality of character representation that is even more problematic: the character who becomes mad or who feigns madness. Duality of perception is challenged when we must witness a character who seems to move in and out of derangement, feigned or real, whose delirium alternates with, or is interrupted by, rational clarity. Hamlet's "pretended 'Wildness,'" Samuel Taylor Coleridge believed, is but half-false. Observing that "subtle trick to pretend to be acting when we are very near being what we act," Coleridge sees but a gradation of intensity that renders "Ophelia's vivid Images nigh akin to and productive of temporary mania."[24] Benjamin West's depiction of the madness of Lear on the heath is acclaimed among the best works contributed to Boydell's Shakespeare Gallery (see Figure 5).

West also painted the madness of Ophelia, which has garnered very little critical praise. Admittedly, his Ophelia lacks the heroic composition of his Lear, but it does use gesture to achieve dramatic complexity (see Figure 6).

Like Fuseli, West sought to intensify the dramatic moment by exhibiting the passions in vehement extremity. He depicted Lear, crossing the heath with Kent and the Fool, encountering Edgar disguised as a madman and Gloucester bearing a torch. West centered Lear in the virtual eye of the storm of passions. The mad dance of Ophelia is also the dramatic center of the composition, providing the leitmotif for the entire scene. But the scene is much confused; the court of King Claudius has become a mad house. Distraught at the affliction that has befallen his sister, Laertes appeals to heaven for divine aid. The guilt-tormented king looks as wild and deranged as Ophelia. The Switzers whom he has sent to guard the door seem, rather, to stare upon the furled banner that leans against the arch. The gentleman who brought Ophelia to court, with the news that "Her mood will needs be pitied" (iv.v.3), seems indeed to pity her strange antics, also watched by the ladies-in-waiting who stand behind the queen's throne. The queen, however, has lapsed into such deep brooding that she seems totally oblivious to those around her.

Engel advocated gesture founded on physiology and psychology. Pantomimic gesture, widely used on the Baroque and Classical stage in France and Italy, had been advocated in Luigi Riccoboni's *Dell'arte rappresentativa* (1725). Engel objected that pantomimic gesture distracted the audience from the actual power of the drama.[25] Metaphoric language may effectively communicate impressions of the sublime, noble, or horrific to the imagination, yet when a player attempts to conjure the same images through gesture, the results, Engel says, may well appear farcical. Pantomimic gesture may work in scenes of comic buffoonery, as does mimic gesture when a character narrates, by re-enacting, a previous event. When pantomimic gesture is used to act out words, not thoughts or feelings, it will inevitably undermine the effects of more serious scenes. Engel cites as example a scene from Noverre's *Les Horaces* (adapted from Corneille's tragedy, which, as Henry Siddons adds, was played as *The Roman Father*, Drury Lane, 1750). Camilla's speech (Horatia in the English version), Engel describes as noble and grand and at the same time terrible for the imagination:

> Quelle-même [Rome] sur soir renverse ses *murailles*,
> Et de ses propres mains déchire ses entrailles! (p. 248)

In the imagination Camilla's curse conjures an immense and profound gulf, which opens like the jaws of some terrible monster to consume and destroy the whole of a vast and puissant people. The terror of the curse is rendered ludicrous, Engel argues, when delivered in pantomimic gesture

False Gesture

Figure 7 Camilla in *Les Horaces*. Siddons, *Practical illustrations*, Plate 34.

(see Figure 7), "pointing to the bottom of the scene (apparently to indicate the spot where we are to imagine the city of Rome); subsequently agitating her hand, directed downwards to the earth; afterwards suddenly opening, not the jaws of a monster, but her own little mouth, and thither conveying her clenched fist, from time to time, as if she meant to swallow it with the greatest avidity."[26] As another example of a false use of pantomimic gesture Engel recalls the scene from Lessing's *Emilia Galotti* (IV.vii), in which Countess Orsina reveals to Odoardo that his daughter's bridegroom has been killed and that his daughter is in danger. Impatient for the Countess to complete the worst of her report, he exclaims, "Weaken not this drop of poison in a large vessel" (p. 225). The scene

False Gesture

Figure 8 Odoardo in *Emilia Galotti*. Siddons, *Practical illustrations*, Plate 32.

calls for Odoardo to express increasing horror at the details the Countess has already revealed together with his eagerness to learn the fate of his daughter. How strangely incongruous was the actor who delivered this speech in pantomime (see Figure 8).

"An exact observer of the rule prescribed by Riccoboni, he lifted up the right arm methodically, and curving his hand, held it down to the ground as if he were pouring something in the earth. This movement was meant to designate the drop of poison.

Figure 9   Odoardo in *Emilia Galotti*. Siddons, *Practical illustrations*, Plate 33.

After this first gesture, stretching out his arms, with the fingers widely scattered, he seemed to wish to embrace something of vast circumference, and this was . . . the painting of the tub" (pp. 225–6. See Figure 9).[27]

As illustrations to his commentary, Engel drew upon contemporary performances on the Berlin stage. Siddons, in the sixty-nine illustrations

Figure 10 Henry Tresham, *Antony and Cleopatra*. Act iii, Scene ix. The Palace in
Alexandria. Antony, Cleopatra, Eros, Charmian, Iras, &c. Engraved by Georg Siegmund
and Johann Gottlieb Facius (1795). Pape and Burwick, eds., *The Boydell Shakespeare
Gallery*, Vol. ii, Plate 31.

that accompanied his translation, substituted poses of John Philip
Kemble and Sarah Siddons, and provided cross-references to the London
stage. The illustrations, of course, are stymied by the same temporal
limitations confronting the history painter. The motion of the player
upon the stage is caught in the stasis of art. The resolution of the frozen
movement, as Lessing described it in his essay on the *Laokoon* (1766), is to
show rising motion just prior to its apex, so that the entire causal sweep is
revealed. Art attains its illusion of temporality by enabling the viewer to
imagine the before and after, the inception and consequence of a depicted
action.[28]

Henry Siddons discusses the exasperation and self-contempt that
overcomes Antony in his doting on the Egyptian queen. It is his own
shame at having been unmanned, Siddons suggests, that explains why
Antony has Thyreus, Caesar's noble ambassador, whipped like an errant
schoolboy (pp. 125–6). The gesture of shame and exasperation (p. 178) is
appropriately adapted by Henry Tresham to his depiction of Antony (see
Figure 10).

Antony has led Cleopatra's expedition against Octavius at sea. In the very midst of the battle, Cleopatra's vessel turns in flight and Antony follows. Tresham depicts the scene in which Cleopatra approaches Antony after this humiliation in battle. As model for Cleopatra he has taken Lady Emma Hamilton, who effectively renders the feminine ploy of feigning a faint.

"Have you reflected on the very great difference which exists between the painter and the actor?" Engel has two answers to this question: a simple answer and an answer that is ingeniously complex. The simple answer is that the actor has merely to modify the features of his own face, while the painter must paint the face and all, besides the difficulty of conforming to all the rules and principles laid down in the art of physiognomy. The one is aided by nature, the other must rely on convention. The matter becomes complex when Engel proposes the need for the actor or actress to know when it is permitted to make use of painting in the play of gesture. Engel, that is, distinguishes between "the veritable gesture . . . which expresses the sentiment of the moment, and the feigned or foreign gesture which is adopted as a mode of pretence or deceit." The natural gesture he calls expression, the feigned gesture he calls painting (pp. 206–11). The painted gesture may be effectively controlled to reveal the duplicities of Iago, but should the actor resort to painted posing when the action requires an exhibition of sincerity, the performance is inevitably undermined.

The painted gesture is appropriate for Cleopatra feigning a faint, but Hero's swoon (*Much Ado about Nothing*, IV.i) must appear as a natural expression (see Figure 11).

Don John, jealous of Hero's affections for Claudio, resorts to slander to break up the match. He first arranges for his man, Borachio, to make love to a waiting-maid in Hero's chamber, then he invites Don Pedro and Claudio to a meeting outside the chamber window. In this scene at church the following morning, Claudio and Don Pedro, deceived by Don John's evil stratagem, reveal to the congregation what they had witnessed, or thought they had witnessed, the night before. The innocent Hero falls in a swoon. Beatrice and Benedick come to her aid, and the compassionate Friar Francis disbelieves the evil report. Hamilton may well have seen the performance of *Much Ado* at Drury Lane between April and May, 1788, just prior to his rendition of this scene. Whether or not he adapted particular details, his setting and gesture reflect contemporary theatrical practice. *Much Ado* played again at Covent Garden in September, 1793, and October, 1797.

Figure 11 William Hamilton, *Much Ado about Nothing*. Act IV, Scene i. Engraved
by Jean Pierre Simon (1790). Pape and Burwick, eds., *The Boydell Shakespeare Gallery*,
Vol. 1, Plate 17.

While the debate stirred by Lessing's essay on the *Laokoon* (1766)
prompted much discussion of the frozen moment, the comparison
between the presumed stasis of the spatially defined visual arts and the
presumed dynamism of the temporally defined visual arts often overlooks
the function of stasis in the drama. There is, after all, a dramatic power in
the frozen moment on stage. As I have already shown with the plates of
Lear and Hamlet (Figures 5 and 6), Engel and Siddons described the pause
as a natural mimismetic gesture. Engel also asserts that the frozen posture
is a natural response to shocking revelation (p. 79. See Figure 12).[29]

Henry Siddons elaborates Engel's assessment of the dramatic efficacy of
the frozen moment, and he notes the instances in which Sarah Siddons
pauses in a striking pose, and allows the motionless gesture to displace
speech (pp. 369–70). Boaden, too, comments on Siddons' silences. As
Belvidera in Otway's *Venice Preserv'd*, "she rises at the bidding of Renault
and the conspirators, the alarmed yet searching survey which she took of
them was one of those expressions in which the actress writes the characters of fire: you felt that there was a language more eloquent than

Figure 12 The smith hears of Prince Arthur's death. *King John*. Siddons,
Practical illustrations, Plate 14.

speech, and saw beauty and intelligence interpret the very silences of the
poet."[30] In speaking of her self-possession, Boaden also notes reliance on
the sustained pause: "In the hurry of distraction she could stop, and in
some frenzied attitude speak wonders to the eye, till a second rush forward brought her to the proper ground on which her utterance might be
trusted."[31]

From Riccoboni, to Lavater, Engel, Bell, and Smirk, theories of gesture
and expression underwent radical change. The legacy of the Enlightenment was its emphasis on empirical observation, scientific method, and
typology. This was also the period that saw the rise of experimental
psychology and reform in the treatment of mental disorders. Playwrights
like Joanna Baillie were strikingly self-conscious about the norms and
aberrant deviations in gesture and expression. Artists and players were

wary of stylized mannerisms, even as they adopted a new set of them that would conform to notions of self-referentiality (an actor's playing a character who is playing another character) and to the pathology of madness and emotional torment.

Gesture, in the review provided by Engel and Siddons, is described both as it accompanies speech and provides a complement or emphasis to the spoken words. In the natural mode, gesture may be deliberate or spontaneous; in the pantomimic mode it is nothing more than playing charades with each and every metaphor. For Henry Siddons there was no greater example of the power of physical presence on the stage than the remarkable Sarah. She, more than any other player, could demonstrate how gesture may construct or annihilate an ideal; how gesture, as expression of powerful feelings, may completely displace speech. Pantomimic gestures, Engel grants, are often used as signs to express defiance or scorn, to refuse to speak, to trespass social or sexual mores, to defy authority. Mimismetic gesture, the struggling with internal thoughts, may well be enacted in silence as if waiting for words that are yet to come. Unlike previous expositions on gesture, the Engel–Siddons account elaborates the differences between expressing an emotion, or dissembling an emotion: dissimulation (shrewd simpleton, naïve seductress, deceptive friend, etc.). *The Practical illustrations* of Engel and Siddons are not informed by the anatomical explanation of nerves and muscles provided by Charles Bell, but they do, with Siddons' additions, consider the aberrational pathology of Kemble's De Monfort or Hamlet, or Sarah's Lady Macbeth or Ophelia. Rather than insist upon theatrical illusion – the actor becoming the character – as an all-or-nothing phenomenon, Henry Siddons fully endorses Engel's appeal to the dual perception of performance. No matter what role she played, as her enthralled viewers always knew, Sarah Siddons was physically present in that character. Engel and Siddons acknowledge the motionless gesture of the frozen moment as at once psychologically natural and dramatically effective, yet as Henry underscores the point, Sarah Siddons made the audience feel the suspended power of that momentary pause. It was the ominous lull before the storm, the hesitation before the outburst that would shatter the ideal. Her reliance on gesture works, Henry Siddons emphasizes, because of her perfect sense of timing. Her control of the moment in the confluent flux of physical and psychological movement defines the greatness of her acting.

In her role as Mrs. Oakley in George Colman's *The Jealous Wife* (April 28, 1792), Sarah Siddons was compelled to discriminate for her audience between the differences in her character's true feelings and the show that she puts on for her husband. In portraying Mrs. Oakley as "a sensible but jealous woman," Siddons contrived to make her feelings seem like natural mistakes rather than pernicious conjurings of a suspicious mind. Once the jealousy has taken root, she takes pains to disguise it. Her dissembling is in full play in Act II, when "she enters into the feelings of her husband for Charles, in order to extract from him all that he knows relative to the object of her jealousy." The comic effect is achieved when Mrs. Oakley's power of dissembling is overtaxed and her true feelings burst forth. "Amazing!" she cries out, revealing to Charles that "he has been only feeding the flame while he thought he was quenching the fire." Another mode of feigning is called for when Mrs. Oakley "falls into practiced fits as a mode for alarming humanity." Crucial to Siddons' performance as Mrs. Oakley is the transparency of her dissembling, the rapid transition from feigned emotions to real feelings. In the penultimate scene, that transition defines Mrs. Oakley's realization of the absurdity of her pretences. Siddons made that revelation appear first in her face and then move through her body. In a speechless moment, the audience could "observe in that most expressive of faces the dawning of conviction that she had been imposing upon herself." With an economy of movement, she slowly rises from her chair in a manner that displays "the growing effects of irresistible evidence reducing her to shame for her violence, and apprehension that she may have trifled with love till it is lost."[32]

Typically, a scene of dissimulation is explicitly revealed to the audience before it occurs. Iago, as previously noted, must cloak his dark pupose with the pretense of subservient care and concern. The victim of Iago's dissembling, the noble Moor, is the character who exhibits the shattering of the ideal. To Kemble's Othello, Siddons played Desdemona (March 8, 1785). Unlike the roles in which she played the shattered ideal – Isabella, Jane Shore, Belvidera, Zara, Calista, Lady Macbeth, Mrs. Beverly, Mrs. Haller[33] – her performance as Desdemona, studiously constant and unchanging, exhibited her mastery of minimalism. When Othello gives abusive voice to his suspicions, she responds with passive incredulity. "If her eye had ever magic power," Boaden said of her resigned turn to the audience, "it then displayed it." Her undeviating love and admiration contrasts with Othello's increasing doubt and despair.[34]

It was Kemble's choice on his benefit night to perform Petruchio to his sister's Katherine (March 13, 1788). In Boaden's opinion (and Boaden freely indulged his superlatives), *The Taming of the Shrew* "was never better acted." But his account also reveals that Siddons imposed her own unique interpretation on the role. "If the bent of mind had once been given, it would not have been possible for the teasing, violent, and harassing discipline of Petruchio to have tamed down such a woman to so absurd an obedience to his pleasure. Of a petulant spoiled girl the transformation might be credited." Siddons' Katherine was no "petulant spoiled girl." She was, rather, an artful and intelligent woman who knew how to deal effectively with her mate. Before responding to each of Petruchio's stratagems to impose his will, Katherine briefly interrupted the action with a silent "aside" to the audience, hand on hip and a look of bemused consternation on her face, to let them know that she was well aware of his motives. She was "taming" Petruchio.[35]

Because lying and dissimulation dominate much of the plotting of Romantic drama, the critical attention to acting such roles naturally followed, and the playwrights, too, became more attentive to the details of physical movement. Characters were made to comment on their motions and poses and to call attention to tell-tale gestures of other characters. Indeed, the characters might even, on occasion, provide instruction on the art of dissimulation and how to discriminate shrewd from clumsy prevarication. To demonstrate the dramatic strategies of dissembling and performative self-reflection, I have selected five very different plays: Hannah Cowley's *A Bold Stroke for a Husband* (1783), Joanna Baillie's *De Monfort* (1800), Richard Cumberland's *The Imposters* (1789), Hannah Brand's *Adelinda* (1798), and Thomas Holcroft's *Deaf and Dumb* (1801). These plays exhibit a nuanced attention to psychological manifestations of grief, jealousy, and anger in physical behavior. All five playwrights involve their characters not simply in situations of disguise or dissimulation calling for false or feigned gestures; they also use these occasions to comment on how to conceal or how to expose the subterfuge.

In the opening of *A Bold Stroke for a Husband*, Hannah Cowley introduces Pedro as a simple rustic newly entered into service and not yet proficient in lying:

SANCHA. There he is: do'st see him? just turning by St. Antony in the corner. Now, do you tell him that your mistress is not at home; and if his jealous Donship should insist on searching the house, as he did yesterday, say that somebody is ill – the black has got a fever, or that –

PEDRO. Pho, pho, get you in. Don't I know that the duty of a lacquey in Madrid is to lie with a good grace? I have been studying it now for a whole week, and I'll defy Don or Devil to surprize me into a truth. Get you in, I say – here he comes.

[*Exit. Sancha. Enter Carlos.*]
[*Pedro struts up to him.*] Donna Laura is not at home, Sir.

CARLOS. Not at home! – come, Sir, what have you received for telling that lie?
PEDRO. Lie! – Lie! – Signor! –
CARLOS. It must be a lie by your promptness in delivering it. – What a fool
does your mistress trust! – (1.i.2–13)

Thoroughly familiar with the ploys of lying servants, Don Carlos exposes
Pedro's lie, but also tells him what he should have done to deliver that lie
successfully: "A clever rascal would have waited my approach, and,
delivering the message with easy coolness, deceived me." He goes on to
explain to Pedro how he has betrayed his ineptitude: "*thou* hast been on
the watch, and runnest towards me with a face of stupid importance,
bawling, that she may hear through the lattice how well thou obeyest
her, – '*Donna Laura is not at home, Sir.*'" Truth and lying are marketable
commodities. Just as servants are paid to lie, truth may also be purchased
at slightly higher rate:

CARLOS. There, take that, [*gives money*] and if thou art faithful I'll treble it.
Now go in, and be a good lad – and, d'ye hear? – you may tell
lies to every body else, but remember you must always speak
truth to me.
PEDRO. I will, Sir, – I will. (1.i.41–4)

This introductory scene is thematic, for all the subsequent disguises
depend upon deception cunning enough to escape detection amongst
those who are themselves experienced in intrigue and who have learned to
exercise an alert wariness. Don Carlos, however, is not as wary of duplicity
as he ought to be. Having abandoned his wife, he has fallen into the
clutches of the wily courtesan Donna Laura, who plies him with liquor
and persuades him to sign over the deed to his wife's estate. To regain her
home and win back her husband, Donna Victoria disguises herself as a
suitor, Don Florio. This clever rationale for a charming "breeches part"
also provides Cowley with an occasion to have her character reveal how she
adjusts her manner to assume masculine identity (see Chapter 5).

In the latter eighteenth century, growing interest in the language
of gesture resulted in the publication of numerous guides, manuals, and
disquisitions on physical movement as crucial to oratory and acting.
As the playwrights, too, became more attentive to the onstage movement
of their characters, they began to insert more detailed stage directions.
With the advent of melodrama, highly nuanced gesture was as super-
fluous as dialogue. An inevitable consequence of melodrama was that

psychological subtleties of characters were abandoned. Villains were expected to be villains, and their victims were duped simply because of their innocence and naïveté.

Because melodrama relied so heavily on body language, a more refined attention to mimic and pantomimic action was asserted in other plays as a countermovement to the reductive stylization of melodramatic gesture. A dramatic theory founded on witnessing aberrational behavior provided the "Introductory Discourse" to Joanna Baillie's *Plays of the Passions* (1798). Her intention was to reveal how a character succumbs to a compulsive emotion, which then wreaks its dramatic consequences. She also emphasized the sympathetic propensities that prompt a strong curiosity to observe the changing moods of others. In her plays, dramatic action involves not just the audience but the characters themselves in watching those changes unfold. She chose to represent dramatic character not in terms of traditional literary models, but rather in relation to the accounts of mental pathology in contemporary medical science.[36] In the effort to comprehend its own nature, the human mind, even in its daily social occupations, seeks to trace the varieties of understanding and temper that constitute the characters of men. Amongst the common occurrences of life, evidence of vanity and weakness put themselves forward to view, more conspicuously than virtues, and behavior that is marked with the whimsical and ludicrous will strike us most forcibly.

Curiosity and sympathy are the driving impulses in Baillie's theory of the drama, and her subject is the exposure of a person in the thrall of strong emotion. The theatre provides an acceptable arena for the voyeurism that can otherwise be satisfied only by chance and stealth. To witness a fellow being in the throes of extreme mental agitation and emotional turmoil holds a powerful attraction for our sympathetic curiosity. Whenever passions are displayed, the gaze must follow. Unlike the momentary sensations of joy or pain, the emotions of fear, despair, hatred, love, jealousy embed themselves deeply into mind and character, influencing all one's thoughts and actions. In our experience of watching the turbulent passions, we soon learn to detect the advanced signs of inner turmoil, the tell-tale facial expressions and physical gestures that indicate the struggle to conceal anxieties or desires.[37] With her insistence that drama should address the power of emotions to dictate behavior and compel the overwrought individual to acts of irrational excess, Joanna Baillie engages aberrational psychology. She seeks to ground her analysis of behavior on empirical observation, and to identify the looks and gestures that foreshadow an emotional crisis: the restless eye, the muttering lip, the half-checked exclamation and the hasty start.

In *De Monfort*, she not only depicts the incremental sway of madness, she thematizes the act of watching. The play opened at Drury Lane in April 1800, with Kemble as De Monfort; Sarah Siddons as Jane De Monfort; and Talbot as Rezenvelt, the object of De Monfort's irrational hatred. From the very opening scene of the play, Baillie reveals that the mind of her central character is unsettled. He is not the man he was, his servant Manuel tells their landlord. He has become difficult, capricious, and distrustful. The audience need not strain to pick up the peculiarities of De Monfort's gestures. They are observed and commented on by the other characters. When Rezenvelt appears, his very presence drives De Monfort into frenzy. They duel, but Rezenvelt, the superior swordsman, easily disarms his opponent with a deft maneuver of his sword. Rezenvelt disarms him, then offers to return the weapon when his opponent is calmer (IV.ii). But no calm comes to De Monfort; rather, he continues to rave in mounting delirium. Rezenvelt is last seen wandering alone in the woods.

Baillie provides the final act with a Gothic setting: a convent in the woods, torches burning over a grave, lightning flashing at the windows, sounds of wind and thunder. A young pensioner, with a wild terrified look, her hair and dress all scattered, rushes in upon the assembled nuns to report hearing horrid cries of "Murder!" echoing from the woods. Found and brought to the convent, De Monfort reacts with violent perturbation when the corpse of Rezenvelt is shown to him. Left alone with his murdered foe, De Monfort is overcome with wild anguish and attempts suicide. In his translation of Engel's work on gesture, it is Henry Siddons who comments on the detailed attention to the physical debility of De Monfort's madness: "the man tormented by his own conscience is the object of self-violence; he is fearful and trembling; a leaf fall, a zephyr whispering fills him with terror, and inclines him to flight."[38]

Baillie founded her theory of the drama on a "sympathetick propensity" that compels individuals to watch fellow human beings, seeking to discern in their outward movements the secret springs of their internal feelings.[39] Although this concern with the behavioral symptoms of extreme emotional duress is articulated more thoroughly by Joanna Baillie than by other playwrights of the period, it is nevertheless true that many others shared her attention to how a person may be saying one thing while their body communicates something very different. The theatricality of asides and *marivaudage*, fondly recalled by Charles Lamb in his essays "Stage Illusion" and "On the Artificial Comedy of the last Century,"[40] initiated the audience into a complex repertory of *dedoublement* in which the actor could move with subtlety and dexterity in and out of character, or shift from one character into another. Lamb praises especially John Bannister for his art of "perpetual subinsinuation" in making the comic coward a laughable rather than a merely pitiable character. The *doubleness* of stepping out of a role or of disguise or dissimulation (Schlegel's *Verkleidung* or *Verstellung*: counterfeiting appearance or attitude) has a venerable tradition dating from Aristophanes, indeed from the very origins of drama. The Romantic contribution was to thematize the activity and have the characters reflect upon the manner and means of their performance.

The title of Cumberland's play, *The Imposters*, gives a clear hint to the plot: the impostors are Harry Singleton and Polycarp. As former valet of Lord Janus, Singleton knows, and can mimic with ease, the habits and quirks of his late master. Polycarp pretends to be financial advisor to Lord Janus. Philbert, a tailor who supplies a suitably aristocratic wardrobe, serves as valet to the former valet. The three arrive at the estate of Sir Solomon Sapient, with Singleton's lucrative design of marrying Sir Solomon's sole heir, his daughter Eleanor. To the advantage of Singleton's scheme, Sir Solomon has never met Lord Janus personally, but is nevertheless impressed with the prestige of having His Illustrious Lordship as his son-in-law. To its disadvantage, however, Sir Charles Freemantle, the present suitor of Eleanor, is a close friend of Lord Janus. Although Eleanor has already confessed her love to him, he is ready to withdraw his pretensions as suitor if Lord Janus should assert a claim to her hand. In his role as His Lordship, Singleton overplays the character with a bit too much arrogance; and Polycarp, as his man of business, is given to unbusinesslike behavior. In attempting to win the anxious Eleanor, Singleton finds his entreaties curtly rebuffed. Polycarp has greater success in his salacious overtures to Sir Solomon's spinster cousin, Mrs. Dorothy.

Sir Solomon's brother, Captain George Sapient, grows suspicious at the lapses he observes in the presumed Lord Janus' character and breeding. When he tries to alert his brother, telling him that "his lordship's suite is not very splendid," Sir Solomon replies that it is simply because "Lord Janus does not affect pomp; he travels as it were incognito" (Act 1, lines 56–8). To his brother's urging that he make enquiries, Sir Solomon responds that the proper source of enquiry would be Collins' *Peerage*, and he need not consult it, because

I have his pedigree by heart; I can trace him from the heptarchy; his very title of Janus proves the circumspection of his ancestors; 'tis as much as to say they had all their eyes about 'em: his armorial bearings are typical of sagacity; two vizors in a wreath of serpents: his supporters are an allegory; on the dexter side a fox, denoting cunning; on the sinister a goose, which is the emblem of wariness. (Act 1, lines 71–8)

The goose, as George suggests, is never wary enough. At stake is the fate of Eleanor, "a very fine girl" with "a fine fortune." In question are the character and motives of the supposedly noble house-guest who endeavors to lay claim to her wealth and person. Dismissing his brother's misgivings about Lord Janus, Sir Solomon tells him that "you have not made human nature your study; you have not been in the world as I have" (Act 1, lines 89–90). Although the younger brother is, in fact, the more cautious observer of human nature, he nevertheless turns upon the worthy suitor, Sir Charles, whom he accuses of lying.

Having successfully deluded Sir Solomon, Singleton continues to play the Lord. Only Sir Charles, his rival for the hand of Eleanor, can expose him. Eleanor, from her very first encounter with the fraudulent Lord, has seen his opportunistic greed. When Sir Charles praises the virtues of his friend – "he is much too modest and well-bred to affect the man of wit and acuteness; he is of the gentlest manners and diffident almost to a failing" (Act II, lines 173–5), Eleanor is quick to quip, "Oh, then I assure you he has effectually got rid of that failing" (lines 176–7). And when the importunate impostor subsequently tries to embrace her, he moves with possessive lust:

ELEANOR. Stand off! Are you the elegant, the accomplished Lord Janus, whom your friend Sir Charles describes in raptures?

LORD JANUS No truly I am not. [*Aside.*]
[SINGLETON].

ELEANOR. The modest, well-bred, gentle peer, whose diffidence is his only failing? – I'll not believe it. (Act III, lines 490–6)

Exposure seems imminent when Sir Charles insists upon an interview with Lord Janus. George tells Singleton that Sir Charles is expecting to meet him – "Lord Janus" – in the woods. For this interview, Singleton reassumes his identity as valet to Lord Janus, who, he explains, has sent him to deliver a message to Sir Charles. The message declares His Lordship's proposal and Eleanor's acceptance. Sir Charles is baffled by the message and distraught at Eleanor's apparent betrayal, and when he tells George that he has not met Lord Janus, each is certain that the other is lying.

GEORGE.   Then why do you presume to the contrary? Did Lord Janus assert he had her consent to marry him?

SIR CHARLES. I have not seen Lord Janus.

GEORGE.   For shame! for shame! I blush to hear you so prevaricate: such
                     meanness let me tell you, scarce deserves a gentleman's
                     resentment.
SIR CHARLES.   Meanness! prevaricate! what language is this? I tell you once
                     again I have not seen Lord Janus.
GEORGE.   'Tis false! I know 'tis false.
SIR CHARLES.   Intolerable insult! Draw! [*they draw.*] (Act IV, lines 454–65)

George, earlier a perceptive observer of human nature, is here blinded to
the possibility that Sir Charles is telling the truth. Indeed, the false Lord
has so far succeeded that his falsehood has almost obliterated the truth. As
the two face off with swords drawn, Eleanor intervenes. Her explanation
reveals at once that Singleton is an impostor. Sir Charles and Eleanor
marry with the blessings of the true Lord Janus.

Like Cowley and Cumberland, Hannah Brand, too, creates dramatic
situations that put deceit and dissembling to the test: are there tell-tale
signs that betray the liar? The plot of *Adelinda* (1798) borrows from
romance the device of exchanged infants: Adelinda, reared by the Marquis
and Marchioness D'Olstan, is really the daughter of a farmer, whose
widow switched the infants, and raised Zella as her own daughter.

The Marquis had betrothed Adelinda to Count D'Olstan, a relative
and heir to his title, but Adelinda is secretly married to Strasbourg, the
Marquis' confidential aide. To conceal the secret love, Strasbourg feigns
an interest in Zella. In the meantime another secret love emerges –
between the Count, although engaged to Adelinda, and Zella. Among
this play's many occasions for dissimulation, one recurring feature is
Brand's reliance on a third-party observer, who functions like a Greek
chorus in weighing the evidence and deliberating on the truth or falsehood of what is spoken. An example is the scene in which the Marchioness upbraids Zella for having attracted the attentions of the Count
and insists that she marry Strasbourg.[41] Zella's replies to the Marchioness
are candidly appraised in the maid's series of asides to the audience: does
Zella "tell lies" or is she "innocent"? "[I]s she angel, or demon?" Or a
"Sorceress" who commands "the art of . . . surprise"? The circumstance of
the two girls having been switched as infants seems to serve no other
purpose than to lend propriety to their apparently having chosen marriage partners out of their social class. The secret loves between Zella and
the Marquis' kinsman, Adelinda and the Marquis' servant, bring to
virtually every scene a game of pretending and subterfuge. In each scene,
Brand introduces an observer to keep the audience alert to such gestures
as downcast eyes, a fluttering hand, or faltering speech.

A final example of the art of telling lies with body language involves a character who, born deaf and mute, can communicate only with body language. Briefly described in Chapter 2, Thomas Holcroft's *Deaf and Dumb* (1801) was translated from Jean Nicolas Bouilly's *L'Abbé de l'Épée* (1800). Upon his death, the Count of Hancour charged that his heir, Julio, was to be reared by the boy's uncle, Darlemont. His guardian, however, wants the estate for himself, so he dresses the child in rags and, with his confederate Dupré, abandons Julio amidst the crowds of Paris. Darlemont builds his claim on a ruthless scheme of lies. The boy, rescued by the Abbé de l'Epée (who names him Theodore), is taught to communicate in signs. The use of sign language on the stage is coincident with the rise of melodrama. Just one year later, again translating from the French, Holcroft brought René-Charles Guilbert de Pixérécourt's *Cœlina* (1800) to the London stage as *A Tale of Mystery* (1802). This play, too, features a mute who must communicate by gestures and by writing. Francisco has been persecuted and severely wounded by assassins hired by his treacherous brother, Count Romaldi. When Romaldi is trapped at the play's end, the noble mute Francisco places himself before his brother to protect him from the arrows of the archers. On the opening performance (Covent Garden, November 13), Genest writes that this "was the first of those Melo-dramas, with which the stage was afterwards inundated – tho' this mixture of dialogue and dumb show, accompanied by music, be an unjustifiable species of the drama, yet it must be acknowledged, that some of the Melo-dramas have considerable merit – the Tale of Mystery was the first and the best."[42] It was not an even mixture, for the "dumb-show," accompanied by music, comprised 80 percent of the performance, the dialogue a scant 20 percent. In his stage directions Holcroft describes the pantomimic action for which he gives seventy musical cues.[43] As previously stated, melodrama gave far greater emphasis to body language on the stage, but it also leveled the psychological subtleties. Because of the apparent kinship to the "dumb-show" of pantomime, the deaf mute became a stock character in melodrama.[44] The mute is the one character for whom gesture is not just a random supplement to spoken language but is the major means of communication. For the mute the language of gesture is the natural language, thus creating the momentary illusion on the stage that pantomime has ceased to be mere artifice.

Holcroft's *Deaf and Dumb* takes a major step toward melodrama in creating a central character whose performance is entirely gestural. In several scenes, the silent revelations are dramatically underscored. Indeed, the play opens with the exposition of the silent accuser: a full-length portrait of Julio, the true heir to the Palace of Hancour, hangs in the main hall. As Dupré passes before the portrait, the servant Pierre observes his furtive movements and notices that he always pauses and fixes his eyes on the painted figure. Questioned by the servant, the guilt-ridden Dupré declares that he has seen the figure "start from his frame, and stand before me" (1.i.42). Dupré seems dangerously close to confessing the crime, when Darlemont interrupts and declares that the picture must be removed. Dupré insists that it must remain in its place. Before the first scene closes, Darlemont's son, St. Alme, explains to the curious Pierre why he so often sees "Dupré gazing on that picture of the young count" (1.i.126). The explanation, however, is only the lie Darlemant has invented to affirm that the boy has died:

> ST. ALME. My father took him to Paris about eight years ago, in hopes that this affliction might be removed; and, whether improper medicines were administered to him, or that his constitution sunk under the efforts for his cure, I know not; but there, in a short time, he died in the arms of Dupré, who accompanied my father on this journey. (1.i.118–24)

In Act III, Scene i, the picture that caused Dupré to creep and stare in the opening scene begins to affect the cruel and calculating usurper as well. Pierre reveals that an abbot and a boy have come to the palace and have asked questions; the boy, he says, is apparently a deaf mute but speaks in signs. He also comments that the boy bears a striking resemblance to the young count in the portrait. Darlemont's extreme agitation at this news increases Pierre's suspicions. When Pierre departs, Darlemont reveals in a soliloquy that, shortly before abandoning the helpless boy, he himself had commissioned the painting, "in order to impress an opinion of my affection for this boy, and so prevent suspicion" (III.i.72–5). Refusing Darlemont's bribes, Dupré leaves Darlemont in a state of panic. To the now alert and watchful Pierre, Darlemont's guilty secret is seen to be increasingly exposed in his nervous pacing and his flailing arms.

A contrary delineation of body language is elaborated in the scenes in which Julio, under de l'Épée's tutelage, masters the silent communication of signs. In the hopes that the boy will perhaps recognize a familiar place, de l'Épée strolls with him through various sections of Paris. One day they pass the Palace of Hancour. Julio ("Theodore"), who has not yet learned more than the rudiments of sign language, manages nevertheless to communicate that he recognizes this as the place of his birth:

DE L'ÉPÉE.   This warm emotion – this sudden change in all his features – convinces me that he recollects this place. Had'st thou the use of speech! [*Theodore, looking round him, observes the church, and gives signs more expressive of his knowing the place.*]

DE L'ÉPÉE.   It is – it must be so; and I am then arrived at the period of my long and painful search! [*Theodore now sees the palace of Hancour; he starts – rivets his eyes to it – advances a step or two to R. – points to the statues – utters a shriek – and drops breathless into the arms of De l'Épée.*]

DE L'ÉPÉE.   Ah, my poor wronged boy – for such I'm sure you are – that sound goes to my very heart! He scarcely breathes. I never saw him so much agitated. There, there – come, come. Why was voice denied to sensibility so eloquent! [*Theodore makes signs, with the utmost rapidity, that he was born in that palace – nursed there – that he lived in it when a child – had seen the statues – come through the gate, &c. &c.*]

DE L'ÉPÉE.   Yes – in that house was he born. Words could not tell it more plainly. The care of Heaven still wakes upon the helpless. [*Theodore makes signs of gratitude to De l'Épée, and fervently kisses his hands. De l'Épée explains that it is not to him, but to Heaven, that he ought to pay his thanks – Theodore instantly drops on his knee, and expresses a prayer for blessings on his benefactor.*] (1.ii)

The stage directions indicate the gestures for the boy's performance, and the words given to de l'Épée repeatedly affirm the eloquence of that language of gesture. Although de l'Épée thus knows from the very outset of the play the place of the boy's birth, he realizes that the boy must have a formidable enemy. He therefore continues to tutor the boy's silent eloquence so that he will be fully prepared to expose the villain. De l'Épée also makes sure that he has secured influential allies on the boy's behalf. In Act III, Scene ii, de l'Épée introduces Julio–Theodore to the Advocate Franval, Franval's sister Marianne, and Franval's mother. They are called upon to test the boy so that he might demonstrate the elaborate and subtle nuances of the silent speech of hand signs:

FRANVAL.   Are you then so perfectly comprehensible to each other?
MAD. FRANVAL.   Are your signs so minutely accurate?
DE L'ÉPÉE.   As speech itself.
MARIANNE.   And does he understand every thing you desire to express?
DE L'ÉPÉE.   You shall have proof of it this moment.
                  [*De l'Épée taps Theodore on the shoulder, to make him observe; rubs his forehead, then points to Marianne, and writes a*

line or two with his finger on the palm of his left hand. Theodore nods to De l'Epée, runs to Franval's table, sits down, snatches up a pen, and shews that he is ready to write.]

DE L'EPÉE.   Now, madam, make what inquiry you please of him, he will copy it down from my action, and immediately give you his reply. He waits for you.

MARIANNE.   [*With timidity.*] I really don't know what to –

FRANVAL.   Any thing – any thing.

MAD. FRANVAL.   Ay, ay, child: the first thing that comes into your head.

MARIANNE.   [*After a moment's reflection.*] In your opinion –

DE L'ÉPÉE.   Speak slowly, and repeat the question, as if you were dictating to him yourself.
                    [*Theodore expresses that he attends to de l'Épée's signs.*]

MARIANNE.   In your opinion –

DE L'ÉPÉE.   [*Makes a sign.*]
                    [*Theodore writes.*]

MARIANNE.   Who is the greatest genius –

DE L'ÉPÉE.   [*Makes a sign.*]
                    [*Theodore writes.*]

MARIANNE.   That France has ever produced

DE L'ÉPÉE.   [*Makes a sign.*]
                    [*Theodore writes.*]

DE L'ÉPÉE.   [*Takes the paper from the table and shews it to Franval.*] You see, he has written the question distinctly. [*De l'Épée returns the paper to Theodore, who for a moment sits motionless and meditating.*]

MARIANNE.   He seems a little at a loss.

DE L'ÉPÉE.   I don't wonder at it – it's a delicate question.
                    [*Theodore starts from his reverie – looks affectionately at de l'Épée – wipes his eyes, and writes with the utmost rapidity.*]

FRANVAL.   Look, look, what fire sparkles in his eyes! What animation in every turn! I dare promise you, this will be the answer of a feeling heart, and an enlightened mind.
                    [*Theodore starts up – presents the paper to Marianne, and desires her to read it to the company. Madame Franval and Franval look eagerly over Marianne, as she reads; – Theodore runs to de l'Épée, and looks at him with fond curiosity.*]

MARIANNE.   [*Reads.*] "In your opinion, who is the greatest genius that France has ever produced?"

MAD. FRANVAL.   Ay; what does he say to that?

MARIANNE.   [*Reads.*] "Science would decide for Pascal, and Nature say, Buffon; Wit and Taste present Boileau; and Sentiment

> pleads for Montesquieu; but Genius and Humanity cry
> out for de l'Épée; and him I call the best and greatest of
> all human creatures."
> [*Marianne drops the paper, and retires to a chair in tears.*
> *Theodore throws himself into de l'Épée's arms. Madame*
> *Franval and Franval look at each other in astonishment.*]
> (III.ii.144–75)

With Franval's assistance, Darlemont is exposed and Julio–Theodore is restored as rightful heir to the Count of Hancour. Although Bouilly may be credited with bringing to the stage the first play in which dialogue is conducted in sign language, Holcroft's English version shifted attention away from the intended tribute to Abbé Charles Michel de l'Épée (1712–1789), who in 1755 founded the first free school for deaf people. De l'Épée developed and taught a system of signs that enabled deaf people to communicate through a system of conventional gestures, hand symbols and finger-spelling. On the other hand, Holcroft recognized, as Bouilly did not, that the emphasis on physical gesture gave the play significant relevance to current developments in a dramaturgy of body language.

Because of the prominence of the acting companies of Drury Lane and Covent Garden, it was inevitable that each performer would shape the manners and actions of the character role he or she assumed. Familiar with the players, theatre-goers would inevitably witness similarities from one role to the next. Maria Theresa De Camp played the deaf mute, and her future husband, Charles Kemble, played St. Alme. Richard Wroughton, who played the salacious rascal Polycarp in *The Imposters*, and the errant Don Carlos in *A Bold Stroke for a Husband*, appeared as the malicious villain Darlemont. Jack Palmer, who was the trickster Singleton in *The Imposters*, became the shrewd and observant Pierre. Elizabeth Pope, who in *The Imposters* failed to fend off Polycarp's overtures, played the more sedately virtuous Madame Flanval. Genest observes that "Kemble was eminently qualified by nature to be the representative of de l'Épée, and his acting was inimitable."[45] Kemble, of course, had played the title role in Baillie's *De Monfort*, opposite Sarah Siddons as Jane De Monfort. And Barrymore, the Count Albert of *De Monfort*, is Franval in *Deaf and Dumb*.

In adapting Engel's work to contemporary practices on the English stage, Henry Siddons gave emphasis to the London stage, and the acting styles of John Philip Kemble and Sarah Siddons, replacing Engel's original attention to Friedrich Ludwig Schröder and August Wilhelm Iffland on the Berlin stage (see note 2 above). As a clue to unstated motives, hidden guilt, mental duress, and as a mode of expression in its own right, body language gained considerable attention from both actors and playwrights. In forwarding models for using body language to communicate moods and passions, Henry Siddons implicated more conflicting issues than he could master in his commentary. For one thing, body language both interprets and is influenced by cultural norms. Henry Siddons had to arbitrate between English and German examples. In advocating effective models, he also had to recognize the peculiar idiosyncrasies of individual style. Not every actress could imitate a pose of Sarah Siddons. A third conflict resided in the way in which the idiom of body language, as in any other language, evolves and changes. Major changes were already at work at the time of Henry Siddons' first edition of 1807, and even more by the time of his revised second edition of 1822. Yet these changes are largely ignored. Henry Siddons does not approve the simplified and radically stylized gestures of melodrama; nor does he, in his revised edition, acknowledge the differences in acting styles that occurred after the era of Kemble and Siddons had passed. Although Fanny Kemble could still win applause in striking a recognizable Siddons pose (for example, as Queen Katherine in *Henry VIII*), Madame Vestris brought an entirely new and different repertory of physical mannerisms to the stage, as did Edmund Kean, whose erratic style was totally at odds with the choreographed precision of John Philip Kemble. Because the criteria for emotional authenticity in physical movement had changed, it was also necessary for the new generation of players to find new strategies for telling lies with body language.

CHAPTER 5

Transvestites, lovers, monsters: character and sexuality

As introduced in earlier chapters, the optical metaphors of the periscope and "Pepper's Ghost" were intended to conjure the experience of being in the theatre and witnessing the characteristic doubleness of performance. With the homosexual critic John Waldie as one periscopic eye-witness and the homophobic William Hazlitt as another, the present chapter may require a bit more effort to filter out present-day attitudes and acknowledge those of the late eighteenth and early nineteenth century. The phenomena of superimposed reflected and refracted images are given yet another metaphorical application in terms of representation of gender norms and transgressions. Members of the audience, then as now, would presumably exercise a high degree of confidence in their ability to recognize on stage the characterizations of dubious or deviant sexuality. Most often it was an easy matter. Gothic villains were readily exposed as sexual predators. Theatrical representations of fops and dandies typically lacked the polish and sophistication that they most probably possessed in the real world and were to acquire on the stage only much later in the century. There were, nevertheless, moments of ambiguity in the construction or constriction of predatory or homoerotic desire. The reflected images might depict a familiar world in which word and gesture conformed to readily recognizable behavior in courtship, but these might be confounded with refracted images of the dark other side, in which the sexual codes were strange and undecipherable.

While Hannah Cowley, in *A Bold Stroke for a Husband* (Covent Garden, February 25, 1783), demonstrates the great ease with which one sex can mimic the other, Elizabeth Inchbald, in *The Widow's Vow* (Haymarket, June 20, 1786), presents the case that it may be impossible to detect whether a person is male or female. In *A Bold Stroke for a Husband*, Carlos, Victoria's wayward husband, has signed over the deed to her home to his mistress Laura. Determined to regain both her husband and her property, Victoria decides to disguise herself as a man and seduce the seductress. In Act II, she explains to her friend how she has performed her role as Don Florio. She has just received a letter from Laura:

VICTORIA. . . . a letter from Donna Laura, my husband's mistress, stiling me her dearest Florio! her life! her soul! and complaining of a twelve hours absence, as the bitterest misfortune.

OLIVIA. Ha, ha, ha! most doughty Don! pray let us see you in your feather and doublet; as a Cavaleiro, it seems, you are formidable. So suddenly to rob your husband of his charmer's heart! you must have us'd some witchery.

VICTORIA. Yes, powerful witchery – the knowledge of my sex. Oh! did the men but know us, as well as we do ourselves; – but thank fate they do not, 'twould be dangerous.

OLIVIA. What, I suppose, you prais'd her understanding, was captivated by her wit, and absolutely struck dumb by the amazing beauties of – *her mind*.

VICTORIA. Oh, no, – that's the mode prescribed by the *Essayists* on the female heart – ha, ha, ha! – Not a woman breathing, from fifteen to fifty, but would rather have a compliment to the tip of her ear, or the turn of her ancle, than a volume in praise of her intellects. (II.ii.7–29)[1]

When Olivia responds that flattery is the "boasted pill" that Victoria has used to drug Laura's sensibilities, Victoria is quick to explain that flattery is "only the occasional gilding." The audience does not see Victoria in her disguise as Don Florio until the beginning of Act IV, so this scene in Act II is a clever piece of anticipatory metatheatre.

With a keen observation of behavior and interaction between the sexes, women had an advantage over men as playwrights of domestic comedy, an advantage demonstrated quite practically in the plays of Hanna Cowley and Elizabeth Inchbald. As telling indication of such power of observation, Victoria proceeds to enact the moods and postures she employs as Don Florio. As a woman, she has acquired a thorough knowledge of what male actions entice and frustrate a female. She gives Olivia a brief sample of her repertory of masculine poses:

VICTORIA. . . . 'tis in vain to attempt a description of what changed its nature with every moment. I was now attentive – now gay – then tender – then careless. I strove rather to convince her that *I was charming*, than that I myself was charm'd; and when I saw love's arrow quivering in her heart, instead of falling at her feet, sung a triumphant air, and remember'd a sudden engagement.

OLIVIA.　　　[*Archly*] Would you have done so, had you been a man?
VICTORIA.　　Assuredly – knowing what I now do as a woman. (II.ii.30–42)

This anticipatory scene is played out while Victoria is still in female dress, not in her costume as cavalier. Even as Victoria assumes her masculine role as Lothario, Cowley has her insistently reassert her motives as a loyal wife:

VICTORIA.　　You, who know me, can judge how I suffered in prosecuting my plan. I have thrown off the delicacy of sex; I have worn the mask of love to the destroyer of my peace – but the object is too great to be abandoned – nothing less than to save my husband from ruin, and to restore him, again a lover, to my faithful bosom. (II.ii.77–83)

In Act IV, when Victoria arrives at Laura's apartment in her disguise as Don Florio, ready to follow through with her seduction of her husband's mistress, Cowley gives her a brief dramatic monologue in which Victoria again reasserts her motivation as a wife:

VICTORIA.　　Now must I, with a mind torn by anxieties, once more assume the lover of my husband's mistress – of the woman who has robb'd me of his heart, and his children of their fortune. Sure my task is hard. – Oh, love! Oh, *married* love assist me! If I can, by any art, obtain from her that fatal deed, I shall save my little ones from ruin – and then – But I hear her step – [*agitated, pressing her hand on her bosom*] – There! I have hid my griefs within my heart, and now for all the impudence of an accomplished cavalier! [*Sings an air – sets her hat in the glass – dances a few steps, &c. then runs to Laura, and seizes her hand*] (IV.i.30–40)

This little prelude concludes with a feminine gesture at the mirror adjusting her cavalier's hat. She is, of course, totally triumphant in deluding Laura. After Laura has torn up the deed to Victoria's property, Carlos comes crashing in ready to attack his presumed rival:

CARLOS.　　Where is this youth? Where is the blooming rival, for whom I have been betray'd? Hold me not, base woman! In vain the stripling flies me; for, by Heav'n, my sword shall in his bosom write its master's wrongs! (V.ii.132–6)

The pun, equating the sword with the pen, is for the reader's, not the auditor's, relish.[2] Carlos once again mistakes his wife's identity. In a stroll with his friend Julio on the Prado they meet with two ladies wearing veils. Julio goes off in one direction with the one, Olivia, and Carlos steps off with the other, only to come dashing back on stage, having discovered to his dismay that he has been "making love to my own wife!" (III.ii.190). Come for his revenge, he again mistakes her identity. The stage direction states that she first turns away from him, "*then returns, takes off her hat, and drops on one knee*":

VICTORIA.   Strike, strike it here! Plunge it deep into that bosom already
             wounded by a thousand stabs, keener and more painful than
             your sword can give. – Here lives all the gnawing anguish of
             love betray'd, here live the pangs of disappointed hopes,
             hopes sanctified by holiest vows, which have been written in
             the book of Heav'n. – Hah! he sinks. – [*She flies to him.*] –
             Oh! my Carlos! My belov'd! my husband! forgive my too
             severe reproaches; thou art dear, yet dear as ever, to
             Victoria's heart! (v.ii.137–46)

From start to finish, Victoria's cross-dressed role as Don Florio is characterized by a doubleness. Laura is fooled. Until Victoria doffs her cavalier's hat, even her husband mistakes her for a man. The audience, however, are constantly reminded of the woman in man's clothing.

Victoria explains that her original motive in disguising herself as Don Florio was not to seduce Laura but to learn the wiles by which the courtesan had ensnared her husband. If there were sexual tricks, she would learn them, "that I might, if possible, be to my Carlos, all he found in her" (II.ii.50–2). Laura, she discovers, has herself been wronged in love. As a courtesan Laura is driven by her desire for revenge to exploit and ruin her lovers. Carlos is only angry, she tells him, because she has rejected him before he rejected her:

LAURA.   I know your sex: the vainest female, in the hour of her exultation and
          power, is still out-done by man in vanity. – 'Tis more your ruling
          passion, than 'tis ours; and 'tis wounded *vanity* that makes you
          thus tremble with rage at being deserted . . . This rage would have
          been all cool insolence, had I waited for your change – the crime
          which now appears so black in me. Then, whilst, with all my sex's
          weakness, I had knelt at your feet, and reproached you only with
          my tears; how *composed* would have been your feelings. – Scarcely
          would you have deigned to form a phrase of pity for me; perhaps
          have bid me forget a man no longer worthy my attachment, and
          recommended me to hartshorn and my women. (ii.i.22–39)

In Don Florio she detects none of the masculine vanity that she has learned to manipulate to her own advantage. Precisely because she thought that she beheld in Don Florio her former innocence, she is roused to anger when she suspects that he too might betray her: "I feel myself on the brink of hatred; and, by all the agonies I have felt, should that passion be once rous'd –" (iv.i.22–4). Still in disguise, Victoria tells Laura that she pities her. Perceiving these words as Don Florio's rejection, Laura responds in fury: "Pity! Oh, villain! and has thy love already snatch'd the form of pity? Base, deceitful – " (v.ii.128–9).

Other than his observation that "Mrs. [Charles] Connor, as Donna Victoria, discovered in her male attire a very pretty figure," and that "her acting in some of the scenes was not without effect and pathos," Hazlitt had nothing to say about Victoria, Laura, and Carlos in his review of the performance at the Haymarket (July 19, 1817);[3] he gave his attention exclusively to the plot involving Olivia's suitors. Hazlitt quoted from the performance lines in which Olivia's maid, pretending to be Olivia, advised Don Julio "how to get rid of the inquiries of her mistress's father – 'Tell him you have been courting the maid – tell him you're the *baker*'" (iv.ii.278–9). The comic effect of these lines, Hazlitt declared, "will do us good for a month to come." Later in the review he referred again to "the interview with her mistress's lover from which we have extracted that inimitable apostrophe – 'Tell him you're the baker'." Hazlitt rightly singled out Mrs. Gibbs' performance as the maid pretending to be Donna Olivia, mentioning specifically how she "affected fine-lady airs, and the natural ebullutions of vulgarity." Mrs. Gibbs excelled in comic roles as the saucy maid and was praised as one of the few actresses who had mastered the art of laughing on stage.[4] The passage Hazlitt recorded, "Tell him you're the baker," was not in Cowley's play. In the original script, Cowley had the maid tell Don Julio, "you may say that you came on a visit to my maid, you know" (iv.iii.279). The line that heartily amused Hazlitt was added for the Haymarket performance.

Hazlitt also referred to Olivia, played by Mrs. Glover, ridding herself of another unwanted suitor, Don Vincentio, played by James Russell. Another of the "the best scenes," as singled out by Hazlitt, was Daniel Terry, as Don Caesar, "with his neighbour's pretty daughter Marcella, whom he does not at all like to marry, but of whom he grows very fond and over sweet upon her, after they have agreed only to make love in jest."[5] Beyond his comment on Mrs. Connor's "pretty figure" in her breeches part, Hazlitt ignored the ingenuity of Cowley's double plot and her multi-layered exploration of sexual attraction and the action.

Elizabeth Inchbald's comedy of gender errors, *The Widow's Vow* (Haymarket, June 20, 1786),[6] involves no cross-dressing: only the belief shared by most of the characters that a brother and sister have traded roles and disguised themselves as the opposite sex. As the servant Jerome explains, the Countess "was only fifteen" when "she fell deep in love with a fine handsome young fellow, inferior to her both in rank and fortune." Her father consented to the marriage, but then died of grief when his son-in-law turned out to be a bad husband. Unable to withstand his wife's hatred, the husband also died of grief (1.i.24–52). The widow then made a vow henceforth to avoid all members of the male sex. Her neighbor, Donna Isabella, promises to assist her brother, the Marquis, as a suitor to the wealthy and beautiful widow. She sends her maid Inis to tell the Countess that Isabella means to visit her dressed as a man. Inis gives this report of her mission:

INIS.   ... now, Madam, says I, I live servant with your neighbour, Donna Isabella, a flighty Lady, who turns every thing serious and sacred into ridicule; and she has resolved to make sport of you for pretending an aversion to men, and for that purpose she has procured recommendations for you to receive the visits of the young Marquis her brother, but instead of him, she purposes to come herself, disguised as a man, prevail on you to consent to be married to her, and then throw off the mask, and make you and your vow the jest of the whole kingdom. (1.ii.72–8)

Angered by her neighbor's rude ploy, the Countess agrees to the visit in order to expose Donna Isabella's presumption. The Countess's uncle, Don Antonio, and her servants are alerted to the cross-dressing masquerade of Donna Isabella disguised as the Marquis. The only one not informed that the Marquis is a woman in disguise is the Marquis himself. Isabella explains that her brother will better act his part if he acts naturally.

ISABELLA.   The Countess, from what you have told her, will suppose him a woman, receive him, and consequently suffer a thousand endearing familiarities; till, charmed by the graces of his mind and person, she shall love him without *knowing* it, and, when she detects the impostor, be unable to part with him.
INIS.   And if she is like me, she'll think it the happiest day of her life – but have you prepared your brother how to act his part?
ISABELLA.   He has nothing to *act*, being the very person he represents, and therefore shall not know of the art by which he is introduced – for, except being a little too attentive to dress and etiquette, a circumstance which, with his youthful appearance, favours our design, he is one of the most amiable young men in the world,

and the least idea of imposition would shock his honour, and put an end to my scheme.

INIS.   Then he is not to know he is to be taken for a woman.
ISABELLA.   Certainly not. (1.ii.98–111)

Before the Marquis arrives, the Countess's servants speculate on the boldness of a woman exposing her body in men's breeches. At a time when Dorothy Jordan drew crowds to see her perform in breeches as Rosalind in *As You Like It* (Drury Lane, 1787) or as Viola in *Twelfth Night*,[7] Inchbald has Flora, the Countess's maid, comment on the naughtiness of a woman thus revealing her leg and *derrière* in tight breeches.

FLORA.   But do you think, Jerome, she'll be drest all over like a man?
JEROME.   To be sure.
FLORA.   What, every thing?
JEROME.   Yes – Every thing – Egad, I long to have a peep at her!
FLORA.   Aye, and so would Antonio too, if he knew. –
JEROME.   Aye, that he would – he'd be so fond of the young Marquis there would be no keeping him away from her – but he does not know of it, you say?
FLORA.   No; no soul knows of it yet but my Lady and I, and now I have told it to you; and I am to tell it to all the servants as soon as she comes, that they may not think my Lady has broken her vow, by admitting a man – Lord, I wonder how I should look in men's clothes!
JEROME.   There's the Priest's old great cloak, doublet, and jack-boots hanging up behind that door, if you have a mind to try, and I'll step out of the way till you have put them on. [*A loud rapping at the door.*]
FLORA.   Here she is! Here she is! Oh dear, Oh dear – how ashamed I am for her. (1.ii.3–28)

The Countess's uncle is a lecherous old man who is, as Jerome says, "for ever running after all the maids" (1.i.79). Once Don Antonio is informed that the Marquis is a woman, he claims to have noticed "her" female gestures:

ANTONIO.   To be sure it is – and I'll be hang'd if it did not strike me to be a woman the moment I laid my eyes on her – for she came up to me slipping and sliding, and tossing her head, just as the fine ladies do. [*Mimicks.*] Well – But what do you intend to do? I know what I intend to do.
COUNTESS   I shall carry on the scheme, and pretend to be deceived, till I turn the joke she designs for me, on herself.
ANTONIO.   Yes; and I intend to have *my* joke too. (1.iii.148–54)

As the plot now unfolds, the Countess allows herself be seduced by a man whom she thinks is a woman, while her uncle begins to ogle, touch, and stroke the presumably disguised impostor. Growing increasingly incensed at Don Antonio's advances, the Marquis at last draws his sword, and the uncle retreats, totally intimidated by this Joan of Arc. Thinking that she can force Isabella to confess her disguise, the Countess declares herself ready to marry the Marquis and calls for the priest. At this moment Donna Isabella arrives wearing a veil. Convinced that the Marquis is Isabella, the Countess and Don Antonio readily assume that her brother has dressed as a woman. In a rapid dénouement, the man is revealed as a man, the woman as a woman.

COUNTESS.   Has the Marquis more sisters than one?
MARQUIS.   No.
ANTONIO.   Then this, I suppose, is your brother?
JEROME.   Aye, in women's clothes – O dear, another fine sight!
COUNTESS.   Oh Heavens, if it is a man, take him out of the room or I shall
             faint.
MARQUIS.   Sister Isabella, when I shall relate to you the strange reception
             I have met with in this house, you will be amazed – but I
             think you will sincerely rejoice at the final event of my visit,
             when I tell you it is a solemn promise from this Lady to
             become my wife.
ISABELLA.   I give you joy most unfeignedly. [*Pulls off her veil.*]
COUNTESS.   It is a woman.
ANTONIO.   Aye, that it is – Madam, let me bid you welcome to the castle.
             [*Goes and salutes her.*]
COUNTESS.   [*To the Marquis.*] Why, what are you – [*After trembling as if much
             terrified.*]
             an't *you* a woman?
ISABELLA.   Countess, I knew you never would have consented to have seen
             the Marquis, had he been introduced into the house as a
             man, therefore I formed this stratagem, unknown to him,
             thus to bring you together.
MARQUIS.   [*To the Countess.*] Do not droop, my dearest wife.
COUNTESS.   And are you really the Marquis? What a strange blunder have I
             made!
MARQUIS.   I am the Marquis – and it shall be my future care to banish
             for ever from your memory, the recollection of that
             marriage which has been the source of so much woe to you.
             (11.ii.220–40).

John Waldie saw *The Widow's Vow* performed at Plymouth (July 30, 1806). This theatre was under the management of Percival Farren, eldest son of the more renowned actor, William Farren, and of special interest to Waldie because his Edinburgh friend and singing-partner Mary Perry had married Farren when both were performing at Hereford.[8] According to Waldie, Farren "acts with great spirit" and plays the Marquis as "a very genteel figure." The two female servants, Inis and Flora, were performed "very well indeed" by Miss Weston and Miss Wentworth. Waldie was especially impressed by Mr. Barnes, who played the lecherous old uncle "with great humour." Unfortunately the crucial role of the widow was given a "most execrable" interpretation by Miss Hague, who had been hired to dance in the ballet but who apparently had no notion how to perform the sexual play between herself and the man whom she thinks is a woman.[9]

By the very fact that Inchbald does *not* use cross-dressing, but only pretends to, she is able to steer the actions of the Countess and Don Antonio much closer to the forbidden boundaries of homosexual touch than most plays of the period. Waldie next saw the play twelve years later, not in Inchbald's adaptation, but in her French source, Joseph Patrat's *L'heureuse erreur* (1783).[10] In this version, as performed in Paris at the Théâtre Français (November 17, 1818), the Countess, performed by Mlle. Levert, was much more responsive. "Hating men," she "is taken in and made to suppose her lover is a woman who is only playing on her – she finds the love so agreeable as to wish it was real – and so it becomes." She undergoes, as it were, a conversion, then, with the revelation that her suitor is indeed a man – a second conversion. Like Mlle. Levert, who "was truth and nature itself" as the Countess, Fermin played the Marquis with corresponding naïve innocence.[11] The play was popular in France, for six months later Waldie reports seeing it yet again at the Grand Théâtre in Bordeaux (April 13, 1819).[12]

Another play of presumed, rather than actual, cross-dressing was *The Secret*, performed on the British stage in adaptations by William Thomas Moncrieff (Adelphi, 29 February 1824 and William Barrymore (Adelphi, May 11, 1824). Waldie knew this play, too, from the original French: François Benoît Hoffmann's *Le secret* (Théâtre de l'Opéra-Comique, April 20, 1796). He saw it first in Amsterdam at the French Comic Opera in 1802. Dupuis helps his friend Valare escape prosecution following a duel. When he hides Valare in his house, Madame Dupuis thinks her husband has smuggled in his mistress disguised as a man. In the opening scene, in which she interrogates a servant, she immediately decides the gender of the unseen stranger must be female. The husband was played by M. de la Forgue, whom Waldie praised for his affable nonchalance in response to his wife's accusations. Remarking the facile way in which gender is mentally constructed, Waldie confesses that he "was highly entertained by the causeless jealousy of Madame Dupuis." The role was "admirably performed by Madame Kuntz, whom I never saw equalled for spirit and propriety of action, both in singing and speaking."[13] In Newcastle, eighteen years later, Waldie saw the English version by Moncrieff, *The Secret; or, The Hole in the Wall*. On this occasion, John Carter and Elizabeth Blanchard played Monsieur and Madame Dupuis, and Samuel Butler played the servant Thomas. Waldie comments on the rising intrigue as Angelica helps her lover Valare hide his belongings in Dupuis's chamber, while the wife and servant spy on them, mistaking first one then the other for Dupuis's mistress (26 January 1821; 47:374).[14]

Restoration comedy frequently employed a pair of street-wise rogues of London to dupe naïve gentry or nobility visiting from the country. Among such perennially popular scoundrels were Archer and Aimwell in George Farquhar's *The Beaux' Stratagem* (Haymarket, March 8, 1707), Dick Amlet and Brass in John Vanbrugh's *Confederacy* (Haymarket, October 30, 1705), and Wheadle and Palmer in George Etherege's *Comical Revenge; or, Love in a Tub* (Lincoln's Inn Fields, 1664). Rascals of the lower class duped their upper-class victims by the expediency of role-playing, pretending to be aristocrats themselves. In *The Town Before You* (Covent Garden, December 6, 1794), Hannah Cowley recreates these staple characters in Tippy and Fancourt, but she restores moral order through a strong affirmation of feminine rectitude. The swindling scams of the men are exposed by the two women whom they have exploited and abused – Tippy's sister and the woman Fancourt has tricked into thinking she is his lawful wife.

Tippy's resemblance to Lord Beechgrove enables him to pass himself off as the Lord. Fancourt introduces him to Sir Robert as such, and the two swindle Sir Robert out of £1,000. The play has two plots: one concerning Sir Robert, his daughter Georgina, and her suitor Conway; another involving Lady Horatia and her admirer Asgill, whose fortunes fail with the bankruptcy of his uncle. Lady Horatia is a sculptor for whom Georgina models. Connections between the two plots are furthered by the scheme of Tippy and Fancourt to arrange a marriage between Georgina and the fraudulent Lord. Fancourt's wife overhears their plan, and, disguised as a fortune-teller, informs Georgina of the false Lord Beechgrove. Needing a different disguise in order to return to Sir Robert's house, Tippy puts on his landlady's gown and becomes "Miss Sally Martin." Angered by her betrayal, Fancourt informs his wife that they are not legally married because the ceremony was performed by Tippy in the disguise of a parson. Mrs. Fancourt is offered shelter by Georgina in her father's house. Similarly, Tippy's sister Jenny exposes his fraud to Sir Robert. Asgill sacrifices his modest wealth in attempting to aid his bankrupt uncle, Sir Simon Asgill, who had only pretended bankruptcy to test his nephew. Lady Horatio learns of Asgill's sacrifice and repents that she has treated him coldly.

Arguing that in order to practice his art of deception he may well have to dress as a woman, Tippy anticipates cross-dressing with ardent relish. Cowley has him establish heroic masculine models for dressing himself as a woman:

TIPPY.   A plan ... sometimes forces me to take shelter, like Hercules, under the disguise of a petticoat. Yes, like him, I exchange my club for a distaff, or like Achilles, transform my surtout to a gauze robe, and my waistcoat to a lace tucker.[15]

Cowley would have found precedence in describing a man's attraction to wearing female garments in Aphra Behn's *The Amorous Prince* (Duke of York's Theatre, February, 1671). Cloris, who has been seduced by Prince Frederick, dresses as a boy so she can travel without being accosted. She is accompanied by a country lad, Guilliam, who eagerly offers to dress as a lass so that they might travel together as a couple. Guilliam fondly recalls how Cloris had dressed him as a "handsom lass" at carnival, where he "simper'd and tript," exciting the amorous attentions of the shepherd Claud. Cloris warns him that such behaviour might be more dangerous at court.[16]

At the opening of Act v of *The Town Before You*, Tippy receives a letter from his "artful sister" Jenny, advising once again to play his female role: "wear the same disguise, and come as Miss Sally Martin." Momentarily baffled because he is without the assistance of "my landlady's maid, who used to lend me that smart dress," he finds that the landlady's gown and bonnet serve the purpose just as well. He is especially pleased that the gown fits him perfectly (v.i.20–8). Once he is inside Sir Robert's household his only stratagem is to abduct Georgina. His sister tells him "to get her *any way* into your power – once get her to your lodgings, and a marriage *must* follow" (v.iii.21–2).

In the penultimate scene of Act v, Sir Robert is baffled by the many deceptions aligned against him:

SIR ROBERT.   Why, what a town this is! A stranger, like me, should go about in leading-strings. Plotters, deceivers in every corner of it. Whether the people one associates with, are what they appear to be, or whether it may not be all one universal masquerade, there is no guessing. (v.vi.1–5)

The deceivers have now invaded his home. Jenny introduces Tippy to Georgina as a lady who "ran into the hall to avoid some gentlemen who were rude to you." Tippy confirms the story, adding that "a modest woman can hardly walk the streets, men are so impertinent." Starting to bow, Tippy catches himself and curtsies. When he trips over his petticoats, he sees that Georgina is not fooled by the disguise. He drops to his knees and declares that he was motivated only by his love for her:

> TIPPY.   Madam I scorn to impose on you – no, Madam, I have a soul above
>   it – I am *not* a lady. I put on this disguise to procure admission
>   here, that I might tell you how I adore you. Madam [*kneeling.*]
>   my passion for you is so great, that if you do not look on
>   me with pity – if you do not listen to me with compassion –
>   (v.vi.43–6)

At this moment, Sir Robert enters with Fancourt; Tippy tries to resume his female identity, but cannot sustain the subterfuge. Georgina recollects what the fortune-teller has revealed to her about the two men plotting against her and her father. Both sharpers are exposed and summarily dismissed:

> SIR ROBERT.   And now, gentlemen, leave my house this moment, or the next
>   you shall be returned into the hands of the constables.
>   (v.vi.123–4)

The restoration of moral order, as Cowley knows, is only a theatrical convenience. The crooks are still free to practice their trade in the streets and in other plays:

> FANCOURT.   We *will* turn out upon the world; so let the world beware! Come,
>   Tippy, the field before us is a wide one – let us erect our
>   banners! *Talents* are our armed forces, with which we
>   encounter Vanity and Folly. Wherever *they* appear, we
>   wage war. Allons! [*to Tippy.*] Be of good heart, my boy!
>   The foe is numerous, but weak. Conquest and pillage are
>   our own! (v.vi.125–30)

Even Sir Robert seems content with this prospect for the future:

> SIR ROBERT.   [*looking after them.*] I am glad you are off! These gentlemen
>   have given me some amusement, together with some
>   experience, and it has cost me only one thousand pounds –
>   a cheap bargain. (v.vi.131–3)

The final scene promises a double marriage to end the comedy: Asgill has his Lady Horatia; Conway his Georgina. John Genest speculated that "Mrs. Cowley would probably have been better pleased, if the applause, which was deservedly bestowed on Tippy, had been given to Asgill, for his romantic conduct and ostentatious display of patriotism."[17] Genest is right, of course, that Cowley has given Asgill the last words, a nationalist tribute to English sailors and English rule. But it is also true that she entertained her audience with more elaborate antics of the transvestite male con artist than were customary on the stage of her period.

Several of W. C. Oulton's farces and comedies make use of cross-dressing and gender confusion.[18] He created great fun out of pairing transvestite females with transvestite males, or exposing them to same-sex overtures and the misperceptions of the "opposite" sex. In Oulton's *The Sleep-walker; or, Which is the Lady?* (Haymarket, June 15, 1812),[19] the question in the play's alternative title refers to confusion over the sexual identity of Sir Patrick Maguire, who is strikingly effeminate, and his bride Sophia, who has disguised herself as a young Irishman. Sir Patrick was played by Richard Jones, Sophia by Mrs. Dalton. Popularly known as "Gentleman Jones" because of his fine manners and gestures, Jones had played such roles as Gossamer in Frederic Reynolds' *Laugh When You Can*, deliberately styling his performances after William Thomas Lewis. When Lewis retired from the stage in 1809, Jones misjudged his own talents in attempting to assume parts that had been the mainstay of Lewis' career: Jeremy Diddler in James Kenney's *Raising the Wind*, and the Copper Captain in the Beaumont and Fletcher comedy, *Rule a Wife, Have a Wife*. Jones succeeded much better when he had occasion to allow his inclination to dandyism to flower.

Jones' performance as Sir Patrick Maguire gave him precisely this sort of opportunity. Because of his long experience at the Crow Street Theatre in Dublin, and throughout Ireland, from 1799 to 1807, Jones acquired great skill as a stage Irishman. His Sir Patrick was an effeminate dandy with an Irish brogue. At the play's opening, Sir Patrick has run away with Sophia, the god-daughter of Mrs. Decorum, played by Mrs. Grove. When Sir Patrick, a young Irishman, and Sophia, pretending to be a young Irishman, stay at inn, the landlord is suspicious of their behavior. The twist in Oulton's plot is that Sir Patrick, who is *not* cross-dressed, is the one identified as a woman.

By means of some jewels that Sophia has left as surety, Mrs. Decorum is able to trace her eloping god-daughter. Upon arriving at the inn, she has her nephew, Squire Rattlepate, present Sophia with a message requesting a private interview. Rattlepate mistakes Sir Patrick for Sophia in disguise. In response to the message, Sir Patrick meets with Mrs. Decorum. She, too, takes him for Sophia, whom she had not seen since her christening. The hour is late, so she offers to share her bed with her presumed goddaughter, Sir Patrick. The nocturnal events are the crux of this farce, but to redirect audience attention away from the consequences of the mistaken identities, Oulton turns the stage over to another bedroom scene, in which Somno, Sir Patrick's servant, begins to stir in his sleep, fancying himself acting upon the stage. Somno was played by Charles Mathews, and the sleep-walking episode was occasion for Mathews' comic routine as mimic. According to John Waldie's eye-witness account, the sleep-walker dreams successively that he is John Philip Kemble, Joseph Shepherd Munden, George Frederick Cooke, Charles Incledon, Samuel Simmons, William Blanchard, John Fawcett, and Richard Suett. Not just his impersonations, but also his sleep-walking and sleep-dancing were hilarious.[20] On the following morning, Mrs. Decorum becomes aware that she was mistaken in her choice of bed-partner for the night. Sophia assures Mrs. Decorum that she will henceforth resume her proper feminine dress, and Sir Patrick makes a point of asserting himself with more masculinity.

After seeing *The Sleep-walker* performed at Covent Garden on June 24, Waldie saw it again sixteen days later in Stamford. The evening programme included both Reynolds' *Laugh When You Can* and Oulton's *The Sleep-walker*, and John Carter played both the roles – Gossamer and Sir Patrick – that Jones had been playing in London. Like Jones, Carter too was under the spell of Lewis in performing Gossamer. Waldie declared that he was "very genteel, elegant, spirited, & unaffected, with something of old Lewis' sprightliness – well suited to the antics of Reynolds' comedy." For his role in Oulton's farce, Waldie added that Carter played Sir Patrick "very finely" with the appropriate modest delicacy.[21]

There is a difference between cross-dressing as a strategy essential to the plot and cross-dressing as an incidental titillation (female as male) or laugh-getter (male as female). In *Love in the East* (Drury Lane, February 25, 1788), a comic opera by James Cobb with music arranged by Thomas Linley, the cross-dressing is a necessity for a young widow who, following an unhappy marriage, has arrived in a military post in Calcutta in search of her true love, Stanmore, played by Charles Dignum. The post is under the command of the lecherous Colonel Batton, played by Robert Baddeley. Eliza, played by Jane Pope, is uncertain whether Stanmore still loves her.

ELIZA. You must know that, in order to conceal myself from my lover the more effectually, I have assumed this disguise, and am at present Alexander M Proteus, at your service.[22]

Eliza manages to avoid entanglements that would expose her, and the lovers find each other in Act III. Another romance in which cross-dressing is the expedient to bring the lovers together is William Dunlap's *Wild-Goose Chase* (Drury Lane, February 1, 1800). In this comedy, adapted from August von Kotzebue, it is the man who disguises himself as a woman. Playing the role of a wronged woman, Frederick gains access to the house of Madame Von Brumbach and then elopes with her daughter, Nanette.

Even when plot and situation did not command the introduction of cross-dressed characters, they were often introduced merely for popular appeal. Just as a female player in tight pants was sure to win the attention of the male members of the audience, a male player wearing a dress was a sure and easy way of gaining a round of laughter. Edward Fitzball's *The Flying Dutchman* (Adelphi, January 1, 1827) has already been described in Chapter 3. No necessity of Fitzball's plot required that Peter von Bummel, played by James Reeve, should emerge from hiding prettily dressed as a shepherdess, in a pink and white gown, with a laced stomacher and a large straw hat. Although only a brief and incidental comic interlude, Fitzball made it anticipate the abduction scene that immediately follows. Peter wears the dress of the dead pirate's bride that has been stored a century in his trunk: the dress that his bride wears in the portrait that hangs on the wall above the trunk, the dress that is identical to that worn by Lestelle Vanhelm, whom the dead pirate intends to keep in his lair beneath the sea. Peter, who thought by means of his shepherdess disguise to escape the rough crew of sailors pursuing him, has naïvely misjudged his predicament. His attempt at flirtatious charm only provokes their leader to reach under the petticoats:

PETER. Oh! Gentlemen of the jury, pity and protect a lovely young creter, who has been set on by ruffians, and compelled to screen her innocence in that cave – I think I had better be off. [*Escapes, but is caught and brought back.*]

PETER. Conduct me to the nearest vessel, if you please; I'm England bound. [*Aside.*]
I wish they were bound neck and heels together. Pity me, sweet gentlemen, good-looking, fair-complexioned gentlemen. I'm only a poor trembling, palpitating little damsel.

SMUTTA.   Is, missy, me pity you ver much – you got dam a large leg, missy;
           fine calf undem petticoats – eh! [*Catching at the petticoat a
           little, and laughing.*] Ha, ha! how funny!
PETER.   O fie! where's your manners? talk of a lady's calves – you might as
           well talk of – bag my books, if this isn't worser than – I'm in
           such a flutter – don't you see I'm going to faint – I – oh!
SMUTTA.   You go with us, massa – you big rogue – Smutta him know all about.
           Come, massa – come!
PETER.   If I do – I'll – I tell ye I'm a gentlewoman, lonely, virtuous, and in
           want! Don't believe, eh? Well, then, I'll show ye a gentle-
           woman's trick for once. [*Snatches a cudgel.*] There! there!
           there![23]

Having beaten off his captors, Peter holds up his dress, and runs across
the stage. In the next scene, the audience sees the heroine of the play,
wearing the identical costume, being carried by the ghostly pirate into his
ocean cave.

As a legacy of Elizabethan drama, in which all female roles were played by
young men, shifts in sexual identity remained a part of character exposition
throughout the following centuries. Cross-dressed characters coexisted with
the representations of effeminate males and masculine females. The fops
and dandies, commonplace in Restoration and eighteenth-century comedies,[24] came under new scrutiny with the cult of society fashion and
mannerisms instigated by George Bryan "Beau" Brummell.[25] The stage
dandy, as modeled after Brummell throughout the Regency period, was a
figure who not only stepped daintily across gender boundaries with pretty
clothes and effeminate gestures, but also across class boundaries. To dress
the part and assume the manners of upper-class refinement was all that was
necessary to move in the highest social circles. Although Brummell set the
trend, the stage dandy had attained that social mobility several decades
earlier. As an early example Susan Staves has pointed to the character Flutter
in Hannah Cowley's *The Belle's Stratagem* (Covent Garden, February 22,
1780). Flutter well illustrated the ease with which the fop could cross the
boundaries of rank and class, as well as gender.[26] In his conversation with
Miss Ogle and Mrs. Rackit, Sir George grumbles that decorum and propriety are out of fashion. Society has become "a mere chaos, in which all
distinction of rank is lost in the same select party; you will often find the
wife of a bishop and a sharper, an earl and a fidler; in short 'tis one universal
masquerade, all disguis'd in the same habit and manners!" At this moment
Flutter enters, and Sir George has his proof. "Now I defy you to tell from his
appearance," he says to Miss Ogle, "whether Flutter is a privy counsellor or a
mercer, a lawyer, or a grocer's 'prentice."[27]

Surveying the dramatic functions of cross-dressing – male as female, the more frequent female as male – reveals only part of the trans-sexual mobility in the theatre. Without changing from a woman's dress, an actress might well assert a strong masculine character. In her role as Lady Macbeth, Sarah Siddons made her audience shudder when she called upon the spirits to "unsex" her, to "come to my woman's breasts, / And take my milk for gall" (*Macbeth*, I.v.41–9). An entirely different category of cross-dressing was the instance of a woman playing a man's part. Siddons was the first woman in the history of the stage to play Hamlet, thus introducing a tradition still followed by Sarah Bernhardt at the close of the nineteenth century.[28] Genest notes that when Siddons played Hamlet in Bristol (July 27, 1781) it was the sixth time that she had performed the role.[29] She continued to play the role for thirty years. Known for her dignity, for her rich and resonant voice, Siddons gave an interpretation of the role that complemented that of her brother. She avoided lending the role any of the boyish or effeminate characteristics adopted by the subsequent generation of actors. In 1805 the thirteen-year-old Master Betty added the role of Hamlet to his novelty performances.

After having played Mistress Quickly, hostess of the Boar's Head Tavern, Mrs. Webb decided to take on the role of the most raucous patron of the Boar's Head, Sir John Falstaff. As I noted in the introduction, Mrs. Webb performed Falstaff in *Henry IV*, Part 1 (Haymarket, July 21, 1786). At an earlier performance in 1784, one critic, outraged that Sir John's dignity had been compromised, found her impersonation a "vile and beastly" transformation that "indelicacy seldom parallels." He granted that Mrs. Webb exhibited herself in the appropriate costume of Falstaff, and even sustained the character word for word throughout the first part of *Henry IV*, but he nevertheless concluded that her sole qualification for the role was obesity.[30] It cannot be claimed that, like Siddons as Hamlet, Mrs. Webb launched a tradition of female Falstaffs, but the role has been repeated by capable actresses, recently by Pat Carroll at the Folger Shakespeare Theatre in Washington in May, 1990. Carroll's performance was praised for investigating the character, "rather than merely as ideological window dressing for a gimmicky production."[31] Mrs. Webb deserved similar credit, for she took on the more challenging role of Falstaff in *Henry IV*; Carroll played the Falstaff of *The Merry Wives of Windsor*, a character who, William Hazlitt declared, was "not the man he was in the two parts of *Henry IV*."[32] Indeed, it was the later Falstaff who compromised his own dignity by hiding in a basket of dirty linen, being dumped into a muddy ditch (III.iii), disguising himself in woman's clothing as Mother Prat (iv.ii), and wearing horns and being tormented with burning tapers (v.v).

A norm of sexual character in dramatic performance is subject to the same approval or disapproval as the norms that regulate social behavior. Indeed, the audience is always a ready arbiter of those norms. Even though a stage romance is no more than a parody of real-life courtship, and the characters often no more than caricatures, yet even they gain their attraction, appeal, and approval because of their recognizable familiarity and their adherence to social norms. Two of the most popular comedies of the period were Thomas Holcroft's *The Road to Ruin* (Covent Garden, February 18, 1792) and James Kenney's *Raising the Wind* (Covent Garden, November 5, 1803). Both plays present the dilemma of marrying for love versus marrying for money: dilemma rather than choice because the young men in both plays are under the duress of financial desperation.

The Road to Ruin is a tale of love, lust, and sculduggery, contrasting youth and age, wealth and poverty, wanton waste and dire need. It is also a tale of social and moral values. The play opens with an exasperated father, the banker Dornton, fretting over the latest exploits of his extravagant son. Harry Dornton returns from Newmarket with a gambling debt of £10,000 (multiply by 92.7 to calculate the amount in current purchasing power).[33] Needless to say, the waste of so huge a sum must have made everyone in the audience, whether merchant or gentry, side with the parent against the improvident son. Equally irresponsible, Harry Dornton's companion, Milford, has squandered a £5,000 inheritance and run up a debt of another £5,000. Holcroft set himself the task as playwright of converting antipathy into sympathy, and he accomplished it primarily by repeated demonstrations of the powerful bond of love between father and son, but also through repeated instances of young Harry's selfless generosity.

Harry's sexual character is defined by his moral integrity and respect for the woman he loves, Sophia Freelove. Sophia's sexual character, in spite of her impetuosity as a seventeen-year-old, is tempered by her respect for her grandmother's advice, which, to be sure, she sometimes finds difficult to follow. "My grandma' has told me a hundred times, it's a sin for any body to be in love before they be a woman grown, full one-and-twenty; and I am not eighteen." She is troubled by the thought that she must wait more than three years and nine months to entertain Harry's interest in her. Even offering a valentine greeting is taboo, because "My grandma' told me I must never mention nor think of such things till I am a woman, full one-and-twenty grown," especially "if I were to find such a thing at my window, or under my pillow, or concealed in a plum-cake." Should such overtures be forthcoming, she tells Harry that he must be willing to wait:

SOPHIA.   Why first he must love me very dearly! – With all his heart and
          soul! – And then he must be willing to wait till I am one-and-
          twenty.
HARRY.   And would not you love in return?
SOPHIA.   N – yes, when I come to be one-and-twenty.
HARRY.   Not sooner?
SOPHIA.   Oh no! – I must not!
HARRY.   Surely you might if you pleased?
SOPHIA.   Oh but you must not persuade me to that! If you do I shall think you
          are a bad man, such as my grandma' warned me of!
HARRY.   And do you think me so?
SOPHIA.   Do I? – No! – I would not think you so for a thousand thousand
          golden guineas!
HARRY.   [*Aside.*] Fascinating purity! – What am I about? To deceive or trifle
          with such unsuspecting affection would indeed be villainy![34]

Raised by her grandmother in Gloucestershire, Sophia now lives in the city with her mother, and her mother's advice, she quickly realizes, would not serve her well at all. The Widow Warren, who dresses herself "like a girl," will not permit her daughter to dress as a woman:

SOPHIA.   . . . she won't let me wear high-heeled shoes! I am sure I am old
          enough! I shall be eighteen next Christmas day at midnight,
          which is only nine months and two days! And since she likes to
          wear slips, and sashes, and ringlets and – nonsense, like a girl,
          why should not I have high heels, and gowns, and sestinis, and
          hoops, and trains, and sweeps [*Mimicking.*] and – like a
          woman? (11.ii.24–8)

The Widow Warren, whose sexual character is driven exclusively by selfish concern for her own pleasures, considers her beautiful young daughter an unwanted rival. Whenever Harry calls, the Widow dismisses her daughter so that she may have him to herself.

Hazlitt, in his *Memoirs of the late Thomas Holcroft* (1816), observed that *The Road to Ruin* moved with a "bustle of the scene," and a "rapidity with which events follow one another." "The wonder seems to be," Hazlitt wrote, "how so many incidents, so regularly connected, and so clearly explained, can be brought together in so small a compass." Neither "the hurry of events" nor "the intricacy of the plot," impede the effective "unfolding of the characters, or the forcible expression of the passions."

Not usually inclined to mistake artifice for nature, Hazlitt declared that "the scenes are replete with the truest pathos, which is expressed without exaggeration, or the least appearance of art," and that the characters expressed themselves "in language so easy and natural, that not only might it be uttered by the persons themselves, but they could scarcely use any other."[35] Neither the characters nor their language can be considered "natural," if that word means "true to life." If Hazlitt meant, however, that the characters speak in a language appropriate to them as characters in a comedy, then they are indeed most thoroughly "natural."

Hazlitt gave special attention to the language of Goldfinch, the character who, as Hazlitt rightly said, "contributed most to the popularity of the piece":

[His] language consists entirely of a few cant words; yet the rapidity with which he glances from object to object, and the evident delight which he takes in introducing his favourite phrases on all occasions, have all the effect of the most brilliant wit. That's your sort comes in at least fifty times, and is just as unexpected and lively the last time as the first, for no other reason than because Goldfinch has just the same pleasure in repeating it.[36]

By Hazlitt's estimation, nine persons out of ten who went to see *The Road to Ruin* went for the sake of seeing Goldfinch. When Goldfinch first appears in Act II, he is announced by Sophia as "that great, ridiculous, horse jockey oaf Goldfinch." His language is nothing more than a recitation of slang and catch-phrases of the race-track and stables. He is an inveterate gambler, "in the heigh-day of youth and thoughtlessness, and who is hurried away by all the vulgar dissipation of fashionable life." Goldfinch serves as an example of what Harry or Milford may soon become. Harry himself recognizes this when he tells Goldfinch: "[the world] says you have got into the hands of jockeys, Jews, and swindlers; and that, though old Goldfinch was in his day one of the richest men on 'Change, his son will shortly become poorer than the poorest black leg at New-market." With a moment's reflection, Harry adds: "damn the world, for it says little better of me" (II.i.421–5).

As the central character of the play, Harry is tested in terms of his relationship to each of the other characters: his love and loyalty to his father, who is worried that his son has fallen into evil ways; his friendship to Milford, whose financial crisis resembles his own; his determination to break from the gambling that is Goldfinch's only purpose; his love for Sophia, whose innocence he is determined to protect; his willingness to forsake Sophia and marry the amorous Widow in order to rescue his father from bankruptcy. The welfare of Milford and Sophia is threatened by an unscrupulous plot. In his summary, Hazlitt untangles the confusion of names that resulted in the will of Widow Warren's late husband falling into the hands of Mr. Silky, a character of "smooth, sleek, fawning knavery," instead of the intended recipient, Mr. Sulky, an honest executor and bank partner of the elder Dornton:

the late Mr. Warren, not being well pleased with the conduct of his wife, and suspecting her violent professions of a determination not to marry again, had made a will, in which, in case such an event should happen, he had left his property to his natural son, Milford, and to his wife's daughter, appointing Mr. Sulky his executor. He died abroad; and the person who brought over the will, being deceived by the name, leaves it in the possession of Mr. Silky, instead of Mr. Sulky. Mr. Silky, knowing the widow's amorous propensities, and willing to profit by them, informs Goldfinch, who is besieging her for her money, that he has a deed in his possession which puts the widow's fortune, should she marry again, entirely in his power; and exacts a promise from him of fifty thousand pounds out of a hundred and fifty, as the price of secrecy, with respect to himself. He then calls on the widow, shews her the conditions of the will, and threatens to make it public unless she marries Goldfinch, and assents to his proposal. She, however, governed by her passion for young Dornton, and relying on the exhaustless wealth of his family, sets Mr. Silky and his secret at defiance; and on his next visit, treats Mr. Goldfinch with very little ceremony. But after she finds herself disappointed of Dornton, and is in the height of her exclamations against the whole sex, Goldfinch is announced. His name at this moment has the effect of suddenly calming her spirits; he is admitted; received with much affected modesty: he makes another offer; the bargain is struck; Mr. Silky is sent for, and Goldfinch sets off post haste for a license. But just as he is going out, he meets Milford; and being more fool than knave, he tells the latter of his marriage, and of the hush-money to Silky, on account of some deed, by which he has the widow's fortune at his command, though he does not know how. This excites suspicion in the mind of Milford, who, supposing it must be his father's will, goes immediately to Sulky to inform him of the circumstance, and they conceal themselves in the widow's apartment. Goldfinch, Silky, and the widow, soon after come in; every thing is settled; and the will is on the point of being committed to the flames, when Milford and Sulky burst upon them, and their whole scheme is unluckily defeated.[37]

At its opening performance, Dornton was played by Munden, Harry by Holman, Sulky by Wilson, Silky by Quick, Goldfinch by Lewis, Milford by Harley, Widow Warren by Mrs. Mattocks, and Sophia by Mrs. Merry.

Eleven years later, Waldie was able to see a performance at Covent Garden with three of the principal players of the original cast. Waldie notes that he was fortunate to find good places in the pit, as the theatre "was immensely full in every part." Goldfinch was played by Lewis, who had made the role very much his own, and was "more comical, spirited, & entertaining" than any other actor could hope to be. Munden was again Old Dornton, "at once ludicrous & affecting: the play of his features was the more effective, as he avoided the buffoonery he sometimes gives way to in farces." Mrs. Mattocks, as the lusty Widow Warren, presented a "complete & irresistibly laughable portrait of an old coquette." Disappointed in Mrs. Mills as Sophia, Waldie granted that she possessed "some spirit in her acting." The problem was that "she does not enter into the character," or, rather, that she kept falling out, so that "when she ought to cry & be miserable, she could not refrain from laughing, which quite spoiled the effect of the scene." How different is her hoyden, Waldie declared, "from the charming & bewitching humor of Mrs. Jordan's romps." Dorothy Jordan, at this very time, was performing as Sophia (Drury Lane, June 6, 1803). "Emery looked very well in the character of Silky, but his voice & action too often betrayed his youth." Sulky, whose one reiterated line in every dialogue is a disgruntled "Humph," ought to have been played with more sedate restraint, and Davenport "replied too fast for so sober a character." Brunton "displayed both feeling & animation in Harry Dornton – he seemed to enter into it completely." Brunton might become a very good actor, Waldie advised, if he could exercise more discrimination in identifying the poignant and passionate moments. He tended to be "too animated on trifling occasions."[38] (8 June 1803; 8:83–5).

Six years later, Waldie again commented on a performance of *The Road to Ruin*. On this occasion, William Augustus Conway, whose career Waldie had been supporting, was playing at the Theatre Royal in Newcastle. As the sly villain Silky, John Grove was "inimitable," especially when he coerces the Widow to surrender to him one-third of her late husband's wealth (III.i.100–234), and when he refuses to help Harry ward off a financial crisis (III.iii.613–713). Miss Simpson (no relation to Elizabeth Inchbald, née Simpson) "was too violent in Sophia," playing her role as if it were a tragedy.

Conway in Harry was really pleasing – he was not equal in every scene, but his mirth & gaiety were natural – & his transitions when convinced of the fatal effect of his folly was admirable – but his finest scene was that with Silky – it was inimitable – it was impossible not to feel every point. I was delighted, and all the audience also.[39]

Waldie had been meeting frequently with Conway, and he shared with Conway his advice and criticism on his performances.

James Kenney's first play, *Raising the Wind*, owed its success to the popularity of the character Jeremy Diddler. As a rogue and scoundrel, Diddler is a contrast with Harry, whose only fault is his careless gambling. The sexual attraction that Sophia feels for Harry is tempered by her refusal to "do amiss." She will not engage in the act of love, even though she feels love.

HARRY.   Love they say cannot be resisted.
SOPHIA.   Ah, but I have been taught better! – It may be resisted – Nobody
          need be in love unless they like: and so I won't be in love, for I
          won't wilfully do amiss. [*With great positiveness.*] No! I won't
          love any person, though I should love him ever dearly!
HARRY.   [*Aside.*] Angelic innocence! [*Aloud.*] Right, lovely Sophia, guard your
          heart against seducers. (11.i.302–9)

For his part, Harry loves Sophia for her "[a]ngelic innocence." At her response to the argument that love "cannot be resisted," he praises her resistance, her determination to guard "against seducers." Although Diddler declares at the end that he has reformed when he marries Peggy, Plainway's daughter and sole heir, he has exercised throughout the play a much more pliable moral code. It is almost as if Goldfinch were to elope with Sophia, especially since both parts, Goldfinch and Diddler, became mainstay roles for Lewis. Goldfinch's catch-phrase, "That's your sort," has its parallel in Diddler's phrase, "raising the wind," which defines Diddler's own name, a trifling cheat and swindler, who is always diddling people out of money.

Having lost the comforts he once possessed, Diddler has adopted wily ways in order to survive. At Bath, he recently met and enjoyed a brief flirtation with Miss Peggy Plainway. His attraction to her seems at first inspired more by her wealth than any abiding fondness. He is quite ready to turn his attentions to any other woman with money enough to pay his debts.

DIDDLER.   How unlucky, that the rich and pretty Miss Plainway, whose heart
           I won at Bath, should take so sudden a departure, that I
           should lose her address, and call myself a foolish romantic
           name, that will prevent her letters from reaching me. A rich
           wife would pay my debts, and heal my wounded pride. But
           the degenerate state of my wardrobe is confoundedly against
           me. There's a warm old rogue, they say, with a pretty
           daughter, lately come to his house at the foot of the hill. –
           I've a great mind – it's damn'd impudent, but, if I had'nt
           surmounted my delicacy, I must have starved long ago.[40]

Unlike Harry, who was prepared to abandoned Sophia and marry Widow Warren only in order to save his father from bankruptcy, Diddler courts a middle-aged spinster, Miss Laurelia Durable (played by Mary Ann Davenport, née Harvey), with no other motive than to regain riches for himself.

Peggy's father, Plainway (William Blanchard), means to marry his daughter (Mrs. Henry Beverly, née Chapman) to the yet unseen suitor, Fainwould (Samuel Simmons). Diddler steals Fainwould's letter of introduction to Plainway, and passes himself off as Fainwould. Although amused by Diddler's roguish cunning, Genest nevertheless declares that the theft of Fainwould's letter was "contemptible." Diddler's courtship of Peggy is thus made to depend, not just on subterfuge, but on stealing. The audience at large, however, happily accepted the deceit, perhaps persuaded that Fainwould is a fool who might be better left to bachelorhood. Fainwould has no objection to the marriage arranged by his father, but he candidly confesses that he does not impress the ladies. "The girls in London don't treat me with proper respect," he tells servant, "I always do some stupid thing or other when I want to be attentive." With a refrain that he gets "no respect," Fainwould describes the ineptitude that afflicts his attempts at gallantry: "The other night, in a large assembly, I picked up the tail of a lady's gown, and gave it to her for her pocket-handkerchief. – Lord, how the people did laugh!" (1.1.129–33).

Fainwould is easy prey, readily falling for Diddler's tricks. On their first encounter at the inn where Fainwould has just arrived, Diddler hustles him by pretending he needs change for postage:

DIDDLER.   A letter for me? desire the man to wait. That bumpkin is the most impertinent – I declare it's enough to – [*Advancing towards Fainwould.*] – You haven't got such a thing as half-a-crown about you, have you, sir? there's a messenger waiting, and I haven't got any change about me.

FAINWOULD.   Certainly – at your service. (1.1.196–200)

The scam works so easily that Diddler decides to ply his trade more vigorously, calling for breakfast at Fainwould's expense, snatching the breadrolls as soon as they are brought, then repeating the very same pretense that he needs to pay for postage:

DIDDLER.   [*Again taking his letter out of his pocket.*] What, another letter by the coach. Might I trouble you again? You haven't got such a thing as tenpence about you, have you? I live close by, sir; I'll send it to you all in the moment I go home. Be glad to see you any time you'll look in, sir. (1.1.231–4)

The comic tradition that gave rise to Archer and Aimwell, Dick Amlet and Brass, Wheadle and Palmer, Tippy and Fancourt, also fostered Jeremy Diddler. And Fainwould is his convenient dupe.

Diddler relies on a letter as the prop of all his scams, and a letter is his undoing. To woo the spinster Laurelia Durable, he sends her a love letter:

DIDDLER.   Here it is, brief, but impressive. If she has but the romantic imagination of my Peggy, the direction alone must win her. [*Reads.*] "*To the Beautiful Maid at the foot of the hill.*" The words are so delicate, the arrangement so poetical, and the tout-ensemble reads with such a languishing cadence, that a blue-stocking gardenwench must feel it! "To the Beautiful Maid at the foot of the hill." She can't resist it! (1.ii.149–53)

Diddler has no notion that Miss Durable is visiting her cousin Plainway, nor that Plainway awaits the arrival of Fainwould as his daughter's suitor. As Diddler strolls beneath the spinster's window, looking for some means of delivering the letter to her, Miss Durable appears and is enchanted to see a prospective suitor of her own:

MISS DURABLE.   What a sweet-looking young gentleman – and his eyes are directed towards me. Oh, my palpitating heart! what can he mean?
DIDDLER.   You're a made man, Jerry. I'll pay off my old scores, and never borrow another sixpence while I live.
MISS DURABLE.   [*Sings.*] "Oh! listen, listen to the voice of love." –
DIDDLER.   Voice indifferent: – but damn music when I've done singing for my dinners. (1.ii.62–7)

Intending to pursue his courtship of the spinster, Diddler gains entrance into her house, but Fainwould, too, arrives just at that moment. Concealing himself, Diddler overhears Fainwould tell of the arranged marriage with Plainway's daughter, expressing his hope that he will "meet with a little more respect." Conveniently, Fainwould has in his hand the letter his father has written to introduce him to Plainway. Now that he knows that there is a younger, prettier, even wealthier object for his affections, Diddler immediately schemes to obtain the letter, get rid of Fainwould, and present himself as Peggy's suitor. He steps out of hiding and introduces himself as a nephew:

DIDDLER.   Well, I'm very glad to see you. Won't you take a seat?
FAINWOULD.   And you live here, do you, sir?
DIDDLER.   At present, sir, I do.

FAINWOULD.   And is your name Plainway?

DIDDLER.   No, sir, I'm Mr. Plainway's nephew. I'd introduce you to my
               uncle, but he's very busy at present with Sir Robert
               Rental, settling preliminaries for his marriage with my
               cousin.

FAINWOULD.   Sir Robert Rental's marriage with Miss Plainway!

DIDDLER.   Oh, you've heard a different report on that subject, perhaps.
               Now, thereby hangs a very diverting tale. If you're not in
               a hurry, sit down, and I'll make you laugh about it.
               [*Diddler goes up and gets a chair, which he brings forward,
               R., and in placing it, he strikes it on Fainwould's foot.*]

FAINWOULD.   [*Aside.*] This is all very odd, upon my soul. [*They sit down, he
               having brought down chair, L.*]

DIDDLER.   You see, my uncle did agree with an old fellow of the name of
               Fainwould, a Londoner, to marry my cousin to his son,
               and expects him down every day for the purpose; but, a
               little while ago, Sir Robert Rental, a baronet, with a
               thumping estate, fell in love with her, and she fell in love
               with him. So my uncle altered his mind, as it was very
               natural he should, you know, and agreed to this new
               match. – And, as he never saw the young cockney, and has
               since heard that he's quite a vulgar, conceited, foolish
               fellow, he hasn't thought it worth his while to send him
               any notice of the affair. So, if he should come down, you
               know, we shall have a damn'd good laugh at his disap-
               pointment. [*Fainwould drops his letter, which Diddler picks
               up unseen.*] Ha! ha! ha! Capital go, isn't it? (1.ii.31–58)

Fainwould, raging at the want of respect at his reception, vows to return
to the house to "expose that Mr. Diddler, blow up all the rest of the
family." Peggy recognizes the lover she left behind in Bath, and Diddler
whispers to her that she should play along with his impersonation. The
spinster, however, is convinced that he is her suitor. Plainway has found
the love letter, Diddler is exposed, and both ladies are angry at Diddler's
deceit. Just as he manages to make peace with Peggy, Fainwould arrives in
a fury. At the conclusion, Diddler receives a legacy of £10,000 left him by
his uncle. Restored to wealth and estate, and thus exonerated from the
suspicion that he would marry Peggy only for her money, the wedding is
approved with her father's blessing.

   For the purpose of the plot, Laurelia Durable is a dramatic counterpart
to Widow Warren. While Miss Durable is a sexually eager but aging
virgin, Widow Warren is well accustomed to sexual adventures and, as her
daughter says, "wants to have all the marriage in the world to herself" and

would "be married every morning that she rises, if any body would have her."[41] Unlike Sophia, Peggy has made no pledges to her grandmother and is quite ready to elope with her lover. Both plays bring the lovers together in financial prosperity. The more important common ground of these two comedies, however, is the character acting of Lewis, who became for the entire age the true Goldfinch, the true Jeremy Diddler.

Raising the Wind is a comedy that Waldie saw repeatedly – in different theatres, with different casts. But even for him, Lewis was the proper Diddler. Upon seeing the play in Newcastle, he granted the rest of the cast performed well, but the entire production failed because of the failure of Thomas Noble in Diddler. "All the effect," Waldie wrote, "depends on Diddler, who was quite out – nothing could be worse." Noble reduced Diddler to "a harlequin."[42] When it was performed again at Newcastle the following year, Waldie enthusiastically pronounced that Betterton made "a most capital Diddler." Indeed, he went so far as to declare that "I never saw it so well before." Betterton did not surpass Lewis; rather he became Lewis. The treat was seeing Betterton, master of mimicry, playing Lewis playing Diddler: "his imitation of Lewis in voice, tone & manner almost, when I shut my eyes, made me believe it was really he. Never any thing was so like." Of the rest of the cast, – "Mrs. Jones in Laurelia, Miss A. De Camp in Peggy, Liston in Sam, Chippendale in Fainwould, & Lindoe in Plainway – all as good as were required." But again he affirmed, "it all hangs on Diddler."[43]

Four years later, in 1809, William Augustus Conway was performing on the Newcastle stage. Waldie was spending a great deal of time with Conway, at private dinners, walks, and, when Conway was not per-forming, at the theatre. Conway seemed pleased with Waldie's attentions:

he seemed most delighted to be noticed – & his manners are most elegant, frank, & genteel. He is really a most amiable young man & certainly has great genius for the tragic art. He is so enthusiastically attached to the stage, that I think there can be no doubt of his success.[44]

Conway declined the invitation to sit in Waldie's box, so the two sat together in the pit. Drury Lane had burned down on February 24, 1809, and Sheridan was financially ruined by the loss:

We [. . .] lamented the dismal news of the burning of Drury Lane on friday night. It was a most sudden & rapid conflagration, being all over in 3 or 4 hours – being a Lent friday there had been no play. I fear no good account of its origin can be given. Nothing was saved – the insurance is but £70,000 – and most terrible will be the loss to every one concerned; & to the public – as certainly in point of cost & size, it was the second building in London. Most melancholy event.[45]

They also talked about the Newcastle theatre, Conway's roles, and his interaction with the other players. Waldie, who in the meantime had seen much more of Betterton on the stage, now described him as an actor who steps in and out of his role, appearing momentarily passive when he appears on stage, and only after a pause allowing himself to be fully swept away with the part that he is playing. Betterton's performance as Diddler especially "suits his vacant, dull style" because the contrast is so great that Betterton appears momentarily harried: "Diddler is so active & alert, that it was amusing to watch the actor try to keep apace with his part."[46]

During the summer of 1809, Waldie frequented the theatres of Tunbridge Wells and Brighton. Sarah Siddons was performing in Brighton. Waldie praised her performance as Lady Randolph in *Douglas*. *Raising the Wind* followed, but Waldie protested that "I paid very little attention, as I was thinking all the time of Mrs. Siddons." Waldie complained that John Brunton made Diddler "too like a Madman" and too bereft of humor. Fainwould was played by William Murray, brother of Mrs. Henry Siddons, and to Waldie he seemed, in appearance as well as acting, "very like his sister." Miss Boyce, whom he acknowledged to be "excellent in pathetic, sentimental parts," was "too grave for Peggy." Mrs. Henry Loveday, "a clever actress," played Miss Durable admirably (August 11, 1809; 20:207).[47]

From Brighton, Waldie traveled on to Arundel, where he again saw the ever popular *Raising the Wind*. This time it was with Daniel Egerton in the role of Jeremy Diddler. Egerton was now with the theatre company in Bath, but Waldie knew him from the Newcastle stage. Upon seeing Egerton again, Waldie observed that "[h]e is not improved in appearance, being got too stout." "His lively comedy is good," Waldie wrote, "but he has no feeling." Waldie did not mean that Egerton failed to bring adequate emotion to his role; rather that he conveyed inappropriate emotion. As Diddler, he "was not animated enough – indeed he is too large & heavy for it – he was not so good as Betterton or Brunton, & far indeed from Lewis or Jones."[48]

Otherwise difficult to document, amateur theatricals, such as Jane Austen described in *Mansfield Park*,[49] are occasionally commented on in Waldie's journal. While traveling in Italy, he joined in Florence with the company of Lord and Lady Normanby, Lord Francis Conyngham, Lady Burghersh, and Lord and Lady Rendlesham, who entertained themselves by renting out the local theatre. The theatre, Waldie observed, was "not so neat as that of the Margravine at Naples," but it suited the purpose of the amateur performance quite well. First the group performed scenes from *Henry VIII*: the trial, Wolsey's fall, and Katherine's death. Waldie was hard on the aristocrats: "Lord Normanby in Wolsey looked it tolerably, and gave some of Kemble's tones, but was monotonous"; Lady Burghesh, who performed as Queen Katherine, "has a fine face and speaks with feeling – but too rapidly – she is much agitated – if she was not, she would be the best"; "Lady Normanby as her attendant looked pretty." King Henry was played by George FitzClarence, later first Earl of Muster. Waldie described him as a "very comic" actor, "so like his mother, Mrs. Jordan, it is quite ridiculous." Were it necessary, he might well pursue a career in acting. He has "great comic powers, but is idle and never perfect." Hobbyn, who played Cromwell "with feeling," was only "indifferent" as Diddler in *Raising the Wind*: "He had animation and no humour – his forte would be genteel comedy or tragedy." Lady Rendlesham as Laurelia Durable conveyed very well the frustrated spinster. Waldie regretted that FitzClarence had not taken a second role that evening, for his "fat figure and real humour in some farces would be capital." In summing up the amateur performance, Waldie pronounced "the acting as good as can be expected."[50]

Diddler and Goldfinch are characters who, under the strain of financial desperation, adhere to the expedient of marrying for money. Goldfinch reveals only a bemused curiosity concerning Widow Warren's sexual energy. Diddler is willing enough to humor Miss Durable's frustrated desires, but he is much happier to reciprocate the love of Peggy. In Gothic melodrama, mutual love and sexual attraction, if present at all, serve as targets of the villain's evil machinations and underscore his malevolence. The melodramatic villain seldom has any other motivation than lust, jealous possessiveness, and/or a thrill of power in his acts of perversion, rape, and excess.

Nowhere in the drama of the period is such perversion taken further than in Percy Bysshe Shelly's *The Cenci* (1819). Although he sought to have it performed, and even recommended that the parts of Cenci and his daughter Beatrice should be acted by Edmund Kean and Liza O'Neill,[51] Shelley's representation of incest, rape, and patricide was too stark for the stage of the period. *The Cenci* was not performed until May 7, 1886.[52] Count Cenci's murder of his sons, his cruel abuse of his wife, his rape of his daughter, are scarcely more outrageous than the perversities of character already stock-in-trade for the Gothic villain. Sexual atrocities of a worse sort had already been depicted in the fiction of the age. In *The Monk* (1796), Matthew Gregory Lewis had described in lurid detail Ambrosio's crimes against his sister and mother. The Marquis de Sade gave graphic accounts of scene after scene of sexual cruelty in *Histoire de Juliette, ou les prospérités du vice* (1797). Unlike Shelley, Horace Walpole had serious reservations about staging *The Mysterious Mother* (1768), for he confessed that he had allowed himself to indulge fantasies that were "revolting" and "disgusting."[53] Contemporary judgment agreed that Walpole had depicted scenes of incest so shocking that "the delicacy of the present age would not permit it to be acted."[54] In Walpole's tragedy, the incest is the secret scheme of a mother who, upon learning that her son sexually desired her maid, secretly takes her maid's place in bed, so that when Edmund comes to her in the night, he does not know that he is making love to his mother, nor does he know, sixteen years later, that the girl whom he takes as his wife is their daughter. In Shelley's tragedy, the violent acts are committed with full awareness. As Count Cenci declares:

> I love the sight of agony, and the sense of joy,
> When this shall be another's, and that mine.
> And I have no remorse and little fear . . . (1.i.82–4)

To inflict suffering is for the Count a source of pleasure. He thrills in the power that he holds over his victim:

>   I the rather
> Look on such pangs as terror ill conceals,
> The dry fixed eyeball; the pale quivering lip,
> Which tell me that the spirit weeps within
> Tears bitterer than the bloody sweat of Christ.
> I rarely kill the body, which preserves,
> Like a strong prison, the soul within my power,
> Wherein I feed it with the breath of fear
> For hourly pain. (1.i.109–17)[55]

Cenci accuses his daughter of insolence; she replies that he deserves no obedience. "I know a charm," he tells her, "shall make thee meek and tame" (1.iii.167). The "charm" stirs her first to madness, then to murder.

Charles Maturin's *Bertram* (Drury Lane, May 9, 1816)[56] is the play that Coleridge denounced as a "superfetation of blasphemy upon nonsense."[57] It is often argued that Coleridge's attack was motivated by his resentment that *Bertram* was chosen over his own *Zapolya* for production at Drury Lane.[58] Even so, there is merit in Coleridge's contention that the cult of the outlaw hero had inverted moral judgment. Satan thus became "the Hero of Paradise Lost." As Shelley also observed, "The character of Satan engenders in the mind a pernicious casuistry which leads us to weigh his faults with his wrongs, and to excuse the former because the latter exceed all measure."[59]

The Don Juan of Thomas Shadwell's *The Libertine* (1675) is, Coleridge asserted, "from beginning to end, an intelligible character: as much so as the Satan of Milton."[60] Don Juan's wickedness, like Satan's, is forgotten in the admiration of his heroic bravado. "The very extravagance of the incidents and the super-human *entireness* of *Don Juan's* agency, prevents the wickedness from shocking our minds."[61] Because it derives from his power of seducing rather than raping innocence, Bertram's moral monstrosity is more like Don Juan's than like Cenci's. Bertram's wickedness is similarly countered by his heroic qualities and his love for Imogine. Forced into exile, Bertram pillaged as a pirate, until being shipwrecked on his native shore, where he discovered that Imogine, his former love, had married Aldobrand, the very man who had driven him forth. Maturin teases the audience with the possibility that Bertram, in his hatred for Aldobrand, will kill the son that Aldobrand sired with his beloved. The scene closes instead with Bertram snatching up the child, blessing and kissing it (11.iii). With her husband absent, Imogine and Bertram reignite their former passion. Coleridge summarized their illicit plans:

[Act 111] introduces Lord Aldobrand on his road homeward, and next Imogine in the convent, confessing the foulness of her heart to the prior, who first indulges his old humour with a fit of senseless scolding, then leaves her alone with her ruffian paramour, with whom she makes at once an infamous appointment, and the curtain drops, that it may be carried into act and consummation.[62]

The ensuing events, when the curtain rises again on Act IV, prompt Coleridge to his most vitriolic condemnation – not of Maturin's play, not of Edmund Kean and Miss Somerville in their performance as the adulterous Bertram and Imogine, but of an audience for having been seduced totally into the topsy-turvy moral approbation against which he warned:

I want words to describe the mingled horror and disgust, with which I witnessed the opening of the fourth act, considering it as a melancholy proof of the depravation of the public mind. The shocking spirit of jacobinism seemed no longer confined to politics. The familiarity with atrocious events and characters appeared to have poisoned the taste, even where it had not directly disorganized the moral principles, and left the feelings callous to all the mild appeals, and craving alone for the grossest and most outrageous stimulants. The very fact then present to our senses, that a British audience could remain passive under such an insult to common decency, nay, receive with a thunder of applause, a human being supposed to have come reeking from the consummation of this complex foulness and baseness, these and the like reflections so pressed as with the weight of lead upon my heart.[63]

Describing the abrupt disjunctures of Romantic irony, Henry Wadsworth Longfellow wrote that it was as if, in the midst of intensity of feeling, "suddenly a friend at your elbow laughs aloud, and offers you a piece of Bologna sausage."[64] At Coleridge's elbow was "a plain elderly man . . . who with a very serious face, that at once expressed surprize and aversion, touched my elbow, and pointing to the actor, said to me in a half-whisper – 'Do you see that little fellow there? he has just been committing adultery!'"[65]

Rather than disrupt Coleridge's attention to the play, the "plain elderly man" brings him back to it. "Relieved by the laugh which this droll address occasioned," Coleridge returns to the action on stage. Michael Tomko recognizes in Coleridge's critique of Bertram in Chapter 23 of *Biographia Literaria* a further exposition of the "willing suspension of disbelief" posited in Chapter 15, but here, Tomko argues, the "poetic faith" is stifled by Coleridge's outrage at the play's moral trespass and his consequent "unwillingness to cooperate with the author in order to make the illusion work." Tomko further posits that the "plain elderly man" is a "British 'everyman,'"[66] responding to the adultery as would most of the audience; that is, with a titillation at the scandal that overrides the moral objection at the act. Tracy Davis, in her response to Tomko, faults him for over-reading "the playgoer's over-reading of Kean/Bertram as adulterer."[67] As Jacky Bratton also points out, the scandal of Kean's affair with Charlotte Cox was still far in Kean's future.[68] Were the private life of the performers to merge often with the perception of their theatrical performance on stage, the "plain elderly man" might well have had a busy time nudging his theatre companions and pointing, for example, to Michael Kelly as he catches Mrs. Crouch leaping from the burning tower in *Lodoiska*: "Do you see that little fellow there? he has just been committing adultery!" Or John Braham with Anna Storace in Dibdin's *Family Quarrels* (Covent Garden, December 2, 1802). Or nudging and pointing to Mary Robinson, or to Dorothy Jordan. Neither could the infamous adultery trial of Queen Caroline have been far from the minds of spectators who watched the tribulations of Mrs. Haller in *The Stranger* at Covent Garden on October 20, 1820.[69]

Adultery had provided the plot of *The Wheel of Fortune* (Drury Lane, February 28, 1795), *The Stranger* (Drury Lane, March 24, 1798), and many more popular plays of the period. In those plays, the sin was accompanied by guilty remorse. In *Bertram*, as Coleridge objected, the sin was accompanied by more sin. Imogine confesses to her husband that unless she perform due penance "black perdition" may "gulf my perjured soul" (IV.ii.59–60). No sooner does Aldobrand leave her to her "penance" than the lovers recommence their adulterous affair:

Well! the husband gone in on the one side, out pops the lover from the other, and for the fiendish purpose of harrowing up the soul of his wretched accomplice in guilt, by announcing to her with most brutal and blasphemous execrations his fixed and deliberate resolve to assassinate her husband; all this too is for no discoverable purpose on the part of the author, but that of introducing a series of super-tragic starts, pauses, screams, struggling, dagger-throwing, falling on the ground, starting up again wildly, swearing, outcries for help, falling again on the ground, rising again, faintly tottering towards the door, and, to end the scene, a most convenient fainting fit of our lady's, just in time to give Bertram an opportunity of seeking the object of his hatred, before she alarms the house, which indeed she has had full time to have done before, but that the author rather chose she should amuse herself and the audience by the above-described ravings and startings.[70]

After murdering Imogine's husband, Bertram conceals himself with the corpse, only to emerge covered with gore when Aldobrand's troops arrive. Imogine, too, goes into hiding with the child, who reminds her of Aldobrand. When she emerges from the cave, the child is dead and she is mad. Imogine dies at the feet of her enchained lover, and Bertram then stabs himself.

As staged at Drury Lane, Edmund Kean as Bertram played opposite Miss Somerville as Imogine. In her first appearance in any theatre, Miss Somerville's inexperience enabled Kean to manipulate her actions on stage, making Bertram's manipulations of Imogine all the more convincing. In his scenes with Miss Somerville Kean persistently upstaged her, either forcing her to turn away from the audience, or attracting the audience's attention to movements and gestures that she could not see. On Kean's deliberately subordinating Somerville's actions, Genest cited O'Keeffe. It was the strategy, wrote O'Keeffe, of an "old stager, who knows the advantageous points of his art."[71]

Maturin's *Bertram*, originally staged with music by Thomas Cooke,[72] was adapted as operatic libretto for Vincenzo Bellini's *Il pirata* (La Scala, October 27, 1827). Waldie arrived in Milan too late for the premiere performance, but attended two weeks later. La Scala, he said, was "as large and dark as night and has its same fine orchestra." Bellini he described as "a young Neapolitan, who has written two operas before, one for the Conservatorio, where he studied under Zingarelli, and one commissioned by Earbaia for the San Carlo at Naples." The musical score he found "sweet and expressive," praising especially "a fine duo & trio in the 1st act, & a still finer solo by Rubini and in the 2d act the solo of Rubini is most exquisite for power and feeling." On the negative side, Waldie objected to the "want of fine concerted pieces" and a lack of "spirit and variety." Nevertheless, "such a work from a man of 25 is most wonderful." The success of the production "owes much to the great talents of Madame Lalande and Rubini" who performed the principal roles. Waldie compared Henriette Méric-Lalande to two of the foremost sopranos in German opera: Henriette Sontag, "for voice and execution" and Anna Schechner "for acting." Madame Lalande (whose name Edgar Allan Poe borrowed in his tale, "The Spectacles"):[73]

is genteel and has fine teeth and an expressive face. She is not handsome, but has a most brilliant voice and fine action and manner, both in singing and acting, and most perfect intonation. She was a pupil of Talma for tragedy, but as a singer is indeed most superior.[74]

Bertram's name was changed to Gualtiero, Imogine became Imogene, but the more significant change is that the lovers are no longer adulterers in the absence of Imogene's husband.[75] The chief moral objection to Maturin's play was thus removed. Giovanni Rubini, up to this time known for his performances in the operas of Gioachino Rossini, found remarkable affinity with the musical character that Bellini had crafted for him. He moved in with Bellini and sang each song as it was being composed ("Rubini in Gualtiero, the Pirate, sung his 2 solos with such power, such astonishing feeling and amazing expression of passion, as well as beautiful tone and execution, that as a tenor and a singer of soul I never heard any but Braham at all to compare to him"). Waldie, who had on a previous night witnessed Rubini's performance in the title role of Rossini's *Mosè in Egitto* (1818), confessed that "I should not have thought from seeing him in Mosè that he had so much soul." Far more effective in the opera than in Maturin's play was the protracted "mad scene of Imogene," in which Madame Lalande was most moving in her song, "Col sorriso d'innocenza . . . Oh sole, ti vela di tenebre oscure."[76]

Drama arouses passions: not just laughter or tears, but the discomfort, hurt, or anger provoked by scenes that may strike personal feelings.

Coleridge's extreme reaction to *Bertram* is a case in point. Another is Hazlitt's repeated ridicule of Conway. In Chapter 1, I called attention to Hazlitt's remarks on Conway's performance as Romeo: "He bestrides the stage like a Colossus, throws his arms into the air like the sails of a windmill, and his motion is as unwieldy as that of a young elephant."[77] Hazlitt went on to declare that there is "no reason why this preposterous phenomenon should not be at once discarded from the stage, but for the suppressed titter of secret satisfaction which circulates through the dress-boxes whenever he appears." He ends with the insinuating query: "Why does he not marry?"[78] The tittering in the dress-boxes and the implication that he was not sexually suited for marriage were insults inappropriate to a theatre review.[79] Having aroused the ire of several of Conway's fans who objected to Hazlitt's not-so-covert innuendos, Hazlitt issued an apology in the *Theatrical Inquisitor* (May, 1818):

Some expressions in my *View of the English Stage* relating to Mr. Conway, having been construed to imply personal disrespect to that gentleman, and to hold him up to ridicule, not as an actor but as a man, I utterly disclaim any such intention or meaning, in the work alluded to, the whole of what is there said being strictly intended to apply to his appearance in certain characters on the stage, and to his qualifications or defects as a candidate for theatrical approbation.[80]

Hazlitt's apology was far too disingenuous to appease. In "Hazlitt Cross-Questioned," *Blackwood's Magazine* (August, 1818), Hazlitt is again charged with having "wantonly and grossly and indecently insulted Mr. Conway the actor, and published a Retracting Lie in order to escape a caning."[81]

In his essay "On Effeminacy of Character," Hazlitt asserted that such weak behavior is a vile disease.[82] He continued to scatter rude hints of Conway's homosexuality throughout his subsequent reviews. When Conway performed as Comus, Hazlitt mocked Covent Garden for staging Milton's masque as a "common pantomime," and scoffed at Conway's "usual felicity." His Comus seemed "as if the genius of a maypole had inspired a human form." Echoing Shakespeare's Richard III referring to his own deformity (*Richard III*, 1 ii 155), Hazlitt deemed Conway to be "a marvellous proper man," but denied that he seemed "the magician, or the son of Bacchus and Circe." Granting that he might "make a very handsome Comus," Hazlitt added, "so he would make a very handsome Caliban; and the common sense of the transformation would be the same."[83] In reviewing Thomas Otway's *Venice Preserv'd*, Hazlitt asserted that he liked "Conway's Polydore not at all," and declared it "impossible that this gentleman should become an actor."[84] Hazlitt again cast doubt on Conway's masculinity by suggesting something amiss with his performance as Theseus in *A Midsummer Night's Dream*, asking "Who would ever have taken this gentleman for the friend and companion of Hercules?"[85]

After news reached him that Conway had drowned himself in the Charleston harbor,[86] Hazlitt issued a half-hearted apology. Without counting himself among the antagonistic critics, Hazlitt acknowledged that Conway's death, "must have occasioned regret to some who had at any time commented freely on his acting."

[T]hose who had at first extolled him to the skies, now swelled the cry against him; and the honey of adulation was naturally turned into gall and bitterness. Young, enthusiastic, and sincere, he attributed to malice and rooted enmity what was owing to accident, and the caprice and levity of the world, who keep up the sense of self-importance and excitement, by loading their thoughtless favourite with caresses one moment, and treating him with every mark of obloquy the next. Poor Conway was not prepared for this; he thought their admiration of him lasting and invaluable, their desertion wounded him to the quick. He did not know that the town was a hardened jilt, whose fondness or aversion are equally suspicious.[87]

Admitting no part in the opposition against Conway, Hazlitt blamed instead Conway's own inclination to "shewiness" and his over-sensitivity to the fickleness of the public. Not the only critic to come to Conway's defense, John Waldie remained a steadfast supporter. Waldie was also among the few to avoid prevailing homophobic prejudices.

Players, playwrights, and audiences all seemed far ahead of critics in coming to terms with the complex gender issues of the drama. The theatre seemed to flourish with comedies of cross-dressing and with romances of conflicted motives and the desperation of love versus money. The villains of melodrama drew bountiful box-office receipts because of, not in spite of, their wickedness. Perhaps the popular response was in fact no more sophisticated than that of the critics, who still wanted a vocabulary, an ethical or aesthetic system capable of evaluating the new social issues already crowding the stage. Certainly something more was needed in deciphering sexual character on the stage than Coleridge's anger, Hazlitt's homophobia, or even the nudge of a "plain elderly man," to point out that a seduction, deception, murder, or adultery has taken place.

CHAPTER 6

Setting: where and elsewhere

The most popular and familiar of border crossings in the Romantic period were marked by the proscenium arch. Theatre was at once an international venue and a showcase for national prejudice toward other countries, other customs. While much is revealed in the dramatic setting and the stage representation of foreign character and intrigue in plays by British writers, even more telling were their translations and adaptations from the drama of other countries. Robert Young, in *White Mythologies* (1990) argued that "the creation of the Orient . . . signifies the West's own dislocation from itself, something inside that is presented, narrativized, as being outside."[1] While "arm-chair travelers" encountered vicariously the foreign and strange in their reading of travel narratives, the drama of the period enhanced such encounters through the vivid impact of theatrical setting and action, yet often replicating the images familiar as book illustrations. The inside–outside disjunctures of heterotopia nourished, and were nourished by, the growing consciousness of Empire in the Romantic period.

The setting of a play (where the action is supposed to take place) determines as well the stage sets (how that setting is visually represented on stage). Whatever is on stage is "other." The era of picture-book stage designs in Britain commenced in 1767 when David Garrick hired Philippe-Jacques de Loutherbourg to create his illusionist renderings of nature and architecture. De Loutherbourg's set designs also used oil lamps to simulate moonlight and nocturnal street scenes.[2] Utilizing the brighter, oxygen-fed oil lamps developed in the early decades of the nineteenth century, David Brewster became the wizard of special effects.[3] The rebuilding of Drury Lane and Covent Garden, as mentioned in the Introduction, resulted in a vaster audience capacity but also vaster stages, and consequently a need for much larger stage settings. The four major components were the backdrop, the wing sliders (angled segments mounted in grooves that could be pushed forward and withdrawn as needed for scene changes), the free-standing flats that could be placed anywhere on stage, and drop flats or canvases suspended from the fly gallery. In costuming as well as stage design the period saw a new emphasis on historical verisimilitude.[4] The source materials for these efforts at authenticity were period paintings, statues, engravings. In their very methods of reconstructing the past, the artists of stage design had committed themselves to replication of picture-books and art galleries.

Even while the Drury Lane theatre was being rebuilt, from 1791 to 1794, John Philip Kemble engaged William Capon as artist for the new sets.[5] Capon was an artist, like Augustus Pugin after him, passionately committed to the Gothic style. He served as chief scenic artist for Drury Lane from 1794 to 1813. His canvas backdrops were exquisitely detailed architectural paintings on a grander scale than ever before attempted. His backdrop of a Gothic cathedral was 56 feet wide (17.07 meters) and 52 feet high (15.85 meters). Although Capon researched his architectural designs to insure historical authenticity, the resulting scenes were often hyper-Gothic: accurate in the parts, overdone in the ensemble. A case in point was Capon's setting for George Colman's *The Iron Chest* (Drury Lane, March 12, 1796). To be discussed in Chapter 7 in terms of its Gothic and anti-Gothic *mélange*, *The Iron Chest* was as thoroughly Gothic as Capon could make it: as Gothic in its interior scenes as Richard Westall's depiction of the conspirators in the house of the Archdeacon of Bangor (*Henry IV, Part 1*, iii.i), or James Northcote's prison scene with Hubert and Arthur (*King John*, iv.i).[6] To represent Sir Edward Mortimer's "ancient baronial hall," his library, and a nearby ruined abbey, Capon painted for *The Iron Chest* three very large scenes, each architecturally accurate with *trompe l'œil* perspective and shading. For the hall, Capon added a correct music gallery and screen from the times of Henry VI and Edward IV; for the library, he created a composite of actual specimens of Gothic architecture, using his sketches of the vaulting of the groined ceiling in the monastic cloister of St. Stephen, Westminster; "the book-cases were from another antique source; and the painted glass from the windows of a time-honoured church in Kent."[7] Capon's scene paintings were impressive, but unwieldy: so unwieldy that the scene changes could not be managed. The play involved ten scenes in all, with five of them in Act II: the forest (ii.i), the hall (ii.ii), Helen's cottage (ii.iii), the library (ii.iv), the ruined abbey (ii.v). The forest and the cottage were managed on wing sliders. Only three hours remained before the play was to begin on opening night, Colman complained, when he was informed of the difficulty of moving the two large pieces – the library and the abbey – at the end of Act II:

the present stage of Drury – where the Architect and Machinist, with the judgment and ingenuity of a Politian and a Wit to assist them, had combined to outdo all former theatrical outdoings – was so bunglingly constructed, that there was not time for the carpenters to place the lumbering frame-work, on which an Abbey was painted, behind the representation of a Library, without leaving a chasm of ten minutes in the action of the Play.[8]

With the keen competition among the theatres to attract audiences with ever more elaborate scenery, it was not surprising that Capon inadvertently designed sets larger than the stage was equipped to handle. Not a play that required period authenticity, *The Iron Chest* was given grand scenery and impressive historical aura simply as *Augenfang* for the audience.

The Gothic settings painted by Westall and Northcote, mentioned above, were representative of contemporary conceptions of the staging of Shakespeare. The Boydell Shakespeare Gallery, on exhibit in Pall Mall from 1789 to 1805, not only responded to actual performances; many of the artists found lucrative commissions in painting stage scenery. William Hodges, a scene painter for a theatre in Derby and later for the London Opera in the former Pantheon, brought his skills as a landscape artist to such scenes as the moonlit grove and lawn before Portia's house in *The Merchant of Venice* (v.i).[9] Adhering closely to his training as a landscape painter, Hodges strove to create a landscape background for the performance. The stage-setting depicting a forest or garden was intended to be something more than merely realistic. The stage was an art gallery, and the scene a fine painting of a forest or garden.[10] The range of representation engaged Gothic supernaturalism and fairy-tale fantasy.[11]

For *Abudah; or, The Talisman of Oromanes* (Drury Lane, April 13, 1819) and *The Caliph and the Cadi; or, Rambles in Bagdad* (August 16, 1819), James Robinson Planché had the scenery copied from William Marshall Craig's illustrations to *The Tales of the Genii*.[12] Similarly, for extravaganzas from the *Arabian Nights*, Planché had his set designers follow the familiar book illustrations by Robert Smirke.[13] Later in his career, when Planché worked under Madame Vestris at the Lyceum Theatre, he collaborated with William Roxbury Beverley, whose breathtaking sets earned him a reputation as "the Watteau of Scene painters," a soubriquet that reaffirmed the art gallery presumption of his stage designs.[14] Another adherent of the art gallery mode, Clarkson Stanfield, was engaged in August, 1816, as a decorator and scene-painter at the Royalty Theatre in Wellclose Square, London. In 1816, David Roberts was taken on as a stage designer's assistant at the Pantheon Theatre in Edinburgh, the beginning of his career as a painter and designer of stage scenery. Roberts and

Stanfield were both employed at the Royal Coburg Theatre. In 1819, Roberts became the scene painter at the Theatre Royal in Glasgow; in 1823 Stanfield became resident scene-painter at Drury Lane, where he rose rapidly to fame through the huge quantity of spectacular scenery that he produced for that house until 1834. He was especially known for his vast "moving dioramas" for Christmas pantomimes.

Whether a Gothic fabrication, a conveniently conjured France or Spain, or a fantastic Orient, dramatic settings exhibit the deceptive dimensions of "elsewhere." In Elizabeth Inchbald's *Animal Magnetism* (Covent Garden, April 29, 1788), the place is ostensibly across the channel in present-day Paris. As the actual city in which Franz Anton Mesmer had established his practice during the previous decade, Paris was a likely and logical setting. But Inchbald's Parisian setting aptly suits, as well, her satire on the domestic constraints for a woman to choose her own husband or to control her own wealth and property. Her satire, of course, also responds to the contemporary controversy over the reputed charlatanry, and sexual exploitation of female patients. By 1788, *Animal Magnetism* had already crossed the Channel and gained a following in England. Inchbald's script reveals her awareness of Pierre Yves Barré's *Les docteurs modernes*, staged in Paris in 1784 and published in 1785. Setting her play in France, she nevertheless implicated similar trespasses that were already stirring a scandal in London. The plot involves a hoax perpetrated on an elderly doctor, who resorts to animal magnetism in order to cast a spell on his young ward, Constance, who has rejected all his overtures to her. He is tricked into thinking that he has mastered the power of magnetism, but his spells all go awry. In the resulting confusion, Constance is able to meet with her lover, a handsome young nobleman, and the two manage to extort the doctor's permission to marry. Since "Paris" is revealed only from the interior of the doctor's house, it is little more than a reflection in a fun-house mirror. But "elsewhere" nevertheless has an important function. Where in the world might a lecherous old doctor keep his beautiful young ward confined in the hopes of compelling her consent in marriage? In London? Heaven forbid! In Paris? Far too enlightened and sophisticated to tolerate such oppression. Where then? Spain! Lisette, maid and companion to Constance, laments their plight:

LISETTE.   . . . is it not a shame the Doctor should dare here in Paris to forbid both you and your servant to stir from home; lock us up, and treat us as women are treated in Spain?

CONSTANCE.   Never mind, Lisette, don't put yourself in a passion, for we can learn to plot and deceive, and treat him as men are treated in Spain. (I.i.33–8)

Whether true or not, it was certainly an established trope that Spain was the place of domestic oppression of women, but also the place where women had mastered the arts of intrigue. *Animal Magnetism* was performed frequently throughout the first half of the nineteenth century, and when it was revived at Tavistock House in January, 1857, Charles Dickens was apparently persuaded by the logic of the trope to move the setting from France to Spain. Paris, after all, had long since lost its relevance as the site of Mesmer's exploits. Dickens himself played the doctor who is tricked into thinking that he can "magnetize," with his sister-in-law Georgina Hogarth as his ward, and his mistress Ellen Ternan as her maid.[15]

That same trope of oppression and intrigue informs the setting in Madrid for Hannah Cowley's *A Bold Stroke for a Husband* (Covent Garden, February 25, 1783). The themes are those I have already observed in Inchbald's play and often repeated by other women authors of the age: the woman's right to choose her own husband and to control her own wealth and property.[16] Olivia and Victoria demonstrate a more ingenious assertion of those rights in the face of greater opposition. Olivia's father, Don Caesar, endeavors to arrange her marriage, but she is determined to have the man of her choice, Don Julio. When told that she might be sent to a convent, Olivia voices her rebellious passion: "Immur'd in a convent! then I'll raise sedition in the sisterhood, depose the abbess, and turn the confessor's chair to a go-cart."[17] Victoria has brought wealth and property into her marriage, but her husband, Don Carlos, forced her to sign over control, then abandoned her in pursuit of a gold-digging courtesan, Laura, who uses quantities of wine and her seductive wiles to wheedle from him the deed to the estate. Victoria disguises herself as a man, seduces the seducer, and gains back from Laura the deed to her own estate. Once again in possession of her wealth and property, she is reconciled with her wayward husband, whom she henceforth keeps under her control. One reviewer noticed that Cowley borrowed aspects of the character of Don Carlos, and some of his language, from the character of Courtine in Thomas Otway's *The Atheist* (1683).[18] But the quibble about her originality does not detract from her own "bold stroke" in empowering the women of her play, who certainly command the trope of learning how "men are treated in Spain."

Spain, of course, was more than simply the code of male dominance and female subterfuge in an era in which women were struggling for rights.

Spain, as the historical site of the Inquisition, also provided a trope for ruthless exercise of authority. When Wordsworth and Coleridge first met in 1797, it was not the *Lyrical Ballads* that were at the center of their collaborative interests. It was Friedrich Schiller's *Die Räuber* (1781), from which Wordsworth drew inspiration in composing *The Borderers*, and Coleridge in writing *Osorio*, performed and published as *Remorse* (Drury Lane, January 23, 1813).[19] Staying closer than Wordsworth to his source in *Die Räuber*, Coleridge kept the setting in Spain; more importantly, he kept the rivalry between the two brothers. The significance of Coleridge's theatrical "elsewhere" is manifold. Spain is the site of ethnic persecution. Coleridge's equivalent to Karl and Franz Moor are Don Alvar and Don Ordonio. The play is set, as Coleridge's opening note explains, on the coast of Granada during "the reign of Philip II, just at the close of the civil wars against the Moors, and during the heat of the persecution which raged against them, shortly after the edict which forbad the wearing of Moresco apparel under the pain of death."[20] Having escaped his brother's attempt to assassinate him, Alvar returns to Spain with his Moorish companion, Zulimez. In spite of the edict, Alvar disguises himself as a Moor, and returns to his father's estate to discover whether his beloved Theresa has been faithful to him or yielded to his brother's overtures. She has rejected all Ordonio's advances, in spite of the fact that he insists that Alvar has perished.

When Alvar presents himself as a Moorish wizard, unrecognized in his disguise, Ordonio decides that this charlatan might be employed to conduct a conjuration that that will convince Theresa that Alvar is dead. The magic scene, a stunning *coup de théâtre*, makes the most of the inside–outside dislocations of "elsewhere." Coleridge appreciated the incredible power of the stage to represent those scenes in which recesses are created within the "elsewhere" of the setting, and a character – Friar Bacon, or Doctor Faustus, or Prospero – reaches into deeper, darker dimensions to snatch an image of the supernatural. Alvar is brought not to the chapel of the castle, but into the armory, where a magical altar is erected for his unholy necromancy.

Accompanied by eerie music, composed by Michael Kelly and performed on glass-harps hidden off stage, the conjuration begins. Alvar – who is and is not Alvar, who is and is not a Moorish wizard – begins his incantation: "I call up the Departed! Soul of Alvar! Hear our soft suit, and heed my milder spell" (111.i.30–2). As a play-within-a-play, the conjuration scene functions, much like "The Murder of Gonzago," to expose guilt. The inside–outside dimensions of the altar/shrine create a Necker Cube illusion of religion as magic, magic as religion. In his lectures on

Shakespeare, delivered at the Surrey Institution (November 1812–January 1813) during the months preceding the opening of *Remorse* at Drury Lane (January 23, 1813), Coleridge had spoken against the prevailing fashion of spectacle as a detriment to the drama. Here he plays directly to the audience's love of spectacle. At the altar, by a bright flash of gunpowder, an image of Alvar is revealed. But this is not the image that Ordonio expected, an image that would convince Theresa that Alvar is dead. No – it is an image that shows the attempted assassination, Alvar being attacked by Ordonio's henchman. Not Alvar's death, but Ordonio's crime is exposed at the altar.

As is well known, August von Kotzebue's plays enjoyed considerable popularity on the London stage. Kotzebue's *Die Spanier in Peru* (1795) was adapted by Richard Brinsley Sheridan as *Pizarro* (Drury Lane, May 24, 1799), the most lucrative box-office success of Sheridan's career.[21] The opening performance featured John Philip Kemble as Rolla, the Peruvian hero; Charles Kemble as Alonzo, Rolla's friend but also his rival in love; Dorothy Jordan as Alonzo's Peruvian wife, Cora; William Barrymore as Pizarro, the ruthless Spanish Conquistador; and Sarah Siddons as Elvira, his mistress. The fact that Sheridan knew no German was no impediment to his effort as translator. He was, in fact, merely the adaptor, and the identity of the true translator remained a mystery.[22] But in his adaptation, he was a shrewd manipulator of "elsewhere." His Spanish Conquistadores may bear a Spanish standard, but they could well be French soldiers in Napoleon's army; his Peruvian natives are (and, yes, they really are!) English. Among the English had spread a prevailing alarm that Napoleon was planning a full-scale invasion of England. Pizarro is a surrogate for the insidious Napoleon; Rolla and the Peruvians are the "noble savages" of Britain. This play fully exploits the doubleness of outside as inside, of there as here, of then as now.

But it was not Sheridan who discovered the doubleness inherent in the historical tale of Pizarro's conquest. Neither was it Kotzebue, nor his source, Jean-François Marmontel's *Les Incas, ou la destruction de l'empire du Perou* (1777). The subtle hints of events in France within a tale of the Spanish overthrow of the Incas had been wrought by the author of the stunning eye-witness account, in the year following the storming of the Bastille, of the Festival of Federation and the debates in the National Assembly, in *Letters Written in France in the Summer of 1790, to a Friend in England*. This account was followed by even more stunning volumes on the events in Paris during the "Bloody Reign of Terror," in the five volumes of *Letters from France* (1791–6). The author, of course, was

Helen Maria Williams. In her narrative poem, *Peru: A Poem; in Six Cantos* (1784), she told the tale of Pizarro's invasion, of Rolla's heroic resistance, of Cora's pleading for his life at the feet of the cruel tyrant. Her sense of doubleness, of course, did not anticipate the French Revolution, or the fears of Napoleonic invasion, but it did indict military occupation and colonial exploitation. In that indictment she departs from her principal source, William Robertson's *History of America* (1770). It was Cora's scene in *Peru* that prompted the young Wordsworth, who had neither met nor even seen Helen Maria Williams, to write his sonnet "On Seeing Helen Maria Williams Weep." She was forthright in expressing her sympathies for the Revolution in her poem "The Bastille, a Vision" (1790), and in *Peru*, she told what was to become an allegory for the age.[23]

Animal Magnetism required only interior scenes, and thus afforded no pictorial challenge to realize the Parisian setting. *A Bold Stroke for a Husband* relied on travel-book backdrops for its Madrid street scenes and the Prado. The Spanish setting of *Remorse* stipulated more complex scene changes, from exterior bluffs and caves to castle terrace and halls. Most complex of all was the Peruvian setting of *Pizarro*, with fourteen scene changes and ten different sets. The Peruvian Andes, to judge from the contemporary depictions of the performance, may have looked more like the fells of Buttermere. The four scenes designated simply *A Landscape* were played downstage with the sliding wings in the first grooves. Other scenes were second- or third-groove sets, and there were several large free-standing flats. Charles Shattuck lists the most elaborate sets and notes the interaction that provided the culminating *coup de théâtre*:

The style of decoration is well suggested by such headings as, at III.i, *A wild Retreat among Stupendous Rocks* or, at v.i, *A thick Forest – In the back Ground, a Hut almost covered by Boughs of Trees – A dreadful Storm, with Thunder and Lightning.* One of the more spectacular sets was the final one of Act II: *A View of the Peruvian Camp, with a distant View of a Peruvian Village. Trees growing from a rocky Eminence on one Side.* In the course of this scene a Boy climbs up the rocks and from there climbs a tree, so that he can report to his blind (!) old father the outcome of the battle. The most famous scene, often drawn or painted, was that of v.ii: *The Outpost of the Spanish Camp. –The back ground wild and rocky, with a Torrent falling down the Precipice, over which a Bridge is formed by a fell'd Tree.* As Rolla crosses the bridge, bearing off Cora's child, a shot from a Spanish rifle strikes him; but with superhuman effort he destroys the bridge by tearing from the rock the tree that supports it.[24]

These scenes of wild and rugged nature were not in Capon's style. Rather, they hearken back to the set designs of de Loutherbourg, who may well have been called back to Drury Lane at age fifty-nine to oversee the preparation of the scenery.[25] The scene on the bridge also provided the setting for the well-known portrait of Kemble as Rolla by Sir Thomas Lawrence, exhibited at the Royal Academy in 1800.[26]

Ten years after *Pizarro* had opened in London, the domestication of the "elsewhere" of the Spaniards in Peru still seemed appropriate to the Newcastle audience when John Waldie persuaded his friends to join him in a "Committee Night" production in April, 1809. A wave of panic had just spread through the town at the sighting of a ship off the coast that was thought to be a lead vessel for a French assault. The ship turned out to be a privateer, but the anxiety about Napoleon's European conquest was widely felt. The plan for the production of *Pizarro* at the Theatre Royal was first presented to John Fawcett on April 20, 1809.[27] To organize the production, Waldie was joined by his actor friend, William Augustus Conway; a fellow member of the Theatre Committee, Joseph Lamb; and their guest at Newcastle, Captain Samuel Edward Widdrington, RN. A naval officer already distinguished for breaking up the French batteries and flotillas near Boulogne, as well as for his service in the West Indies, Captain Widdrington was the unanimous choice for playing the heroic Rolla.[28] Conway was to play Alonzo, and the rest of the *dramatis personae* included both regular cast members of the Theatre, as well as amateur performers from the Theatre Committee. When rehearsals commenced the following day, Waldie regretted that he was to serve "merely as Conductor of the business, for I promised my father not to take part, as he is much against it." At least he could "stand at the wing and sing all the Choruses."[29] On the same bill with *Pizarro*, Conway was to read "Alexander's Feast" by John Dryden, to be followed by Thomas Holcroft's *Tale of Mystery* (Covent Garden, November 13, 1802).[30]

On opening night, Waldie was pleased to have a full house. "The play went off uncommonly well," but he was disappointed in Captain Widdrington's acting. Having assumed that a decorated naval officer would naturally bring an heroic presence to the role, Waldie regretted that Widdrington's real-life accomplishments were not manifest in his stage performance. Life and art are not the same. "There was a sad want of energy in Rolla – very tame – the other amateurs got thro' much better than I expected." Eager to give him deserved credit for his willingness to perform for the Newcastle Theatre, Waldie granted that Widdrington knew his lines, his entrances and exits, and managed "Rolla's stage business" well. In the final act "he died finely." In *The Tale of Mystery*, Widdrington played the lead as Francisco. His acting "was graceful &

affecting: but he has no fire, no spirit." Miss Macaulay of the Newcastle company played Elvira "better than any other part"; Miss Simpson was "tolerable in Cora"; Conway was "impassioned & animated" and "made a great deal of Alonzo."[31]

Immediately after the entertainment in Newcastle, Captain Widdrington departed for Cayenne and Surinam, and Waldie headed south for London. During the three days of rehearsals, Waldie enjoyed the company of both Conway and Widdrington. With Conway he had been especially close: "He is the best creature in the world & so amiable, unaffected, & good humoured – so happy & gay yet modest & respectful – & has such a fund of agreeable conversation that I never met with any one who suited me so well."[32] Waldie claimed that a shared interest in Conway was his bond with Widdrington: "He seems so much taken with me that I cannot fail to like him – & we are both so attached, I by long acquaintance, & he by sudden admiration, to Conway that he is a bond of union." Before his departure for the theatres of London, Waldie spent a final evening with Conway,

> & had a most agreeable conversation about every thing interesting to the drama. Conway is to write to me in London. I took leave of him with the deepest regret. I feel now from our intimacy so attached to him, & am so delighted with his temper, manners, & genius that I shall feel a sad loss in the want of his society. I shall be delighted to hear that he succeeds in the world, & hope sincerely that he may always be as happy as he is at present.[33]

One week later, just arrived in London, Waldie visited the Haymarket to see the great Charles Mayne Young[34] perform as the heroic Rolla. The energy and authority that Widdrington doubtless commanded as a naval officer, had not become apparent in his actions as Rolla; the experienced actor, who might well falter and fail in actual battle, exhibited the appropriate illusion of strength against the ruthless Spaniards. Six years earlier, on January 23, 1802, Waldie had first seen Young perform on the Edinburgh stage as Doricourt in Hannah Cowley's *The Belle's Stratagem* (1800).

Having admired Young as an actor in comedy, Waldie was impressed to see how "natural" he appeared as the Peruvian leader. Because Young was stepping into the role made familiar by John Philip Kemble, comparisons to Kemble were inevitable. Young was one of the most successful tragedians, prior to Edmund Kean, to break from Kemble's declamatory style. Kemble himself tried to vary the rhythms of blank verse with rapid bursts. The challenge, of course, was in making tempo and volume express the emotional content of the lines. Young had a resonant voice and was masterful in the stage-whisper, but he needed more effective modulation. The difficulties of delivery prompted Waldie also to compare Young to Joseph George Holman, an actor whose breaks were criticized as being too rapid.

Rolla by Mr. Young was the attraction. He is indeed a first rate actor. His neck & head are Roman, His figure very fine – he has just enough of dignity & action, & his walk is the most beautiful I ever saw – his voice grand & capacious – his solemn declamation inimitable: – his energy when called forth, as in his calling back the Peruvians to rescue of Ataliba, is most affecting & astonishingly powerful. There he is far before Mr. Kemble – but in the prison scene & with the sentinel, he is much inferior – he is too solemn & measured, & wants that persuasive feeling, those sudden bursts that Kemble shines in – his "Did Rolla ever counsel" [IV.i.172] was exquisite in a fine whisper – & his aside whisper at the end of "Then was this sword Heaven's gift" [V.ii.77] were very judicious – he has the highest judgement, voice, & manner & action – & in solemn or energetic parts is truly great – but in the softer, nicer touches of the soul he fails – he is altogether much like Mr. Holman, but has less flourish, more dignity, a finer figure & face – & a more tragic air. I was highly pleased, tho' I expected more feeling & find pathos is his great want.[35]

The scenery for the Haymarket production was "beautifully got up," but, with the exception of Young as Rolla, "not well acted." Charles Kemble in Alonzo "was very tame indeed – he sadly wanted some of Conway's fire."[36]

Pizarro was performed again at Newcastle in February, 1815, this time with Rolla played by Meggett, who was visiting from London. In August, 1815, Meggett's performance at the Haymarket as Sir Edward Mortimer in Colman's *The Iron Chest* was denounced by Hazlitt as "too hard and dry."[37] Waldie described Meggett's Rolla as "extravagant & violent & unnatural." Meggett "has great powers which he might make a great deal of, if he would only be natural." Instead, Waldie wrote, he exhibited only "affected tones and extravagant action." Waldie said nothing about the stage sets for this performance except to confirm that it "was got up with care."[38]

Kotzebue's source for *Die Spanier in Peru* (1796), as noted above, was Marmontel's *Les Incas* (1777). Even earlier, Kotzebue had drawn previous events from Marmontel's narrative as the plot for *Die Sonnenjungfrau* (Liebhabertheater zu Reval, December 19, 1789). This earlier episode told how Cora, consecrated as a virgin to the Incan sun god, fell in love with Alonso, a Spanish soldier, and became pregnant. In punishment for violating her vow, Cora is to be buried alive. The Incan king spares her life and permits her to marry Alonso. This plot was adapted several times for opera: Giuseppe Maria Foppa wrote the libretto for Francesco

Bianchi's *Alonso e Cora* (Vienna, February 7, 1786); Giuseppe Bernardoni wrote the libretto for Johann Simon Mayr's *Alonso e Cora* (La Scala, Milan, December 26, 1803). Waldie remarked that the Bernardoni–Mayr plot compared not to Sheridan's *Pizarro*, but to Frederic Reynolds' *Virgin of the Sun* (Covent Garden, January 31, 1812).[39] Reynolds' version, as libretto to the music of Sir Henry Bishop,[40] was spliced together from Anne Plumptre's translation of Kotzebue[41] and an anonymous translation of Marmontel.[42] Young performed Rolla, Francis Huntley was Alonso, Sarah Smith was Cora, Elizabeth Powell (née Harrison) was the High Priestess, and William Barrymore (who had played Pizarro) was the king of the Incas. Just as *Pizarro* worked upon fears of French invasion, *The Virgin of the Sun* played to the xenophobia of the nation's daughters being seduced by foreigners. Reynolds made the most of sets and stage-effects, including a tremendous earthquake in Act 1, a grand temple, and elaborate costumes for the Incan priests and priestess.[43] As in *The Stranger* (Drury Lane, March 24, 1798; from *Menschenhaβ und Reue*), Kotzebue dramatized the violation of moral codes of sexual behavior (German, Incan, English) in a way that recommend forgiving the transgressor, yet keeping the codes intact.[44]

The performance of Mayr's *Alonso e Cora* at the Teatro di San Carlo, Naples, in 1817 featured Giacomo Davide as Alonso and Isabella Colbran as Cora. The scenery was exceptionally fine and, among the special effects, "the storm and earthquake and destruction of the temple, and the volcano, were beautifully done." Waldie makes it clear that he considers Mayr a less gifted composer than Rossini:

Colbran was very good in Cora. I never heard her sing so well as she sung a grand bravura in the beautiful finale of the last act, after the King, moved by the restoration of his child, agrees to the marriage of Cora and Alonzo, instead of her sacrifice for breaking her vows of becoming a Virgin of the Sun . . . Davide's part is the best and he sung most delightfully and with great spirit, but was drest like a postillion. Colbran does not look the interesting Cora (Elizabeth is her great part), but she sung delightfully . . . Altogether I was very much pleased, tho' not so much as with *Otello* & *Elizabeth* by Rossini. The music of this is by Mayr: it is like all his, very unequal, and often very limping and unexpected and unsatisfactory, yet is noble in some parts, especially the duet of Davide and Colbran in the 2nd act and the quartett at the end of the 2nd act; the whole of the last act is good, and the finale is a most exquisite quintetto.[45]

Waldie found further evidence of the popularity of the story of Alonzo and Cora in the Teatro de Marionette, where *The Virgin of the Sun* was performed "by marionettes mixed with Polichinello, indispensable in all popular Neapolitan Theatres, and who beat and kicked about the Priests most terribly."⁴⁶

How a play might project the inside–outside doubleness of "elsewhere" is complicated, as just seen in the case of the narrative, poetic, dramatic, and operatic representations of Peru under the Spanish Conquistadores. Translation, in and of itself, requires a cultural shift that inevitably complicates representation of people and place. That complication is even more extreme when the adaptation from a source also involves a shift in place. Consider what happens, for example, when setting is radically relocated. Edward Jerningham's *The Siege of Berwick* (1793) tells of a major battle in the Scottish War of Independence against Edward III, when Sir Alexander Seaton refused to surrender Berwick-upon-Tweed, even at the peril of losing his two sons, Archibald and Valentine. In the opening scene, the sons persuade their father to allow them to make a sally against the enemy. They are captured, and the English general informs Seaton that, unless he surrenders, his sons will be bound to pillars and exposed to arrows shot by Seaton's own troops. When Seaton resolves not to surrender, his wife, Ethelberta, goes to the English camp to plead for their release. The general rejects her plea, but Seaton's troop successfully attack the English camp, kill the general, and secure the release of the two sons unharmed. The plot ought to be familiar: this is the source for Felicia Hemans' *Siege of Valencia* (1823), and she replicates the dilemma of the father, the anguish of the mother, the desperate predicament of the sons, and the uncompromising aggression of the enemy general. But what is the implication of moving the "elsewhere" of the stage from the northeastern coast of Britain to the Mediterranean coast of Spain? Situated in medieval Spain, amidst the Moorish–Christian conflicts that provided the setting to Coleridge's *Remorse*, Hemans has constructed a tragedy that pits more emphatically maternal passions against masculine war-mongering. Her management of theatrical doubleness, too, is almost as shrewd as Sheridan's *Pizarro*, for she allows her historical narrative, imbued with the valor of the legendary *El Cid Compeador*, to serve as a matrix through which an audience might glimpse the turmoil of post-Napoleonic conflict and the impact of the French invasion of Spain and the Battle of Trocadero (August 31, 1823).

Felicia Hemans was not the first to shift the "elsewhere" of the *Siege* far from the Scottish–English borderlands on the North Sea. Preceding both Jerningham's *Siege of Berwick* (1793) and Hemans' *Siege of Valencia* (1823) was John Home's *Siege of Aquileia* (1760), which takes the historical account of Sir Alexander Seaton's defense of Berwick-upon-Tweed, and relocates that story in ancient Rome, with Aemilius, a Roman Consul, defending Aquileia from attack by the tyrant Maximin. When Aemelius' sons, Paulus and Titus, are captured, Cornelia, his wife, pleads for their release. Home may have loosely founded his play on Roman history, but, as Genest observes, "he has borrowed his plot chiefly from what really happened at the Siege of Berwick." While it is clear that Home used the historical sources on Edward III and the Scottish War of Independence, it is also clear that Jerningham has "borrowed considerable from Home."[47] Hemans' version is closer to Jerningham. Why has Home indulged his radical and rather peculiar shift of "elsewhere"? Having just gained theatrical success with his *Douglas* (1757), it may be that Home wanted to show that he had a historical range that could take him far beyond Scottish nationalism. If that was his strategy, then he might have sought a plot that would better disguise the fact he was still relying on Scottish Border history.

In recent criticism of the Romantic representations of "elsewhere," led especially by Edward Said's influential *Orientalism*,[48] the exotic East has attracted much attention. Certainly the inside–outside doubleness of those representations is shaped by such factors as colonialism, the investments of the East India Company, the opium trade, and other military and mercantile ventures. The East had also entered into the popular imagination with great conjuring power as a site of exotic, erotic, and magical "otherness." *The Tales of Arabian Nights* were introduced to Europe by Antoine Galland between 1704 and 1717; the earliest English version, from Galland's French, came almost immediately (1706–8). During the eighteenth century the tales of "Sinbad," "Aladdin," and "Ali Baba" were published in numerous popular editions. William Wordsworth and Thomas De Quincey were among the many authors who record their childhood delight in these tales. The plots were also adapted in English pantomime, and occasionally appeared in the entertainments at Drury Lane and Covent Garden.

Recalling his response to the tales of the *Arabian Nights* as a five-and-a-half-year-old child, De Quincey had "pronounced Aladdin to be pretty nearly the worst" because of "the advantage given to the magician by the inconceivable stupidity of Aladdin in regard to the lamp."[49] The contest between trust and trickery is the source of intrigue that made this tale especially popular on the stage, but intrigue and action were always supported by the visual opulence of the oriental set designs. First performed as *Harlequinade*, a pantomime of Aladdin was staged at Covent Garden in 1788. "A new dramatic spectacle, called *Aladdin*," opened in Norwich in 1810.[50] The version that was to become a great sensation was the work of Charles Farley,[51] supported by an overture and, by all accounts, a rousing and rollicking musical score by William Ware.[52] With several years' experience in preparing the annual pantomimes at Covent Garden, Farley created the picturesque groupings for *Aladdin; or, The Wonderful lamp* (Covent Garden, April 19, 1813).

Already well known for his performances as Timour and as the dumb Francisco in *Tale of Mystery*, Farley played Abanazar, the African Magician. The boy, Aladdin, was played by Marie Thérèse Kemble (née De Camp). And the inimitably comic Joe Grimaldi played Kazrac, the magician's Chinese servant. The ingénue love interest was provided by Miss Bolton as the beautiful Princess, in comic contrast to Mary Ann Davenport in the role of the lusty widow of Ching Mustapha. "This Melodramatic Romance had considerable merit," Genest granted rather begrudgingly, "for this sort of thing." It ran for thirty-six performances and owed its success to its rich musical score, its wonderful "Oriental" backdrops and costumes, its "magical" effects with projected images, and back-lighting designed by Farley. The scenes of innocent love between Mrs. Kemble and Bolton were effectively contrasted to the raunchy worldly-wise exchanges between the Magician and the Widow.[53]

When Waldie saw the spectacle on the thirty-second night of its popular run at Covent Garden, he declared that *Aladdin* had fulfilled his expectations. Just as "the duty of a golden coin is to be as florid as it can,"[54] the duty of a spectacle is to be as spectacular as it can. The "elsewhere" of the setting had no need of cultural accuracy, no need of meeting any preconditions other than those set in the minds of young readers by Robert Smirke in his well-known illustrations of the *Arabian Nights*.[55] Smirke, who also contributed thirty-two of the scenes from Shakespeare subsequently engraved in the *Boydell Shakespeare Gallery*,[56] set the standard of visual "correctness" for the staging of these Arabian fantasies. Waldie could therefore declare that the stage design was "correct" and that script and scenery were "exactly like the Arabian tale":

The scenery & machinery far exceed any thing I ever saw before, especially the scene where the marriage palace & all the parties are carried up supported by cupids &c. to the skies. The golden garden & cave &c. are most lovely – the Persian & Chinese views, correct & grand. I was delighted with the scenery . . .

Waldie went on to delineate the particular excellencies:

The Procession of Aladdin – the Bridges & Towers, & the last scene – all most splendid indeed. Mrs. C. Kemble is interesting & elegant in Aladdin, & Miss

Bolton in the Princess Badroulbodour. Mrs. Parker looked & danced most enchantingly in Zobeid & Miss E. Bolton in Amron was good – Mrs. Davenport in Aladdin's mother excellent – Farley in the Magician – Grimaldi in Kasrac the Chinese slave was excellent – as was Bolton in the Vizier's son or Lover. It is a most charming & interesting piece . . . & most splendid in all respects.[57]

The setting of the magical, oriental "elsewhere" involved a mixing of Chinese and Arab elements, a geographical juxtaposition that was to become firmly established in the minds of London audiences and per- sisted in subsequent adaptations.[58]

Thirteen years passed before there was a successful rival production, but even it was accused of taking its subject too seriously. George Soane's *Aladdin, a Fairy Opera* (Drury Lane, April 29, 1826)[59] featured sumptuous stage designs and a musical score by Sir Henry R Bishop.[60] James Kenney, whose *Raising the Wind* (Covent Garden, November 5, 1803) was discussed in Chapter 5, also wrote a version, *Aladdin and the Wonderful Lamp; or, New Lamps for Old Ones*, with music by Albert Smith.[61] In subsequent adaptations the widow of Ching Mustapha was transformed into Widow Twankey (named after a brand of Chinese tea), who became the central character.[62]

In contrast to his enthusiasm for the Covent Garden production of *Aladdin*, Waldie's reaction to George Colman's *The Forty Thieves* (Drury Lane, April 8, 1806) was utterly dismissive. The visual effect was grand, but the story was boring:

It is the dullest thing I ever saw in point of story – Miss De Camp in Morgiana the slave has one charming scene. She looks & acts divinely and sings with great feeling – a duet by her & Mrs. Bland is beautiful – but the music on the whole is poor. Mrs. Bland in Cogia – Mrs. Mathews in Lelia – Mrs. Dormer in Cassim's wife – Siddons in Abdallah – De Camp in Hasencar, Mathews in the Cobbler, Kelly in Ganem, &c., did as much as possible – but Bannister in the Woodman is the life of the piece. He & Miss De Camp support it. The Scenery is profusely splendid & in general very beautiful. It is deficient in interest, but the Robbers, dancing girls, &c., and all the dresses & scenery have a grand effect.[63]

A week later, when *The Forty Thieves* was again performed as the after- piece, Waldie said that he left in the middle, "being quite tired of its dullness . . . having seen it before, it would not bear a second performance."[64]

Not overly impressed by other attempts at staging oriental splendor and opulence, Waldie wrote that the scenery of *Aladdin* "is far finer than that of *Timour*." Matthew Gregory Lewis' last play, *Timour the Tartar*

(Covent Garden, April 29, 1811), was intended to rival the oriental splendor of Colman's *Blue-Beard; or, Female Curiosity!* (Covent Garden, January 23, 1798). Back then, the procession of Abomelique was managed with "pasteboard horses operated by the mechanists."[65] When revived at Covent Garden in 1811, it was performed with live horses on stage. Accepting the challenge to rival his own play, Lewis brought to the stage not only a grand eastern fortress and battlements, but an elaborate equestrian procession.[66]

In addition to the horses, and the oriental display, the production of *Timour* also featured impressive gymnastic feats. Waldie saw *Timour* when revived at Covent Garden in 1813, 1814, and 1815. He recorded that it was played "with all its original horses & splendour." The only change was that the role of Zorilda, originally played by Nannette Johnstone (née Parker) had been taken over by Sarah Egerton (née Fisher), who "played with much more feeling, though she did not give up some of the points so well as Mrs. H. Johnson." Zorilda, not Timour, is the great heroine of this piece, and commands the stage from her first entrance, when she arrives on horseback costumed as an Amazon warrior. The young Prince Agib has been imprisoned by the conquering Timour, and Zorilda undertakes his rescue. The action "is indeed most magnificent."[67] Waldie also witnessed *Timour the Tartar* performed without horses on the Edinburgh stage. The acting and the stage décor were not as impressive as the London production. What saved the performance was the remarkably athletic display, as in the tournament battle between Kerim and Sanballat, played by William Murray and John Duff (1.iii), and the daring but agile leaping and climbing in the last scene (11.iii).[68]

Although Waldie had enjoyed the *Tales of Arabian Nights* as much as most readers, he was not therefore smitten by any stage adaptation, nor was he ready to accept either musical fanfare or opulent stage design as adequate substitutes for plot and character. In *The Forty Thieves* Colman was obviously trying to recapture the success of his early production of *Blue-Beard* (see Chapter 8), but he had not bothered to develop interest in the characters.[69] In *The Travellers, or Music's Fascination* (Drury Lane, January 22, 1806), Andrew Cherry had created a spectacle that depended on appropriate musical motifs, provided by Dominico Corri,[70] and, act by act, visually exciting travel scenarios to unfold his story of a Chinese prince on his way to England. Act 1 is set in China, where the emperor decides that his son must travel; Act 11 is in Turkey, where the prince falls in love with a harem girl, is imprisoned, and manages to escape; Act 111 is in Italy, where the prince falls in love with a marchioness; Act 1v, still in

Italy, presents the prince escaping the assassins sent by the jealous duke; ACT V features a stage transformed into the quarterdeck of a man-of-war as the ship arrives off the English coast. Genest denounced the clap-traps as "contemptible."[71] Acted twenty-six times, it was seen on the twenty-sixth night by Waldie: "the music very fine, tho' it is not like Storace's. It is far superior as a spectacle to the *Forty Thieves* and much better as a play."[72]

As the playbills confirm, the representation of foreign sites was often justified as educational, a means to provide understanding and familiarity with the "other." It might be objected, however, that such displays served rather as self-aggrandizement, to assert superiority over it. Pedagogic pretense was intermixed with chauvinistic opportunism. Such displays as William Bullock's Egyptian Hall, which opened in 1812 and offered 15,000 artifacts in dimly lit rooms and labyrinthine halls, transformed the presentation of the archeological object into a theatrical experience. At the same time, the theatrical exposition sought more and more to replicate the latest archeological findings.

There are numerous plays of the period that provide further evidence of the ways in which the oriental setting gives context to themes of colonial and domestic exploitation. Moncrieff's *The Cataract of the Ganges!* (1823) directly engages the public concerns with Britain's military campaigns in India. The play's English soldier, Robinson, who is friend to the Rajah, helps him overthrow the Grand Brahmin. The Grand Brahmin has raised a rebellion against the Rajah who has been friendly to the English troops, and he has kidnapped the Rajah's daughter. Once his rule has been restored and his daughter rescued, the Rajah declares at the plays conclusion: "Generous Britons – greatest of mortal conquerors, your battle is ever on virtue's side – your aim is charity – your victory peace. You spread your sway o'er your opponent's hearts, and carry the Christian spirit of your race through every clime to civilize and bless!"[73] Those in the audience who may well have wanted to believe this chauvinism could surely manage to ignore any possible doubleness – to ignore, as well, the fact that these were Moncrieff's words spoken by a stage Rajah.

Byron, in *Sardanapalus* (1821; first performed Drury Lane, April 10, 1834), uses orientalism to lay claim to luxurious opulence in a climate of treachery and intrigue. For the historical details of his play, Byron acknowledges his debt to Diodorus Siculus, the Greek historian. As "grandson of Semiramis, the man-queen" (subject of a play by Voltaire), Sardanapalus is haunted in his nightmare by her incestuous kiss. A self-indulgent voluptuary, he finds the cruelty of conquest repugnant. He rejects Zelima, his queen, and prefers the company and comfort of Myrrha, his Ionian slave. Byron has situated

his character in the dramatic tradition of the "effete king" with such fore-
bears as Marlowe's Edward II and Shakespeare's Richard II. Among those
who have sought a contemporary model, some have recognized it as yet
another autographical projection of the author himself and his estranged
wife, Lady Annabelle Milbanke Byron; others have seen in the monarch/
voluptuary a representation of George IV who, at the close of his Regency,
came into kingship with the scandal of his divorce from Queen Caroline.[74]
In his final moment, however, Byron's Assyrian monarch ascends his own
funeral pyre with a resignation that sets him apart from his historical lineage
(Nimrod and Semiramis), from his literary lineage (Edward II, Richard II),
and, most radically, from any resemblance to George IV. As Myrrha holds
the torch ready to ignite their bed of flames, Sardanapalus declares:

> Adieu, Assyria
> I loved thee well, my own, my father's land,
> And better as my country than my kingdom.
> I satiated thee with peace and joys; and this
> Is my reward! And now I owe thee nothing,
> Not even a grave. (v. i.492–7)

Eugène Delacroix, in his painting "The Death of Sardanapalus" (1827–8),
has rendered the scene more as a sacrificial orgy, as Sardanapalus witnesses
the slaughter of his naked concubines. Byron gives more dignity to his
hero, who expresses love for his country even while he persists in pro-
claiming "peace and joys." He does so without resorting to the bald
chauvinism of Moncrieff's tribute to "Generous Britons."

The multiple refractions of then and now, there and here, amid the
representational matrices of Byron's play, reveal yet another variation on
the matrices of doubleness in Romantic drama. The survey of examples
could go on, but the purpose of this sampling is not simply to exhibit that
the "elsewhere" of the Romantic stage was historically and geographically
wide-ranging; that range might be confirmed just by consulting a catalogue of titles. What is important is that "elsewhere" on the stage, from
the conquest of Peru to the remoter ranges of the Orient, provides a
matrix for authorial manipulation of levels of reference and representation, and brings into play a complexity of social and cultural interaction
that explores, exploits, explodes audience fears and desires.

CHAPTER 7

Gothic and anti-Gothic: comedy and horror

In the Romantic literature of Britain, the influence of Donatien-Alphonse François, Marquis de Sade (1740–1814) has sustained continued interest since it was first examined in Mario Praz's *The Romantic Agony*.[1] Both Matthew Gregory Lewis (1775–1818) and George Gordon, Lord Byron (1788–1824), were among those who fell under "the shadow of the divine marquis." In his scurrilous Gothic romance, *The Monk* (1796), Lewis described how Ambrosio, a saintly Capuchin monk, is seduced by the beautiful demon Matilda into a life of depravity, committing rape, incest, and murder. In Lewis' Gothic tragedy, *The Castle Spectre* (1797), Osmond lusts after Evelina, his brother's wife, whom he kills in a struggle with his brother; years later, he holds their daughter imprisoned to force her to submission. Byron, when he departed from England in 1816 amidst the scandal over his relationship with his half-sister Augusta Leigh, left behind in his trunk a bottle of laudanum and a copy of Sade's *Justine*. According to Leslie Marchand, her discovery of the contents of her husband's trunk convinced Lady Byron that he was seriously deranged.[2] Her discovery is re-enacted in the character of Donna Inez: "She kept a journal, where his faults were noted, / And open'd certain trunks of books and letters."[3] The obscure but suggestively incestuous sins between Manfred and Astarte in the dark tower demonstrate how Byron, like Lewis, could conjure with Sade's themes.[4]

Not only was Lewis a reader of Sade, Sade was a reader of Lewis. Among those novels "whose only merit, more or less, consists of their reliance on witchcraft and phantasmagoria," Sade wrote in his *Reflections on the Novel*, the best of them is Lewis' *The Monk*, "which is superior in every respect to the strange outpourings of the brilliant imagination of Mrs. Radcliffe." This type of novel, Sade declares, "is the necessary offspring of the revolutionary upheaval which afflicted all of Europe," necessary because fiction had fallen woefully behind actual experience in depicting "all the evil which the wicked can bring down on the heads of the good." In spite of the license of fantasy, there were nevertheless obstacles in depicting the true conditions of cruelty and depravity: "The author of *The Monk* was no more successful in overcoming them than Mrs. Radcliffe." The author must choose "either to develop the supernatural and risk forfeiting the reader's credulity, or to explain nothing and fall into the most ludicrous implausibility."[5]

Lewis' *The Castle Spectre* (1797) was promptly followed by *The Minister* (1797), a translation from Friedrich Schiller's *Kabale und Liebe*, and *Rolla* (1799), a translation from August von Kotzebue's *Die Spanier in Peru*. Lewis' debt in *The Castle Spectre* to Schiller's *Die Räuber* has long been acknowledged.[6] But there are other debts, so complex and manifold that the play is a tapestry of intertextuality. As discussed in Chapter 3, cross-referencing and layering of sources provided for coded dialogue between playwright and those savvy members of the audience who could follow the allusions. In recognizing an allusion, a person feels a conspiratorial bond with the author: the sense that something secret has been shared not accessible to everyone. This may not be transgressive, but can easily become so when the playwright has thus triggered awareness of another text or play that might well be forbidden by censorship.

Like George Colman's *Blue-Beard*, to be discussed in Chapter 8, *The Castle Spectre* exposes a sadistic villain's cruel and ruthless treatment of women. The manner of the exposé could not be more different. *The Castle Spectre* is a Gothic drama; *Blue-Beard* is a fairy-tale spectacle. Both, however, feature the music of Michael Kelly; both make effective psychological use of the comic; and both draw upon multiple sources. The latter two, the use of the comic and the appropriation of sources, are especially relevant to the examination of Gothic and anti-Gothic in the present chapter.

In the published edition of *The Castle Spectre* (1798), Lewis added ten footnotes in which he identified eight sources for specific lines and scenes; then, in his afterword "To the Reader," he named four more. "The situations of Angela, Osmond and Percy," he acknowledged, "so closely resemble those of Isabella, Manfred, and the animate portrait in *The Castle of Otranto*, that I am convinced that the idea must have been suggested by that beautiful Romance." Lewis phrases this identification of source to make it seem as if the borrowing was not at all conscious and that he recognized it only afterwards. He continues with the same sort of apology for his use of other sources: "Wherever I can trace any plagiarisms, whether wilful or involuntary, I shall continue to point them out to the reader without reserve."[7] Lewis keeps this promise when he comes to Act II, Scene ii. Motley's Song, "Sing Megen-oh! Oh! Megen-Ee!", is intended to let Percy know that his friends have prepared for his escape. "Now is the fittest time for flight / ... / Beneath the window of your tower / A boat now waits to set you free,"[8] are lines that echo the stratagem from Michel-Jean Sédaine's *Richard Cœur de Léon* (1784), whence Lewis also admits borrowing the idea of Saib and Muley playing dice. Percy's leap from the tower window is based on a scene from Ludwig Wilhelm Langenau's *Ludwig der Springer* (1782). In two different translations, *Richard Cœur de Léon* appeared at Covent Garden and Drury Lane in 1786.[9] At the end of Act III, Lewis confesses that he has taken from Ann Radcliffe's *The Mysteries of Udolpho* the scene in which Angela and Alice discover the concealed chamber of Evelina.[10]

Another scene for which Lewis acknowledges a source is Osmond's dream in Act IV, Scene i. The review in the *Monthly Mirror* cites this passage as an example of the play's suspicious "German" tendencies:[11] "Rolls not my eye, as if still gazing in the Spectre? Are not my lips convulsed, as if they were yet prest by the kiss of corruption?"[12] The reviewer may not have guessed wrong, for the nightmare vision of being kissed by the corpse of Evelina is indeed similar to the widowed Count Sponheim's dream of being kissed by his dead wife in August Kindler's *Die feindliche Brüder* (1788). Lewis may not have known Kindler's play, but he certainly knew the nocturnal love scene between the dead bride and her living groom in Goethe's *Die Braut von Korinth* (1797).[13] In Chapter 9 further attention will be given to the female vampire in Goethe's ballad, but for the moment it is enough to point out the similarities to both Osmond's dream and the dream of Sardanapalus in the play that Byron published in 1821, and then dedicated to Goethe in the second edition of 1823. Awakening from a ghastly nightmare, Sardanapalus tells Myrrha of the charnel embrace of Semiramis: "she flew upon me, / And burnt my lips with her noisome kisses" (IV.i.149–50).[14] Readers of *The Monk* might well have anticipated the putrid yet lurid imagery as Osmond continues to relate his dream of the lusting corpse:

"We meet again this night!" murmured her hollow voice! "Now rush to my arms, but first see what you have made me! – Embrace me, my bridegroom! We must never part again!" – While speaking, her form withered away: the flesh fell from her bones; her eyes burst from their sockets: a skeleton, loathsome and meagre, clasped me in her mouldering arms! – . . . Her infected breath was mingled with mine; her rotting fingers pressed my hand, and my face was covered with her kisses! (IV.I, p. 97)[15]

For repugnantly vivid detail, Lewis has far outdone Goethe in describing the sexual embrace of the dead bride. In documenting his source for Osmond's dream, Lewis does not acknowledge a German parallel. He thinks it likely that his audience would have been reminded of Clarence's dream in *Richard III* (i.iv), or Richard's own dream (v.iii). His immediate source, Lewis claims, was not Shakespeare but Schiller: Franz's dream in *Die Räuber* (v.i), in which the villainous brother confronts the ghost of his dead father.

By this point, it should be growing increasingly obvious that Lewis shared with many other playwrights of the period a mode of composition that wove together numerous thematically kindred materials. Radcliffe's Gothic novels were a treasure-trove. The Shakespearean Gothic, as Anne Williams and Christy Desmet argue, was important in the effort to endow the popular Gothic mode with a degree of literary prestige and historical elegance.[16] In his afterword "To the Reader," Lewis reveals that he conceived of Alice as a copy of the Nurse in Shakespeare's *Romeo and Juliet*, and Father Philip as a copy of Father Paul in Sheridan's *The Duenna*.[17] Schiller's *Die Räuber* (1781), translated as *The Robbers* (1792) by Alexander F. Tytler, engendered many plays of rival brothers: an evil brother who lusted after the good brother's betrothed; a good brother forced into exile and assuming a disguised identity in order to return and rescue his bride. Coleridge's *Osorio* (1798), revised as *Remorse* (1813), is thus wrought from same source as Lewis' *The Castle Spectre*. Lewis, of course, lays claim to many sources, yet conceals the extent to which Schiller's Karl and Franz were his principal models in defining the rivalry of Osmond and Reginald. The tale of rival brothers is as old as the story of Cain and Abel – a story that had its Romantic reverberations in Coleridge's "The Wanderings of Cain" (1797, 1807), an "imitation" of Solomon Gessner's *Der Tod Abels* (1758) and Byron's mystery play *Cain* (1821). Unlike the rivalry of Cain and Abel, the rivalry between Karl and Franz Moor is instigated by their love for a woman, Amalia. In Coleridge's *Remorse*, Alvar and Ordonio want the love of Teresa. Lewis has rendered the tale supernatural by having his villain pursue his lust into a second generation: having lusted after, and slain, Evelina, he then, eighteen years later, attempts to rape Angela, Evelina's daughter. Several plays featuring rival brothers caught in a fatal love rivalry were staged in the years following Schiller's play.[18]

When *The Castle Spectre* opened at Drury Lane (December 14, 1797), the play-goers were without the author's pledge to point out the plagiarisms. Even without the notes, many would have recognized scenes from Radcliffe and a few of the suspicious "German" tendencies; many, too, would have been familiar with Tytler's translation of *The Robbers*; virtually all would have presumed the presence of the far more transgressive character of Ambrosio lurking within the performance of Osmond, whose enactment of depraved desires was constrained by censorship. Lewis grants that Hassam and the African attendants may be an "anachronism," but, a Jamaican slave-holder himself, he uses them effectively to speak for the anti-slavery movement of the 1790s. Osmond, like Schiller's Franz Moor and Coleridge's Don Ordonio, is depicted as a villain tormented by a guilty conscience. Not all villains are bothered by such pangs. Shelley's Cenci is free of remorse, and Colman's Bluebeard conducts his trials of female curiosity with no serious regrets about their outcome.

The most important Shakespearean character in the play is Motley, the fool. While Motley shares characteristics with several of his Shakespearean predecessors, his active role in the plot makes him most similar to the Fool in *King Lear*. Having introduced a comic character who remained a favorite with audiences, Lewis can afford to be dismissively cavalier about his real achievement.

> I may . . . boldly, and without vanity, assert that *Motley* is quite new to the Stage. In other plays the Fool has always been a sharp knave, quick in repartee, and full of whim, fancy, and entertainment: whereas *my* Fool (but I own I did not intend to make him so) is a dull, flat, good sort of plain fellow, as in the course of the performance Mr. Bannister discovered to his great sorrow.[19]

Bannister's success in the role made it abundantly evident that Motley was far from dull and flat. Lewis' reputation as author of *The Monk* prompted Larpent to exercise rigorous vigilance in censoring Lewis' religious and political indiscretions in the play, but even Larpent was unusually liberal in allowing Motley to retain much of his sauciness, most noticeably transgressive in his dialogues with Father Philip. In his sacrilegious praise of sins, Father Philip provided additional evidence that "Lewis' mind was strangely warped."[20]

Warped or not, Lewis as a playwright had to conform to censorship. Presumably, however, the depravity of Osmond and the sauciness of Motley might have been more fully expressed in the body language of such accomplished actors as William Barrymore and John Bannister. From one actor to the next, from Barrymore to Robert William Elliston to Thomas Potter Cooke, the wickedness of Osmond was indeed variously interpreted. The boundaries between Gothic and anti-Gothic might be sought not just in the contrast between the fool and the villain, but also in the varying interpretations of the villain himself. Among the actors who performed the evil Osmond was "the Infant Roscius."

As mentioned in the Introduction, William Henry West Betty made his debut at age eleven as Osman in Aaron Hill's adaptation of Voltaire's *Zara* (Belfast, August 19, 1803). From 1804 through 1806 he attracted huge audiences to his performances at Covent Garden. During the peak of his success at age thirteen, Master Betty arrived for an engagement of twelve performances at Newcastle. On August 21, 1805, he played Tancred in James Thomson's *Tancred and Sigismunda* (1745); on August 22 the title role in *Hamlet*; on August 23 Achmet in John Brown's *Barbarossa* (1754); on August 26 the title role in *Richard III*; on August 28 Romeo in *Romeo and Juliet*; on August 29 Frederick in Elizabeth Inchbald's *Lover's Vows* (1798); on August 30 Osman in *Zara* (1736); on September 2 Osmond in Lewis' *The Castle Spectre* (1797); on September 4 Zanga in Edward Young's *The Revenge* (1721); on September 5 again Achmet in *Barbarossa*; on September 6 the title role in Henry Brooke's *Gustavus Vasa* (1739); and on September 8, for his final night benefit, Rolla in Sheridan's *Pizarro* (1799).

What did the audience see in Master Betty's portrayal of Osmond? Innocence pretending to be evil? A child prematurely aware of dark sexual desires? Capable of miming depraved lust after a brother's wife, after his own niece? The question, here, is not simply the extent to which an actor identifies with the character he plays, but also how the audience witnessed the child actor in such a role.[21] Distancing himself from the critics who ridiculed the public adulation of Master Betty in his tragic roles, William Hazlitt found occasion in his *Table-Talk* to praise Betty's performance in the title role of John Home's *Douglas* (1757).

Master Betty's acting was a singular phenomenon, but it was also as beautiful as it was singular. I saw him in the part of Douglas, and he seemed almost like "some gay creature of the element," moving about gracefully, with all the flexibility of youth, and murmuring Aeolian sounds with plaintive tenderness. I shall never forget the way in which he repeated the line in which Young Norval says, speaking of the fate of two brothers: "And in my mind happy was he that died!" The tones fell and seemed to linger prophetic on my ear. Perhaps the wonder was made greater than it was. Boys at that age can often read remarkably well, and certainly are not without natural grace and sweetness of voice. The Westminster school-boys are a better company of comedians than we find at most of our theatres. As to the understanding a part like Douglas, at least, I see no difficulty on that score.[22]

Hazlitt may be right in affirming a twelve-year-old's capacity of "understanding a part like Douglas." But understanding a part like Osmond poses a significantly different challenge. Osmond's character is defined by his perverse sexual obsession. Reflecting on the sixteen long years that have passed since he stabbed Evelina, his brother's wife, in the very moment he meant to ravish her, Osmond anticipates the opportunity at last to consummate his lurid passion by ravishing Evelina's daughter. "Evelina revives in her daughter, and soon shall the fires which consume me be quenched in Angela's arms." He feels no remorse for his murder or cruelty, but only self-pity at being "tortured by desires which I never hoped to satisfy" (ii.i.74–91).[23]

Part of Hazlitt's purpose in declaring his own interest in Betty's performance was to highlight Coleridge's caustic response. When Coleridge returned from Malta, he was incensed to learn that Betty had become the sensation of the theatres:

he got one day into a long *tirade* to explain what a ridiculous farce the whole was, and how all the people abroad were shocked at the gullibility of the English nation, who on this and every other occasion were open to the artifices of all sorts of quacks, wondering how any persons with the smallest pretensions to common sense could for a moment suppose that a boy could act the characters of men without any of their knowledge, their experience, or their passions.[24]

Hazlitt's account of Coleridge's tirade corresponds closely with Coleridge's comments five years later, when he was lecturing on *Love's Labour's Lost*. He cited Biron's lines on things having their proper season:

> Why should proud summer boast
> Before the birds have any cause to sing?
> Why should I joy in any abortive birth?
> At Christmas I no more desire a rose
> Than wish a snow in May's new-fangled mirth;
> But like of each thing that in season grows. (*Love's Labour's Lost*, I.i.102–7)

As a comment on these lines, Coleridge referred to "this age of prodigies when the young Roscii of the times had been followed as superior beings, wonderment always taking the place of sense."[25]

Waldie readily confessed his wonderment but did not see it as usurping sense. An impassioned admirer, he nevertheless gave close attention to performance. He watched Betty in rehearsal, visited Betty's parents, even pocketed one of Betty's gloves "as a relic."[26] His accounts reveal details of Master Betty's acting not found elsewhere. With a far more "willing suspension of disbelief" than Coleridge could muster, Waldie saw no incongruity in the child actor playing the adult role. For his performances at Newcastle, Betty played opposite Elizabeth Satchell Kemble, wife of the theatre manager Stephen Kemble, and the most accomplished performer of the Newcastle cast. She was twenty-eight years older than Betty, old enough – even then a cliché – to be his mother. She played Sigismunda to his Tancred, Juliet to his Romeo, Ophelia to his Hamlet, Lady Anne to his Richard III, and Angela to his Osmond. She played these roles convincingly. In a dramatic representation of a forty-year-old lecher assaulting an eighteen-year-old girl, the audience did *not* see a thirteen-year-old boy grabbing hold of a forty-one-year-old woman. They saw Osmond threatening to rape Angela.

OSMOND.   Angela! I love you!
ANGELA.   [*starting.*] My Lord!
OSMOND.   [*passionately.*] Love you to madness! – My bosom is a gulph of devouring flames! I must quench them in your arms, or perish! – Nay, strive not to escape: Remain, and hear me! I offer you my hand: If you accept it, mistress of these fair and rich domains, your days shall glide away in happiness and honour; but if you refuse and scorn my offer, force shall this instant –
ANGELA.   Force? Oh! No! – You dare not be so base!
OSMOND.   Reflect on your situation, Angela; you are in my power – remember it, and be wise! (II.i.192–200)[27]

As Waldie described this scene, Betty had entered fully into the part: "His scene with Angela where he declares his passion was astonishingly great – the transitions from pride to love [were] nature itself & his action so suited to the vindictive raging part of Osmond." Waldie confirmed that Betty expressed all "the violent rage & fire, which seemed to reign in Osmond's soul – his disturbed & guilty mind was never so portrayed before." He regretted that Pritchard and Bellamy did not make the most of their comic roles as Father Philip and Motley, and he regretted, too, that Newcastle failed to construct the castle hall and haunted chamber as effectively as the stage settings at Drury Lane or Covent Garden. But Betty's acting more than made up for the deficiencies. Waldie mentioned the action with Kenric and Saib (III.ii) and Osmand's nightmare of the spectre (IV.i):

and in the scene with Kenric, at first he promises with freedom, but after the latter's preventing Saib's death, his exit at "you who could so well succeed in saving others – now look to yourself" was admirable. The dream scene was powerful horror – his gasping for breath, his roving eyes, his seizing on Hassan to save him, his agony on relating what he has suffered were beyond belief: but his description of the horrid dream brought every image of it to the soul – one felt the shuddering he describes – every word was given with that sort of expression which best suited it & all the horrid images – his face, voice, & action completely brought to view the agony & torment of mind & soul – any one ignorant of the language would from the tone & manner have known that he described some horrid unaccustomed sight. – I shall never forget it.

Although Waldie gave primary attention to the emotional power of Betty's acting, pausing to comment on his monologues, he also argued that Betty interacted effectively with the other players, and that he still commanded great energy at the play's conclusion.

His scenes with Percy & Angela were also truly great – indeed nothing can exceed him in this part, & in the frantic violence of the last act, where he is going to kill his brother & the Ghost intervenes – nothing could be finer – also his attitude & adjuration of the figure of Percy, disguised in Reginald's armour, exceed belief.[28]

Betty's acting, in Waldie's estimation, was no mere novelty, and his performance as Osmond was "one of his finest parts."

Eight years before the first performance of *The Castle Spectre*, seven years before *The Monk*, twenty-eight years before *Manfred*, Sade's play, *La tour enchantée* (1788), had already been adapted for the London stage as *The Haunted Tower* (1789) and had been welcomed with stunning box-office success. The theme of "the unfortunate, persecuted maiden," Praz noted, ". . . is as old as the world," but he went on to point out that its peculiar refurbishing in the eighteenth century emphasized the eroticism of that persecution. As examples of the refurbishing, Praz cited Samuel Richardson's *Clarissa*, Darles de Montigny's pornographic *Thérèse philosophe* (both published in 1742), and Choderlos de Laclos's *Les liaisons dangereuses* (1782).[29] After acting in amateur theatricals on the provincial stages of Evry, Nazan, and La Coste, Sade commenced his career as a playwright with *Le philosophe soi-disant* and *Le mariage du siècle* (both written in 1772).[30] By the 1780s, he was regularly sending his comedies and tragedies to the leading theatres of Paris. Among these, the comedy *L'inconstant* was completed in 1781, the comedy *Le prévaricateur* and the tragedy *Jeanne Laisné* in 1783. After he was imprisoned in the Bastille in 1784, he commenced *Les 120 journées de Sodom*, with its "inside–outside" narrative re-enactment: in the "inside" text Madame Duclos tells of her own sexual encounters, which are then, in the "outside" text, acted out by her auditors.[31] Still a prisoner in the Bastille in 1787, he wrote the first version of *Justine*. His philosophical novel, *Aline et Valcour*, was written between 1786 and 1789.

During these years, too, he began to assemble the series of tales later published as *Les crimes de l'amour* (1800). In some of these tales he used the same characters and incidents that he had developed in the plays of the same period. For example, in "Rodrigue, ou la tour enchantée," the cruel king of Spain forces all the men of court to surrender their daughters to his pleasure. One of his victims, Florinde, returns from the dead to avenge herself when the lecherous king is trapped in the enchanted tower of Toledo. Although this story has little in common with the play, *La tour enchantée*, there are telling parallels: in the tale, the lecherous king meets his fate in the tower; in the play, the baron, angered by a remark concerning his current love interest, kills his friend in the tower. In "Ernestine," another tale in *Les crimes de l'amour*, Sade tells the story of Count Oxtiern, a rebellious libertine who led a revolution in Sweden against King Gustavus. This was also the subject of *Le compte Oxtiern ou les malheurs du libertinage*, the play that opened at the Théâtre Molière on October 22, 1791, and remained Sade's only success on the public stage in his own country. The year previously his comedies *Le boudoir ou le mari crédule* and *Le misanthrope par amour* were both rejected at the Comédie Français. Sade was unaware, however, of another, even grander success. Among the plays that he submitted to the Parisian theatres in 1788 was *La tour enchantée, un opéra-comique*, described in his *Catalogue raisonné* (October 1, 1788) as the concluding episode to a sequence of six plays entitled *L'union des arts*. On February 27, 1791, Monsieur Framery, agent for playwrights, informed Sade that several of the plays had been accepted for performance.[32] They remained unstaged, but *La tour enchantée, un opéra-comique* made its way from Paris to London.

On November 24, 1789, *The Haunted Tower, a Comic Opera*, with a musical score by Stephen Storace (1763–96) and libretto by James Cobb (1756–1818), opened at Drury Lane. It was a significant success, with eighty-four performances in its first two seasons,[33] many more throughout the 1790s, and frequent revivals for the next half century. Sade, imprisoned in the Bastille, wrote his version a year earlier. On July 2, 1789, Sade shouted from his cell window that the prisoners were being murdered; on July 4, he was transferred from the Bastille to the lunatic asylum at Charenton; on July 14, the citizens of Paris stormed the Bastille, beginning the French Revolution. The advent of the French Revolution contributed to Cobb's rewriting and to the English reception of the play. Because Sade frequently described revolution and the downfall of corrupt aristocracy, it may well be that the original version of *La tour enchantée* provided the politically charged context missing from the surviving version, a transcription made in 1810 during Sade's final years at the Charenton Hospital.[34] In "Roderigue, ou la tour enchantée," Sade describes the decadence of the Spanish king at the time of the Moorish Conquest.[35] In Cobb's adaptation, the play depicts treacherous rivalry among the English Barons after the Norman Conquest under King William.

Storace's musical education took him from the Conservatorio di Sant' Onofrio in Naples to Vienna, where he produced two operas, from 1783 to 1787. Returning to London with his sister, Anna Storace, and Michael Kelly, he met with James Cobb and promptly commenced a series of collaborations that made him the master of comic opera in London. Cobb and Storace produced *The Doctor and the Apothecary* (Drury Lane, October 25, 1788), *The Haunted Tower* (Drury Lane, November 24, 1789), *The Siege of Belgrade* (Drury Lane, January 1, 1791), *The Pirates* (Drury Lane, November 21, 1792), and *The Cherokee* (Drury Lane, December 20, 1794).[36] In many of these, Kelly and Anna Storace played leading roles: as Lord William and Adela in *The Haunted Tower*, as Seraskier and Lilla in *The Siege of Belgrade*, as Don Altador and Fabulina in *The Pirates*, and as Colonel Blandford and Elinor in *The Cherokee* (for more on Kelly's career, see Chapter 8). For a libretto that John Philip Kemble pieced together from French and Italian sources, Storace in similar fashion pieced together a score for *Lodoiska* (Drury Lane, June 9, 1794).[37] It was performed by Kelly as Count Floreski and Anna Maria Crouch as his love, Lodoiska. In addition to his collaboration with Cobb, Storace also wrote the score for *No Song, No Supper*, an opera in two acts by Prince Hoare (Drury Lane, April 16, 1790). For Hoare's libretto Storace introduced some of the music that he had written in Venice for his opera, *Gli equivoci* (December 27, 1786), based on Shakespeare's *Comedy of Errors*. Storace then provided the music to George Colman's play, *The Iron Chest* (Drury Lane, March 12, 1796), based on William Godwin's *Caleb Williams*. This production created an even greater sensation than *The Haunted Tower*, but it was to be the end of Storace's career. During the rehearsals he caught cold and died on March 19, 1796.

Whether or not the historical context of Cobb's libretto derived from Sade's original version, it was particularly apt for the period of its reception, when sympathy for, and opposition to, the French Revolution grew intense. In their response to Sheridan's *Pizarro* (1799), as described in Chapter 6, British audiences readily identified with the suffering

Peruvians and perceived in Pizarro's campaign the threat of French invasion.[38] Similar reminders of the current turmoil in France were built into the cross-channel plot of *The Haunted Tower*. Set on the coast of Kent in the time of William the Conqueror,[39] the first scene commences with the arrival, after a stormy crossing, of Lady Elinor de Courcey and her attendants. She has been sent by her father, Lord de Courcey of Normandy, who, at the behest of King William, has arranged her marriage to the son and heir of the Baron of Oakland. In a flashback provided by the cottager Maud, it is revealed that the present Baron is but "plain Edmund, the ploughman," a local villager who happened to be remotely related to the true Baron:

about ten years ago, the old Baron, Lord William, was accused of being in a plot, and conspiring against the life of our good King William, the conqueror, and was banished . . . He took with him his only son, a fine youth, about twelve years of age; but, alas! sir, he has not been heard of since . . . about a year ago, Lord William's wicked accuser died, and declared the good baron innocent . . . The king willing to make reparation for the wrongs he had done him, endeavoured to find him, but all in vain, therefore his lands and estates have been in possession of a distant relation of the family. (1.i.71–80)

Ten years have passed. The usurping Baron lives in fear of the ghost of the old Baron, who is said to haunt the tower awaiting the return of the true heir of Oakland. That heir had been sent to France, where now, as a young man he is known as Sir Palamede (Sir Lorville in Sade's version). He has found protection in the court of Lord de Courcey, has fallen in love with Lady Elinor, De Courcey's daughter, and she is in love with him. When Lady Elinor is sent to England by her father to be married to the heir of Oakland, she has no notion that Sir Palamede is the true heir. She thinks she is to be married to Edward, son of the false Baron. Edward is in love with a village girl, Adela, and both would be much happier to continue life in the country rather than in court, a theme well suited to the times. In the hope of fulfilling his father's expectation, Edward persuades Adela to assume the character of Lady Elinor. With a similar motive to delay her impending marriage, Lady Elinor assumes the character of one of her own attendants along with her maid Cicely. Meeting with Hugo, a loyal servant of his father, Sir Palamede reveals himself as Lord William. He declares that he expects letters from the king, acknowledging him as Baron of Oakland. From Hugo he receives a key to the tower, supposed to be haunted by the old Baron's ghost. Lord Hubert, a neighboring nobleman, sends his army to assist Lord William in reclaiming his estate. Restored to his title and lands, Lord William marries Lady Elinor, and Edward marries Adela. The double marriage plot may have been Cobb's addition, but both Sade and Cobb rely on a haunting to enable true love to succeed.

In spite of discrepancies in the plotting, both works use Gothic supernaturalism as a convenient ruse, psychologically effective because of the Baron's guilt. The version of *La tour enchantée* that survives in the transcription of 1810 has a much simpler plot. The old Baron, although he similarly fears an avenging ghost haunting his castle tower, has no son whom he is eager to see married into nobility. He has, instead, a daughter, whose hand in marriage he has promised to whomever succeeds in exorcising the ghost. Thirty have tried and failed. The daughter, Juliette, and her companion, Louise, correspond to Lady Elinor and Cicely, and her young lover, Lorville, corresponds to Sir Palamede/Lord William in Cobb's version. Although Lorville is the son of an old friend, the Baron rejects him as a suitor and attempts to discredit him as profligate and unprincipled. Juliette, however, remains attracted to him. To her father's account of Lorville having abducted a burgomaster's daughter, Juliette responds: "Ah! the monster! That's why he hasn't written to me" (Scene iii). The Baron wants to be rid of the ghost, but he also wants to marry his daughter profitably. Thus he promotes as suitor the elderly Grouffignac, a tax collector. Juliette and Louise conspire to arouse Grouffignac's superstitious fears of the haunted tower and to assist Lorville in his successful "exorcism."

How different this version of 1810 might have been from Sade's missing version of 1788 is impossible to ascertain. The simplification of plot may have been prompted by Sade's effort to make the play suitable for the more limited means of production at the Charenton Hospital, where patients performed the plays that Sade himself directed. Evidence that Cobb may have adhered fairly closely to the earlier manuscript can be derived from a comparison of another instance of early and late revisions: *Le prévaricateur*, originally written in 1783, was also among those transcribed at the Charenton Hospital by Monsieur Donge, head of the Lottery Office.[40] A copy of the early manuscript was recovered by Sade in May, 1793, after his estate in La Coste had been pillaged by villagers.[41] The version of 1810 establishes political distance by emphasizing that the magistrate, whose dishonesty is identified in the play's title, belongs to a time "long ago." The original inscription was a denunciation of corrupt judges: "They ought to regulate public morality, and they corrupt it; they're supposed to be guardians of virtue, and they become the helpmates of vice." In 1810, this indictment was replaced by a less pointed statement on evil people avoiding exposure: "In general, men are so evil and ridiculous that their most pressing interest lies in rising against the malicious philosophy that gives them a glimpse of getting caught."[42] Another difference was Sade's five-page introductory essay, in which he compares the hostility he has incurred in his efforts to stage *Le prévaricateur*, with that experienced by Molière when he tried to stage *Tartuffe*. Sade's argument is that, like Molière, he is met with opposition from those who wish to conceal the very sort of behavior that the play exposes. Sade then goes on to describe his two principal characters.[43] The Marquis, who repudiated his aristocratic title and became "Citoyen" Sade with the advent of the Revolution, clearly knew the advantages of adjusting his politics to the temper of the times. Adjusting his morality, or immorality, was a completely different matter. As he did in the second version of *Le prévaricateur*, in the 1810 version of *La tour enchantée* he may have excised earlier political references. An outspoken critic of British commerce and British imperialism, Sade accused the English of draining the economies of other nations. In "Ernestine," for example, he blames the failure of the Swedish mines at Taperg on English banking:

Mines, for so long the state's major source of revenue, soon became dependent on the English, because of the debts contracted by their owners with a nation which is always quick to extend a helping hand to those it believes it can some day gobble up, once it has wrecked their trade or undermined their power through loans made at extortionate rates.[44]

The 1810 version of *La tour enchantée* is without any direct historical or political reference. Grouffignac, the tax collector, is a character who might well have served as a target for Sade's critique of corrupt government and greedy public officials, yet in this version of the play he is guilty only of cowardice and sexual inadequacy.

The task of rendering *La tour enchantée* palatable to an English audience was far more complicated than simply excising Sade's comments about the English. Cobb had to tell the story from an English rather than a French perspective. He was greatly assisted in this task by Storace, who provided several set pieces to reinforce a sense of British tradition: an opening chorus "To Albion's Genius," a hunting song, a chorus to the "Roast Beef of Old England," and a drinking song praising English ale.[45] Storace made far more extensive use of choral or group numbers than was typical of the period. In *The Haunted Tower*, there are six choral numbers, two trios, and three duets, leaving fourteen solos. Further, Cobb's libretto, with its marriage between Lady Elinor de Courcey and Lord William – restored to his estate as the true Baron of Oakland – re-establishes harmony between France and England. The division between the aristocracy and the common folk is not overcome, but the virtues and advantages of the commoners are repeatedly affirmed. Indeed, the significant contribution of the subplot, the love of Edward and Adela, was to emphasize the sincerity and integrity of the lower classes. Michael Kelly declares that the subplot "was taken from an Italian intermezzo opera," and it was clear that Stephen Storace intended the role of Adela as a showcase for his sister Anna's accomplishments, "both as a singer and an actress."[46]

Revolutionary themes are incorporated but controverted: the corrupt aristocracy is overthrown, but the usurping Baron was only a fake aristocrat. The class hierarchy is topsy-turvy. In his endeavor to fulfill his father's expectations as heir to the Baron's estate, "plain Edward the ploughman" introduces his beloved Adela, a cottager, into court disguised as Lady Elinor. Meanwhile, to avoid the unwanted marriage, Lady Elinor pretends to be her own maid-in-waiting and Lord William passes himself off as a court jester. As jester, Lord William mocks the false Baron, who, lacking the sexual attraction and prowess to which he pretends, is still rich enough to pay for flattery and other services. As the male lead, Lord William, Kelly had three solos, a duet, and a sestetto, as well as his part in the grand finale. Lord William's father, the true Baron, has been falsely accused of treason and then secretly murdered in the tower. The usurper has taken over castle and land, forcing the son to flee to France. He now returns a grown man to reclaim his rights, but must remain in disguise until he can secure the support of his father's friends. With his first solo, "From hope's fond dream" (I.i), he reveals his plan upon the moment of his return to England. Disguised as a court jester, he has the opportunity to express his scorn to the wicked usurper in a satirical song, "Tho' time has from your lordship's face" (II.ii), in which he tells the false Baron that he is old, ugly, and despised, and must therefore remove his care by purchasing love and favors.

> Whate'er your faults, in person, mind,
> (However gross) you chance to find,
> Yet why should you despair?
> Of flattery you must buy advice,
> You're rich enough to pay the price,
> So that removes your care. (II.ii)

Lord William must enter the "haunted tower" to prepare himself for battle. When he steps forth, wearing his father's armor, he sings "Spirit of my sainted sire" (iii.iv), which Kelly declares to be "one of the most difficult songs ever composed for tenor voice."[47] Thirteen measures in, on the words "raise, raise, raise," the voice must rise from D, to E, to A above the staff. Stephen Storace also gave Kelly an appoggiatura that would allow a C above the staff, and in the final line a cadenza, doubtless falsetto, rising to F above the staff.

Several songs express the honesty and freedom of the lower class. Cicely, for example, sings of her freedom "From high birth and all its fetters," which allows her, in contrast to Lady Elinor who is bound in an arranged marriage, to choose the "youth I love" (iii.iii). Edward and Adela ridicule aristocratic pretensions in their duet, "Will great lords and ladies" (i.iii). The conflict between upper and lower class is given full expression in the sestetto, "Alas! behold the silly maid" (ii.iv), and more directly in the duet with Adela and Lady Elinor, "Begone! I discharge you!" (iii.iii).

Throughout Storace's score, the musical numbers are well integrated into the dramatic action of the play.[48] Operatic conventions of the time put all the drama into the spoken lines or sung recitative, while arias are reserved for reflection on the events that have transpired. Storace's ensembles are not only musically complex, but also progress dramatically rather than remaining static.[49] The most stunning, perhaps, is the sestetto "Mutual Love Delighted," in which Adela and Edward express their confusion at being treated like nobility by these strangers (Elinor, William, and Cicely). Charles encourages Adela to continue her disguise, and Adela reflects upon it. The trading off of actual dialogue in an aria, rather than in recitative, was highly unusual. There are, of course, other instances: "Albion's Genius" introduces Elinor and Cicely to England, as well as describing the storm they have just escaped; the roast beef and hunting songs contextualize the action, and the drinking trio "And Now We're Met a Jolly Set" provides a line of music for Lord William to echo as he pretends to be the ghost in the tower, scaring the false Baron.

However, the music in *The Haunted Tower* plays a much more important role than simply contextualizing and allowing characters to express emotion. *The Haunted Tower*, after all, is a French story about a marriage between a Frenchwoman and an Englishman, as well as a tale about a usurping baron. When the play was staged in London in 1789, audiences shared in the concerns about the French Revolution. Conventions of social class and social hierarchy were undergoing change. Storace's music and Cobb's lyrics reflect each character's awareness of social position. At the end of the story the usurping Baron is defeated and order is re-established, so that social order seems to have restored the old status quo, but the finale, dismissing forever "The banished ills of heretofore" suggests that enduring change has been achieved.[50]

In the Cobb–Storace comic opera, *The Haunted Tower* (1789), Anna Storace sang three solos, in addition to her part in several multi-voiced songs. Her first solo is a simple air, "Whither my love" (1.iii), with a melody adapted from Paisiello. Her halting syllabic lilt, further accented with her punctuated "No, no, no," progresses into a more extended range with her rising passion. In the last thirteen measures, she rises to a high G, touches it lightly, then returns to the simple melody suited to her country life. Her second solo, "Be Mine Tender Passion" (11.i), is sung right after Adela enters disguised as Lady Elinor. The aria starts modestly, but quickly moves above the staff as Adela tries to express her aristocratic role more completely. Stephan Storace has, of course, composed the song to show off his sister's abilities. Adela seems to work up her courage in the song, so that as she approaches the end, she is able to hold out a high B for seventeen beats. Reasserting her confidence after she finishes that long high note, she touches on it four more times before the end of the song. Kelly declared that Anna Storace "was greatly received as Adela, both as a singer and an actress," and "Mrs. Crouch, as Lady Elinor, was in the full bloom of beauty, and the richest voice."[51]

As John and Ben Franceschino argue in the headnote to their translation, a more persistent evidence of Cobb's reliance on his source is "in the lyrics and situations of several songs that seem to serve parallel functions in both shows."[52] Indeed, *La tour enchantée* provides prime evidence of Sade's skill as lyricist, and Cobb followed Sade's lead in his English adaptation. It was also to Cobb's great advantage that he had the collaboration of Stephen Storace, whose score has been judged "the most successful full-length opera that Drury Lane staged in the entire century."[53]

In trying to determine how similar Cobb's adaptation might have been to Sade's original version of 1788, another problem is the inevitable "drift" in subsequent performances. It is the nature of all performative arts to alter with each performance, with the interpretation of each new actor, each new director. The text too would be altered whenever new music was interpolated, and new singers often wanted new music. "Attune the Pipe," to a melody by Ignaz Joseph Pleyel (1757–1831), was not in Storace's original score,[54] yet it was sung by Anna Maria Crouch (1763–1805), who performed in the original performance as Lady Elinor. It may have been added for the second season in 1790, but more likely in 1791

when Pleyel arrived in London to take charge of the Professional Concerts for the 1792 season. The song brings with it a bolder attribute to
Lady Elinor's character, for it is a very open invitation to be kissed:

> A kiss from Laura shall thy music pay.
> Let other swains to praise or fame aspire,
> Thou from her lips the sweet reward require.

There is, of course, no Laura in the play. Lady Elinor's reference to
Laura's kiss is a poetic trope, an allusion to Petrarch's Laura, who in this
instance satisfies her lover's longing. The presence of Petrarch's Laura,
however, introduces an odd coincidence. Because Cobb apparently knew
little or nothing about the author of the play, it was unlikely that Cobb
knew that Sade was a direct descendent of Petrarch's beloved Laura de
Novis, married to Hugues de Sade.[55]

"Come tell me where the maid is found" is another song introduced in a
later performance of *The Haunted Tower*. The song was a setting by Sir
John Stevenson (1761–1833) of "The Wonder," a ballad by Thomas Moore
(1779–1852). Added for the performance in 1816 to show off John Braham's
virtuoso tenor style, the song declares a quest for an ideal woman.

> Come, tell me where the maid is found,
> Whose heart can love without deceit,
> And I will range the world around,
> To sigh one moment at her feet.[56]

The quest is appropriate only if Sir Palamede is supposed to imagine
himself still searching for the ideal love that he has already found in Lady
Elinor.

How evil or how lecherous was the Baron, either in Sade's version or in
Cobb's? Both, of course, are burdened by guilt and fear the tower is
haunted by a ghost seeking vengeance. In the French text of 1810, Juliette
explains her father's crime:

one of his friends made a remark about some woman the Baron was courting at
the time. It was only a joke, but little by little the conversation heated up and
they started fighting. My father had the misfortune of killing his friend. Dying,
the man looked at my father to assure him of his forgiveness, and to ask him to
embrace him one last time. This frightening image never leaves my father's head.
Every time he turns around, he imagines seeing his friend. (Scene ii, lines 46–52)

In Cobb's adaptation of the earlier text, the circumstance of the ghost in
the tower is shrouded in mystery. It is the faithful servant Hugo who first

reveals that "the good Baron ... now haunts the old Tower" (II.i.12). Sade's Baron is greedy and conniving, eager to secure the profit to be gained by marrying his sixteen-year-old daughter to the sixty-year-old tax collector, and quite willing to vilify her true love's character with his lie about Lorville losing 25,000 francs in gambling and abducting the burgomaster's daughter. In cunning and deceit, however, he is no match for his daughter's maid-in-waiting. Like Cobb's Cicely, Sade's Louise is an adept schemer. She readily declares that she would have no objection to a marriage-for-profit to the sixty-year-old tax collector. In terms of vulgarity, Cobb's Baron outdoes Sade's: "Nature; why, look at me, do you see any thing like nature about me? No, no: yet I, myself, am as vulgarly and naturally pleased as any body; but I'll not show it, I'll defy the best friend I have to say I have given him a civil word since I have been Baron of Oakland – an't I the terror of the neighbourhood?" Cobb's Baron imprisons unjustly a "poor fellow for catching a hare" (I.iii.50–6), and, when Lady Elinor is introduced to him as a favorite maid-in-waiting, he comments on her sexual attraction: "She must be a great favourite of every body's, for she's a monstrous pretty girl." And in his very next breath the Baron suggests that Sir Palamede, also in disguise, must enjoy sexual privileges as "a favourite of your ladyship's" (II.ii.25–7).

In the first few seasons of *The Haunted Tower*, the Baron was played by Robert Baddeley (1732–94), who was often cast as a comic villain. Michael Kelly, who performed opposite him as Sir Palamede/Lord William, observed that Baddeley "had a habit of smacking his lips always when speaking."[57] His manner of "tasting his words" gave an impression of salacious lechery no matter what he was saying. For his part, Michael Kelly had earlier joined Anna Storace in Vienna for the premiere of Mozart's *Nozze di Figaro* (1786), in which he performed both as Basilio and as Don Curzio. He returned to London with the Storaces in March of 1787, and soon moved in with Anna Maria Crouch and became her partner in spite of her marriage to Rawlings Crouch, a Navy lieutenant. As a handsome young tenor, Kelly usually played the role of the lover. He was also a talented composer of theatre songs, and wrote the music for Lewis' *Castle Spectre* and Joanna Baillie's *De Monfort*. Before the war was declared between Britain and revolutionary France in February, 1793, Kelly often made visits to the theatres in Paris and brought back whatever he thought might suit the London stage.[58] He describes seeing in Paris in 1791 the rival versions of *Lodoiska*: Kreutzer's at the Théâtre des Italiens and Cherubini's at the Feydeau. Kelly provided the libretto from which Kemble made his adaptation, and Storace borrowed from both scores and added original music of his own for Kemble's English version, which opened at Drury Lane on June 9, 1794.[59] At the Comédie-Italienne in Paris, Kelly saw in 1790 *Raoul Barbe Bleue*, a comic opera by Ernest Modeste Grétry (1741–1813), with libretto by Michel-Jean Sédaine (1719–97). Kelly subsequently wrote the score for George Colman's *Blue-Beard; or, Female Curiosity!* (Drury Lane, January 16, 1798).[60]

Kelly, as Sir Palamede in *The Haunted Tower*, played lover to his real-life partner, Anna Maria Crouch, as Lady Elinor. They were also paired together as the lovers, Selim and Fatima, in Colman's *Blue-Beard*. As already mentioned, Adela was played by Anna Storace. Cicely, her maid, was played by then nineteen-year-old Maria Theresa Romanzini (1769–1838), known later in her career as Mrs. Bland, popular as a "sweet-voiced ... ballad singer," and effective in pert and saucy roles.[61] In the role of Beda, a pretty slave and dancing girl owned by Blue-Beard, Maria Bland also performed with Kelly and Anna Crouch in Colman's "Grand Dramatick Romance."

The affinity with Cobb's 1789 adaptation is still evident in Sade's 1810 version: the characters of the Baron, Lady Elinor, Cicely, and Sir Palamede are clearly aligned with their French counterparts, the Baron, Juliette, Louise, and Lorville. Sadistic villains, to be sure, are more obvious in other Gothic drama of the period. Apparently intending, instead, a degree of self-parody in creating the character of the Baron, Sade has given that character such a large measure of buffoonery that the wicked lechery is rendered impotent. In his commentary, Genest calls attention to the concluding scene, where "the Baron enters with his sword drawn, and some old armour awkwardly put on," and he goes on to cite Hanna Cowley's observations in her preface to *The Town before You*. Making his last hopeless stand as the false Baron, Baddeley "holding a sword in his left hand, and making awkward passes with it, charms the audience; and brings down such applauses as the bewitching dialogue of Farquhar pants for in vain."[62] Granting that Cowley meant to emphasize that *The Haunted Tower* attained its success with song and comic action, rather than with the "bewitching dialogue" of the gifted playwright, she nevertheless called attention to the effective ingredient of the Gothic spoof: the Sadistic villain is utterly emasculated, as harmless as the "toothless mastiff bitch" in Coleridge's "Christabel." Waving his sword in a grandly ineffectual dramatic gesture, the Baron becomes precisely the sort of eunuch jester that he has presumed Sir Palamede to be, or that Grouffignac is revealed to be.

John Braham, who had been engaged by Storace at Drury Lane in 1796, was soon to assume Kelly's role as Lord William. Drury Lane, which controlled the rights to Storace's works, granted permission to Covent Garden to perform *The Haunted Tower* for Margaret Martyr's benefit in May, 1803.[63] Mrs. Martyr (née Thornton) played the role of Cicely. As Waldie noted in his account of this and other performances, Storace's musical score was expanded with interpolated songs, several not at all appropriate to the dramatic context. As Lord William, Braham sang "From hope's fond dream," "Though time has from your Lordship's face," and "Spirit of my sainted sire," then introduced the "Pollacca."[64] Although he was encored in "Spirit," which he "executed . . . with great spirit," Waldie argued that it was "too noisy" for Braham's "delicate powers" and provided too little occasion for Braham to introduce the "beautiful decoration which he bestows on ad libitum passages."[65] The great performance of the evening was Adela, as performed by the "truly comic" *soprano buffa*, Anna Storace:

her dress, air, & manner are very ludicrous & she seems so happy acting, & so much at her ease. She is most charming, and in the song of the "Carpet weaver"[66] & "Whither my love" was delightful; tho' in that of "Be mine tender passion" I liked her best – she was melting in the slow part, & in the quick part ran thro' the passages in a most charming & spirited manner; her upper notes are clear & beautiful.

Waldie lamented, however, that she was losing her command of "her lower tones," which now had an unpleasant "grating sharpness."[67]

In the production for Braham's benefit on May 12, 1806, he was again Lord William and Anna Storace again Adela. Waldie praised her as "the life of the piece":

She sung charmingly all her songs which were very numerous and "Together let us range" with Braham. He sung, "From Hope's fond dream," "When time has from" & "Spirit of my sainted sire" – also "The Pollacca," the "Death of the Abercrombie," "Oft on a plat," "Sally in our alley"[68] – every one better than the last. He was in exquisite voice and sung divinely to a bumper. Catches & Glees were sung by Dignum, Kelly, & Welsh, & Braham and Dignum sung "All's Well."[69]

Maintaining a personal as well as professional relationship with Anna Storace, Braham continued to perform with her until she retired from the stage in 1808. Braham, who kept his voice well throughout his long career, performed in the concert series at Newcastle with Angelica Catalani in January, 1822, and again played his accustomed roles in Storace's *Siege of Belgrade* and *The Haunted Tower*. Even though the florid virtuoso style of performance was falling out of fashion, Braham continued to introduce long cadenzas. No matter that they were dramatically out of place, Braham also insisted on introducing songs of his own composition, such as "The Death of Nelson." From Waldie's perspective, the script of Cobb's Gothic spoof had become less important than the music, and, more importantly, "the house was crammed – above £110."[70]

Waldie provided frequent reminders that the musical score and the singing were major elements in production. Indeed, in the musical farce, *No Song, No Supper* (Drury Lane, April 16, 1790), a collaboration between Stephen Storace and Prince Hoare, the music is as crucial as the title indicates. The premiere performance featured Michael Kelly, Richard Dignum, Anna Maria Crouch, Anna Storace, and Maria Theresa Romanzini. Waldie said that the local players in Edinburgh, especially Mrs. Kemble, Mrs. Bland (née Romanzini), and Miss Perry, performed it almost as well as Drury Lane's remarkable cast of singers. The plot: a farmer's wife invites a lawyer to dinner; just as the roast leg of lamb is served her husband returns; dinner and lawyer are quickly hidden. The songs lament the lack of food, not restored until the finale. "The last scene – of the supper, the song, & the lawyer in the poke – set the house in a roar – it is an excellent farce."[71]

The hint of a flirtatious, if not adulterous, indiscretion, brings the plot of the farce very close to circumstances that might be reworked with more dire conclusion. *The Haunted Tower* is an anti-Gothic comedy with all the trappings of a Gothic melodrama. *The Siege of Belgrade* (Drury Lane, January 1, 1791), the third of James Cobb's five collaborative productions with Storace, bring the circumstances even closer to tragedy. Kelly played the Seraskier, the leader of the Turks who have laid siege to Belgrade; Mrs. Crouch played Katherine, the wife of Colonel Cohenberg of the Austrian army; and Anna Storace played Lilla, in love with Leopold, also of the Austrian army. The Seraskier manages to capture both women and make love to them before they can be rescued by the Austrians. It is not the mere fact that Cohenberg spares the life of the Seraskier that shifts the plot from tragedy; rather it is the interplay of comedy throughout. The Seraskier is very much a wanton seducer, a Don Juan rather than a Gothic villain, but his debauchery of the women seems to follow, not from an irresistible seduction, but rather a helpless sort of compliance. The comedy is provided principally through the frantic actions of Leopold as played by John Bannister, and by Yusuph, the rascally and opportunistic Mayor of Belgrade, played by Richard Suett.

Fifteen years after *The Siege of Belgrade* had first opened, Waldie witnessed a performance at Drury Lane that retained only a few of the original cast. Anna Storace was still in her role as the abducted Lilla, Bannister still performed as her comic lover. Braham had taken over Kelly's role as the Seraskier, and Dignum played the Mayor. Waldie notes that many new songs were interpolated. Braham and Storace were excellent in their duet, as were Braham and Dignum in the comic song, "All's Well." Waldie gave principal attention to Braham's solos,

Sung with such force & expression, & such grandeur of style, I never saw him to appear to greater advantage. He seemed to enjoy the beauty of the music. Indeed, other than bits of historic pretense & histrionic fanfare, the Siege of Belgrade offers little else for enjoyment, Storace sung as well as she can do – & with great effect in several parts: they cut out a sweet duet . . . & several other exquisite morceaux: which I regretted much. On the whole we had some delightful music.[72]

Instead of the music supporting or enhancing the dramatic performance, as Waldie often observed, the dramatic plot seemed to exist only to provide a context for the music. A year earlier he had attended the comic opera, *Una cosa rara* (1786), by Vicente Martín y Soler with a libretto by Lorenzo da Ponte.[73] The "great part of it," Waldie recognized, was the same as *The Siege of Belgrade*, "which was partly taken from this opera." Braham and Elizabeth Billington (née Weichsell) performed the lead roles, Anna Storace was Lilla, and Kelly Corrado.[74]

John Philip Kemble's *Lodoiska* (Drury Lane, June 9, 1794) had the elements of a Gothic melodrama. Lodoiska is in love with Count Floreski, but her father sends her to Baron Lovinski, who, determined to make her his bride, "either by fraud or force,"[75] holds her captive in his castle tower. A bit of comedy is provided by Varbel, Floreski's servant, played by Suett. Kemble collaborated with Stephen Storace in creating this musical adaptation from the opera by Rodolphe Kreutzer, libretto by Jean Claude Bédéno Dejaure (Comédie-Italienne, August 1, 1791). Kreutzer's version premiered shortly after the version by Luigi Cherubini, libretto by Claude François Filette Loraux (Théâtre Feydeau, July 18, 1791). Michael Kelly brought both scores from Paris to London,[76] and Storace set to work constructing a composite musical score using the overture and three orchestral pieces from Kreutzer, the quintet and trio in Act 1 from Cherubini, and a song from Gaetano Andreozzi.[77]

Waldie recorded seeing *Lodoiska* twice. On the first occasion, the performance had been condensed to an "entertainment," retaining all its spectacular scenery. "It is admirably acted," Waldie said, "except by Dignum who is not at all adapted for Count Floreski which is Kelly's part, but he is ill at present." The evil Baron was played by James Raymond, and the captive maiden in the tower was Maria Theresa De Camp. Raymond performed several years in Belfast, then made his London debut as Osmond in *The Castle Spectre* (Drury Lane, September 26, 1799).[78] As the villain, his very manner and movement aroused dislike and distrust. Waldie was especially impressed by Miss De Camp in both her singing and acting: "She is a beautiful girl & very pleasing in her manner." The rescue scene from the burning tower he pronounced a grand *coup de théâtre*.[79]

Waldie again saw *Lodoiska* during his visit to Brussels, where he arrived with his sisters, Charlotte and Jane, on June 15, 1815, the very eve of Napoleon's last four desperate campaigns: Quatre Bras and Ligny (June 16), Waterloo (June 18), and Wavre (June 18–19). Although both his sisters published best-selling accounts of the battles,[80] Waldie kept only his personal notes of discussions with citizens and soldiers during the confusion. He related the fear and anxiety over rumors of Brunswick's death and the mistaken report that the Prussian army had been defeated. Waldie much preferred the horrors of the stage to the horrors of war. Even the horrors of a bad performance could be laughed at, but not the wagonloads of the wounded and dead.[81] Sickened in heart and mind, he welcomed the arrival of Angelica Catalani and Captain Valabrègue. Together with Valabrègue and Catalani he saw the performance of Kreutzer's *Lodoiska* in the Brussels Theatre, which he described as "an ugly shape – and ill lighted – not unlike the old Covent Garden." Concerning the unnamed tenor who played the wicked Baron Lovinski, Waldie reported that his voice was flat "and his action was not elegant – he is but a beginner, has little voice and no ear." Mlle. Terneaux,[82] who performed the title role, was "nearly as bad." In all, "they made dreadful screaming and bawling out of tune, which was a great pity for the music is long, full, and exquisite – 3 times as much as there is on the same piece in English." The saving grace of the performance was a superbly conducted thirty-piece orchestra.[83]

Mentioned earlier in this chapter as the last play in Storace's career as a stage composer, *The Iron Chest* (Drury Lane, March 12, 1796) has always stood out as a strange pastiche. In his summary of the play, Genest described it as "one of those jumbles of Tragedy, Comedy, and Opera of which Colman Jun. was so fond." After granting that "Sir Edward Mortimer is a striking character, and one well calculated to show off a good actor,"[84] Genest went on to quote several pages of Colman's angry indictment of Kemble for his "feeble" performance as Mortimer:

I found Mr. Kemble, in his dressing room, a short time before the curtain was drawn up, taking *Opium Pills*: and, nobody who is acquainted with that gentleman will doubt me when I assert, that, they are a medicine which he has long been in the habit of swallowing. He appear'd to me very unwell; and seemed, indeed, to have imbibed,

> Poppy and Mandragora,
> And all the drowsy syrups of the world.[85]

Colman blamed Kemble's drugged condition for everything that went wrong with the opening performance, not just Kemble's own slurred speech and stumbling movements on stage, but for the failure as manager to conduct proper rehearsals, so that the comic scenes were flat and Storace's songs were ill-prepared. Somehow it was also Kemble's fault that the delightfully comic role of Adam Winterton, Mortimer's aged servant, was badly performed by James William Dodd. Although he had often displayed his mastery in comic roles as elderly gentleman or servant, Dodd's health was failing. He died before the end of the 1796 season. Colman was nevertheless right in blaming Kemble's soporific performance. Described in Act I as a melancholy recluse yet generous to the poor and suffering, Mortimer does not appear on stage until Act II. Colman intended the character to be charged with a turmoil of guilt. Kemble, perhaps numbed by opium, played him as morose and lethargic:

the great actor was discover'd, as *Sir Edward Mortimer*, in his library. Gloom and desolation sat upon his brow; and he was habited, from the wig to the shoe-string, with the most studied exactness. Had one of King Charles the First's portraits walk'd from it's frame, upon the boards of the Theatre, it could not have afforded a truer representation of ancient and melancholy dignity . . . The spectators, who gaped with expectation at his first appearance, yawn'd with lassitude before his first *exit*. It seem'd, however, that illness had totally incapacitated him from performing the business he had undertaken.[86]

As Genest cautiously phrased it, "this piece is professedly founded on the novel of Caleb Williams."[87] Colman was equally cautious in defining the debt: "Much of Mr. Godwin's story I have omitted; much, which I have adopted, I have compress'd; much I have added; and much I have taken the liberty to alter."[88] Although Colman could not have created the guilt-ridden character of Mortimer without Godwin's Ferdinando Falkland as his model, the character of Wilford has little in common with Caleb Williams. The psychological complexity of their relationship is tempered down. Wilford is not driven by vindictiveness. Even his curiosity is of a much tamer species.[89] Colman made the most of the Gothic elements.

The murder, the mystery of the trunk, and above all Mortimer's tormented behavior, are crucial, but so too are the comic scenes and the romance. The comedy is provided primarily by Samson in the cottage scenes, by the robbers, and by the bantering of Winterton. Storace's songs, especially "Sweet Barbara," sustain the scenes of Wilford's courtship of Barbara, the poacher's daughter.

Once Winterton revealed that a murder had taken place, Wilford became obsessed with unraveling the mystery. Marjean Purinton has provided valuable insight into the dramatic unfolding of Wilford's actions by relating the mysterious trunk to the forbidden chamber in Colman's *Blue-Beard, or, Female Curiosity!* (Covent Garden, January 23, 1798). Colman's earlier play might have had a parallel subtitle: *The Iron Chest, or, Male Curiosity!* Colman uses both the mysterious trunk and the forbidden chamber to excite the curiosity, not just of the characters in the respective plays, but of the audience. Purinton argued that trunk and chamber were "curiosity cabinets"; more specifically they were correlates of the Temple, the "curiosity cabinet" of entrepreneurial mountebank and sexologist Dr. James Graham. With the teasing possibility of something lurid and forbidden hidden within, trunk and chamber became thematic focal points for theatrical peeping.[90] Because it contains Mortimer's written account of the murder, the trunk serves the theatrical function of keeping the age-old dramatic device of the concealed letter visually prominent on stage.[91]

Hazlitt, who praised Godwin's *Things as They Are: The Adventures of Caleb Williams* (1794) as "unquestionably the best modern novel,"[92] readily acknowledged the vast difference between Falkland and Colman's Mortimer. The latter has "much less genius and elevation." Although "forcible and affecting," Mortimer is "harsh, heavy, fierce, and painfully irritable." Hazlitt reported twice on performances of *The Iron Chest*, first at the Haymarket in August, 1815, with Meggett in the role of Mortimer, then at Drury Lane in November, 1816, with Edmund Kean. It has been speculated that Meggett had only a short career because of hostility from Edmund Kean's supporters, known as "the Wolves."[93] Hazlitt, himself a strong supporter of Kean, explains that Meggett's acting was cramped, and barren of "genial expression":

His habitual manner is too hard and dry – he makes too dead a set at every thing. He grinds his words out between his teeth as if he had a lockjaw, and his action is clenched till it resembles the commencement of a fit of the epilepsy. He strains his muscles till he seems to have lost the use of them. If Mr. Kemble was hard, Mr. Meggett is rigid, to a petrifying degree. We however think that he gave considerable force and feeling to the part, by the justness of his conception, and by the energy of his execution. But neither energy nor good sense is sufficient to make the great actor.

The character of Wilford, the Caleb Williams of the piece; was played by Barnard. Hazlitt granted the actor "considerable merit," but complained that the part had been so diminished from Godwin's conception that "he seemed somewhat too insignificant an instrument to produce such terrible effects."[94]

   The passion that was missing in Meggett's performance was provided in abundance by Edmund Kean. Hazlitt praised Kean's delivery of Mortimer's "soliloquy on honour" (1.iii.34–54), but also the confession of his crime to Wilford. In the first he hoped that his secret might remain undiscovered so that "my pure flame of Honour [may] shine in story." In the latter speech, Honor becomes a "blood-stain'd God!" Hazlitt was impressed by the vehemence with which Kean expressed the ghastly deed: "I stab'd him to the heart: – and my oppressor / Roll'd, lifeless, at my foot" (11.iv.113–14).

In the picturesque expression of passion, by outward action, Mr. Kean is unrivalled. The transitions in this play, from calmness to deep despair, from concealed suspicion to open rage, from smooth decorous indifference to the convulsive agonies of remorse, gave Mr. Kean frequent opportunities for the display of his peculiar talents. The mixture of common-place familiarity and solemn injunction in his speeches to Wilford when in the presence of others, was what no other actor could give with the same felicity and force. The last scene of all – his coming to life again after his swooning at the fatal discovery of his guilt, and then falling back after a ghastly struggle, like a man waked from the tomb, into despair and death in the arms of his mistress, was one of those consummations of the art, which those who have seen and have not felt them in this actor, may be assured that they have never seen or felt any thing in the course of their lives, and never will to the end of them.[95]

Hazlitt's major complaint against *The Iron Chest* is not simply that it is "a melange of the tragic and comic," but that the opposing elements never work in concert, neither to inform nor to accentuate one another. Colman's tragedies lack "force and depth in the impassioned parts," which are further impeded by the counter-effect of the comic.

The two plots (the serious and ludicrous) do not seem going on and gaining ground at the same time, but each part is intersected and crossed by the other, and has to set out again in the next scene, after being thwarted in the former one, like a person who has to begin a story over again in which he has been interrupted.

Because there is no "high-wrought" tragedy, there is no need for "comic relief." Indeed, it is never clear "whether the comedy or tragedy is principal," whether Colman introduced "the comic for the sake of the tragic, or the tragic for the sake of the comic." In this confusion, there is only a jostling of the dark Gothic pretensions with anti-Gothic buffoonery.[96]

Waldie held much the same opinion of *The Iron Chest*. "I think it one of the worst of Colman's plays," he wrote, first because "the Catastrophe is not satisfactory," and secondly because "the author himself has thwarted the dramatic effects by clumsily juggling his comic and tragic plots."[97] The comic scenes with Blanch, Samson, and Winterton take on a life of their own, almost as if a comedy had been tucked into the tragic tale of Mortimer's crime and guilty remorse. Even the tragic plot seems split, just as Mortimer's character is split. More complex than the usual Gothic villain, such as Lewis' Osmond, who is evil through and through, Mortimer is known for his charity and good deeds. His brooding melancholy arouses sympathy rather than fear. Colman has even altered Falkland's persecution of Caleb, so that Mortimer's outbreaks against Wilford express more anxiety than anger. As that anxiety grows, Mortimer reveals an impulsive violence otherwise restrained by his strong code of propriety. The audience is given hints of a covert tale of domestic abuse in a character who "protects" the woman "left an orphan" because he has murdered her uncle. Although she had "long been enamour'd of him," Helen has felt more than any other his aloof reserve.

Waldie's objections to an unsatisfactory "Catastrophe" point to Colman's difficulty in managing a reconciliation between Mortimer and Wilford as well as between Mortimer and Helen. Although Wilford, like Caleb, is falsely charged with stealing jewels, he is not chained and imprisoned many months in a dungeon, but declared innocent even before the officers are called. With his expedient addition of Mortimer's brother, Fitzharding, Colman has provided an "arbiter" to exonerate Wilford. Unlike Falkland, Mortimer is not charged for his crime. The murder is kept a family secret. In his dying convulsions, he cannot confess the deed even to Helen:

HELEN.   Where is he? Ill! and on the ground! Oh, Mortimer!
              Oh, Heaven! my Mortimer. O, raise him. – Gently.
              Speak to me, love. He cannot!
MORTIMER.   Helen – 'Twas I that – [*he struggles to speak, but appears
              unable to utter.*]
HELEN.   Oh, he's convulsed!

FITZHARDING. Say nothing. We must lead him to his chamber.
          Beseech you to say nothing! Come, good lady.
          [*Fitzharding and Helen lead Mortimer out.*] (III.ii.841–7)

Although Mortimer shares with the Gothic villain the character of
dark, brooding melancholy, Colman has drawn from his Godwinian
source the exposition of "the good man turned bad," or, rather, of the
lurking violence that "the good man" struggles to keep hidden and under
control.

Among the several performances that he witnessed, Waldie saw it twice
with Robert William Elliston as Mortimer. The first time was at the
Haymarket. In managing the contrasting moods of Mortimer, "every
working of passion, doubt, fear, guilt, deceit, shame, & rage, were astonishingly depicted." Elliston's manner was "animation & fire, tempered by
propriety – the dignity of his action is natural, easy, & unaffected." Waldie
praised the supporting cast, especially the role of Wilford as performed by
Henry Kelly, a very pleasant young actor, whose inexperience was an asset
in representing the character's naïve innocence. John Burton was a dithering
Adam Winterton. Charlotte Goodall was not well cast as Helen: "she is
much more pleasing in men's clothes than her own dress – she is too large
for a girlish character." Mrs. Gibbs (née Logan) "was charming in Blanch";
Mrs. Atkins (née Warrell) "sung sweetly in Barbara."[98]

At Drury Lane three years later, Elliston was again in the leading
role. His performance exhibited "some inimitable turns of feeling in his
manner, & his more violent parts are most impressive." Vincent De Camp
"was hardly inferior to him in Wilford." In assuming a role, De Camp
"always takes so much pains, & gives so much pains, is so animated, &
gives so much interest to it that nothing could be more affecting." The best
scenes of the production were those between De Camp and Elliston.
Waldie also declared that the music was beautiful, praising especially
Maria Theresa Bland (née Romanzini) in her songs as Barbara. Andrew
Cherry, "a much better actor . . . in old parts" than William Dowton,
made an "excellent Adam Winterton."[99]

As previously noted, Waldie formed a close friendship with William
Augustus Conway at Newcastle in 1809. When *The Iron Chest* was performed, Conway took the role of Wilford opposite John Fawcett in
Mortimer. In Waldie's estimation, "Fawcett was truly ridiculous in Sir
Edward – all rant, folly, & absurdity – it was impossible not to laugh." On
the other hand, Conway "was charming in Wilford" and made "much of
the part."[100] In September of the same year, Waldie attended the performance at the Haymarket. The tragic roles with Charles Mayne Young

as Mortimer and Richard Jones as Wilford were, respectively, misinterpreted and miscast:

Young played Sir Edward with great force & effect – in the violent agonies, & half smothered nervous irritability of the part, he was truly great & shewed himself to have great powers & greater sense & judgement but wherever he was to be pathetic and feeling, he was too measured & solemn, & commanded no sympathy. His face is terrible – certainly. Jones has a great deal of energy –but no variety – & a total want of softness. His Wilford was poor indeed – lively comedy is his forte. How much I longed for C. Kemble, or Conway! Mathews was perfection in Samson, so natural & easy, yet comic. Mrs. Glover will soon be in the straw – but she is a most elegant charming lovely woman & all she does is marked by sense & elegance – there is a peculiar charm in her countenance & manner admirably adapted for the first line of comedy. She is as much superior to Miss Duncan as that lady to Miss Norton or Mrs. H. Johnston – or any other of the wretched set they have at C. G. theatre . . . On the whole the comic scenes were well done – I must not forget Grove in Adam. He was capital. Eyre in Fitzharding, very well – but I longed for Elliston in Sir Ed & C. Kemble or Conway – or even De Camp in Wilford.[101]

During March and April of 1815, Waldie was in Bath to witness the performances of William Henry West Betty. Earlier in this chapter, I summarized Waldie's account of Betty's performances at Newcastle in 1805, including his role as Osmond in *The Castle Spectre*. He was then thirteen. In 1808 he made his final appearance as a boy actor. After his four years at Christ's College, Cambridge, Betty returned to the stage in 1812. Many accounts said that Betty's performances were ill received, but Waldie provided a markedly different perspective on Betty's attempt to revive his acting career.

When James Prescott Warde commenced his acting career at Bath, he found himself playing many of the roles that had been a part of Betty's repertory. His first appearance on the Bath stage was as Achmet in Browne's *Barbarossa* (December 28, 1813). In the meantime, Betty had also begun playing at Bath, and the management seems to have deliberately set up a competition between the two actors. Interestingly enough, Warde was engaged in a similar competition in 1817 playing against Conway.[102] Two things become evident: Betty was indeed Warde's superior in acting, but he was coerced into a disadvantage that was probably more extreme at Bath than elsewhere. That disadvantage at Bath was in playing to an audience who expected to see Betty playing Betty. All his old roles were revived, even the role of Osman in *Zara*, the role that he had played in his very first stage performance in Belfast at age eleven. Betty was thus caught in a time-warp as a twenty-four-year-old adult booked for a series of reprises of roles for which he had been applauded and adulated as a child. Because he had already seen Betty perform during the 1814 season at Bath, Waldie was quite prepared to compare and denounce Warde's performance as Mortimer as "weak & no dignity & little nature," adding that "nothing in that part can go down after Betty."[103] Three weeks later he said of the performance, "Betty was very great & gave some points of Sir Edward with inimitable effect," with the added note: "Every body was delighted with Betty's acting."[104]

The Iron Chest, Genest wrote, was "one of those jumbles of Tragedy, Comedy, and Opera of which Colman Jun. was so fond." Hazlitt called it "a melange of the tragic and comic." Waldie said that Colman had "thwarted the dramatic effects by clumsily juggling his comic and tragic plots." The plays discussed in this chapter were selected because they well illustrate the contrasting presence of the comic in plays of dark melodrama. Hazlitt insisted that it was inappropriate in *The Iron Chest* to regard as "comic relief" what was actually a comic countermovement to Mortimer's morbid brooding. In their oblivious disregard for the horrific, Lewis' Motley in *The Castle Spectre*, and, as we will see in Chapter 9, McSwill in Planché's *The Vampire*, bring a comic nonchalance that is not a "relief," but an essential heightening of the prevailing doom. The audience is made more aware of the impending danger by the total disregard or incompetence of the comic figures. In *The Siege of Belgrade*, the frantic Leopold is of no use in the rescue, and the rascally Mayor cares more about his own profit than about liberation. Varbel, the Count's servant in *Lodoiska*, the poacher's son Samson, and the old servant Adam Winterton in *The Iron Chest* are characters who engage the audience in frivolity even while the grim causality of Gothic evil is unfolding.

In *The Haunted Tower* the entire Gothic structure might be said to have collapsed into parody, for the Gothic villain himself is a clown. The false Baron is a lecherous buffoon, and the plot is carried forward by Cicely as saucy maid; Palamede in his sub-role as ironic Fool; Lewis as lazy, lusting servant. Cobb and Storace produced a musical comedy of errors with the confusions of the true and disguised Adela, the true and disguised Lady Elinor, the true and disguised Lord William. The evil is abjured, and the haunted tower exorcised – at least for that brief moment when the curtain falls. Storace's Grand Finale promises that with the restoration of peace and the double marriage of the comic opera's "happy ending," past conflict will be forgotten.

> The banished ills of heretofore
> At happy distance viewing;
> Of the past we'll think no more,
> While future bliss pursuing. (III.vi)

Whether "future bliss" might be hoped for from the Revolution in France, *The Haunted Tower* continued a major success throughout the 1790s. Storace died of a severe attack of gout and fever on March 19, 1796; Anna Storace left London to travel abroad with the young tenor, John Braham; Michael Kelly's beloved Anna Crouch succumbed to alcoholism; James Cobb continued to enjoy popularity for his unabashed celebration of "Anglo-Saxon liberty" but gradually ceased to write after the turn of the century. In subsequent revivals of *The Haunted Tower*, Cobb's script became increasingly subservient to the musical performance. In France, the Marquis de Sade spent his final years in the mental hospital at Charenton, directing and revising his earlier plays.

Among the examples of theatrical "clap-trap," one often thinks of James M. Barrie's *Peter Pan*, when Peter, at the close of Act IV, tells the audience that Tinker Bell is dying and that she could be saved only "if children believed in fairies!"

> Do you believe in fairies? Say quick that you believe!
> If you believe, clap your hands![105]

The Marquis de Sade's "clap-trap" is more ominous: we applaud to break the spell of dramatic illusion. *La tour enchantée* may be a comedy, but whether it is performed in an insane asylum or in the city's finest theatre, it sets loose all the antic madness of the imagination.

JULIETTE.   [*To the audience.*] Ah! If the haunted tower
            Was successful where you're sitting,
            To render it less dangerous,
            Gentlemen, please applaud.
            The author will think there's something wrong
            If you all happen to agree with him!
            But, hurry up, do what he suggests
            'Cause the Devil is in his house.

CHAPTER 8

Blue-Beard's castle: mischief and misogyny

At odds with the popular concept of "romantic love" is the pervasive presence of misogyny in Romantic drama. Although it has been acknowledged that the Gothic in Romantic literature provided a fictive disguise for exposing issues of domestic abuse of women,[1] little attention has yet been addressed to the presumed rationale for the abuse or for the punishment of the perpetrator. Nor was violence against women a theme confined exclusively to Gothic drama. While some works may have been intended as a moral corrective, others seem to indulge a sadistic male fantasy. Indeed, in some plays the moral retribution in the final scene seems no more than a belated excuse for the sexual fantasy that dominates throughout the preceding scenes. Even the women playwrights (Joanna Baillie, Charlotte Birch-Pfeiffer, Mary Mitford) modulate the relative transparency/opacity of the disguise in depicting male hypocrisy. The representation of a fatal "female curiosity" in the staging of *Blue-Beard* – in the theatrical versions by Jean Michael Sédaine and André Grétry (1789), Ludwig Tieck (1797), George Colman (1798), William Dunlap (1811), Reginald Heber (1812), and James Robinson Planché (1839) – reveal marked variations in the strategies of sadistic eroticism, displaced culpability, and pretenses of moral rectitude. Although similar patterns of misogyny and disguise could be observed in plays as different as Wordsworth's *The Borderers*, Lewis' *The Castle Spectre*, Baillie's *Orra*, and Shelley's *The Cenci*, the attention here will be given exclusively to the identity and motives of the blue-bearded villain, to the circumstances of his victim's entrapment, and to the ethical ground of her rescue.

The murderous lust of Blue-Beard, as Maria Tatar points out in *Secrets beyond the Door*, is only part of the story. The other part is the curiosity of his wife. Tatar observes how female inquisitiveness has been represented through the past three centuries. Like Eve, who succumbed to the temptation of the serpent and plucked fruit from the sole forbidden tree (Genesis 3:1–6), Blue-Beard's wife similarly opens the sole forbidden door.

As disobedient wife, her curiosity and her inability to resist temptation make her fully culpable, perhaps even deserving her punishment. "Some wives of Blue-Beard," Tatar declares, "are treacherous deceivers, guilty of moral and sexual betrayal; others are resourceful instigators who use their wits to get to the bottom of the dark secrets haunting their marriages." There has been, Tatar adds, a moral shift from the former to the latter perspective, from an earlier time in which Blue-Beard's wife was denounced "for her 'reckless curiosity' and her 'uncontrolled appetite,'" to an age in which "her problem-solving skills and psychological finesse make her a shrewd detective" and heroine of the tale.[2] In tracing that shift, Tatar grants a broad range of reinvention that includes not only such variations as Anatole France's *The Seven Wives of Bluebeard* ("Les Sept Femmes de Barbe-Bleue," 1909), Angela Carter's *The Bloody Chamber* (1979), Margaret Atwood's *Bluebeard's Egg* (1983), and Joyce Carol Oates' *Blue-Bearded Lover* (1988), but also such narrative parallels as Jane Eyre and the forbidden attic in Charlotte Brontë's novel (1847), or Danny Torrance and the forbidden room 217 in Steven King's *The Shining* (1978). She finds further similarities in Frances Hodgson Burnett's *The Secret Garden* (1888) and Daphne du Maurier's *Rebecca* (1938). Although she begins with the folk tales as told by Charles Perrault (1697)[3] and the Brothers Grimm (1812),[4] and goes on to survey another eighty works, she leaves the Romantic period untouched, except for a glance at Mary Shelley's *Frankenstein* (1818) and a single paragraph on Tieck's *Ritter Blaubart* (1797).[5]

A first step in tracing the identity and motives of Blue-Beard is to determine whence he comes and where he has built his castle. In Richard Burton's account of the "Fans, or the so-called cannibal tribes of the Gaboon country," the practice of cannibalism in each village he visits seems always to be deferred to the tribes of villages further off.[6] So too the practice of wife-killing: it is not done in our village, but by violent misogynists who dwell elsewhere.[7] The Aarne–Thompson index of folk-tales[8] identifies "Blue-Beard" among types 312 and 312A, about women whose brothers rescue them from their ruthless husbands or abductors. Because versions of the tale are told among many cultures, including a tale from India of "The Brahmin Girl who Married a Tiger,"[9] the setting of domestic violence, the location of Blue-Beard's castle, might presumably be anywhere. But prevailing social denial insisted that Blue-Beard could not be one of us. He belonged to another time or another place. He was an alien, and his otherness was fully exposed in the color of his beard. Within the European tradition, "Blue-Beard" was certainly best known in the version of Charles Perrault in France,[10] which influenced the version included in the folk tales of the Brothers Grimm,[11] and yet again in Ernst Meier's collection of Swabian folk tales.[12] An Eastern setting occurs in none of these versions.

When did Blue-Beard become an Eastern tyrant? Among the illustrations that she reprints in her book, Maria Tatar calls attention to the depiction of the wife in the forbidden chamber in *Bluebeard, or the Fatal Effects of Curiosity and Disobedience* (1808).[13] The wife, dressed in a feathered turban and harem pantaloons, looks aghast at the decapitated heads of her six predecessors, each with an identifying tag around her neck, with European hairstyles and with demure or smiling faces. In the very title the wife's action is already judged as "Disobedience," and that judgment is repeated in the motto: "Inquisitive tempers to mischief may lead / But placid obedience will always succeed." Also among Tatar's illustrations is a Blue-Beard in a bejeweled Eastern turban on the title-page of *The Popular Story of Blue Beard; or, Female Curiosity* (1850). Not until Arthur Quiller-Couch's version in 1910, Tatar declares, was the bride of Blue-Beard "finally given a name."[14] Quiller-Couch calls her Fatima,[15] the name of the daughter (616?–33) of the Islamic prophet Muhammad, regarded by Muslims as one of the Four Perfect Women. If Tatar had looked at the theatrical versions produced by Tieck and Colman in the 1790s, she would have known that the setting had already been moved to Istanbul, and that 110 years before Quiller-Couch the bride of Blue-Beard had already been named Fatima.

Andrew Lang (1844–1912), the poet, novelist, anthropologist, and folklorist who edited the *Arabian Nights* and a dozen volumes of folk tales, vehemently protested the Easternizing of Perrault's tale: "Monsieur de la Barbe Bleue was *not* a Turk!" Perrault's version contained no reference to Turkey or the East: "One of the ladies' brothers was a Dragoon, the other a Mousquetaire, of M. d'Artagnan's company perhaps." Lang denounced the oriental fashions of the illustrations as totally inappropriate: "They were all French folk and Christians; had he been a Turk, Blue Beard need not have wedded one wife at a time."[16] Nor was there any hint of the Orient in the version published by the Brothers Grimm, nor in Meier's Swabian version. Although there were significant variants among these three early versions, the more striking changes appeared in the theatrical performances. Certainly the most emphatic change was the Eastern setting that Lang denounced a full century later. And it was on the stage, too, and not in Quiller-Couch's text of 1910, that the bride of Blue-Beard first became Fatima.

The Easternizing did not commence with the first of the stage versions. André Grétry's opera, *Raoul, Barbe Bleue*, with libretto by Jean Michel

Sédaine,[17] was performed at the Comédie-Italienne in Paris (March 2, 1789) just a few months before the storming of the Bastille (July 14, 1789), and its success had much to do with Sédaine's politicizing of the plot as a protest against exploitation of the underprivileged classes by the aristocracy. In contrast to later theatrical versions, the central conflict, the sadistic passion of Blue-Beard to force his bride into terrified submission, presented that brutal lust as symptomatic of the relationship between the feudal aristocracy and the citizenry.

While it is only a coincidence of history that the Marquis de Sade, incarcerated in the Bastille, was at work on *Justine* at the very time that Sédaine was composing *Raoul, Barbe Bleue*, that coincidence is compounded by the fact that both Sade and Sédaine turned to the historical record of Gilles de Rais (1404–40) in constructing the character of libertine depravity.[18] Although the possibility exists, there is no evidence that Perrault himself may have modeled his Barbe-Bleue on the notorious crimes of Gilles. A Marshal of France serving under Joan of Arc before her execution, Gilles became a national hero for helping drive the English out of France. After the crowning of the Dauphin and the death of Joan of Arc, Gilles returned to his castle in Brittany and indulged his pleasures in sexual cruelty. He lured young boys to his castle, sodomized and then beheaded them. When a local militia finally responded to protests and stormed the castle, they found the decapitated bodies of 50 boys. At his trial he confessed to 140 killings, but it was estimated that the number might have been in excess of 300. He was executed on October 26, 1440.[19] The story of Blue-Beard might not have been invented in response to the sexual brutality of Gilles, but its telling in Brittany must have seemed more urgent than a mere cautionary fable. Praised by Sade and condemned by Sédaine, Gilles represented the depravity of the *ancien régime*. Sédaine's setting and characters, like Perrault's, are French. Isaure is the name of the latest bride to be brought to the castle of the blue-bearded Raoul. Grétry's music reveals the fervor of his sympathy with the Republican ideals. With a happy ending and virtue rewarded, the libretto is clearly constructed as *comédie*; on this eve of Revolution, however, the musical score has somber reminders of the prevailing tragedy of an abusive aristocracy.

Even in its politically charged version, the retelling of "Blue-Beard" retains its essential ambiguity. How confident were Sédaine and Grétry at the advent of the Revolution that the tyranny would cease? In all versions, Blue-Beard's sword is impatiently poised to slice through his bride's neck before the much-delayed rescue. In Perrault's version, the bride calls three times to her sister Anne atop the tower to ask whether their brothers may yet be seen approaching the castle. The delay, to be sure, functions to heighten suspense, but it also sustains the ambiguity as to whether the bride will indeed be punished for having disobeyed her husband and violated his trust. Does the wife's trespass justify the punishment? Although the forbidden lock and bloody key were readily interpreted as symbols for sexual infidelity, Perrault adopted a frivolous tone in giving his tale not one but two morals:

> Moral:
> Ladies, you should never pry –
> You'll repent it by and by!
> 'Tis the silliest of sins;
> Trouble in a trice begins.
> There are, surely – more's the woe! –
> Lots of things you need not know.
> Come, forswear it now and here –
> Joy so brief, that costs so dear!
> Another Moral:
> You can tell this tale is old
> By the very way it's told.
> Those were days of derring-do;
> Man was lord, and master too.
> Then the husband ruled as king.
> Now it's quite a different thing;
> Be his beard what hue it may –
> Madam has a word to say.[20]

Readily assuming that women are indeed apt to be guilty of curiosity, Perrault in his first moral repeats the warning that the ladies will "repent it by and by," but his chastisement is no more than idle tongue-clucking disapproval of this "silliest of sins." Even if the sin should be infidelity, it is unwise to indulge "joy so brief, that costs so dear." The first moral addresses the wife, and reduces the fatal "curiosity" to a sin deserving no worse than a light-hearted scold. The second moral addresses the husband, noting that by the enlightened year of 1697 the good old days have passed and men have long since relinquished domestic rule. As in the later operatic comedy of Sédaine and Grétry, however, the disturbing tragedy of the slain wives was not easily dispelled.

When Ludwig Tieck commenced writing his fairy-tale comedies his source was Perrault, but his model was Carlo Gozzi. In his contest as playwright with Carlo Goldoni, Gozzi achieved fame by reviving *commedia dell'arte* improvisation and bringing popular folk tales to the stage. Among his successes were *L'amore delle tre melarance* (1761, *Love of Three Oranges*), *Il re cervo* (1762, *The King Stag*), *Turandot* (1762, from the *Arabian Nights*), *La donna serpente* (1762, *The Serpent Woman*), and *L'augellino belverde* (1765, *The Green Bird*). Tieck saw the possibility of replicating this theatrical coup against neo-classical drama. To be sure, the Germans had no tradition of *commedia dell'arte*, but they did have Hanswurst, the raucous clown whom Johann Christoph Gottsched had banished from the stage in 1730,[21] and there were folk tales in abundance. As a companion volume to his Shandyesque novel, *Peter Lebrecht: A Story without Adventures* (1795, *Peter Lebrecht. Eine Geschichte ohne Abentheuerlichkeiten*), Tieck published in 1797 a collection of folk tales. Fifteen years before the Brothers Grimm published their collection, Tieck's source was Perrault. For his stage adaptations of *Knight Bluebeard* and *Puss-in-Boots* (*Ritter Blaubart* and *Der gestiefelte Kater*), Tieck introduced the irony of play-within-a-play and play-about-a-play, of illusionist and anti-illusionist complexity. Tieck actually penned two different versions of the Blue-Beard story, one as tale, another as play, reprinting the play version sixteen years later in the second of the three volumes of *Phantasus* (1812–16).

Tieck's *Der gestiefelte Kater* is frequently cited as the foremost theatrical example of Romantic irony; similarly, his *Ritter Blaubart* shows how the comic and tragic, already key ingredients in Perrault's tale and the comic opera of Sédaine and Grétry, could be fused into the grotesque.[22] As part of the satire against the campaigns of Napoleon, Tieck introduces a fool and a wise man to discuss military policy. In addition to the two brothers of Perrault's tale, he has also introduced two cousins, who add to the debate on the virtues and vices of the battlefield. Although Peter Berner, the knight known as Blue-Beard,[23] is represented primarily as a ruthless warrior, in his wooing of Agnes his seductive manner has all the effusive charm that Béla Lugosi lent to his film role as Count Dracula.[24] More grotesque than the Knight is his seventy-year-old housekeeper, Mechtilde, whom he fondly calls his dragon. She is Tieck's invention, her character made up of the "terror and dear folly" ("Schreck und liebe Albernheit") that he identified as his play's major ingredients.[25] Her "dear folly" lies in instigating the bride's fatal curiosity. She has a counterpart in Matilda, the diabolical female in Matthew Gregory Lewis' *The Monk* (1796), who pushes Ambrosio forward to rape and stab Antonia, his sister, and to strangle Elvira, their mother. Her role provides a clever twist in the misogynist plot: yes, a male commits the brutal crimes against women, but their trespasses are encouraged by another woman. The idea, of course, was by no means original with Tieck: he had the example of Lady Macbeth who screws her husband's "courage to the sticking place" in his act of regicide; or Eve, who induces Adam to bite the forbidden fruit. Indeed, more like the Serpent, she piques Agnes' curiosity to explore the forbidden chamber.

Mechtilde tells Agnes of her master's vast riches and encourages her to explore the rooms in her master's absence (IV.i).[26] At nightfall, when Mechtilde announces that she is going to bed, she cautions Agnes to be wary of the bats should she ascend the balcony to the forbidden seventh room. Agnes quickly protests: "It has never occurred to me to look into the seventh room, about which the Knight was so concerned." Mechtilde grants the possibility that the room "contains nothing remarkable," explaining that she has never seen inside. The old servant's revelation that not even she has seen the mysterious room further arouses Agnes' curiosity. After a long monologue in which Agnes weighs the pros and cons of looking into the room, she finally decides that if she were not to go into the room, the Knight should have kept the key himself. Tieck does not stage her entrance into the forbidden chamber. Instead, he shows her on the following morning, pale, distraught, and raving about the blood-stained key (IV.iii, pp. 459–62). The lines in which she expresses her frenzied anxiety echo Macbeth's lines about having "murdered sleep," and Lady Macbeth's "Out damned spot!" Reveling in her *Schadenfreude*, Mechtilde, "uncanny, and appareled with all the terrors of hell,"[27] pretends to calm Agnes by telling her a fairy-tale. It is a tale about an old hunter and his children who lived in the dark forest. He warned the children never to stray outside on a certain night of the year. While the father was absent, a daughter forgot his command and ventured out into the night. Strange noises surround her in the darkness. She sees before her a lake, and from the lake there appear three gory hands, and each hand points a blood-dripping finger at the young girl. "Bloody?" cries Agnes, realizing that Mechtilde knows that she has used the seventh key, the bloody key. "Look at the old witch!" she shouts to her sister Anne, "look at the face she is making." Agnes calls her a monster and murderer, but Mechtilde calmly walks off commenting that Agnes has acquired strange ideas (V.ii, pp. 469–70).

The character of Mechtilde was a bold addition to the play, and the fairy-tale within a fairy-tale was an effective *coup de théâtre*. Following Perrault, Tieck kept the bride's sister, Anne, adds a third brother, and a dozen minor characters. He took pride in his appropriation of Gozzi's Fiabesque drama, and readily acknowledged his indebtedness to

Shakespeare. He had translated Shakespeare's *The Tempest*, and had written a critical essay on "Shakespeare's Treatment of the Marvelous."[28] Tieck had studied Orientalism at Göttingen, and between 1789 and 1793 had penned two oriental tales and an oriental play: *Almansur, Abdallah*, and *Alla-Moddin*.[29] He nevertheless kept a German setting in both the play and the tale of Blue-Beard. But there is a strange displacement. Tieck pointed to Turkey in the publication of the tale, "The Seven Wives of Bluebeard: A True Family Story" (*Die sieben Weiber des Blaubart: Eine wahre Familiengeschichte*). The title-page identifies the author as "Peter Lebrecht" and the editor as "Gottlieb Färber."[30] The title-page also gives the place and date of publication as "Istambul, 1212." The work was, in fact, published in Berlin by Friedrich Nicolai in 1797. Here is an artful dodge that anticipates, but by no means pre-empts, the Turkish version that was soon to appear on the London stage. "A True Family Story" indicates immediate domestic relevance, but that relevance is then relocated, dislocated, to "Istambul, 1212."

When George Colman, the Younger, adapted *Blue-Beard* for his Drury Lane production (opening on January 16, 1798), he gave it an opulent Eastern setting: "A Turkish Village – A Romantik Mountainous Country beyond it" (1.i). There is no evidence that he had looked at Tieck's version in choosing a Turkish settting; nevertheless, the Easternizing of Blue-Beard, so vigorously decried by Andrew Lang, commenced with Colman. In British nurseries of the preceding generations children learned the lessons of Perrault's tales from the English translation by Robert Samber, first published in 1729.[31] Samber was a scurrilous translator and, not the same thing, a translator of scurrilous texts. Among his other translations were Ancillon's *Eunuchism Display'd* (1718), pondering whether eunuchs are "capable of marriage" and concluding that it happens all the time; de La Motte's *Court Fables* (1721), offering young princes "a true knowledge of the world"; Longeville's *Long Livers* (1722), revealing, with the necessary recipes, "the rare secret of rejuvenescency"; and Sallengre's *Praise of Drunkenness* (1723), presenting a persuasive case on "the necessity of frequently getting drunk."[32] Samber's keen sense of satire made him well suited to the task of translating Perrault. Maria Tatar has called attention to scurrilous attributes of "Little Red Riding Hood" and "Rapunzel": "the one story had featured a striptease performed for a lecherous wolf, and the other young woman wondering why her clothes were too tight after indulging in daily romps with a prince up in her tower."[33] Samber's English version retains the sly hints, and in telling the story of "Blue-Beard" subtly reminds readers that power brings the privilege of a succession of wives, and beheading them for reputed infidelity was not without precedence. Samber does not explicitly equate Blue-Beard with Henry VIII, but he left that association lurking in his text. Samber's translation appeared in the early years of the reign of George II, a king who was lax in his morals and unregal in his behavior, but had the good fortune to rule during a period of British prosperity. There was little chance in 1729 that Samber might be charged with sedition for promulgating anti-monarchical sentiments. The situation in 1798 was very different. What-ever else Colman might do in staging *Blue-Beard*, he would have to avoid pro-revolutionary implications.

But pro-revolutionary implications were embedded in the sources, subtle and teasing in Samber's translation, more strident in *Raoul, Barbe Bleue* by Sédaine and Grétry. Michael Kelly, a London theatre composer, had seen the opera in Paris in 1789. Kelly brought back a theatre programme and begged Colman to collaborate with him on an English version.[34] Eight years later, Colman and Kelly had their musical extravaganza. Whether or not influenced by Tieck's theatrical version, which had also been published in the interim, Colman transported Blue-Beard's castle far from France, or Germany, or England, and, like Tieck, placed it in Turkey. His reasons were doubtless based on his sense of the economics and politics of the box-office. It might be discomforting to his audience to confront them with local versions of misogyny; less upsetting would be the xenophobic attribution to a foreign brutality. Besides, Colman intended to stage it for a special occasion, the annual Christmas extravaganza. In order to emphasize the magical appeal of the fairy-tale, Colman thought of that other favorite of the nursery, the *Arabian Nights*. The association was obvious: in addition to Blue-Beard and Henry VIII, the other popular beheader of wives was Sultan Shahryar, who, convinced that all women are inherently unfaithful, insured his honor by beheading each wife immediately after the wedding night. As this practice continued, the sultan's wazir found it more and more difficult to recruit new brides. When he confessed this difficulty to his daughter Scheherazade, she promptly offered herself as bride for the night. Through her skill as a storyteller, she succeeded in forestalling her execution night after night. When a thousand and one nights had passed, Sultan Shahryar abandoned all pretense to beheading and determined to live happily ever after with Scheherazade. Between 1704 and 1717 twelve volumes of these tales were translated by Antoine Galland from Arabic into French. From France they quickly made their way into England, serialized in 455 install-ments over a three-year period in the *London News*. By the end of the eighteenth century there were eighty English versions.[35]

In his introduction to *Blue-Beard; or, Female Curiosity!* Colman declared that "The following Trifle is not a Translation from the French, nor from any other Language: – I have exclusive right to all its imperfections."[36] As manager at Covent Garden, Colman spent liberally to provide an elaborate stage extravaganza.[37] Indeed, he declared that he had deliberately made "the Dialogue and Songs . . . subservient to the . . . Artists" who prepared the spectacular sets and stage machinery.[38] "Over £2,000 was expended on the sets, including the huge animated panorama [of galloping horses] that showed the advance of Abomelique's party and the 'Blue Chamber,' complete with moving skeleton and bleeding walls."[39] Rather than show the bloody chamber on the stage, Tieck relied on Agnes' fear and the bloody fingers of accusation in Mechtilde's fairy-tale. Colman, as he acknowledged in his Introduction, relied on the visual splendor and horror of stage display.

Although he had taken notes on Grétry's score to *Raoul, Barbe Bleue,* Michael Kelly's songs had no debt to the French composer. The opening duet sung by Fatima and Selim, the Grand Chorus accompanying Abomelique's March, and Fatima's song in Abomelique's Castle found an enduring place in subsequent revivals. Occasionally a popular song reaches very deep into the popular consciousness, not only enduring much longer than the usual ephemeral lifetime of the genre, but also penetrating deeper into the culture. Such permanence involves more than a song being revived in nostalgic mood, or to amuse the grandparents with a "golden oldie." The echoing functions much like literary allusion with the confidence that tune or phrase will be immediately recognized. Such a song was Kelly's musical adaptation of Thomas Moore's "Ballad Stanzas," written on his American tour of 1804 and published in 1806.[40] Michael Kelly – actor, stage tenor, stage manager, and prolific composer – set Moore's poem to music in 1814.[41] Popularly known as "The Wood-Pecker," the musical version transformed the final lines of the second stanza into a repeated refrain:

> It was noon, and on flowers that languish'd around
> In silence repos'd the voluptuous bee;
> Every leaf was at rest, and I heard not a sound
> But the woodpecker tapping the hollow beech tree.
> (Moore, *Poetical Works*, Vol. 11, p. 155, lines 5–8)

Typical of Moore's lyrics, the stanza enhances the final rhyme with echoing assonantal patterns: "the voluptuous bee" and "the hollow beech tree." Kelly gave the stresses in the final line a strong rhythmic beat, with the result that the refrain of "the woodpecker tapping" refused to go away even after the song was ended. Twelve years later, in 1826, W. T. Moncrieff put together a comic "Three Part Medley" for a stage entertainment at the Royal Coburg. The comic effects of the medley were wrought by the unexpected, incongruous, and, at a couple of junctures, suggestively naughty transitions from one song to the next. Thus the intrusion of Kelly's song comes at the moment in which the lover of the preceding song seems to be promising a nocturnal visit to his beloved:

> Oh, hush thee, my darling, the hour will soon come,
> When thy sleep shall be broken, by –
> The wood-pecker tapping the hollow beech tree,
> The wood-pecker tapping –[42]

The refrain is still echoing in the mind of Charles Dickens[43] as he writes *Sketches by Boz* (1836).[44] Dickens gives his allusion a macabre turn in *Martin Chuzzlewit* (1843–4), when Mrs. Mould alters the verse to refer to the coffin-maker's trade:

"Quite the buzz of insects," said Mr. Mould, closing his eyes in a perfect luxury. "It puts one in mind of the sound of animated nature in the agricultural districts. It's exactly like the woodpecker tapping."

   "The woodpecker tapping the hollow ELM tree," observed Mrs. Mould, adapting the words of the popular melody to the description of wood commonly used in the trade.

   "Ha, ha!" laughed Mr. Mould. "Not at all bad, my dear. We shall be glad to hear from you again, Mrs. M. Hollow elm tree, eh! Ha, ha! Very good indeed. I've seen worse than that in the Sunday papers, my love." . . . "Hollow ELM tree, eh?" said Mr. Mould, making a slight motion with his legs in his enjoyment of the joke. "It's beech in the song. Elm, eh? Yes, to be sure. Ha, ha, ha! Upon my soul, that's one of the best things I know?"[45]

Dickens again conjures Kelly's song in Chapter 36 of *David Copperfield* (1850). Mr. Micawber tells David that he intends to educate his twelve-year-old son for the Church:

"For the Church?" said I . . . "Yes," said Mr. Micawber. "He has a remarkable head-voice, and will commence as a chorister. Our residence at Canterbury, and our local connexion, will, no doubt, enable him to take advantage of any vacancy that may arise in the Cathedral corps." On looking at Master Micawber again, I saw that he had a certain expression of face, as if his voice were behind his eyebrows; where it presently appeared to be, on his singing us (as an alternative between that and bed) "The Wood-Pecker tapping."[46]

From the elder Micawber anticipating his son singing in the church choir to young Master Miacawber giving an impromptu rendition of "The Wood-Pecker" is as incongruous a shift as that in Moncrieff's "Medley," and again demonstrates the author's assurance that his readers knew the song as well as Master Micawber. A similar confidence in the persistent popularity of the song is still readily assumed many years later by W. S. Gilbert in his play *The Wedding March*, which debuted at the Court Theatre on November 15, 1873. The play was a free adaptation of Eugène Marin Labiche's *Un chapeau de paille d'Italie* ("An Italian Straw Hat"), but Gilbert introduces his native English joke by naming his hero Woodpecker Tapping.

It is not particularly remarkable that Moncrieff, or Dickens, or Gilbert are familiar with one of Kelly's songs twelve, twenty-two, thirty, thirty-six, or fifty-nine years after it was composed. What is significant is that their entire audience or readership share that familiarity. Nor was that familiarity confined to just one song. Kelly composed hundreds of songs, including other settings to the lyrics of Thomas Moore. He even wrote the music and performed the title role for Moore's comic opera, *The Gipsy Prince*, which premiered at the Haymarket on July 24, 1801. It would be easy to build an even more complex case for the enduring persistence of any number of Moore's lyrics set to music. But the case that I want to make here is not for Michael Kelly as composer of incidental songs, nor as the period's famous Irish tenor. I wish to show, rather, how Michael Kelly shaped the reception of *Blue-Beard* and influenced subsequent theatre music.

With musical training in Dublin, Venice, and Vienna, Kelly composed the music for sixty-two dramatic pieces, including several of the most successful plays performed on the London stage during the Romantic era. He composed the music for Richard Brinsley Sheridan's *Pizarro* (1799), Joanna Baillie's *De Monfort* (1800), and Samuel Taylor Coleridge's *Remorse* (1814). Among the box-office attractions featuring his music were also Matthew Gregory Lewis' *The Castle Spectre* (1797) and George Colman's *Blue-Beard* (1798), in both of which Kelly sang the lead tenor role. In defining and documenting Kelly's informing contribution to musical theatre, I will take my examples from these latter two pieces, *The Castle Spectre* and *Blue-Beard*, as well as from his earlier part in *The Haunted Tower* (1789), which had a libretto by James Cobb and score by Stephen Storace.

Kelly commenced his career early. Clearly intending his son for the stage, his father, Thomas Kelly, a dancing-master, arranged his music

lessons and guided him to theatrical opportunities in Dublin. Acknowledging that his father was also "a wine merchant of considerable
reputation," Michael Kelly identified his father's role as Master of
Ceremonies at the castle and emphasized his "elegant and graceful
deportment." "No lady," he added, "would be presented at the Irish
Court, who had not previously had the advantage of his tuition" (*R* 1: 1–2).
His parents "were both excessively fond of music" and he and his thirteen
siblings all "evinced musical capabilities." From ages seven to nine
(1770–2), Kelly received pianoforte lessons from "a wonderful genius"
named Morland, a gifted teacher, who unfortunately "was continually in a
state of whiskey-punch intoxication." He later received further keyboard
instruction from Michael Arne (1777–8) and then Dr. Cogan (1778–9). He
benefited from several singing-masters: Passerini, Peretti, Santo Giorgio,
and briefly the renowned Matteo Rauzzini. His first public performance,
when his boyhood voice was still soprano, was in the part of Daphne in
Kane O'Hara's puppet-theatre in Capel Street. In his sixteenth year, Kelly
was invited to perform at the newly opened theatre on Fishamble Street.
He appeared as the Count in Piccinni's *La buona figliuola*. Then, at the
Crow Street Theatre, he performed for three nights as the title character in
Michael Arne's *Cymon*, and on the fourth night as Lionel in Charles
Dibdin's *Lionel and Clarissa*. This last performance was a benefit, which
provided the money to pay for his trip to Naples, where Rauzzini had
prepared for his further instruction. On May 1, 1779 he left Dublin, and
on May 30 he arrived in Naples.

At Naples he attended the venerable Conservatorio di Santa Maria di
Loreto under the master tutelage of Fedele Fenaroli. Upon discovering
that the boys studying composition at the Conservatorio were expected to
perform their lessons amidst a "Babel" of vocal and instrumental
rehearsals, Kelly complained. He was granted a separate apartment and
considerable independence (*R* 1: 42–3). Fenaroli introduced Kelly to the
operatic composers and performers of Naples, so that his days of study
were embellished by evenings in the theatres. He subsequently studied in
Palermo under the legendary castrato, Giuseppe Aprile. From Palermo he
sailed to Leghorn (Livorno). His landing was greeted by truly serendip-
itous good fortune. At the docks were a pair of Londoners, Stephen and
Anna (Nancy) Storace. "*He* was well known afterwards, as one of the best
of English composers; and *she* was at that time, though only fifteen, the
prima donna of the Comic Opera at Leghorn." Stephen had begun his
study of composition at the Conservatorio San Onofrio in 1775. Brought
by their parents to Italy in 1778, Anna made her first Italian performance

at the Teatro alla Pergola in Florence in 1780. The Storaces were to remain Kelly's close friends throughout the ensuing decades (*R*1: 94–5).[47]

In Leghorn he was able to assemble a concert at which his singing "was very much approved" and his finances replenished. When Stephen Storace returned to London, Kelly traveled on to Lucca, Pisa, and Florence. In Florence, he performed at the Teatro Nuovo from April to June, 1781 (*R*1: 107–11). Promised an engagement in Venice, Kelly arrived to find his expectation delayed. In Verona, Kelly again refurbished his impoverished finances with a concert (*R*1: 176). Returning to Venice, with Count Vidiman's engagement, he met again with Anna Storace, who drew overflowing audiences to her performances (*R*1: 188). Kelly had been performing with Anna and the Italian baritone Francesco Benucci when all three were offered an engagement by Count Deluzzo, the Austrian Ambassador, who had been sent by Emperor Joseph II of Vienna to hire singers for his newly formed Italian Opera Company (*R*1: 193).

For the next five years, 1783 to 1787, Kelly remained in Vienna, again joined by Stephen Storace, and enjoying the friendship of Mozart. All three of the singers from Venice performed in the premiere production of Mozart's *Le nozze di Figaro* (May 1, 1786): Kelly sang as Don Basilio and Don Curzio, Anna as Susanna, and Benucci as Figaro. At the end of February, 1787, Kelly and the Storaces left Vienna, arriving in London on March 18. Kelly was now twenty-four, Stephen twenty-three, and Anna twenty-one. Even before their departure from Vienna, Kelly had been assured of engagement at Drury Lane by Thomas Linley and Richard Brinsley Sheridan (*R* 1: 255–62). Anna opened in London as the black slave in Paisiello's *Gli schiavi per amore* (*The Slaves of Love*) on April 25, 1787. Kelly's first performance in London, opening at Drury Lane on April 20, 1787, was as Lionel in *Lionel and Clarissa* (*School for Fathers*), the same role he had performed before his departure from Dublin eight years earlier (*R* 1: 291–2, 297).

Kelly continued as first tenor at Drury Lane from 1787 until he retired from the stage in 1811. In 1793 he was also engaged at the King's Theatre, where for many years he was the acting manager. Appreciating Stephen Storace as a superior composer, Kelly was content with his role as lead stage tenor. When Kelly, together with Anna and Stephen Storace returned from Vienna, Stephen Storace quickly launched the series of collaborations with James Cobb that made him the master of comic opera in London (see Chapter 7). George Colman's *The Iron Chest* (Drury Lane, March 12, 1796), adapted from William Godwin's *Caleb Williams*, featured Storace's musical score, but he did not live see its premiere performance. During rehearsals he caught cold and died on March 19, 1796. Storace left behind an incomplete score to a libretto by Prince Hoare, *Mahmoud, Prince of Persia*, which, in a benefit for his widow and children, premiered the following month (Drury Lane, April 30, 1796). With adaptations from Giuseppe Sarti, the music was "vamped up" by Anna Storace,[48] and Kelly contributed to completing the work. In spite of the makeshift nature of the completed version, "all the performers took the greatest pains to do justice to the posthumous work of the composer" (*R* 11: 77–81). Richard Suett played the Sultan, who, fearing a prophecy of patricide, imprisons his son, Mahmoud, played by John Philip Kemble. Other cast members included John Braham, performing for the first time at Drury Lane, as well as Anna Storace, Kelly, and Mrs. Bland (Maria Theresa Romanzini).[49]

Already by 1789 Kelly had written songs for Henry Seymour Conway's *False Appearances* (Drury Lane, April 20, 1789) and, at the request of the Earl of Orford, the songs for *Fashionable Friends* (first performed thirteen years later, Drury Lane, April 22, 1802). Following Storace's death, Kelly set to work industriously, providing music to as many as three or four plays a year. In 1797, he prepared the stage music for Prince Hoare's *A Friend in Need* (Drury Lane, February 9, 1797) and Matthew Gregory Lewis' *The Castle Spectre* (Drury Lane, December 14, 1797). One month later his big success was the musical score to Colman's *Blue-Beard* (Drury Lane, January 16, 1798). The year following it was the musical score to Sheridan's *Pizarro* (Drury Lane, May 24, 1798). By this time Kelly was as much sought after as composer as he was as stage tenor and actor. Among the sixty-two dramatic works for which he composed, thirteen were for William Dimond, including an adaptation from Byron's *The Bride of Abydos* (Drury Lane, May 2, 1818); seven were for Matthew Gregory Lewis;[50] and six were for George Colman. Twice he teamed up with Charles Dibdin, and twice with James Cobb, including a revision of the Cobb–Storace production of *The Cherokee*. The Cobb–Kelly version was entitled *Algonah* (Drury Lane, April 30, 1802).[51]

In Dublin, on October 1, 1811, Kelly made his farewell appearance on the stage. He sang "The Bard of Erin," composed by himself for the occasion. No longer acting, he continued as a prolific composer throughout the ensuing decade. Kelly's goals as a song writer were strongly influenced by his own experience as actor and stage tenor. He cared little for virtuoso display, yet retained characteristic traits of his Italian training. Although he emphasized melody over ornamentation, he often introduced catchy rhythmic effects. He strove to create songs that would fully exploit the emotions of the dramatic situation but would also be memorable as melodies. He crafted songs with repetitive phrases that he hoped would continue to haunt his audience on their way home from the theatre.

Kelly found a great opportunity to test his skills as a composer in his settings for Matthew Gregory Lewis' *The Castle Spectre* (Drury Lane, December 14, 1797).[52] For Dorothy Jordan, in the role of Angela, he composed two songs, "Return, return, sweet Peace!" (I.ii, p. 167) and "How slow the lingering moments wear!" (IV.ii, p. 200), but she found the second one too strenuous to sing at the opening. As he leads a band of peasants to rescue Percy (John Philip Kemble) from the tower, Motley (John Bannister) sang, 'Sing Megen-oh! Oh! Megen-Ee!' (II.iii, pp. 178–9), a rousing comic song with chorus. Motley also sang a grotesque elegy on his lost love, the castle cook:

> Baked be the pies to coals! Burn, roast-meat, burn!
> Boil o'er, ye pots! Ye spits, forget to turn!
> Cindrelia's death – (v.i, p. 208)

The villain Osmond (William Barrymore) was given an opportunity to express his misanthropic bitterness upon hearing at his window the happy song of the peasants returning from their labours:

CHORUS   [*Without.*]
         Pleased the toils of day to leave,
         Home we haste with foot-steps light:
         Oh! how gay the cotter's eve!
         Oh! how calm the cotter's night!

OSMOND.   [*Closing the window with violence.*] – Curses upon them – I
         will look, I will listen no more! I sicken at the sight of
         happiness. (III.ii, p. 185)

At the very end of the play, Reginald (Richard Wroughton), rescued from his long years in prison, has the final song, "And, Oh thou wretch! whom hopeless woes oppress," (v.iii, p. 220).

In his *Reminiscences*, Kelly simply asserted "I composed the music for the piece," (*R* II: 126), describing in detail only one scene. That scene was the *coup de théâtre*, thrilling every audience in the play's incredibly long run.[53] It was, however, a scene for which Lewis had written no dialogue and for which Kelly merely interpolated a slow dance by Niccolò Jommelli. It was a scene of pure melodramatic pantomime. At the end of

Act IV, Angela hears the sound of a guitar and someone singing a lullaby. The doors to the closed chamber that once belonged to her long-dead mother swing open:

(*The folding doors unclose, and the oratory is seen illuminated. In its centre, stands a tall female figure, her white and flowing garments spotted with blood; her veil is thrown back, and discovers a pale and melancholy countenance; her eyes are lifted upwards, her arms extended towards heaven, and a large wound appears on her bosom. Angela sinks upon her knees, with her eyes riveted upon the figure, which, for some moments, remains motionless. At length, the spectre advances slowly to a soft and plaintive strain; she stops opposite Reginald's picture, and gazes upon it in silence. She then turns, approaches Angela, seems to invoke a blessing upon her, points to the picture, and retires to the oratory. The music ceases, Angela rises with a wild look, and follows the vision, extending her arms towards it. The spectre waves her hand, as bidding her farewell. Instantly the organ's swell is heard; a full chorus of female voices chants, "Jubilate!" a blaze of light flashes through the oratory, and the folding doors close with a loud noise.*) (IV.ii, p. 206)

The scene, of course, is very much like the *coup de théâtre* that Kelly provided for Coleridge's *Remorse* (Drury Lane, January 23, 1813),[54] when Alvar (Robert William Elliston), disguised as a Moorish sorcerer, conjures at the altar to the eerie music played upon a glass-harp. Following the incantation sung by Maria Theresa [Romanzini] Bland, there is a chorus of boatmen, sung beneath the convent wall. The conjuration concludes with the chorus, "Wandering Demon hear the spell," and the entire scene is engulfed in a blazing flash of light (*R* 11: 277). In *The Castle Spectre*, Jane Powell performed as the spirit of the dead mother. Kelly described the scene:

[F]or the situation in which the Ghost first appears in the oratory to her daughter, and in which the acting both of Mrs. Powell and Mrs. Jordan, without speaking, riveted the audience, I selected the chaconne of Jomellis, as an accompaniment to the action. This chaconne had been danced at Stuttgard, by [Lucia Elizabetta] Vestris, and was thought an odd choice of mine for so solemn a scene; but the effect which it produced warranted the experiment. (*R* 11: 126–8)

In *The Siege of Belgrade*, the duet "Of Plighted Faith" was sung by Kelly and Anna Maria Crouch, playing the roles of Seraskier and Catherine. Lovers in real life, as were Anna Storace and John Braham, Kelly and Crouch were again stage lovers in their roles as Selim and Fatima in George Colman's *Blue-Beard* (1798). Kelly admitted that he was inspired by seeing the performance of Grétry's *Raoul, Barbe Bleue* in Paris in 1790, but he insisted that in his own production at Drury Lane he "did not introduce a single bar from Grétry."[55] Kelly needed no defense against borrowings from Grétry, for the entire production, both score and libretto, are radically different. In their opening duet (1.i.1–17), Selim and Fatima attempt to elope. As she climbs from her window on a ladder of silken ropes, their song mimics her descending steps, "Pit a pat, pit a pat," down the ladder:

SELIM.   Twilight glimmers o'er the Steep:
             Fatima! Fatima! wakest thou, dear?
             Grey-eyed Morn begins to peep:
             Fatima! Fatima! Selim's here!
             Here are true-love's cords attaching
             To your window. – List! List!
             [*Fatima opens the Window.*]
FATIMA. Dearest Selim! I've been watching;
             Yes, I see the silken twist.
SELIM.   Down, Down, Down, Down, Down!
             Down the Ladder gently trip;
             Pit a pat, pit a pat, – haste thee, dear!
FATIMA. O! I'm sure my foot will slip!
             [*With one foot out of the Window.*]
SELIM.   Fatima! –
FATIMA. Well Selim? –
SELIM.   Do not fear!
             [*She gets upon the Ladder – they keep time in singing to her*
                 steps as she descends, towards the end of the last line
                 she reaches the ground and they embrace.]
BOTH.   Pit a pat, pit a pat, Pit a pat,
             Pit a pat, pit a pat – Pat, Pat, Pat.

Fatima's father, Ibrahim, foils the lovers' attempt to elope. He drives off Selim, and tells Fatima that she must marry the powerful and wealthy Bashaw, Abomelique. Kelly provides a strident Turkish March and Chorus for the arrival of Abomelique (1.i.135–42; 204–15).

As in the opening duet, with its "Pit a pat, pit a pat" of Fatima's descent, Kelly reveals in subsequent songs his recurrent fascination with musical mimicry: the instrumental echoing of natural sounds and the vocal echoing of instrumental sounds. This, of course, is the feature that made Kelly's "Woodpecker Tapping" so memorable.[56] In the duet of Shacabac and Beda (1.i.58–76; 30–3), Kelly plays with the tinking, clinking sounds of the guitar.

SHACABAC. Yes, Beda, – This, Beda, when I melancholy grow,
             This tinking heart-sinking soon can drive away.

BEDA.   When hearing sounds cheering, then we blythe and
                 jolly grow;
                 How do you, while to you, Shacabac, I play?
                 Tink, tinka, tinka, tink – the sweet Guittar shall cheer
                 you.
                 Clink, clinka, clinka, clink – So gaily let us sing!
SHACABAC.   Tink, tinka, tinka, tink – A pleasure 'tis to hear you,
                 While, neatly, you sweetly, sweetly touch the string!
BOTH.   Tink, tinka, &c.
SHACABAC.   Once sighing, sick, dying, Sorrow hanging over me,
                 Faint, weary, sad, dreary, on the ground I lay;
                 There moaning, deep groaning, Beda did discover
                 me –
BEDA.   Strains soothing, Care smoothing, I began to play.
                 Tink, tinka, tinka, tink, – the sweet Guittar could
                 cheer you:
                 Clink, clinka, clinka, clink, so gaily did I sing!
SHACABAC.   Tink, tinka, tinka, tink, – A pleasure 'twas to hear you,
                 While, neatly, You sweetly, sweetly touch'd the string!
BOTH.   Tink, tinka, &c.

In the Glee at the opening of Act II, a band of Turkish soldiers prepare
an ambush, plotting to give their signal with the "tapping on the drum"
(II.ii.1–10; 49–53):

> Stand close! – Our Comrade is not come:
> Ere this, he must be hovering near; –
> Give him a Signal we are here,
> By gently tapping on the Drum.
> Rub, Dub, Dub.
> A Comrade's wrong'd: Revenge shall work:
> Thus, till our project's ripe, we lurk; –
> And still, to mark that we are here,
> Yet not alarm the distant ear,
> With caution, ever and anon,
> The Drum we gently tap upon.
> Rub, Dub, Dub.

Poets and composers have often attempted to echo the hoof-beats
of horses. The familiar galloping of Gioachino Rossini's Overture to
Guillaume Tell or Franz von Suppé's "Light Calvary Overture" were
nineteenth-century versions of an echoic game that dates back at least
as far as Virgil's onomatopoeia in the *Aeneid*: "Quadrupedante putrem
sonitu quitit ungula campum," translated by Dryden as "Then struck the

hoofs of the steed on the ground with a four-footed trampling." While Abomelique threatens to behead her with his scimitar, Fatima, her sister Irene, and the slave Shacabac hold look-out from the turret for the arrival of Selim and his comrades. Just as the rescue seems too late, they hear the galloping, galloping:

IRENE, SHACABAC. I see them galloping, they're spurring on amain!
Now, faster galloping, they skim along the plain!
(II.vi.101–2)

Genest lists revivals of *Blue-Beard* at Covent Garden on February 18, 1811, and on June 2, 1825. Thirty-one years after its opening in 1798, James Robinson Planché produced a parody, *Blue Beard; A Grand Musical, Comi-Tragical, Melo-Dramatic, Burlesque Burletta, in One Act* (Olympic Theatre, January 1, 1839).[57] Planché's *Blue Beard* closely parodies Colman's from start to finish. While he gives French names to other characters, Abomelique retains the name Colman had adapted from the *Arabian Nights*, and the slave Shacabac becomes O'Shac O'Back, from "the Land of the West." Fatima becomes Fleurette, whose character is transformed from modesty to coquetry. No longer timidly curious, Fleurette is playfully naughty (especially as originally performed by Madame Vestris). Only because of the enduring popularity of Kelly's songs could Planché construct much of his humor on his parody of the original lyrics. Parody, after all, does not work unless the audience recognizes the original. The Grand March at Abomelique's entrance, "Our Life and Death / Hang on his breath: – / Hail to the great Bashaw!" becomes "Here to choose a wife, / It's true, upon my life, / So without more rout, / Trot your daughter out."[58] Fatima's song, "While pensive I thought on my Love," ceases to be her melancholy thoughts on her absent lover, and is turned into her greedy speculation on the contents of the forbidden room. Among his additions, Planché borrowed from *Guillaume Tell* to enhance the galloping of the rescue scene.

Like the persistence of "The Woodpecker Tapping," Michael Kelly's theatre music shaped the style and manner of theatrical music throughout the age. His pieces were often more permanently embedded in the play than either the character or dialogue that they were designed to enhance. Kelly's major concerns were that the songs should arise directly from the action and contribute to it, and that the melodies should stay with the audience long after the curtain fell. With his contributions to sixty-two of the plays of the period, Kelly personally shaped the theatrical experience for it. Beyond those sixty-two plays, however, were the many imitators

among his contemporaries, and the influential legacy still reverberating at
the time of Gilbert and Sullivan.

Among the impressive effects provided by Colman's stage machinist was
a grand cavalcade across the mountains in which, at each successive
appearance, larger model figures were used so that the animals appeared to
be coming closer and closer. At a revival of *Blue-Beard* at Covent Garden
(February 18, 1811), "thunders of applause" greeted sixteen white horses
as they crossed the stage in Abomelique's March. The playbill for the return
of the Christmas spectacle (December 9, 1816) again announced the
performance of an Equestrian Troop; although it would introduce "New
Scenes and Embellishments" it would feature "the Original Musick by
Michael Kelly, esq." That music was also heard in the American performances, adapted with additional songs by William Dunlap. This version was
first performed at Park Theater, New York, March 5, 1802.[59] It was one of
Kelly's songs, however, that was echoed in Samuel Woodworth's poem "To
Mary, On hearing her sing the air, from *Blue Beard*, of 'When pensive I
thought on my love.'"[60] John Genest, who is usually reserved in his comments on musical spectacles, was pleased that *Blue-Beard* replaced the usual
Harlequinade: "as a substitute for a Pantomime this piece has great merit –
it was very successful."[61] Although the reviews were mixed, the work
remained popular with audiences, and it was revived yet again at Covent
Garden on June 2, 1825.

The play, as Cox and Gamer observe, "challenges us to think about the
ramifications of this fairy tale of misogyny – where a tyrannical husband
kills his wives when they inevitably display an essentialized 'female
curiosity.'" They go on to suggest that "Colman's play could be seen either
as re-enacting masculine stereotypes or as using conventional orientalist
imagery to decry the subjugation of women to oppressive men."[62] The
latter alternative seems exceptionally generous to Colman. To be sure, as
in the several versions of the folk tale, the present bride is rescued, even in
the face of gory evidence that previous brides have been brutally tortured
and killed. If Colman is to be defended against the charge of misogyny,
then the defense must take its evidence from the intelligence and integrity
he has lent his women to counterbalance their emotional whims. As it is,
Colman has it both ways. Fatima maintains her moral integrity; her sister
Irene is swayed by irrepressible female curiosity. The Turkish setting –
opulent, elaborate, exotic – is at best a means of displaying masculine
wealth and power while distracting attention from the cruelty it covers.

To be sure, Selim rescues his Fatima from the cruel blue-beard
Abomelique, and there is poetic justice in the death of Abomelique, slain

by the skeleton in his torture chamber. But the order of masculine dominance and female subservience is not overcome, not even in the final embrace of Selim and Fatima. That Blue-Beard's bride is rescued not by her brothers but by her faithful lover, is an important change to the plot and, at least potentially, to the meaning of her trial. Her father had blessed her engagement to Selim, but withdrew that blessing when bribed by the riches of Abomelique. In her first interview with this new suitor, Fatima confesses to him that she still loves Selim. When her husband departs and leaves her the key to the forbidden door, he warns Fatima that the door is as sacred as her marriage vows: "A Wife were unworthy of my love, could I not confide in her discretion." As soon as he departs, her sister Irene urges her "just to take one peep." Fatima is fully aware of what is at stake:

Tempt me not to a breach of faith, Irene. When we betray the confidence reposed in us, to gratify our curiosity, our crime is coupled to a failing, and we employ a vice to feed a weakness. – The door within the blue apartment must remain untouch'd. (ii.ii.79–82)

The door, of course, is opened. But Colman gives Fatima a just motive: the sisters hear a "deep groan" issuing from the chamber. Not curiosity, not infidelity, but an act of humanity to rescue an unknown victim trapped within prompts Fatima to use the key. The eunuch slave Shacabac, whom Abomelique leaves to watch over the sisters in his absence, may seem to be a character parallel to Tieck's Mechtilde, and for a moment Fatima perceives him to be the agent in the slaughter of the previous wives:

Begone! – You knew of this! Your look, when late Abomelique left me, now is explained. – You are an accomplice in this bloody business . . . My Death, no doubt, is certain, – and, in you, perhaps, I see my executioner. (ii.iv.61–6)

Shacabac, however, has nothing of Mechtilde's malevolence. Had he the will or the power he would rebel against his master. As it is, he can do no more than join Irene in the tower to signal to Selim. Missing from Colman's theatricality is Tieck's ironic *dédoublement* of immediacy ("a true family story") and distance ("Istambul, 1212"). Colman uses the legerdemain of his Oriental splendors to distract attention from any serious confrontation with domestic violence.

Genest, who was not concerned whether the play seriously addressed issues of misogyny, made a valid point: Colman and Kelly produced a musical spectacle that was indeed of greater merit that the usual

Harlequinade. Blue-Beard had indeed already appeared in pantomime. William Reeve's *Blue Beard, or, The Flight of Harlequn*, first produced December 21, 1791, at Covent Garden,[63] allows the villainy to be fully usurped by the clownery. How seriously should one take these stage adaptations of a folk tale? Entertainment and a good laugh ought to be justification enough. The problem is in the disturbing matter of the tale itself. For all of his light-hearted bantering and jesting, Perrault closed his narrative with a double moral that could not draw closure on the issues of a wife's curiosity and infidelity or a husband's presumption of domestic authority.

These issues continued to be examined and challenged in subsequent theatrical versions. One of the funniest and strangest is Reginald Heber's *Blue-Beard. A Serio-Comic Oriental Romance* (1812): funniest because Heber's dialogue is in rhymed couplets, and the comic rhymes tilt what is being said with persistent irony; strangest because of the paradoxical syntheses of those "serio-comic" elements announced in its title. As its title also reveals, Heber follows Colman in maintaining an oriental setting. Colman's orientalism was no more than a plaything of theatrical spectacle; Heber's orientalism was informed by his studies at Brasenose College, Oxford. In 1805 he was elected Fellow of All Souls College, Oxford, and spent the next two years traveling through Germany, Russia, and the Crimea. From 1807 to 1812 he served as parish priest in Hodnet; was appointed prebendary at St. Asaph in 1812; Brampton lecturer at Oxford in 1815;[64] and Bishop of Calcutta in 1822. His biography of Jeremy Taylor and his edition of Taylor's works went through many editions. His travels in India, his sermons, and his poetry appeared posthumously.[65] He had published only a few of his literary works during his lifetime; among these were his narrative poems, *Palestine* (1803, 1807) and *Europe* (1809), and his play, *Blue-Beard* (1812).[66]

Heber has reduced *Blue-Beard* to one act of four scenes, and to a cast of six characters: Abou Malek, the Blue-Beard; Fadlallah, an old Turk; Fatima and Ayesha, his daughters; Selim, a young Turk in love with Fatima; the Shekh of Mount Hor, uncle of Selim. As a sample of the strident pace of his mock-heroic couplets, here are a few lines from the scene in which Selim petitions the aid of his uncle in rescuing Fatima:

SELIM.   But now for protection, dear uncle, I sue –
         You know the Bashaw of Damascus?
SHEKH.   I do. –
SELIM.   The monster has borne off my beautiful bride.
SHEKH.   He's perfectly right for himself to provide.

SELIM.   Is my uncle in earnest?
SHEKH.   I am, my Selim:
         And, thou wilt do right to assassinate him!
SELIM.   By my beard! I intend it, – but how shall I do it?
SHEKH.   Oh just as thou wilt, so thou fairly goest through it. –
         Thou mayst shoot him, or stab him, or beat out his
              brain.
SELIM.   But how to get at him? – your meaning explain.
SHEKH.   I have spoken! – and he who hath purpose to slay,
         If he have but the courage, will find out the way!
         If thou diest, I'll avenge thee.
SELIM.   Far rather defend me!
         I hoped that the spears of Mount Hor would befriend
              me!
         You have eaten our salt, have been warm'd at our fire,
         And there flows in my veins of the blood of your sire.
         To a castle in Hauran, if truth is in fame,
         Abou Malek has borne my disconsolate dame.
         The walls are not strong, and the garrison few.
         What say you to singeing those whiskers of blue?
              (Scene iii, 52–71)

Reverend Heber gives emphasis to the tender morality with which Selim
and his uncle ponder the value of Abou Malek's life. He also shows
the similar moral constraint with which Fatima and Ayesha subdue their
curiosity and resist the temptation to approach the forbidden blue chamber:

AYESHA.   Thank Heaven he is off! I have heard your dispute –
          He a Bashaw, indeed! A fantastic old brute.
FATIMA.   You heard it?
AYESHA.   I listen'd, my love, at the door –
          I never have met such a monster before.
          Kill a woman for peeping! why here's a to-do!
          I wonder what's in that same chamber – Don't you?
FATIMA.   Oh talk not of prying!
AYESHA.   The Prophet forbid!
          But – he never could know it, my dear, if we did.
          And – now that I look, what a beautiful key!
          Do, Fatima, trust it a moment with me.
               [*Snatching the key.*]
FATIMA.   What, what are you doing?
          [*Ayesha tries the key in the lock of the door.*]
AYESHA.   I want to be sure
          If this is the key which belongs to the door –
          It fits I declare like a finger and glove!

FATIMA.   In mercy, return it!
AYESHA.   *Return* it, my love!
I have not yet *turn'd* it, – nor do I intend.
No, child, on my prudence you well may depend!
I would not for the world – Oh, my stars! it is done!
[*The door flies open with a tremendous sound, several*
    Skeletons seen within.]
The chamber is open, as sure as a gun,
And oh! what an object! See, Fatima, see!
Oh shut-to the door! turn the key, turn the key!
Run! Run for your life – Oh!
[*Fatima closes the door.*]
FATIMA.   Wretched girl! we're undone!
The key is all bloody!
AYESHA.   Run, Fatima, run! (Scene ii, 69–90)

In the final scene, Abou Malek, having received a death wound from the
Shekh, declares that Fatima, his thirteenth bride, is the only one whom he
has loved, and in his dying breath grants her his estate. The Shekh advises
his nephew to give Abou Malek a handsome burial before he rushes into his
own marriage to Fatima. The Shekh then offers his final pronouncement on
the fate of Blue-Beard: "'tis always unlucky to marry *thirteen*!" Heber has
raised the count. The fate of the six wives of Henry VIII, or the six wives of
Perrault's Blue-Beard, is no longer enough to shock.

In the version by James Robinson Planché, the count continued to rise:
his Blue Beard has done away with nineteen and is now flirting with his
prospective twentieth. Planché, one of the most prolific authors of musical
comedies in the period, collaborated on this one with Charles Dance, a
writer of light comedies and farces who had worked with Planché for
several years. Although Planché had a gift for lively dialogue, he would rely
on Dance to set up the comic situations. Like Tieck, Planché frequently
turned to folk tales for his subject-matter: *Beauty and the Beast, Puss in
Boots, The Sleeping Beauty*. In a prefatory note, Planché pretended to
distance himself from Colman's oriental precedent:

The Melo-Dramatists of the past century converted "Blue Beard" into an Eastern
story, but every child knows that the old nursery tale, by Mons. Charles Perrault,
is nothing of the sort. At Nantes, in Brittany, is preserved amongst the records
of the Duchy the entire process of a nobleman (the original of the portrait of
Blue Beard) who was tried and executed in that city for the murder of several
wives, A.D. 1440. In accordance, therefore, with the laudable spirit of critical

inquiry and antiquarian research, which distinguishes the present era, the scene of the Drama has been restored to Brittany, and the Costumes selected from authorities of the period above mentioned. But, at the same time, in order not to wound the feelings of a noble family, the last of whom has been dead scarcely three hundred years, the real name of the criminal has been carefully suppressed, and that under which he first obtained dramatic notoriety substituted.[67]

This statement is a red herring. Yes, Planché has rid his characters of the oriental pretense. But he has incorporated nothing from the story of Gilles de Rais, nothing to conjure the age of Joan of Arc, Henry VI, or Margaret of Anjou. In fashion and manners, his characters are contemporary, as much a part of the 1830s as possible for any characters in a burlesque.

In addition to the songs of Michael Kelly, Planché borrowed from Rossini's *La Cenerentola* and *Guillaume Tell*, and from a variety of other sources. Just before Fleurette opens the forbidden door, she sings a comic version of "Son vergin vezzosa" ("I am a charming virgin") from Bellini's *I Puritani*. The song may invite parody – Maria Callas once sang it as "Son vergin viziosa" ("I am a vicious virgin"). Like Reginald Heber, Planché adds to the burlesque incongruity with his use of comic couplets. Here are Fleurette's lines as she approaches the Blue Chamber and sings her "charming virgin" song made up of a bit of nursery rhyme with mock Italian endings (Scene iv):

> Well, I think now I've been in every corner,
> And ate as much minced pie as young Jack Horner.
> I'm dressed as fine as any princess, too,
> And haven't got a single thing to do;
> Yet I'm not happy – no, 'midst all these revels,
> I'm troubled by a touch of the blue devils.
> I've used my ten toes so
> They need some repose, so
> I'll seek in a doze – O
>   My senses to steep.
> My Blue-bearded sposo
> Objects to "peep-bo," so
>   I'll go to "bo-peep."

To express her repentance when Blue-Beard returns and she must show him the bloody key, Planché has Fleurette sing a parody of the cavatina from Meyerbeer's *Robert le diable* ("Robert, toi que j'aime"): "Ah! sir, Ah! sir – I was not to blame sir! / Oh, don't, sir! I won't, sir, do so any more."

As Blue-Beard raises his sword above her neck, Fleurette once more breaks into song, this time a parody of the popular air, "How can you smile at my despair" (Scene v).

> How can you think my head I'll spare?
>   As if I'd others by the score.
> 'Stead of my head, cut off my hair,
>   And I will trouble you no more.
> Pray be so kind to grant my prayer,
>   Hair grows again just as before;
> But my poor head, unlike my hair,
>   If once cut off will grow no more!

In Colman's version, it was the father who urged the marriage to Bluebeard for financial gain. There is no father in Planché's cast. He has substituted the mother, Dame Perroquet, "a Widow Lady of a certain age – with an uncertain income, two unmarried Daughters, and two Sons in the Army." Her motives and actions are much the same, exept that she urges her daughter's true love, Joli Cœur, "a worthy and noble-minded young man," to await an opportune occasion. The most significant difference in Planché's production is the persistent anti-illusionism. This is all parody, pretending, and play-acting; nothing can possibly be taken seriously. Not a trace of guilt or grief is left of abuse or violence. Abomelique is no sooner stabbed by the brothers than he sits up again and declares that no more damage has been done than a couple of holes in his wedding-clothes. Colman's production had a bloody chamber of horrors with a clockwork skeleton. When the Blue Chamber is opened in Planché's production, out comes a chorus of "Nineteen Female Curiosities,"

> Each with her noddle,
> Nid, nid noddle,
> Each with her noddle
> Underneath her arm.

The moral of Planché's version in 1839 is much the same as the double moral of Perrault's version in 1697. It is told with smile and laughter, even while domestic abuse within the hidden chamber persists.

Not just in the theatre for adults, but in the nursery for children, it is the telling of the story that remains important. This is why the folk tale had been widely dispersed. Eliza Lee Cabot Follen, the American educator, adapted Colman's version for children's performance.[68] Unlike the tale of "Cupid and Psyche," which John Keats retells from *The Golden Ass* of Apuleius, unlike the tale of "Pandora's Box," the story is not just about "female curiosity." It is about covert violence against women, the violence that lurks within "the Blue-beard room of the house" where Thomas De Quincey sought shelter with a young girl of the streets, as described in his *Confessions* (1822).[69] Or, as Thomas Carlyle observed, the frightening experience hidden within the Blue-Beard Chamber of a woman's mind, "into which no eye but her own must ever look."[70] What is striking about these plays of the Romantic era – the works of Sédaine and Grétry, of Tieck, Colman, Dunlap, Heber, and Planché – is that the cautionary tales from earlier eras, already given their satirical edge by Perrault and Sembler, found a place in comedy and musical extravaganza, were made the subject of irony and jests, and continued to stir up troubled laughter wherever the fictions of a remote region of the Orient did not seem remote enough.

CHAPTER 9

Vampires in kilts

Just as the transgressive acts of domestic violence were conveniently displaced far from contemporary Britain in some historically/geographically
remote castle, themes of dark eroticism and ruthless seduction were also
distanced by transforming them into demonic fantasies. As sexual predator
Blue-Beard is thus closely related to the Vampire. In assuming this
new role as one who first debauches then sucks the blood of his victims,
the vampire underwent a considerable transformation from his earlier
eighteenth-century identity to his peculiarly urbane post-Revolutionary
character. Once no more than a resurrected corpse that preyed upon the
living, the new vampire was a nobleman of the *ancien régime*. In the figure
of the sophisticated vampire, sexual transgressions were blended with
the Sadistic themes of the sexual libertinism of a decadent aristocracy. In
addition, the stage vampire was an evil antagonist and defiler of religious
orthodoxy, whose worship of Satan included the blasphemous parody of
drinking the blood, not of Christ, but of a victim or new "convert" to the
dark ways of the living dead.

The vampire melodrama performed during the 1820s introduced a
disturbingly different transgressive behavior.[1] In imposing his spell on his
victims, male as well as female, the stage vampire controlled all witnesses
to his act. Members of the audience, no less than characters on the stage,
succumbed to the *Wirkungsästhetik* of the vampire's gaze.[2] The viewer of
the play, as another "convert," is presumed to fall under the vampire's
thrall. This concluding chapter provides an opportunity to discuss the
presumptions of transgressive theatre: not simply to reveal the trespasses
against established norms, but to provoke audience tensions of participation and repudiation.

As manifestation of the "Byronic hero," the character of this Romantic
vampire was sketched by Lord Byron himself. The traditional vampire,
as abundantly documented in Augustin Calmet's *Treatise on Vampires*
(1746),[3] was a hungry corpse who rose from the grave. The new vampire
combined the wickedness and the charm of Byron himself, an aristocrat

at ease in high society, oblivious to moral constraints, and readily seducing women to feed an insatiable lust. The Byronic vampire that gained prominence on the European stage in the 1820s, ultimately known as Lord Ruthven, came into being one night in Switzerland. At Villa Diodati on Lake Geneva in 1816, Byron, Shelley, Mary Shelley, and John Polidori engaged in a "ghost story" competition. Mary Shelley commenced her tale of Victor Frankenstein and his creature. "Poor Polidori," Mary later recalled, "had some terrible idea about a skull-headed lady, who was so punished for peeping through a keyhole – what to see I forget – something very shocking and wrong, of course."[4] Byron told of Augustus Darvell, who is guided by a companion to an ancient burial ground in Smyrna, where he asked to be buried according to a prescribed ritual. Enough of the story is told to make it apparent that Darvell is returning to his own tomb. Abandoning his story of the "skull-headed lady," Polidori transformed Byron's hints about Augustus Darvell into a full-length narrative entitled "The Vampyre," introduced by "A Letter from Geneva, with Anecdotes of Lord Byron" and published in Henry Colburn's *New Monthly Magazine* (April, 1819).[5]

The author of the introductory letter referred to himself throughout in the third person, leaving the reader to surmise that the story was Byron's.[6] Many were fooled; even Byron's publisher. Byron promptly wrote to John Murray (May 15, 1819): "I have got yr. extract, & the 'Vampire.' I need not say that it is *not mine* – there is a rule to go by – you are my publisher (till we quarrel) and what is not published by you is not written by me."[7] Byron vigorously denied that he was the author of *The Vampyre*, but he granted that most of Polidori's account of writing ghost stories at Villa Diodati was true. Byron enclosed a copy of his fragment on Augustus Darvell, so that Murray might see for himself "how far it resembles Mr. Colburn's publication" in *The New Monthly Review*. Byron also told Murray that he might publish the tale in Blackwood's *Edinburgh Magazine* – "*stating why*." Instead, Murray published "A Fragment," along with "Venice: An Ode" following the title poem, *Mazeppa* (1819).[8]

Trying to dispel the notion that *The Vampyre* was his creation, Byron also wrote to the editor of Galignani's *Messenger* (April 27, 1819):

Sir, – In various numbers of your Journal – I have seen mentioned a work entitled "the Vampire" with addition of my name as that of the Author – I am not the author and never heard of the work until now ... I have besides a personal dislike to "Vampires" and the little acquaintance I have with them would by no means induce me to divulge their secrets.[9]

Byron, of course, did know something of vampires, and had even conjured the vampire's spell several years earlier in his *Giaour* (1812):

> But first on earth, as Vampyre sent,
> Thy corpse shall from its tomb be rent;
> Then ghastly haunt thy native place,
> And suck the blood of all thy race;
> There from thy daughter, sister, wife,
> At midnight drain the stream of life;
> Yet loathe the banquet which perforce
> Must feed thy livid living corpse,
> Thy victims, ere they yet expire,
> Shall know the demon for their sire;
> As cursing thee, thou cursing them,
> Thy flowers are withered on the stem.
> Then stalking to thy sullen grave
> Go – and with Ghouls and Afrits rave,
> Till these in horror shrink away
> From spectre more accursed than they. (lines 755–86)[10]

In a letter addressed to the editor of the *New Monthly Magazine* and published in the *Courier* (May 5, 1819), Polidori acknowledged that he was the author of *The Vampyre*. By this time, however, Byron had already been accepted as both the author and the title character of the tale. Johann Wolfgang von Goethe declared that it was Byron's finest work.[11] E. T. A. Hoffmann praised "vampiric Byron" for his vivid conjuring of the weird and the horrible.[12]

Polidori did more than adapt Byron's tale and confound authorial identity. He also utilized the most thoroughly delineated satirical representation of Byron in the literature of the age, Ruthven Glenarvon, the title character in Lady Caroline Lamb's *roman à clef* on her tempestuous love affair with the man she declared to be "mad, bad and dangerous to know."[13] She cast herself in the role of Calantha, and created Dr. Jeckyll and Mr. Hyde personae for Lord Byron: his good side in the character of Lord Avondale, his dark side in Lord Glenarvon (dale = glen; avon = arvon; the name as well as the personality are reversed). Lord Ruthven Glenarvon is a literary descendent of the historical Lord Ruthven, marauder, murderer, reputed warlock, and dabbler in witchcraft.[14] Lady Caroline described the countenance of Lord Glenarvon:

It was one of those faces which, having once beheld, we never afterwards forget. It seemed as if the soul of passion had been stamped and printed upon every feature. The eye beamed into life as it threw up its dark ardent gaze, with a look nearly of inspiration, while the proud curl of the lip expressed haughtiness and bitter contempt; yet, even mixed with these fierce characteristic feelings, an air of melancholy and dejection shaded and softened every harsher expression.[15]

Lord Glenarvon's personality is made up of irresolvable contrasts, and the woman who loves him is made to feel his sadistic disdain:

Glenarvon seized Calantha's hand, which he wrung with violence. Passion in him was very terrible: it forced no fierce word from his lips; no rush of blood suffused his cheek and forehead; but the livid pale of suppressed rage spread itself over every feature: even his hands bore witness to the convulsive effort which the blood receding to his heart occasioned. Thus pale, thus fierce, he gazed on Calantha with disdain. (Vol. II, pp. 292–3)

In creating the character of his Byronic vampire, Polidori took the character from her novel and even the name. Polidori gave to Lord Ruthven a similar pale countenance, cold reserve, and piercing eye:

... a cold grey eye, which, fixing upon the object's face, did not seem to penetrate, and yet at one glance to pierce through to the inward workings of the heart, but fell upon the cheek with a leaden ray that weighed upon the skin it could not pass ... In spite of the deadly hue, which never gained a warmer tint, either from the blush of modesty, or from the strong emotion of passion, though its form and outlines were beautiful, many of the female hunters after notoriety attempted to win his attentions. (pp. 27–8)

Lord Ruthven, like Lord Glenarvon and Lord Byron himself, was "mad, bad and dangerous to know." With this Byronic character, the vampire gained new stature in the nineteenth century. No longer a lurking night-stalker, who rises from the grave to feed upon the blood of the living, the new vampire is a handsome and sophisticated aristocrat, and his "irresistible powers of seduction" (p. 37) serve his thirst for blood. According to Lady Caroline as well as Polidori, he seems to possess mesmeric power in his piercing eye. He transcends death, yet becomes bored with mortal humanity. His aloof arrogance is tempered by ennui and a melancholy sense of the futility of life.

Not just the fatal seduction of his female victim, but also his strange thrall over a male companion is a feature of the vampire's ability to control others. The male "bonding" is more pronounced in Polidori's version than in Byron's. In Byron's "Fragment," the unnamed narrator ardently pursues the mysterious Darvell:

My advances were received with sufficient coldness; but I was young, and not easily discouraged, and at length succeeded in obtaining, to a certain degree, that common-place intercourse and moderate confidence of common and every day concerns, created, and cemented by similarity of pursuit and frequency of meeting, which is called intimacy, or friendship. (p. 60)

At the graveyard in Smyrna where Darvell has returned to die, he compels his companion to swear an oath that he will fling Darvell's signet ring on the ninth of the month "into the salt springs which run into the Bay of Eleusis" and will bury him in a designated plot. Byron's "Fragment" ends with this burial, leaving untold the consequences of Darvell's insistence that his companion must then immediately "repair to the ruins of the temple of Ceres, and wait one hour." "Why?" asks the narrator. "You will see," replies Darvell (p. 67). In Polidori's version, Lord Ruthven's companion, Aubrey, becomes far more deeply ensnared by his oath, even to the point that his health and sanity are undermined, and he must silently witness his sister become another of the vampire's victims.

No less than the audiences of the twentieth century were enthralled by cinematic representations of Bram Stoker's Count Dracula, the theatre audiences of the nineteenth century were captivated by the first stage adaptations of Polidori's Lord Ruthven. The craze for stage vampires commenced in France. Following the publication of Cyprien Bérard's sequel, *Lord Ruthven ou les Vampires* (1820), Charles Nodier was quick to adapt the novel to the stage.[16] Nodier's *Le Vampire* was performed at the Théâtre de la Porte-Saint-Martin on June 13, 1820. Two days later Nodier's play was burlesqued by Eugène Scribe and Mélésville in the comic *Le Vampire* staged at the Théâtre de Vaudeville, June 15, 1820. A week later, June 22, 1820, *Les trois Vampires, ou le clair de la lune*, a collaboration by Nicholas Brazier, Gabriel De Lurieu, and Armand d'Artois, opened at the Théâtre de Variétés. Nodier's version was then adapted for the English stage by James Robinson Planché, who acknowledged his debt to the French play and apologized "for the liberty which has been taken with a Levantic Superstition, by transplanting it to the Scottish Isles." In Polidori's novel Lord Ruthven's tomb was in Greece. Nodier's melodrama moved the setting to Staffa's Cave in Scotland. Planché declared that "the unprecedented success of the French Piece" persuaded him "to hazard the same experiment, for the sake of the same Dramatic effect."[17]

The experiment, of course, brought Lord Ruthven closer to home, and increased the association with Lord Byron, who was born in London, reared in Aberdeen, and held his ancestral estate at Newstead Abbey, near Nottingham. In contrast to George Colman's *Blue-Beard*, which deliberately moves the setting to a Turkish village, Nodier and Planché wanted their vampire nearby. In the burlesque of Nodier's play, *Les trois Vampires*, the characters imply that England regularly sends vampires to suck French blood:

GOBETOUT. I've read in the *Paris Journal* that a vampire appeared at the Porte-St.-Martin Theatre. So there is no reason for one not to come to Pantin . . .
MME. G. From what country could they have come? From Switzerland? Russia? Indochina?
GOBETOUT. The vampires . . . they come to us from England . . . It's another kindness of these gentlemen . . . They give us such nice presents![18]

Nodier's motives may also have been political, an opportunity to chide the British, just as the Marquis de Sade had done in *La tour enchantée*. Rather than making the play pro-British as James Cobb and Stephen Storace had done in their adaptation from the French, Planché used the experiment to insist that the vampire lurked amidst Britain's own mists and shadows. Most importantly, the experiment took the audience to the site of the bloody exploits sung by MacPherson's Ossian. The action is transposed to the Western Isles of Scotland, using Fingal's Cave on Staffa as the setting of the supernatural death and resurrection.[19] In the opening Vision, Lady Margaret slumbers in Fingal's Cave, where she has sought shelter from a storm. Two spirits, Ariel and Unda, explain that the vampire spirit of Cromal, "the bloody,"[20] has taken possession of the body of Lord Ruthven:

UNDA. . . . wicked souls
Are, for wise purposes, permitted oft
To enter the dead forms of other men;
Assume their speech, their habits, and their knowledge,
And thus roam o'er the earth. But subject still,
At stated periods, to a dreadful tribute.
ARIEL. Aye, they must wed some fair and virtuous maiden,
Whom they do after kill, and from her veins
Drain eagerly the purple stream of life;
Which horrid draught alone hath pow'r to save them
From swift extermination. (lines 42–52)

In Nodier's version Oscar Montcalm, a superannuated bard of super-natural tales, appears in the cave and prophesies the danger about to befall Lady Malvina, sister of Sir Aubrey. Because Rutwen apparently died in rescuing Sir Aubrey from attacking banditti, Aubrey promises his sister's hand in marriage to Rutwen's younger brother, Lord Marsden. The supposed younger brother, of course, is none other than the resurrected Rutwen.

Although Nodier secured a degree of sympathy for Rutwen for having saved Aubrey's life, that sympathy is progressively undermined as Rutwen reveals his ruthless predatory lust. In Act II, a marriage is arranged for Rutwen's servant, Edgar, and a peasant girl, Lovette. Thirsting for the virgin's blood, Rutwen attempts to ravage Lovette, but is shot by her vigilant groom. As in Polidori's novel, Rutwen exacts from Aubrey an oath that he will not reveal the fact of his death to his sister for twelve hours (Polidori: "for a year and a day" [p. 55]) and that he will expose his body to the moonlight. In Act III, Aubrey realizes Rutwen's true nature as a vampire when, now for a second time, he beholds Rutwen, again risen from the dead, come to claim Lady Malvina for his bride. The distraught Aubrey is declared to be mad and is taken away by servants. He escapes, however, and returns to confront Rutwen at the altar. Rutwen attacks Aubrey with a knife; Malvina faints; the church bell rings the passing of the last hour allotted the vampire to preserve himself from "swift extermination" by drinking the blood of his bride. The ghosts of the vampire's victims arise and an Exterminating Angel descends to destroy the body of the fiend.

In Polidori's tale, Aubrey attends to the dying Ruthven and performs the final rites. Nodier repeats this scene twice, once in the flashback in which Aubrey recollects the attack in Greece, then again in the scene following the vampire's attempted rape of Lovette. Planché, perhaps responding to contemporary rumors about Byron's homosexual relationships,[21] makes much more of the implication of Ruthven's power over a male companion. Planché's Ruthven "had contracted an intimacy" in Athens with the son of Ronald, Baron of the Isles. Under Ruthven's care, the son grows weaker. The father arrives too late to save his son:

Would that I could harbour a doubt on the subject; but, alas! the fatal scene of his death is ever present to my imagination. When called, as you know, by the sudden illness of my now lost son to Athens, I found Lord Ruthven, with whom he had contracted an intimacy, hanging over his sick couch, and bestowing on him the attentions of a brother. Such behaviour naturally endear'd him to me; and after my poor boy's death, his lordship being, like myself, an enthusiastic admirer of the beauties of nature, and the works of art, became the constant companion of my excursions. The more I saw of him, the more I admired his extraordinary talents. In my eyes he appear'd something more than human, and seem'd destin'd to fill that place in my affections which had become void by my son's decease. I shew'd him your miniature. – Never shall I forget his emotion on beholding it. "By heavens!" he exclaim'd, "'tis the precise image my fancy has created as the only being who could ever constitute my happiness." (p. 15)

The father sees only compassion in Ruthwen's intimacy with the dying boy, and he is touched by Ruthwen's immediate response to the portrait of his daughter. Shortly thereafter, as Sir Ronald goes on to relate, Ruthwen saved his life. In his dying breath, he repeats his attraction to Sir Ronald's daughter:

Returning to Athens then – one evening, after a short excursion, we were attack'd by some banditti. I was disarm'd. Ruthven threw himself before me, and received the ruffian's sabre on his own breast. Our attendants, however, succeeded in overcoming the villains. I threw myself into the arms of my expiring friend – he press'd my hand – "Lord Ronald," said he, "I have sav'd your life – I die content – my only regret is, that fate has prevented me from becoming your son." Gallant, unfortunate Ruthven! what a destiny was thine to fall in a foreign land, in the flower of thy youth, deprived of sepulchre (p. 16)

In explaining why Ruthven had no sepulcher, Planché follows Nodier rather than Polidori:

An extraordinary circumstance prevented my fulfilling that last melancholy duty. In his dying agonies he conjur'd me to quit the spot, lest the assassins should return in number. The moon was rising in unclouded majesty. "Place me," said he, "on yonder mound, so that my fleeting spirit may be sooth'd by the soft and tranquil light of yon chaste luminary." I did so – he expired. I left the body to collect our servants who were in pursuit of the defeated villains, and 'ere we could return to the spot, it had disappeared. (p. 16)

Like Nodier, Planché also shifted the oath of silence from Ruthven's death at the hands of the bandits, to the later scene in which he is shot while attempting to rape the peasant girl: "Conceal my death from every human being, till yonder moon, which now sails in her meridian splendour, shall be set this night; and 'ere an hour shall elapse after I have expired, throw this ring into the waves that wash the tomb of Fingal" (p. 24). Tossing Ruthven's ring into the waters of Fingal's Cave is a detail that follows Ruthven's request, in Polidori's novel, to throw the ring "into the salt springs which run into the Bay of Eleusis." Although Planché claimed to be unhappy with Nodier's setting in Scotland, rather than in some Levantine or Eastern European country where belief in vampires prevailed, he certainly used Scottish elements to advantage.

Samuel J. Arnold, manager of the English Opera House, insisted on the Scottish setting because Scottish music was popular and Scottish costumes were available.[22] Planché's most significant change in the cast of characters was his addition of the Scottish drunkard, McSwill. With no comic moments, Nodier's *Le Vampire* took itself all too seriously. Thus it was an easy target for the comic parodies that followed it: *Le Vampire* by Scribe and *Les trois Vampires, ou le clair de la lune*, by Brazier, De Lurieu, and d'Artois.

Planché has given McSwill, as the "comic drunk," a role that may seem merely a familiar stage and literary stereotype. But his presence is far more complicated. Thomas De Quincey, in his well-known essay "On the Knocking at the Gate in Macbeth" (1823), asked why the interlude with the drunken porter "reflected back upon the murderer a peculiar awfulness and a depth of solemnity."[23] Disregarding the concept of "comic relief," De Quincey argues that, in order for "the world of devils" to "be conveyed and made palpable" the ordinary human "world must for a time disappear." Nor is it enough that the deeds of murder be "insulated"; it is also necessary that the audience "be made sensible that the world of ordinary life is suddenly arrested." Once "the world of darkness passes away," De Quincey asserts, the human world must again make "its reflux upon the fiendish." The "re-establishment of the goings-on of the world in which we live," as provided by the grumblings of the porter, "first makes us profoundly sensible of the awful parenthesis that had suspended them."[24]

Similarly, Planché's drunken Scotsman provides something other than "comic relief." He appears in the opening scene, immediately following the "Vision" in Fingal's Cave. His comic exchange with Bridget and Robert (housekeeper and servant to Sir Ronald) does not mitigate, but rather heightens the anticipation of the supernatural fiend. De Quincey acknowledges the dramatic "opposition and contrast" and the way in which these contrasts also play into the tensions of the intellectual vs. the emotional.[25] Without suggesting that Planché's melodrama begins to rival Shakespeare's *Macbeth*, it may nevertheless be observed that Planché was effective in modulating the oppositions of comedy and terror, and, as Sir Walter Scott often did,[26] heightening supernatural effects through the beliefs of the common folk. The "Vision" reveals the secret of the vampire's life beyond death: he must drink the blood of a virgin bride. That story is told again in the opening scene. McSwill stumbles into the kitchen after a night of drinking, crawls under a table, then crawls forth again when he hears that Robert spent the night searching around the haunted cave for Lady Margaret. With frequent interruptions, McSwill tells the tale of Lady Blanch, long ago murdered by the vampire:

MCSWILL.   Once on a time, there lived a lady named Blanch, in this very castle, and she was betrothed to a rich Scotch nobleman; all the preparations for the wedding were finished, when, on the evening before it was to take place, the lovers strolled into the forest –

BRIDGET.   Alone?

MCSWILL.   No; together to be sure.

BRIDGET.   Well, sot, I mean that; and I think it was highly improper.

MCSWILL.   Well, they were seen to enter the grotto, and –

ROBERT.   And what?

MCSWILL.   They never came out again.

ROBERT.   Bravo! – an excellent story.

MCSWILL.   But that isn't all. – The next morning the body of the lady was found covered with blood, and the marks of human teeth on her throat, but no trace of the nobleman could be discovered, and from that time to this he has never been heard of; and they do say, (I hope nobody hears us) they do say that the nobleman was a *Vampire*, for a friar afterwards confessed on his death bed, that he had privately married them in the morning by the nobleman's request, and that he fully believed it some fiend incarnate, for he could not say the responses without stuttering.

ROBERT.   Better and better! and how came you by this precious legend?

MCSWILL.   The great uncle of my grandfather had it from the great grandfather of the steward's cousin, by the mother's side, who lived with a branch of the family when the accident happened; and moreover, I've heard my great uncle say, that these horrible spirits, call'd Vampires, kill and suck the blood of beautiful young maidens, whom they are obliged to marry before they can destroy. – And they do say that such is the condition of their existence, that if, at stated periods, they should fail to obtain a virgin bride, whose life blood may sustain them, they would instantly perish. Oh, the beautiful young maidens! (p. 11)

Before the action commences, the nature of the vampire's blood-thirst is twice revealed. When Ruthven, Earl of Marsden, reappears after his presumed death in Greece, the ever-tippling McSwill insists that the dead man lives still:

MCSWILL.   My master's gone mad – there's a pretty job. If he had been going to be married, instead of the Earl, I shouldn't have wonder'd so much; but for an old man to go mad, who can sit and drink all day, without any one to snub him for it, is the most ridiculous thing that ever came under my observation. Old mother Bridget never lets me drink in quiet at home, so I carry a pocket pistol about with me [*Pulls out a Flask.*] Now this is what I call my "Young Man's Best Companion"; it's a great consolation on a night excursion, to one who has so respectful a belief in bogles and warlocks, as I have. – Whiskey's the only spirit I feel a wish to be intimately acquainted with . . .

ANDREW.   The Earl of Marsden sent you?

MCSWILL.   Yes, to be sure; he's in the Castle there, and just going to be married to my Lady Margaret.

ROBERT.   Fool! the Earl of Marsden is dead.

MCSWILL.   Nay, now you're mad. My master's been telling the same story this half hour; but the Earl says it's no such thing; that he is not dead, and never was dead; that my master's out of his wits; – and off he sends me for Father Francis, to come and talk to my master, and marry my mistress.

ROBERT.   What mystery is this? There is some foul play towards – At any rate, the Lady Margaret must know her danger. Is the friar gone?

MCSWILL.   Oh yes, he's there before now. The very name of a wedding made him chuckle, and waddle off at a rate, which obliged me to stop so many times for refreshment, that he has been out of sight these some minutes. (p. 32)

The comic ploy, much the same as those scenes which Bud Abbot and Lou Costello played with Béla Lugosi,[27] is that the audience is fully aware of the impending danger but the characters fail to realize it.

MCSWILL.   It appears there is something wrong, but I can't positively pretend to say what it is; and as my flask seems as much exhausted as my speculations, I'll make the best of my way home, and ruminate how much whiskey I shall drink at the wedding. (p. 33)

McSwill has all the evidence that Ruthven is the vampire, but in his drunken stupor, he cannot put the facts together. Instead, he thinks of the wedding and staggers off singing "Fy, let us awa' to the Bridal."

For the first run of *The Vampire* J. P. Harley played the role of McSwill. Harley began his acting career at Drury Lane in 1815, performing as Edward in William Macready's *Irishman in London* (October 27, 1815), as Filch in John Gay's *The Beggar's Opera* (October 28, 1815), and as Frank in John O'Keefe's *Modern Antiques, or The Merry Mourners* (November 1, 1815). He had already established his reputation as a comic character in Gothic melodrama, appearing as Motley in Matthew G. Lewis' *The Castle Spectre* (April 16, 1816) and as Edward in James Cobb's *The Haunted Tower* (February 24, 1816). Comic skills that served him particularly well as McSwill were Harley's gift in dialects, his comic timing, and his mastery of the double-take. Also to his credit was his comic restraint. Rather than play McSwill as a mere buffoon, Harley kept the character grounded in rustic realism.[28] McSwill's account of the supernatural was all the more convincing because of the earnestness with which he upheld his belief.

The popular plays of London usually made it to the provinces within the season. Planché's *The Vampire* (English Opera House, August 9, 1820) was performed in Newcastle on January 5, 1821, and in Bath on January 10, 1821. Genest, who often scoffed at Gothic melodrama, generously granted that this play "has considerable merit."[29] The loci of merit resided in the characters of Lord Ruthven, as master of a power to make his intended victims love him, and in the struggling thralldom of two of those victims, Lady Margaret and Ronald. In the original London cast, Lord Ruthven was played by Thomas Potter Cooke, popular as the villain in numerous Gothic melodramas; as Dirk Hatteraick in *The Witch of Derncleugh* (English Opera House, 1821), adapted from Scott's *Guy Mannering*; and most notably as the Monster in Richard Brinsley Peake's *Presumption; or, The Fate of Frankenstein* (English Opera House, July 28, 1823). When John Waldie saw *The Vampire* in Newcastle, he too granted that "it was excellent, & well acted, & more interesting than one could expect from such extreme impossibility." In spite of the fiction that "a Vampire dies & comes to live, & nearly gets the 2 females of the piece to feed his dreadful necessity of devouring young women," the intrigue carries the performance. "The escapes & interest are clever & well managed." The local cast included Thomas Sowerby Hamblin as Lord Ruthven, Elizabeth Blanchard as Lady Margaret, and Samuel Butler as the drunken McSwill (5 January 1821; 47:360–1).[30]

The interactions of comedy and horror, as well as eroticism and horror, are reworked in the vampire plays that follow: first came William Thomas Moncrieff's *The Vampire, a drama in three acts* (Royal Coburg, August 22, 1820); then Planché's *Giovanni the vampire!!! or, How shall we get rid of him?* (Adelphi, January 15, 1821); then Moncrieff once more with the *Spectre Bridegroom; or, A Ghost in spite of himself* (Drury Lane, February 7, 1821); and Planché yet again with his adaptation from the German opera, Heinrich Marschner's *Der Vampyr* (English Opera House, August 25, 1829).

In his first attempt at a vampire melodrama, Moncrieff seemed at a loss on how to use comedy to intensify the horror. Within the previous five years he had written a dozen plays, performed at the Olympia, the Lyceum, the Adelphi, and during the past year at the Royal Coburg he had turned to melodrama. *The Shipwreck of the Medusa; or, The Fatal Raft*, a clever combination of documentary and melodrama,[31] opened at the Coburg on June 19, 1820. He followed this with a historical melo-drama, *The Ravens of Orleans; or, The Forest of Cercotte*, on July 3, 1820. For the following month Moncrieff completed *The Vampire*. He drew from Nodier and Planché, but he also turned back to Polidori's tale, repeating in his prefatory "Remarks" for the 1829 edition of the play "the report of its being from the pen of the noblest poet of the day."[32] In these "Remarks" he also cited "Sir Walter Scott's translation of the Eyrbyggia Saga" as evidence that vampires were not just a part of the lore of Eastern Europe and the Levant, but were also known in the North. Nodier was therefore not wrong in setting the tale in Scotland.[33] The only character in Moncrieff's version who slightly corresponds to Planché's McSwill is the servant Davie. Unlike McSwill, Davie reveals nothing of the lore of the vampire. McSwill's song, "Fy, let us awa' to the Bridal," anticipated the wedding. Davie's song, on how women chatter, prattle, gossip, and scold, is a song fitting to the character of the comic Scotsman, but it has no bearing on the dramatic situation. Moncrieff's major change was to emphasize romance rather than comedy.

In Nodier's version, the lady's defender against the vampire was her brother; in Planché's, her father. Moncrieff retains the brother, but introduces Edgar, Chief of the Lorn, as her defender. He is in love with Lady Malvina, but withdraws his suit when Ruthwold arrives to ask her hand in marriage. In the opening vision, the cave is crowded with a chorus of vampires, then spirits announce that before twenty-four hours pass and the clock strikes one, Ruthwold must drink the blood of his bride or forever perish. Recognizing him as the monster of her dream, Malvina screams when she first beholds her betrothed. The weakness of the romance plot is that Moncrieff's Ruthwold has no seductive powers and is never a serious rival. Edgar suspects his evil nature from the very beginning, so that the plot involves nothing of Ruthwold's mesmeric entrancement of the fair sex, but only the brute force with which he intends to capture his victim. The plot therefore must focus on Edgar's vigilance and his exposure of Ruthwold's villainy. Borrowing the character of Oscar, the aged bard, from Nodier, Moncrieff has Edgar disguised as an old minstrel. Jeannie, the bride in the peasant marriage (Nodier's Lovette, Planché's Effie), is deliberately exposed as vampire-bait while Edgar and Sandy, her bridegroom, hide in the shadows to protect her. Ruthwold threatens her with a knife and tries to force his ring onto her finger. He is about to carry her off when Sandy and Edgar intervene. In the swordfight between Edgar and Ruthwold, the villain is killed. He rises again in the final act to claim Malvina as his bride. The ceremony is interrupted by Edgar. Just as Ruthwold draws his sword, the clock strikes one. Malvina faints into the arms of Edgar. Amidst thunder and the red glow of hell, the Phantoms and their invisible leader gather round him, and all vanish. A window opens above the altar, and Edgar, Malvina, and her father are bathed in the light of the moon.

In France, the melodrama of Nodier was quickly satirized in burlesque and farce. In England, the same pattern was repeated, with the significant difference that Planché and Moncrieff provided their own comic parodies of vampire melodrama. The first of these was Planché's "operatic burlesque burletta," *Giovanni the vampire!!! or, How shall we get rid of him?* Only the songs, not the text, were published,[34] but Roxana Stuart found that the songs and the names of the characters provided an adequate basis for her to reconstruct the plot.[35] The names of the characters made it apparent that Planché had combined the plot that he had already used from Polidori and Nodier with characters from Mozart's *Don Giovanni*.[36]

As Byron observed in the opening Canto of *Don Juan* (1819), his hero was an "ancient friend . . . / We have all seen him in the pantomime, / Sent to the devil somewhat ere his time" (lines 6–8). *Don Juan, or the Libertine Destroyed* (Drury Lane, May 10, 1782) was a popular pantomime, revived several times. George Cruikshank's scurrilous cartoon, "Fare Thee Well" (1816), depicted Byron, embraced by three actresses of Drury Lane, being rowed out to the ship that is to carry him in his exile from England. This well-known cartoon provided the idea for Moncrieff's *Giovanni in London: or The Libertine Reclaimed* (Olympia, December 26, 1817): having proved himself a nuisance even in the Underworld, the wicked seducer is sent into exile. He seizes Charon's boat at the River Styx and carries three women off with him. From the Styx onto the Thames, he arrives in London, attends a masquerade, makes love to Constantia, and, swearing to reform, marries her.[37] In *Don Giovanni, or the Spectre on Horseback* (Bath, May 19, 1819), Thomas Dibdin took a hint from Gottfried August Bürger's *Lenore* (1773):[38] he had the Statue Spectre arrive on horseback to seize the wicked seducer and toss him to the demons who leap with his body into the stage-trap.

Borrowing from Lady Caroline Lamb's depiction of the Byronic Lord Ruthven Glenarvon as a cunning seducer, Polidori had introduced into literature a vampire with mesmeric sexual prowess. How fitting, then, that Planché created a hybrid of these two ruthless ravagers of female innocence – *Giovanni the vampire!!!* – how inevitable, too, having brought such a sexual predator into society, that Planché must then answer the question, *How shall we get rid of him?* As commentators on Bram Stoker's *Dracula* (1897) have observed, the vampire represents uncontrolled sexual appetite. The pursuit of the vampire is driven by male anxiety over female sexuality and a superior sexual rival. The jeopardized men must thwart the unbridled erotic force. In Bram Stoker's version, driving the stake through the vampire's heart to exorcise the demon replicates the act of sexual penetration.[39]

Planché's Giovanni is introduced as "an old acquaintance considered in a new light," and it matters little whether we understand that "old acquaintance" to be the vampire now appearing as the playboy of Seville, or the playboy of Seville now become a blood-thirsty as well as sexually voracious predator. Compounding the irony already implicit in the self-parody, Planché stages this piece as a play about a play. Included in the case are three playwrights – Cabbage, Cribb, and Fudge – whose names suggest the modus operandi of their inspiration and composition. They are uninspired by Tragedy and Comedy, characters introduced as "Melancholy representatives of two Species of composition nearly obsolete." Although the curtain rises upon "Vision" in the Cave of Fingal, the familiar scene is comically distorted. The Spirits who gather are Imagination and Burlesque. In mock-lament, Imagination observes that Giovanni is an irrepressible theatrical interloper:

> That many-
> Liv'd Libertine! – that monster – Don Giovanni:
> At every house in turn he rears his head;
> In vain, alas! you think him damn'd and dead.
> When first the Opera Italian burn'd him,
> Into a pantomime some author turn'd him;
> At Covent Garden, and at Drury Lane,
> The cry was, "Curse him! There he is again."[40]

It does not require Planché to turn him into a vampire. His repeated resurrections reveal that he already is one. Imagination reveals to

Burlesque that a playwright has arrived to "threaten the Adelphi" with yet another Giovanni. "What's to be done?" asks Burlesque. Imagination replies, "Why, let the Vampire be annihilated." Even as they speak the sleeping figure in the cave begins to stir. It is neither Lady Malvina nor Lady Margaret, but rather Mr. Bustle, the manager of the Adelphi. The two spirits begin their incantation to conjure the monster, "Appear! Appear!" Up springs the Vampire, played by a shapely actress in a breeches part, shouting "I would appear – at the Adelphi!" Roxana Stuart observes that "the borrowed tunes are an eclectic and playful collection," recycling songs that Planché had used in *The Vampire*, and giving new lyrics to Ophelia's mad song from *Hamlet* (iv.vii), the deer-killing song from *As You Like It* (iv.ii), the popular Burns ballad, "My love is like a red, red rose" (sung by Leoporello to his drunkard wife), and two tunes from Mozart's *Don Giovanni* (sung as part of a debate on toasted cheese). When the frolicsome Giovanni Vampire is finally vanquished by the indefatigable Mrs. Bustle, who apparently has such a vast store of vital energy that she could satiate several vampires, the cast gathers for a Grand Finale on his demise, sung to the tune of "Rob Roy Macgregor, O!"[41]

While it is certainly true that Moncrieff's melodrama was inferior to Planché's, his satirical spoof is a superiorly crafted play with a clever plot of mistaken identity. Nor could it scarcely matter, among such contemporary playwrights as Cabbage, Crib, and Fudge, that the plot was borrowed. As Moncrieff acknowledges in his introductory "Advertisement," he has taken his plot from "a story of the same name, in that beautiful piece of enamel writing (if I may be allowed the expression) 'The Sketch Book.'"[42] He refers, of course, to Washington Irving's "The Spectre Bridegroom, a Traveller's Tale," in *The Sketch-Book of Geoffrey Crayon Gent* (1819–20), a volume containing as well "The Legend of Sleepy Hollow" and "Rip Van Winkle," and recently published by John Murray in London.[43] Irving's tale is set in the Odenwald at the Castle of the convivial, garrulous, but impoverished Baron von Landshort, who has arranged the marriage of his daughter to a wealthy young heir, Count von Altenburg. Released from military duty, Altenburg sets forth on horseback from Würzburg to meet for the first time his destined bride. On the way he meets a companion-in-arms, Herman von Starkenfaust, who agrees to ride with him through the Odenwald. In the depths of the forest, they are beset by robbers, and Altenburg is mortally wounded. Starkenfaust readily consents to his friend's dying request that he proceed to the castle and inform the Baron von Landshort of the fatal event. "'Unless this is done,' said he, 'I shall not sleep quietly in my grave.' He repeated these last words with peculiar solemnity." Starkenfaust arrives at the castle and is mistaken for Altenburg. Because his host never pauses in telling "his best and longest stories," Starkenfaust finds no time to identify himself and deliver his tragic message. In the meantime, he grows increasingly fascinated with the Baron's beautiful daughter. The Baron has just finished telling the tale "of the goblin horseman that carried away the fair Leonora – a dreadful story which has since been put into excellent verse, and is read and believed by all the world." When the Baron gives his guest a moment's silence to appreciate the horror of Leonora's abduction, Starkenfaust suddenly rises to his feet and solemnly announces that he must go.

> "Ay," said the baron, plucking up spirit, "but not until to-morrow – to-morrow you shall take your bride there."
> "No! no!" replied the stranger, with tenfold solemnity, "my engagement is with no bride – the worms! the worms expect me! I am a dead man – I have been slain by robbers – my body lies at Wurtzburg – at midnight I am to be buried – the grave is waiting for me – I must keep my appointment!" (p. 129)

Having fallen in love with the Baron's daughter, Starkenfaust decides to play the role of the ghostly rider in Bürger's ballad. The news that Altenburg had been slain convinces the Baron that his guest was indeed the resurrected phantom come to claim his bride. In the meantime, Starkenfaust "had repeated his visits by stealth – had haunted the garden beneath the young lady's window – had wooed – had won – had borne away in triumph – and, in a word, had wedded the fair" (p. 132).

Moncrieff's alterations to Irving's tale effectively enhance its theatricality.[44] First, he makes more of the mistaken identity by transforming the friends into look-alike cousins, Gaspar and Abraham Nicodemus, and adding the detail that a portrait of the prospective bridegroom had already been sent to the castle. Second, he adds a romantic subplot: Miss Georgiana Aldwinkle, whose hand in marriage has been promised to Gaspar Nicodemus, is secretly in love with Captain Vauntington. Her cousin Lavinia, however, is attracted to Abraham Nicodemus, who arrives at the castle intending to report Gaspar's death. With his subplot, Moncrieff deftly complicates the ensuing comedy of errors: Lavinia welcomes her nighttime visitor, and Georgiana is free to encourage Captain Vauntington. Third, while Irving's Starkenfaust deliberately assumes the role of vampire lover, Moncrieff's Nicodemus is completely unaware that everyone perceives him to be a blood-lusting corpse. Fourth, he borrows more details from Bürger's well-known ballad. Fifth, he introduces both Squire Aldwinkle (who has the marriageable daughter) and Abraham Nicodemus as deeply involved in the lore of vampires: Nicodemus as a matter of scholarly research, and the Squire out of superstitious fascination. As comic contrast to the superstitious Squire Aldwinkle, Moncrieff has given him a servant, Dickory, as fond of drink as McSwill but more pragmatic in his response to supernatural visitations.

In the opening scene, Abraham Nicodemus is alone in his study when his cousin's servant Paul arrives to inform him that his master has died in "an apoplectic fit." He agrees to fulfill the mission to Aldwinkle Hall, even though it means that he must interrupt his work on vampires:

> Then his wishes shall be complied with. I'll lock up my grand treatise on Vampires, hasten to Aldwinkle Hall this very moment, and return here the first thing to-morrow morning, to make preparations for the funeral. Unhappy Gaspar! he was the last of the Nicodemus family, except myself. What a pity he was'nt as like me in other things as he was in person. But, drink! drink was the ruin of him. I'll go directly and break out the melancholy news to Miss and the Old Gentleman. (p. 7)

Moncrieff thus sets the study of vampire lore in opposition to the supernatural belief in vampires. In contrast to his carefree and carousing cousin, Abraham Nicodemus has lived as a scholarly recluse. In Aldwinkle Hall, where he is mistaken for the expected bridegroom, he is embarrassed by the exuberant attentions and finds no opportunity to reveal the death of his cousin. Ushered into the banquet that has been prepared to welcome the bridegroom, he feels out of place amidst the social bustle. Seated at the table with Georgiana and Lavinia, he shyly retreats from their conversation. As an aside, he declares: "Methinks that I cut but a very foolish figure here; I neither know what to do or say; I believe my best refuge is in silence – Heigho! would I were at home continuing my treatise on Vampires" (p. 13). He realizes that the mistaken identity may soon be exposed when it is known that his cousin is dead, yet it never occurs to him that he may be seen as a resurrected corpse. When Paul arrives to relate the funeral and burial arrangements for his master, Abraham Nicodemus does not realize that Dickory and Aldwinkle are eavesdropping. When they hear him speak of his research, they become all the more convinced that Nicodemus is a vampire: "I will now go and continue my researches in the Domestic History of Vampires, that I may be completely au fait to my task, and not prove myself a novice, and by the time I've married old Aldwinkle's daughter, I shall be able to put my theory in practice" (pp. 23–4). If it was assumed that Nicodemus was writing his own extension of Augustin Calmet's *Treatise on Vampires* (1746),[45] his reference

here to a "Domestic History of Vampires" places the purpose of his study
in a different context. The possibilities of a vampire's household practices
are certainly enough to alarm the eavesdroppers:

DICKORY.   Dang me, if this bain't the first time I ever heard of a dead man
                being asked when he liked to be buried.
ALDWINKLE.   I am perfectly perforated in every part with horror – going to
                marry my daughter and turn Vampire – Ah! no doubt to
                practise on her. But, thank Heaven, he'll be buried
                to-morrow. Dickory, go you the first thing to-morrow
                and see him box'd up, and d'ye hear, bribe the sexton to
                dig his grave a foot or two deeper, and put one of the
                heaviest and largest stones he can get upon it. (p. 24)

Dickory does his job well, making sure that the body is securely entombed:
"He be earth'd down, safe enough now, sur. I did'nt come away till I'd
seen sexton fill up every crack there were – he'll be cunning to get out this
time" (p. 28). Still unaware that Squire Aldwinkle has warned the entire
household of a prowling vampire, Nicodemus continues his attempt to
meet secretly with Georgiana. At first he seems unsettled by the reception
he receives when he returns to Aldwinkle Hall. But the wooing of
Georgiana happily suits his occult research:

NICODEMUS.   Zounds, one would think I was a spectre, where ever I go I
                frighten every body away. Surely it can't be this suit of
                black – no matter, the melancholy ceremony over, I have
                now time to return to the soft duties of love and my
                grand work on Vampires. (p. 29)

Squire Aldwinkle fears that his is about to lose his daughter as Nicodemus
re-enacts from Bürger's ballad the nightly visitations of Wilhelm to his
Lenore. To protect Georgiana from the vampire, and hoping thus to win
her father's permission to marry her, Vauntington bravely holds a midnight watch, his courage bolstered by pistols and brandy.

VAUNTINGTON.   [*looking at his watch.*] 'Tis very near twelve – I don't half like
                this job. I must take a little more brandy. – [*Drinks.*] –
                It would be no use firing at him, he'd no more mind
                having the contents of a pistol in his body than if they
                were only so many force meat balls; I must take
                another bumper. – [*Drinks.*] (p. 29)

Unfortunately, the brandy puts him to sleep. When Nicodemus arrives,
he thinks that Vauntington has merely fallen asleep without making it to

bed. Failing to awaken him, he fires one of the pistols. Startled out of his sleep, Vauntington sees the monster before him and runs off in terror. Only afterwards does he realize that in his cowardice he has lost his one chance to win Georgiana as his bride. Alarmed by the gunshot, Aldwinkle, Dickory, Georgiana, and Lavinia nervously inquire over the fate of the vampire. The pistol shot, Vauntington tells them, was useless, so he assaulted the vampire with abjuring spells.

VAUNTINGTON.   What the deuce shall I say? If I confess my defeat, I lose my Georgiana. I must brazen it out. – [*aside.*] – Oh! I've had desperate work – we've been at it tooth and nail for the last half hour, but I think the business is settled now. Firing was of no use, one might as well have shot at the air for all the wounds it created, so I had at him with the Latin, Friar Bacon, Doctor Faustus, and Agrippa. (p. 31)

Puzzled by Vauntington's frightened response, Nicodemus wonders whether he has somehow changed. From these reflections, he returns to his principal preoccupation, his "grand work" on vampires. He begins to realize that, like vampires, mortal men too can "prolong their existence" by union in marriage.

NICODEMUS.   This is more and more extraordinary. Surely I must have been metamorphosed unknown to myself; transmogrified into some monster, or – But I have more important things to occupy my mind.
[*Aldwinkle, Lavinia, &c. appear listening.*]
The great and conclusive truth at which I have arrived in my grand work, renders my mind sufficiently disengaged to think of love. There is no doubt that Vampires seek an union with mortal beings expressly to prolong their existence on this earth. I shall instantly, therefore, seek the fair Aldwinkle, and achieve our marriage. After what I have endured, meanwhile, a walk in the soft moonlight will revive me. (p. 32)

Once more his soliloquy is misunderstood by the listening eavesdroppers. Or rather it is misunderstood by all but one. Lavinia has a good inkling what has stirred the young man's nocturnal visits and prompted his moonlight walks:

LAVINIA.   There, sir, you hear what he said, he is a Vampire, and merely seeks an union with my cousin to prolong his existence.

GEORGIANA.   Oh, I'm sure I'll never marry a Vampire, pa; he'd eat me up if I
did. (p. 32)

Knowing that Georgiana has all along been in love with Vauntington,
Lavinia sees an opportunity for herself:

LAVINIA.   Listen to me, sir – Guarantee that the captain shall have my cousin,
and settle a small fortune on me, and I undertake to keep Mr.
Nicodemus from ever troubling you at night again; I'll make
him rest, I'll warrant him. (p. 32)

Her strategy for dispelling the phantom that nightly threatens the Hall is
to secure the wandering creature in bed.

NICODEMUS.   Can it be possible, that the moon beaming such cool pure
lustre can entrance men's minds to madness – She bathes
me in her filmy light like dew, refreshing and allaying –
melting me into softness, and attuning each sterner chord
of heart to love and harmony – Heigho! [*Enter Lavinia.*]
By heavens, responsive to my feelings comes this angelic
girl, to captivate and charm.

LAVINIA.   My good sir, if you have no particular wish to be knock'd o'the
head for an evil spirit, you will give over these nightly
wanderings; hit upon some decisive method of proving
yourself an ipso facto man, and rest quietly in your bed at
night.

NICODEMUS.   How admirably she will assist me in my learned labors.

LAVINIA.   I fear I am more likely to disturb his learned labors, than to
assist him in them.

NICODEMUS.   An evil spirit – nightly wanderings – knock me o'the head. A
light begins to break in upon me – how better can I
prove myself a man, sweet girl, than by uniting my life's
fate with thine.

LAVINIA.   Marry me! – that will be one way, certainly.

NICODEMUS.   Thus on my knees – (p. 33)

Moncrieff's farce is a departure from the previous representations on the
stage of vampires, for his play demonstrates the *Wirkungsästhetik* as effect
without cause. There is no vampire, only the belief in a vampire. Nicodemus
himself has no notion that others think him to be a vampire come to fetch his
bride. Only Lavinia has insight into a primary psychological urge in the
"Domestic History of Vampires," and she uses that urge to her own
advantage.

It may seem that Planché and Moncrieff held between them an exclusive
contract for vampires on the London stage of the 1820s. Not just Planché

and Moncrieff, other authors of the period exploited the popular interest in vampires: Edward Fitzball, who had numerous stage successes and St. John Dorset, who had none.[46] Before considering these two, however, it is useful to turn yet again to Planché, this time not as importer of Polidori via France, but of Nodier via Germany. Ruthven, not a player in Moncrieff's farce, was restored by the Germans fully empowered as suave and seductive predator. For its English premiere at the Lyceum (English Opera House), August 25, 1829, Planché adapted Heinrich Marschner's *Der Vampyr*. The German libretto was by Marschner's brother-in-law, Wilhelm August Wohlbrück, theatre director in Magdeburg. During Marschner's visit to Magdeburg in April, 1827, the two read Nodier's *Le Vampire* as well the first German adaptation, Heinrich Ludwig Ritter's *Der Vampyr oder Die Todten-Braut*, performed in Karlsruhe, March 1, 1821.[47] The success of Carl Maria von Weber's *Der Freischütz* influenced their choice of work with similar demonic themes.[48] Wohlbrück commenced work on the libretto, and before he left Magdeburg, Marschner composed the music for the first scene.[49] The opera was completed within the year, with its premiere performance on March 29, 1828, at the Leipzig Stadttheater.

In adapting Wohlbrück's libretto for an English audience, Planché felt that he must temper the explicit sexuality. Wohlbrück's libretto presents a Rutwen whose lust is obsessively sensual. Yes, he must drink the virgin's blood to survive, but his thirst is driven by a passion that sates itself only in the excesses of physical intercourse. His mouth, teeth, tongue are all involved in the multiple acts of penetration. Wohlbrück has turned back to Polidori's version for Rutwen's first victim, Ianthe. Although she had not appeared in any of the previous stage adaptations, she is needed here to demonstrate the cruelty of Rutwen's sexual passion. She has lost her way in the woods when Rutwen finds her and takes her to the cave. He easily has his way with her, and as he witnesses her passion gradually twisted into pain, he becomes sadistically aroused by her cries.

> Ah, what pleasure from beautiful eyes,
> From flowering breasts, new life
> In a wondrous drink,
> To suck all this in with one kiss!
> With lustful daring
> To coaxingly nip
> The sweetest blood
> Like nectar of roses
> From crimson lips!
> And when the burning thirst is quenched,

And when the blood has flowed from the heart,
And when they groan, filled with terror,
Ha ha, what delight!
What pleasure, with new lust,
Their death agony is fresh life!
Poor darling, white as snow,
No doubt you feel pain in your heart.
Ah, once I felt these pangs
Of fear in my warm heart
Which heaven created for feeling.
Don't remind me in these fresh tones
Of the curse of the heavens!
I understand your cry!
Ah, what pleasure![50]

Because Rutwen lost the once warm heart that a merciful Heaven had given him, Ianthe's screams brazenly scorn the Heaven he has denounced. Relevant here is another of Wohlbrück's significant changes. As in the Faust tradition revived by Goethe and re-invoked in Weber's *Der Freischütz*, Wohlbrück introduces Rutwen making his pact with the Vampire Master:

MASTER VAMPIRE. This creature here is already
One of our slaves.
He wishes for a short time
To be among free men.
His desire will be granted
When he fulfills his vow:
Before midnight to bring
Three sacrifices before us.
For three brides delicate and pure,
A year shall be given to the vampire.
RUTWEN. By all-powerful evil
I swear to keep my word.
But fly this place,
Because the first of the sacrifices
Will soon be here.
[*The master disappears, then moon shines again.*][51]

Ianthe is the first victim, Emmy (the peasant bride) is the second, and Lady Malwina is intended as the third. In the previous stage adaptation, Rutwen is always stopped before he manages to suck the blood of his victims. In the German opera, these are the major scenes. In Act 1, Ianthe has just collapsed lifeless in Rutwen's arms, when her father, Sir Berkeley, arrives in the cave and takes his revenge on the vampire. No sooner has Sir Berkeley departed, bearing the corpse of his daughter, than Aubrey arrives at the cave. In the strange intimacy between the two characters, one witnesses for the first time since Polidori hints of Aubrey's homosexual dependency. To be sure, Rutwen has saved Aubrey's life, but that debt alone does not fully explain Aubrey's subservience. In the cave, the dying Rutwen requests that Aubrey place his body in the moonlight at the top of the bluff. He also demands that Aubrey swear an oath not to reveal Rutwen's secret for twenty-four hours.[52] The next scene begins with Malwina's confession of her love for Aubrey, but her father, Sir Humphry, has granted the suit of the wealthy Rutwen, Earl Marsden, to be her husband. In spite of feeling sorry for Aubrey, the audience can scarcely have much confidence is his capacity to rescue Malwina.

Act II begins, in preparation for the peasant wedding, with a rousing drinking song: "In Autumn one must drink" ("Im Herbst, da muß man trinken"). George Dibdin, Sir Humphry's servant, is to marry the peasant girl, Emmy (Nodier's Lovette, Planché's Effie, Moncrieff's Jeannie). In all three of the earlier versions, Ruthven is slain in his attempt to seduce the bride-to-be. In Wohlbrück's libretto, he wins her passionate compliance. Before she meets with Rutwen, Emmy is warned by her mother:

> Child, do not look upon that pale man,
> Because he will destroy you.
> Stay away from him!
> Many a beautiful young maiden
> Looked too deeply into his eyes
> And had to pay with bitter anguish
> And her life blood,
> Because, secretly and softly I tell you:
> The pale man is a vampire!
> God save all of us on earth
> From ever becoming like him.[53]

Not heeding her mother, Emmy is flattered by the nobleman's attentions and aroused by his kisses. Like Ianthe, she is the victim of her own desire. The emphasis in her mother's warning is that looking into the vampire's eyes will end with the loss of her life blood. But the warning also adds the possibility that others may become like him. How does one become a vampire? Vampire lore identifies many causes: a curse, perverted desire, unstilled longing for revenge, reanimating the dead, tasting human blood or the blood of a vampire. In Wohlbrück's libretto, Rutwen assures Aubrey that he will himself become a vampire if he violates his oath.

Effectively situated, a variation on De Quincey's theory, between the scene in which the passionate Emmy follows Rutwen into the wood, and the scene in which George finds her ravished body, is the comic scene where four young wedding guests drink too much and are scolded by Emmy's mother. Her scolding is interrupted by pistol shots, as George races after the fiend.

The final scene commences with Aubrey and Malwina appealing for Heaven's protection. Rutwen demands that the wedding be performed before the midnight hour. Aubrey watches the ceremony helplessly: if he reveals the vampire's secret, he breaks his oath and becomes himself a vampire; if he keeps the secret, she becomes the vampire's bride and victim. Breaking the oath and sacrificing himself is the only way to save her. Fortunately, just as Aubrey shouts out, "This monster is a vampire!" ("Dies Scheusal hier ist ein Vampyr!"), the clock strikes one. The twenty-four hours have passed. Amidst thunder and lightning, the disempowered Rutwen is claimed by the Vampire Master.

When he adapted Wohlbrück's libretto for the performance of Marschner's *Der Vampyr* at the Lyceum, Planché took the opportunity to make changes "in accordance with my own ideas of propriety." His notions of "propriety" did not involve eliminating or even reducing the vampire's violent lust. Indeed, his main concern seemed to be shifting the setting from Scotland to Hungary, "where the superstition exists to this day."[54] Londoners were exposed to several other stage vampires during the 1820s. The melodrama *The Vampire* was the collaborative work of Hugo John Belfour and George Stephens.[55] Although not performed, it went through a second edition. The reviewer for the *London Magazine* observed that the character of the vampire exhibited "the revolting egotism . . . of Lord Byron's works." These exhibitions of the "Byronic hero," the reviewer went on to say, were "the children of a diseased imagination."[56] Edward Fitzball, a prolific author of melodrama, adapted Robert Southey's poem, *Thalaba the Destroyer* (1801) for the stage.[57] It was performed with spectacular oriental scenery at the Royal Coburg, August 18, 1823. In Southey's poem, Thalaba's bride, Oneiza, dies on her wedding day. She is transformed into a vampire, and Thalaba accompanies her father, Moath, to the tomb, where he dispatches her with his lance. Fitzball has changed the plot, giving Oneiza a rather different role. He therefore has Thalaba's mother, Zeinah, transformed into a dangerous vampire who preys on the living. There are two significant features of Fitzball's melodrama: first, he has brought to stage a female vampire; and second, he has given the vampire a double character, evil only because caught in a transitional state between physical and spiritual being. Her former goodness is restored when her captive spirit is released from her vampiric corpse. She then becomes a protective spirit who guides Thalaba's subsequent deeds. Lord Ruthven was dangerous because his polished manners and urbane charm concealed his ruthless appetite for virgin blood; he never pretends to the role of husband and father. The double character of Southey's Oneiza and Fitzball's Zeinah is more threatening, because they transform the loving bride and the nurturing mother into a murderous demon.

During those twenty-two years from Southey's *Thalaba* to Fitzball's adaptation as melodrama, other female vampires were featured prominently in the poetry of the period, but none were brought on stage until the popularity of Polidori's Lord Ruthven made vampires a box-office attraction. The male vampire wielded a mesmeric spell over his innocent victims. He is at once the embodiment of male fantasy and male fear. A sexually superior rival, demonized as utterly ruthless in his lust, the male vampire is a threat to social and domestic order. He must be permanently vanquished so that he can no longer rise from death. His counterpart, the female vampire, seems also to be the invention of male fantasy and male fear. The vampiric woman, erotic and dominating, retains youth and beauty by drawing life-energy from her lovers. Several German poets had taken up the theme of the female vampire, notably Goethe, who in 1797 portrayed an ancient Greek vampire in *The Bride of Corinth*. Erroneously attributed to Ludwig Tieck, "Wake not the dead" (1802) was doubtless the work of another German writer of tales. E. T. A. Hoffmann showed his mastery of the genre in "Aurelia" ["Vampirismus"], one of the tales in *Die Serapions-Brüder* (1820). The two parts of Samuel Taylor Coleridge's "Christabel", often considered the first English vampire poem, were written in 1797 and 1801, but not published until 1816. The serpent woman of John Keats' *Lamia* (1820) derived from a Roman tale of a blood-sucking creature, and his "La Belle Dame sans Merci" (1820) told of a beautiful lady who cast a spell over men. Among the most compelling vampires in the literature of the earlier nineteenth century are Nodier's *Smarra, ou les démons de la nuit* (1821), Théophile Gauthier's "La morte amoureuse" (1836), and Edgar Allen Poe's "Ligeia" (1838). Later in the century, Sheridan Le Fanu created a haunting female vampire in "Carmilla" (1872). In *The Leaving Dead*, James Twitchell devotes a thorough and insightful chapter to the female vampire in poetry and prose fiction.[58] Perhaps with good reason, he gives no attention to the female vampire on stage. In spite of such horrific literary models as Geraldine, Lamia, or Smarra, none of these characters were introduced into the theatre. During the period that witnessed the rise of the Byronic vampire in melodrama, there emerged no corresponding demonic femme fatal. Or, rather, they emerged in such a minority that Roxana Stuart is compelled to refer to the melodrama of the female vampire as a "subspecies."[59]

C. Z. Barnett, who wrote dozens of Gothic melodramas, including *The Skeleton Hand; or, The Demon Statue* (1833), provided an eerie example of the avenging female in *Phantom Bride; or, The Castilian Bandit* (1830).[60] The play that most fully exploits the double character of the wife become vampire is George Blink's *Vampire Bride, or the Tenant of the Tomb* (1834), adapted from the anonymous German tale falsely attributed to Ludwig Tieck. After Brunhilde, his first wife, died, Walter took a second wife, Swanhilde, who bears him two children. Still longing for his first wife, Walter visits a necromancer. Revived from the grave, Brunhilde is incapable of feeling any emotional bond, and she must nourish herself on the blood of the living. Swanhilde commits suicide when she discovers that the vampire has killed her infant babes. Walter is awakened from his sleep to discover Brunhilde sucking his blood. Again aided by the sorcerer, he slays the vampire with a consecrated knife. Still obsessed with the memory of his vampire bride, he later meets another woman whom he brings home. Just when he thinks that his domestic happiness is restored, his third bride reveals that she is the indestructible vampire. Transforming into a serpent, she crushes him to death. For the stage, Blink omits the metamorphosis and emphasizes the contrast between the evil Brunhilde and the good Swanhilde.[61] Roxana Stuart objects that Blink gives too much stage time to the comic subplot with the wedded servant couple, Annetta and Jansen, and the cobbler, Kibbitz, who provides a running commentary on their marital spats.[62] Parallel to the major plot, the subplot exposes false expectations of marital bliss and provides an effective reminder that the vampire plot plays out on the level of fantasy and terror the same familiar themes of domestic conflict and exploitation, the psychic vampirism in which one partner drains the energy of the other.

Throughout this study of Romantic drama, I have emphasized performance and audience response. In documenting the reciprocity between the two, I have stressed that spectators were aware of the theatre as a showplace in which singing, acting, costuming, lighting, stage-designing, all contributed to the grand illusion-making, whether that illusion be domestic, historical, documentary, or fantastic. Performers vied with one another to gain audience favor for their particular manner of interpreting a familiar role, and at the same time they sought to reveal their own distinctive character in and through the roles they played. Illusionism always went hand-in-hand with anti-illusionism. With the optical metaphor of a periscopic perspective, I have relied frequently on eye-witness accounts in an effort to recreate the theatre experience of the time. And with the optical metaphor of "Pepper's Ghost," I have sought to explain the pervasive doubleness, the reflective and refractive nature of the pretend world of theatrical performance. The central chapter described the sexual shifts from transvestites, to lovers, to monsters, and the subsequent chapters examined geographic displacement, a theatrical "elsewhere," as a rationale of moral displacement. Beginning with the account of the Gothic and anti-Gothic, and the interaction of comedy and horror, the final chapters have examined that dialectic in presentations of two memorable monsters of the Romantic stage, the wife-killing Blue-Beard and the blood-sucking Vampire.

The vampire melodrama of the 1820s, and the advent of the female vampire on the London stage of the 1830s, may well have relied for their success on the audience pleasure in the affective aesthetics of eroticism and terror. But a part of the attraction to the vampire theme was certainly the sense, even if it were only subliminal, that the entropy of vampire and victim played out recognizable transgressive acts of domestic domination and subservience. The acts of seduction and rape were distanced by transforming them into demonic fantasies. Yet by weaving in comic action that contrasted with the supernatural fantasy, the comic characters reminded the audience of the perceptive wisdom in folk beliefs. The comic reaffirmed the world of reality that is suspended in the scenes of nightmare fears and taboos. The vampire melodrama provided an apt post-Revolutionary commentary on an aristocracy feeding upon the lower classes. As a nobleman of the old order, Lord Ruthven served as model for the sophisticated vampire of the century that followed and was direct predecessor of the aristocratic vampire than succeeded him, Count Dracula.

Notes

INTRODUCTION

1 John Keats to Richard Woodhouse (October 27, 1818), *Selected Letters*, pp. 194–5.

2 Burwick, *Illusion and the Drama*, pp. 5, 6, 9, 11, 61, 123–4, 232.

3 Richard Cumberland, *The Wheel of Fortune* (Drury Lane, February 28, 1795), in Kemble, *Kemble Promptbooks*, Vol. XI, pp. 15–16. The plays in each volume of the *Promptbooks* retain original pagination.

4 Kotzebue, *The Stranger* (Drury Lane, March 24, 1798), trans. Benjamin Thompson, in *Kemble Promptbooks*, Vol. XI, p. 27 (I.ii).

5 Adams, *A Dictionary of the Drama*, Vol. I, p. 306.

6 Harley, *William Henry West Betty*, p. 136.

7 Davis, "Self-Portraiture On and Off the Stage," pp. 177–200; Davis, "They Shew Me Off in Every Form and Way," pp. 243–56.

8 Adolphus, *Memoirs of John Bannister*, p. 62.

9 Mathews, *Memoirs of Charles Mathews*, Vol. I, pp. 49–52.

10 Grimaldi, *The Memoirs of Joseph Grimaldi*.

11 Hannah Cowley, *The Town Before You*, p. x.

12 The Haymarket was one of the most prominent centres of prostitution in London. See Henderson, *Disorderly Women*, and Clark, ed., *The Cambridge Urban History of Britain*, Vol. II: *1540–1840*.

13 Watson, *Sheridan to Robertson*, p. 429.

14 Thomson, "Drury Lane, Theatre Royal," in *The Cambridge Guide to Theatre*, pp. 309–11.

15 Iain Mackintosh, *Architecture, Actor and Audience*, p. 34.

16 Boaden, *Memoirs of Mrs. Siddons*, Vol. II, p. 250.

17 *Ibid.*, p. 251.

18 Byng, *The Torrington diaries*, Vol. IV, p. 261; also cited in Mackintosh, *Architecture, Actor and Audience*, p. 35.

19 Kemble, *Lodoiska* (1794).

20 Kelly, *Reminiscences*, Vol. II, pp. 59–60.

21 Genest, *Some account of the English Stage*, Vol. VII, p. 151. See also this volume, Chapter 7.

22 Auburn, "Theatre in the Age of Garrick and Sheridan," pp. 7–46.

23 Handley and Kinna, *Royal Opera House Covent Garden*, pp. 37–9.
24 Rees, *Theatre Lighting in the Age of Gas*; Burwick, "Romantic Drama: from Optics to Illusion," pp. 167–208.
25 Nicoll, *A History of English Drama*; on Sadler's Wells: pp. 43, 231–2; on Astley's: pp. 37, 230.
26 *Ibid.*, p. 41.
27 Kemble, *Kemble Promptbooks*, Vol. v, pp. ii–iii.
28 Planché, *Blue Beard*, in *The Extravaganzas of J. R. Planché*, Vol. ii, p. 35.
29 Schlegel, *Vorlesungen über dramatische Kunst und Literatur*; Burwick, *Illusion and the Drama*, pp. 164–5.
30 Percec, "Transvestism as Bricolage," pp. 7–13; Howard, "Crossdressing, the Theatre, and Gender Struggle," pp. 418–40.
31 Staves, "A Few Kind Words for the Fop," pp. 413–28.
32 Wolfson, "A Problem Few Dare Imitate," pp. 867–902.
33 Burwick, "The Grotesque in the Romantic Movement," pp. 37–57.
34 Praz, *The Romantic Agony*, pp. 95–186.
35 Cox and Gamer, eds., *The Broadview Anthology of Romantic Drama*, Introduction, pp. 75–6.

1 PERISCOPES INTO THE THEATRE

1 Küster, ed., *Theatrum mundi*, pp. 60–100.
2 John Waldie, Journals and letters. In Paris on June 15, 1831 (LVIII: 14), Waldie attended the Opéra Comique to see again a performance of François Devienne's *Les Visitandines* (Théâtre Feydeau, July 7, 1792), which he vividly remembered from the performance he had seen thirty-nine years earlier as a boy in Kelso: "I wished to see again [*Les Visitandines*] to remind me of the French theatre at Kelso, Joubert, Lebas, Dupuy, & c., who performed it nearly as well as this great theatre." For other references to the French theatre in Kelso, see July 30, 1816 (xxv: 3); November 19, 1818 (txvLii: 72 ["t" before the volume number indicates a transcribed volume]).
3 Hunt, "Performers of the English Stage" (1807), in *Leigh Hunt's Dramatic Criticism*, p. 87.
4 Hazlitt, "On Play-going and On Some of Our Old Actors."
5 Lamb, "Stage Illusion," in *Life and Works*, Vol. iii, pp. 29–34; Lamb refers to Bannister's performances as Young Wilding in Samuel Foote's *The Liar* (1762), and Joseph Surface in Richard Brinsley Sheridan's *The School for Scandal* (1777).
6 Kelly, *Reminiscences*, Vol. i, pp. 318–20, 348.
7 Inchbald, *The British theatre*, Vol. xxiv, pp. 2–5.
8 Kotzebue, *Pizarro*; Kemble, *Kemble Promptbooks*, Vol. xi.
9 Hunt, *Selected Writings*, Vol. iii, pp. 186–7.
10 Hazlitt, *Complete Works*, Vol. v, pp. 174–6, 180, 200–2, 223, 378; Vol. viii, 277–8; Vol. xx, iii.

11 Boaden, *Memoirs of Mrs. Siddons*: as Lady Macbeth, Vol. II, pp. 87–99; as Desdemona, Vol. II, pp. 106–7; as Ophelia, Vol. II, pp. 156–9; as Imogen, Vol. II, p. 165; as Cordelia, Vol. II, p. 183; as Katharine in *Taming of the Shrew*, Vol. II, pp. 185–6; as Cleopatra, Vol. II, pp. 189–91; as Queen Katharine in *Henry VIII*, Vol. II, pp. 205–11; as Mrs. Haller in *The Stranger*, Vol. II, pp. 261–3.

12 Genest, *Some account of the English Stage*; Baker, Reed, and Jones, *Biographia dramatica*.

13 Coleridge, *Biographia Literaria*, Vol. II, p. 6.

14 Stendahl (= Henri Beyle), *Racine et Shakespeare* (1823), reprinted in *Œuvres complètes*, Vol. XIII, pp. 15–16.

15 von Arnim, *Hollins Liebeleben* (1802), in *Werke*, Vol. I, pp. 1–116.

16 Burwick, *Illusion and the Drama*, pp. 33–6, 196–7, 268–70.

17 Waldie, Lectures on chemistry, moral philosophy, and universal history, MSS Dc 5: 118–20; Dc 6: 113–15.

18 Scott, Letter to Charlotte Ann Waldie Eaton. In addition to his recollection of the Waldie family, Scott advised Charlotte: "I am afraid you have not well chosen your turn for lighter literature, which is at present quite strangled by politics. But they must take turns around and I make no doubt that the taste of folks will return for cakes & ale and that ginger will be red hot in the mouth too." Scott attended school at Kelso with Robert Waldie and was welcomed to the Waldie library, where Mrs. Waldie, a Quaker, would always include a few religious tracts among the books he borrowed. She had the same concern for the "Temporal and Eternal welfare" of his parents, to whom she also sent pamphlets (Jane Ormston Waldie, Letter to Walter Scott). The characters too were drawn, in John Lockhart's words, from "what Walter witnessed under Mrs. Waldie's hospitable roof," (Lockhart, *Life of Sir Walter Scott*, Vol. I, 146–7). Scott himself appended a note to *Redgauntlet*, Letter VII, on his experience with the Waldies. See also Johnson, *Sir Walter Scott: The Great Unknown*, Vol. I, p. 54; Smith, *History of Kelso Grammar School*, pp. 51, 56.

19 In addition to the entries in the *Dictionary of National Biography* (*DNB*) and *Burke's Landed Gentry* (1846 edition), information on the Waldie family has been taken from the following: Anderson, *The Scottish Nation*, Vol. III, p. 596; Burleigh, *Ednam and Its Indwellers*, pp. 180–3; Jeffrey, *The History and Antiquities of Roxburghshire*, pp. 116–18; Mason, *Kelso Records*, pp. 139, 193–4; Rutherford, *Kelso Past and Present*, pp. 33–5, 65; Tancred, *The Annals of a Border Club*, pp. 248–50.

20 Byron to John Murray (September 29, 1820), *Byron's Letters and Journals*, Vol. VII, pp. 183–4.

21 Waldie, Journals and letters, journal entry of July 3, 1809 (XIX: 331).

22 *Ibid.*, journal entry of June 26, 1809 (XIX: 307).

23 *The Monthly Mirror*, n.s. (July 6, 1809).

24 Piozzi, *Love Letters*. Her letters were written at Bath in 1810; see also Tearle, *Mrs. Piozzi's Tall Young Beau*.

25 William Augustus Conway, letter to John Waldie, July 24, 1809. Waldie, Journals and letters, MS 169, Vol. II, no. 17.

26 Hazlitt, "Miss O'Neill's Juliet," *The Champion* (October 16, 1814), in *A View of the English Stage* (1818), in *Complete Works*, Vol. v, p. 200.

27 *Dramatic Magazine* (December 1, 1830) 2: 297.

28 Waldie, "Musical Report of the Newcastle Theatre," p. 3.

29 Waldie, Journals, journal entry of June 24, 1799 (IV: 50).

30 Madame Frederick, celebrated dancer of the Theatre Royal, Edinburgh, was known for her performance of the Scottish Strathspey, including pieces especially composed for her by William Marshall (1748–1833).

31 Cumberland, *The Brothers* (1769).

32 Cumberland, *The Wheel of Fortune* (1795).

33 Kelly, *Reminiscences*, Vol. II, p. 84.

34 Hazlitt, *A View of the English Stage* (1818), in *Complete Works*, 5: 376.

35 Hunt, *Dramatic Criticism*, pp. 5–6.

36 Inchbald, *The British theatre*, Vol. XVIII, p. 4.

37 *Ibid.*, p. 2.

38 Kotzebue, *The Stranger*, in *The German Theatre*, Vol. I.

39 For the argument that even in Germany Kotzebue was considered by some as propagating immorality, see Williamson, "What Killed August von Kotzebue?".

40 Genest, *Some account of the English Stage*, Vol. VII, p. 336.

41 Thompson, *Kotzebue*, p. 25.

42 Waldie, Journals, journal entry of February 22, 1800 (IV: 189).

43 Barker, *The Theatre Royal Bristol*. On p. 65, she describes the structure of the stage and boxes; in her index of plays, she lists performances of *The Stranger* at Bristol Theatre Royal on Monday, February 24, 1803 and Wednesday, October 5, 1803; in her transcripts of local newspaper reports, she documents Kemble's appearances in *Macbeth* at the Bristol Theatre Royal and Bath Theatre Royal between April 12 and 19, 1803.

44 *Ibid.*, p. 33.

45 Burwick, "Ideal Shattered."

46 Hazlitt, "The Drama: II," *London Magazine* (February, 1820), in *Complete Works*, Vol. XVIII, p. 283.

47 Winkelmann, *Reflections on the Painting and Sculpture of the Greeks* (1765), p. 86: "eine edele Einfalt und eine stille Grosse, sowohl in der Stellung als im Ausdruck" ("a noble simplicity and calm grandeur, both in pose and in expression").

48 Walker, *Wallace: an Historical Tragedy in five acts* (1820).

2 NATIONALISM AND NATIONAL CHARACTER

1 Conolly, *The Censorship of English Drama 1737–1824*; Kinservik, *Disciplining Satire*.

2 O'Quinn, "Mercantile Deformities"; Hamilton, "*Inkle and Yarico* and the Discourse of Slavery"; Troost, "Social Reform in Comic Opera."

3 Lindfors, "Ira Aldridge's London Debut"; Marshall and Stock, *Ira Aldridge: The Negro Tragedian*.

4 Page, "Hath not a jew eyes?".
5 On John Braham and Isaac Nathan, see Introduction to Nathan and Byron, *A Selection of Hebrew Melodies*, pp. 4–10.
6 Brewer, "This monstrous tragic-comic scene"; Carlson, *The Theatre of the French Revolution*; Cox, "The French Revolution in the English Theater"; Friedland, *Political Actors*; Maslan, *Revolutionary Acts*; Taylor, *The French Revolution and the London Stage*; Wray, "English Adaptations of French Drama between 1780 and 1815."
7 O'Neill, *The Burke–Wollstonecraft Debate*.
8 Philp, ed., *Resisting Napoleon*.
9 Holcroft, *Memoirs of the late Thomas Holcroft*.
10 Beaumarchais, *The Follies of a Day; or, the Marriage of Figaro*.
11 Charles Bonnor collaborated with Robert Merry on "The Picture of Paris"; see Hargreaves-Mawdsley, *The English Della Cruscans and Their Time*, pp. 221–3; Hauger, "William Shield."
12 Clarke, *The Georgian Era*, Vol. IV, pp. 384–5.
13 Dryden, *The Satires of Dryden: Absalom and Achitophel*, pp. 7–10.
14 Engels, *Der Ursprung der Familie*, in Marx, Engels, *Werke*, pp. 130–1:

> Daß aber in Schottland früher Mutterrecht herrschte, beweist die Tatsache, daß in der königlichen Familie der Pikten, nach Beda, weibliche Erbfolge galt. Ja selbst ein Stück Punaluafamilie hatte sich, wie bei den Walisern, so bei den Skoten, bis ins Mittelalter bewahrt in dem Recht der ersten Nacht, das der Clanhäuptling oder der König als letzter Vertreter der früheren gemeinsamen Ehemänner bei jeder Braut auszuüben berechtigt war, sofern es nicht abgekauft wurde.

> (That maternal right dominated earlier in Scotland is proven by the fact that in the royal families of the Picts, according to Bede, the succession of inheritance followed the female line. Even a part of the Punalua family, as with the Welsh so also with the Scots, had upheld until the Middle Ages the right of the first night: that the chief of the clan or the king, as last representative of the earlier community husband, held the right to use every bride if he did not sell that right.)

> The imposition of the "right of the first night" is among the motivating factors in the movie *Braveheart*. Gibson portrayed a legendary Scot, William Wallace, who led the First War of Scottish Independence by opposing Edward I of England.

15 Richardson, *Pamela* (1740). In the stage adaptation by James Dance, performed at Goodman's Fields on November 9, 1741, the plot is focused on the marriage to Colebrand that Belvile has arranged for Pamela, with the understanding that Colebrand is to immediately surrender his bride to Belvile. Mrs. Jewkes, the house-keeper, takes a perverse delight in aiding Belvile's plot. The plot is exposed when Pamela receives a letter intended for Mrs. Jewkes. When she confronts Belvile, he attempts to ravish her but is prevented by the arrival of Chaplain Williams. The play ends with a lawful marriage of Pamela and Belvile.
16 Orwell, *1984*, Part I, Chapter 7, p. 106: "There was also something called the *jus primae noctis* which would probably not be mentioned in a textbook for

children. It was the law by which every capitalist had the right to sleep with any woman working in one of his factories."

17 Boureau, *The Lord's First Night*: see especially the chronological bibliography, pp. 277–88; Gutberlet, *Irrtümer und Legenden der deutschen Geschichte*; Wettlaufer, *Das Herrenrecht der ersten Nacht*; Wettlaufer, "The *Jus primae noctis* as a Male Power Display."

18 Voltaire, *Le droit du seigneur*; See Stackelberg, "Voltaire, Beaumarchais und das ius primae noctis."

19 Howarth, "The Theme of the 'Droit du Seigneur' in Eighteenth-Century Theatre."

20 Vulpius, *Rinaldo Rinaldini, der Räuber-Hauptmann*, p. 458.

21 Schiller, *Wilhelm Tell* (1804).

22 Genest, *Some account of the English Stage*, Vol. VI, pp. 357–8.

23 Beaumarchais, *The Follies of a Day*, I.i, pp. 2–3.

24 Taylor, *The French Revolution and the London Stage*, pp. 40–1.

25 Humble, "Liberty and/or Equality." Humble discusses Heinrich Mann's *Madame Legros* (1913).

26 Written in collaboration with Pierre-Jacques Bonhomme de Comreyras, an account of Latude's imprisonment and escapes was published as *Histoire d'une détention de trente-neuf ans, dans les prisons d'Etat* (1787). Latude then published *Mémoire de M. Delatude, ingénieur* (1789). Three English translations were published: *Memoirs of Mr. Henry Masers de La Tude, containing an account of his confinement thirty-five years in the state prisons of France; and of the stratagems he adopted to escape, once from the Bastille, and twice from the Castel of Vincennes; with the sequel of those adventures* (1787), *Memoirs of Henry Masers de Latude during a confinement of thirty-five years in the state prisons of France. Of the means he used to escape once from the Bastile, and twice from the dungeon of Vincennes, with the consequences of those events* (1787), and a third edition with the same title (also 1787). Among the later translations: *Memoirs of Henry Masers de Latude: who was confined during thirty-five years in the different state prisons of France*, trans. John William Cole (1834).

27 The Convention in France, made up of the constitutional and legislative assembly, convened from September 20, 1792 to October 26, 1795 (4 Brumaire in the year IV under the French Republican Calendar adopted by the Convention). It held executive power in France during the first years of the French First Republic.

28 Quétel, *Escape from the Bastille*. Quétel draws from original documents of the period to correct the lies and misrepresentations of Latude's *Memoirs*.

29 François Lolonois, notorious pirate who plundered Nicaragua and killed hundreds of villagers; Alexander Exquemelin, *The Buccaneers of America* (1678). D'Arcy, in *Some Passages in the Life of an Adventurer*, p. 24, reported that O. Smith's melodrama, *Lolonois; or, The Bucaniers of 1660* (Royal Coburg, August 21, 1818) "abounded ... in trap-doors, rope-ladders, impossible combats, and sickly sentimentalism."

30 Raymond, *The Old Oak Tree*, I.ii, p. 16.

31 Andrews, *Fire and Water!*; *Dissipation*.

32 Miles Peter Andrews shared little of the Della Cruscan sentimentality and none of their cosmopolitan pretensions, but he was in close alliance with the flamboyant Edward Topham (1751–1820) and often in the company of Robert Merry (1755–98), founder of the Della Cruscan circle: (Hargreaves-Mawdsley, *The English Della Cruscans and Their Time*, pp. 156–8). On Andrews as Della Cruscan, see Rosenfeld, "A Della Cruscan Poet," *Times Literary Supplement*, p. 345; and Rosenfeld again, "A Della Cruscan Poet," *Notes and Queries* CXCVII.

33 Bernard, *Retrospections of the Stage*, Vol. II, p. 92; Lennox, *Celebrities I Have Known*, Vol. I, pp. 233–8.

34 Bernard, *Retrospections of the Stage*, Vol. II, p. 92. For an example of Andrews' craft, see below his epilogue to Reynolds' *Notoriety* (Covent Garden, November 5, 1791).

35 Andrews, *Dissipation*, p. iii.

36 Bernard, *Retrospections of the Stage*, Vol. I, pp. 318–20.

37 *Ibid.*

38 Smith, *Nollekens and his Times*, Vol. II, p. 366, states that "the most fascinating of all the lovely women painted by Ozias Humphrey, was the famous Kitty Frederick," adding that she lived in a house provided by the Duke of Queensberry.

39 Bernard, *Retrospections of the Stage*, Vol. I, p. 320.

40 Andrews, *Fire and Water!*, I.i, p. 3.

41 Knight, "Webb, Mrs. (d. 1793)"; Doran, *"Their Majesties' Servants,"* Vol. II, p. 204. Referring to roles in which she used her weight effectively on stage, Doran mentions her performance as Cowslip in *A Midsummer Night's Dream* and as Falstaff in *The Merry Wives of Windsor*.

42 Knight, "Wewitzer, Ralph (1748–1825)"; Wewitzer, *Dramatic Reminiscences*.

43 Reynolds, *Notoriety*, I.i, pp. 7–8.

44 Genest, *Some account of the English Stage*, Vol. VII, p. 65.

45 Reynolds, *Delays and Blunders*, I.iii, p. 14.

46 *Ibid.*, pp. 576–8.

47 Saint-Fond, *Description des expériences de la machine aerostatique* (1784); Fauré, *Les frères Montgolfier et la conquête de l'air* (1983). Developed by the brothers Joseph-Michel and Jacques-Etienne Montgolfier in Annonay, France, the first balloon flight with humans on board took place at the *Folie Titon* in Paris on October 19, 1783, with the scientist Jean-François Pilâtre de Rozier; the manufacture manager, Jean-Baptiste Réveillon; and Giroud de Villette. The first public exposition of balloon flight was made one month later on November 21, 1783, in Paris by Jean-François Pilâtre de Rozier and François Laurent d'Arlandes.

48 Reynolds, *The Blind Bargain*, I.i, v.i.

49 Genest, *Some account of the English Stage*, Vol. VII, pp. 658–9.

50 "Mrs. Orger" [Mary Ann Orger, *née* Ivers, 1788–1849], in Anon., *The Biography of the British Stage*, pp. 203–6.

51 Poole, *Simpson and Co.*, I.i, p. 9.

52 Genest, *Some account of the English Stage*, Vol. IX, p. 266, and Vol. VIII, pp. 695–6.

53 Voltaire, *The History of Peter the Great*.

54 "Coveney, 1790–1881," in Adams, *A Dictionary of the Drama*, Vol. I, p. 346.

55 Raker, "Liston, John (*c.*1776–1846)"; Doran, *"Their Majesties' Servants,"* Vol. II, p. 351.

56 *Le Vampire* (1820) was actually a collaboration: Charles Nodier wrote together with Achille Jouffrey and Pierre Carmouche. See Hemmings, "Co-authorship in French Plays of the Nineteenth Century."

57 Genest, *Some account of the English Stage*, Vol. VIII, pp. 116–19.

58 Elliston, "Advertisement" in Payne, *Adeline*, p. 4.

59 Genest, *Some account of the English Stage*, Vol. IX, pp. 146–7.

60 *Ibid.*

61 Payne, *Richelieu*, 1.1.33–40.

62 *Ibid.*, pp. 5–6.

63 *Ibid.*

64 Among the many discussions of Inchbald's play in Austen's novel, see Jordan, "Pulpit, Stage, and Novel"; Gay, "Theatricals and Theatricality in *Mansfield Park*"; Conger, "Reading *Lovers' Vows*"; Ford, "'It Is about Lovers' Vows.'"

65 Bode, "Unfit for an English Stage?"

66 Inchbald, *The Plays of Elizabeth Inchbald*. Of her twenty-one plays, two were adapted from German, eight from French sources: *The Widow's Vow* (1786) from Patrat, *L'heureuse erreur* (1783; see also Patrat, *L'Anglois; ou, Le fou raisonnable* [1784]); *The Midnight Hour* (1787) from Dumaniant, *Guerre ouverte; ou, Ruse contre ruse* (1787); *Animal Magnetism* (1788) from Berre and Radet, *Les Docteurs modernes* (1784); *The Child of Nature* (1788) from de Genlis, *Zélie ou l'ingénue* (1781); and *Next Door Neighbours* (1791) from Mercier, *L'Indigent* (1772) and Destouches, *Le Dissipateur* (1745).

67 O'Quinn, *Staging Governance*, pp. 125–63. Noting that five of Inchbald's plays are set in India, O'Quinn makes the point that she "deploys India and related spaces throughout her work as part of a complex critique of late eighteenth-century British masculinity and statecraft" (p. 126).

68 Clancy, "Mme de Genlis, Elizabeth Inchbald and *The Child of Nature*."

3 GENRE: THE REALISM OF FANTASY, THE FANTASY OF REALISM

1 For the first performance of Charles Dickens' *The Haunted Man* (Adelphi, December, 1848) many special effects were scripted. On Pepper's illusion, see Steinmeyer, *Two Lectures on Theatrical Illusion*, pp. 1–86.

2 Coleridge, *The Friend*, Vol. II, p. 117 (No. 8, October 5, 1809):

The Window of my Library at Keswick is opposite to the Fire-place, and looks out on the very large Garden that occupies the whole slope of the Hill on which the *House* stands. Consequently, the rays of Light transmitted *through* the Glass, (i.e. the Rays from the Garden, the opposite Mountains, and the Bridge, River, Lake, and Vale interjacent) and the rays reflected *from* it, (of the Fire-place, &c.) enter the eye at the same moment. At the coming on of Evening, it was my frequent amusement to watch the image or reflection of the Fire, that seemed burning in the bushes or between the trees in different parts of the Garden or the Fields beyond it, according as there was more or less Light; and which still arranged itself among the real objects of Vision, with a distance and magnitude proportioned to its greater or less faintness. For still as the darkness encreased, the Image of the Fire lessened and grew nearer and more distinct; till the twilight had deepened into perfect night, when all outward objects being excluded, the window became a perfect Looking-glass: save only that my Books on the side shelves of the Room were lettered, as it were, on their Backs with Stars, more or fewer as the sky was more or less clouded (the rays of the stars being at that time the only ones transmitted.) Now substitute the Phantom from the brain for the Images of *reflected* light (the Fire for instance) and the Forms of the room and its furniture for the *transmitted* rays, and you have a fair resemblance of an Apparition, and a just conception of the manner in which it is seen together with real objects.

3 Coleridge, *Marginalia*, Vol. III, p. 212; Coleridge, *The Notebooks of Samuel Taylor Coleridge*, Vol. I (1794–1804), pp. 145n, 894, and 1737.
4 Keats, letter to George and Georgiana Keats, September 17–27, 1819, in Keats, *The Letters*, Vol. II, p. 200.
5 McFarland, *Romanticism and the Forms of Ruin*, p. 384; on mimetic vs. meontic, see pp. 384–418 *passim*.
6 Hugo, "Préface de *Cromwell*," in *Œuvres dramatiques et critiques complètes*, p. 145; Ives, English translation of "Préface de *Cromwell*" in Hugo, *Dramatic Works*, Vol. III.
7 Wordsworth, *The Prelude*, VII, 302, 309 (p. 266).
8 As first performed, the cast for *The Apparition* (Haymarket, September 3, 1794) included Glanville, Mr. C. Kemble; Baron Fitz-Allen, Mr. Usher; Earl Egbert, Mr. Cooke; Larry, Mr. Johnstone; Chearly, Mr. Bannister, Jun.; Peter, Mr. Suet; Hubert, Mr. Benson; Friar, Mr. Pindar; Lady Lauretta, Miss Leake; Polly, Mrs. Harlowe; Elinor, Miss De Camp.
9 Genest, *Some Account of the English Stage*, Vol. IX, p. 496.
10 Fitzball, *The Flying Dutchman* (1827). On the performance, see Fitzball, *Thirty-Five Years of a Dramatic Author's Life*, Vol. II, pp. v–vi.
11 Fitzball, *The Flying Dutchman*, pp. 9–11. Opening at the Adelphi, January 1, 1827, the cast of characters were:

Captain Peppercoal, formerly Captain of a Trade Ship, Mr. Butler
Lieutenant Mowdrey, a young Sea Officer, Mr. Hemmings.
Peter Von Bummel, a Cockney Dutchman, a Dabbler in Law, alias a benighted Shepherdess, Mr. J. Reeve.
Toby Varnish, his Friend, a physical Marine Painter, and a Bear. Mr. Yates.
Tom Willis, Mate of the Enterprise, Mr. Smith.
Mynheer Von Swiggs, Purser of the same Vessel, Mr. Saunders.
Smutta, a Slave Signor Paulo.

Vanderdecken, Captain of the Phantom-Ship, the Flying Dutchman.
Mr. O. Smith.
Rockalda, an Evil Spirit of the Deep, Mr. Morris.
Lestelle Vanhelm, Niece to Captain Pepper-coal, Mrs. Fitzwilliam
Lucy, her Attendant, Miss Apjohn.
Sailors, Slaves, Water-Imps, &c. &c.

12 G. Daniel, Preface, *The Flying Dutchman*, p. 2.
13 Foote, *Companion to the Theatres*, p. 26.
14 Daniel, Preface, *The Flying Dutchman*, p. 4.
15 Burwick, "Romantic Drama: from Optics to Illusion"; Burwick, "Science and Supernaturalism."
16 Brewster, *Letters on Natural Magic*, pp. 56–97.
17 Fitzball and Rodwell, *The Devil's Elixir* (1829); Hoffmann, *Die Elixiere des Teufels* (1815–16); Chamisso, *Peter Schlemihls wundersame Geschichte* (1814).
18 Genest, *Some account of the English Stage*, Vol. IX, pp. 482–3.
19 Waldie, Journals, journal entry of May 23, 1829 (LVI:344). Robert Keeley (1793–1869) performed as the original Jemmy Green in W. T. Moncrieff's *Tom and Jerry* (Adelphi, November 26, 1821); as Rumfit, the tailor, in Peake's *Duel, or, My Two Nephews* (Covent Garden, February 18, 1823); as the original Fritz in Peake's *Presumption, or the Fate of Frankenstein* (English Opera House, July 28, 1823); as the gardener in Planché's *The Frozen Lake* (English Opera House, September 3, 1824); and as Master Innocent Lambskin in Planché's *A Woman Never Vext, or, The Widow of Cornhill* (Covent Garden, November 9, 1824).
20 Waldie, Journals, journal entry of May 23, 1829 (LVI: 334): "I don't know when I've laughed so much," of Keeley's performance in Richard Brinsley Peake's *Master's Rival* (Covent Garden, May 6, 1829), adding that "this farce is 'rather vulgar', tho' no way offensive, & Keeley is irresistible." After several years of playing comic roles together, Keeley and Mary Ann Goward (1805–99) were married at the close of this season on June 26, 1829.
21 Baillie, "Introductory Discourse" (1798), in *Plays of the Passions*, in *The Dramatic and Poetical Works*, pp. 1–18.
22 Diderot, *Les Bijoux indiscrets* (1748), in *Œuvres complètes*, Vol. IV, pp. 286–7.
23 *Morning Post* (October 11 and 22, November 5 and 20, December 31, 1802).
24 Nicoll, *A History of English Drama*, p. 465. In his list of plays by unknown authors, Nicoll notes that a play with the same title, *The Gamblers*, opened on the same date, November 17, 1823, at the Surrey Theatre. If not the same play, this was most probably another dramatization of Thurtall's crime.
25 A summary of reports in *The Times, Morning Chronicle* and *The Observer* appeared in the *Mannheimer Zeitung* 336 (December 4, 1823) and 342 (December 10, 1823).
26 Kant, *Kritik der Urteilskraft*, §6, in *Werke*, Vol. V, p. 288.
27 De Quincey, "On Murder Considered as a Fine Art" (*Blackwood's Magazine* [1827]), in *Works*, Vol. VI, pp. 110–13; "Peter Anthony Fonk" (1827), in *Works*,

Vol. VI, pp. 279–93; "Second Paper on Murder Considered as One of the Fine Arts" (*Blackwood's Magazine* [1839]), in *Works*, Vol. IX, pp. 397–408.

28 Burwick, "Mimesis and the *idem et alter*," in *Mimesis and Its Romantic Reflections*, pp. 45–76.

29 Freud, "Das Unheimliche" (1919), in *Psychologische Schriften*, Vol. IV, pp. 241–74.

30 Foucault, *Discipline and Punish*, pp. 2–69.

31 Hindley, "The Confession and Execution of John Thurtell at Hartford Gaol," in *Curiosities of Street Literature*, p. 187; Altick, *Victorian Studies in Scarlet*, p. 36.

32 Even in responding to and replicating the sensationalism of newspaper and periodical journalism, the docu-drama of the Romantic stage could achieve a more powerful illusion of realism, but at the same time it constrained that realism within the accustomed artifices of theatrical performance. The actuality of headline news was converted into the alterity of dramatic art. Thus the news of the Battle of Leipzig (also known as the "Battle of the Nations"), October 16–18, 1813, was immediately adapted as *Buonaparte Burnt Out; or, The Allies Victorious* in the extravaganza that opened at the Surrey on October 18, 1813 (playwright unknown). Or again, when Arthur Thistlewood, William Davidson, James Ings, Richard Tidd, and John Brunt were executed for high treason on April 28, 1820, the Royal Coburg used the occasion to draw in crowds to see a re-enactment of *The Cato Street Conspiracy*, showing the conspirators plotting in a hayloft, their arrest by the squad led by George Ruthven, Thistlewood firing his pistol point-blank at Richard Smithers, the trial for treason and murder, and the comic–heroic scene on the gallows in which Ings was loudly singing *Death or Liberty* until Thistlewood told him "Be quiet, Ings; we can die without all this noise." The comic moment then turned grotesque when neither Ings nor Brunt would die when the platform dropped and they were left dangling in twitching convulsions at the end of the rope so that several of the executioner's assistants had to pull on their legs until their agonies at last ended. See Wilkinson, *An Authentic History of the Cato Street Conspiracy* (1820).

33 Kant, *Kritik der Urteilskraft*, §13 (*Werke*, Vol. V, pp. 302–3), §48 (*Werke*, Vol. V, pp. 410–12).

34 See, for example, the three volumes of Moncrieff, *Selections from the dramatic works*.

35 Moncrieff, *Shipwreck of the Medusa*. Because this text has no line references, passages will be cited parenthetically by page number. For many of her insights, I am indebted to Kristin Crawford, UCLA undergraduate student, who submitted in May, 2006, a close reading of the play.

36 Alexander McKee, *Death Raft: the Human Drama of the Medusa Shipwreck*.

37 Moncrieff, *Shipwreck of the Medusa*, refers only once to this circumstance; Jack states, "What, though we didn't win Waterloo, damme, we led the way to it; – we won the Nile and Trafalgar, aye, and single handed too, and we will win again whatever old England chooses to give the world, for British heart of oak stands firm forever," p. 16.

38 Savigny and Correard, *Narrative of a Voyage to Senegal*, p. 103.
39 Moncrieff, *Shipwreck of the Medusa*, p. 14.
40 Bolton, "Saving the Rajah's Daughter."
41 Jackson and Morrow, "Aqua Scenes at Sadler's Wells Theatre, 1804–1824," and "Handlist of Aqua-Dramas Produced at Sadler's Wells, 1804–1824"; Rosenfeld, "A Sadler's Wells Scene Book."
42 Kelly, *Reminiscences*, Vol. II, p. 63, describes the "grand sea-fight" featuring model ships capable of firing at each other.
43 Forbes, "Water Drama"; Van der Merwe, "Stage Sailors: Theatrical Material in the National Maritime Museum."

4 ACTING: HISTRIONICS AND DISSIMULATION

1 Sharp, "Essay on Gesture." In Sharp's theatre paintings, the exaggerated attention to gesture suggests more the flailing of the "silent movies" than the subtleties of accomplished stage performance. See especially his scene from Shakespeare's *King John* with Eliza O'Neill as *Queen Constance before the Tents of the English and Foreign Sovereigns* (1819). A more intriguing study of gesture is his *An Author Reading his Drama to an Assemblage of the Performers in the Green Room of Drury Lane*, which depicts the ways in which the players imagine themselves entering into the action.
2 Engel, *Ideen zu einer Mimik*, observations based primarily on the performances of Friedrich Ludwig Schröder and August Wilhelm Iffland. Engel, contemporary with Lessing, Mendelssohn, Goethe, and Schiller, was a recognized critic of the drama. Following his work, *Über Handlung, Gespräch und Erzählung* ("On Plot, Dialogue, and Narrative" [1774]), his study of gesture was the major work on mimic, mimetic, and mimismetic expression.
3 Austin, *Chironomia*.
4 Siddons, *Practical illustrations*.
5 Thomas De Quincey, "The Apparition of the Brocken," in *Suspiria de profundis* (1845), in *Works*, Vol. XV, pp. 182–5.
6 Diderot, *The Paradox of Acting*, p. xii. See also Diderot, *Paradoxe sur le comédien*, pp. 79–137.
7 Hobson, *The Object of Art* (1982), p. 18; Burwick, *Illusion and the Drama* (1991), p. 26.
8 Diderot refers to the acting of David Garrick and Claire-Josèphe Clairon as examples of this paradoxical doctrine of the illusion of overwhelming emotion achieved through emotional constraint. Garrick, *Private Correspondence*. in his letter to Jean-Baptiste-Antoine Suard, March 7, 1776 (pp. 36–9), Garrick promises a commentary on Diderot's *Paradoxe sur le comédien*; Clairon, *Mémoires d'Hippolyte Clairon*. On La Clairon's acting, see Lancaster, *French Tragedy in the Time of Louis XV and Voltaire*, pp. 186–91.
9 In the *Entretiens sur le Fils naturel* (1757), Diderot had declared that actors, like all artists, must possess an exquisite sensibility: "The poets, the actors, the musicians, the painters, the singers of the first order, the great dancers, the

tender lovers, the truly devout, all this enthusiastic and passionate troop feel vividly but think very little." (*Œuvres complètes*, Vol. vii, p. 108: "Les poëtes, les acteurs, les musiciens, les peintres, les chanteurs de premier ordre, les grands danseurs, les amants tendres, les vrais dévots, toute cette troupe enthousiaste et passionnée sent vivement, et réfléchit peu.")

10 Goethe, *Wilhelm Meisters Lehrjahre*.

11 Jagemann, *Erinnerungen*, p. 26.

12 See, for example, Nierenberg and Calero, *How to Read a Person Like a Book* (1980); Delmar, *Winning Moves: The Body Language of Selling* (1985); Fast, *Body Language in the Workplace* (1988); Ekman, *Telling Lies* (1992); Wainwright, *Body Language* (1993); Lloyd-Elliott, *Secrets of Sexual Body Language* (1996); Quilliam, *Body Language Secrets* (1997).

13 Birdwhistell, *Kinesics and Context* (1970); Blacking, ed., *The Anthropology of the Body* (1977); Bull, *Body Movement and Interpersonal Communication* (1983); Buck, *The Communication of Emotion* (1984); Bull, *Posture and Gesture* (1987); Burgoon, Buller, and Woodall, *Nonverbal Communication* (1996); Knapp and Hall, *Nonverbal Communication in Human Interaction* (1997).

14 Siddons, *Practical illustrations*, p. 70.

15 *Ibid.*, p. 53: "Lavater is a book which I have not ready at hand, and even if I had, I should not consult him very frequently. Strange notions, whose depth and value I have not thoroughly fathomed, might perplex my own ideas. If you happen to have the book, I beseech you to read what is there said concerning attitudes."

16 *Ibid.* Figures 1, 2, 3, 7, 8, 9, and 12 are from this edition, with original plate numbers.

17 Hazlitt, "Mr. Kean's Richard" (*Morning Chronicle* [February 15 and 21, 1814]), in *A View of the English Stage* (1818, reprinted in Hazlitt, *Works*, Vol. v, pp. 180–4); "Richard III," in *Characters of Shakespear's Plays* (1818, reprinted in Hazlitt, *Works*, Vol. iv, pp. 298–303).

18 Pape and Burwick, eds., *The Boydell Shakespeare Gallery*, p. 264. Figures 4, 5, 6, 10, and 11 are from this edition, with reference to the volume and plate number in the original two-volume edition of 1805.

19 Hazlitt, "Mr. Kean's Richard," pp. 180, 182, 184.

20 Lessing, *Hamburgische Dramaturgie*, in *Werke*, Vol. iv, pp. 461–6; Schlegel, *Vorlesungen über dramatische Kunst und Literatur* (1809–11), pp. 146–51.

21 Lessing, *Hamburgische Dramaturgie*, Section 42 (September 22, 1767): "Dem komischen Dichter ist es eher erlaubt, auf diese Weise seiner Vorstellung Vorstellungen entgegen zu setzen; denn unser Lachen zu erregen, braucht es des Grades der Täuschung nicht, den unser Mitleiden erfordert" (Lessing, *Werke*, Vol. iv, p. 428). See also Siddons, *Practical illustrations*, p. 87.

22 Lessing, *Hamburgische Dramaturgie*, Section 57 (November 17, 1767): "Ohne Verstellung fällt der Charakter Weg; bei der Verstellung die Würde desselben" (Lessing, *Werke*, Vol. iv, p. 494).

23 Burwick, *Illusion and the Drama*, p. 164. The first aspect of dual perception is readily achieved in theatre painting. In Johann Zoffany's *David Garrick*

as Abel Drugger in Ben Jonson's 'The Alchymist', for example, we recognize David Garrick even before we begin imaginatively to reconstruct his role in the play. Zoffany has not neglected to give us the lifted shoulders, the wry expression, that we can recognize from other portraits of Garrick. The second aspect of dual perception is more difficult to realize, but surely Zoffany has also succeeded in revealing the confidence game, as Subtle and Face watch with amusement the entrapment of Drugger. Subtle – pretending to be an alchemist, and wearing the doctor's cap and gown – and Face, a servant who has decked himself out as master of the house, have just succeeded in duping Dapper; and Drugger, their second gull, has entered bringing tobacco in payment for promised revelations in alchemy. To the extent that we can see Garrick as Abel Drugger, and Abel Drugger as the dupe of Subtle and Face, Zoffany's painting effectively solicits the dual perception of the ruse being played out at the close of Act II.

24 Coleridge, lecture of November 11, 1813 (*Lectures 1808–1819*, Vol. I, pp. 541–2).

25 Siddons, *Practical illustrations*, pp. 29–30. Redressing the bad effects of requiring an actor to give sole attention to attitudes of gesture and posture, Engel gives an example from the pedantic rules of Riccoboni. On the motion of the hand, Riccoboni asserts: "'In lifting up the arm, the superior part, *i.e.* that from the shoulder to the elbow, ought to be first elevated: the hand ought to be the last part in action,' &c. &c.," to which Engel responds "Is not all this a species of pedantry, as Engel, and more adapted to complete a set of puppets than to form a race of great orators and accomplished comedians?"

26 Siddons, *Practical illustrations*, pp. 248–9, Plate 34.

27 *Ibid.*, pp. 225–6, Plates 32 and 33.

28 Lessing, *Laokoon*, in *Werke*, Vol. VI, pp. 23–8.

29 The illustration depicts Hubert de Burgh's description of the response to Prince Arthur's death (*King John*, IV.iii.193–5):

> I saw a smith stand with his hammer, thus,
> The whilst his iron did on the anvil cool,
> With open mouth swallowing a tailor's news.

30 Boaden, *Memoirs of Mrs. Siddons*, Vol. I, p. 321.

31 *Ibid.*, Vol. II, p. 231.

32 *Ibid.*, pp. 241–2.

33 Isabella in Garrick, *Isabella* (1757); Jane Shore in Rowe, *Jane Shore* (1714); Belvidera in Otway, *Venice Preserved* (1682); Zara in Congreve, *The Mourning Bride* (1697); Calista in Rowe, *The Fair Penitent* (1703); Mrs. Beverley in Moore, *The Gamester* (1753). Siddons established a repertory of roles during the first three seasons after her return from Bath to London. For lists of the number of times each role was performed, see Boaden, *Memoirs of Mrs. Siddons*, Vol. I, p. 361 [1782–3, her first season], Vol. II, p. 51 [1783–4, her second season]; and Vol. II, pp. 123–4 [1784–5, her third season, and her first appearance as Lady Macbeth]. Her popular role as Mrs. Haller in *The*

Stranger (translated by A. Schink from August von Kozebue's *Menschenhaß und Reue*) was first performed in 1798.

34 Boaden, *Memoirs of Mrs. Siddons*, Vol. II, pp. 106–8.
35 *Ibid.*, pp. 185–6.
36 Burwick, *Poetic Madness and the Romantic Imagination* (1996), p. 11; see: Matthew Baillie's Gulstonian Lectures (read before the Royal College of Physicians, May 1794), in *Lectures and Observations on Medicine*, pp. 123–9; the supplements to *Morbid Anatomy* (1795), including the symptomatology added to the second edition (1797) and published separately as *An Appendix to the first edition of the Morbid Anatomy* (1798); and *A series of engravings, . . . intended to illustrate the morbid anatomy* (1799–1802).
37 Joanna Baillie, "Introductory Discourse," in *A Series of Plays in which it is attempted to delineate the stronger passions of the mind* (1798), in *Dramatic and Poetical Works*:

> It is not merely under the violent agitations of passion, that man so arouses and interests us; even the smallest indications of an unquiet mind, will set our attention as anxiously on watch, as the first distant flashes of a gathering storm. When some great explosion of passion bursts forth, and some consequent catastrophe happens, if we are at all acquainted with the unhappy perpetrator, how minutely shall we endeavour to remember every circumstance of his past behaviour! and with what avidity shall we seize upon every recollected word or gesture, that is in the smallest degree indicative of the supposed state of his mind, at the time when they took place." (p. 3b)

38 Siddons, *Practical illustrations*, p. 82.
39 Baillie, "Introductory Discourse," p. 4.
40 Lamb, "Stage Illusion," in *Life and Works*, Vol. III, pp. 29–34, and "On the Artificial Comedy of the last Century," in *Works*, Vol. IV, pp. 275–87; see also "On Some of the Old Actors" (*Life and Works*, Vol. IV, pp. 257–74), and "On the Acting of Munden" (*Life and Works*, Vol. IV, pp. 288–91).
41 Brand, *Adelinda*, III. iv. 24–100.
42 Genest, *Some account of the English Stage*, Vol. VII, p. 579.
43 Smith, *Melodrama*, pp. 4–5: in *A Tale of Mystery* Thomas Holcroft "calls for extensive background music to heighten entrances, indicate character, and underline the mood of a scene. The first act alone asks for '*soft music*', '*sweet and cheerful music*', '*confused music*', '*threatening music*', '*music to express discontent and alarm*', '*music of doubt and terror*', and much more besides."
44 Brooks, *The Melodramatic Imagination*. In Chapter 3, "The Text of Muteness," pp. 56–80, Brooks argues that muteness gained a "privileged position . . . in melodrama" because of "the genre's own derivation . . . from pantomime" (p. 62).
45 Genest, *Some account of the English Stage*, Vol. VII, p. 502.

5 TRANSVESTITES, LOVERS, MONSTERS: CHARACTER AND SEXUALITY

1 Transvestites, lovers, monsters: character and sexuality Cowley, *A Bold Stroke for a Husband* (1784). Quoted from the 1784 edition.

2 *Ibid.*; also in Cox and Gamer, eds., *The Broadview Anthology of Romantic Drama*, p. 32.

3 Hazlitt, *Complete Works*, Vol. XVIII, pp. 239–40.

4 Baron-Wilson, "Memoir of Mrs. Gibbs, now Mrs. Colman," in *Our Actresses*, Vol. I, pp. 83–90.

5 Hazlitt, *Complete Works*, Vol. I, p. 240.

6 Inchbald, *The Widow's Vow.*

7 Tomalin, *Mrs. Jordan's Profession*, pp. 6, 20, 52–3, 66, 77–8. On Leigh Hunt's criticism of Dorothy Jordan, see Marsden," Modesty Unshackled."

8 Marriage of Percival Farren and Mary Perry in the City of Hereford, All Saints Parish Church at the top end of Broad Street, on September 21, 1801. Percival Farren was an actor. Mary Perry was an actress and singer. The clergyman: Rev. Henry William Barry: witnesses Robert Hoy, J. Richer, Louisa Richer and Mary Hoy. The *Hereford Journal* (September 25, 1801): "On Monday last [. . .] was married, at All Saints Church in this city, Mr. Percival Farren, to Miss Perry, both of our Theatre" (*Hereford Journal* [September 25, 1801]).

9 Waldie, Journals, journal entry of July 30, 1806 (XIII: 258–9).

10 Inchbald, *The Widow's Vow*, adapted from Joseph Patrat (1732–1801), *L'heureuse erreur* (1783).

11 Waldie, Journals, journal entry of November 17, 1818 (TXLII: 70–1).

12 *Ibid.*, journal entry of April 3, 1819 (TXLII: 269–70).

13 *Ibid.*, journal entry of May 15, 1802 (V: 107).

14 *Ibid.*, journal entry of January 26, 1821 (XLVII: 374).

15 Cowley, *The Town Before You*, II.ii.82–4.

16 Behn, *The Amorous Prince*, III.iii.21–31.

17 Genest, *Some account of the English Stage*, Vol. VII, p. 206.

18 Oulton, *The Happy Disguise* (Capel Street, Dublin, January 7, 1784); *The Irish Tar* (Haymarket, August 24, 1797); *My Landlady's Gown* (Haymarket, August 10, 1816).

19 Oulton, *The Sleep-Walker* (Haymarket, June 15, 1812); published as *The Twin Sisters; or, Forgery in Love*, in Cumberland, ed., *The British Drama*, Vol. XI, pp. 1–28. Each play has a separate title-page and pagination.

20 Waldie, Journals, journal entry of June 24, 1813 (XXVIII: 191a).

21 *Ibid.*, journal entry of July 10, 1813 (XXVIII: 236).

22 Cobb, *Love in the East*, I.i.196–7.

23 Fitzball, *The Flying Dutchman*, III.i.72–84.

24 For Restoration comedy, see Heilman, "Some Fops and Some Versions of Foppery." For early eighteenth-century comedy, see Campbell, "When Men Women Turn."

25 Lewis, *Beau Brummell: His Life and Letters*; Jesse, *The Life of Beau Brummell*; Campbell, *Beau Brummell*; Kelly, *Beau Brummell: The Ultimate Man of Style.*

26 Staves, "A Few Kind Words for the Fop."

27 Cowley, *The Belle's Stratagem*, II.i.278–83.

28 Russell, "Tragedy, Gender, Performance," and "Gender, Passion, and Performance in Nineteenth-Century Women Romeos." Olga Nethersole (1870–1957) played Romeo in 1897; Charlotte Cushman (1816–76) performed many male roles, and in 1839 starred as Romeo with younger sister Susan Cushman as Juliet. The two sisters frequently played *Romeo and Juliet* together; see Lisa Merrill, *When Romeo Was a Woman*.

29 Genest, *Some account of the English Stage*, Vol. VIII, p. 310.

30 Douglas, "Mrs Webb."

31 Rich, "Pat Carroll as Falstaff in 'Merry Wives' at Folger."

32 Hazlitt, "The Merry Wives of Windsor," in *Characters of Shakespear's Plays* (1817), in *Complete Works*, Vol. IV, p. 350.

33 Based on the retail price index, £10,000 from 1792 would have been worth about £927,830 in 2006. Conversion tool for calculating purchasing power of British pounds in 1792 available at www.measuringworth.com/ppoweruk/.

34 Holcroft, *The Road to Ruin*, II.ii.349–63.

35 Hazlitt, *Complete Works*, Vol. III, p. 124.

36 *Ibid.*, pp. 122–3.

37 *Ibid.*, pp. 123–4.

38 Waldie, Journals, journal entry of June 8, 1803 (VIII: 83–5).

39 *Ibid.*, journal entry of March 22, 1809 (XIX: 745). Although Waldie has little to say about the performance at Kelso eleven years later, his appraisal is worth quoting for the description of theatrical conditions in the provinces:

> [W]ent to the play at Kelso – bespoke by the Duchess of Roxburgh . . . I sat with the Duchess's party – some men were noisy & quarrelsome – it was hot & crowded – & the play (the Road to Ruin) very stupid. I have so often seen it performed by the best players, yet 3 or 4 actors were decent – Calcraft in Harry, Jones in Goldfinch, Loveday in Silky, & Mrs. Eyre in the Widow – the rest were poor – but altogether it was not worse than the companies we have seen at Newcastle. Mrs. Eyre, Calcraft, & Jones are of the Edinburgh Company. (Journals, journal entry of September 25, 1820 [XLVII: 264])

40 Kenney, *Raising the Wind*, I.i.99–105.

41 Holcroft, *The Road to Ruin*, II.I.278–9.

42 Waldie, Journals, journal entry of February 10, 1804 (IX: 167).

43 *Ibid.*, journal entry of February 8, 1805 (X: 333).

44 *Ibid.*, journal entry of February 20, 1809 (XIX: 22).

45 *Ibid.*, journal entry of February 27, 1809 (XIX: 31).

46 *Ibid.*, journal entry of February 20, 1809 (XIX: 24).

47 *Ibid.*, journal entry of August 11, 1809 (XX: 207).

48 *Ibid.*, journal entry of August 24, 1809 (XX: 263).

49 Gay, "Theatricals and Theatricality in *Mansfield Park*"; Ford, "It Is about Lovers' Vows."

50 Waldie, Journals, journal entry of April 27, 18020 (TXLV: 238–9).

51 Letter to Thomas Love Peacock, July [20?], 1819, in *Letters of Percy Bysshe Shelley*, Vol. II, pp. 102–3; see also Peacock, *Memoirs of Shelley*, in Peacock, *Works*, Vol. VIII, pp. 81–2. Shelley's attention to contemporary theatre in his

composition of *The Cenci* is discussed in Curran, *Shelley's Cenci*; see especially the chapters "Shelley and the Romantic Theater" (pp. 157–82), and "Singularly Fitted for the Stage" (pp. 183–256).

52 *The Cenci*, sponsored by the Shelley Society, was performed in the Grand Theatre, Islington, London on May 7, 1886, with Miss Alma Murray as Beatrice, Miss Maud Brennan as the Countess Cenci, Hermann Vezin as Count Cenci, L. S. Outra as Orsino, and W. Farren, Jr. as Cardinal Camillo. It was also performed at the New Theatre (1920–1), directed by Lewis Casson, with Sybil Thorndike as Beatrice; at the Old Vic (April, 1959), directed by Michael Benthall; at the Bristol Old Vic (1985); at the People's Theatre, Newcastle (February, 1935), and again at the People's Theatre, Newcastle (May 22–6, 2001). It was performed in a fringe venue in London by the "Swinish Multitude" (London, 1997). As *Cenci*, it was performed in Frankfurt-am-Main (1924–5). Antonin Artaud directed his French adaptation, *Les Cenci* (1935) for the "Theatre of Cruelty." The opera by Alberto Ginastera, *Beatrix Cenci*, was performed at the Kennedy Center for the Performing Arts (September, 1971), and at the New York City Opera (March, 1973). *The Cenci* was also performed at the Shelley Bicentenary, celebrated in New York in 1992. Concluding a course on Shelley led by Professor Lilla Maria Crisafulli at the University of Bologna in June, 1999, *The Cenci* was performed as a collaborative project between exchange students from the University of York and students of Bologna.

53 Clery, "Horace Walpole's *The Mysterious Mother*."

54 Genest, *Some account of the English Stage*, Vol. x, p. 185. The play was performed in Glasgow in February, 2001. In her review, Elisabeth Mahoney asserted that the production was a good argument "for leaving things undisturbed in the cupboard full of unperformed stinkers" (*The Guardian* [February 3, 2001]).

55 Shelley, *The Cenci*, in *Poetical Works*, pp. 274–333.

56 Maturin, *Bertram*. Originally published by John Murray in 1816.

57 Coleridge's critique of *Bertram* first appeared in five issues of the *Courier* (1816), later published as Chapter 23 of *Biographia Literaria*, Vol. 11, pp. 207–23. See Hayter, "Coleridge, Maturin's *Bertram*, and Drury Lane."

58 Published as *Zapolya: A Christmas Tale* (1817), it was recast as a three-act melodrama by Thomas Dibdin and performed as *Zapolya; or, The War Wolf* (Surrey, February 9, 1818). See Coleridge, *Poetical Works* (Part 11: *Plays*), Vol. 111, pp. 1330–2.

59 Shelley, Preface to *Prometheus Unbound*, in *Poetical Works*, p. 205.

60 Coleridge, *Biographia Literaria*, Vol. 11, p. 214.

61 *Ibid.*, p. 216; Holland, "The Present State of the Stage."

62 Coleridge, *Biographia Literaria*, Vol. 11, p. 229.

63 *Ibid.*

64 Longfellow, *Hyperion and Kavanaugh*, p. 38.

65 Coleridge, *Biographia Literaria*, Vol. 11, p. 229.

66 Tomko, "Politics, Performance, and Coleridge's 'Suspension of Disbelief,'" *passim*.

67 Davis, "Response: Drama in Practice," pp. 268–76.
68 Bratton, "The Celebrity of Edmund Kean," pp. 90–106.
69 Waldie, Journals, journal entry of November 14, 1820 (XLVII: 306).
70 Coleridge, *Biographia Literaria*, Vol. II, p. 230.
71 O'Keeffe, *Recollections of the life of John O'Keeffe*, Vol. I, p. 329, cited in Genest, *Some account of the English Stage*, Vol. VIII, pp. 532–3.
72 Thomas Simpson Cooke, Irish singer and composer, performed at Drury Lane from the early 1810s. "The new musick incidental to the tragedy, composed by Mr. T. Cooke" is acknowledged in the published libretto. See Fenner, *Opera in London*, pp. 463–6, 470–2, 478–80, 497–8, 506–7.
73 Pollin, "'The Spectacles' of Poe."
74 Waldie, Journals, journal entry of November 15, 1827 (TLIV: 258).
75 Willier, "Madness, the Gothic, and Bellini's *Il pirata*."
76 Waldie, Journals, journal entry of November 15, 1827 (TLIV: 257–9).
77 Hazlitt, "Miss O'Neill's Juliet," *The Champion* (October 16, 1814), in *A View of the English Stage* (1818), in *Complete Works*, Vol. V, p. 200.
78 Hazlitt, *Complete Works*, Vol. V, pp. 404–5; review in *The Champion* (16 Oct 1814), in *ibid.*, p. 200.
79 On the prevailing response to homosexuality, see Goldsmith, *The Worst of Crimes*.
80 Hazlitt, *Complete Works*, Vol. V, p. 405.
81 Z., "Hazlitt Cross-Questioned," *Blackwood's Magazine* (August, 1818); quoted in *ibid.*, Vol. V, p. 405.
82 Hazlitt, "On Effeminacy of Character," in *Table-Talk* (1821–2), in *ibid.*, Vol. VIII, pp. 248–55.
83 Hazlitt, review in *The Examiner* (June 11, 1815), in *ibid.*, Vol. V, p. 230.
84 Hazlitt, review in *The Examiner* (December 10, 1815), in *ibid.*, Vol. V, p. 261.
85 Hazlitt, review in *The Examiner* (January 21, 1816), in *ibid.*, Vol. V, p. 275.
86 *Dramatic Magazine* (December 1, 1830) 2: 297.
87 Hazlitt, *The Examiner* (April 6, 1828), in *ibid.*, Vol. XVIII, pp. 386–7.

6 SETTING: WHERE AND ELSEWHERE

1 Young, *White Mythologies*, p. 6
2 Lawrence, "The Pioneers of Modern English Stage Mounting: Philippe Jacques de Loutherbourg, R. A."
3 Burwick, "Romantic Drama: from Optics to Illusion," and "Science and Supernaturalism: Sir David Brewster and Sir Walter Scott."
4 Hazelton, *Historical Consciousness in Nineteenth-Century Shakespearean Staging*. See also Rosenfeld, *A Short History of Scene Design in Great Britain*.
5 Allen, "Kemble and Capon at Drury Lane."
6 Pape and Burwick, eds., *The Boydell Shakespeare Gallery*, Vol. II, Plates 1 (pp. 244–5) and 6 (pp. 250–1).
7 Lawrence, "The Pioneers of Modem English Stage Mounting: William Capon."

8 Colman, *The Iron Chest*, p. vii.

9 Pape and Burwick, eds., *The Boydell Shakespeare Gallery*, Vol. 1, Plate 23 (p. 225). Burwick, "John Boydell's *Shakespeare Gallery* and the Stage."

10 For example, Hodges' "Jacques and the Wounded Stag" (*As You Like It* [II.i]), in Pape and Burwick, eds., *The Boydell Shakespeare Gallery*, Vol. 1, Plate 25 (p. 227).

11 To cite once again *The Boydell Shakespeare Gallery*, Henry Fuseli provided examples of the fantastic (far too fantastic for the stage) in his scenes from *A Midsummer Night's Dream* (IV.i): Vol. 1, Plates 20 and 21 (pp. 222–4). Sir Joshua Reynolds depicted the supernatural in his cave scene with the three witches and Hecate, in *Macbeth* (IV.i): Vol. 1, Plate 39 (p. 240).

12 Morell, *The Tales of the Genii*. Twelve plates drawn by William Marshall Craig.

13 Forster, *The Arabian Nights*.

14 Finkel, *Romantic Stages*, p. 26.

15 The artist Augustus Egg played the rival lover, and the novelist Wilkie Collins played his rival's servant.

16 Anderson, *Female Playwrights and Eighteenth-Century Comedy*.

17 Cowley, *A Bold Stroke for a Husband* (1784), II.ii.109–11.

18 Genest, *Some account of the English Stage*, Vol. VI, p. 271.

19 Schiller, *The Robbers* (1792). Metzger, *The Role of Feeling*; Stilz, "Robbers, Borderers, Millers and Men."

20 Coleridge, *Remorse*, in *Poetical Works*, Vol. III, Part 2, p. 1073.

21 Sheridan's *Pizarro* is estimated "to have brought £15,000 to the treasury of Drury Lane." Sheridan, *The Plays*, p. vi.

22 Richard Brinsley Sheridan, Introduction to *Pizarro*, in Kemble, *Kemble Promptbooks*, Vol. XI, pp. i–vi. In his note on possible translators, Kemble's editor, Charles H. Shattuck, cites both James Boaden and Crompton Rhodes, attributing the work to Constantin Geisweiler. That the translation might have been made by Anne Plumptre is rendered unlikely by Rhodes' "account of Sheridan's dealings with Mrs. Plumptre" (Rhodes, *Harlequin Sheridan*, pp. 136–8).

23 Williams, *Letters*; *Peru*; Adams, "Helen Maria Williams and the French Revolution," p. 96.

24 Shattuck, Introduction to Sheridan's *Pizarro*, in Kemble, *Kemble Promptbooks*, Vol. XI, pp. v–vi.

25 Donohue, Jr., *Dramatic Character in the English Romantic Age*, Illustrations 20 and 21; Oliver and Saunders, "De Loutherbourg and *Pizarro*, 1799," Plate 1; Mander and Mitchenson, "De Loutherbourg and *Pizarro*, 1799," p. 160, and Plates 1 and 2; Jackson, "*Pizarro*, Bridges and the Gothic Scene."

26 Williams, *Life and Correspondence of Sir Thomas Lawrence*, Vol. 1, p. 207.

27 Waldie, Journals, journal entry of April 24, 1809 (XIX: 104–7).

28 Drake, "Knight of the Tower and Sword"; Carlyle, "Samuel Edward Widdrington."

29 Waldie, Journals, journal entry of April 21, 1809 (XIX: 100).

30 For Waldie's comments on Holcroft's *Tale of Mystery*, see Waldie, Journals, journal entries of April 30, 1803 (VII: 156); May 27, 1803 (VIII: 48); March 17, 1806 (XII: 227); May 9, 1806 (XII: 321); March 17, 1809 (XIX: 66); March 24, 1809 (XIX: 80–1); April 21, 1809 (XIX: 100); April 24, 1809 (XIX: 107); June 16, 1809 (XIX: 284).

31 *Ibid.*, journal entry of April 24, 1809 (XIX: 107).

32 *Ibid.*, pp. 104–5.

33 *Ibid.*, journal entry of April 25, 1809 (XIX: 109–10).

34 Stephen, "Charles Mayne Young."

35 Waldie, Journals, journal entry of May 2, 1809 (XIX: 130–1).

36 *Ibid.*, p. 129.

37 Hazlitt, *The Examiner* (August 6, 1815), in *Works*, Vol. V, pp. 240–2.

38 Waldie, Journals, journal entry of February 13, 1815 (XXXI: 213–14).

39 Reynolds, *The Virgin of the Sun* (1812). Waldie, Journals, journal entry of March 9, 1817 (TXXXVIII: 67–8).

40 Bishop, *The Virgin of the Sun!* (1812).

41 Plumptre, *The Virgin of the Sun* (1799).

42 Marmontel, *The Incas; or, The destruction of the empire of Peru* (1777).

43 Kewes, "[A] play, which I presume to call original."

44 Williamson, "What Killed August von Kotzebue?"

45 Waldie, Journals, journal entry of March 9, 1817 (TXXXVIII: 67–9).

46 *Ibid.*, journal entry of February 26, 1820 (TXLV: 154).

47 Genest, *Some account of the English Stage*, Vol. IV, pp. 582–3, and Vol. VII, pp. 156–7. Genest delineates further similarities between Jerningham's *Siege of Berwick* and Home's *Siege of Aquileia*. See Lopez, "Recovered Voices: The Sources of *The Siege of Valencia*."

48 Said, *Orientalism* (1978).

49 De Quincey, "A Sketch from Childhood," in *Works*, Vol. XVII, p. 130.

50 O'Keefe, *Aladdin*.

51 Doran, "Charles Farley."

52 The musical score is untraced, but sheet music is available for one of the popular songs: Ware, *Every face looks cheerily* (1813).

53 Genest, *Some account of the English Stage*, Vol. VIII, p. 378.

54 De Quincey, "Elements of Rhetoric," in *Works*, Vol. VI, p. 188.

55 Forster, *The Arabian Nights*. A prolific book illustrator, Smirke was the first English artist to tackle in any quantity interpretations of the tales. His fine detailed work depicted rather English-looking characters in diaphanous robes and turbans.

56 Pape and Burwick, eds., *The Boydell Shakespeare Gallery*, pp. 192–3.

57 Waldie, Journals, journal entry of June 10, 1813 (XXVII: 165a–166a).

58 Intended for private performances: Webb, *Aladdin; or, The wonderful lamp* (1813).

59 Soane, *Aladdin, a Fairy Opera in Three Acts*. Music by Sir Henry R. Bishop. On George Soane, see my Introduction to his translation from Goethe, in *Faustus, translated by Samuel Taylor Coleridge*, pp. 141–4.

60 Bishop, *Aladdin; or, The Wonderful Lamp* (1826).

61 James Kenney, *Aladdin and the Wonderful Lamp*. Music by Albert Smith (1844).

62 The first Widow Twankey, in *Aladdin and the Wonderful Lamp* (Strand Theatre, 1861), was played by James Rogers. More recently, Widow Twankey has been played by Sir Ian McKellen (Old Vic, 2004 and 2005).

63 Waldie, Journals, journal entry of April 25, 1806 (xii: 287).

64 *Ibid.*, journal entry of June 2, 1806 (xiii: 2).

65 Kelly, *Reminiscences*, Vol. ii, pp. 131–3. Quoted in Cox and Gamer, eds., *The Broadview Anthology of Romantic Drama*, p. 80.

66 Genest, *Some account of the English Stage*, Vol. viii, pp. 234–6.

67 Waldie, Journals, journal entry of June 24, 1813 (xxviii: 191a–192a).

68 *Ibid.*, journal entry of December 10, 1814 (xxxi: 131).

69 Cox and Gamer, eds., *The Broadview Anthology of Romantic Drama*, include both Colman's *Blue-Beard* and Lewis' *Timour the Tartar* in their anthology. They print not Colman's *The Forty Thieves* but rather his *The Quarupeds of Quedlingburgh* (Haymarket, July 26, 1811): a spectacular parody of Lewis' *Timour.*

70 Fenner, *Opera in London*, pp. 433–5.

71 Genest *Some account of the English Stage*, Vol. vii, pp. 704–5.

72 Waldie, Journals, journal entry of May 3, 1806 (xii: 303).

73 Moncrieff, *The Cataract of the Ganges* (Drury Lane, October 27, 1823). The role of the Rajah, who recites this grand tribute to British soldiers, was played by Young.

74 Wolfson, "A Problem Few Dare Imitate"; Biggs, "Notes on Performing *Sardanapalus*"; Judson, "Tragicomedy, Bisexuality, and Byronism."

7 GOTHIC AND ANTI-GOTHIC: COMEDY AND HORROR

1 Praz, *The Romantic Agony*, pp. 95–186.

2 Marchand, *Byron: A Biography*, Vol. ii, p. 559.

3 Byron, *Don Juan*, 1.xxix, in *Poetical Works*, 5: 61.

4 Burwick, "The Grotesque in the Romantic Movement," p. 44.

5 Sade, *Les crimes de l'amour; The Crimes of Love*, pp. 13–14.

6 See Ewen, *The Prestige of Schiller in England*, pp. 28–33.

7 Lewis, *The Castle Spectre*, in Cox, ed., *Seven Gothic Dramas*, p. 172.

8 *Ibid.*, pp. 178–9.

9 *Richard Cœur de Léon* appeared at Covent Garden in a version translated by Leonard MacNally (October 16, 1786), and at Drury Lane in a version translated by Lieutenant General John Burgoyne (October 24, 1786). Both versions retained the musical score from the French original by André Ernest Modeste Grétry, but Genest judged MacNally's version "considerably inferior." Of the two adaptations, only Burgoyne's enjoyed a continuing success, with a run of thirty-three performances following its opening, two

subsequent revivals at Drury Lane (October 19, 1796; October 6, 1804), and a third at Covent Garden (May 24, 1814): Genest, *Some account of the English Stage*, Vol. VI, pp. 424–5, 438. As librettist, Michel-Jean Sédaine also collaborated with Grétry on *Amphitryon* (1788) and *Raoul Barbe-Bleue* (1789). For more on the latter, see Chapter 8.

10 Lewis, *The Castle Spectre*, pp. 191–2.

11 *Monthly Mirror* (December, 1797), cited in Cox, *Seven Gothic Dramas*, p. 197.

12 Lewis, *The Castle Spectre*, p. 197.

13 Franklin, "The Influence of Madame de Staël's Account of Goethe's *Die Braut von Korinth*.

14 *Sardanapalus*, in Cox and Gamer, eds., *The Broadview Anthology of Romantic Drama*, p. 295.

15 Lewis, *The Castle Spectre*, p. 197.

16 Desmet and Williams, eds., *Shakespearean Gothic*.

17 Lewis, *The Castle Spectre*, p. 222.

18 Frenzel, *Motive der Weltliteratur* lists the following works with similar plots: Christian Friedrich Daniel Schubart, *Zur Geschichte des menschlichen Herzens* (1775), a short tale that was a source for *Die Räuber*; J. A. Leisewitz, *Julius von Tarent* (1776); F. M. Klinger: *Die Zwillinge* (1777); Friedrich Schiller, *Die Räuber* (1781); A. W. Iffland, *Die Mündel* (1784); August Kindler, *Die feindliche Brüder* (1788); August von Kotzebue, *Die Versöhnung oder der Bruderzwist* (1798); Schiller, *Die Braut von Messina* (1803); Christian Grabbe, *Herzog Theodor von Gothland* (1827).

19 Lewis, *The Castle Spectre*, p. 223.

20 Genest, *Some account of the English Stage*, Vol. VII, p. 333.

21 Slout and Rudisill, "The Enigma of the Master Betty Mania."

22 Hazlitt, *Complete Works*, Vol. VIII, pp. 294–5.

23 Lewis, *The Castle Spectre*, p. 168–9.

24 Hazlitt, *Complete Works*, Vol. VIII, p. 295.

25 Coleridge, *Lectures 1808–1819: On Literature*, Vol. I, p. 277.

26 Waldie, Journals, journal entry of August 28, 1805 (XI: 19–20).

27 Lewis, *The Castle Spectre*, p. 171.

28 Waldie, Journals, journal entry of September 2, 1805 (XI: 331–3).

29 Praz, *The Romantic Agony*, p. 95–107.

30 Sade, *Plays*, Vol. III, pp. viii–xii. See also Rabenalt, *Theatrum sadicum*; and Foster, "The Place of the Theater and Drama in the Life of the Marquis de Sade."

31 Burwick, "The Grotesque in the Romantic Movement," p. 44.

32 Sade, *Plays*, Vol. III, pp. 1, 95–6.

33 Genest, *Some account of the English Stage*, Vol. VI, pp. 586–8.

34 Sade, "La tour mystérieuse." This is the only surviving manuscript of this play, written in secretarial hand, with corrections in Sade's own.

35 Sade, "Rodrigue, ou la tour enchantée, conte allégorique," in *Les crimes de l'amour*.

36 Girdham, *English Opera in Late Eighteenth-Century London*, pp. 137–53.

37 Baker, *John Philip Kemble*, pp. 187–9. The sources were Luigi Cherubini's *Lodoiska* (1791), libretto by Claude-François Fillette-Loraux, from the novel *Les Amours du chevalier de Faublas* by Jean-Baptiste Louvet de Couvrai; and Simone Mayr's *Lodoiska* (1796), libretto by Francesco Gonella. Storace also adapted songs from Kreutzer and Andreozzi.

38 See the chapter on *Pizarro* in Loftis, *Sheridan and the Drama of Georgian England*; Darby, "Spectacle and Revolution in 1790s Tragedy"; Cox, "Romantic Drama and the French Revolution."

39 In directing the production of *The Haunted Tower* at UCLA (March 3, 4, and 5, 2006), and at Cal State Long Beach (March 9, 2006), I changed the setting from the time of William the Conqueror to the time of George III in order to make the references to the French Revolution more evident. Among other changes, I restored the opening dialogue between Juliette and Louise (Lady Elinor and Cicely), which provides at the very beginning of the play the explanation of the haunting. I also restored the scene in which an attempt is made to persuade Grouffignac, the tax collector, to enter the haunted tower. Here I made the further change of giving the task of seducing the tax collector to two village girls rather than to Juliette and Louise.

40 Plays transcribed at the Charenton include *Le prévaricateur*, *La tour enchantée*, *Le capricieur*, and *Comte Oxtiern*.

41 Sade, *Plays*, Vol. i, pp. 145–6.

42 Sade has taken this epigraph from Claude-Joseph, Chevalier Dorat (1734–80), *Avis aux sages du siècle*.

43 Sade, *Le prévaricateur* (1810).

44 Sade, "Ernestine," in *The Crimes of Love*, p. 160.

45 Storace, *The Haunted Tower*, i.i, i.iii, ii.vii, iii.iv.

46 Kelly, *Reminiscences*, Vol. i, p. 319.

47 *Ibid.*, Vol. i, p. 320.

48 White, *A History of English Opera*, p. 410.

49 Ottenberg, *Die Entwicklung des theoretisch-ästhetischen Denkens*, p. 36.

50 Storace, *The Haunted Tower*, pp. 44–7. A vocal–instrumental performance of the songs of Storace's entire score is available on the website, *Romantic-Era Songs*: www.sjsu.edu/faculty/douglass/music/index.html.

51 Kelly, *Reminiscences*, Vol. i, pp. 318–20.

52 Sade, *Plays*, Vol. iii, pp. 4. "For example, Juliette's opening air, 'Love, listen to my sorrow' evokes Adela's 'Whither, my love!' in Cobb's libretto. Both pieces depict long-suffering heroines yearning to be reunited with their long-lost lovers in lyrics that evoke images of bondage, lovers' tokens, and an obsession with the lover's image. Lorville's lament recalling his leaving his lover behind, 'Oh! Juliette,' is echoed in Cobb's libretto with Charles' 'My native land I bade adieu,' in which the noble servant character philosophizes about the girl he left behind. In both airs, the characters singing imagine that the intensity of emotion has changed on the part of the women involved. In the English work, Charles accepts the situation with wry humor; in the French, Lorville responds melodramatically in images of bondage and death."

53 Fiske, *English Theatre Music in the Eighteenth Century*, p. 501; cited in Sade, *Plays*, p. 3; see also Fiske, "The Operas of Stephen Storace."

54 Storace, *The Haunted Tower*. I added "Attune the Pipe" from the sheet music and reinstated from Sade's play a scene with the tax collector omitted from Cobb's version.

55 Lennig, *Marquis de Sade in Selbstzeugnissen und Bilddokumenten*, pp. 12–13.

56 Stevenson, "Come tell me where the maid is found" (1816).

57 Kelly, *Reminiscences*, Vol. II, p. 59.

58 Even before war was declared against France, Kelly acknowledged threats against English travelers: "In the summer of 1792, I went to Paris to seek what I could pick up in the way of dramatic novelty for Drury Lane, and a most interesting period it certainly was, and not to be forgotten by those who were there." When his party was accosted at Ecouen on his departure from Paris, he attributed his escape to the fact that he wore a national cockade in his hat as a precaution, and was facile in claiming Republican sympathies (*Ibid.*, Vol. I, pp. 284–7, 342–9).

59 *Ibid.*, Vol. II, p. 61.

60 *Ibid.*, pp. 130–4.

61 On the singing and acting of Anna Maria Crouch, see Thornbury and Walford, *Old and New London*, Vol. IV, p. 448; from the The Vauxhall Gardens Archive at the Minet Library in Lambeth V, fo. 82: "even in common speech [Mrs Crouch's voice] is touching and harmonious."

62 Cowley, Preface to *The Town Before You*, p. iv.

63 Anonymous, "Mrs. Martyr, Singer and Actress." She married John Martyr on May 6, 1780; performed "breeches" roles at Drury Lane (for example Cherubino); lived with the oboist W. T. Parke from 1784; and had three children with him in 1792, 1799, and 1803.

64 Adapted from the pollacca, "La donna," in *La capricciosa corretta, o la scuola dei maritati* by Vicente Martín y Soler (1754–1806). For the published sheet music, see Dibdin and Braham, *No More By Sorrow*.

65 On Braham's elaborate cadenzas, see Nathan and Byron, *A Selection of Hebrew Melodies, Ancient and Modern*, pp. 6, 8, 12, 16.

66 "Don't you remember a carpet-weaver?" is a song from Stephen Storace's *Mahmoud* (Drury Lane, April 30, 1796). Incongruously out of place in *The Haunted Tower*, it was obviously interpolated by Anna Storace to show off her *buffa* repertory. Graves, in "The Comic Operas of Stephen Storace," calls it "attractive in a mildly folky way, despite its unlikely title."

67 Waldie, Journals, journal entry of May 17, 1803 (VII: 226–8).

68 Not a part of *The Haunted Tower* but introduced by John Braham: "The Pollacca," see n. 64 above; "Death of Abercrombie" (1805), ballad by Charles Dibdin, to the tune of "Admiral Benbow"; "Oft on a plat," a musical setting to John Milton's "Il penseroso" (1645); "Sally in our Alley" (1715), a popular ballad by Henry Carey.

69 Waldie, Journals, journal entry of May 12, 1806 (XII: 327).

70 *Ibid.*, journal entry of January 25, 1822 (XLVIII: 300–1).

71 *Ibid.*, journal entry of February 19, 1800 (IV: 184). For his comments on additional performances of *No Song, No Supper*, see *ibid.*, journal entries of November 19, 1803 (IX: 81); March 13, 1809 (XIX: 59); June 12, 1815 (XXXI: 177); January 16, 1817(TXXXVII: 150).

72 *Ibid.*, journal entry of June 4, 1806 (XII: 8–9).

73 Lorenzo da Ponte is best known for his libretti to three Mozart operas, *Le nozze di Figaro*, *Don Giovanni*, and *Così fan tutte*. See Holden, *The Man who Wrote Mozart*.

74 *Ibid.*, journal entry of June 13, 1805 (XI: 195).

75 Genest, *Some account of the English Stage*, Vol. VII, p. 151.

76 Kelly, *Reminiscences*, Vol. II, p. 59.

77 Fenner, *Opera in London*, p. 417.

78 Greene, *Theatre in Belfast*, pp. 276–7.

79 Waldie, Journals, journal entry of May 20, 1803 (VIII: 2–3).

80 Charlotte Waldie's *Narrative of a Residence in Belgium, during the Campaign of 1815* (1817) was popularly received and twice revived later in the century (as *The Days of Battle* [1853], and *Waterloo Days* [1888]). After the grand tour of 1818–20, Charlotte published, in three volumes, *Rome in the Nineteenth Century* (1820). In spite of its numerous inaccuracies, this work was long popular as a travel-guide and went through six subsequent editions by 1860. Charlotte also wrote three novels based on travels with her brother: *Continental Adventures* (1826), *Vittoria Colonna* (1827), and *At Home and Abroad* (1831). Jane Waldie, who exhibited many of her paintings at the Royal Academy and the British Gallery, had her panoramic sketch of the battlefield of Waterloo published with a prose description, *Waterloo, by a Near Observer* (1817), which enjoyed ten editions within a few months. Jane was also the author of *Sketches Descriptive of Italy in the years 1816 and 1817* in 4 volumes (1820).

81 Burwick, "Manuscript Journal of John Waldie."

82 Mlle. Terneaux is not Mme. Terneaux, stage name for Rosine Stolze, the mezzo-soprano who debuted in Brussels in 1832. Remy, ed., *Baker's Biographical Dictionary of Musicians* 3rd edn., p. 914.

83 Waldie, Journals, journal entry of July 12, 1815 (TXXXII: 148).

84 Genest, *Some account of the English Stage*, Vol. VII, p. 233.

85 Colman, *The Iron Chest*, p. vii. Colman's charges against Kemble were suppressed in subsequent editions of *The Iron Chest*, but were later reprinted as "Suppressed Preface on Mr. John Kemble's alleged improper conduct." Genest quoted from this later version. The lines on "drowsy syrups" are adapted from *Othello*, III.iii.330–1.

86 Colman, *The Iron Chest*, p. x.

87 Genest, *Some account of the English Stage*, Vol. VII, p. 233.

88 Colman, *The Iron Chest*, p. xxi.

89 Cox, *Reading Adaptations*, pp. 16–24.

90 Purinton, "George Colman's *The Iron Chest* and *Blue-Beard*."

91 Verhoeven, "Opening the Text."

92 Hazlitt, *Complete Works*, Vol. v, p. 241; Hazlitt also refers to *Caleb Williams* as "one of the best novels in the language, and the very best of the modern school" (*ibid.*, p. 342).

93 Wood, *The Stage History of Shakespear's King Richard the Third*, p. 118 n. 43. Genest, *Some account of the English Stage*, Vol. viii, p. 486, offers the same explanation of the opposition to Meggett.

94 Hazlitt, *The Examiner* (August 6, 1815), in *Complete Works*, Vol. v, pp. 240–2.

95 Hazlitt, *The Examiner* (December 1, 1816), in *ibid.*, Vol. v, p. 344.

96 *Ibid.*, p. 343.

97 Waldie, Journals, journal entry of June 15, 1083 (viii: 100).

98 *Ibid.*, p. 101.

99 *Ibid.*, journal entry of June 2, 1806 (xiii: 4).

100 *Ibid.*, journal entry of April 10, 1809 (xix: 78a).

101 *Ibid.*, journal entry of September 2, 1809 (xx: 326–7).

102 Cole, *The Life and Theatrical Times of Charles Kean*, Vol. i, p. 94. See also Cook, "Mr. Conway and Mrs. Piozzi."

103 Waldie, Journals, journal entry of March 16, 1815 (xxxi: 271–2).

104 *Ibid.*, journal entry of April 8, 1815 (xxxi: 314–15).

105 Barrie, *Peter Pan*, pp. 503–76.

8 BLUE-BEARD'S CASTLE: MISCHIEF AND MISOGYNY

1 Among recent books exploring aspects of domestic abuse in Gothic fiction, see especially Ellis, *The Contested Castle* (1989); Clery, *Women's Gothic* (2000); Massé, *In the Name of Love* (1992); and Roberts, *The Gothic Romance* (1980).

2 Tatar, *Secrets beyond the Door*, pp. 2–4.

3 Perrault, "La Barbe Bleue," in *Histoires ou contes du temps passé* (1697; rpt. 1980).

4 Grimm and Grimm, "Blaubart," in *Kinder- und Hausmärchen* (1812, 1815), Vol. i, pp. 285–9, as no. 62 of eighty-six numbered folk tales. The second volume of *Kinder- und Hausmärchen* was published in 1814 (dated 1815), adding seventy stories to the previous collection. Six additional editions were prepared by the Brothers Grimm. "Blaubart" was omitted in 1819 and the subsequent editions. The final version contained two hundred numbered stories plus ten "Children's Legends."

5 Tatar, *Secrets beyond the Door*, p. 69 (on Mary Shelley); p. 134 (on Tieck).

6 Burton, "A Day amongst the Fans," in *Selected Papers on Anthropology*, pp. 92–106. See Bode, "Distasteful Customs," pp. 147–58.

7 The ethical deferral to "elsewhere" in *Bluebeard* is described in Burwick, "Gateway to Heterotopia," pp. 27–39.

8 Thompson, *Motif-Index of Folk Literature* (1993).

9 Kingscote and Sástrî, *Tales of the Sun*, no. 10, pp. 119–30. Another story of the same type (AT-312) is "Conomor and Triphine" (King Komor from the

Breton legend of Saint Trophime). Yet another is the Italian tale of "Don Firriulieddu," translated in Crane, *Italian Popular Tales.*

10 Perrault, *Histoires ou contes du temps passé*; *The original Mother Goose Melody* (1892).

11 Grimm and Grimm, "Blaubart."

12 Meier, *Deutsche Volksmärchen aus Schwaben*, no. 38, pp. 134–7.

13 Tatar, *Secrets beyond the Door*, p. 17; Perrault, *Bluebeard, or the Fatal Effects of Curiosity and Disobedience.*

14 Tatar, *Secrets beyond the Door*, p. 40.

15 Not until 1917, with the apparitions at the Church of Our Lady of Fatima, a village in Portugal near Lisbon, did the name Fatima become associated with the Virgin Mary. See Ryan, *Our Lady of Fátima.*

16 Lang, ed., *The Blue Fairy Book* (1889).

17 Sédaine, *Raoul, Barbe-Bleue* (1791). The musical score was published at the time of the opening performance in Paris (1789).

18 Sade, *Justine* (1791), Vol. 11, p. 127, on Gilles de Rais and other monsters:

> C'étaient des monstres, m'objectent les sots. Oui, selon nos mœurs et notre façon de penser; mais relativement aux grandes vues de la nature sur nous, ils n'étaient que les instruments de ses desseins; c'était pour accomplir ses lois qu'elle les avait doués de ces caractères féroces et sanguinaires.
>
> (But these were monsters, fools might object. Yes, but only according to our customs and our ways of thinking. Relative to the grand plans nature has for us, they were but instruments of her design; it was in order to achieve her laws that she endowed them with such ferocity and bloodthirstiness.)

See also *Histoire de Juliette*, Vol. 11, p. 111.

19 Praz, *The Romantic Agony*, pp. 310–11. In discussing the relevance of the crimes of Gilles de Rais to versions of the Blue-Beard tale, Praz cites the detailed account by Abbé Eugène Bossard and René de Maulde, *Gilles de Rais*, pp. 10, 12. Claiming to have been inspired by Suetonius' account of Nero and Caligula, Gilles stated: "Ces voluptés abjectes, ces crimes atroces, j'en ai conçu Suetonius la pensée. J'ai tué par plaisir, pour ma propre délectance et sans le conseil de qui que ce soit." Presenting evidence that Gilles's crimes were not the source of the Blue Beard folk tale, Gabory (*La Vie et la mort de Gilles de Raiz*, p. 135) argues that the two characters were fused in the popular imagination after Gilles's execution in 1440.

20 Perrault, *Histoires ou contes du temps passé*, p. 36:

> Moralité
> La curiosité malgré tous ses attraits,
> Coûte souvent bien des regrets;
> On en voit tous les jours mille exemples paraître.
> C'est, n'en déplaise au sexe, un plaisir bien léger;
> Dès qu'on le prend il cesse d'être,
> Et toujours il coûte trop cher.
> *Autre moralité*
> Pour peu qu'on ait l'esprit sensé,

> Et que du Monde on sache le grimoire,
> On voit bientôt que cette histoire
> Est un conte du temps passé;
> Il n'est plus d'Epoux si terrible,
> Ni qui demande l'impossible, Fût-il malcontent et jaloux.
> Près de sa femme on le voit filer doux;
> Et de quelque couleur que sa barbe puisse être,
> On a peine à juger qui des deux est le maître.

The translation is by S. T. Littlewood, in Perrault, *Perrault's Fairy Tales*.

21 Gottsched. *Versuch einer critischen Dichtkunst.* (1730; rpt. 1977).

22 Burwick, "Phantastisch-groteske Literatur."

23 In the version published in *Phantasus* (1812), Blue Beard is renamed Hugo von Wolfbrunn.

24 The film *Dracula* (1931), with Béla Lugosi in the title role, was directed by Tod Browning.

25 Prologue to Tieck, *Ritter Blaubart*, pp. 6–15.

26 Tieck, *Phantasus* (1812), Vol. VI, pp. 445–6. Quotations are from the text of *Phantasus* in Tieck, *Ludwig Tieck Schriften*, Vol. VI, pp. 394–483.

27 "[D]ie unheimliche, mit allem Grauen der Hölle umkleidete Mechtildis": Hebbel, "Ein Stern in Menschengestalt"(1853), p. 464. Günzel also prints the testimony of Karl Leberecht Immermann, theatre director in Düsseldorf, who brought *Ritter Blaubart* to the stage in 1835 and for a second successful run two years later (p. 414); it was also directed by Philipp Eduard Devrient in Dresden (p. 440).

28 Tieck, "Shakespeare's Behandlung des Wunderbaren" (1793), in *Ludwig Tieck Schriften*, Vol. I, pp. 685–722.

29 Bosse, *Orientalismus im Frühwerk Ludwig Tiecks*; Hamm-Ehsani, "Ex Oriente Lux."

30 Tieck, *Peter Lebrecht* (1795–6); *Ritter Blaubart* (1797); *Der Blaubart* (1812).

31 Thomas and Perrault, *The original Mother Goose*.

32 Ancillon, *Eunuchism display'd* (1718); La Motte, *One hundred new court fables* (1721); Longeville, *Long livers* (1722); Sallengre, *Ebrietatis encomium* (1723).

33 Tatar, *Secrets beyond the Door*, pp. 15–16.

34 Kelly, *Reminiscences*, Vol. I, p. 348.

35 Galland, *Les Mille et une nuits, contes arabes*. The first volume appeared in 1704; by 1706 seven volumes had been published; Vol. VIII was published in 1709; Vols. IX and X in 1712; and Vols. XI and XII in 1717, two years after Galland's death. The most recent English edition at the time of Colman's *Blue-Beard* was the *Arabian nights entertainments* (1798). Burton, *The Thousand Nights and a Night*, has become the most widely read English translation.

36 Colman, *Blue-Beard; or, Female Curiosity!* (1798), pp. 75–96.

37 Kelly, *The Grand Dramatic Romance of Blue Beard* (1798).

38 Colman, "Introduction," in *Blue-Beard: or, Female Curiosity!*, pp. 7–8.

39 The name "Abomelique" might also be transliterated as "Abu Malek" or "Abd-el-Melik ." Although there are several Caliphs after whom he might

have named his Blue Beard, Colman has taken his names from the *Arabian Nights*, such as the tale of "El Malik and the Sixteen Officers of the Police."

40 Moore, *Poetical Works* (1852).

41 Biographical details of the career of Michael Kelly (1762–1826) are derived primarily from his *Reminiscences* (1826), cited parenthetically in the text as "*R*".

42 Moncrieff, "Three Part Medley," Second Part, lines 20–3 (1826), in *An Original Collection of Songs*, pp. 28–31.

43 Thomas, "The Music and Musicians of Dickens"; Lightwood, *Charles Dickens and Music*. See also Lockwood, "Jane Austen and Some Drawing-Room Music of Her Time."

44 Dickens, *Sketches by Boz*, Tales, Ch. 1, in *Works*, Vol. I, p. 298.

> "Ah! you have done it nicely now, sir," sobbed the frightened Agnes, as a tapping was heard at Mrs. Tibbs's bedroom door, which would have beaten any dozen woodpeckers hollow.
>
> "Mrs. Tibbs! Mrs. Tibbs!" called out Mrs. Bloss. "Mrs. Tibbs, pray get up." (Here the imitation of a woodpecker was resumed with tenfold violence.)

45 Dickens, *Martin Chuzzlewit*, Ch. 25, in *Works*, Vol. VIII, p. 417.

> The premises of Mr. Mould were hard of hearing to the boisterous noises in the great main streets, and nestled in a quiet corner, where the City strife became a drowsy hum, that sometimes rose and sometimes fell and sometimes altogether ceased; suggesting to a thoughtful mind a stoppage in Cheapside. The light came sparkling in among the scarlet runners, as if the churchyard winked at Mr. Mould, and said, "We understand each other"; and from the distant shop a pleasant sound arose of coffin-making with a low melodious hammer, rat, tat, tat, tat, alike promoting slumber and digestion.
>
> "Quite the buzz of insects," said Mr. Mould, closing his eyes in a perfect luxury. "It puts one in mind of the sound of animated nature in the agricultural districts. It's exactly like the woodpecker tapping."
>
> "The woodpecker tapping the hollow ELM tree," observed Mrs. Mould, adapting the words of the popular melody to the description of wood commonly used in the trade.
>
> "Ha, ha!" laughed Mr. Mould. "Not at all bad, my dear. We shall be glad to hear from you again, Mrs. M. Hollow elm tree, eh! Ha, ha! Very good indeed. I've seen worse than that in the Sunday papers, my love."
>
> Mrs. Mould, thus encouraged, took a little more of the punch, and handed it to her daughters, who dutifully followed the example of their mother.
>
> "Hollow ELM tree, eh?" said Mr. Mould, making a slight motion with his legs in his enjoyment of the joke. "It's beech in the song. Elm, eh? Yes, to be sure. Ha, ha, ha! Upon my soul, that's one of the best things I know!" He was so excessively tickled by the jest that he couldn't forget it, but repeated twenty times, "Elm, eh? Yes, to be sure. Elm, of course. Ha, ha, ha! Upon my life, you know, that ought to be sent to somebody who could make use of it. It's one of the smartest things that ever was said. Hollow ELM tree, eh? of course. Very hollow. Ha, ha, ha!"

46 Dickens, *David Copperfield*, Ch. 36, in *Works*, Vol. XVIII, p. 534.

47 Husk and Sands, "Storace, Anna."

48 Knight, "Storace, Anna"; see also Knight, *A History of the Stage during the Victorian Era* (1901); and *Theatrical Notes* (1893).

49 Storace, *Songs, Duets, Trios, Finales*. Among the songs: "Oh hapless youth," sung by Anne Miller; "Toll, toll the knell," sung by Anna Storace; "Though pleasure swell the jovial cry" and "From shades of night," sung by John Braham; "Where jealous misers starve," sung by Mrs. [Maria Theresa Romanzini] Bland.

50 Kelly, *Reminiscences*, Vol. 11, p.127. The plays by Matthew Gregory Lewis for which Kelly composed the music are: *The Castle Spectre* (1798), *Adelmorn the Outlaw* (1801), *The Wood Daemon* (1807), *Adelgitha* (1807), *Venoni* (1808), "all for Drury Lane"; *Zoroaster*, "a romantic drama, which he never brought forward"; and *One o'Clock* (1811), "produced at the Lyceum."

51 Fenner, *Opera in London*, pp. 407–8. His music for Colman's *Blue-Beard* (1798), *Feudal Times* (1799), *Love Laughs at Locksmiths* (1803), *We Fly by Night* (1806), *The Forty Thieves* (1806) [originally written by Charles Ward, but thoroughly revised by Colman], *Africans* (1808), pp. 408–9; his music for William Dimond's plays, pp. 425–7. His other collaboration with Cobb was the music for *A House to be Sold* (1802), pp. 416–17.

52 Lewis, *The Castle Spectre*, in Cox, *Seven Gothic Dramas*, pp. 149–224. Quotations from *The Castle Spectre* are documented parenthetically with act, scene, and pagination from this edition.

53 On the reception of *The Castle Spectre*, see Peck, *A Life of Matthew G. Lewis*, pp. 73–4: "Years later James Boaden wrote, 'I yet bring before me, with delight, the waving form of Mrs. Powell, advancing from the suddenly illuminated chapel, and bending over Angela (Mrs. Jordan) in maternal benediction; during which slow and solemn action, the band played a few bars of 'unearthly music' [*The Life of Mrs. Jordan*]." The music was the chaconne of Jommelli, chosen by Michael Kelly, who records that the scene "rivetted the audience" (*Reminiscences*, Vol. 11, p. 126). This scene, presumably, led a newspaper critic of one of the early performances to testify that there was "literally a magic" in *The Castle Spectre*, which "recalled every solemn remembrance of the spectator and appealed directly to the heart" (*Morning Herald*, December 16, 1797). See also Ranger, *"Terror and Pity Reign in Every Breast"*, pp. 121–5. Boaden (*The Life of Mrs. Jordan*, p. 168), described the mime:

. . . the figure began slowly to advance; it was the spirit of Angela's mother, Mrs. Powell, in all her beauty, with long sweeping envelopments of muslin attached to the wrist . . . Mrs. Jordan cowered down motionless with terror, and Mrs. Powell bent over her prostrate duty, in maternal benediction: in a few minutes she entered the oratory again, the doors closed, and darkness once more enveloped the heroine and the scene.

54 Coleridge, *Remorse* (iii.ii), in *Poetical Works*, Vol. iii, Part 2, pp. 1101–7. Among the reviews of *Remorse* cited by J. C. C. Mays are *Morning Chronicle* and *The Courier* (January 25, 1813), which described the conjuration scene as "one of the most novel and picturesque we remember to have witnessed"; Thomas Barnes in *The Examiner* (January 31, 1813): "We never saw more

interest excited in a theatre than was expressed at the sorcery-scene in the third act. The altar flaming in the distance, the solemn invocation, the pealing music of the mysterious song, altogether produced a combination so awful, as nearly to overpower reality, and to make one half believe the enchantment which delighted our senses" (Introduction to *Remorse*, in Coleridge, *Poetical Works*, Vol. III, Part 2, pp. 1031–5, 1041).

55 Kelly, *Reminiscences*, Vol. I, p. 348:

[W]e saw the opera of 'Blue Beard.' 'Raoule Barbe Bleu;' is the French title of it: the fine bass singer, Chenard, was famous in 'Barbe Bleue;' Madame Dugazzon, in Fatima [= Isaure], and Mademoiselle Cretue, in Irène, were both excellent: the music, by Grétry, was very good; but so different are the tastes of the French and English audience, that when I produced my 'Blue Beard' at Drury Lane, I did not introduce a single bar from Grétry. Mrs. C[rouch] was struck by the subject, and wrote down the programme of the drama, with a view to get it dramatized at Drury Lane; [Jack] Johnstone got the music copied to bring to Mr. Harris at Covent garden, and it was got up at that theatre as a pantomime, I believe by Delpini; I never was [= saw] it in that shape, but I have heard that it was not successful.

56 Earlier examples of echoing instrumental sounds may be found in John Dryden's "Alexander's Feast" or "St. Cecilia's Day Ode" in the musical settings by Charles Purcell. Kelly doubtless knew the use of echoic passages in the *opera buffa* of Giovanni Battista Pergolesi. In the final number of *La serva padrona* (*The Servant Mistress* [1733]), Pandolphe, in love with his servant girl Serpina, sings of his beating heart which is loudly heard as a beating drum. The influence of Pergolesi's *La serva padrona* on English opera is evident in the works Storace, Sr., and Storace, Jr. Only the final duet is blatantly onomatopoeic, although much of the musical language of *opera buffa* is mimetic in more subtle ways: plodding rhythms for the comic characters, ornaments in the continuo that suggest laughter, etc.

57 Planché, *Blue Beard*, in *The Extravaganzas of J. R. Planché*, Vol. II, pp. 35–62.

58 *Ibid.*, pp. 39–40.

59 Dunlap, *Blue Beard; or, Female Curiosity* (1806; 2nd edn. 1811).

60 Woodworth, *The Poems, Odes, Songs, and other Metrical Effusions*, p. 63.

61 Genest, *Some account of the English Stage*, Vol. VII, p. 394; Genest's entry is for the sixth performance: January 23, 1798.

62 Cox and Gamer, eds., *The Broadview Anthology of Romantic Drama*, editors' introduction, pp. 75–6.

63 William Reeve, *Blue Beard, or, The Flight of Harlequin* [*sic*].

64 Heber, *Personality and office of the Christian comforter* (1818).

65 Heber, *The Lay of the Purple Falcon* (1812); *Palestine, a Prize Poem* (1803); *Palestine ... To which is added, The passage of the Red Sea* (1809); *Europe: Lines on the Present War* (1809); *Poems and Translations* (1812). Published posthumously: *The Poetical Works of Reginald Heber* (1841; 2nd edn. 1875); *Europe: Lines on the Present War; Palestine: With The Passage of the Red Sea* (1978).

66 Heber, *The whole works of the Right Rev. Jeremy Taylor* (1839); *Narrative of a journey through the upper provinces of India* (1828; 2nd edn. 1843–4); *The Life of Reginald Heber* (1830).
67 Planché, *Blue Beard*, pp. 35–62.
68 Follen, "Blue Beard. Charade" (1859).
69 De Quincey, *Confessions of an English Opium Eater*, in *Works*, Vol. 11, p. 23.
70 Carlyle, on the "edited" correspondence in the *Memoirs of Sophia Dorothea* (1845), Vol. 11, pp. 385, 393: "A dark tragedy of Sophie's, this; the Bluebeard Chamber of her mind, into which no eye but her own must ever look." From *History of Friedrich II*, Vol. 1, Book v, Chapter 1. *Complete Works of Thomas Carlyle*, Vol. v, p. 437.

9 VAMPIRES IN KILTS

1 This entire chapter is indebted, as any study of stage vampires must be, to the thoroughly researched commentary in Roxana Stuart, *Stage Blood*.
2 Burwick, "Vampir-Ästhetik."
3 Calmet, *Dissertations sur les apparitions des anges*.
4 Mary Shelley, Introduction to the 3rd edn. (1831): *Frankenstein, or the Modern Prometheus*, ed. James Rieger, p. 225.
5 The version printed in *New Monthly Magazine* was subsequently published anonymously: see [Polidori], *The Vampyr*.
6 McDonald, *Poor Polidori*, pp. 178–87.
7 Byron's *Letters & Journals*, Vol. 6, p. 125.
8 Byron, "A Fragment," appended to *Mazeppa: A Poem*, pp. 57–69.
9 Byron, *Letters and Journals*, Vol. vi, pp. 118–19. Galignani's *Messenger* was the English-language newspaper in Paris, established in 1814.
10 Byron, *Poetical Works*, p. 317. Byron also refers to vampires in "On Sam Rogers" (line 17); "Windsor Poetics" (line 8); *Don Juan*, Canto ii (line 485); "On a Royal Visit to theVaults" (line 8); and *Marino Faliero*, Act iii (line 603).
11 Eckermann, *Gespräche mit Goethe in den letzten Jahren seines Lebens*, ed. Woldemar von Biedermann, in Goethe, *Werke*, Fünfte Abteilung, Bd. 4, S. 18–19: [February 25, 1820]. "Bei Goethe ... kam dann auf Byron zu sprechen, gegen den er sich vielleicht in einem halben Jahre erklären werde, übrigens »Vampyr« als Byrons bestes Product erklärte." ("With Goethe ... we began to discuss Byron, concerning whom in six months he would have something to say; moreover he declared *The Vampyre* as Byron's best work.")
12 Hoffmann, "Die Serapionsbrüder: Der Zusammenhang," in *Poetische Werke*:

> "Sehr merkwürdig," nahm Sylvester das Wort, "ist es doch, daß, irre ich nicht, mit Walter Scott beinahe zu gleicher Zeit ein englischer Dichter auftrat, der in ganz anderer Tendenz das Große, Herrliche leistet. Es ist Lord Byron, den ich meine, und der mir kräftiger und gediegener scheint als Thomas Moore. Seine 'Belagerung von Korinth' ist ein Meisterwerk voll der lebendigsten Bilder, der genialsten Gedanken. Vorherrschend soll sein Hang zum Düstern, ja Grauenhaften und Entsetzlichen sein, und seinen 'Vampir' hab' ich gar nicht lesen mögen, da mir die bloße Idee eines

Vampirs, habe ich sie richtig aufgefaßt, schon eiskalte Schauer erregt. Soviel ich weiß, ist ein Vampir nämlich nichts anders als ein lebendiger Toter, der Lebendigen das Blut aussaugt." (Vol. IV, p. 526)

("It is indeed very remarkable," interposed Sylvester, "that an English writer, if I am not mistaken, emerged at the very same time as Walter Scott, and achieved greatness and grandeur in a completely different direction. It is Lord Byron whom I mean, and who seems to me more powerful and splendid than Thomas Moore. His *Siege of Corinth* is a masterpiece of the most lively images and the most genial thoughts. Predominant is his inclination to the gloomy, horrible and terrifying, and I couldn't even read his *Vampyre*, because the very idea of a vampire, if I have rightly understood it, excites an ice-cold spasm. I know this much: a vampire is nothing other than a living corpse that sucks the blood from the living.")

Hoffmann, "Die Serapionsbrüder [Vampirismus]," in *Poetische Werke*: "sei düster, schrecklich, ja entsetzlich, trotz dem vampirischen Lord Byron" ("... is dark, terrible, frightening, notwithstanding the vampiric Lord Byron") (Vol. IV, p. 531).

13 Douglass, *Lady Caroline Lamb*, p. 186.
14 William Ruthven, 4th Lord Ruthven and 1st Earl of Gowrie (*c.* 1543–84). Along with his father, Patrick Ruthven (3rd Lord Ruthven, *c.* 1520–66), William took part in the murder of Queen Mary of Scots' secretary/favorite, David Riccio, on March 9, 1566. He later took part in the so-called "Ruthven Raid," on August 23, 1582, in which the young James VI was kidnapped. After James escaped, in June, 1583, Ruthven was initially given a full pardon, but the next year he was arrested and, as the *DNB* puts it:

He was brought first to Edinburgh, then to Kinneill, before being taken to Stirling where he was tried at the beginning of May. In addition to treason he was accused of witchcraft and conferring with a sorcerer, charges which he denied and which were not pursued. Condemned for treason, Gowrie was beheaded at Stirling on 4 May 1584 and his lands were forfeited. He died with impressive fortitude.

The family got their lands back in 1586, but two of William's sons, John Ruthven, 3rd Earl of Gowrie (1577/8–1600) and Alexander Ruthven (1580?–1600), were then involved in the "Gowrie Conspiracy" of August, 1600, which appears to have been an attempt to assassinate the king. Both brothers died in the attempt. After this, the family was irrevocably disinherited, and the name was banned from James' court: no-one with the name Ruthven was allowed within ten miles of the king. Further details can be found in the *DNB* entries for the above. I thank Ian Blyth, University of St. Andrews, for drawing my attention to the historical Lord Ruthven.

15 Lamb, *Glenarvon*, Vol. II, pp. 31–2.
16 *Le Vampire* (1820) was a collaboration: Charles Nodier wrote it together with Achille Jouffrey and Pierre Carmouche. See Hemmings, "Co-authorship in French Plays of the Nineteenth Century."
17 Planché, *The Vampire* (1986).

18 Brazier, De Lurieu, and d'Artois, *Les Trois Vampires* (1820):

GOBETOUT.   J'ai lu dans le Journal de Paris q'il en a paru un à la Porte-
              Saint-Martin. Ainsi il n'y a pas de raison pour qu'il
              n'en vienne pas à Pantin . . .
MME G.   Mais enfin, de quel pays peuvent-ils venire? . . . de la Suisse?
              . . . de la Russie? de la Cochinchine?
GOBETOUT.   Les vampires . . . Ils nous viennent d'Angleterre . . . C'est
              encore une gentilesse de ces messieurs . . . il nous font
              de jolis cadeaux! (1.iii.4)

Quoted in Stuart, *Stage Blood*, p. 274.

19 Fingal's Cave is the famous basaltic landmark on the Island of Staffa. For the
   bloody exploits of Fingal, see MacPherson, *The Poems of Ossian* (1796). For
   example, 1: 29:

"Annir," said Starno of lakes, "was a fire that consumed of old. He poured death from
his eyes along the striving fields. His joy was in the fall of men. Blood to him was a
summer stream, that brings joy to the withered vales, from its own mossy rock. He
came forth to the lake Luth-cormo, to meet the tall Corman-trunar, he from Urlor of
streams, dweller of battle's wing."

20 The name Cromal is adapted from MacPherson, *The Poems of Ossian*; see
   "Croma" (1: 113–24); and "Calthon and Comal" (1: 125–36).
21 Crompton, *Byron and Greek Love* (1985).
22 Buczkowski, "James Robinson Planché (1794–1880)."
23 De Quincey, *Works*, Vol. III, p. 150.
24 *Ibid.*, p. 153.
25 *Ibid.*, pp. 153–4 and 439 n. 10.
26 Burwick, "Competing Histories in the Waverley Novels."
27 The combination of horror and comedy in early nineteenth-century melodrama was belatedly rediscovered in twentieth-century cinema. *Abbott and
   Costello Meet Frankenstein* (1948), featured Chick Young (Bud Abbbott) and
   Wilbur Grey (Lou Costello) as two freight handlers hired to deliver baggage.
   Unaware of the contents, they transport crates with the coffins of Count
   Dracula (Béla Lugosi) and Frankenstein's monster (Glenn Strange) to an
   eerie castle. Dracula has enlisted a mad scientist, Sandra Mornay (Lenore
   Aubert), to reanimate the monster using Wilbur's brain. Pretending her
   love for him, she lures Wilbur to their laboratory in the castle. Larry Talbot
   (Lon Chaney) tries to stop Dracula, but his efforts go awry when he is
   intermittently transformed into the Wolf Man.
28 As George Bernard Shaw observed in the "Epistle Dedicatory" to *Man and
   Superman* (1903), when "comic characters walk with their feet on solid
   ground, vivid and amusing, you know that the author has much to shew and
   nothing to teach."
29 Genest, *Some account of the English Stage*, Vol. IX, pp. 123–4 (January 10,
   1821).

30 Waldie, *Journals*, journal entry of January 5, 1821 (XLVII: 360–1).
31 Savigny and Correard, *Narrative of a Voyage to Senegal* (1986). For an account of the voyage of the *Medusa*, see Chapter 3, p. 78.
32 Moncrieff, *The Vampire*, p. vii.
33 *Ibid.*, p. vi; cf. Mallet, *Northern antiquities*.
34 Planché, *Songs, duets, glees, chorusses*, p. 821.
35 Stuart, *Stage Blood*, pp. 281–3.
36 *Don Giovanni* (1787), the opera by Wolfgang Amadeus Mozart with libretto by Lorenzo da Ponte, was based on the comedy *Dom Juan* (1665) by Jean Baptiste Poquelin de Molière, borrowed, in turn, from Tirso de Molina's *Don Juan, El burlador de Sevilla* (1635). Weinstein, *The Metamorphoses of Don Juan*.
37 Moncrieff, *Giovanni in London*, rev. edn. (1825).
38 Dibdin, *Don Giovanni*. Gottfried Bürger's *Lenore* was first written in 1773; his revised version appeared in the *Musenalmanach* in 1774. The ballad became well known in English through translations by Sir Walter Scott and others, including Dante Gabriel Rossetti.
39 Commentaries on the sexual implications of vampire narratives are too numerous to list here; among those that I have found useful: Twitchell, *The Living Dead*; Wolf, *A Dream of Dracula*, Chapter 6; Bentley, "The Monster in the Bedroom"; Roth, "Suddenly Sexual Women in Bram Stoker's *Dracula*"; Fry, "Fictional Connections and Sexuality in *Dracula*"; Eltis, "Corruption of the Blood and Degeneration of the Race"; Rottenbucher, "From Undead Monster to Sexy Seducer"; Wyman and Dionisopulos, "Primal Urges and Civilized Sensibilities"; Gagnier, "Evolution and Information"; Demetrakopoulos, "Feminism, Sex Role Exchanges, and Other Subliminal Fantasies in Bram Stoker's *Dracula*."
40 Planché, "Introductory Vision," in *Songs, duets, glees, chorusses*, p. 4.
41 Stuart, *Stage Blood*, p. 283.
42 Moncrieff, *The Spectre Bridegroom* (1821), p. v.
43 Irving, "The Spectre Bridegroom, a Traveller's Tale" (1819–20).
44 Moncrieff, in suggesting that his alterations may have been made "possibly from remembering the Original French Story," is responding to Irving's own footnote on his source for the tale: "The erudite reader, well versed in good-for-nothing lore, will perceive that the above Tale must have been suggested to the old Swiss by a little French anecdote, a circumstance said to have taken place in Paris" (*ibid.*, p. 119).
45 See note 3 above.
46 "St. John Dorset" is a *nom de plume* used by the two young authors, Hugo John Belfour (1802–27) and George Stephens (1800–51), for their collaborative authorship of *The Vampire* (1821).
47 Ritter, *Der Vampyr oder die Todten-Braut* (1822); also the author of *Der Weibermagistrat in Klatschhausen· Lustspiel in einem Aufzuge*, and *Meine Stiefkinder* in *Possen und Lustspiele für die deutsche Bühne* (1818).

48 The original tale, "Der Freischütz" by Johann August Apel, appeared in *Das Gespensterbuch* (1810). Friedrich Kind adapted the tale as libretto to Carl Maria von Weber's *Der Freischütz*, which was first performed at the Schauspielhaus in Berlin on June 8, 1821. Apel's tale was translated by De Quincey, as "The Fatal Marksman."

49 Even before the success of Weber's *Der Freischütz*, Marschner had previously experimented with the combination of magic and folk themes in *Der Kiff-häuser Berg*, a comic opera (1816; Stadttheater Zittau, January 2, 1822), with libretto by August von Kotzebue, based on a Thuringian legend. Following *Der Vampyr*, Wohlbrück subsequently collaborated with Marschner as author of three additional librettos: *Der Templer und die Jüdin* (1829), from a play by Johann Reinhold von Lenz; *Das Gericht der Templer* (1823) – based on Sir Walter Scott's *Ivanhoe* (1819) – a romantic opera (1829; Stadttheater Leipzig, December 22, 1829. Rev. Sommer, 1830); *Des Falkners Braut*, a comic opera (1830; Stadttheater Leipzig, March 10, 1832), from a story by Alexander Julius Carl Spindler; and *Der Bäbu*, a comic opera (Hoftheater Hannover, February 19, 1838).

50   Ha, welche Lust aus schönen Augen
                An blühender Brust neues Leben
                In wonnigem Beben
                Mit einem Kusse in sich zu saugen.
                Ha, welche Lust in liebendem Kosen
                Mit lüsternem Mut
                Das süsseste Blut
                Wie Saft der Rosen
                Von purpurnen Lippen
                Schmeichelnd zu nippen!
                Und wenn der brennende Durst sich stillt,
                Und wenn das Blut dem Herzen entquillt,
                Und wenn sie stöhnen, voll Entsetzen,
                Ha, ha, welch' Ergötzen,
                Welche Lust!
                Mit neuem Mut
                Ihr Todesbeben
                Ist frisches Leben.
                Armes Liebchen, bleich wie Schnee,
                Tat dir wohl im Herzen weh.
                Ach, einst fühlt' ich selbst die Schmerzen
                Ihrer Angst im warmen Herzen,
                Das der Himmel fühlend schuf.
                Mahnt mich nicht in diesen Tönen,
                Die den Himmel frech verhöhnen.
                Ich verstehe euern Ruf!
                Ha, welche Lust. (I, no. 2)

51 VAMPYRMEISTER: Dieser hier, des schon verfallen
                     Unsrem Dienste ist.
                     Wünscht Noch eine kurze Frist

Unter den freien Menschen zu wallen. Sein Begehren
  sei bewilligt,
Wenn er seinen Schwur erfüllt,
Wenn er bis Mitternacht
Drei Opfer für uns gebracht:
Für drei Bräute, zart und rein
Soll dem Vampyr ein Jahr bewilligt sein.

LORD RUTWEN: Bei der Urkraft alles Bösen
Schwör' ich euch, mein Wort zu lösen.
Doch fliehet diesen Aufenthalt
Denn eins der Opfer naht sich bald. (Der Meister
  verschhwindet, der Mond scheint wider.)

52 Schumann, *Handbuch der Opern*, pp. 174–6.

53   Kind, sieh den bleichen Mann nicht an,
Sonst ist es bald um dich getan,
Weich schnell von ihm zurück!
Schon manches Mägdlein jung und schön
Tät ihm zu tief ins Auge sehn,
Musst' es mit bittern Qualen
Und seinem Blut bezahlen,
Denn still und heimlich sag ich dir:
Der bleiche Mann ist ein Vampyr!
Bewahr'uns Gott auf Erden,
Ihm jemals gleich zu werden. (II, no. 12)

54 Planché, *The Recollections and Reflections of J. R. Planché*, Vol. 1, p. 151.

55 See note 46 above.

56 The review in the *London Magazine* is quoted in Stuart, *Stage Blood*, p. 96, who quoted it from Frayling, *The Vampyre: Lord Ruthven to Count Dracula*, p. 10.

57 Southey, *Thalaba the Destroyer*; Fitzball, *Thalaba, the destroyer*.

58 Twitchell, "The Female Vampire," in *The Living Dead*, Chapter 2, pp. 39–73.

59 Stuart, *Stage Blood*, p. 22.

60 C. Z. Barnett, *Phantom Bride*, which opened at the Royal Pavilion, Mile-End, on September 6, 1830. "The only edition, correctly marked, by permission, from the prompter's book. To which is added, a description of the costume, cast of the characters, the whole of the stage business, situations, entrances, exits, properties and directions" (title-page).

61 George Blink, *Vampire Bride, or the Tenant of the Tomb* (1834). The tale on which it is based, "Wake not the Dead," appeared in, *Popular Tales and Romances of the Northern Nations* (1823), Vol. 1. For reference to the false attribution to Tieck, see Stableford, "Sang for Supper," p. 72.

62 Stuart, *Stage Blood*, pp. 121–2.

Bibliography

Adams, M. Ray. "Helen Maria Williams and the French Revolution," in *Wordsworth and Coleridge: Studies in Honor of George McLean Harper*. Ed. Earl Leslie Griggs. Princeton: Princeton University Press, 1939; rpt. New York: Russell & Russell, 1962.

Adams, William Davenport. *A Dictionary of the Drama: a guide to the plays, playwrights, players, and playhouses of the United Kingdom and America, from the earliest times to the present*, Vol. 1: A–G. London: Chatto & Windus, 1904.

Adolphus, John. *Memoirs of John Bannister, Comedian*, 2 vols. London: R. Bentley, 1839.

Allen, Ralph G. "Kemble and Capon at Drury Lane, 1794–1802," *Educational Theatre Journal* 23(1) (March, 1971), 22–35.

Altick, Richard D. *Victorian Studies in Scarlet*. Toronto: Norton, 1970.

Ancillon, Charles. *Eunuchism display'd, describing all the different sorts of eunuchs. Wherein principally is examin'd, whether they are capable of marriage, and if they ought to be suffer'd to enter into that state. The whole confirm'd by the authority of civil, canon, and common law, and illustrated with many remarkable cases by way of precedent*. London: E. Curll, 1718.

Anderson, Misty G. *Female Playwrights and Eighteenth-Century Comedy: Negotiating Marriage on the London Stage*. New York: Palgrave, 2002.

Anderson, William. *The Scottish Nation*, 3 vols. Edinburgh: Fullarton, 1866.

Andrews, Miles Peter. *Dissipation. A comedy, in five acts: As it is performed at the Theatre-Royal, In Drury-Lane*. London: printed for T. Becket [etc.], 1781.

Fire and Water! A Comic Opera: in Two Acts. Performed at the Theatre-Royal in the Hay-Market. London: printed for T. Cadell, 1780.

Anonymous [falsely attributed to Ludwig Tieck]. "Wake not the Dead," in *Popular Tales and Romances of the Northern Nations*, 3 vols. London: W. Simpkin, R. Marshall, and J.H. Bohte (1823), pp. 233–91.

Anonymous. *The Biography of the British stage: being correct narratives of the lives of all the principal actors & actresses ... Interspersed with original anecdotes and choice and illustrative poetry. To which is added, a comic poem, entitled "The actress."* London: printed for Sherwood and Jones, 1824.

Anonymous. "Mrs. Martyr, Singer and Actress," *Notes and Queries*, s. 9–XII, no. 293 (1903): 107.

Apel, Johann August. "Der Freischütz," in *Das Gespensterbuch*, 2 vols. Ed. Apel and Friedrich Laun. Leipzig: Goschen, 1810.

Arnim, Achim von. *Werke*, 6 vols. Ed. Roswitha Burwick, Jürgen Knaack, Paul Michael Lützeler, Renate Moering, Ulfert Ricklefs, and Hermann F. Weiss. Frankfurt-am-Main: Deutsche Klassiker Verlag, 1989–92.

Auburn, Mark S. "Theatre in the Age of Garrick and Sheridan," in *Sheridan Studies*. Ed. James Morwood and David Crane. Cambridge: Cambridge University Press, 1995, pp. 7–46.

Austin, Gilbert. *Chironomia; or, A Treatise on rhetorical delivery: comprehending many precepts, both ancient and modern, for the proper regulation of the voice, the countenance, and gesture.* London: printed for T. Cadell and W. Davies in the Strand; by W. Bulmer, Cleveland-Row, St. James, 1806.

Baillie, Joanna. *The Dramatic and Poetical Works of Joanna Baillie.* London: Longman, Brown, Green, and Longmans, 1853.

Baillie, Matthew. *An Appendix to the first edition of Morbid Anatomy of some of the most important parts of the human body.* London: J. Johnson and G. Nicol, 1798.

A series of engravings, accompanied with explanations, which are intended to illustrate the morbid anatomy of some of the most important parts of the human body: divided into ten fasculi. London: printed by W. Bulmer for J. Johnson and G. and W. Nicol, 1799–1802.

Lectures and Observations on Medicine. London: Richard Taylor, 1825.

The Morbid Anatomy of some of the most important parts of the human body. London: J. Johnson and G. Nicol, 1793.

The Morbid Anatomy of some of the most important parts of the human body. Second edition, corrected and considerably enlarged. London: J. Johnson and G. Nicol, 1797.

The Works of Matthew Baillie, M.D. to which is prefixed an Account of his Life, collected from authentic sources, 2 vols. Ed. James Wardrop. London: Longman, Hurst, Orme, Brown, and Green, 1825.

Baker, David Erskine, Isaac Reed, and Stephen Jones. *Biographia dramatica.* London: Longman, Hurst, Rees, Orme, and Brown [etc.], 1812.

Baker, Herschel. *John Philip Kemble: The Actor in His Theatre.* Cambridge, MA: Harvard University Press, 1942.

Banham, Martin, ed. *The Cambridge Guide to Theatre.* Cambridge: Cambridge University Press, 1995.

Barker, Kathleen. *The Theatre Royal Bristol, 1766–1966: Two Centuries of Stage History.* London: Society for Theatre Research, 1974.

Barnett, C. Z. *Phantom Bride; or, The Castilian Bandit a melo-drama in two acts.* London: J. Duncombe, 1830.

Baron-Wilson, Mrs. Cornwell. *Our Actresses; or, Glances at stage favourites, past and present*, 2 vols. London: Smith, Elder, and Co., 65, Cornhill, 1844.

Barrie, James Matthew. *Peter Pan; or, The Boy who Would Not Grow Up*, in *The Plays of J. M. Barrie in One Volume.* Ed. Albert Edward Wilson. London: Hodder & Stoughton, 1942.

Barrymore, William. *The Secret, as Performed at the Royal Adelphi Theatre, 11 May 1824*. London: J. Cumberland & Son, 1824.

Beaumarchais, Pierre-Augustin Caron de. *The Follies of a Day; or, the Marriage of Figaro. A Comedy, as it is now performing at the Theatre-Royal, Covent-Garden. From the French of M. de Beaumarchais by Thomas Holcroft*. London: G. G. and J. J. Robinson, 1785.

Behn, Aphra. *The Amorous Prince; or, the Curious Husband. A Comedy, As it is Acted at his Royal Highness, the Duke of York's Theatre*. London: printed by J. M. for Thomas Dring [etc.], 1671.

Bell, Charles. *Essays on the anatomy and philosophy of expression*. 2nd edn. London: John Murray, 1824.

Bentley, C. F. "The Monster in the Bedroom: Sexual Symbolism in Bram Stoker's *Dracula*," *Literature and Psychology* 22 (1972): 27–34.

Bernard, John. *Retrospections of the Stage*, 2 vols. Boston: Carter and Hendee, 1832.

Berre, Pierre-Yon and Jean Baptiste Radet. *Les Docteurs modernes. Représentée pour la premiere fois, à Paris, par les Comédiens italiens, 16 Novembre 1784*. 3rd edn. Paris: Chez Gastelier, Libraire, Parvis Notre-Dame, No. 15, 1785.

Biggs, Murray. "Notes on Performing *Sardanapalus*," *Studies in Romanticism* 31(3) (Fall, 1992): 373–85.

Birdwhistell, Ray L. *Kinesics and Context: Essays on Body Motion Communication*. Philadelphia: University of Pennsylvania Press, 1970.

Bishop, Sir Henry R. *The overture, and the whole of the music in Aladdin; or, The Wonderful Lamp: a fairy opera in three acts, performed at the Theatre Royal Drury Lane* [musical score]. London: Goulding, D'Almaine, & Co., 1826.

The overture, chorusses, and whole of the music as performed at the Theatre Royal Covent Garden, to the grand melo dramatic opera, called The Virgin of the Sun! London: printed by Goulding, D'Almaine, Potter, & Co., 1812.

Blacking, John, ed. *The Anthropology of the Body*. London, New York: Academic Press, 1977.

Blink, George. *Vampire Bride, or the Tenant of the Tomb*. London: J. Duncombe, 1834; T. H. Lacy, 1854.

Boaden, James. *The Life of Mrs. Jordan: including original private correspondence, and numerous anecdotes of her contemporaries*. London: E. Bull, 1831.

Memoirs of Mrs. Siddons: interspersed with Anecdotes of Authors and Actors, 2 vols. London: H. Colburn and R. Bentley, 1831; London: Grolier Society [1900–?].

Bode, Christoph. "'Distasteful Customs': Richard F. Burton über den Kannibalismus der Fan," in *Das andere Essen: Kannibalismus als Motiv und Metapher in der Literatur*. Ed. Daniel Fulda and Walter Pape. Freiburg-im-Breisgau: Rombach Verlag, 2001, pp. 147–58.

"Unfit for an English Stage? Inchbald's *Lovers' Vows* and Kotzebue's *Das Kind der Liebe*." *European Romantic Review* 16(3) (July, 2005): 297–309.

Bolton, Betsy. "Saving the Rajah's Daughter: Spectacular Logic in Moncrieff's *Cataract of the Ganges*," *European Romantic Review* 17(4) (Fall, 2006): 477–93.

Bonnor, Charles and Robert Merry. "The Picture of Paris taken in the year 1790," Huntington Library, MS Larpent 886; dated by Larpent "11th Decr. 1790 Covent Garden"; first performed Covent Garden, 20 December 1790; cf. MacMillan, *Catalogue of the Larpent Plays.*

Bossard, Abbé Eugène and René de Maulde. *Gilles de Rais, maréchal de France, dit Barbe-bleue.* Paris: Champion, 1886.

Bosse, Anke. *Orientalismus im Frühwerk Ludwig Tiecks.* Tübingen: Niemeyer, 1998.

Boureau, Alain. *The Lord's First Night: The Myth of the Droit de cuissage* [*Le droit de cuissage: la fabrication d'un mythe, XIIIe–XXe siècle.* Paris: Albin Michel, 1995]. Trans. Lydia G. Cochrane. Chicago: University of Chicago Press, 1998.

Brand, Hannah. *Adelinda*, in *Plays and Poems.* Norwich: printed by Beatniffe and Payne, 1798.

Bratton, Jacky. "The Celebrity of Edmund Kean: An Institutional Story," in *Theatre and Celebrity in Britain, 1660–2000.* Ed. Mary Luckhurst and Jane Moody. New York: Palgrave Macmillan, 2005, pp. 90–106.

Brazier, Nicholas, Gabriel De Lurieu, and Armand d'Artois. *Les Trois Vampires, ou le clair de la lune, folie-vaudeville en un acte; par mm. Brazier, Gabriel et Armand. Représentée pour la 1re. fois à Paris, sur le théâtre des Variétés, le 22 juin 1820.* Paris: J.-N. Barba, 1820.

Brewer, John. "'This monstrous tragic-comic scene': British Reactions to the French Revolution," in *In the Shadow of the Guillotine: British Reactions to the French Revolution.* Ed. David Bindman. London: British Museum, 1989, pp. 9–25.

Brewster, Sir David. *Letters on Natural Magic, addressed to Sir Walter Scott.* London: John Murray, 1832.

Brooks, Peter. *The Melodramatic Imagination: Balzac, Henry James, Melodrama, and the Mode of Excess.* New Haven: Yale University Press, 1976; 2nd edn. with new Preface, 1995.

Buck, Ross. *The Communication of Emotion*, The Guilford Social Psychology Series. New York: Guilford Press, 1984.

Buczkowski, Paul J. "James Robinson Planché (1794–1880)" www-personal.umd. umich.edu/~nainjaun/#Contents, www-personal.umd.umich.edu/~nain-jaun/drama.html.

Bull, Peter. *Body Movement and Interpersonal Communication.* Chichester, New York: Wiley, 1983.

Posture and Gesture, International Series in Experimental Social Psychology 16. Oxford, New York: Pergamon Press, 1987.

Burgoon, Judee K., David B. Buller, and W. Gill Woodall. *Nonverbal Communication: The Unspoken Dialogue.* 3rd edn. New York: McGraw-Hill, 1996.

Burleigh, John. *Ednam and Its Indwellers.* Glasgow: Fraser, Asher, & Co., 1912.

Burton, Richard Francis. "A Day amongst the Fans," *Anthropological Review* 1 (1863): 43–54, 285–7; reprinted in Burton, *Selected Papers on Anthropology, Travel, and Exploration.* Ed. Norman Mosley Penzer. London: Philipot, 1924; rpt., New York: Blom, 1972.

The Thousand Nights and a Night: a plain and literal translation of the Arabian Nights entertainments, 16 vols. (10 vols. 1885; 6 supplementary vols. 1886–8). [S.l.]: printed by the Burton Club for private subscribers only, 1885–8.

Burwick, Frederick. "Competing Histories in the Waverley Novels," in *Romantic Enlightenment: Sir Walter Scott and the Politics of History*. Ed. Bruce Beiderwell, special issue of *European Romantic Review* 13(3) (September, 2002): 261–71.

"Gateway to Heterotopia: The Staging of Elsewhere," in *Heterotopia and Romantic Border Crossings*. Ed. Jeffry Cass and Larry Peer. Burlington, VT: Ashgate, 2008, pp. 27–39.

"The Grotesque in the Romantic Movement," in *European Romanticism: Literary Cross-Currents, Modes, and Models*. Ed. Gerhart Hoffmeister. Detroit: Wayne State University Press, 1990, pp. 37–57.

"Ideal Shattered: Sarah Siddons, Madness, and the Dynamics of Gesture," in *Notorious Muse: The Actress in British Art and Culture 1776–1812*. Ed. Robyn Asleson. New Haven: Yale University Press, 2003, pp. 129–49.

Illusion and the Drama: Critical Theory of the Enlightenment and Romantic Era. University Park, PA: Penn State University Press, 1991.

"John Boydell's *Shakespeare Gallery* and the Stage," *Shakespeare Jahrbuch* 133 (1997): 54–76.

"Manuscript Journal of John Waldie," *UCLA Librarian* 23(1) (January, 1970): 1–3.

Mimesis and Its Romantic Reflections. University Park: Penn State University Press, 2001.

"Phantastisch-groteske Literatur," in *Fischer Lexikon Literatur*, 3 vols. Ed. Ulfert Ricklefs. Frankfurt-am-Main: Fischer Bücherei, 1996. Vol. III, pp. 1478–94.

Poetic Madness and the Romantic Imagination. University Park, PA: Pennsylvania State University Press, 1996.

"Romantic Drama: from Optics to Illusion," in *Literature and Science: Theory and Practice*. Ed. Stuart Peterfreund. Boston: Northeastern University Press, 1990, pp. 167–208.

"Science and Supernaturalism: Sir David Brewster and Sir Walter Scott," *Comparative Criticism* 13 (1991): 82–114.

"Vampir-Ästhetik," in *Das andere Essen: Kannibalismus als Motif und Metapher in der Literatur*. Ed. Walter Pape and Daniel Fulda. Freiburg-im-Breisgau: Rombach Verlag, 2001, pp. 341–67.

Byng, John, *The Torrington diaries, containing the tours through England and Wales of the Hon. John Byng (later fifth viscount Torrington) between the years 1781 and 1794*, 4 vols. Ed. with an introduction by C. Bruyn Andrews, with a general introduction by John Beresford. London: Eyre & Spottiswoode, 1934–8.

Byron, Lord George Gordon. *Byron's Letters and Journals*, 12 vols. Ed. Leslie A. Marchand. Cambridge, MA: Belknap Press of Harvard University Press, 1973–82.

The Complete Poetical Works of Lord Byron. Ed. Paul Elmer More. Boston, NY: Houghton Mifflin, 1933.

"A Fragment," appended to *Mazeppa: A Poem.* London: John Murray, 1819.

Byron, Lord George Gordon and Isaac Nathan. *A Selection of Hebrew Melodies, Ancient and Modern.* Ed. Frederick Burwick and Paul Douglass. Tuscaloosa: University of Alabama Press, 1988.

Calmet, Augustin. *Dissertations sur les apparitions des anges, des démons & des esprits. Et sur les revenans et vampires. De Hongrie, de Boheme, de Moravie & de Silesie.* Paris: Chez De Bure l'aîné, 1746.

Campbell, Jill. "'When Men Women Turn': Gender Reversals in Fielding's Plays," in *Crossing the Stage: Controversies on Cross-Dressing.* Ed. Lesley Ferris. London: Routledge, 1993, pp. 58–79.

Campbell, Kathleen. *Beau Brummell.* London: Hammond, 1948.

Carlson, Marvin. *The Theatre of the French Revolution.* Ithaca, NY: Cornell University Press, 1966.

Carlyle, Edward Irving. "Samuel Edward Widdrington," in *Dictionary of National Biography.* London: Oxford University Press, 1901.

Carlyle, Thomas. *Complete Works of Thomas Carlyle,* 20 vols. New York: P. F. Collier & Son, 1901.

Chamisso, Adelbert von. *Peter Schlemihls wundersame Geschichte.* Nürnberg: J. L. Schrag, 1814.

Clairon, Claire-Josèphe-Hippolyte Léris de la Tude. *Mémoires d'Hippolyte Clairon et reflexions sur l'art dramatique.* Paris: Buisson, 1799.

Clancy, Patricia. "Mme de Genlis, Elizabeth Inchbald and *The Child of Nature,*" *Australian Journal of French Studies* 30(3) (September, 1993): 324–40.

Clark, Peter, ed. *The Cambridge Urban History of Britain,* 3 vols. Vol. 11: *1540–1840.* Cambridge: Cambridge University Press, 2000.

Clarke, –. *The Georgian Era: Memoirs of the Most Eminent Persons, who have flourished in Great Britain, from the accession of George the First to the demise of George the Fourth,* 4 vols. London: Vizetelly, Branston and Co., 1832–4.

Clery, Emma Juliet. "Horace Walpole's *The Mysterious Mother* and the Impossibility of Female Desire," in *The Gothic, Essays and Studies,* new series 54 (2001). Ed. Fred Botting for the English Association. Woodbridge: D. S. Brewer, 2001, pp. 23–46.

Women's Gothic: From Clara Reeve to Mary Shelley. Plymouth, UK: Northcote House Publishers Ltd., 2000.

Cobb, James. *Love in the East; or, Adventures of Twelve Hours: a Comic Opera, in Three Acts.* Music arranged by Thomas Linley. London: printed for W. Lowndes [etc.], 1788.

Cole, John William. *The Life and Theatrical Times of Charles Kean, F.S.A., including a Summary of the English stage for the last Fifty Years,* 2 vols. London: R. Bentley, 1859.

Coleridge, Samuel Taylor. *Biographia Literaria* [= *BL*], 2 vols. Ed. Walter Jackson Bate and James Engell, *The Collected Works of Samuel Taylor Coleridge* 7. Princeton: Princeton University Press, 1983.

Faustus, translated by Samuel Taylor Coleridge from the German of Goethe. Ed. Frederick Burwick and James McKusick. Oxford: Oxford University Press, 2007.

The Friend, 2 vols. Ed. Barbara E. Rooke, *The Collected Works of Samuel Taylor Coleridge* 4. Princeton: Bollingen, 1969.

Lectures 1808–1819: On Literature, 2 vols. Ed. Reginald A. Foakes, *The Collected Works of Samuel Taylor Coleridge* 5. London: Routledge & Kegan Paul; Princeton: Princeton University Press, 1987.

Marginalia, 6 vols. Ed. H. J Jackson and G. Whalley, *The Collected Works of Samuel Taylor Coleridge* 12. Princeton: Bollingen, 1980–2001.

The Notebooks of Samuel Taylor Coleridge, 5 vols. Ed. Kathleen Coburn, Merton Christensen, and Anthony Harding. Princeton: Bollingen, 1957–2002.

Poetical Works, 6 vols. Ed. J. C. C. Mays, *The Collected Works of Samuel Taylor Coleridge* 16. Princeton: Princeton University Press, 2001.

Zapolya: A Christmas Tale, in Two Parts. London: Rest Fenner, 1817.

Colman, George, the Younger. *Blue-Beard; or, Female Curiosity!* London: printed by T. Woodfall, for Messrs. Cadell and Davies [etc.], 1798.

The Iron Chest: A Play: in Three Acts. With a Preface. First represented at the Theatre-Royal, in Drury-Lane, On Saturday, 12th March, 1796. London: printed by W. Woodfall, for Messrs. Cadell and Davies [etc.], 1796.

"Suppressed Preface on Mr. John Kemble's alleged improper conduct," *Theatrical John Bull and Weekly Journal of Amusement* IV–VI (November, 1822): [25]–7, [33]–5, 42–3.

Conger, Syndy McMillen. "Reading *Lovers' Vows*: Jane Austen's Reflections on English Sense and German Sensibility," *Studies in Philology* 85(1) (Winter, 1988): 92–113.

Congreve, William. *The Mourning Bride, a Tragedy: as it is acted at the theatre in Lincoln's-Inn-Fields by His Majesty's servants*. London: printed for Jacob Tonson, 1697.

Conolly, Leonard W. *The Censorship of English Drama 1737–1824*. San Marino, CA: Huntington Library, 1976.

Cook, Dutton. "Mr. Conway and Mrs. Piozzi," *The Gentleman's Magazine* 251(2) (July–December, 1881): 538–50.

Cowley, Hannah. *The Belle's Stratagem: a comedy, as acted at the Theatre-Royal in Covent-Garden*. London: printed for T. Cadell, 1781.

A Bold Stroke for a Husband. A Comedy. Written by the ingenious Mrs. Cowley . . . and performed forty nights last season at the Theatre-Royal, Covent-Garden. Dublin: printed, and sold by all the booksellers, 1783.

A Bold Stroke for a Husband, a comedy, as acted at the Theatre Royal, in Covent Garden. London: printed by M. Scott . . . for T. Evans [etc.], 1784.

The Town Before You, a comedy, as acted at the Theatre-Royal, Covent-Garden. London: printed by G. Woodfall, for T. N. Longman [etc.], 1795.

Cox, Jeffrey N. "The French Revolution in the English Theater," *History & Myth: Essays on English Romantic Literature*. Ed. Stephen Behrendt. Detroit: Wayne State University Press, 1990, pp. 33–52.

"Romantic Drama and the French Revolution," in *Revolution and English Romanticism: Politics and Rhetoric*. Ed. Keith Hanley and Raman Selden. Hertfordshire: Harvester Wheatsheaf, 1990, pp. 241–60

ed. *Seven Gothic Dramas, 1789–1825*. Athens, OH: Ohio University Press, 1992.

Cox, Jeffrey N. and Michael Gamer, eds. *The Broadview Anthology of Romantic Drama*. Peterborough, ON; Orchard Park, NY: Broadview Press, 2003.

Cox, Philip. *Reading Adaptations: Novels and Verse Narratives on the Stage, 1790–1840*. Manchester: Manchester University Press, 2000.

Crane, Thomas Frederick, ed. *Italian Popular Tales*. Boston: Houghton Mifflin Company, 1885.

Crompton, Louis. *Byron and Greek Love: Homophobia in 19th-century England*. Berkeley: University of California Press, 1985.

Cross, James C. *The Apparition*. London: printed for J. Barker [etc.], 1794.

Cumberland, Richard, ed. *The British Drama, a collection of the most esteemed dramatic productions with biography of the respective authors and critique of each play*, 14 vols. London: printed for C. Cooke, 1817.

The Brothers: a comedy. As it is performed at the Theatre Royal in Covent-Garden, 2 December 1769. London: printed for W. Griffin [etc.], 1770.

The Imposters: a Comedy. Performed at the Theatre Royal, Drury Lane. London: printed for C. Dilly, in the Poultry, 1789.

The Wheel of Fortune: A Comedy. Performed at the Theatre-Royal, Drury-Lane, 28 February 1795. London: printed for C. Dilly, 1795.

Curran, Stuart. *Shelley's Cenci: Scorpions Ringed with Fire*. Princeton: Princeton University Press, 1970.

Dance, James. *Pamela: a comedy, performed at Goodman's Fields 9 November 1741*. London: printed for Joseph Miller, 1741.

Darby, Barbara. "Spectacle and Revolution in 1790s Tragedy," *Studies in English Literature* 39(3) (1999): 575–96.

D'Arcy, Douglas. *Some Passages in the Life of an Adventurer*. London: F. J. Mason, 1834.

Davis, Jim. "Self-Portraiture On and Off the Stage: The Low Comedian as Iconographer," *Theatre Survey* 43 (2002): 177–200.

"They Shew Me Off in Every Form and Way: The Iconography of English Comic Acting in the Late Eighteenth and Early Nineteenth Centuries," *Theatre Research International* 26(3) (October, 2001): 243–56.

Davis, Tracy C. "Response: Drama in Practice," *Victorian Studies: An Interdisciplinary Journal of Social, Political, and Cultural Studies*, 49(2) (2007): 268–76.

Delmar, Ken. *Winning Moves: The Body Language of Selling*. New York: Warner Books, 1985.

Demetrakopoulos, Stephanie. "Feminism, Sex Role Exchanges, and Other Subliminal Fantasies in Bram Stoker's *Dracula*," *Frontiers: A Journal of Women Studies* 2(3) (1977): 104–13.

De Quincey, Thomas. "The Fatal Marksman," in *Popular Tales and Romances of the Northern Nations*, 3 vols. London: W. Simpkin, R. Marshall, and J. H. Bohte, 1823, Vol. III, pp. 141–98.

The Works of Thomas De Quincey, 21 vols. Ed. Grevel Lindop, *et. al.* London: Pickering and Chatto, 2000–3.

Desmet, Christy and Anne Williams, eds. *Shakespearean Gothic*. Cardiff: University of Wales Press, 2008.

Destouches, Néricault. *Le Dissipateur; ou L'honnette-friponne*. Paris: Prault Père, 1745.

Devienne, François. *Les visitandines: comédie en deux actes et en prose*. Paris: Cousineau, Père et Fils, gravée par Huguet, 1792.

Dibdin, Thomas. *Don Giovanni; or, A spectre on horseback! a comic, heroic, operatic, tragic, pantomimic, burletta-spectacular extravaganza in two acts*. London: printed for J. Miller by B. McMillan, 1818.

Edward and Susan; or, The Beauty of Buttermere. London: W. Glendinning, 1803.

Family Quarrels, a comic opera. London: Longman, Hurst, Rees, and Orme, 1805.

Dibdin, Thomas and John Braham. *No More By Sorrow, Pollacca as Sung by Mr. Braham at the Theatre Royal Covent Garden in the Comic Opera of the Cabinet. The Words by T. Dibdin & the Music by I. Braham*. London: printed for J. Dale [*c.* 1809–10].

Dickens, Charles. *Complete Works*, 20 vols. Temple Edition De Luxe. Philadelphia: John D. Morris and Company, 1900.

The Haunted Man (Adelphi, December, 1848). British Library, Lord Chamberlain's Collection (1824–1968). Add. MS 43015, fos. 558–96. Licensed 14 December, 1848.

Diderot, Denis. *Œuvres complètes*, 20 vols. Ed. J. Assézat and M. Tourneaux. Paris: Garnier, 1875–7.

The Paradox of Acting, by Denis Diderot [trans. Walter Herries Pollock] *and Masks or Faces? by William Archer*. Introduction by Lee Strasberg. New York: Hill and Wang, 1957.

Paradoxe sur le comédien, avec recueilles et présentées sur l'art du comédien. Ed. Marc Blanquet. Paris: Librairie Théatrale, 1958.

Donohue, Joseph W., Jr. *Dramatic Character in the English Romantic Age*. Princeton: Princeton University Press, 1970.

Doran, John. "Charles Farley," *Notes and Queries*, s. 2–VII, no. 164 (1859): 143–4.

"Their Majesties' Servants," Annals of the English Stage, from Thomas Betterton to Edmund Kean, 2 vols. New York: W. J. Widdleton, 1865.

Dorset, St. John [= Hugo John Belfour and George Stephens], *The Vampire*. London: C. & J. Ollier, 1821.

Douglas, William. "Mrs Webb," *Notes and Queries*, s. 9–i, no. 10 (1898): 192–3.

Douglass, Paul. *Lady Caroline Lamb: A Biography*. Houndmills, Basingstoke: Palgrave 2004.

Drake, Wilfred. "Knight of the Tower and Sword," *Notes and Queries* CLII (March 12, 1927): 192.

Dramatic Magazine, embellished with numerous engravings of the principal performers. v. 1–3: no.3 (March, 1829–April, 1831). Original in Yale University

Library. University microfilms, Ann Arbor, Michigan. English literary periodicals (75E, reel 1).

Dryden, John. *The Satires of Dryden: Absalom and Achitophel, The Medal, Mac Flecknoe.* Ed. John Churton Collins. London: Macmillan, 1905.

Dumaniant, Antoine-Jean. *Guerre ouverte; ou, Ruse contre ruse.* Paris: Cailleau, 1787.

Dunlap, William. *Blue Beard; or, Female Curiosity: A Dramatic Romance, in Three Acts by G. Colman, the younger; as altered for the New York theatre, with additional songs, by W. Dunlap.* New York: David Longworth, 1806; 2nd edn. 1811.

Wild-Goose Chace: A Play, in Four Acts. With Songs. From the German of Augustus Von Kotzebue. With Notes Marking the Variations from the Original. New York: G. F. Hopkins, 1800.

Duval, Alexandre. *La jeunesse du duc de Richelieu ou Le Lovelace français, comédie en prose et en 5 actes; présentée, pour la 1. fois, au Théâtre de la République, en nivôse, an V [1796].* Paris: Barba, 1797.

Eaton, Charlotte [Waldie]. *At Home and Abroad; or, Memoirs of Emily de Cardonnell,* 3 vols. London: John Murray, 1831.

Continental Adventures, 3 vols. London: Hurst, Robinson, 1826.

The Days of Battle. London: Bohn, 1853.

Narrative of a Residence in Belgium, during the Campaign of 1815. London: John Murray, 1817.

Rome in the Nineteenth. Century, 3 vols. Edinburgh: printed by James Ballantyne, for Archibald Constable, 1820.

Vittoria Colonna: a tale of Rome, in the nineteenth century, 3 vols. Edinburgh, W. Blackwood; London: T. Cadell, 1827.

Waterloo Days. London: George Bell, 1888.

Ekman, Paul. *Telling Lies: Clues to Deceit in the Marketplace, Politics, and Marriage.* New York: W. W. Norton, 1992.

Ellis, Kate Ferguson. *The Contested Castle: Gothic Novels and the Subdivision of Domestic Ideology.* Urbana: University of Illinois Press, 1989.

Eltis, Sos. "Corruption of the Blood and Degeneration of the Race: Dracula and Policing the Borders of Gender," in Bram Stoker, *Dracula.* Ed. John Paul Riquelme. New York: Palgrave, 2002, pp. 450–65.

Engel, Johann Jakob. *Ideen zu einer Mimik,* 2 vols. Berlin: August Mylius, 1785–6.

Über Handlung, Gespräch und Erzählung. Facsimile rpt. of 1st edn. (1774): *Neuen Bibliothek der schönen Wissenschaften und der freyen Künste,* Ed. E. T. Voss. Stuttgart: Metzler, 1964.

Engels, Friedrich. *Der Ursprung der Familie,* in Karl Marx and Friedrich Engels, *Werke,* 39 vols. [Vols. 1–26: *Works*; Vols. 27–39: *Correspondence.*] Vol. XXI. Berlin: Dietz, 1957–68.

Etherege, George. *Comical Revenge: or, Love in a Tub, acted at His Highness the Duke of York's Theatre in Lincolns-Inn-Fields.* London: printed for Henry Herringman, 1664.

Ewen, Frederic. *The Prestige of Schiller in England: 1788–1859*. New York: Columbia University Press, 1932.

Exquemelin, Alexander. *The Buccaneers of America* [1678], trans. Alexis Brown. Harmondsworth: Penguin, 1969; rpt. Mineola, NY: Dover Publications, Inc., 2000.

Farquhar, George. *The Beaux' Stratagem, a comedy; as it is acted at the Queen's theatre in the Hay-market; by Her Majesty's sworn comedians*. London: Printed for Bernard Lintott, 1707.

Fast, Julius. *Body Language in the Workplace*. New York: Penguin, 1994.

Body Language of Sex, Power, and Aggression. New York: M. Evans, 1977.

Fauré, Michel. *Les frères Montgolfier et la conquête de l'air*. Aix-en-Provence: Edisud, 1983.

Fenner, Theodore. *Opera in London: Views of the Press, 1785–1830*. Carbondale: Southern Illinois University Press, 1994.

Finkel, Alicia. *Romantic Stages: Set and Costume Design in Victorian England*. Jefferson, NC and London: McFarland & Company, 1996.

Fiske, Roger. *English Theatre Music in the Eighteenth Century*. Oxford: Oxford University Press, 1986.

"The Operas of Stephen Storace," *Journal of the Royal Musical Association* 86(1) (1959): 29–44.

Fitzball, Edward. *The Flying Dutchman. Printed from the acting copy, with remarks biographical and critical, by D.-G.* [= George Daniel, 1789–1864, of Canonbury Square]: *To which are added, a description of the costume, – cast of the characters, – entrances and exits, – relative positions of the performers on the stage, – and the whole of the stage business. As now performed at the Adelphi Theatre*. London: John Cumberland, 1829.

Thalaba, the destroyer a melo-drama in three acts. London: John Lowndes, 1826.

Thirty-Five Years of a Dramatic Author's Life, 2 vols. London: T. C. Newby, 1859.

Fitzball, Edward and George Herbert Rodwell. *The Devil's Elixir; or, The Shadowless Man, a musical romance in two acts*. London: J. Cumberland, 1829.

Follen, Eliza Lee Cabot. "Blue Beard. Charade. In Two Syllables, and Three Scenes," in *Home Dramas for Young People*. Boston: James Munroe & Company, 1859.

Foote, Horace. *Companion to the Theatres; and Manual of the British Drama*. London: printed for Edward Philip Sanger, 1829.

Forbes, Derek. "Water Drama," *Performance and Politics in Popular Drama: Aspects of Popular Entertainment in Theatre, Film and Television 1800–1976*. Ed. David Bradby, Louis James, and Bernard Sharratt. Cambridge: Cambridge University Press, 1980, pp. 91–107.

Ford, Susan Allen. "'It Is about Lovers' Vows': Kotzebue, Inchbald, and the Players of Mansfield Park," *Persuasions: The Jane Austen Journal On-Line* 27(1) (Winter, 2006), www.jasna.org/persuasions/on-line/vol27no1/index. html.

Forster; Edward. *The Arabian Nights*, 5 vols. Translated from the French of Antoine Galland; illustrated by Robert Smirke [24 engravings]. London: printed for W. Miller, by W. Bulmer and Co., 1802.

Fort, Garrett. *Dracula*. Screenplay, filmed at Universal Studios, 1931. Produced by Carl Laemmle, Jr. and Tod Browning; directed by Tod Browning, with Bela Lugosi in the title role. Based on the novel by Bram Stoker (1897) and the stage play by Hamilton Deane and John L. Balderston.

Foster, Annetta. "The Place of the Theater and Drama in the Life of the Marquis de Sade," Ph.D. dissertation. University of California, 1975.

Foucault, Michel. *Discipline and Punish: The Birth of the Prison* [*Surveiller et punir: naissance de la prison* (Paris: Gallimard, 1975)], trans. Alan Sheridan. New York: Vintage, 1995.

Franklin, Caroline. "The Influence of Madame de Staël's Account of Goethe's *Die Braut von Korinth* in *De l'Allemagne* on the Heroine of Byron's *Siege of Corinth*," *Notes and Queries* 35(3) (1988): 307–10.

Frayling, Christopher *The Vampyre: Lord Ruthven to Count Dracula*. London: Gollancz, 1978.

Frenzel, Elisabeth. *Motive der Weltliteratur: ein Lexikon dichtungsgeschichtlicher Längsschnitte*, Kröners Taschenausgabe 300. Stuttgart: A. Kröner, 1998.

Freud, Sigmund. *Psychologische Schriften*. Ed. Alexander Mitscherlich, Angela Richards, and James Strachey. Frankfurt-am-Main: Fischer Verlag, 1970.

Friedland, Paul. *Political Actors: Representative Bodies and Theatricality in the Age of the French Revolution*. New York: Cornell University Press, 2002.

Fry, Carrol L. "Fictional Connections and Sexuality in *Dracula*," *Victorian Newsletter* 42 (Fall, 1972): 20–2.

Gabory, Emile. *Alias Bluebeard*, trans. Alvah Bessie. New York: Brewer & Warren, 1930.

La vie et la mort de Gilles de Raiz dit – à tort – Barbebleue. Paris: Perrin, 1926.

Gagnier, Regenia. "Evolution and Information; or, Eroticism and Everyday Life, in *Dracula* and Late Victorian Aestheticism," in *Sex and Death in Victorian Literature*. Ed. Regina Barreca. Bloomington: Indiana University Press, 1990, pp. 140–57.

Galignani, Giovanni Antonio, ed. *Messenger*. Paris: A. and W. Galignani, 1814–46.

Galland, Antoine. *Arabian nights entertainments: being a collection of stories, told by the Sultaness of the Indies to divert the Sultan from the execution of a bloody vow he had made to marry a lady every day, and have her head cut off next morning, to avenge himself for the disloyalty of the first Sultaness: Containing a better account of the customs, manners, and religion of the Eastern nations, viz. Tartars, Persians, and Indians, than hitherto published. Translated into French from the Arabian mss. by M. Galland, of the Royal Academy; and now done in English from the Paris edition*. London: printed for T. N. Longman, 1798.

Les Mille et une nuits, contes arabes, 12 vols. Paris: chez la veuve de Claude Barbin, 1704–17.

Garrick, David. *Isabella*, adapted from Thomas Southerne, *The Fatal Marriage* (1694). London: printed for J. and R. Tonson, 1758.

Private Correspondence of David Garrick, with most celebrated persons of his time. London: H. Colburn and R. Bentley, 1831–2.

Gay, Penelope. "Theatricals and Theatricality in *Mansfield Park*," *Sydney Studies in English* 13 (1987): 61–73.

Genest, John. *Some account of the English Stage: from the Restoration in 1660 to 1830*, 10 vols. Bath: H. E. Carrington, 1832.

Genlis, Stéphanie Félicité, Comtesse de. *Théâtre de société*, 2 vols. Paris: Chez M. Lambert & F. J. Baudouin, impr.-librairies, 1781.

Zélie ou l'ingénue. Paris: M. Lambert & F. J. Baudouin, 1781.

Gilbert, William Schwenck. *The Wedding March (Le chapeau de paille d'Italie), an Eccentricity in Three Acts*. London, New York: S. French, 1873.

Girdham, Jane. *English Opera in Late Eighteenth-Century London: Stephen Storace at Drury Lane*. Oxford: Clarendon Press; New York: Oxford University Press, 1997.

Goethe, Johann Wolfgang von. *Werke, Weimarer Ausgabe, herausgegeben im Auftrage der Grossherzogin Sophie von Sachsen*, 146 vols. Ed. Gustav von Loeper *et al*. Weimar: H. Böhlau, 1887–1919.

Wilhelm Meisters Lehrjahre. Berlin: Johann Friedrich Unger, 1795–6.

Goldsmith, Netta Murray. *The Worst of Crimes: Homosexuality and the Law in Eighteenth-Century London*. Aldershot: Ashgate, 1998.

Gottsched, Johann Christoph. *Versuch einer critischen Dichtkunst*. Leipzig, 1730; rpt. Darmstadt: Wissenschaftliche Buchgesellschaft, 1977.

Graves, Richard. "The Comic Operas of Stephen Storace," *The Musical Times* 95(1340) (October, 1954): 530–2.

Greene, John C. *Theatre in Belfast, 1736–1800*. Bethlehem, PA: Lehigh University Press, 2000.

Grétry, André. *Raoul, Barbe-Bleue*. Paris: Chez l'auteur, 1789.

Grimaldi, Joseph. *The Memoirs of Joseph Grimaldi*, 2 vols. Ed. "Boz" [Charles Dickens]. London: R. Bentley, 1838.

Grimm, Jacob and Wilhelm. *Kinder- und Hausmärchen*. Berlin: in der Real-schulbuchhandlung, 1812, 1815; facsimile rpt. Ed. Ulrike Marquardt and Heinz Rölleke. Göttingen: Vandenhoeck & Ruprecht, 1986.

Günzel, Klaus, ed. *König der Romantik. Das Leben des Dichters Ludwig Tieck in Briefen, Selbstzeugnissen und Berichten*. Tübingen: Wunderlich, 1891.

Gutberlet, Bernd Ingmar. *Irrtümer und Legenden der deutschen Geschichte*. Hamburg: Europa Verlag, 2002.

Hamilton, Joan. "*Inkle and Yarico* and the Discourse of Slavery," *Restoration and Eighteenth-Century Theatre Research* 9(1) (Summer, 1994): 17–33.

Hamm-Ehsani, Karin. "Ex Oriente Lux: Cosmopolitics of Orientalism in Ludwig Tieck's Play *Alla-Moddin*," *Acta Germanica: German Studies in Africa* 32 (2004): 27–41.

Handley, Ellenor and Martin Kinna. *Royal Opera House Covent Garden: A History from 1732*. West Wickham: Fourlance Books, 1978.

Hargreaves-Mawdsley, W. N. *The English Della Cruscans and Their Time, 1783–1828*. The Hague: Martinus Nijhoff, 1967.

Harley, George Davies. *An Authentic Biographical Sketch of the Life, Education, and personal Character of William Henry West Betty: the celebrated Young Roscius.* London: printed for Richard Phillips, T. Gillet, 1804.

Hauger, George. "William Shield," *Music & Letters* 31(4) (October, 1950): 337–42.

Hayter, Alethea. "Coleridge, Maturin's *Bertram*, and Drury Lane," in *New Approaches to Coleridge: Biographical and Critical Essays.* Ed. Donald Sultana. London: Vision, 1981, pp. 17–37.

Hazelton, Nancy J. Doran. *Historical Consciousness in Nineteenth-Century Shakespearean Staging.* Ann Arbor: UMI Research Press, 1987.

Hazlitt, William. *The Complete Works of William Hazlitt,* 21 vols. Ed. P. P. Howe, after the edition of A. R. Waller and Arnold Glover. London, Toronto: J. M. Dent and Sons, Ltd., 1930–4.

"On Play-going and On Some of Our Old Actors," No. 1, *London Magazine* (January, 1820), in *Hazlitt on Theatre* [selections from *A View of the English Stage,* and *Criticisms and Dramatic Essays*]. Ed. William Archer and Robert Lowe. Introduction by William Archer. New York: Hill and Wang, 1957.

Hebbel, Friedrich. "Ein Stern in Menschengestalt" [1853], in *König der Romantik. Das Leben des Dichters Ludwig Tieck in Briefen, Selbstzeugnissen und Berichten.* Ed. Klaus Günzel. Tübingen: Wunderlich, 1891, pp. 462–5.

Heber, Reginald. *Europe: lines on the present war.* London: printed for J. Hatchard, bookseller to Her Majesty, 1809.

Europe: Lines on the Present War; Palestine: With the Passage of the Red Sea. Rpt. with introduction by Donald H. Reiman. New York: Garland, 1978.

The Lay of the Purple Falcon. London: Longman, Hurst, Rees, and Orme; J. Hatchard, 1812.

The Life of Reginald Heber, D.D., Lord Bishop of Calcutta: with selections from his correspondence, unpublished poems, and private papers; together with a Journal of his tour in Norway, Sweden, Russia, Hungary, and Germany, and a History of the Cossacks. Ed. Amelia Heber. London: John Murray, 1830.

Narrative of a journey through the upper provinces of India: from Calcutta to Bombay, 1824–1825, (with notes upon Ceylon,) an account of a journey to Madras and the southern provinces, 1826, and letters written in India. Ed. Amelia Heber. London: John Murray, 1828; 2nd edn. 1843–4.

Palestine, a Prize Poem. Oxford: S. Collingwood, 1803.

Palestine, a poem, recited in the theatre, Oxford, 1803. To which is added, The passage of the Red Sea. A fragment. London: Longman, Hurst, Rees, and Orme; J. Hatchard, 1809.

Personality and office of the Christian comforter: asserted and explained: in a course of sermons on John XVI, 7; *preached before the University of Oxford, in the year* MDCCCXV, *at the lecture founded by the Late Rev. John Bampton.* London: printed for J. Hatchard, 1818.

Poems and Translations. London: printed for Longman, Hurst, Rees, Orme, and Brown, 1812.

The Poetical Works of Reginald Heber. London: John Murray, 1841; 2nd edn. 1875.

The whole works of the Right Rev. Jeremy Taylor, with a life of the author, and a critical examination of his writings. London: Longman, Orme, Brown, Green, and Longmans, 1839.

Heilman, Robert B. "Some Fops and Some Versions of Foppery." *ELH* 49(2) (Summer, 1982): 363–95.

Hemans, Felicia. *Siege of Valencia, a dramatic poem; The last Constantine: with other poems.* London: John Murray, 1823.

Hemmings, F. W. J. "Co-authorship in French Plays of the Nineteenth Century," *French Studies: A Quarterly Review* 41(1) (Winter, 1987): 37–51.

Henderson, Tony. *Disorderly Women in Eighteenth-Century London: Prostitution and Control in the Metropolis, 1730–1830.* London: Longman, 1999.

Hereford Journal (September 25, 1801). Available at http://newspaperarchive.com.

Hindley, Charles. *Curiosities of Street Literature, comprising "cocks," or "catch pennies": a large and curious assortment of street-drolleries, squibs, histories, comic tales in prose and verse, broadsides on the royal family, political litanies, dialogues, catechisms, acts of Parliament, street political papers, a variety of "ballads on a subject," dying speeches and confessions.* London: Reeves and Turner, 1871.

Hoare, Prince. "Mahmoud." Huntington Library, MS Larpent 1126. Application for license dated April 27, 1796; first performed Drury Lane, April 30, 1796; cf. MacMillan, *Catalogue of the Larpent Plays.*

Hobson, Marian. *The Object of Art: The Theory of Illusion in Eighteenth-Century France.* Cambridge: Cambridge University Press, 1982.

Hoffmann, Ernst Theodor Wilhelm [Amadeus]. *Die Elixiere des Teufels. Nachgelassene Papiere des Bruders Medardus, eines Kapuziners,* 2 vols. Berlin: [s.n.], 1815–16.

Poetische Werke, 6 vols. Berlin: Aufbau-Verlag, 1958.

Hoffmann, François Benoît. *Le secret, comédie en un acte et en prose, mêlée de musique. Représentée sur le Théâtre de l'opéra-comique, ci-devant théâtre italien, le premier Floréal, l'an iv (20 avril 1796, vieux style).* Music by Jean Baptiste Soulier. Paris: Vente, 1803.

Holcroft, Thomas. *Deaf And Dumb; or, The Abbé de l'Épée, an historical play in five acts.* London: printed by C. Whittingham for T. N. Longman and O. Rees, 1801.

Memoirs of the late Thomas Holcroft, written by Himself and continued down to the Time of his Death, from his Diary, Notes and other Papers. Ed. William Hazlitt. London: printed for Longman, Hurst, Rees, Orme and Brown, 1816.

The Road to Ruin: A comedy. As it is acted at the Theatre Royal, Covent-Garden. London: printed for J. Debrett [etc.], 1792.

A Tale of Mystery, a Melo-drame; as performed at the Theatre-Royal Covent Garden. 2nd edn. London: R. Phillips, 1802.

Holden, Anthony. *The Man who Wrote Mozart: The Extraordinary Life of Lorenzo Da Ponte.* London: Weidenfeld & Nicolson, 2006.

Holland, Patrick. "'The Present State of the Stage': Coleridge's Diabolization of C. R. Maturin's *Bertram.*" *Essays in Theatre/Etudes Théâtrales* 18(2) (May, 2000): 119–29.

Home, John. *Siege of Aquileia, a tragedy: As it is acted at the Theatre-Royal, in Drury-Lane.* London: Printed for A. Millar, 1760.

Howard, Jean E. "Crossdressing, the Theatre, and Gender Struggle in Early Modern England," *Shakespeare Quarterly* 39(4) (Winter, 1988): 418–40.

Howarth, W. D. "The Theme of the 'Droit du Seigneur' in Eighteenth-Century Theatre," *French Studies* 15(3) (1961): 228–40.

Hugo, Victor. *Dramatic Works of Victor Hugo.* Ed. George Burnham Ives, 3 vols. Boston: Little, Brown, 1909.

    Oeuvres dramatiques et critiques complètes. Ed. Francis Bouvet. Paris: Jean-Jacques Pauvert, 1963.

Humble, Malcolm. "Liberty and/or Equality: The Theme of the French Revolution in German Literature of the Twentieth Century," *Forum for Modern Language Studies* 25(3) (Summer, 1989): 191–208.

Hunt, Leigh. *Critical Essays on the Performers of the London Theatres including general observations on the practise and genius of the stage.* London: printed by and for John Hunt, 1807.

    Leigh Hunt's Dramatic Criticism, 1808–1831. Ed. Lawrence Huston Houtchens and Carolyn Washburn Houtchens. New York: Columbia University Press, 1949.

    The Selected Writings of Leigh Hunt, 6 vols. Ed. Greg Kucich, Jeffrey N. Cox, Robert Morrison, Charles Mahoney, Michael Eberle-Sinatra, and John Strachan. London and Brookfield, VT: Pickering & Chatto, 2003.

Husk, William H. and Mollie Sands. "Storace, Anna," in *Grove's Dictionary of Music and Musicians.* Ed. Eric Blom, 10 vols. 5th edn. New York: St. Martin's Press, 1961. Vol. VIII, pp. 102–3.

Inchbald, Elizabeth. *The British theatre; or, A collection of plays: which are acted at the Theatres Royal, Drury Lane, Covent Garden, and Haymarket . . . with biographical and critical remarks by Mrs. Inchbald,* 25 vols. London: Longman, Hurst, Rees, and Orme, 1808.

    The Child of Nature. A dramatic piece, in four acts. From the French of Madame the Marchioness of Sillery, formerly Countess of Genlis. Performing at the Theatre Royal, Covent Garden. London: printed for G. G. J. and J. Robinson [etc.], 1788.

    The Plays of Elizabeth Inchbald [Photo-reprint edn. of 21 plays published 1785–1833. Includes bibliographical references], 2 vols. Ed. Paula R. Backscheider. New York: Garland, 1980.

    The Widow's Vow. A Farce, in two acts, as it is acted at the Theatre Royal, Hay-Market. London: printed for C. G. J. and J. Robinson [etc.], 1786.

Irving, Washington. "The Spectre Bridegroom, a Traveller's Tale," in *The Sketch-Book of Geoffrey Crayon Gent* [1819–20]. London: John Murray, 1823.

Jackson, Allan S. "*Pizarro,* Bridges and the Gothic Scene," *Theatre Notebook: A Journal of the History and Technique of the British Theatre* 51(2) (1997): 81–91.

Jackson, Allan S. and John C. Morrow. "Aqua Scenes at Sadler's Wells Theatre, 1804–1824," *Ohio State University Theatre Collection Bulletin* 9 (1962): 22–37.

'Handlist of Aqua-Dramas Produced at Sadler's Wells, 1804–1824,'" *Ohio State University Theatre Collection Bulletin* 9 (1962): 38–47.

Jagemann, Karoline. *Die Erinnerungen der Karoline Jagemann, nebst zahlreichen unveröffentlichten Dokumenten aus der Goethezeit.* Ed. Eduard von Bamberg. Dresden: Sibyllen Verlag, 1926.

Jeffrey, Alexander. *The History and Antiquities of Roxburghshire.* Edinburgh: Thomas C. Jack, 1859.

Jerningham, Edward. *The Siege of Berwick, a Tragedy: as performed at the Theatre-Royal, Covent-Garden* [November 13, 1793]. London: printed for J. Robson, 1794.

Jesse, Captain William. *The Life of Beau Brummell.* London: The Navarre Society Limited, 1927.

Johnson, Edgar. *Sir Walter Scott: The Great Unknown,* 2 vols. New York: Macmillan, 1970.

Jordan, Elaine. "Pulpit, Stage, and Novel: *Mansfield Park* and Mrs. Inchbald's *Lovers' Vows.*" *Novel: A Forum on Fiction* 20(2) (Winter, 1987): 138–48.

Judson, Barbara. "Tragicomedy, Bisexuality, and Byronism; or, Jokes and Their Relation to *Sardanapalus,*" *Texas Studies in Literature and Language* 45(3) (Fall, 2003): 245–61

Kant, Immanuel. *Werke,* 6 vols. Ed. Wilhelm Weischedel. Darmstadt: Wissenschaftliche Buchgesellschaft, 1957.

Keats, John. *The Letters of John Keats,* 2 vols. Ed. Hyder Edward Rollins. Cambridge, MA: Harvard University Press, 1958.

Selected Letters of John Keats. Ed. Grant Scott. Cambridge, MA: Harvard University Press, 2002.

Kelly, Ian. *Beau Brummell: The Ultimate Man of Style.* London: Hodder & Stoughton, 2005.

Kelly, Michael. *The Grand Dramatic Romance of Blue Beard; or, Female Curiosity.* Playbill. London, Edinburgh: printed for Corri, Dussek, & Co. [1798].

Reminiscences of Michael Kelly, of the King's theatre, and Theatre royal Drury lane, including a period of nearly half a century; with original anecdotes of many distinguished persons, political, literary, and musical, 2 vols. London: H. Colburn, 1826.

Kemble, John Philip. *John Philip Kemble Promptbooks,* 11 vols. Ed. Charles H. Shattuck. Charlottesville: published for the Folger Shakespeare Library by the University Press of Virginia, 1974.

Lodoiska; an opera, in three acts, performed, for the first time, by His Majesty's Servants, at the Theatre Royal, Drury-Lane. The Music composed, and selected from Cherubini, Kreutzer, and Andreozzi, by Mr. Storace. London: printed for G. G. and J. Robinson [etc.] [1794].

Kenney, James. *Aladdin and the Wonderful Lamp; or, New Lamps for Old Ones, in Two Acts.* Music by Albert Smith. London: W. S. Johnson, 1844.

The Alcaid; or, The secrets of office; a comic opera in three acts. London: T. Dolby, 1824.

Raising the Wind A Farce, In Two Acts. Printed from the acting copy, with remarks, biographical and critical. To which are added, a description of the costume, – cast of the characters, entrances and exits, – relative positions of the performers on the stage, – and the whole of the stage business. As now performed at the Theatres Royal, London. Embellished with a fine wood engraving, By Mr. Bonner, from a Drawing taken in the Theatre, by Mr. R. Cruikshank. London: John Cumberland [1828].

Sweethearts and wives: a popular comedietta, in two acts. London: J. Dicks, 1823.

Kewes, Paulina. "'[A] play, which I presume to call original': Appropriation, Creative Genius, and Eighteenth-Century Playwriting." *Studies in the Literary Imagination* 34(1) (Spring, 2001): 17–47.

Kingscote, Mrs. Howard and Pandit Natêsá Sástrî. *Tales of the Sun; or, Folklore of Southern India.* London: W. H. Allen and Company, 1890.

Kinservik, Matthew J. *Disciplining Satire: The Censorship of Satiric Comedy on the Eighteenth-Century London Stage.* Lewisburg, PA: Bucknell University Press, 2002.

Knapp, Mark L. and Judith A. Hall. *Nonverbal Communication in Human Interaction.* 6th edn. Belmont, CA: Wadsworth/Thomson Learning, 2006.

Knight, Joseph. *A History of the Stage during the Victorian Era.* London: Spottiswood, 1901; rpt. New York: Garland, 1986.

"Storace, Anna," in *Dictionary of National Biography.* New York: Macmillan; London: Smith Elder & Co., 1899.

Theatrical Notes. London: Lawrence and Bullen, 1893.

"Webb, Mrs. (d. 1793)," in *Dictionary of National Biography,* Vol. LX (Watson–Whewell). New York: Macmillan; London: Smith Elder & Co., 1899, pp. 94–5.

"Wewitzer, Ralph (1748–1825)," in *Dictionary of National Biography,* Vol. LX (Watson–Whewell). New York: Macmillan; London: Smith Elder & Co., 1899, pp. 388–9.

Kotzebue, August von. *Pizarro; a Tragedy in Five Acts; as performed at the Theatre Royal in Drury-Lane; taken from the German Drama of Kotzebue; and adapted to the English Stage by Richard Brinsley Sheridan.* 3rd edn. London: printed for James Ridgway, York Street, St. James's Square, 1799.

Die Sonnenjungfrau: ein Schauspiel in fünf Aufzügen. Leipzig: Paul Gotthelf Kummer, 1791.

Die Spanier in Peru oder Rollas Tod. Ein romantisches Trauerspiel in fünf Akten. Leipzig: Paul Gotthelf Kummer, 1796.

The Stranger. A drama. In five acts. As performed at the Theatre Royal Drury-Lane, in *The German Theatre,* 6 vols. Vol. 1. Trans. Benjamin Thompson. London: printed by J. Wright . . . for Vernor and Hood [etc.], 1801.

The Stranger. Trans. Benjamin Thompson. London: printed by A. Strahan for T. N. Longman & O. Rees, 1802.

Küster, Ulf, ed. *Theatrum mundi: die Welt als Bühne*. Wolfratshausen: Edition Minerva, 2003.

Lamb, Charles. *Life and Works of Charles Lamb*, 12 vols. Ed. Alfred Ainger. Boston, MA: Merrymount Press, 1888.

Lamb, Lady Caroline. *Glenarvon*. 3 vols. London: printed for Henry Colburn, 1816; facsimile rpt. Oxford: Woodstock Books, 1993.

La Motte, M. de [= Antoine Houdar]. *One hundred new court fables, written for the instruction of princes, and a true knowledge of the world . . . With a discourse on fable. By the Sieur de la Motte*. London: printed for E. Curll [etc.], 1721.

Lancaster, Henry Carrington. *French Tragedy in the Reign of Louis XVI and the early years of the French Revolution, 1774–1792*. Baltimore: Johns Hopkins University Press, 1953.

French Tragedy in the Time of Louis XV and Voltaire, 1715–1774. Baltimore: Johns Hopkins University Press, 1950.

Lang, Andrew, ed. *The Blue Fairy Book, with numerous illustrations by H. J. Ford and G. P. Jacomb Hood*. London, New York: Longmans, Green, 1889.

Latude, Henri Masers de. *Mémoire de M. Delatude, ingénieur*. Paris: Gueffier, 1789.

Memoirs of Mr. Henry Masers de La Tude, containing an account of his confinement thirty-five years in the state prisons of France; and of the stratagems he adopted to escape, once from the Bastille, and twice from the Castel of Vincennes; with the sequel of those adventures. London: J. Johnson, 1787.

Memoirs of Henry Masers de Latude during a confinement of thirty-five years in the state prisons of France. Of the means he used to escape once from the Bastile, and twice from the dungeon of Vincennes, with the consequences of those events. London: Logographic Press, 1787.

Memoirs of Henry Masers de Latude during a confinement of thirty-five years in the state prisons of France. Of the means he used to escape once from the Bastile, and twice from the dungeon of Vincennes, with the consequences of those events. London: Robson and Clarke, 1787.

Memoirs of Henry Masers de Latude: who was confined during thirty-five years in the different state prisons of France. Trans. John William Cole. Dublin: printed for W. F. Wakeman; London: Simpkin and Marshall, 1834.

Latude, Henri Masers de and Pierre-Jacques Bonhomme de Comreyras, *Histoire d'une détention de trente-neuf ans, dans les prisons d'Etat*. Amsterdam: n.p., 1787.

Lavater, Johann Caspar. *Physiognomische Fragmente: zur Beförderung der Menschenkenntniss und Menschenliebe*. Leipzig: Weidmanns Erben und Reich; Winterthur: Heinrich Steiner, 1775–80.

Lawrence, W. J. "The Pioneers of Modern English Stage Mounting: Philippe Jacques De Loutherbourg, R.A." *The Magazine of Art* (1895): 172–7.

"The Pioneers of Modern English Stage Mounting: William Capon," *The Magazine of Art* (1895): 289–92.

Lees, Robert, Frederic I. Rinaldo, and John Grant. *Abbott and Costello Meet Frankenstein*. Screenplay. Directed by Charles T. Barton; produced by Robert Arthur. Universal International, 1948.

Lennig, Walter. *Marquis de Sade in Selbstzeugnissen und Bilddokumenten.* Hamburg: Rowohlt, 1965.

Lennox, William Pitt. *Celebrities I Have Known: With Episodes, Political, Social, Sporting, and Theatrical,* 2 vols. London: Hurst and Blackett, 1876.

Lessing, Gotthold Ephraim. *Werke,* 8 vols. Ed. Herbert G. Göpfert, with Karl Eibl *et al.* Munich: Carl Hanser, 1970–9.

Lewis, Matthew Gregory. *The Castle Spectre; a drama in five acts.* London: printed for J. Bell, 1798.

The Monk: A Romance, 3 vols. 2nd edn. London: printed for J. Bell, 1796.

Venoni; or, The Novice of St. Mark's: A Drama, in three acts. London: printed for D. N. Shury . . . for Longman, Hurst, Rees, and Orme [etc.], 1809.

Lewis, Melville. *Beau Brummell: His Life and Letters.* New York: Doran, 1925.

Lightwood, James T. *Charles Dickens and Music.* New York: Haskell House Publishers, 1970.

Lindfors, Bernth. "Ira Aldridge's London Debut," *Theatre Notebook: A Journal of the History and Technique of the British Theatre* 60(1) (2006): 30–44.

Lloyd-Elliott, Martin. *Secrets of Sexual Body Language.* London: Hamlyn, 2005.

Lockhart, John Gibson, *Life of Sir Walter Scott,* 8 vols. Boston: Ticknor and Fields, 1861.

Lockwood, Elisabeth M. "Jane Austen and Some Drawing-Room Music of Her Time," *Music & Letters* 15(2) (April, 1934): 112–19.

Loftis, John. *Sheridan and the Drama of Georgian England.* Cambridge, MA: Harvard University Press, 1977.

Longeville, Harcouet de. *Long livers: A curious history of such persons of both sexes who have liv'd several ages, and grown young again: with the rare secret of rejuvenescency of Arnoldus de Villa Nova, and a great many approv'd and invaluable rules to prolong life: as also, how to prepare the universal medicine.* London: printed for J. Holland at the Bible and Ball in St. Paul's Church-Yard, and L. Stokoe at Charing-Cross, 1722.

Longfellow, Henry Wadsworth. *Hyperion and Kavanaugh.* London: George Routledge and Sons, 1886.

Lopez, John David. "Recovered Voices: The Sources of *The Siege of Valencia*," *European Romantic Review* 17(1) (January, 2006): 69–72.

Mackintosh, Iain. *Architecture, Actor and Audience.* London: Routledge, 1993.

MacMillan, Dougald, comp. *Catalogue of the Larpent Plays in the Huntington Library.* San Marino, CA: Henry E. Huntington Library and Art Gallery, 1939.

MacPherson, James. *The Poems of Ossian.* 2 vols. London: printed for A. Strahan and T. Cadell: And sold by T. Cadell, Jun. and W. Davies, Successors to Mr. Cadell, in the Strand, 1796.

Maffei, Marchese Scipione. *Merope: a tragedy; translated from the original Italian by Mr. Ayre.* London: Sold by J. Chrichley, 1740.

Mahoney, Elisabeth. Review: "The Cenci," *The Guardian* (February 3, 2001).

Mallet, Paul Henri. *Northern antiquities; or, An historical account of the manners, customs, religion and laws, maritime expeditions and discoveries, language and literature of the ancient Scandinavians.* Trans. Bishop Percy, with translation of the Prose Edda, and notes by J. A. Blackwell. Also an Abstract of the 'Eyrbyggia Saga' by Sir Walter Scott (1809). London: H. G. Bohn, 1847.

Mander, Raymond and Joe Mitchenson, "De Loutherbourg and *Pizarro*, 1799," *Theatre Notebook: A Journal of the History and Technique of the British Theatre* 20 (Summer, 1966): 158–66.

Mann, Heinrich. *Madame Legros.* Leipzig: Kurt Wolff, 1913; 2nd edn. 1917.

Mannheimer Zeitung 336 (December 4, 1823); 342 (December 10, 1823).

Marchand, Leslie. *Byron: A Biography,* 3 vols. New York: Knopf, 1957.

Marmontel, Jean-François. *The Incas; or, The destruction of the empire of Peru,* 2 vols. Dublin: printed by A. Stewart, for Price & the Company of booksellers, 1777.

Les Incas, ou la destruction de l'empire du Perou. Liège: Bassompierre, 1777.

Marsden, Jean I. "Modesty Unshackled: Dorothy Jordan and the Dangers of Cross-Dressing." *Studies in Eighteenth-Century Culture* 22 (1992): 21–35.

Marshall, Herbert and Mildred Stock. *Ira Aldridge: The Negro Tragedian.* London: Rockliff, 1958.

Maslan, Susan. *Revolutionary Acts: Theater, Democracy, and the French Revolution.* Baltimore: Johns Hopkins University Press, 2005.

Mason, John. *Kelso Records.* Edinburgh: Peter Brown, 1839.

Massé, Michelle A. *In the Name of Love: Women, Masochism, and the Gothic.* Ithaca, NY: Cornell University Press, 1992.

Mathews, Anne Jackson. *Memoirs of Charles Mathews, Comedian.* 4 vols. London: R. Bentley, 1838.

Maturin, Charles Robert. *Bertram; or, The Castle of St. Aldobrand.* London: John Murray, 1816.

Bertram; or, The Castle of St. Aldobrand, in *Seven Gothic Dramas.* Ed. Jeffrey N. Cox. Athens, OH: Ohio University Press, 1991, pp. 315–84.

McDonald, D. L. *Poor Polidori: A Critical Biography of the Author of "The Vampyre."* Toronto: University of Toronto Press, 1991.

McFarland, Thomas. *Romanticism and the Forms of Ruin: Wordsworth, Coleridge, and Modalities of Fragmentation.* Princeton: Princeton University Press, 1981.

McKee, Alexander. *Death Raft: The Human Drama of the Medusa Shipwreck.* New York: Scribner, 1976.

Meier, Ernst. *Deutsche Volksmärchen aus Schwaben.* Stuttgart: C. P. Scheitlin's Verlagshandlung, 1852.

Mercier, Louis-Sébastien. *L'Indigent: drame en quatre actes, en prose.* Paris: Chez Lejay, 1772.

Merrill, Lisa. *When Romeo Was a Woman.* Ann Arbor: University of Michigan Press, 1999.

Metzger, Lore. *The Role of Feeling in the Formation of Romantic Ideology: The Poetics of Schiller and Wordsworth.* Rutherford: Fairleigh Dickinson University Press, 1990.

Moncrieff, William Thomas. *The Cataract of the Ganges! or, The Rajah's Daughter, a grand romantic melo-drama in two acts.* London: Simpkin & Marshall, 1823.

Giovanni in London: or the Libertine Reclaimed, A Grand Moral, Satirical, Comical, Tragical, Melo-Dramatical, Pantomimical, Critical, Infernal, Terrestrial, Celestial, in one word for all, Gallymaufrical-ollapodridacal Operatic Extravaganza, in Two Acts, as performed at the Theatres Royal Drury Lane and Covent Garden. The Music Selected and Adapted by the Author of the Piece. Rev. edn. London: W. T. Moncrieff, 1825.

An Original Collection of Songs, sung at the theatres royal, public concerts &c. &c. London: John Duncombe, 1850.

The Secret; or, The Hole in the Wall. London, J. Cumberland & Son, 1823.

Selections from the dramatic works of William T. Moncrieff. Chosen for their extreme popularity from between two and three hundred dramas, &c. produced and performed at the Theatres Royal, Drury Lane, Covent Garden, the Haymarket. 3 vols. London: H. Lacy, 1851.

Shipwreck of the Medusa; or, The Fatal Raft!: a drama, in three acts. London: T. Richardson, 1830.

The Spectre Bridegroom; or, A Ghost in Spite of Himself. A Farce, in Two Acts. First performed at the Theatre Royal, Drury Lane. Monday, July 2, 1821. London: printed by J. Tabby, 1821.

Tom and Jerry: or, Life in London: an operatic extravaganza, in three acts, founded on Pierce Egan's well-known and highly popular work of the same name. London: printed for John Lowndes, by S. G. Fairbrother, 1821.

The Vampire, a drama in three acts. London: T. Richardson, 1829.

Monthly Mirror (December, 1797). London: printed for the proprietors, 1795–1811.

Moore, Edward. *The Gamester. A Tragedy. As it is acted at the Theatre-Royal in Drury-Lane.* London: R. Francklin [etc.], 1753.

Moore, Thomas. *The Poetical Works of Thomas Moore as corrected by himself in 1843; to which is added, an original memoir, by M[ary] Balmanno.* 2 vols. in 1. New York: D. & J. Sadlier, 1852.

Morell, Sir Charles [= James Ridley]. *The Tales of the Genii,* 2 vols. London: printed for J. Wilkie, 1764; London: printed for James Wallis ... by Thomas Davison, 1805.

Morwood, James and David Crane, eds. *Sheridan Studies.* Cambridge: Cambridge University Press, 1995.

Nathan, Isaac. *The Alcaid; or, The secrets of office; a comic opera in three acts.* London: T. Dolby, 1824.

Songs, duets, chorusses, &c. &c. in the new operatic comedy of Sweethearts & wives. London: J. Miller, 1823.

Nathan, Isaac and Lord Byron, *A Selection of Hebrew Melodies, Ancient and Modern.* Ed. Frederick Burwick and Paul Douglass. Tuscaloosa: University of Alabama Press, 1988.

Nicoll, Allardyce. *A History of English Drama, 1660–1900*, 6 vols. Vol. IV: *Early Nineteenth-Century Drama, 1800–1850*. Cambridge: Cambridge University Press, 1965–7.

Nierenberg, Gerald I. and Henry H. Calero. *How to Read a Person like a Book*. New York: Cornerstone Library, 1980.

Nodier, Charles, Achille Jouffrey, and Pierre Carmouche. *Le Vampire: mélodrame en trois actes, avec un prologue; représenté, pour la première fois, à Paris, sur le théâtre de la Porte-Saint-Martin, le 13 juin 1820*. Paris: Barba, 1820.

O'Keefe, John. *Aladdin; or, The Wonderful Lamp*. Music by William Shield. Covent Garden, December 26, 1788. First published in Hannah Brand, *Plays and Poems*. Norwich: printed by Beatniffe and Payne, 1798).

Recollections of the life of John O'Keeffe, written by himself, 2 vols. London: H. Coburn, 1826; rpt. New York: B. Blom, 1969.

Oliver, Anthony and John Saunders, "De Loutherbourg and *Pizarro*, 1799," *Theatre Notebook: A Journal of the History and Technique of the British Theatre* 20 (Fall, 1965): 30–2.

O'Neill, Daniel I. *The Burke–Wollstonecraft Debate: Savagery, Civilization, and Democracy*. University Park, PA: Penn State University Press, 2007.

O'Quinn, Daniel. "Mercantile Deformities: George Colman's *Inkle and Yarico* and the Racialization of Class Relations," *Theatre Journal* 54(3) (Fall, 2002): 389–409.

Staging Governance: Theatrical Imperialism in London, 1770–1800. Baltimore: Johns Hopkins University Press, 2005.

Orwell, George. *1984: A Novel*. New York: New American Library, 1950.

Ottenberg, Hans-Günter. *Die Entwicklung des theoretisch- ästhetischen Denkens innerhalb der Berliner Musikkultur von den Anfängen der Aufklärung bis Reichardt*. Leipzig: VEB Deutscher Verlag für Musik, 1978.

Otway, Thomas. *Venice Preserv'd* [1682]. London: printed for J. Miller, 1814.

Oulton, Walley Chamberlaine. *The Happy Disguise; or, Love in a Meadow* [Capel Street, Dublin, January 7, 1784]. N.p.

The Irish Tar; or, Which is the Girl? Huntington Library, MS Larpent 1178. Application for license dated August 18, 1797; first produced August 24, 1797, at the Little Theatre, Haymarket. George Colman the Younger: manager. Dated by Larpent August 19; cf. MacMillan, *Catalogue of the Larpent Plays*.

My Landlady's Gown: a farce, in two acts [Haymarket, August 10, 1816]. London: printed for W. Simpkin and R. Marshall, 1816.

The Sleep-Walker; or, Which is the Lady? London: printed by and for J. Roach, 1812.

Page, Judith W. "'Hath not a jew eyes?': Edmund Kean and the Sympathetic Shylock," *Wordsworth Circle* 34(2) (Spring, 2003): 116–19.

Pape, Walter and Frederick Burwick, eds. *The Boydell Shakespeare Gallery*. Bottrop: Peter Pomp, 1996.

Patrat, Joseph. *L'Anglois; ou, Le fou raisonnable: comédie en un acte et en prose*. Paris: Au bureau de la Petite bibliothèque des théâtres, 1784.

L'heureuse erreur. Toulouse: Broulhiet, 1783.

Payne, John Howard. *Adeline, the Victim of Seduction: A Melo-Dramatic Serious Drama, in Three Acts: Altered from the French of Monsieur R. C. Guilbert Pixérécourt, and Adapted to the English Stage. First Performed at the Theatre Royal, Drury Lane, Saturday Evening, February 9, 1822.* London: J. Tabby, 1822.

————. *Richelieu: A Domestic Tragedy, Founded on Fact: As Accepted for Performance at the Theatre Royal, Covent Garden, London; Before it Was Altered by Order of the Lord Chamberlain, and Produced Under a New Name. In Five Acts. Now First Printed from the Author's Manuscript.* New York: E. M. Murden, 1826.

Peacock, Thomas Love. *The Works of Thomas Love Peacock,* 10 vols. Ed. H. F. B. Brett-Smith and C. E. Jones. Rpt. of the Halliford edition, 1924–34. New York: AMS Press, 1967.

Peake, Richard Brinsley. *Duel, or, My Two Nephews: a farce in two acts* [first performed on Tuesday, February 18, 1823, at the Theatre Royal, Covent Garden]. London: Printed for John Miller, 1823.

————. *Master's Rival; or, A day at Boulogne a farce in two acts.* Adapted from Alain René Le Sage, *Crispin rival de son maître,* with a Preface by George Daniel. London: John Cumberland, 1830.

————. *Presumption, or the Fate of Frankenstein* [English Opera House, July 28, 1823]. London: J. Duncombe, 1824.

Peck, Louis F. *A Life of Matthew G. Lewis.* Cambridge, MA: Harvard University Press, 1961.

Percec, Dana. "Transvestism as Bricolage: A Reading of Shakespeare's *Twelfth Night* and *As You Like It,*" *BAS: British and American Studies/Revista de Studii Britanice si Americane* 9 (2003): 7–13.

Perrault, Charles. *Bluebeard, or the Fatal Effects of Curiosity and Disobedience.* London: printed and sold by J. Pitts, 14, Great St. Andrew-street, Seven Dials, 1808.

————. *Histoires ou contes du temps passé avec des moralités* [*Les contes de ma mère l'oye*] [Paris: Claude Barbin, 1697]; facsimile rpt. with preface by Jacques Barchilon. Geneva: Slatkine Reprints, 1980.

————. *Perrault's Fairy Tales.* Translation of verse morals by S. T. Littlewood. London: Herbert & Daniel, 1912.

————. *The original Mother Goose Melody.* Ed. William H. Whitmore. London: Damrell & Upham, 1892.

Philp, Mark, ed. *Resisting Napoleon: The British Response to the Threat of Invasion, 1797–1815.* Aldershot: Ashgate, 2006.

Piozzi, Hester Lynch. *Love Letters of Mrs. Piozzi, Written When She Was Eighty to William Augustus Conway.* London: John Russell Smith, 1843.

Pixérécourt, Guilbert. *Valentine, ou la séduction, mélodrame en trois actes.* Paris: J. N. Barba, 1822.

Planché, James Robinson. *Blue Beard: an extravaganza.* London: S. G. Fairbrother, 1839.

The Extravaganzas of J. R. Planché, Esq. (Somerset Herald) 1825–1871. 5 vols. Ed. T. F. Dillon Croker and Stephen Tucker. London: Samuel French, 1879.

The Frozen Lake [English Opera House, September 3, 1824]. Adapted from E. Scribe and G. Delavigne, *La neige*. Music by Daniel Auber. London: [s.n.], 1824.

The Recollections and Reflections of J. R. Planché, (Somerset herald). A professional autobiography, 2 vols. London: Tinsley Brothers, 1872.

Songs, duets, glees, chorusses, &c in the new, operatic burlesque burletta entitled, Giovanni the vampire!!! or, How shall we get rid of him? with the whole of the introductory Vision (performed at the Adelphi theatre . . . Jan 15th, 1821). London: printed for John Lowndes, 1821.

The Vampire; or, The Bride of the Isles. A Romantic Melo-Drama, in two acts: preceded by an introductory Vision (performed at the Theatre Royal English Opera House, August 9th, 1820), in *Plays*. Ed. Donald Roy. Cambridge: Cambridge University Press, 1986.

A Woman Never Vext, or, The Widow of Cornhill [Covent Garden, November 9, 1824]. Adapted from William Rowley, *A New Wonder, a Woman Never Vext* (1632). London: Dolby, 1824.

Plumptre, Anne. *The Virgin of the Sun, a play in five acts*. London: printed for R. Phillips, 1799.

[Polidori, John]. *The Vampyr; A Tale*. London: printed for Sherwood, Neely, and Jones, Paternoster-Row, 1819.

Pollin, Burton R. "'The Spectacles' of Poe – Sources and Significance," *American Literature: A Journal of Literary History, Criticism, and Bibliography* 37 (1965): 185–90.

Poole, John. *Simpson And Co. A comedy, in two acts. As Performed At The Theatre Royal, Drury Lane*. London: printed by J. Tabby . . . published by Mr. Miller, 1823.

'Twould Puzzle a Conjuror! A comic drama, in two acts. London: Thomas Hailes Lacy [1824].

Praz, Mario, *The Romantic Agony* [*La carne, la morte e il diavolo nella letteratura romantica*. Milan, Rome: Soc. Editrice "La Cultura," 1930]. Trans. Angus Davidson. London: Oxford University Press, 1933; 2nd edn. 1951.

Purinton, Marjean D. "George Colman's *The Iron Chest* and *Blue-Beard* and the Pseudoscience of Curiosity Cabinets," *Victorian Studies* 49(2) (2007): 250–7.

Quétel, Claude. *Escape from the Bastille: The Life and Legend of Latude* [*Les évasions de Latude*, 1986]. Trans. Christopher Sharp. New York: St. Martin's, 1990.

Quilliam, Susan. *Body Language Secrets: Read the Signals and Find Love, Wealth and Happiness*. London: Thorsons, 1997.

Rabenalt, Arthur Maria. *Theatrum sadicum. Der Marquis de Sade und das Theater*. Emsdetten: Verlag Lechte, 1963.

Raker, R. J. "Liston, John (*c.* 1776–1846)," in *Encyclopaedia Britannica*, 29 vols. New York: The Encyclopaedia Britannica Co., 1910–11. Vol. xvi, p. 780.

Ranger, Paul. *"Terror and Pity Reign in Every Breast": Gothic Drama in the London Patent Theatres, 1750–1820.* London: Society for Theatre Research, 1991.

Raymond, Richard John. *The Castle of Paluzzi; or, the Extorted Oath.* London: W. Sams, 1818.

The Old Oak Tree. London: J. Duncombe, 1835.

The State Prisoner. London: W. Sams, 1819.

Rees, Terence. *Theatre Lighting in the Age of Gas.* London: The Society for Theatre Research, 1978.

Reeve, William. *Blue Beard, or, The Flight of Harlequn.* Huntington Library, MS Larpent 923. Application for license dated December 19, 1791; first produced December 21, 1791, at Covent Garden Theatre; cf. MacMillan, *Catalogue of the Larpent Plays.*

Remy, Alfred, ed. *Baker's Biographical Dictionary of Musicians.* 3rd edn., revised and enlarged. New York: G. Schirmer, 1919.

Reynolds, Frederic. *The Blind Bargain; or, Hear It Out; a comedy, in five acts. As performed at the Theatre-Royal, Covent-Garden.* London: printed for Longman, Hurst, Rees, and Orme, 1805.

Delays and Blunders: A comedy, in Five Acts. As performed at the Theatre-Royal, Covent-Garden. London: printed by A. Strahan . . . for T. N. Longman and O. Rees, 1803.

Notoriety: a comedy. Dublin: printed by P. Byend, 1792.

The Virgin of the Sun, an Operatic Drama. London: printed for C. Chapple, 1812.

Rhodes, Raymond Crompton. *Harlequin Sheridan, the Man and the Legends, with a Bibliography and Appendices.* Oxford: Blackwell, 1933.

Rich, Frank. "Pat Carroll as Falstaff in 'Merry Wives' at Folger," *New York Times* (May 30, 1990).

Richardson, Samuel. *Pamela; or, Virtue Rewarded.* London: printed for C. Rivington and J. Osborn, 1741.

Ritter, Heinrich Ludwig. *Possen und Lustspiele für die deutsche Bühne.* Heidelberg: Gedruckt auf Kosten des Verfassers in der Engelmannschen Officin, 1818.

Der Weibermagistrat in Klatschhausen: Lutspiel in einem Aufzuge. Hiedelberg: Gedruckt auf Kosten des Verfassers in der Engelmannschen Officin, 1818.

Der Vampyr oder die Todten-Braut: romantisches Schauspiel in drei Acten, deutsch bearbeitet von L. Ritter. Braunschweig: Meyer, 1822.

Roberts, Bette B. *The Gothic Romance: Its Appeal to Women Writers and Readers in Late Eighteenth-Century England.* New York: Arno Press, 1980.

Rosenfeld, Sybil. "A Della Cruscan Poet." *Times Literary Supplement* (May 23, 1952): 345.

"A Della Cruscan Poet." *Notes and Queries* CXCVII (December 6, 1952): 533–4.

"A Sadler's Wells Scene Book," *Theatre Notebook* 25 (1961): 57–62.

A Short History of Scene Design in Great Britain. Oxford: Blackwell, 1973.

Roth, Phyllis R. "Suddenly Sexual Women in Bram Stoker's *Dracula,*" *Literature and Psychology* 27 (1977): 113–21.

Rottenbucher, Donald. "From Undead Monster to Sexy Seducer: Physical Sex Appeal in Contemporary Dracula Films," *Journal of Dracula Studies* 6 (2004): 34–6.

Rowe, Nicolas. *The Fair Penitent, a Tragedy; as it is acted at the new theatre in Little Lincolns-Inn-Fields; by Her Majesty's servants.* London: printed for Jacob Tonson, 1703.

The Tragedy of Jane Shore. London: printed for Bernard Lintott, 1714.

Russell, Anne. "Gender, Passion, and Performance in Nineteenth-Century Women Romeos," *Essays in Theatre/Etudes Théâtrales* 11(2) (May, 1993): 153–66.

"Tragedy, Gender, Performance: Women as Tragic Heroes on the Nineteenth-Century Stage," *Comparative Drama* 30(2) (Summer, 1996): 135–57.

Rutherford, J. H. *Kelso Past and Present.* Kelso: Rutherford, 1880.

Ryan, Finbar Patrick. *Our Lady of Fátima.* 3rd edn. Dublin: Browne & Nolan, 1943.

Sade, Donatien Alphonse François, Marquis de. *Les crimes de l'amour. Nouvelles héroïques et tragiques, précédés d'une "Idée sur les romans."* Paris: Massé, an viii [1800].

The Crimes of Love. Heroic and Tragic Tales, preceded by an Essay on Novels. Trans. David Coward. Oxford: Oxford University Press, 2005.

Histoire de Juliette ou les prospérités du vice. Paris: Massé, 1797.

Justine ou les malheurs de la Vertu. 2 vols. in 1. En Hollande: Chez les Libraires Associés 1791.

The Plays of the Marquis de Sade, 3 vols. Trans. and ed. John and Ben Franceschina. Lincoln, NE: Writers Club Press, 2000.

Le prévaricateur: 5 actes. UCLA Clark Library, f MSS S125M2 p94.

"La tour mystérieuse: opéra comique en un acte." UCLA Clark Library, MSS S125M2 t72.

Said, Edward. *Orientalism.* New York: Pantheon Books, 1978.

Saint-Fond, Barthélemy Faujas de. *Description des expériences de la machine aerostatique de MM De Montgolfier: et de celles auxquelles cette découverte a donné lieu.* Paris: Cuchet, 1784.

Sallengre, Albert-Henri de. *Ebrietatis encomium; or, The praise of drunkenness: wherein is authentically and most evidently proved the necessity of frequently getting drunk, and that the practice of getting drunk is most antient, primitive, and catholic: confirmed by the example of heathens, Turks, infidels, primitive Christians, saints, popes, bishops, doctors, philosophers, poets, Free Masons, and other men of learning in all ages.* London: printed for E. Curl [etc.], 1723.

Savigny, Henry J.-B. and Alexander Correard. *Narrative of a Voyage to Senegal.* Marlboro, VT: Marlboro Press, 1986.

Schiller, Friedrich. *The Robbers.* Trans. Alexander F. Tytler. [London: printed for G. G. J. & J. Robinson, *Paternoster-Row,* 1792]; facsimile rpt. introduced by Jonathan Wordsworth. Oxford: Woodstock Books, 1989.

Wilhelm Tell: Schauspiel. Ed. with commentary by Wilhelm Grosse. Frankfurt-am-Main: Suhrkamp, 2002.

William Tell: a Drama. First performed in English at Drury Lane, 11 May 1825. Trans. Samuel Robinson. London: printed for Hurst, Robinson; Manchester: Robinson & Bent, 1825.

Schlegel, August Wilhelm. *Vorlesungen über dramatische Kunst und Literatur [1809–11], in Kritische Schriften und Briefe*, 7 vols. Ed. Edgar Lohner. Stuttgart: Kohlhammer, 1962–74.

Schumann, Otto. *Handbuch der Opern*. Wilhelmshaven: Heinrichshofen, 1972.

Scott, Sir Walter. Letter to Charlotte Ann Waldie Eaton, June 8, 1831. National Library of Scotland, MS 98.

Sédaine, Jean Michael. *Richard Cœur de Lion: an historical romance in three acts* [Drury Lane, October 24, 1786]. Adapted from the French by General John Burgoyne. London: J. Dicks, 1786.

Amphitron: Opéra en 3 actes. Musical score by André-Ernest-Modeste Gréty. Paris: Ballard, 1786.

Raoul, Barbe-Bleue, comédie en trois actes et en prose, représentée pour la première fois, par les Comédiens Italiens ordinaires du Roi, le lundi 2 mars 1789. Paroles de m. Sédaine; musique de M. Grétry. Avignon: chez Jacques Garrigan, 1791.

Sharp, Michael William. "Essay on Gesture," *Annals of the Fine Arts* 4 (1820) and 5 (1821). London: Sherwood, Neely, and Jones, 1817–21.

Shaw, Bernard. *Man and Superman: a Comedy and a Philosophy*. Westminster: Archibald Constable & Co., 1903.

Shelley, Mary. *Frankenstein; or, the Modern Prometheus*. Ed. James Rieger. New York: Bobbs-Merrill, 1974.

Shelley, Percy Bysshe. *The Complete Poetical Works of Shelley*. London: Oxford University Press, 1905; rpt. 1970.

The Letters of Percy Bysshe Shelley, 2 vols. Ed. Frederick L. Jones. Oxford: Clarendon Press, 1964.

Sheridan, Richard Brinsley. *The Plays of Richard Brinsley Sheridan*. London: Macmillan, 1900.

Siddons, Henry. *Practical illustrations of rhetorical gesture and action /adapted to the English drama from a work on the same subject by M. Engel With sixty-nine engravings*. London: printed for Richard Phillips, 1807; 2nd edn. London: Sherwood, Neely, and Jones, 1822.

Slout, William L. and Sue Rudisill. "The Enigma of the Master Betty Mania," *The Journal of Popular Culture* 8(1) (Summer, 1974): 80–90.

Smith, James. *History of Kelso Grammar School*. Kelso: Rutherford, 1909.

Smith, James L. *Melodrama*. London: Methuen, 1973.

Smith, John Thomas. *Nollekens and his Times; a life of that celebrated sculptor and memoirs of several contemporary artists, from the time of Roubiliac, Hogarth and Reynolds to that of Fuseli, Flaxman and Blake*, 2 vols. London: H. Colburn, 1828.

Soane, George. *Aladdin, a Fairy Opera in Three Acts*. Music by Sir Henry R. Bishop. London: printed for the proprietors by A. J. Valpy, 1826.

Southey, Robert. *Thalaba the Destroyer*, 2 vols. London: T. N. Longman and O. Rees, 1801.

Stableford, Brian. "*Sang* for Supper: Notes on the Metaphorical use of Vampires in *Empire of Fear* and *Young Blood*," in *Blood Read: The Vampire as Metaphor in Contemporary Culture*. Ed. Joan Gordon and Veronica Hollinger. Philadelphia: University of Pennsylvania Press, 1997, pp. 69–84.

Stackelberg, Jürgen von. "Voltaire, Beaumarchais und das ius primae noctis," in *Der unfertige Garten: Essays zur französischen Literatur*. Bonn: Romanistischer Verlag. 2007.

Staves, Susan. "A Few Kind Words for the Fop," *Studies in English Literature, 1500–1900* 22(3) (Summer, 1982): 413–28.

Steinmeyer, Jim. *Two Lectures on Theatrical Illusion*. Burbank, CA: Hahne, 2001.

Stendahl (= Henri Beyle). *Œuvres complètes*, 79 vols. Ed. Henri Martineau. Paris: Le Divan, 1927–37.

 Racine et Shakespeare. Paris: Bossange,1823.

Stephen, Leslie. "Charles Mayne Young (1777–1856)," in *Dictionary of National Biography*. London: Oxford University Press, 1901.

Stevenson, Sir John. *Come tell me where the maid is found: introduced in the opera of the Haunted Tower by Mr. Braham; composed by Sir John Stevenson*. London: J. Power, 1816.

Stilz, Gerhard. "Robbers, Borderers, Millers and Men: Englische Räuberstücke zwischen Revolutionstragödie und melodramatischer Restauration," *Deutsche Vierteljahrsschrift für Literaturwissenschaft und Geistesgeschichte* 65(1) (March, 1991): 117–31.

Stoker, Bram. *Dracula*. Westminster: A. Constable, 1897.

Storace, Stephen. *The Haunted Tower: a comic opera in three acts, as performed at the Theatre-Royal Drury Lane, music selected adapted & composed by Stephen Storace*. London: Longman & Broderip, 1789.

 The Songs, Duets, Trios, Finales, &c. in Mahmoud, a Musical Romance. London: Joseph Dale, 1796.

Stuart, Roxana. *Stage Blood: Vampires of the 19th Century Stage*. Bowling Green, OH: Bowling Green State University Popular Press, 1994.

Tancred, George. *The Annals of a Border Club*. Edinburgh, Glasgow: John Menzies & Co., 1903.

Tatar, Maria. *Secrets beyond the Door. The Story of Bluebeard and his Wives*. Princeton: Princeton University Press, 2004.

Taylor, George. *The French Revolution and the London Stage, 1789–1805*. Cambridge: Cambridge University Press, 2000.

Tearle, John. *Mrs. Piozzi's Tall Young Beau: William Augustus Conway*. Cranbury, NJ: Associated University Presses, 1992.

Thomas, C. Edgar. "The Music and Musicians of Dickens. 11 (Concluded)," *The Musical Times* 61(931) (September 1, 1920): 608–10.

Thomas, Isaiah and Charles Perrault. *The original Mother Goose Melody: as issued by John Newbery, of London, circa 1760, Isaiah Thomas, of Worcester, Mass., circa 1785, and Munroe & Francis, of Boston, circa 1825*. Reproduced in facsimile, from the first Worcester edition, with introductory notes by William H. Whitmore; to which are added the fairy tales of Mother Goose

[*Les contes de ma mère l'oye*], *first collected by Perrault in 1696 reprinted from the original translation into English, by R. Samber in 1729.* Boston: Damrell & Upham; London: Griffith Farran & Co., 1892.

Thompson, L. F. *Kotzebue: A Survey of his Progress in France, and England, preceded by a consideration of the critical attitude to him in Germany.* Paris: Champion, 1928.

Thompson, Stith. *Motif-Index of Folk Literature: A Classification of Narrative Elements in Folk Tales, Ballads, Myths, Fables, Mediaeval Romances, Exempla, Fabliaux, Jest-Books and Local Legends* [CD-ROM edn.]. Bloomington: Indiana University Press, 1993.

Thomson, Peter. "Drury Lane, Theatre Royal," in *The Cambridge Guide to Theatre.* Ed. Martin Banham. Cambridge: Cambridge University Press, 1995.

Thornbury, Walter (Vols. I–II) and Edward Walford (Vols. III–VI). *Old and New London: A Narrative of its History, its People and its Places,* 6 vols. London: Cassell Petter & Galpin, 1873–8.

Tieck, Ludwig. *Der Blaubart. Drama in fünf Akten.* Berlin: Reimer, 1812.

Ludwig Tieck Schriften, 12 vols. Ed. Manfred Frank *et al.* Frankfurt-am-Main: Deutsche Klassiker Verlag, 1985–91.

Peter Lebrecht. Eine Geschichte ohne Abenteuerlichkeiten. Berlin, Leipzig: C. A. Nicolai, 1795–6.

Phantasus. Berlin: Realschulbuchhandlung, 1812.

Ritter Blaubart. Ein Ammenmährchen von Peter Lebrecht. Berlin, Leipzig: Friedrich Nicolai, 1797.

Tomalin, Claire. *Mrs. Jordan's Profession.* London: Viking, 1994.

Tomko, Michael. "Politics, Performance, and Coleridge's 'Suspension of Disbelief.'" *Victorian Studies: An Interdisciplinary Journal of Social, Political, and Cultural Studies* 49(2) (Winter, 2007): 241–9.

Troost, Linda V. "Social Reform in Comic Opera: Colman's *Inkle and Yarico,*" *Studies on Voltaire and the Eighteenth Century* 305 (1992): 1427–9.

Twitchell, James B. *The Living Dead: A Study of the Vampire in Romantic Literature.* Durham, NC: Duke University Press, 1981.

Vanbrugh, John. *Confederacy, a comedy; as it is acted at the Queen's theatre in the Hay-market; by Her Majesty's sworn servants.* London: printed for Jacob Tonson, 1705.

Van der Merwe, Pieter. "Stage Sailors: Theatrical Material in the National Maritime Museum," *Theatre Notebook: A Journal of the History and Technique of the British Theatre* 34(3) (1980): 123–5.

Verhoeven, Wil M. "Opening the Text: The Locked-Trunk Motif in Late Eighteenth-Century British and American Gothic Fiction," in *Exhibited by Candlelight: Sources and Developments in the Gothic Tradition.* Ed. Valeria Tinkler-Villani, Peter Davidson, and Jane Stevenson. Amsterdam: Rodopi, 1995, pp. 205–19.

Voltaire, François-Marie Arouet de. *Le droit du seigneur ou L'écueil du sage: comédie, 1762–1779.* Vijon: Lampsaque, 2002.

The History of Peter the Great, Emperor of Russia [*Histoire de l'empire de Russie sous Pierre le Grand*]. Trans. Tobias Smollett. London: printed for J. Nourse & P. Vaillant in the Strand and L. Davis & C. Reymers in Holborn, 1763.

Vulpius, Christian August. *Rinaldo Rinaldini, der Räuber-Hauptmann*. Leipzig: 1799–1801; rpt. Hildesheim: Olms, 1974.

Wainwright, Gordon R. *Body Language*. Chicago: Contemporary Books, 2003.

Waldie, Jane. *Sketches Descriptive of Italy in the years 1816 and 1817, with a brief account of travels in various parts of France and Switzerland in the same years*, 4 vols. London: John Murray, 1820.

Waterloo, by a near Observer. London: John Murray, 1817.

Waldie, Jane Ormston. Letter to Walter Scott ("For his spouse with a small Parcel"), June 19, 1780. National Library of Scotland, MS 1549, fos. 84–5.

Waldie, John. *The Journal of John Waldie: Theatre Commentaries*, 1799–1830. Ed. Frederick Burwick, assisted by Lucinda Newsome. e-Scholarship Repository. California Digital Library. 2008. http://repositories.cdlib.org/uclalib/dsc/waldie/.

Journals and letters of John Waldie. D. Litt., of Hendersyde Park, Kelso, Scotland. University of California, Los Angeles. Collection MSS 169 (MC4973228), 74 journal vols., 11 vols. on travels transcribed from the journals, and 1 vol. of passports (1827–37).

Lectures on chemistry, moral philosophy, and universal history, 1798–1801. University of Edinburgh, MSS Dc 5 and Dc 6.

"Musical Report of the Newcastle Theatre," *Newcastle Chronicle* (February 2, 1822): 3.

Walker, Charles Edward. *Wallace: an Historical Tragedy in five acts, Covent Garden 14 November 1820*. London: printed for John Miller, 1820.

Wallace, Randall. *Braveheart* [screenplay; videorecording]. Produced by Mel Gibson, Alan Ladd, Jr., and Bruce Davey; directed by Mel Gibson. Hollywood, CA: Paramount Pictures, 1996.

Ware, William. *Every face looks cheerily: the favorite glee in the new melo dramatic romance of Aladdin or the Wonderful lamp, performed at the Theatre Royal Covent Garden*. London: printed & sold by William Hodsoll, 1813.

Watson, Ernest Bradlee. *Sheridan to Robertson: A Study of the Nineteenth Century London Stage*. Cambridge, MA: Harvard University Press, 1926.

Watts, Jane Waldie. *Sketches Descriptive of Italy in 1816–1817*, 4 vols. London: John Murray, 1820.

Waterloo, by a near Observer. London: John Murray, 1817.

Webb, W. *Aladdin; or, The wonderful lamp a romantic drama, in two acts, written expressly for, and adapted only to Webb's characters & scenes in the same*. London: printed and published by W. Webb, 1813.

Weinstein, Leo. *The Metamorphoses of Don Juan*. Stanford: Stanford University Press, 1959.

Wettlaufer, Jörg. *Das Herrenrecht der ersten Nacht: Hochzeit, Herrschaft und Heiratszins im Mittelalter und in der frühen Neuzeit*, Campus historische Studien 27. Frankfurt-am-Main, New York: Campus, 1999.

"The *Jus primae noctis* as a Male Power Display: A Review of Historic Sources with Evolutionary Interpretation," *Evolution and Human Behavior* 21(2) (2000): 111–23.

Wewitzer, Ralph. *Dramatic Reminiscences, anecdotes, comical sayings and doings.* London: Thomas Hailes Lacy, 1826.

White, Eric Walter. *A History of English Opera.* London: Faber and Faber, 1983.

Wilkinson, George Theodore. *An Authentic History of the Cato Street Conspiracy.* London: T. Kelly, 1820; rpt. New York: Arno Press, 1972.

Williams, D. E. *Life and Correspondence of Sir Thomas Lawrence*, 2 vols. London: H. Colburn and R. Bentley, 1831.

Williams, Helen Maria. *Letters Written in France in the Summer of 1790, to a Friend in England*, 4 vols. Dublin: printed by J. Chambers, 1794.

Peru: A Poem; in Six Cantos. London: printed for T. Cadell, 1784.

Williamson, George S. "What Killed August von Kotzebue? The Temptations of Virtue and the Political Theology of German Nationalism, 1789–1819," *The Journal of Modern History* 72 (December, 2000): 890–943.

Willier, Stephen A. "Madness, the Gothic, and Bellini's *Il pirata*," *The Opera Quarterly* 6 (1989): 7–23.

Winkelmann, Johann Joachim. *Reflections on the Painting and Sculpture of the Greeks* [*Gedanken über die Nachahmung der griechischen Werke in der Malerei und Bildhauerkunst* (1755)]. Trans. Henry Fusseli [*sic*]. London: printed for the Translator, and sold by A. Millar, 1765; rpt. Menston: Scholar Press, 1972.

Wolf, Leonard. *A Dream of Dracula, in Search of the Living Dead.* Boston: Little, Brown, 1972.

Wolfson, Susan J. "'A Problem Few Dare Imitate': *Sardanapalus* and 'Effeminate Character,'" *ELH* 58(4) (Winter, 1991): 867–902.

Wood, Alice Ida Perry. *The Stage History of Shakespear's King Richard the Third.* New York: Columbia University Press, 1909.

Woodworth, Samuel. *The Poems, Odes, Songs, and other Metrical Effusions.* New York: Abraham Asten and Matthias Lopez, 1818.

Wordsworth, William. *The Prelude: The Four Texts (1798, 1799, 1804, 1850).* Ed. Jonathan Wordsworth. Harmondsworth: Penguin, 1995.

Wray, Edith. "English Adaptations of French Drama between 1780 and 1815," *Modern Language Notes* 43(2) (February, 1928): 87–90.

Wyman, Leah M. and George N. Dionisopulos. "Primal Urges and Civilized Sensibilities: The Rhetoric of Gendered Archetypes, Seduction, and Resistance in Bram Stoker's *Dracula*," *Journal of Popular Film and Television* 27(2) (Summer, 1999): 32–9.

Young, Robert. *White Mythologies: Writing History and the West.* London: Routledge, 1990.

Index

Abbot, Bud, and Lou Costello,
  Abbott and Costello Meet Frankenstein, 240
Adelphi, 5, 9, 57, 60, 62, 123, 129, 241,
  242, 245
Aldridge, Ira,
  as Hamlet and Othello, 33
  in anti-slavery plays, 33
amateur theatricals, 142, 159
Ancillon, Charles,
  Eunuchism Display'd, 209
Andrews, Miles Peter, 34, 47, 54
  Dissipation, 40, 41, 43, 45
  epilogue to *Delays and Blunders*, 48
  epilogue to The Child of Nature, 54
  Fire and Water, 40, 45, 46
anon.,
  Bluebeard, or the Fatal Effects of Curiosity
    and Disobedience, 204
  Don Juan, or the Libertine Destroyed, 243
  The Popular Story of Blue Beard or, Female
    Curiosity, 204
Aprile, Giuseppi, 214
Apuleius,
  The Golden Ass, 229
Archer, William, 82
Aristophanes, 106
Aristotle, 32
Arne, Michael, 214
  Cymon, 24
Arnim, Achim von,
  Hollins Liebeleben, 16
Arnold, Samuel J., 238
Arundel Theatre, 142
Astley's Amphitheatre, 7
Atkins, Mrs., née Warrell,
  as Barbara in *The Iron Chest*, 198
Atwood, Margaret, Bluebeard's Egg, 203
Austen, Jane,
  Mansfield Park, 54, 142
Austin, Gilbert,
  Chironomia, 81

Baddeley, Robert,
  as Colonel Batton in *Love in the East*, 128
  as the Baron in *The Haunted Tower*, 188
Baillie, Joanna, 32, 99, 202
  De Monfort, 102, 105, 113, 188, 213
  Introductory Discourse, 32, 104, 105
  Orra, 202
  Plays of the Passions, 32
Baillie, Matthew,
  mental pathology, 104
Banks, John,
  Earl of Essex, The, 90
Bannister, John, 3, 4, 15, 106
  as Ali Baba in *The Forty Thieves*, 166
  as Daggerwood in *Bannister's Budget*, 4
  as Joseph Surface in Sheridan's *The School for
    Scandal*,
  as Leopold in *Siege of Belgrade*, 191, 192
  as Motley in *The Castle Spectre*, 174, 217
  as Sylvester Daggerwood in *New Hay at the
    Old Market*, 3
  as Young Wilding in Foote's *The Liar*, 15
Barnard,
  as Wilford in *The Iron Chest*, 196
Barnes, John,
  as the Don Antonio in *The Widow's Vow*, 123
Barnett, C. Z.,
  Phantom Bride, 256
  Skeleton Hand, The, 256
Barrie, James M.,
  Peter Pan, 201
Barrymore, William,
  as Count Albert in *De Monfort*, 113
  as Franval in *Deaf and Dumb*, 113
  as King of the Incas in *Virgin of the Sun*, 162
  as Osmond in *The Castle Spectre*, 174, 217
  as Pizarro, 157
  as Steinfort in *The Stranger*, 28
  Secret, The, 123
Bath Theatre, 199, 241
Beaumarchais, Pierre-Augustin Caron de, 35

La Mère coupable, 35
Le Barbier de Séville, 34
Le Mariage de Figaro, 35, 37
Beaumont, Francis and John Fletcher,
  Rule a Wife, Have a Wife, 127
Beethoven, Ludwig van,
  Fidelio, 37
Behn, Aphra,
  Amorous Prince, The, 125
Belfour, Hugo John, and George Stephens,
  Vampire, The, 251, 254
Bell, Charles,
  Anatomy and *Philosophy of Expression, The*, 83,
    99, 100
Bellamy,
  as Motley in *The Castle Spectre*, 177
Bellini, Vincenzo,
  Il Pirata, 147
  I Puritani, 227
Benucci, Francesco, 215
  as Figaro in *Le Nozze di Figaro*, 215
Bérard, Cyprien,
  Lord Ruthven ou les Vampires, 51, 234
Bernard, John,
  Retrospections, 40, 41, 43, 47
Bernardoni, Giuseppe,
  Alonso e Cora, libretto for Mayr, 162
Bernhardt, Sarah,
  as Hamlet, 131
Berré, Pierre-Yon, and Jean Baptiste Radet,
  La Docteurs moderne, 54, 154
Betterton, Thomas,
  as Diddler in *Raising the Wind*, 141, 142
Betty, William Henry West, 4
  as Achmet in *Barbarossa*, 3, 175
  as Frederick in *Lover's Vows*, 175
  as Hamlet, 134, 175
  as Mortimer in *The Iron Chest*, 200
  as Osman in *Zara*, 3, 575, 199
  as Osmond in *The Castle Spectre*, 3, 175
  as Richard III, 175
  as Rolla in *Pizarro*, 3, 175
  as Romeo in *Romeo and Juliet*, 3, 175
  as Tancred in *Tancred and Sigismunda*, 175
  title role in Brooke's *Gustavus Vasa*, 175
  title role in Home's *Douglas*, 3, 175, 176
Beverley, William Roxbury,
  Watteau of Scene painters, 553
Beverly, Mrs. Henry, née Chapman,
  as Peggy in *Raising the Wind*, 138
Bianchi, Francesco,
  Alonso e Cora, 162
Diggs, Mariana, 21, 22, 25
  as Charlotte in *The Stranger*, 26
  as lady Dove in *The Brothers*, 21

as Lappet in *The Miser*, 21
as Miranda in *Busy Body*, 23
Billington, Elizabeth, née Weichsell,
  as Queen Isabella in *Una cosa rara*, 192
Birch-Pfeiffer, Charlotte, 202
Bishop, Sir Henry R., 166
  Virgin of the Sun, music, 162
Blackwood's *Edinburgh Magazine*, 231
  Hazlitt Cross-Questioned, 149
Blanchard, Elizabeth,
  as Lady Margaret in Planche's *The Vampire*,
    241
  as Madame Dupuis in Moncrieff's *The Secret*,
    124
Blanchard, William, 128
  as Plainway in *Raising the Wind*, 138
Bland, Maria Thérèsa, née Romanzini,
  as Barbara in *The Iron Chest*, 198
  as Beda in *Blue-Beard*, 189
  as Cicely in *The Haunted Tower*, 189
  as Cogia in *The Forty Thieves*, 166
  as Dorothy in *No Song No Supper*, 191
  in *Mahmoud*, 216
  sings incantation in *Remorse*, 218
Blink, George,
  Vampire Bride, 256
Blue-Beard,
  misogyny and domestic violence, 2
Boaden, James, 5
  Memoirs of Mrs. Siddons, 16, 20, 98, 99, 101,
    102
Bolton, Miss,
  as Princess Badroulbodour, *Aladdin*, 165, 166
Bolton, Miss E.,
  as Amron in *Aladdin*, 166
Bonnor, Charles,
  as Figaro in *The Follies of a Day*, 35
Bouilly, Jean Nicolas,
  L'Abbé de L'Épée, adapted by Holcroft, *Deaf
    and Dumb*, 37, 72, 109, 113
  Leonore, ou L'amour Conjugal, adapted as
    libretto to Beethoven's *Fidelio*, 37
Boyce, Miss,
  as Peggy in *Raising the Wind*, 42
Boydell, John,
  Shakespeare Gallery, 91, 153, 165
Brackenridge, Hugh Henry,
  Death of General Montgomery, The, 72
Braham, John, 18, 19, 33, 148, 190, 191, 201, 218
  as Don Giovanni in *Una cosa rara*, 192
  as Charles in *Family Quarrels*, 46
  as Lord William in *The Haunted Tower*, 187,
    189, 190
  as Serkasier in *Siege of Belgrade*, 192
  in *Mahmoud*, 216

Brand, Hannah,
  Adelinda, 102, 108
Brazier, Nicholas, Gabriel De Lurieu, and
  Armand d'Artois,
  Les Trois Vampires, 234, 238
Brewster, Sir David,
  Letters on Natural Magic, 67, 151
Brighton Theatre, 42
Bristol Theatre Royal, 27, 131
Brontë, Charlotte,
  Jane Eyre, 205
Brooke, Henry,
  Gustavus Vasa, 175
Brown, John,
  Barbarossa, 3, 175, 199
Brummell, George Bryan, Beau, 130
Brunton, John,
  as Diddler in *Raising the Wind*, 142
  as Harry Dornton in *The Road to Ruin*, 136
Brussels Theatre, 193
Bullock, William,
  Egyptian Hall, 168
Bürger, Gottfried August,
  Lenore, 243
Burghersh, Lady, 142
Burke, Edmund,
  Reflections on the Revolution in France, 34
Burke, William, and William Hare,
  delivered corpses to Edinburgh College, 68
Burnett, Frances Hodgson,
  Secret Garden, The, 203
Burns, Robert,
  My love is like a red, red rose, 245
Burton, John,
  as Adam Winterton in *The Iron Chest*, 198
Burton, Richard,
  Day Amongst the Fans, A, 203
Burwick, Frederick,
  Illusion and the Drama, 1
Butler, Samuel,
  as McSwill in Planché's *The Vampire*, 241
  as Thomas in Moncrieff's *The Secret*, 124
Byng, John, 6
Byron, Annabelle Milbanke, Lady, 169
Byron, George Gordon, Lord, 18, 57, 170, 234,
  254
  Bride of Abydos, The, 217
  Cain, 173
  Don Juan, 170, 243
  Fare Thee Well, 243
  Fragment, 232
  Giaour, 232
  Hebrew Melodies, see Nathan, Isaac
  Manfred, 170, 178
  Sardanapalus, 168, 169, 172

Calmet, Augustin,
  Treatise on Vampires, 230, 247
Capon, William,
  setting for *The Iron Chest*, 152
  stage designs, 152, 158
Carlyle, Thomas,
  Memoirs of Sophia Dorothea, 229
Caroline, Queen, divorce trial, 169
Carroll, Pat,
  as Falstaff in *Merry Wives of Windsor*, 131
Carter, Angela,
  Bloody Chamber, The, 203
Carter, John,
  as Gossamer in *Laugh When You Can*, 128
  as Monsieur Dupuis in Moncrieff's *The
  Secret*, 124
  as Sir Patrick in *Sleep-walker, or Which is the
  Lady*, 128
Catalani, Angelica, 18, 190, 193
Cato Street Conspiracy, 68
Caufield, John,
  as Apewell in *New Hay at the Old Market*, 3
Centlivre, Susanna,
  Bury Body, 23
Chamisso, Adelbert von, *Peter Schlemihl*, 67
Chapman, Master,
  as Prince Agib in *Timour the Tartar*, 167
Cherry, Andrew,
  as Adam Winterton in *The Iron Chest*, 198
  Travellers, or Music's Fascination, The, 167
Cherubim, Luigi,
  Lodoiska, musical score, 188, 192
Chippendale, William Henry,
  as Fainwould in *Raising the Wind*, 141
chirologia, 83
chironomia, 83
clap-trap, 168, 201
Coats, Robert,
  his bad acting, 3, 4
Cobb, James, 201, 216
  Cherokee, The, libretto, 180
  Haunted Tower, The, libretto, 11, 12, 15, 178,
  179, 180, 181, 182, 184, 186, 187, 188, 189,
  190, 191, 200, 213, 235
  Love in the East, 128
  Pirates, The, libretto, 180
  Siege of Belgrade, The, libretto, 12, 46, 180,
  190, 191, 192, 200, 218
Cogan, Philip, 214
Colbran, Isabella,
  as Cora in Mayr's *Alonso e Cora*, 162
Colburn, Henry, 231
Coleridge, Samuel Taylor,
  Biographia Literaria, 16, 146
  Christabel, 189, 255

lectures on Shakespeare, 157
Maid of Buttermere, 69
on Hamlet's madness, 91
Love's Labour's Lost, 19
on Master Betty, 176
on Maturin's *Bertram*, 144, 145, 146, 147, 149, 150
on Milton's Satan, 45
on Shadwell's *The* Libertine, 45
optical illusion, 57
Osorio, 24, 156, 173
Picture, The, 57
Remorse, 24, 156, 157, 158, 163, 173, 174, 213, 218
Wanderings of Cain, The, 173
willing suspension of disbelief, 16, 56, 46, 177
Zapolya, 144
Colman, George, the Younger, 216
accuses Kemble of drugged performance in *The Iron Chest*, 194
Blue-Beard libretto, 12, 15, 51, 72, 167, 171, 174, 189, 195, 202, 209, 210, 211, 213, 218, 221, 222, 224, 223, 229, 234
Examiner of Plays, 38
Forty Thieves, The, 166, 167, 168
Inkle and Yarico, 33
Iron Chest, The, 11, 12, 152, 153, 161, 180, 193, 194, 195, 196, 197, 198, 199, 200, 215
Jealous Wife, The, 100
New Hay at the Old Market, 3
Comédie Français, 179
Comédie Italienne, 189, 192, 205
Commedia dell'arte, 4, 207
Congreve, William, 4
Mourning Bride, The, 20
Connor, Mrs. [Charles],
as Donna Victoria in *Bold Stroke for a Husband*, 119
Conway, Henry Seymour,
False Appearances, 216
Conway, William Augustus, 18, 19, 136, 49, 150, 159, 160, 198, 199
as Alonzo in *Pizarro*, 159, 160, 161
as Harry Dornton in *The Road to Ruin*, 136
as Polydore in *Venice Preserv'd*, 149
as Romeo, 149
as Theseus in *Midsummer Night's Dream*, 150
as Wilford in *The Iron Chest*, 198, 199
his suicide, 19, 150
recites Dryden's Alexander's Feast, 159
roles at Newcastle, 41, 142
Conyngham, Lord Francis, 142
Cooke, George Frederick, 128
as Mr. Sullen in *The Beaux' Stratagem*, 23
Cooke, Thomas,
music to Maturin's *Bertram*, 147

Cooke, Thomas Potter,
as Dirk Hatteraick in *The Witch of Derncleugh*, 241
as Lord Ruthven in Planché's *The Vampire*, 241
as Osmond in *The Castle Spectre*, 174
as the Monster in *Presumption*, 241
Copeau, Jacques, 82
Corneille, Pierre,
Les Horaces, 92
Corri, Dominico,
music for Cherry's *The Travellers*, 167
Courier, 232
Coveney, Mr.,
as Count Marville in *'Twould Puzzle a Conjuror*, 51
Covent Garden, 3, 4, 7, 9, 15, 22, 24, 28, 29, 31, 35, 47, 48, 49, 51, 53, 54, 67, 68, 97, 109, 115, 124, 128, 130, 132, 135, 137, 146, 149, 151, 154, 155, 159, 162, 164, 165, 166, 167, 172, 175, 177, 190, 193, 195, 199, 211, 221, 222, 224
Cowley, Hannah,
Belle's Stratagem, The, 130, 160
Bold Stroke for a Husband A, 102, 103, 113, 115, 116, 117, 118, 119, 155, 158
Town Before You, The, 4, 124, 125, 126, 127, 189
Cox, Jeffrey, and Michael Gamer,
Broadview Romantic Drama, 222
Craig, William Marshall,
illustrations to *Tales of the Genii*, 153
Cross, James C.,
Apparition, The, 59, 60
cross-dressing,
sexual identity, 2, 10, 32, 120, 123, 124, 125, 127, 128, 129, 130, 131, 150
Crouch, Anna Maria, née Phillips, 6, 46, 188, 201
as Fatima in *Blue-Beard*, 189, 218
as Katherine in *Siege of Belgrade*, 191, 218
as Lady Elinor in *The Haunted Tower*, 186, 189
as Lodoiska, 6, 180
as Louisa in *No Song No Supper*, 191
Cruikshank, George,
Fare Thee Well, 243
Cumberland, Richard,
Brothers, The, 21, 24
Importers, The, 102, 106, 107, 108
Joanna of Montfaucon, 29
Wheel of Fortune, The, 2, 16, 24, 25, 47

da Ponte, Lorenzo,
Una cosa rara, libretto, 192

Dalton, Mrs. Richard,
  as Sophia in *Sleep-walker, or Which is the Lady*, 127
Dance, Charles,
  collaboration on Planché's *Blue Beard*, 226
Daniels, Miss, 23
Davenport,
  as Sulky in *The Road to Ruin*, 136
Davenport, Mary Ann,
  as widow of Ching Mustapha in *Aladdin*, 165, 166
Davide, Giacomo,
  as Alonso in Mayr's *Alonso e Cora*, 162
Davis, Tracy, 146
Dazincourt, Joseph-Jean-Baptiste Albouy,
  as Figaro in *Le Mariage de Figaro*, 35
De Camp, Miss A.,
  as Peggy in *Raising the Wind*, 141
De Camp, Maria Theresa, *see* Kemble, Mrs Charles
  as Lodoiska,
  as Theodore in *Deaf and Dumb*, 113
De Camp, Marie Therese,
  as Morgiana in *The Forty Thieves*, 166
De Camp, Vincent, 17
  as Hasencar in *The Forty Thieves*, 166
  as Wilford in *The Iron Chest*, 198, 199
de L'Épée, Abbé Charles Michel, 37
de la Forgue, Monsieur,
  as Dupuis in Hoffmann's *Le secret*, 123
De Loutherbourg, Philippe Jacques,
  stage designs, 151, 158
De Quincey, Thomas,
  as reader of *Arabian Nights*, 164
  Brocken Spectre, 8
  Confessions, 229
  Murder Considered as a Fine Art, 70
  On the Knocking at the Gate in Macbeth, 238, 254
Dejaure, Jean Claude Bedeno,
  Lodoiska, libretto, 192
Delacroix, Eugene,
  Death of Sardanapalus, The, 169
Deluzzo, Count, 215
Desfontaines-Lavallee, Francois-Georges,
  Le droit du Seigneur, adapted as opera by Jean Paul Egide Martini, 36
Dibdin, Charles, 216
  Edward and Susan, or The Beauty of Buttermere, 69, 70, 72
  Lionel and Clarissa, 214, 215
Dibdin, Thomas,
  Don Giovanni, or the Spectre on Horseback, 243
Dickens, Charles,
  Animal Magnetism at Tavistock House, 155

David Copperfield, 212
  Haunted Man, The, 57
  Martin Chuzzlewit, 212
  Sketches by Boz, 212
Diderot, Denis, 68
  Le Paradoxe sur le comedien, 8, 82
Dignum, Charles, 190
  as Count Floreski in *Lodoiska*, 192
  as Crop in *No Song, No Supper*, 191
  as Stanmore in *Love in the East*,
  as Yusuph in *Siege of Belgrade*, 192
Dimond, William,
  Bride of Abydos, The, 216
documentary drama, 68
Dodd, James William,
  as Adam Winterton in *The Iron Chest*, 194
Dorset, St. John, nom de plume, Hugo John Belfour and George Stephens, 251
Dowton, William, 198
Drury Lane, 3, 4, 5, 7, 11, 12, 15, 16, 20, 24, 25, 28, 31, 40, 41, 43, 49, 52, 77, 79, 87, 92, 97, 105, 113, 121, 128, 129, 136, 144, 147, 151, 152, 153, 156, 157, 159, 162, 164, 166, 167, 168, 172, 173, 177, 179, 180, 186, 189, 191, 192, 193, 195, 198, 209, 215, 216, 217, 218, 240, 241, 243
  dimensions and capacity, 5
  fire of, 1809, 141
Dryden, John,
  Aeneid, translation, 220
du Maurier, Daphne,
  Rebecca, 203
Duke of York's Theatre, 125
Dumas, Alexander,
  Man in the Iron Mask, The, 39
Duncan, Maria, 199
Dunlap, William,
  Blue Beard, 202, 222, 229
  Wild-Goose Chase, adapted from Kotzebue's *Der Wildfang*, 129
Dussane, Béatrix, 82
Duval, Alexandre,
  La jeunesse du duc de Richelieu, 53

Eaton, Charlotte Ann Waldie,
  At Home and Abroad, 18
  Continental Adventures, 18
  Narrative of a Residence in Belgium, during the Campaign of 1815, 18
  Rome in the Nineteenth Century, 18
  novelist, sister to John Waldie, 17
Edinburgh Theatre, 160, 167, 191
Egerton, Daniel,
  as Capt. Faulkner in *The Way to Get Married*, 22
  as Diddler in *Raising the Wind*, 142

as Steinfort in *The Stranger*, 26
as the Marquis in *Animal Magnetism*, 22
Egerton, Sarah, née Fisher,
　as the Countess in *The Stranger*, 28
　as Zorilda in *Timour the Tartar*, 167
El Cid Compeador,
　anon. poem (1207), 163
Elliston, Robert,
　as Lothario in *The Fair Penitent*, 3
Elliston, Robert William,
　as Alvar in *Remorse*, 218
　as Hamlet, 7
　as Mortimer in *The Iron Chest*, 198, 199
　as Osmond in *The Castle Spectre*, 174
　as Penruddock, 25
　Preface to *Adeline*, 52
Emery, John,
　as Silky in *The Road to Ruin*, 136
　as Solomon in *The Stranger*, 28
Engel, Johann Jacob,
　Ideen zu einer Mimik, 80
Engels, Frederick,
　on *jus de primae noctis*, 36
English Opera House, 38, 238, 241, 242
equestrian drama, 7, 167, 222
Etherege, George,
　Comical Revenge, 124
Examiner, The, 38

Farley, Charles,
　as Abanazar in *Aladdin*, 165, 166
　as Francisco in *A Tale of Mystery*, 165
　as Timour, in *Timour the Tartar*, 165, 167
　stage designs for Aladdin or the Wonderful
　　Lamp, 165
Farquhar, George,
　Beaux' Stratagem, The, 22, 124
Farren, Percival,
　as the Marquis in *The Widow's Vow*, 123
　manager of Plymouth Theatre, 122
Farren, William, 123
Fawcett, John, 48, 159
　as Mortimer in *The Iron Chest*, 198
Fenaroli, Fedele, 24
Fermin, Monsieur,
　as the Marquis in Patrat's *L'heureuse erreur*,
　　123
Fitzball, Edward, 251
　Devil's Elixir, The, 67
　Flying Dutchman, The, 9, 60, 61, 62, 63, 64,
　　65, 66, 67, 68, 72, 129, 130
　Thalaba, the Destroyer, adapted from Southey,
　　254, 255
FitzClarence, George,
　son of Dorothy Jordan, 143

Fletcher, John,
　Monsieur Thew, 47
Florence Theatre, 142
Folger Shakespeare Theatre, 131
'Rob Roy Macgregor, O!', 245
Follen, Eliza Lee Cabot,
　Blue Beard, 228
Foppa, Giuseppe Maria,
　Alonso e Cora, 161
Foucault, Michel,
　Discipline and Punish, 71, 72
France, Anatole,
　Seven Wives of Bluebeard, The, 203
Franceschino, John and Ben, 186
Frederick, Kitty, 43
Frederick, Madame, 21
Freud, Sigmund,
　Das Unheimliche, 70
Fullerton, Mr.,
　Waldie's theatre companion, 22, 23
Fuseli, Johann Heinrich,
　Essays on Physiognomy, trans. Lavater, 83

Galignani's *Messenger*, 231
Galland, Antoine,
　Arabian Nights, 164, 210
Garrick, David, 3, 5, 9, 80
1st portrait of, 21
Gautier, Théophile,
　La morte amoureuse, 255
Gay, John,
　Beggars' Opera, 38, 240
Genest, John, 26, 31, 36, 47, 51, 52, 53, 60,
　68, 109, 113, 127, 131, 138, 147, 164,
　165, 168, 189, 193, 194, 200, 221, 222,
　223, 241
Geniis, Elizabeth de,
　Zelie ou l'ingenue, 54
George IV, 169
Géricault, Theodore,
　Raft of Medusa, The, 74
Gessner, Solomon,
　Der Tod Abels, 173
Gibbs, Maria, née Logan,
　as Blanch in *The Iron Chest*, 198
　as Charlotte in *The Stranger*, 28
　as Minette in *Bold Stroke for a Husband*,
　　119
Gilbert, William Schwendt,
　Wedding March, The, 213
Gilbert, William Schwenck, and Sir Arthur
　Sullivan,
　librettist and composer at D'Oyle Carte's
　　Opera, 1871–1896, 222
Glasgow Theatre Royal, 154

Glover, Juliana, née Betterton,
  as Blanch in *The Iron Chest*, 199
  as Olivia in *Bold Stroke for a Husband*, 119
Godwin, William,
  Caleb Williams, as source for *The Iron Chest*,
    180, 194, 195, 198, 215
Goethe, Johann Wolfgang von, 232
  Die Braut von Korinth, 172, 255
  Faust, 252
  Wilhelm Meister's Apprenticeship, 82
Goldoni, Carlo, 206
Goodall, Charlotte,
  as Helen in *The Iron Chest*, 198
Gothic melodrama,
  and Anti-Gothic, 2
Gottsched, Johann Christoph, 207
Goward, Mary Ann,
  as Urika in *The Devil's Elixir*, 68
Gozzi, Carlo, 206, 208
  Il re cervo, 207
  L'amere delle tre melarance, 207
  L'augellino belverde, 207
  La Donna Serpente, 207
  Turandot, 207
Graham, Dr. James, 195
Grand Théâtre, Bordeaux, 123
Grétry, André Ernest Modeste,
  Raoul, Barbe Bleue, musical score, 51, 189, 202,
    204, 205, 206, 207, 210, 211, 218, 229
Griffeth, Maria Jane Waldie,
  sister to John Waldie, 17
Grimaldi, Joseph, 3, 4
  as Kazrac in *Aladdin*, 165, 166
  *Harlequin and Mother Goose, or the Golden
    Egg*, 4
Grimm, Jakob and Wilhelm,
  Blue Beard, 203, 204, 207
Grove, John,
  as Silky in *The Road to Ruin*, 136
Grove, Mrs.,
  as Mrs. Decorum in *Sleep-walker, or Which is
    the Lady*, 127

Hague, Miss,
  as Countess in *The Widow's Vow*, 123
Hamblin, Thomas Sowerby,
  as Lord Ruthven in Planché's *The Vampire*,
    241
Hamerton, Mr.,
  as the Count in *The Stranger*, 28
Hamilton, William,
  Much Ado About Nothing. IV,i, 97
Harlequinade, 4, 164, 222, 224
Harley, George Davies,
  as Milford in *The Road to Ruin*, 135

Harley, J. P., 240
  as Edward in Macready's *Irishman in London*,
    240
  as Edward in *The Haunted Tower*, 241
  as Frank in O'Keefe's *Modern Antiques*, 241
  as McSwill in Planché's *The Vampire*, 240
  as Motley in *The Castle Spectre*, 241
Hatfield, John, 69
Haymarket, 3, 5, 33, 38, 40, 45, 50, 115, 119, 124,
    127, 131, 160, 161, 195, 198, 213
Hazlitt, William, 8, 31, 85, 115
  homophobia, 19, 149
  in the *Theatrical Inquisitor*, 149
  Memoirs of the late Thomas Holcroft, 133
  on Barnard as Wilford in *The Iron Chest*, 196
  on *Bold Stroke for a Husband*, 119
  on Conway as Comus, 149
  on Conway as Polydore, 149
  on Conway as Romeo, 19, 149
  on Conway as Theseus *Midsummer Night's
    Dream*, 150
  on Conway's death, 150
  on Edmund Kean, 16
  On Effeminacy of Character, 149
  on Falstaff, 131
  on Godwin's *Caleb Williams*, 195
  on Goldfinch, 134
  on John Bannister, 15
  on Kean as Mortimer in *The Iron Chest*, 195,
    196
  on Kean as Richard III, 89
  on Kemble as Mortimer in *The Iron Chest*, 195
  on Kemble as Penruddock, 24
  on Master Betty, 175, 176
  on Meggett as Mortimer in *The Iron Chest*,
    161, 195
  on Sarah Siddons, 29
  on *The Iron Chest*, 195, 196, 197, 200
  on *The Road to Ruin*, 133, 134, 135
  View of the English Stage, 149
Heber, Reginald,
  Blue-Beard, A Serio-Comic Oriental
    Romance, 202, 224, 225, 226, 227, 229
  Europe, 224
  Palestine, 224
Hemans, Felicia,
  Siege of Valencia, 163
Henry VIII,
  six wives of, 210
Hill, Aaron,
  Zara, adapted from Voltaire, 3, 175
Hoare, Prince,
  Friend in Need, A, 216
  Mahmoud, libretto, 216
  No Song No Supper, libretto, 180, 191

Hodges, William,
  depiction of *The Merchant of Venice* (V.i), 153
Hoffmann, E. T. A., 232
  Aurelia [Vampirismus], 255
  Die Elixiere des Teufels, 67
Hoffmann, Francois Benoit,
  Le secret, 123
Hogarth, Georgina,
  as Constance in *Animal Magnetism*, 155
Holcroft, Thomas, 34, 35, 36, 40, 46, 54, 102, 133
  adapts Pixérécourt's *Coelina*, 109
  as Figaro, 35
  Deaf and Dumb, 37, 72, 102, 109, 110, 111, 112, 113
  Road to Ruin, The, 15, 132, 133, 134, 135, 136, 143
  Tale of Mystery, A, 35, 37, 109, 159, 165
Holman, Joseph George, 161
  as Harry in *The Road to Ruin*, 135
Home, John,
  Douglas, 3, 20, 142, 164
  Siege of Aquileia, 163
Hugo, Victor,
  Preface to *Cromwell*, 58
Hunt, Leigh, 8, 31
  meets John Waldie, 18
  on Edmund Kean, 85
  on John Bannister, 15
  on John Philip Kemble, 6
  on Kemble as Penruddock, 24

Iffland, August Wilhelm, 113
illusionism,
  anti-illusionism, 1
Inchbald, Elizabeth, 22, 24, 25, 34, 54, 116, 121
  adaptations from the French, 54
  Animal Magnetism, 24, 22, 54, 154, 155, 158
  Child of Nature, The, 54
  Lovers' Vows, 175, *see* Kotzebue; *Das* Kind der Liebe
  on Kemble as Penruddock, 24
  on *The Road to Ruin*, 15
  on *Wheel of Fortune*, 25
  Widow's Vow, The, 14, 119, 120, 121, 122, 123, *see* Patrat; *L'heureuse erreur*
Incledon, Charles, 128
Irving, Washington,
  Spectre Bridegroom, The, 245, 246
Isherwood, Christopher, *Goodbye to Berlin*, 32
Italian Opera Company, Vienna, 215

Jagemann, Karoline,
  Die Erinnerungen, 82
Jerningham, Edward,
  Siege of Berwick, 163, 164

Johnstone [or Johnston], Mrs. Henry Erskine, Nanette, née Parker, 199
  as Mrs. Haller in *The Stranger*, 28
  as Zorilda in *Timour the Tartar*, 167
Johnstone[or Johnston], Henry Erskine, 28
  as O'Whack in *Notoriety*, 47
Jommelli, Niccolò,
  chaconne adapted for *The Castle Spectre*, 217, 218
Jones, Mrs., née Field,
  as Laurelia in *Raising the Wind*, 141
Jones, Richard,
  as Diddler in *Raising the Wind*, 142
  as Gossamer in Laugh When You Can, 127
  as Sir Patrick in *Sleep-walker, or Which is the Lady*, 127
  as stage Irishman or Dandy, 127
Jordan, Dorothy, 46
  as Angela in *The Castle Spectre*, 217, 218
  as Cora in *Pizarro*, 157
  as Sophia in *The Road to Ruin*, 136
Journal de Paris, 235
jus primae noctis,
  in *The Follies of a Day*, 35, 36

Kant, Immanuel,
  Critique of Judgment, 73
  disinterestedness, 70
Kean, Edmund, 9, 6, 29, 33, 114, 143, 160
  affair with Charlotte Cox, 46
  as Bertram, 145, 147
  as Mortimer in *The Iron Chest*, 195, 196
  as Richard III, 85, 88
Keats, John, 57
  La Belle Dame sans Merci, 255
  Lamia, 255
  letter to Richard Woodhouse, 1
  no identity, 1
  Ode on a Grecian Urn, 57
  Ode to Psyche, 228
Keeley, Robert,
  as Nicholas in *The Devil's Elixir*, 68
Kelly, Henry,
  as Wilford in *The Iron Chest*, 198
Kelly, Michael, 12, 18, 24, 46, 180, 190, 192, 201, 218
  Algonah, 216
  as Armstrong in *The Iron Chest*, 12
  as Basilio and Don Curzio in *Nozze di Figaro*, 188
  as Colonel Blandford in *The Cherokee*, 80
  as Corrado in *Una cosa rare*, 192
  as Count Floreski in *Lodoiska*, 6, 180, 192
  as Daphne in puppet theatre, 214
  as Don Altador in *The Pirates*, 180

Kelly, Michael (*cont.*),
  as Don Basilio and Don Curzio in *Le Nozze di Figaro*, 215
  as Frederick in *No Song, No Supper*, 191
  as Ganem in *The Forty Thieves*, 166
  as Lionel in *Lionel and Clarissa*, 214, 215
  as Lord William in *The Haunted Tower*, 180, 184, 188, 189
  as Selim in *Blue-Beard*, 189, 218
  as Seraskier in *The Siege of Belgrade*, 180, 191, 218
  as the Count in Puccini's La Buona *figliuola*, 214
  Bard of Erin, The, 216
  Blue-Beard, The, musical score, 15, 171, 189, 210, 211, 213, 218, 222, 227
  Castle Spectre, The, musical score, 171, 188, 213, 216, 217
  De Monfort, musical score, 188, 213
  echoic musical effects, 219, 220
  Gipsy Prince, The, musical score, 213
  Mahmoud, additions to, 216
  meets Stephen and Anna Storace,
  Pizarro, musical score, 213, 216
  Reminiscences, 6, 15, 184, 185, 186, 188, 189, 210, 214, 215, 216, 217, 218
  songs for Seymour's False *Appearances*, 216
  songs for Walpole's *Fashionable Friends*, 216
  stage music to Coleridge's *Remorse*, 156, 213, 218
  stage music for Hoare's *A Friend in Need*, 216
  stage music for sixty-two plays, 216
  title role in Arne's *Cymon*, 24
  Woodpecker, The, 211, 212, 213, 219, 221
Kelly, Thomas,
  dancing master, father of Michael Kelly, 213
Kemble, Charles, 199
  alterations to Payne's *Richelieu*, 53
  as Alonzo in *Pizarro*, 157
  as Richelieu, 53
  as St. Alme in *Deaf and Dumb*, 113
  as Wilford in *The Iron Chest*, 599
Kemble, Elisabeth, Mrs,
  as Louisa in *No Song No Supper*, 191
Kemble, Elizabeth,
  as Lisette in *Animal Magnetism*, 21, 22
  as Mrs. Haller in *The Stranger*, 26, 27
  portrait of, 21
Kemble, Elizabeth Satchell, 20
  as Angela in *The Castle Spectre*, 177
  playing opposite Master Betty, 177
Kemble, Fanny, 114
  portrait of, 21

Kemble, John Philip, 1, 4, 9, 20, 80, 113, 114, 128, 152
  acting in Bristol Theatre, 28
  as Coriolanus, life-size medallion by Sarah Siddons, 21
  as De l'Épée in *Deaf and Dumb*, 113
  as De Monfort, 100, 105
  as Hamlet, 100
  as Macbeth, 2, 5
  as Mortimer in *The Iron Chest*, 193
  as Othello, 101
  as Pendruddock in The Wheel of Fortune, 2, 24
  as Percy in *The Castle Spectre*, 217
  as Petruchio in *The Taming of the Shrew*, 101
  as Richard III, 83, 86
  as Rolla in *Pizarro*, 157, 161
  as the Stranger, 28
  Lodoiska, libretto, 6, 12, 79, 180, 188, 192
  portrait of, 21
  promptbooks, 16
  title role in *Mahmoud*, 216
Kemble, Mrs. Charles, Marie Thérèse, née De Camp, *see* De Camp, Marie Thérèse,
  as Aladdin, 165
Kemble, Stephen, 17
  as manager of the Theatre Royal in Newcastle, 25
  as Penruddock,
  as the Stranger, 27
  manager, Newcastle Theatre Royal, 20
  portrait of, 21
Kenney, James,
  Aladdin and the Wonderful Lamp, 166
  Alcaid, The, *see* Nathan, Isaac composer
  Raising the Wind, 127, 132, 137, 139, 140, 141, 142, 143, 166
  Sweethearts and Wives, *see* Nathan, Isaac composer,
Kindler, August,
  Die feindliche Brueder, 172
King, Steven,
  Shining, The, 203
Kotzebue, August von, 26, 30, 32
  Joanna of Montfaucon, 29, 30
  Menschenhaß und Reue, Italian translation as *Misantropia e Pentimento*, 30
  Das Kind der Liebe, 54
  Der Wildfang, 129
  Die Sonnenjungfrau, 161
  Die Spanier in Peru, 157, 161, 171
  Menschenhaß und Reue, 25, *see* Thompson *The Stranger*, 2
Kreutzer, Rodolphe,
  Lodoiska, musical score, 188, 192

Kuntz, Madame,
 as Madame Dupuis in Hoffmann's *Le secret*,
 124
Kuester, Ulf,
 Theatrum Mundi, 14

La Mash, Monsieur, 43, 47
 as Coquin in *Dissipation*, 41, 43, 44
 as ladies' man, 43
La Motu, Antoine Houdar de,
 Court Fables, 209
La Scala, 47, 162
Labiche, Eugène Marin,
 Un Chapeau de Paille d'Italie, 213
Laclos, Choderlos de,
 Les liaisons dangereueses, 178
Lalande, Madame, *see* Méric-Lalande,
 Henriette,
Lamb, Charles,
 on John Bannister, 15
 On the Artificial Comedy of the last Century,
 105
 Stage Illusion, 105
Lamb, Lady Caroline,
 Glenarvon, 232, 44
Lang, Andrew, 204, 209
Langenau, Ludwig Wilhelm,
 Ludwig der Springer, 172
Larpent, John,
 Examiner of Plays, 33, 38, 57, 174
Latude, Henri Masers de, 38
 escape from Bastille, 38
 Memoirs, 39
Lavater, Johann Caspar, *Physiognomische
 Fragmente*, 83, 99
Lawrence, Sir Thomas,
 portrait of Kemble as Rolla, 159
Le Brun, Charles,
 Method to Learn to Design the Passim, A,
 83
Le Fanu, Sheridan,
 Carmilla, 255
Legros, Madame, 39
Leipzig Stadttheater, 251
Lesage, Alain-René,
 Le Diable boiteux, 32
Lessing, Gotthold Ephraim,
 Emilia Galotti, 93
 Hamburgische Dramaturgie, 90
 Laokoon, 96, 98
 on disguise and dissimulation in acting,
 89, 90
Levert, Mlle,
 as Countess in Patrat's *L'heureuse erreur*,
 123

Lewis, Matthew Gregory, 216
 Castle Spectre, The, 3, 11, 58, 170, 171, 173, 175,
 178, 188, 193, 197, 199, 200, 202, 213, 216,
 217, 218, 241
 Minister, The, 171
 Monk, The, 11, 52, 144, 170, 172, 174, 178, 207
 Rolla trans. from Kotzebue's Die Spanier in
 Peru, 171
 Timour the Tartar, 165, 166
 Venoni, 52
Lewis, William Thomas,
 as Count Almaviva in *The Follies of a Day*, 35
 as Diddler in *Raising the Wind*, 127,
 141, 142
 as Goldfinch in *The Road to Ruin*, 15, 135, 136,
 137, 141
 as the Copper Captain in *Rule a Have a Wife*,
 127
Liebhabertheater zu Reval, 161
Lincoln's Inn Fields, 124
Lindoe, Benjamin,
 as Plainway in *Raising the Wind*, 141
Linley, Thomas,
 music for *Love in the Fast*, 128
Liston, John,
 as Sam in *Raising the Wind*, 141
 as Van Dunder in *'Twould Puzzle a Conjuror*,
 51
Liston, Mrs.,
 as Annette in *The Stranger*, 28
Livorno (Leghorn) Comic Opera, 214
London,
 population (1750, 1800, 1821), 5
Longeville, Harcouet de,
 Long Livers, 209
Loraux, Claude Francois Filette,
 Lodoiska, libretto,
Loveday, Mrs. Henry,
 as Miss Durable in *Raising the Wind*, 142
Lugosi, Bela,
 as Count Dracula, 207
 as Count Dracula in *Abbott and Costello Meet
 Frankenstein*, 240
Lyceum Theatre, 4, 153, 242
 English Opera, 18

Macaulay, Miss,
 as Elvira in *Pizarro*, 160
MacPherson, James,
 Ossian, 235
Macready, William, 17, 19
 as Archer in The Beaux' Stratagem, 23
 as La Fleur in Animal Magnetism, 22
 Irishman in London, 240
Macready, William Charles, 9

Maffei, Francesco Scipioni di,
  Merope, 89
Marchand, Leslie, 170
Margravine Theatre, Naples, 143
Marlowe, Christopher,
  Edward II, 169
Marmontel, Jean-François,
  Les Incas, ou la destruction de l'empire du
    Perou, 157, 161
  Les Incas, trans. *The Incas*, 162
Marschner, Heinrich,
  Der Vampyr, 242, 251
Martin y Soler, Vicente,
  Una cosa rara, musical score, 192
Martini, Jean Paul Egide,
  Le droit du Seigneur, comic opera, 36
Martyr, Margaret, née Thornton,
  as Cicely in *The Haunted Tower*, 190
Mathews, Charles, 3, 4
  as Mustapha in *The Forty Thieves*, 166
  as Samson in *The Iron Chest*, 199
  as Somno in Sleep-walker, or Which it the
    Lady, 128
  At Home, 4
  Dissertation on Hobbies, 3
Mathews, Mrs. Charles,
  as Lelia in *The Forty Thieves*, 166
Mattocks, Isabella, née Hallam,
  as Widow Warren in *The Road to Ruin*,
    135, 136
Maturin, Charles,
  Bertram, 144, 145, 146, 147
Mayr, Johann Simon,
  Alonso e Cora, 162
McFarland, Thomas,
  Romanticism and the Forms of Ruin, 57
Meggett,
  as Mortimer in *The Iron Chest*, 161, 195
  as Rolla in *Pizarro*, 161
Méric-Lalande, Henriette,
  as Imogine in Bellini's *Il Pirata*, 148
Merry, Anne, née Brunton,
  as Sophia in *The Road to Ruin*, 135
Mesmer, Franz Anton, 154
Miller, James, and John Hoadley,
  Mahomet the Imposter, see Voltaire; *Mahomet*,
Mills, Mrs., née Burchill,
  as Sophia in *The Road to Ruin*, 136
Milton, John,
  Comus, 149
  Paradise Lost, 145
misogyny,
  as dramatic theme, 2
Mitford, Mary Russell, 202
  Charles I, 38

Molière, Jean-Baptiste Poquelin,
  Tartuffe, 183
Moncrieff, William Thomas, 250
  Cataract of the Ganges, The, 77, 168, 169
  Gamblers, The, 69, 70, 71, 72
  Giovanni in London, 243
  Ravens of Orleans, The, 242
  Secret, The, adapted from Hoffmann,
    Le secret, 123
  Shipwreck of the Medusa, The, 9, 73, 74, 75,
    76, 77, 78, 242
  Spectre Bridegroom, The, 241, 245, 246, 247,
    248, 249, 250
  Three Part Medley, 212
  Vampire, The, 241, 242, 243, 245, 253
Monthly Magazine, 172
Monthly Mirror, 18
Montigny, Darles de,
  Thérèse philosophe, 178
Moore, Edward,
  Gamester, The, 20
Moore, Thomas,
  Ballad Stanzas, 211
  Gipsy Prince, The, libretto, 213
  Wonder, The, a ballad, 187
Morton, Thomas,
  Way to Get Married, The, 22
Mozart, Wolfgang Amadeus,
  Don Giovanni, 243, 245
  Le Nozze di Figaro, 188, 215
Munden, Joseph Shepherd, 128
  as Dornton in *The Road to Ruin*, 15,
    135, 136
Murphy, Arthur,
  Grecian Daughter, The, 20
  Way to Keep Him, The, 22
Murray, John, 231, 245
Murray, William,
  as Fainwould in *Raising the Wind*, 142

Napoleon Bonaparte, 8, 33, 34, 37, 73, 157,
    193, 207
  threat of invasion, 11, 157, 158, 159
Nathan, Isaac,
  music to Byron's *Hebrew Melodies*, 33
  music to Kenney's *Sweethearts and Wives*, 33
  music to Kenney's *The Alcaid*, 33
New Monthly Magazine, 231, 232
New Monthly Review, 231
Newcastle Chronicle, 19
Newcastle Theatre Royal, 8, 19, 20, 21, 25, 30, 31,
    124, 136, 141, 142, 159, 160, 161, 175, 177, 190,
    1914, 199, 241
Noble, Thomas,
  as Diddler in *Raising the Wind*, 141

Nodier, Charles,
  Smarra, ou les Demons de la Nuit, 255
Nodier, Charles, Achille Jouffley, and Pierre
  Carmouche,
  Le Vampire, mélodrame en trois actes, 51, 234,
    235, 236, 237, 238, 242, 243, 251, 253
Normanby, Lord and Lady, 142
Northcote, James,
  painting of King John (IV.i), 152, 153
  painting of Kemble as Richard III, 88
Norton, Miss, 199
Norwich Theatre Royal, 164

O'Keefe, John, 147
  Modern Antiques, 241
O'Neill, Eliza, 29, 143
  as Juliet, 19
  as Mrs. Haller in *The Stranger*, 28
Oates, Joyce Carol,
  Blue-Bearded Lover, 203
Olympic Theatre, 221, 226, 242, 243
Orger, Mary Ann,
  as Madame La Trappe in *Simpson and Co*,
    49
Ormston, Charles,
  great grandfather of John Waldie, 17
Ormston, Jean,
  grandmother of John Waldie, 17
Otway, Thomas,
  Atheist, The, 155
  Venice Preserv'd, 20, 149
Oulton, W. C.,
  Sleep-walker, or *Which is the Lady*, 127, 128

Paisiello, Giovanni,
  Gli schiavi per amore, 215
Palmer, Jack,
  as Pierre in *Deaf and Dumb*, 113
  as Singleton in *The Imposters*, 113
Pantheon Theatre, Edinburgh, 153
parabasis, 13
Parker, Mrs.,
  as Zobeid in *Aladdin*, 166
Pasquin, Anthony, 46
Passerini,
  singing master in Dublin, 214
Patrat, Joseph,
  L'heureuse erreur, 123
Payne, John Howard, 34, 54
  Adeline, 52, 53
  Richelieu, altered as *The French Libertine*, 53
Peake, Richard Brinsley,
  Presumption, 241
Pepper, John Henry,
  Pepper's Ghost, 56, 57, 81, 115, 257

Peretti,
  male contralto in Dublin, 214
performance,
  duality of, 2
Perrault, Charles,
  Blue-Beard, 12, 203, 204, 205, 206, 207, 208,
    209, 224, 226, 228, 229
  Les contes de ma mère l'oye, 209
Perry, Mary, 21, 22, 23, 123
  as Constance in *Animal Magnetism*, 22
  as Julia Faulkner in *The Way to Get Married*,
    22
  as Margaretta in *No Song No Supper*, 191
  as Marian in *The Miser*, 22
  as Mrs. Sullen *in The Beaux' Stratagem*,
  as Sophia Dove in *The Brothers*, 21
  as the Countess in *The Stranger*, 26
  as Widow Belmore in *The Way to Keep Him*,
    22
Petrarch, Francesco,
  Laura de Sade, née de Novis, 187
Piozzi, Hester Lynch, 19
Pixérécourt, René-Charles Guilbert de, 32, 54
  Coelina, 109
  Valentine, 52
Planché, James Robinson, 227, 228, 250, 251
  Abudah, 153
  at the Lyceum Theatre, 153
  Blue Beard, 9, 202, 221, 226, 227, 228, 229
  Caliph and the Cadi, The, 153
  Giovanni the vampire, 241, 243, 244, 245
  Der Vampyr, 241, 251, 252, 253, 254
  Vampire, The, 51, 60, 200, 234, 235, 236, 237,
    238, 239, 240, 241, 242, 243, 245, 253
  Witch of Derncleugh, The, 241
Pleyel, Ignaz Joseph, 186
Plumptre, Anne,
  trans. Kotzebue, *Die Sonnenjungfrau*, 162
Plymouth Theatre, 122
Poe, Edgar Allan,
  Ligeia, 255
  Spectacles, The, 148
Polidori, John, 12
  Vampire, The, 13, 51, 231, 232, 233, 234, 236,
    237, 242, 243, 244, 251, 253, 255, 257
Pompadour, Jeanne-Antoinette Poisson,
  Madame de, 38, 39, 40
Poole, John, 34, 40, 54
  'Twould Puzzle a Conjuror, 50, 51
  Simpson and Co, 49, 50
Pope, Elizabeth,
  as Madame Flanval in *Deaf and Dumb*, 113
  as Mrs. Dorothy in *The Imposters*, 113
Pope, Jane,
  as Eliza in *Love in the East*, 128

Powell, Jane,
  as Alhedra in *Remorse*, 218
  as Evelina in *The Castle Spectre*, 218
Praz, Mario, 11
  Romantic Agony, The, 170, 178
Pritchard,
  as Father Philip in *The Castle Spectre*, 177
Puccini, Niccolò,
  La Buona figliuola, 214
Pugin, Augustus,
  Gothic designs, 151
Purinton, Marjean, 195

Queen Charlotte,
  adultery trial, 146
Quick, Thomas, 44
  as Silky in *The Road to Ruin*, 135
  as Sir Benjamin Dove in *The Brothers*, 21
  as the Doctor in *Animal Magnetism*, 22
Quller-Couch, Arthur,
  Blue Beard, 204

Radcliffe, Ann, 170, 173
  Mysteries of Udolpho, The, 172
Rais, Gilles de, 12, 51, 205, 227
Ratcliff Street murders, 68
Rauzzini, Matteo, 214
Raymond, James,
  as Lovinski in *Lodoiska*, 193
  as Osmond in *The Castle Spectre*, 193
Raymond, Richard John, 46, 54
  Castle of Paluzzi, The, 38
  Old Oak Tree, The, 38, 39, 40, 72
  State Prisoner, The, 38
Reeve, James,
  as Peter von Bummel in *The Flying
    Dutchman*, 129
Reeve, William,
  Blue Beard, or, The Flight of Harlequin, 224
Rendlesham, Lord and Lady, 142
Reynolds, Frederic, 54
  Blind Bargain, The, 49
  Burgomaster of Saardam, or the Two Peters,
    The, 51
  Delays and Blunders, 48
  Laugh When You Can, 127, 128
  Notoriety, 47
  Virgin of the Sun, libretto, 162
Riccoboni, Luigi,
  Dell arte rappresentativa, 92, 94, 99
Richard Jones,
  as Wilford in *The Iron Chest*, 199
Richardson, Samuel,
  Clarissa, 178
Ritter, Heinrich Ludwig,

Der Vampir oder Die Todte-Braut, 251
Roberts, David,
  stage designs, 153
Robertson, William,
  History of America, 158
Robinson, Mary, actress, 146
Robinson, Mary, Maid of Buttermere, 69, 70
Rodwell, George,
  musical score, *The Devil's Elixir*, 67
  musical score, *The Flying Dutchman*, 60
Romanzini, Maria Thérèsa, *see* Bland,
    Mrs. George
  as Dorothy in *No Song, No Supper*, 191
Rossini, Gioachino, 148, 162
  Elisabetta regina d'Inghilterra, 162
  Guillaume Tell, 220, 227
  La Cenerentola, 227
  Mose in Egitto, 148
  Otello, 162
Rowe, Nicholas,
  Fair Penitent, The, 3
  Jane Shore, 20
Royal Coburg, 5, 9, 39, 69, 73, 74, 78, 154, 212,
    241, 242, 254
Royalty Theatre, Wellclose Square, 153
Rubini, Giovanni Battista,
  as Gualtiero in Bellini's *Il Pirata*, 148
Russell, James,
  as Don Vincentio in *Bold Stroke for a
    Husband*, 119
Ruthven, William, 4th Lord Ruthven and 1st
    Earl of Gowrie (c. 1543–84), 232

Sade, Donatien Alphonse François, Marquis de,
    11, 12, 170, 179, 201, 205
  Aline and Valcour, 179
  amateur theatricals, 178
  Catalogue raisonné, 179
  descendent of Petrarch's Laura, 187
  Ernestine, 183
  Histoire de Juliette, ou les Prosperités du vice,
    144
  Jeanne Laisne, 178
  Justine, 170
  L'Inconstant, 178
  L'union des arts, 179
  La tour enchantée, 11, 12, 178, 179, 180, 181, 182,
    183, 186, 187, 188, 189, 201, 235
  Le Boudoir on le mari crédule, 179
  *Le Compte Oxtiern ou Les Malheurs du
    Libertinage*, 179
  Le Mariage du siecle, 178
  Le Misanthrope par amour, 179
  Le Philosephe soi-disant, 178
  Le prévaricateur, 178, 182, 183

Let *120 journées de Sodom*, 178
Les Crimes de l'amour, 179
Reflections on the Novel, 170
Roderigue, ou la tour enchantée,
Sade, Hugues de, 187
Sade, Laura de, née de Novis, 187
Sadler's Wells, 7, 69, 78
Said, Edward,
  Orientalism, 164
Sallengre, Albert-Henri de,
  Praise of Drunkenness, 209
Samba, Robert,
  trans. Perrault's *Tales*, 209
  trans. Ancillon's *Eurruchism Display'd*, 209
  trans. La Motte's *Court Fables*, 209
  trans. Longeville's *Long Livers*, 209
  trans. Sallengre's *Praise of Drunkenness*, 209
Sarti, Giuseppe, 216
Savigny, Henry J.-B., and Alexander Correard,
  Narrative of a Voyage to Senegal, 74, 78
Schechner, Anna, 148
Scheherazade, 210
Schelgel, August Wilhelm, 206
Schiller, Friedrich, 8, 16
  Die Räuber, 156, 171, 173, 174
  Kabale und Liebe, 171
  Maria Stuart, 16
  Wilhelm Tell, 36
Schlegel, August Wilhelm,
  on disguise and dissimulation in acting, 89
  Vorlesungen über dramatische Kunst and Literatur, 90
Schröder, Friedrich Ludwig, 113
Scott, Sir Walter, 238
  at Waldie estate, 17
  Eyrbyggia Saga, 242
  Guy Mannering, 241
Scribe et Mélesville, Eugène,
  Le Vampire, 234
Seaton, Sir Alexander,
  defense of Berwick-upon-Tweed, 163
Sédaine, Michel-Jean,
  Raoul, Barbe Bleue, libretto, 12, 189, 202, 204, 205, 206, 207, 210, 229
  Richard Coeur de Leon, 172
Semper Opera House, 60
Seele, Thomas James,
  as Latude in *The Old Oak Tree*, 39
  Man in the Iron Mask, The, adapted from Dumas, 39
Shadwell, Thomas,
  Libertine, The, 145
Shakespeare, William,
  Antony and Cleopatra, 96
  As You Like It, 245

Comedy of Errors, 180
Cymbeline, Imogen, 1
Hamlet, 85, 91, 131, 175, 245
Henry IV, Part I, 4, 13, 131, 151
Henry VIII, 143
King John, 152
King Lear, 85, 91, 174
Love's Labour's Lost, 176
Macbeth, 1, 5, 131, 208, 238
Merchant of Venice, The, 153
Merry Wives of Windsor, The, 131
Midsummer Night's Dream, 150
Much Ado About Nothing, 97
Othello, 16, 20, 85
Othello, Iago's dissimulation, 1, 83, 97, 101
  portrait of, 21
Richard II, 169
Richard III, 37, 83, 85, 173, 175
Romeo and Juliet, 3, 173, 175
Taming of the Shrew, 20
Tempest, The, 209
Twelfth Night, 13
Sharp, Michael William,
  Essay on Gesture, 99
Shattuck, Charles,
  Kemble Promptbooks, 158
Shelley, Mary,
  Frankenstein, 13, 203, 231
Shelley, Percy Bysshe, 13, 231
  Cenci, The, 143, 144, 174, 202
Sheridan, Richard Brinsley, 5, 7
  Drury Lane fire, 141
  Duenne, The, 173
  Pizarro, 31, 157, 10, 159, 162, 163, 175, 180, 213, 216
  from Kotzebue, *Die Spanier in Peru*, 3
  School for Scandal, The, 15
Siddons, Henry, 20
  as Abdallah in *The Forty Thieves*, 166
  as Douglas, 26
  as the Stranger, 26
  Practical Illustrations of Rhetorical Gesture and Action, adapted from Engel, *Ideen einer Mimik*, 80, 83, 85, 92, 93, 95, 96, 97, 98, 99, 100, 105, 113, 114
Siddons, Sarah, 1, 4, 9, 20, 29, 80, 113
  as Belvidera in *Venice Preserv'd*, 20, 101
  as Calista in *The Fair Penitent*, 271
  as Desdemona in *Othello*, 20, 101
  as Elvira in *Pizarro*, 157
  as Euphrasia in *The Grecian Daughter*, 20
  as Hamlet, 131
  as Isabella in *The Fatal Marriage*, 20
  as Jane De Monfort, 105
  as Jane Shore, 20, 101

Siddons, Sarah (*cont.*),
  as Katherina in *Taming of the Shrew*, 20, 101
  as Lady Macbeth, 2, 4, 5, 100, 101, 131
  as Lady Randolph in *Douglas*, 20, 26, 142
  as Mrs. Beverley in *The Gamester*, 20, 101
  as Mrs. Haller in *The Stranger*, 2, 25, 101
  as Mrs. Oakley in *The Jealous Wife*, 100, 101
  as Ophelia, 100
  as Palmira in *Mahomet*, 20
  as Queen Katherine in *Henry VIII*, 114
  as Sara in *The Mourning Bride*, 20
  portrait of, 21
Siege of Gibraltar,
  at Sadler's Wells, 7, 78
Simmons, Samuel, 28, 128
  as Fainwould in *Raising the Wind*, 138
Simpson, Miss,
  as Cora in *Pizarro*, 60
  as Sophia in *The Road to Ruin*, 136
Smirke, Robert,
  illustrations to *Arabian Nights*, 153, 165
  paintings for the Boydell Shakespeare Gallery, 165
Smith, Albert,
  music to *Aladdin and the Wonderful Lamp*, 166
Smith, O.,
  as Mouchard in *The Old Oak Tree*, 39
  Lolonois, or, The Buccaniers of 1660, 39
Soane, George,
  Aladdin, a Fairy Opera, 166
Somerville, Miss,
  as Imogine in Maturin's *Bertram*, 45, 147
Sontag, Henriette, 148
Southerne, Thomas,
  Fatal Marriage, The, 20
Southey, Robert,
  Thalaba, the Destroyer, 254, 255
stage designs,
  special effects, 151
Stanfield, Clarkson,
  stage designs, 153
Stanislayski, Konstantin, 82
Staves, Susan, 130
Stendahl [Henri Beyle],
  Racine et Shakespeare, 16
Stevenson, Sir John,
  musical setting of Moore's ballad, The Wonder, 187
Stewart, Dugald,
  lectures in philosophy, 17
Stoker, Bran,
  Dracula, 234, 244, 257
Storace, Anna, 180, 190, 214, 218
  as Adela in *The Haunted Tower*, 180, 184, 186, 189, 190

as Caroline in *Family Quarrels*, 146
as Elinor in *The Cherokee*, 180
as Fabulina in *The Pirates*, 180
as Lilla in *The Siege* of *Belgrade*, 180, 191, 192
as Lilla in *Una cosa rara*, 192
as Margaretta in *No Son, No Supper*, 191
as Susanna in *Le Nozzi di Figaro*, 188, 215
as the black slave in Paisiello's *Gli schiavi per amore*, 215
in *Mahmoud*, 216
Mahmoud additions to, 216
Storace, Stephen, 168, 180, 201, 214, 215
  Cherokee, The, musical score, 180
  collaboration with James Cobb, 215
  Doctor and The Apothecary, The, musical score, 180
  Gli equivoci, opera based on *Comedy of Errors*, 180
  Haunted Tower, The, musical score, 11, 12, 15, 178, 179, 183, 185, 186, 190, 200, 213, 235
  Iron Chest, The, musical score, 12, 180, 193, 194, 195, 215
  Lodoiska, musical score, 12, 188, 192
  Mahmoud, musical score, 216
  No Song, No Supper, musical score, 180, 191
  Pirates, The, musical score, 180
  Siege of Belgrade, The, musical score, 46, 180, 190, 191, 218
Stuart, Roxana,
  Stage Blood, 245, 256
Suett, Richard, 128
  as Sultan in *Mahmoud*, 216
  as Varbel in *Lodoiska*, 192
  as Yusuph in *Siege of Belgrade*, 191
Suppé, Franz von,
  Light Calvary Overture, 220
Surrey Institution, 157

Talbot, Richard,
  as Rezenfelt in *De Monfort*, 105
Talma, Francois-Joseph, 148
Tatar, Maria,
  Secrets beyond the Door, 202, 203, 204, 209
Teatro allo Pergola, Florence, 215
Teatro de Marionette, Naples,
  Polichinello in *The Virgin of the Sun*, 162
Teatro Nuovo, Florence, 215
Teatro San Carlo, 162
Ternan, Ellen,
  as Lisette in *Animal Magnetism*, 155
Terneaux, Madlle.,
  as Lodoiska in Kreutzer's opera, 193
Terry, Daniel,
  as Don Caesar in *Bold Stroke for a Husband*, 119

Théâtre de l'Odéon, 35
Théâtre de l'opera-comique, 123
Théâtre de la Gaîté, 52
Théâtre de la Porte-Saint-Martin, 52, 234
Théâtre de Vaudeville, 234
Théâtre des Italiens, 188
Théâtre Feydau, 118, 192
Théâtre Francaise, 123
Théâtre Molière, 179
Thompson, Benjamin,
    The Stranger, from Kotzebue, *Menschenhaß
    und Reue*, 2, 16, 25, 26, 27, 28, 30, 146,
    147, 162
Thompson, Stith,
    Motif-index of Folk Literature, 203
Thomson, James,
    Tancred and Sigismunda, 175
Thurtell, John,
    murderer, 70
    execution, 71
Tieck, Ludwig, 206, 226
    Almansur, Abdallah, and *Alla-Moddin*, 209
    Der Blaubart. Drama in fünf Akten, 202, 244,
        210, 211
    Der gestiefelte Kater, 207
    Die sieben weiber des Blaubart, 209
    Mechthilde in *Ritter Blaubart*, 207, 208
    *Peter Lebrecht. Eine Gechichte ohne
        Abentheuerlichkeiten*, 207
    Phantasm, 207
    Ritter Blaubart, 202, 203, 207, 208, 209, 223, 229
    Shakespeare's Behandlung des Wunderbaren,
        209
    trans. *The Tempest, Der Sturm*, 209
Tomko, Michael, 46
Tresham, Henry,
    Antony and Cleopatra. II.ix, 96, 97
Tunbridge Wells Theatre, 42
Tussaud, Madame,
    wax works, 72
Twitchell, James,
    Living Dead, The, 255
Tytler, Alexander F.,
    lectures on cultural history, 17
    Robbers, The, trans. from Schiller, 173, 174

Valabrègue, Paul de, Captain,
    husband of Angelica Catalani, 193
Vampire,
    misogyny and domestic violence, 2
Vanbrugh, John,
    Confederacy, 124
Vestris, Lucia Elizabeth, née Bartolozzi, 114,
    153, 218
    as Flourette in Planché's *Blue Beard*, 227

Victoria Theatre, 38
villain,
    as sexual predator, 2
violence, domestic,
    as dramatic theme, 2
Virgil,
    Aeneid onomatopoeia, 220
Voltaire, François-Marie Arouet,
    *Histoire de l'Empire de Russie sous Pierre le
        Grand*, 51
    Le droit du seigneur, 36
    Le Fanatisme, ou Mahomet le Prophets, 20
    Semiramis, 168
    Zara, 175
Vulpius, Christian August,
    Rinaldo Rinaldini, 36

Wagner, Ricard,
    Flying Dutchman, The, 60
Wake not the dead, anon., 255, 256
Waldie, Ann Ormston,
    mother of John Waldie, 17
Waldie, George,
    father of John Waldie, 17, 21
Waldie, John, 8, 14, 17, 18, 19, 20, 21, 22, 23, 24,
    25, 26, 17, 29, 30, 31, 32, 68, 115, 136, 161
    Alexander Tytler's lectures, 17
    amateur theatricals, 42, 159
    as singer (tenor), 18
    on *Alonso e Cora*, 162
    comparison of *Wallace* and *Pizarro*, 31
    Dugald Stewart's lectures, 17
    estate at Hendersyde Park, 17
    fluent in French and Italian, with
        conversational German, 29
    his companion Giacomo, 17
    Journal of Waldie, 4
    morality or immorality of the drama, 27
    Musical Report, *Newcastle Chronicle*, 19
    on adaptations of *Arabian Nights*, 167
    on adultery in *The Stranger*, 27
    on *Aladdin*, 165
    on amateur performance of *Henry VIII*, 43
    on amateur performance of *Raising the Wind*,
        143
    on amateur production of *Pizarro*, 159
    on amateur production of *The Tale of
        Mystery*, 159
    on Anna Storace as Adela in *The Haunted
        Tower*, 190
    on Bellini's *Pirata*,
    on Betterton as Diddler in *Raising the Wind*,
        141, 142
    on Braham as Serkasier in *Siege of Belgrade*,
        192

Waldie, John (*cont.*),
  on Bristol Theatre, effect of small size on
    acting, 28
  on Brunton as Diddler in *Raising the Wind*,
    142
  on Carter as Gossamer in *Laugh When You
    Can*, 128
  on Carter as Sir Patrick in *Sleep-walker, or
    Which is the Lady*, 128
  on Conway, 141, 150, 160
  on Daniel Egerton, 142
  on Eliza O'Neill as Mrs. Haller in *The
    Stranger*, 28
  on Elizabeth Kemble as Mrs. Haller in *The
    Stanger*, 26
  on Henry Siddons as the Stranger, 26
  on Hoffmann's *Le secret*, 123
  on John Philip Kemble as the Stranger, 28
  on Kemble as Penruddock, 24
  on *Lodoiska*, 192, 193
  on Maria Thérèsa De Camp as Lodoiska, 193
  on Master Betty, 176, 199
    as Osmond in *The Castle Spectre*, 177, 178
    return to the stage, 199, 200
  on Mayr's *Alonso e Cora*, 162
  on Meggett as as Rolla in *Pizarro*, 161
  on Moncrieff's *The Secret*, 124
  on Mrs. Johnstone as Mrs. Haller in *The
    Stranger*, 28
  on Mrs. Johnstone's excess of passion, 28
  on *No Song, No Supper*, 191
  on Noble as Diddler in *Raising the Wind*, 141
  on Patrat's *L'heureuse* erreur, 123
  on Planché's *The Vampire*, 241
  on prostitutes in the theatres, 30
  on *Raising the Wind*, 141, 142
  on Rubini in Rossini's *Mosè in Egitto*, 148
  on Siddons as Lady Randolph in *Douglas*, 142
  on *Sleep-walker, or Which is the Lady*, 128
  on stage designs of *Aladdin*, 165, 166
  on *The Devil's Elixir*, 68
  on *The Forty Thieves*, 166
  on *The Haunted Tower*, 190, 191
  on *The Iron Chest*, 197, 198, 200
  on *The Road to Ruin*, 135, 136
  on *The Siege of Belgrade*, 191, 192
  on *The Travellers*, 168
  on *The Widow's Vow*, 122
  on *Timour the Tartar*, 167
  on *Una cosa rara* as source for *The Siege of
    Belgrade*, 192
  on *Waterloo*, 193
  on *Wheel of Fortune*, 25
  on Young as Doricourt in *The Belle's
    Stratagem*, 160

  on Young as Rolla in *Pizarro*, 160
  prompter's box, 29
  shareholder of Theatre Royal in Newcastle, 17
  to sing the Choruses in *Pizarro*, 159
Waldie, William,
  brother to John Waldie, 17
Walker, Charles Edward,
  Wallace, 31
Walpole, Horace,
  Castle of Otranto, The, 171
  Mysterious Mother, The, 144
Walpole, Horace, 4th Earl of Orford,
  Fashionable Friends, 216
Warde, James Prescott,
  as Achmet in *Barbarossa*, 199
  as Mortimer *in The Iron Chest*, 200
Ware, William,
  musical score for *Aladdin or the Wonderful
    Lamp*, 165
Watts, Jane Waldie, 28
  novelist, artist, sister to John Waldie, 17
  Sketches Descriptive of Italy in 1816–1817, 18
  Waterloo, by a near Observer, 18
Weave, William,
  murder victim, 70
Webb, Mrs. née Child,
  as Commode in *Fire and Water*, 46, 49
  as Falstaff in *Henry IV, Part 1*, 4, 131
  as Lady Acid in *Notoriety*, 47
  as Mistress Quickley in *Henry IV. Part I*, 131
Webb, W.,
  Aladdin or the Wonderful Lamp, 165
Weber, Carl Maria von,
  Der Freischütz, 251, 252
Wentworth, Miss,
  as Flora in *The Widow's Vow*, 113
West, Benjamin,
  Lear on the Heath III.iv, 91, 92
  Ophelia's Madness IV.iv, 91, 92
Westall, Richard,
  depiction of Henry IV, Part I (III.i),
    151, 153
Weston, Miss,
  as Inis in *The Widow's Vow*, 123
Wewitzer, Ralph,
  as Fripon in *Fire and Water*, 46
Whitbread, Samuel, 7
Whitehead, William,
  The Roman Father, adapted from Corneille,
    Les Horaces, 92
Widdrington, Samuel Edward, Captain, 160
  as Francisco in *The Tale of Mystery*, 159
  as Rolla in *Pizarro*, 159
Williams, Anne, and Christy Desmet,
  Shakespearean Gothic, 173

Williams, Helen Maria,
Bastille, A Vision, The, 158
Letters From France, 158
Peru, A Poem in Six Cantos, 158
Wohlbrück, Wilhelm August,
Der Vampyr, libretto, 251, 252, 253, 254
Wollstonecraft, Mary, 54
A Vindication of the Rights of Men, 34
Woodhouse, Richard, *see* Keats, John,
Woodworth, Samuel,
To Mary, 222
Wordsworth, William,
as reader of *Arabian Nights*, 164
Borderers, The, 156
on Dibdin's *Beauty of Buttermere*, 69
On Seeing Helen Maria Williams Weep, 158
Prelude, The, 58
Wroughton, Richard,
as Darlemont in *Deaf and Dumb*, 113

as Don Carlos in *A Bold Stroke for a Husband*,
113
as Polycarp in *The Imposters*, 113
as Reginald in *The Castle Spectre*, 217
Wyatt, Benjamin Dean,
Drury Lane architect, 7

Young, Charles Mayne, 29, 160, 161, 162
as Doricourt in *The Belle's Stratagem*, 160
as Rolla in *Pizarro*, 160, 161
as the Stranger, 28
on Mortimer in *The Iron Chest*, 198, 199
Young, Edward,
Revenge, The, 175
Young, Robert,
White Mythologies, 151
Younger, Mr.,
as Baron Von Clump in *'Twould Puzzle a
Conjuror*, 51